Frances Fyfield is a criminal lawyer, practising in London, the setting for many of her books. She also lives by the sea which, aside from the love of London, is her passion. *Deep Sleep* won the CWA Silver Dagger Award in 1991 and *A Clear Conscience* was nominated for the CWA Gold Dagger Award and won the Grand Prix de Littérature Policière in 1998. She has also written three novels as Frances Hegarty and her books are widely translated. Her most recent novel, *The Nature of the Beast*, is available in Little, Brown hardback.

HELEN WEST OMNIBUS

DEEP SLEEP
SHADOW PLAY
A CLEAR CONSCIENCE

Three Novels in One Volume

FRANCES FYFIELD

A *Time Warner* Book

First published in Great Britain by Time Warner Paperbacks in 2002
Reprinted in 2002

Helen West Omnibus copyright © Frances Fyfield 2002
Deep Sleep copyright © Frances Fyfield 1991
Shadow Play copyright © Frances Fyfield 1993
A Clear Conscience copyright © Frances Fyfield 1994

A CIP catalogue record for this book
is available from the British Library.

ISBN 0 7515 3283 5

Typeset in Plantin Light by M Rules
Printed and bound in Great Britain by
Clays Ltd, St Ives plc

Time Warner Paperbacks
An imprint of
Time Warner Books UK
Brettenham House
Lancaster Place
London WC2E 7EN

www.TimeWarnerBooks.co.uk

HELEN WEST OMNIBUS

DEEP SLEEP

PROLOGUE

SINCE she had shut the window, the room was stuffy. She liked the central heating fierce, imagined the night air would infect her. Please, she said, I know you prefer it open, but ugh, winter cold out there, honestly. And all the dust from the building works, please . . . She had a way of drawing out the 'please' to make a whole sentence, a series of pleas which ascended to a whine. He should have been sorry for her; but all he could summon up was a rage as hot as heartburn, a furious discomfort which made him smaller and smaller until he felt he might disappear in the smoke of his own anger. One free weekend in a hotel, the chance to breathe and open his own window, but she had called him back, saying Pleeeas, come home, I'm frightened, don't leave me. I'm not leaving you, he had said down the phone; I'm simply staying here, talking, drinking, sleeping, at someone else's expense, for Christ's sake, I can come back tomorrow afternoon if you want, for an hour. I shan't half look a fool . . .

And even then, back across the city with his teeth gritted, very slightly sloshed, he did not think of how angry he could be. Thought of nothing but keeping the peace while she nagged him about the stock, told him how to run the place, and then finally on top of everything else, Will you please close the window?

He could not breathe. Mother had once bound him so closely into his bedclothes that he had lain like a swaddled baby, his face purple. Now Mother was dead and still he could not breathe.

She had settled herself in all right, his little wife. Drew clearly for him, with the blunt pencil of her voice, the extent of his reliance and her control. She had moved the settee, and an ugly cushion had been added to destroy the effect of the worn, Edwardian brocade; two of his favourite pictures had been removed; there was a coffee ring on his mahogany table. All of it so old-fashioned, she said. Why can't we ever get anything new? Like your waist-coats, precious one, light of my life, that make you look like a fella from *My Fair Lady*. I sometimes think you live in that age, hmm? But I do love you, sweet pea, oh, I do. Do you love me? Go on, tell me you do, 'cos I really love you.

And she did, of course. Couldn't live without him, neither he without her since she owned so much of the business. Though he never resented that since greed was not his weakness. Standards slipped, that was all, in the loneliness of relief after Mother's death, that vacuum filled by no one until this woman appeared, like a miracle, offering position, self respect, the chance of popularity and influence, all gifts Mama had denied. He had leapt into these skinny arms. Never mind the love; love grows like roses, don't you know, with desire blooming up among the weeds. Or not.

Oh, my love, my dear love. He closed his eyes to see that other womanly girl, standing in the shop all day, with her gorgeous, worried face; big in front, big behind; so fabulous from every angle he wished he could see each facet at once. Tight cotton shirts in summer, a scent he could smell from fifty paces: worse in winter when she wore bright sweaters stretched over a generous bosom. She never even saw him looking and never guessed how much she visited his dreams. Respectful, undemanding, an angel.

Oh my love . . . If I do not find out about love, I shall die. I shall never know it here.

Ostensibly, wife slept. Please, dear, please, go to sleep, wife, you've done enough damage for one day. Especially mentioning the window in the same breath as the plan to clear out his back room, the only place where he could exist alone, reigning supreme with his secret knowledge. No, not that. Please. Leave me alone, sometimes, please.

She had no idea what he had in mind as he brushed his teeth, looking in the old mirror. Finding her there alongside his own, tired reflection, a tiny, startling vision, scantily dressed in a translucent nylon negligée which gave a view of nothing, no hills, no valleys, but sagging muscles and a face made up with black eyebrows, dyed hair in curls and a very red mouth, smiling. Crimson lipstick disfiguring large teeth, the only things in that face she could call her own.

C'mon, she said. You're being so mumbly. I love you, sweety pie. Give us a kiss.

Not now, darling. Pleees. Had a bit too much to drink, see?

She was always ordering, even before the window was shut while he himself wanted to scream, and clutch his own throat in suffocation. Soundless, in case she awoke and asked silly, obvious questions such as, what's the matter? A man was not even allowed to claim a headache. She would talk; she was going to shame him. She talked too much, was bound to tell soon.

Oh, my love; wait for me. Let me know what love is.

'You awake, sweetheart?' A simpering, anxious voice in the dark. He kept his lips pursed shut, breathed in and out with less speed and more noise through his mouth, counting between each breath to keep the sound regular. She sighed, adjusted, breathed louder herself.

So many nights like these. Days in which work achieved for him those irresistible rewards of love and authority, trust and credibility, nights where that alternative manhood was crushed in this dreadful intimacy. Sweat began again. The negligée generated heat, and in his pretend sleep, clutching his own side of the bed, he realised she was crying, little snuffling sounds without dignity, pathetic as a puppy shown rejection. She could cry in this fashion for hours, knew only the gross comfort she had anticipated when donning the nylon nightie. The reassurance of sex was what she wanted, that bloodless pleasure she mistook for love, and believed in, no matter what aid he employed. Making love fun for both of them, he had said, and she had laughed, immoderate but co-operative. A waft of sickly perfume filled his nostrils. Rage exploded like a quiet set of fireworks in his head, no noise, simply a terrible intimation, a crystal clear picture of what he was going to do.

'What's the matter?' he mumbled. The bird body lay rigid.

'That window's not properly shut. Please shut it. Like I said.'

He checked the window, but the unbearable sobbing continued and suddenly the idea was fully formed, plucked out of cold storage into the stuffy heat. The window was shut. No ventilation, no moving air as he returned to bed and took her stiff little body in his arms.

'Come on, sweetheart, there, there, there.' She clutched him so hard he could feel her long nails digging into his shoulders. His sweating had stopped and his skin to her touch felt as cold as ice.

'Come on, sweetheart, come on then. I'm here. Let's have a bit of fun, shall we? Come on, like last week, eh? You liked that, didn't you? You know what gets me going.' Her head, buried against his chest, nodded gratefully. As long as he loved her she would put up with all the incentives he seemed to need, and if his needs were insulting she did not mind. Do as your husband does: that way you keep him.

'There we are, sweetheart. Deep breath . . . Oh nice, nice . . . Hold me . . .'

When he opened the bedroom window some time later, there was a vague suggestion of light in the sky. Looking out over the back road, leaning right out in order to breathe long and deep, he watched the lamps on the watchman's hut in the building site glow weaker as a cloudy pink grew visible on the horizon behind the crane. Man-made city lights, a false dawn. He watched the buildings come into blurred focus, a hotch-potch of ugly styles, the view marred by experiment and the destruction of a global war which had coincided with the more important event of his birth. The site below lay empty, a vast muddy field, scratched out for a new square, new houses, new people, more customers; a brave new world. For once, this scene of desolation made him shiver with joy. Beneath a jungle of foundations and piecemeal plans, high rise in the distance, low rise next door, there might have been hell and destruction, but at that moment, he found the view perfectly beautiful.

Then, in strict accordance with his plan, he closed the window carefully as his wife would have done, seeing under his outstretched hand a brief hint of familiar movement in the street below: someone else stirring too early, even for market day, a shape in the distance which was disturbingly recognisable, shuffling along by the hoardings which protected road from mud. Let them crawl, let them shuffle like crabs: he did not care. He was jubilant, pushed the window back wider, tempted to shout greetings, then shut it quietly instead. He moved to the next room, where his clothes lay folded precisely over a chair, dressed carefully, exactly as he had been dressed the night before, taking nothing new from any cupboard. He crossed to the opposite window, tidying away all traces of the recent present, careful this time to remain out of view while he heard a familiar rumble in the street below. Market day; one old man beginning at five-thirty to drag out the wheeled stalls. A grand time to leave, the whole of London an empty shell and himself buoyant, brave and free. There was in these movements nothing of the small man schooled to perfection in all domestic tasks: he was a tiger, full of mysterious power. Rejoice, said the radio. Christmas cometh. Rejoice in rebirth.

Ice cold outside, but rejoice; the saviour is born; a tune bubbling out of his throat. The car was parked one whole street hence, near enough still for the building site dust to freeze on the screen. As he sat inside, turned on the lights, and leant forward to straighten his hair, he saw how his face was smiling serene, like a carol singer on the sleeve of a record, mischief still in the face. And also, fat, wet tears, stinging his cold cheeks and descending slowly and steadily into the mouth which smiled and smiled.

Oh my love. Wait for me.

CHAPTER ONE

HELEN West lay in a big, high bed, slightly too wide for one: passenger on an institutional mattress which could perform contortions. Despite the ungainliness of her couch and in the haze of post-anaesthetic, she could envisage the stainless steel framework dancing across the floor, this way and that to the tune of a Strauss waltz, drawn by the company of other beds swishing in the corridor outside. Her own bed could be wheeled, raised, lowered in whole or part for anything but titillation; an expensive couch, but never sexy. The thought of the word, a very fleeting thought, made her shudder as she might at the mention of necrophilia. Helen found it very difficult indeed to see how a person could feel as bad as this without being dead; and if anyone entered now, it would have to be an undertaker. In which case, the bed would be able to spill her into a box and take her away, quietly.

The door opened on oiled hinges as she closed her eyes, denying the existence of anyone who might wish her to respond. But manners did not take wings, even *in extremis*. They remained buried in the bones, forcing her to follow some bloody-minded instinct for politeness even in the face of an impulse to tell the visitor to . . . She surely had the right to be rude? But, although resentful, Helen began to haul herself upwards, out of the fog and the imprisonment of the stiff sheets. Smiling.

'Well! Well! Well! And how are we feeling then? Fighting fit? Ho ho ho. Sorry about that. Had to do a little more than we intended. Oh dearie, dearie me. Nasty little cyst, left ovary. No, the other one. Had to take it off.'

'What, the ovary?'

He laughed as if he had been told an extraordinary joke. 'Oh, my dear me, no, only the cyst. Jolly good.'

The goodness of anything remained beyond Helen's comprehension, but she battled with the question of why she should be so
protective about an unemployed ovary. Odd, the human response,
and oh how painful intellect, in a subdued form, coming back, and
why did they all talk like imbeciles? He was so loud, and why did
he have to speak to her as if she were deaf, while the nurse towered
above his shoulder with a face like a smiling but slightly apologetic
sphinx, professionally concerned. The surgeon reminded her of
the small boy at school who drilled holes from the boys' to the
girls' lavatory out of curiosity, but the nurse leant forward with
surprising tact.

'You'll feel better soon,' she said. 'You might not think so, but
you will, believe me. Your husband called five minutes ago. I told
him to go away.'

'Thank you,' said Helen. 'Thanks very much.'

For all small mercies. The one portion of brain which would
appreciate her hand being held and her blankets tucked was
absurdly disappointed, the rest enormously relieved, sinking, eyes
closing, still smiling. 'Thank you.' For nothing. Push off, whoever
you are. Leave me alone.

Comforting darkness after they left. Nestling into it, descending slowly again into the mattress of that bed, all of her a strange
feeling shape, tiny and large in silly proportions and nothing to do
with real life. The buzz of distant traffic a comfort to the ear,
warm in here, deliciously warm, almost comfortable as long as she
did not move, and a smell, tugging at distaste. Something there
was, scrabbling for entry, while somewhere, shortly after this
descent, there was a dim memory of a kiss on her hair, soft steps,
someone going away. I happen to love you, darling. Very much.
You do look small.

Geoffrey Bailey, Detective Chief Superintendent, squeaked back
down the polished corridor in what his sergeant called his brothel-
creeping shoes, away from Helen's room, his heart thumping
lightly. Of course she would survive; women were tough, but they
looked so vulnerable when asleep he always wondered if they

would wake or shrink away. All right, said the Sister, not proof against his second attempt to visit. But only for a minute, mind, and don't wake her, she won't like that. I have to go in, you see, he had said humbly. Seeing her unconscious brings such memories my sleep will disappear if I don't, and I must work tomorrow. His long frame was bent charmingly, recognisably a copper for all his distinction, something of the watcher evident in the eyes and the lines, the accent perhaps, but not in the cut of the suit. Oh go on then, but mind you behave.

What exactly did Sister think he might do? Scream? Weep? Create a scene? But then strange things happened in hospitals, even private hospitals like this, an abnormal situation for the likes of Helen and him, except for the prudence of her almost forgotten insurance policy. The shiny efficiency of the place sniffed of privilege without any adornment and for once, Bailey approved. The sick should be fêted, although in his experience they rarely were, while all his own waiting behind screens for persons recovering from gunshot wounds, stab wounds, accidents or simply hiding, had rarely been in places like this. There was nothing here of the abattoir smell of the ordinary Casualty. A passing nurse caught his eye, smiled as he smiled back. He would have preferred sleep in the chair by Helen's bed: discomfort was second nature.

Out in the street, the cold struck like a cannonshot to the chest. His car, indifferently parked, felt icy to the touch. Going home alone, he mused on the business of being referred to as Helen's husband and wondered how long it would be before she corrected that glib supposition. Wished, at the same time, that his borrowed status was real.

The precious sleep was short-lived. Helen surfaced like a diver from muddy water granted only a confused glimpse of light. Thrashing through a dream of being in a chemist's shop where music played while she searched for painkillers, finding nothing on the overcrowded shelves but cosmetics, hairbrushes, stockings, gift-wrapped powders. Moving to one side, the pain increased sharply and she was horribly aware of where she was. Four a.m., winter darkness seen through flimsy curtains, a face by the bed, her nostrils filled with the antiseptic hospital smell, but this time, a scent lightly flavoured with a different kind of alcohol and a whiff of nicotine which made her eyes open wide. Not a face poised to mouth clichés, but an old, disreputable face, quite different from the surgeon who looked as if he washed on the hour and shaved three times a day.

'God, you look awful, woman. If looks could kill, I'd be dead.' The face moved round the other side of the bed and examined the drip. 'I put you to sleep,' he went on. 'Like a baby. You wake up without any trace of nausea and then look at me as if I were a gibbon. Gratitude. This is your bloody anaesthetist, if you don't remember. Do you hurt?'

The head by the bed was grizzled and wrinkled, grey hair sticking out on end and large eyebrows arched in a permanent question.

'Well . . . A bit . . .'

'Don't sound so bloody apologetic; so you bloody should. Only surgeons say otherwise. Operations hurt, also dangerous to health, they don't seem to mention that either. Thank your God you're alive, but never mind. One more injection in a minute, but the longer we leave it, the longer it lasts. Hurt? That you should be so lucky. Want a cigarette?' There was a clipped Irish in the voice; platitudes were clearly anathema.

'Oh, please.' Despite herself and the ache, Helen grinned, full of that sense of the ridiculous which was never far from the surface. How idiotic to be thus, hung over, half alive and wanting nothing more than the cigarette proffered by a doctor, of all people. He read her mind and sighed.

'The very height and depth of foolishness, like all addiction. Plus life in general. Sister'll skin me; we'll open the window after. Here.' He passed her one lit cigarette. Helen knew why they used to be called gaspers. The right hand which took it felt spongy: the taste delicious.

'How do you feel?'

'I don't really know. Unwell. Disgustingly disembowelled. Lower end of me resembles an Easter egg wearing a goatee beard.'

He chuckled softly. 'I like that, now. Poetic description of post-laporotomy surgery as endured by the patient. Not a suicidal patient at the moment. I hope?'

'Earlier, yes, but not now. Her friends would shoot her if she so much as thought of it.' She gestured vaguely with the cigarette.

'Easier ways, are there not, to bring oneself to the door of heaven or hell? No point in suicide, really.' He did not sound entirely convinced. 'Now, let me tell you; there's a fellow down the corridor, poor bastard, had a circumcision earlier. Can't get his thing down lower than a flagpole for six hours. And you think you females have problems. How's the cigarette?'

'Wonderful. Awful.'

'You'll be purified yet. Time for the needle. Then you're fit for heaven.'

'Oh no, not heaven. Hate white clothes.'

His chuckle, amazingly comforting and infectious, emerged from beyond the bed. Something signified the presence of a nurse, presenting a dish towards hands which now smelled of soap. After a split second's sharpness, the injection spread into a warm glow from behind her hip, pushing out pain, closing the eyes. The picture of the chemist's shop came back, unthreateningly, something in there teasing at her memory, the haunting smell of medicine. Dr Hazel looked down at the sallow and attractive features of his patient, distinguished by thick, dark hair, a faded scar to her forehead, then folded Helen's arms across her chest. He turned the strong face to one side to aid breathing, wondered objectively if he could describe her as beautiful, decided he could, uncrossed the ankles to aid circulation and pulled the single sheet to chest height, all with a swift economy of light movement at variance with his age.

'You'd make a good nurse, doctor,' said the voice of the acolyte nurse. He sighed and patted her shoulder.

'Pity I wasn't. All very well for a boy today, but in my own time, darling, it just wasn't the done thing.'

★

Four-thirty in the morning and this was certainly no task for a man. Geoffrey Bailey, without a single witness to his activities, felt silly, and because of the three whiskies he had used to dose his sleeplessness, slightly elated. The fact that Helen's persistent pain had proved curable, albeit by the savage means of surgery, made him enormously relieved. He was fiddling, far from efficiently, in the cheerful, chipped kitchen of her basement flat. On the draining board was a block of what he could only think of as flower-arranging foam, into which he understood he had only to stick stems of things in order to obtain a perfect result every time, according to the instructions. 'Destructions,' he corrected. Bailey had crept out to the garden like a thief, careful not to alarm the neighbours, found two large and frayed winter roses, but otherwise sparse foliage for his purpose, and the result was looking bare and crooked, jaunty in defiance of ever becoming elegant. He was only attempting to translate part of Helen's precious but untidy garden into her hospital ward, but this was pathetic; looked like the work of a person too mean to buy a bunch of proper flowers. Which, swathed in polythene, he would hate as much as she. Little failures loomed large and this was not his forte. Geoffrey crossed from kitchen to living-room in pursuit of the Irish whiskey.

Living in Helen's flat without Helen's presence was an odd sensation which he rather liked as long as he knew she was safe. They had keys to each other's apartments, his in the East London warehouse so very different from her own, an eyrie as light and bare as this was comfortably full of mahogany, pictures and colour. The fire in the living-room lit the red walls, casting shadows from the overflowing plant in a brass urn standing to one side as if needing the heat. Helen's daily books were stacked to one side where she sometimes worked; Archbold *Criminal Pleadings*, forty-fourth edition: Stone's *Justices' Manual*, Wilkinson on *Road Traffic Offences*, Cross on *Evidence*, referred to as necessary in preparation for the next day along with an untidy heap of law reports which he longed to straighten and give some sort of index, but he would never presume. Stock in trade to a criminal lawyer, perhaps more especially a prosecutor, although it was impossible to imagine her in that guise now, not quite stripped of the dignity she never quite lost, even playing the fool. Bailey liked this frail Helen as well as her strong counterpart, the one with a will of iron and a useful tongue, though he conceded liking was a weak description of their mutual condition. Why else would he be in her place in her absence, touching her things with such affection? He rarely expressed sentiment in her presence: but here alone he could feel as he pleased. They spent the weekends vacillating between their two abodes, half the week as well, but this was different. An unmarried married couple, he had often said, sometimes with more grace than others. There might have been a better formula, but for now there was not, since one year living together out of London had been no improvement on this status quo. He knew better than to question any arrangement which worked, most of the time.

Bailey stepped away from the fire, went into the bedroom where sleep had evaded him, sorted a few items into an overnight bag. She would need things, such as the clean nighties she did not possess, face cream, a dressing-gown and a couple of books. The selection of these he could manage, packing quickly, jealous of her privacy. Then he settled back by the fire with one of the hundreds of books, ready to wait for morning. No visitors a.m., Sister had said. To hell with that; he wasn't a policeman for nothing. Helen, darling, I may rarely say it, but I do love you; miss you like my right arm and I must not have any more of this whiskey. Thank God I believe you love me back, though there are times when I do wonder.

'Lerve . . . is a many splendoured thing . . .' Oh yeah? At six-fifteen, Duncan Perry, Detective Constable, Met Police, leered away from his own reflection in the cracked mirror of the tiny bathroom, avoiding an expression flushed by alcohol with eyes puffed from lack of sleep. The face was one of which he had once thoroughly approved, but he no longer thought it handsome as he pulled his chin into a better shape for the blunt razor. Overused blades were better for the early morning shave since there was less chance of small nicks to the skin covered with salmon pink toilet paper, adornments he tended to forget until reminded in public, but the current disposable left his chin feeling scraped. The place was overwarm, largely the result of his failure to turn off the gas oven in the kitchenette cheek by jowl with the bathroom. Inside the oven lay a desiccated steak and kidney pie, forgotten the night before.

Tiptoeing out of his flat although there was no need, the quiet steps a result of constant training and an endless sensation of defending his back, Duncan broke into a jerky sprint for his car, the slight sweat freezing on his forehead as he stuffed his hands in the pocket of his suit. He sat inside at the wheel for the few minutes it took for the windscreen to clear, conscious of the solidity of the car around him; it was one of his few remaining possessions, one of the few things which had not gone the same way as his wife, his family and his face, all of which were cheaper to maintain. Kim never asked for a bloody penny, and while that was a relief, it was also insulting. He would get used to living in one and a half rooms sooner or later, but he was not reconciled, not yet.

Six-forty-five, too early for early turn, parade at seven-thirty and not his first task. Duncan drove south from Highbury where he lived, skirting the emptiness of the City, through Shoreditch and into Whitechapel. Jack the Ripper country, now known as little Bengal, hit for the third time in a century by the newest wave of immigration. The first Chinatown, then the Jewish capital, and now dusky, full of spices, coronaries and striving poverty. Hit by a thousand bombs in the war, rebuilt and rebuilt again. Where did they all go when they moved on, he thought. Where am I supposed to go? Nowhere in particular but just Somewhere Else, where you won't be an embarrassment. Well he wouldn't. You didn't treat a dustbin like Kim had treated him, fuck it.

He turned the car into a service road behind a parade of shops, stopped and looked up expectantly. There were flats above the shops, nasty concrete structures of the boom-building sixties, at odds with the wider pre-war stuff, their only advantage the reasonable space inside that offset the stained exteriors and cumbersome balconies, the ugly steps from the street. He was looking for a light in the third one from the end, the unconscious early-morning signal of his wife's presence as she got ready for her own long day. If he could stay where he was until seven-thirty, he might just see the animal arrive, something supposed to be a childminder, a grunting, yawning, shambling man who, to Duncan's anxiety, seemed to take his effeminate child to school. Detective Constable Perry did not like any of the choices made by his wife, but there was nothing he could do.

OK, estranged wife as his solicitor so nicely put it, pompous bastard. Also estranged, one smallish package of truculent child named Tom, whose parentage Duncan had questioned in the course of a blazing row with Kim, a row that ended with her saying, yes, she was going now, leading to the door the boy who was Duncan's spitting image, as if he had ever seriously believed otherwise. The eyes, green eyes, remained with him still, in accusation, along with many other regrets.

Perry could see the shape of her head, or what he hoped was her head and not the skull of some unknown overnight visitor, framed against the frosted glass of the bathroom window. He clenched his fist on the wheel of the car, shut his eyes for an instant. A man in residence might just send him over the edge; the thought made him want to vomit, but she wouldn't, no she wouldn't. Not until she'd qualified, got what she wanted from that poxy shop where she started work so early. She wasn't half determined, he had to hand it to her, worked like she fought, no holds barred. Perry started the car and crept down the street, aggressive, holstering his energies and his jealousy by slanging her under his breath, ashamed.

Helen awoke by seven, not exactly refreshed but considering herself far from dead. Her customary gesture of pushing the hair out of her eyes with her left hand was defeated by the tube attached to the back of the wrist, such a surprise that she looked at it in consternation, swore softly. She also looked at the clock on the wall, remembered that today and on several succeeding days, she would not be in her office by nine o'clock. The thought was a mixed blessing. Work did not evaporate, it simply accumulated, but the hospital cocoon was suddenly appealing, all wrapped up like this and waiting for someone to bring tea. But then the nurse came with her whiff of antiseptic and Helen, remembering some of the files on her desk, groaned out loud.

'Sister's gone off,' the nurse hissed in conspiracy. 'So I'm letting your husband in for a second. OK?'

'He's not sterilised,' Helen said, 'not for dust, anyway, not in my place . . . And he's not my . . .' she began, ever a stickler for detail, but was stopped by her desire to laugh at the picture of Bailey being let into the room like a lion into a pen. There he was, sidling round the door almost shyly, a broad smile on a tired-looking face and in his hand two decadent winter roses.

CHAPTER TWO

'Oh come on, Tom, please, lovey. What's the matter with you?'
Kimberley Perry knew her voice was sharp, and was sorry, without being able to do anything about the edge. Or about the fact that Tom was only ten years old, with a face far older, a large head on thin shoulders. Nothing ever fitted Tombo, even today's stained tracksuit which she privately considered too cold for December but which was de rigueur in his school, or so he insisted. The material bunched at the waist and hung over training shoes which had been the subject of intense pride when new: the exact make, the flashes on the side, the colour of the laces all of paramount importance and he had worn them as if they were silk shot with gold. And similar expense, his mother had considered wryly. Tombo knew more about the rules of dress and behaviour than he did about the school curriculum, she thought as she fought the impulse to empty pockets where the marbles and other invaluable detritus looked like twin hernias. She also yearned to brush his spiky hair for him, but both actions would have been insults. Tombo might look like a baby on more endearing days, or behave like one, flicking his toast across the table as if firing a gun, Kchoo! Kchoo! a bullet imitation noise which sounded like a sneeze, but he was not a baby in his needs. Kim's early morning glances were full of guilt, irritation and a very brusque love. She might have killed for him, but at the moment he was unlovely.

She got up, shoved the dishes in the sink, splashing the front of her sweater with hot soapy water, making Tombo giggle provocatively at her swearing. You should have better clothes, lovey, she was telling him under her breath; better school and better mummy. Only a month or two more till I'm qualified and I'll make it all up to you. Don't look so sulky, please. You little sod.

'Is Daddy coming today?'

'You know very well he isn't. Next weekend.' Sharp, again.

Kim smoothed her skirt. Maybe it was a little too tight for the shop but she could not resist that colour. Life was dull enough. Duncan had always laughed at her tight skirts, high heels, big bosom, big behind, but then he had laughed at everything. All her years of study met with nothing but scorn. 'A chemist, love? You? Oh, ha, ha, ha . . . Sorry about that, sweetheart, didn't mean to laugh, but ho, ho, ho; Kim the Chemist? See, it rhymes! Kim the Chemist who can't even take cough medicine.' So what if it was a big change from happy-go-lucky, down the disco Kimberley with punk hairdo and micro skirt, a person quite grateful to be pregnant, married and apparently out of it all by the age of nineteen. Until Tombo was two and she found herself bored out of her skull, the brain her teachers had despaired of idle and frustrated. Working part-time in a pharmacy, beginning to think, why not me, why shouldn't I learn how to do this? Duncan would have been forgiven anything (since she did not have high expectations of the married state) if he could have begun to understand her excitement. Kimberley from the East End, cheeky girl without an A level, ex school truant making good. Almost a proper pharmacist all these years later, a new kind of rebellion channelled into hard, hard work, rewarded by the kind of love which tried to thwart her in case she should grow up and escape. Taunting all the time, always putting her down.

Great big handsome ape. So she snapped the leash between them, already frayed by argument. He thought her walk-out was spontaneous, but she had planned it. Don't ever laugh at me, she told him: I've got a place, a job. I mean what I bloody say. Don't you laugh at me.

'You'll turn that boy into a pansy,' he had shouted.

'Better than a pig,' she shouted back. Repeating that cold comfort in her mind as she watched him now.

'Don't want to go to school. Kchoo! Kchoo! Kchoo!' More crumbs flew into Tom's milk.

'Oh come on, yes you do, lovey. You like it really.'

He gave her a look of withering scorn and the silence was ominous. Then a noise on the stairs, a groan announcing the arrival of Daniel. Daft Daniel was another worry with his empty morning face and that sickly pale skin. Duncan would kill her if he knew what Daniel was and it was only a matter of time before he found out from Tom. Just a bloke, this Daniel, she had informed Duncan. Just a man, helps in the shop with boxes and things, helps up and down the street, takes Tom to school and meets him sometimes when I can't; stop interfering. She did not say how Daniel was simply omnipresent in the Parade, calling in at all the shops in one endless perambulation, but invariably at the pharmacy for his daily prescription of methadone. Daniel was twenty-five going on sixty, sweet-natured, curious, argumentative about his drugs, but Duncan could not see any strange man, especially a stabilised drug addict, as harmless. Kim was defensive about Daniel, reacted to him as one lonely and truculent soul to another, even fed him sometimes (beans and chips, their favourite fare), and also reckoned that beggars could not be choosers. Daniel was big enough to stop Tom getting thumped and that alone made him better than nothing.

'How are you doing, Dan?'

'OK.'

''Lo, Danny.' A surly greeting from Tom. Dan was a sort of a friend, but not much fun.

''Lo.'

Daniel was designed to sit without much movement, and take Tom to school with a tribe of others whose rude remarks passed over his head like clouds. Standing there now, puffing the cold out, smiling a stupid smile while Kim snatched her bag, planted a kiss on the time bomb that was her son and hurried away, guilty, but relieved.

'Don't let him go on the site, will you? Or pick up rubbish, will you?'

'Nope.'

There was no direct access from the shops of Herringbone Parade to the flats above. Some of the shopkeepers owned the upstairs accommodation, including Philip Carlton the pharmacist who owned his own larger flat and the one next door, rented out to Kim. To get into the street, upstairs occupants had to descend their steps, turn left or right through the litter of the service road which served their own front doors and then turn back. In Kim's case, she arrived beneath her own bedroom windows. The Carltons had been generous in letting Kim rent the flat: she knew they could have got more, and while wages were low, the arrangement suited her well. She reminded herself not to think of 'the Carltons' plural. Since that frothy, bossy little Margaret had died in her sleep four weeks ago without anyone understanding why, there was only one. Kim tried to push this out of her mind along with the vision of dead Margaret in bed, not for lack of rough sympathy, but because she could not afford her concentration to be rocked. Life was far too complicated as it was: death and sentiment presented crises she could not afford.

As she clattered down the steps, knowing she would regret the high heels later in the day, a workman en route to the site whistled. Kim stuck her nose in the air, ignored the compliment, but her large backside wiggled as she walked, unconsciously, blissfully sexy. Gruff and irritated she may have been, but Kimberley Perry in the morning was a sight which glowed in winter.

Seven-forty-five, and only three lights glowed in Herringbone Parade. The view here was an improvement on what she saw from the back, a dirty service road, feeding the back of the shops and flanked by a building site. An improvement zone, old houses, left damaged since the war, finally coming down. You could hear the rumbling of a cement mixer creating filling for foundations, and, some time next year, there would be two dozen new homes which people in the Parade were unlikely to afford. Bitter for those who could remember the bombs which had put their neighbourhood into a twilight zone for two generations. Never mind, the Parade was proud. There were twenty small shops in one unbroken row, and, whenever she thought about anything not related to the minute she was in, Kim thought that was plenty. The lights which glowed so long before conventional opening hours were those of Carlton's Caring Chemist, while three doors down Mr Oza's newsagent and tobacconist was already doing trade. Five doors beyond was Cyril's Caff, renowned for bacon rolls and lorry drivers' breakfasts, the inside windows already steaming. Next to that, though not yet open, was Sylvie's Hair Salon, half-price to pensioners Thursdays only, hotbed of gossip. The other shops included a greengrocer, a butcher, two Indian takeaways open only at night and one slightly famous Chinese restaurant on the other side. There was also a baker's, an emporium of discount electrical goods run by Ahmed, and a toy shop which Tombo scorned as hopelessly untrendy. Alongside that was an off-licence and on the other side of the hardware store, the boutique and shoe shop, selling discontinued lines from shopping catalogues and a few other things besides. No shop was streamlined; there were socks in the hardware store, videos for hire in the off-licence, and everything under the sun on the two days a week when the street outside became a market. Herringbone Parade was an enclave against the world, providing all the urban soul could ever require, filling a gap wherever a gap was mentioned, ordering anything which might sell. Pip Carlton, the Caring Chemist, was easily the worst at this game. He could not bear to be found lacking and the shop burst at the seams in tribute to his passion for pleasing. No wonder Margaret had complained.

Kim closed the door behind her, blinking in the bright strip lighting which illuminated everything on display. Behind the corner at the far end lay Pip's dispensary, always in half light by contrast despite the close work they did in there. Here, stock ran wild, escaping from shelves to be thrust back hourly and even then Kim swore everything got up at night to change places. There were all the conventional shampoos, toothpastes, soaps, patent medicines as well as the homoeopathic range in one corner along with the vitamins, a perfume bar under lock and key, a section devoted to babies' bottoms, one to handcreams and festooned among it all, underwear, cheap jewellery and fourteen different brands of cosmetics. The underwear, nylon dreams of black lace,

frills, suspenders, knickers and multicoloured stockings, somehow spilled across the shop to lend it a raffish air. All this had been
Margaret's sideline, while the rest of her strove to bring order into
the chaos. She had wanted such changes, Margaret, such as less
ordering and the closing of the back dispensary, a room beyond
the room he shared with Kim and where Pip insisted, like a good,
old-fashioned pharmacist, on making some of his own preparations. In strict privacy. Not commercial, Margaret had said
loudly, get rid of it. God rest her soul, said Pip piously, forgetting
the arguments.

'Morning, Pip. Are you winning?' Kim shouted as she edged
her way through the crowded shelves which customers would
rearrange and upset with their various bulks throughout the day as
they made their way to the counter where Pip was endeavouring
to hang a tinfoil sign bearing the legend 'A Happy Xmas to all our
Customers'. Really, she thought, this shop was made for midgets,
not someone of her statuesque build, a sharp contrast to Margaret
who had been built like a pixie. Hence the nature of all Mrs
Carlton's favourite underwear, best worn by persons of miniature proportions and chiefly bought for a joke. Kim loved it.

'Course I'm winning. I have winning ways.' Pip was perched on
the counter, posed like a coquette, one hand spread fan-like in
greeting. 'My, you're a sight for sore eyes. By which I don't mean
an eyesore, ha, ha, oh dear me, no. You look very pretty.' He
scrambled down, the decoration trailing after him. Pip never quite
finished most tasks, all of them started with boyish enthusiasm.
'Here, let me take your coat. How's Tombo?'

His puns and his civilities were engaging and irritating by
turn, but Pip's energy was always infectious. He was a thin,
sprightly man, forty with the bounce of twenty, kept trim by the
lonely jogging which he undertook with obsessive zeal, the way
he did almost everything. The old customers loved Pip; Kim
said they would eat cat food if he told them it was good for them.
This morning, after breakfast, she was disposed to like him,
forget that undertone to his affectionate manner which was ever
so slightly disturbing. The hand on her arm pressed the elbow

unnecessarily as he removed the coat: she was not sure if she understood that or not.

'Tombo's fine,' she said hurriedly. 'Sulking, though.'

'Never mind,' he said. 'I'll send him home something nice. Health-giving lollipops, new order.'

'Oh, Pip,' she said, looking at an open box on the floor, full of sugar-free sweets, a new line when there was no room for the old, 'where on earth are we going to put them?'

'We'll find a place. We'll find places where we didn't know we had places. Tea?'

His glance was rather too intent in its admiration, but for once, she was buoyed by his artless optimism. He was such a kind man and you had to make allowances for grief. 'All right, Lord and Master,' she said grinning back. 'But I'll make it.'

'Ready to tee off, are we?' He roared at his own pun, ready for the day. Silly git, she thought with weary affection, ready for a day full of more of the same and a dozen cups of tea. Kim hung her coat on the hook Pip had placed too high. The red skirt rode up, revealing an acre of sheer-coated thigh. Only one of them noticed.

'Would you like tea, Dr Hazel?' the nurse asked, reconciled to the doctor staying longer than anyone usually did with a patient.

'No, I would not. I'd like an extra large belt of whisky, but I doubt if you could arrange it, darling. Then I'll go on and breathe my glorious fumes over the princess next door.' He sighed. 'OK, then, I'll have tea with my favourite patient. Who has a little colour in the cheeks today and a little light reading matter. Good God, what's this?'

After Helen's third day in hospital, the room had begun to look more like an office. The place was full of flowers, not arranged with any great care or skill, but extravagantly admired; there was a pile of books on the bedside locker and three files spread from the bed to the floor where they had fallen and she had not bothered to retrieve them.

'That's never work, woman, is it?' he gestured, horrified. 'A little something from your office, along with the blooms? Blackmail.'

'Doctor, that is one of my words, not yours. And not accurately used in this context, if I may say so. Blackmail is the obtaining of a pecuniary advantage by threats. There are no threats, only flowers, and I am impecunious.'

'Oh you and your legal words. I meant the emotional sort of a bargain. I'd have anaesthetised your tongue if I'd known you were a lawyer. Always know a lawyer's health by the state of his mouth. When it's shut, he's dead.'

'Sit down for heaven's sake, you make me even more restless *and* you owe me fifty pence. Have a glass of wine since you can't have whisky. You can rinse your mouth out after. Tell me about the world outside.' They had become very comfortable together, dark Helen West and grizzled old Dr Hazel whose flecked eyes regarded her with affection. A tough customer physically, Miss West. Her recovery had been swift, and the thought of her itching to go filled him with an unidentified sadness. But then no patient of right mind ever wanted to stay inside a hospital, even if they were allowed to drink and smoke. In mute conspiracy, each lit a cigarette, his a Players full strength, hers milder.

'The world outside? Oh glory be to God, what do you want to know about that for? They've just lit the lights in Regent Street, the shops are awash with Christmas carols already. It's murder out there. The rest you'll find from your newspaper and why on earth did your bloody office send you files? Don't they know you're sick?'

She laughed. 'And since when, in your career, did a surgeon ever take any notice of that? Even when you were my age as opposed to the rude old man you are now? Physician, heal thyself; get to work.'

'The buggers wouldn't think twice. Bring out your needle, Hazel, my lad: we'll give you a chair if you faint and a mask to keep germs off the patient.'

'So. I get files in here because no one else can read my hand-writing. If I hadn't volunteered, they'd find out how stupid I am. Can I pick your brains?'

'You'll be lucky.'

'Right.' She motioned to the file half on, half off the bed. 'I'm not really working, you know, I'm playing at it. Reading a report where there could be a question of homicide, but I haven't managed more than page one. Tell me, why should a woman of forty-six, non-drinker, non-smoker, healthy, until she dies in bed, simply die? No obvious physical cause at all.'

'She could have been very, very tired,' he suggested flippantly. 'Or she might have been contemplating Christmas. Known to kill many, the mere thought of it. Blood pressure? Heart attack?' He leant forward and leered comically. 'Poison?'

'No evidence of anything in a routine post-mortem. Blood test awaits. I've only half the report. Sleeping like an infant, she was, curled to one side.'

'Even less likely for asphyxia. I don't know why she died. And I don't care. Leave it to the coroner.'

Helen put aside the half-complete Police Report on the death of Mrs Margaret Carlton, relieved to do so, and the talk fell happily to more palatable reading matter. A glass of wine was poured while Dr Hazel scoffed at other books now littering the room. The wine in her veins was preferable to the drip which had left in the removal no trace of a bruise or needle mark, sure sign of a clever anaesthetist. A little alcohol went a long way towards the recovery of the patient, but the verbal fencing was better. The merits of a favourite novelist were under attack. Hazel enjoyed an argument.

'How can you say this is a heap of rubbish, or is your eyesight bad?'

'Oh, get on with you; the woman is indecipherable . . .'

Exactly the kind of conversation which Bailey, that most literary of police officers, should have been able to join with ease, but his coming upon them ended the camaraderie, as Helen could have predicted without quite knowing why, his quiet arrival in that hospital room signalling Hazel's abrupt departure. Quite different from the nurses who simpered in Bailey's presence, there was something in Hazel which obviously disliked the aura of policeman inherent in his mild appearance, shied from it like a nervous pony about to throw the rider. A familiar syndrome which nevertheless provoked in Helen a sharp irritation. He often had this effect on people; the talking cadaver at the feast, as if he reminded them suddenly of a cold outside, conscience, and all sorts of old ghosts. He held the door for Hazel. The doctor neglected to thank him.

The irritation was reciprocal. Tearing across London from the grubby east to the smarter west, Bailey might have expected her to be surrounded with other visitors – Helen attracted nice and nasty without turning any way – but he had not expected to find the patient looking weak but well, wine in one hand and cigarette in the other, deep in conversation with some scruffy male party who was obviously besotted. Last evening he had found Helen scarcely mobile, but playing draughts with the same Dr Hazel: there was something vaguely insulting about it, as if his own protective, companionable role had been usurped. Then he sniffed. The air was full of flowers, tobacco; the sanctity of hospital lost, and the knowledge of that restored his mood. The hackles of insecurity rose and sank back while he registered the beginnings of a mess in the room, secretly rejoicing in this sign of recovery. His own two winter roses were thoroughly dead in a vase by the bed; she had a strange liking for half dead petals and was always reluctant to throw out flowers. Helen might be a peculiar kind of civil servant, but she was clearly impossible to institutionalise.

'Files,' he said caustically, lifting them from the floor. 'What's this, darling?'

'You may look,' she said with mock primness. 'That one comes from somewhere near you, not your manor exactly but near your flat. A chemist.'

'Mrs Carlton,' he read, before putting it down, sitting close to the bed in the chair still warm from Dr Hazel. 'Bugger Mrs Carlton. How are you? When are you coming home?'

'I've got four massive stitches,' said Helen conspiratorially as he bent to kiss her, 'on my Easter egg.'

★

Bailey drove straight back east into the dim car park of the police station where he worked most of the time. He was not seeking the panacea of work: nor was such available since his tasks were now the delegation of tasks, the current investigations run by remote control. He relied on the self-motivation of most of his men; no immediate panics, despite the unexplained deaths, the missing lorry loads, the Asian bride burnt in some feud they would never understand, the armed robbery of the wages van, and all the other weekly hazards of East Central London. Bailey had become a manager by default, controlled three teams of detectives, although control was not always the appropriate word. Respect was what they showed, co-operation forthcoming as often as not while, rather to his own surprise, they could be prevailed upon to confide both professionally and privately, allowing him to circumvent some of the worst disasters before they actually occurred. Such as refusing to authorise a search warrant requested without a shred of evidence, or deflecting the young sergeant about to punch a rival. Sometimes Bailey thought that his present post, his role as the near but still distant wise old man of the division, was a role designed to do no more than save the Commissioner embarrass-ment. For some time he had felt he was suffering from a new version of an old malaise, a growing disinterest in life, and he wondered if this managerial appointment was the cause or result of despair. For months now, ever since he and Helen had returned from outside London, ever since he had seen and heard a boy burn to death, he had felt he was slipping. Did not want to know any more the ingredients of these tragedies, see bodies or hear screaming. All in all, even while resenting many of his current tasks, he preferred welfare and discipline. He had lost touch with his streets; here, there was just enough to keep his mind ticking over, and the patience he displayed did not have to touch his heart. The role called for silence, contemplation, passive intelli-gence, and while Bailey would not have admitted to boredom he hoped that was all that ailed him.

Fog blanketed the ugly building that was East Ham station, Victorian brick-built, solid, but without the fortress appearance of

more modern equivalents, oddly and quite invariably ill lit inside
and out. Spotlights relieved the gloom of the car park, but once
inside the back door, gloom prevailed on painted walls and everyone, uniformed or not, looked as sallow as the mustard of the
decor. Bailey had a separate, although tiny, office with a door leading through into the CID room where several detectives sat by day,
teasing a harassed secretary.

Some wag had stuck a Christmas decoration on Bailey's door,
a loud Santa Claus with frogging on the shoulders and a tie in
Bailey's favourite claret colour round the neck. He liked that: it
indicated a measure of the popularity he never courted since that
way lay madness. There were times when he would have liked to
be hail fellow well met, able to drink with the team, share their
outlook and be fêted as one of them, but, being himself, was rarely
the subject of jokes, perceived as dry, stern, innovative without
ever being revolutionary, the cynicism hidden and the intelligence
far too acute for most people's liking. Bailey's own officers wanted
to please, almost blushed at his praise, but they did not slap him
on the shoulder.

Empty offices always reminded Bailey of empty schools,
deserted markets; places which bore no resemblance whatever at
night to what they were by day, so lonely he would have the feeling each time of having arrived at the wrong place. As he sat at the
desk and dealt briskly with his in-tray, transferring most of it to
OUT, the odd sensation of the quietness, punctuated by cars in
the yard, murmurings from the front desk, became odder as he
heard sounds from the room next door, strange little snorting
noises, masked into anonymity by the constant murmuring of the
antiquated heating which gave all occupants of this unsympathetic space the sensation of water on the brain. Bailey's long
hands, as well equipped for the mending of his clocks as they
were for the writing of clipped phrases in elegantly official prose,
paused, lay flat on the desk as he raised his head, immobile with
curiosity, invisible antennae ready for action although instinct told
him there was no threat in these sounds. Burglars do not come
into police stations for the purposes of burglary, but what crossed

his mind was the unlikely prospect of one of his men working late, or, as likely, staying away from home. The last possibility was more illicit; some male with female officer, taking advantage of an empty room. In which case, best not to interfere: such delicate matters were not his concern. But just as he debated whether or not to move, or at least to clear his throat in signal, the noise became definable. Snoring: unrhythmical snores, falling and dying, ragged sounds not orchestrated or controlled. As soon as Bailey identified the snores, he knew who it was next door. Duncan, back from the pub. If he had driven here in his car, Bailey would skin him. Duncan Perry, Detective Constable, the muscle of the squad, the door breaker, *el machismo* incarnate.

As Bailey opened the door between his room and the next Duncan stirred, not woken, but reaching the natural end of what must have been an uncomfortable sleep. His bulky body, that of an athlete going to seed, was slumped into a chair, one leg extended, the other curled, maintaining his seat by a miracle, while his torso was precariously supported on the desk, head on one arm, the other arm dangling free and dragging him slowly towards the floor. As he woke, the elbow slipped, and Bailey saw him slide out of sight, his face transfixed with surprise. Reaching the floor, he let out a grunt of astonishment. Bailey, looking at the controlled mess of the room, reckoned a little more litter would make no difference, and also reckoned that although Duncan had fallen with quite a thump, he was beyond pain.

'Get up, man,' he said sharply. 'What the hell are you doing here this time of night? Ten o'clock, Duncan. Bedtime by the look of you. Is your car in the yard?'

'No, sir.' Duncan had struggled upright. 'I walked, sir. I'm not quite that stupid.' He was running his hand through his hair as if trying to discover if his head was attached. The words were humble, without a touch of defiance, and, rather to his own alarm, Bailey could see that the man's eyes were filling with tears. 'Didn't even have that much, sir, honest. I went and got some shopping.' He pointed at two supermarket bags in the corner, toilet rolls and tins spilling from the mouths. 'Very tired, sir. Bloody tired.' Bailey looked closer. Maybe Duncan was telling the truth and the manner of his sleeping, as well as the choice of venue, owed more to exhaustion than to alcohol although the latter certainly played a part. There was not a day in Duncan's life when alcohol did not play a part, but he was always disposed to be truthful. Work, truth, silly bravery, obsession and booze, the keys to a character that only appeared simple on the surface. Bailey liked Duncan, but not all of the time. Sometimes, even as men went, he was revolting. Lack of sympathy with Duncans was part of Bailey's condition, carefully hidden from mankind.

'You were supposed to be off duty at six. What the hell have you been doing between then and now?'

Duncan dragged himself straight, yanked up his trousers, and looked at the coat he was still wearing as if he did not recognise it.

'Had a couple of drinks, sir. Late-night shopping.' He pointed towards the carrier bags again. 'Then hung around a bit.'

Bailey sighed inaudibly. He might not join in the gossip, but it was his business to hear enough to have a shrewd notion of what hanging around meant in Duncan's case. Uniformed officers had slipped him the word once or twice about DC Perry's distinctive car being parked in the slip road behind Herringbone Parade early in the morning or evening, watching for his wife, and even without that, Duncan's distress had bleated itself into a dozen ears, month after month. Kimberley Perry was different. Bailey remembered her clearly from an annual party when he had talked to her for a full fifteen minutes, delighted to find an independent woman among the spouses, while Duncan showed her off like a prize bloom at a flower show. She had been brave enough not to run off with someone else. That alone made her uncommon. Christ, Bailey thought to himself. I'm getting cynical.

'I suppose,' he said gently, 'you were checking up on Kimberley. Seeing she was OK? And the boy, Tom, isn't it? Must be a big lad now.'

Duncan looked like a dumb ox, nodding his head in affirmation. 'Any chance you'll make up, you two?' Bailey ventured even more delicately, as if his remarks concerned nothing more than the weather. 'I mean, there comes a time, doesn't there, when you either have to make up or give up. Been a whole year, Duncan, long time.'

'She won't even talk about it,' Duncan muttered through clenched teeth. 'Never a word. I collect the kid, take him back, she smiles, shuts the door, won't let me do anything for her. Cold as ice, the bitch.'

'She's not a bitch,' Bailey interrupted quietly. Duncan turned on him one belligerent eye, sank back against the desk.

'No, sir, she's not a bitch. I almost wish she was.'

'Nor a fool. She can think for herself. Seems to have made up her mind, doesn't she? Got someone else, has she?' He was deliberately harsh.

'Yes. No. I don't know. I love her,' said Duncan with sudden intensity. 'I think she might be having it off with her boss. She can't do this to me, I bloody love her.'

This time Bailey's sigh was not disguised. How often these words were used as cudgels. I love her, therefore she must love me: therefore I must have her and no one else must . . . That obdurate hope, born and dying in stupidity, of love extracting its own reward. He felt a wave of impatience with Duncan. In front of him there stood a man intelligent enough to know that he could not force a prisoner to talk, make a horse drink or a car start, still thinking he could make a woman love him. There was nothing for Bailey to say.

'Well, you mustn't make a nuisance of yourself, or there'll be trouble. Won't do, you know. Come on, I'll run you home. You're on my way,' he added. Duncan hated favours as much as advice. One did only what one could, accepting that people could not be changed.

'Thank you, sir.' Bailey turned away to his own room before the man bent to retrieve his shopping. He had no wish to see what his lone, wilfully miserable officers ate for their suppers; wanted to help without being involved. Wandering outside to wait, he thought bitterly how this had become habit. Stopping people from talking, turning his eyes from suffering which might be stupid, but was still real. Seeing only what he needed to see.

'I'll have to talk to someone, just must. Oh God, I can't go on. Is he going mad, or am I?' Kimberley Perry stifled the feeling of panic, stopped herself running to the phone, running from one room to the other. Nothing to be achieved by that apart from waking fractious Tombo, who had sulked into sleep. There was no one to tell: Kim's stance on the subject of her own marriage alienated her family, pride made them the least likely of chosen confidants, and her thoughts turned to Pip. No, far too personal to tell Pip, as well as unfair, no extra burdens for such a new, if brave widower. Which meant that she could really do nothing at all if Pip were not to know, because even changing the locks on what was, after all, his flat, would be a signal of alarm. She knew what he would do, kind Pip: call me, he would say, whenever you're worried; I'll be round in two seconds. Pip was everybody's helper. For Christ's sake, it was not as if she had done anything wrong in coming back reasonably late, not as if she'd been out dancing till dawn with a rose between her teeth – only out for a drink, for God's sake. But it was the very fact of her being somewhere out of sight that Duncan seemed to dislike so much. Wanted to punish, so he must have crept into the flat with the keys they had agreed he keep against any emergencies on the understanding he never used them otherwise. Crept in here like an alley cat as he brought Tom home from an outing, sniffed around, marking her territory. Taken souvenirs, crept away. Bastard.

'Oh shit. Fucking hell.' Her voice, deep and strident, better suited for joking but no stranger to swearing, sounded harsh and defeated to her own ears, the fury in her tinged with guilt. She need never have suffered this if she hadn't been such a silly cow. Flitting round the flat, feeling sorry for herself, wanting a reminder of being a girl and not a motherly drudge. Searching for that special nightie, a thing of gossamer and satin, bought in headier days, honeymoon stuff, so frivolous it befitted a trousseau. Wanting it now to make herself feel lighter, prettier, even to an audience of no one. A reminder that she was getting out of this hole, going up some day soon and although she tried to pretend the nightie might not have been there in the bottom drawer where she had left it, she knew there was no mistake and it was gone. Along with two pairs of sheer stockings, and, left in place, a single small bottle of the type of perfume Duncan had unfailingly produced on Christmas and birthday. Looking into the drawer, Kim was afraid to look anywhere else, at least until daylight. The evidence of his obsession made her sick.

Who to tell, then, when all this became too much? There were few reserves of fortitude left to manage this new departure of Duncan's, the watchful jealousy worse since she had let him stay, just that once. The night after she found Margaret. Who to tell? There was no reporting policeman Duncan to his fellows and having him jeered down the street. Then an idea illuminated the darkness of the panic, a face swam hopefully into vision and her brow cleared slightly. Bailey, that man Bailey, Duncan's boss. The one she had talked to at the last Christmas party, the only one who listened to what she wanted to do and seemed to know by instinct how tough a time she had with a bleeding drunk spouse like Duncan. A man who had said, let me know if I can help, I doubt if I can, but talking is better than silence. And a man who might, just might be able to exert some control.

'No. Stuff it.' No one helped. No one ever had and no one ever would. You're on your own, gal, silly bitch. Broken all the rules. You, a chemist, don't make me laugh. She scrubbed at her face in the mirror. I'll handle this, sod you all, you wankers. I don't want nothing so leave me alone. Twenty-fucking-nine with eyebags and a maniac husband. Oh Christ. Kim thrust her bosom forward through her pyjamas to intimidate her reflection, the way she would with an awkward customer. She would cope. She would have to.

She knew her silhouette was visible from the window and did not care. The building site was empty, a newly established crane swinging silent. No one whistled and she missed the sound.

CHAPTER THREE

'ANY signs of life in here? Yes? No. Oh well.'

How easy to feel extremely silly. In the atmosphere of soporific indifference which pervaded Helen's office, there had been no point in staggering beyond the portals wearing at the time a flashing bow-tie provided by one of her godchildren; pretending not to be tired while repeating a few thoughts. How awful to be here. No; I think I like it here some of the time. Possibly not today. The ten days' absence felt more like a decade, and in a minute someone would come in that door, look a little sheepish and say, Nice to see you and now you're better would you like to go to court this afternoon? She wanted to be able to say, look, buster, I could have swung the lead on the strength of one small operation and stayed off till after Christmas according to Civil Service rules; as it is, conscience got the upper hand so here I am, but don't push your luck. Seen this tie? Wish it was me with the spare battery. If it weren't for having only half a file on Mrs Carlton, I would have stayed home. Where the hell is everybody?

Helen recognised that talking to oneself had all the ingredients of eccentricity, just as expecting some sort of welcome from her colleagues bore witness to an optimism which was futile at eleven a.m., most other times too. She dropped on a chair one polythene-wrapped hanger bearing newly collected dry cleaning, breathed in the dust with appreciation.

The emptiness was not surprising. There were never enough staff in any inner city office of the Crown Prosecution Service, such a romantic, well-chosen name, she had always thought. Made them sound remarkably like the firm which cleaned the towels, King's Laundry, or any other syndicate which happened to sweep up rubbish. At your service, sir, Prosecutions Incorporated, imprisonments recommended, also cheap eats and good excuses. Helen's untidiness hid her efficiency, and, though the office would have liked to make the same claim it found itself famous instead for failing expectations and losing papers. Justice on a shoestring, poor pay and lousy prospects. Being indifferent to ambition and careless about money, Helen had been in her post far longer than most, and was relied upon by beleaguered colleagues to do the work which no one else had ever done before, the big cases no one else knew how to tackle, the tedious dribs and drabs which had no real place anywhere and precious little interest either. She also supplied shoulders on which to cry (her own excuse for wearing shoulder pads), and, sometimes, the silly jokes.

The battery for the flashing bow-tie was uncomfortable against her skin and the effort of the tube journey more tiring than she expected. Rubbish, she was tired of being tired. One of the reasons for this pretend complete recovery was to avoid solicitude, far worse than any illness. Only as an adolescent had she craved to be pale and interesting like the consumptive heroine of a novel, but now when feeling fragile, she applied the maquillage of perfect health. Bailey had been so kind, so instinctively sensitive, that the attention provoked little but guilt. She was also sick of the idea of resting herself into boredom and drinking nothing but barley water. The door opened. Into the room staggered the case clerk, Mika, under a weight of files.

'Oh. 'Lo, Miss West. Where you been? Got some stuff for you. Redwood thought you might be back. Going to court this afternoon are you? Been poorly? Oh, look.' She pointed to the bow-tie, smiling but bewildered, as if the tie had nothing to do with Helen herself. Mika did not understand jokes. 'What's that?'

'It monitors my heart beat, Mika. How are you?'

'You joking, miss? Oh yes you are. Oh yes, yes, yes. Joke. Shall I tell him you're in? Oh here, Darren wants to see you. And Lefty. Shall I tell . . .'

'Give us a minute, Mika. Don't tell Red Squirrel until after lunch, right? I want to do a bit of reading before he catches me.'

'Right. Gotcha.' Mika grinned, to accompany an elaborate

stage whisper, and pushed off to the clerk's room with the good news and her own bustle.

'Well, well, cover blown,' said Helen aloud, not waiting for the queue to form, but knowing, without self-congratulation, that it would. Case clerks, typists not suffering from flu, disgruntled doorman *et al* would all sidle in, one way or another. They did because they knew how much they could widen her eyes with their gossip or their problems. She could do nothing but listen, of course, but that was maybe better than nothing. The same way she listened to witnesses, defendants in waiting who tended to trust her more than their own representatives, and anyone else with a voice. Helen was a time-waster, Redwood said: appalling subject for a time and motion study. What's more she encourages the others.

Silence fell, the silence of the office inside court hours, an interlude for contemplative study. Helen did not want to contemplate, would have preferred to talk, but reading was mandatory and she had flogged in here purely to read. What had puzzled her so much about the Carlton file, blurred over in hospital, was the fact that it was incomplete. Tantalisingly so. A fine case of a Chief Inspector doing his beleaguered best with a bad grace. There was neither the need nor the official requirement to report an unnatural death to the Crown Prosecutor for the area, but if one did so, long before he read of it in the paper over breakfast and called for a report, then at least no officer of the law could say his back was not clear and he had not done his duty. But the indifference of this particular report was evident, an exercise in writing a few paragraphs to a person in whose existence he did not entirely believe and whom he certainly disliked. A little like the mad letters they got quite often, copied to the Queen.

'Sir. (The fact that the addressee may have been a woman did not enter into the rough calculations of politeness.)

'I beg to report the following incident . . .'

Who begs, thought Helen. I beg, you beg. To be heard, understood or have enough for dinner, he has no need to beg.

'Mrs Margaret Carlton (deceased) was found dead in bed on

Nov third 1990. Her husband had been away for the forty-eight hours before the discovery of her death, he being a pharmacist, attending a drugs symposium/ conference at a central London hotel. Since he had been unable to raise Mrs Carlton by telephone, he had alerted first his assistant, who lives next-door to the flat the couple occupied; she in turn alerted the local police the next morning, at his request. Police Constable Jones forced entry into the flat with Mrs Perry and they found Mrs Carlton dead in bed, but looking quite normally asleep. Since there were no signs, other than those caused by PC Jones himself, of forced entry – here Helen paused and smiled: Jones had obviously entered with all the gentle force of a battering ram – nor were there any signs of struggle or burglary, it was assumed that Mrs Carlton had died in her sleep of natural causes and her doctor was called. He confirmed that she was who she was, a woman of forty-six with no health problems apparent from his own records. She had been married to Philip Carlton, proprietor of the chemist's shop below the flat, for five years prior to her death, and by all local accounts, the marriage had been very happy. Mr Carlton was a bachelor who had spent many years nursing his own mother. The deceased owned the freehold of the shop and assisted in it. Routine post-mortem carried out, mindful of the fact that the deceased was living above a stock of drugs, but nothing untoward was found. Her husband says that on the probable night of her death they had consumed a meal cooked by himself: he then left for the conference. The departure is confirmed by his assistant. The deceased was not missed until the following evening, when Mr Carlton tried to phone her and got no reply. (Continues page two . . .)

There was no page two. The rest of the file consisted of a statement from the doctor and PC Jones, plus one from another doctor at the local hospital who had done the post-mortem, plus two bald descriptions from two ambulancemen, and a statement from someone who watched Mr P. Carlton identify the body of his wife. Helen could see the reason for the report, or thought she could. Chief Inspector whatever he was had some reason to believe there was something wrong here somewhere, didn't like chemists for the good reason that chemists had dealings with drugs, so a certain bad smell must always follow the unexpected demise of anyone near. Or whatever it was, this chemist was not to be taken lightly, according to information received, but all the same, the report, its bitty if formal preparation with all the crossings out, the case itself, starring PC Jones, had never been given the status of any kind of homicide. So where was the rest, if there was any rest. And why, apart from hospital nightmares, did it bother her so much? Slop, rubbish, voluminous, time-wasting things, were the stuff of daily life here; who picked whose pocket. Anyone who thought they joined to deal all the time with real crime etc., soon found out to the difference. But it was that damned shop, or a shop so like this shop, which fixed an uncomfortable, immovable image in her mind.

To say that Helen liked shops was an understatement. Shops and markets without discrimination. The liking was more of an addiction and one which Bailey failed to understand. Shop, she said to herself. Not necessarily the same shop, but she was sure she had remembered the ugly lettering on the outside, 'Carlton's Caring Chemist', with a market outside. Some weeks before hospital, which now seemed another life, driving back from Bailey's flat on a Saturday morning, a journey she could manage with her eyes half-closed and often did, she had found the market, stopped mid-stall with a pair of green tights in hand, arrested by the pain, walked into that shop, and up to the counter, muttering, 'Nurofen, please, anything that works.' Only then did she notice the dizzy interior of the place. Socks hung above the counter, frilly undies, every patent medicine under the sun, one poster showing flossed teeth in a wide smile, another showing the state of a smoker's lungs. The effect of this brightly illuminated variety, plus all the posters, warnings and directions, as well as the condescension of the proprietor – 'Got a headache, have we?' – had the same effect on Helen as psychedelic décor inflicted on a hangover. So much so she had only mumbled her thanks, taken her purchase and fled to the car. Swallowing pills and pulling faces at the taste, she forgot the image, the funny smell which was talcum powder, vitamins, bleach, dispensary scents, all mixed up with the sugary, bitter taste in the mouth. Then, in hospital nightmares, the same scents carried in by nurses and impregnated in the sheets, reminded her again.

So. A chemist's wife may die, sadly alone, like any other wife (Helen was alternately happy and sad not to be a wife), without the faintest suggestion of crime since tragedy and crime do not always go hand in hand, and if there was no sufficient suggestion of crime, then Helen had no business to linger over this or any file, because she was not paid for idle curiosity, only for the prosecution of those who were criminal by accident or design in some incident already established.

All the same, she dived into the in-tray, searching for the addendum or any additions to this scrappy and preliminary report which somehow held the imagination. Ahh. Page two emerged from the internal memos, notes on Christmas leave, law reports, other reports and letters which she allowed to fall to the floor, one way of forcing herself to examine them. An in-tray was a magnet for the meaningless, but full of hazards.

'Mrs Perry, the pharmacist's assistant, was questioned about the death, she being apparently well acquainted with the deceased and the person who found the body. She could contribute no information to explain the cause. However, Mr Carlton volunteered the fact that his wife was in the occasional habit of sniffing chloroform to induce sleep and/or well-being. Small bottle of same found in bathroom, but the dose found in the body was not enough to kill, being only half that necessary (see Pathologist's report). There were no other drugs on the premises at all, no chemicals, apart from the usual domestic range, bleach, dry-cleaning fluid, etcetera. Same have been kept. There were no stimulants. I seek your guidance on how much further this matter should be investigated . . . The family would like the body released for burial . . .'

Well, I can see his point, Helen thought. No murder suspect, no misadventure but the simple and unacceptable fact of death. Chloroform, self-administered, well, well. Twelve milligrammes, she read, not lethal. How did anyone know, since no modern doctor used the stuff any more? The arrogance of all this infuriated her. Why sniff chloroform when you live upstairs from a stockpile of pills you could drink in your tea? She rummaged in the top right-hand drawer of her desk, looking for the familiar store of apples kept to impose limits on her cigarette consumption, forgot there would be none, and found instead a packet of cough sweets which she ate, absently. She jotted on the blotter, phone . . . retest blood – for what? Chloroform in bathroom, body in bed. How? I hate facts, she complained to herself. I hate facts and smells.

Smells, obnoxious scents. She lived by visual images, second to words heard and things smelled, all of these senses acute and long-remembered. The cough sweet tasted of eucalyptus, but alongside that was another smell, reminiscent of a dentist, the mask coming down over the face, a sickly smell inhaled in mute protest. A little like the smell of the dry-cleaning she had placed over the spare chair on the other side of the desk, the polythene covering disturbed to release that waft of cutting scent, so suggestive of aggressive cleanliness. The smells in a pharmacy, as clear as a notice saying we have cleaned everything twice. She jotted on the pad again, 'Dry cleaning fluid: test . . .' How weird was the association of smells, worse, oh far worse than the association of words.

No, she did not believe. No one willingly dumped such cloying smells over their faces simply to sleep. Not if they had ever been to a dentist. Somewhere this report contained a lie.

Helen stirred, felt the still swollen abdomen, wished someone would come in to talk. She felt lazy, resented the prospect of effort; wanted back her hospital bed, tea and sympathy, but not this faint and dangerous scent of anaesthesia.

Tombo hated the smell for a start, nearly as much as he hated the whole occasion. Rotten fruit, not rotten but overripe, suppurating somewhere, ready to burst from boxes and dribble to the floor, fruit worse than the kind his mother packed for him every day and

DE

which he threw, extravagantly, towards the playground
they all did. He joined in, afraid, as he always was, that so
from Herringbone Parade would hit him. A party like this, fu
these kids who tormented him whenever they saw him for reason
none of them could have defined, was the worst possible thing
about living in Herringbone Parade. Life was better with Daddy –
or maybe not. Daddy was better to think about and shout about, as
in, You leave me alone, my daddy's a copper, between class, scuffling shouts repeated and rehearsed to perfection, losing their
potency now. Boasting about Daddy was better than the actual
experience of him every other Saturday when he didn't really
know what to do and didn't really know where to go, apart from
the pictures where he fell asleep and Tombo sat on, eating popcorn
until he felt as sick as he was bored by the characters on the screen.
Or playing inept football with Dad, even worse, since Dad was
always so disappointed in him. Dad? Can we go and see *Omen
Three*? Jimmy's dad took him to that and he said it was great. No,
you can't. Here, catch. Got to make a man of you. Can't have you
turning out a cissy, but no nightmare films either.

What a joke. As if anything was more of a nightmare than this
party. Tombo had not been given the choice of refusing the party
organised by Mrs Bum from the grocer's on her premises, but
sponsored and bossed by Mrs Bosom from the clothes shop,
names he had coined for the satisfaction of giggling himself silly.
But while he was there, knew very well what a nightmare was. He
felt the symptoms: a flush in the chest, a little sweat on the forehead, a feeling of hot and urgent panic, and only because he was
strictly, if imperfectly, tutored about his manners, did he stay,
suffering like a soul in torment.

They did this every year, Mrs Bum and Mrs Bosom, whatever
they were really called, both in competition with one another,
which ensured the continuation of this time-battered ritual. Mrs
Bosom could not let Mrs Bum take the accolades for what had
once been a philanthropic idea in harder times; nor could Mrs
Bum stop donating her larger shop one afternoon a year for a
ritual she privately loathed (although she always said otherwise, in

case anyone should consider her mean and a person who did not like little kiddies, which she emphatically did not). So far, only the little kiddies could tell, and the compromise she had managed to make was to insist that this party, for all the children in Herringbone Parade, as well as all the children of the Parade's customers, be held at the very beginning of December, to inaugurate the whole festive season and at least not waste as much trading time as it might if she held it during Christmas week when everyone else had a party anyhow and their own efforts would not be noticed. She cleared the front of the shop as well as one of the large rooms at the back where they kept the new stock along with the old, now all piled against the wall, awaiting trimming and rejuvenation before sale. Her husband did not hump the sacks of sprouts because of his ulcer: Daniel did that. Daniel was useful, tolerantly despised. Never mind him being an addict; he was nice enough, not always reliable, but cheap at the price, without ever being comfortable. There were several cartons of melons he had carried indoors, a mistake, those melons, but the fairy lights were sound, tested here before Mrs Beale moved them to the window the week after next. Sod the little bastards, get them organised. Tombo heard her voice, but all he was really registering, by deliberately removing himself from all the other children around him, was the smell of the rotting melons, the dankness of the room, the unaccustomed sweat of his own terror.

'We're all going to play pass the parcel,' shrieked Mrs Bosom, who despite the alarming nature of her appearance, all shiny stuff and so big on top, entered fully into the spirit of this gathering. Mrs Bosom did not have children and still preserved the body beautiful, as well as a belief in childish fun. Currently, her voice was hoarse. 'And after that, boys and girls, hide and seek! With prizes!'

Tombo was quite beyond wanting a prize, the only carrot to be found in a grocer's shop: the disgrace of not getting one of the many prizes progressively less important, and besides, they had all been given a bar of chocolate already. They were ushered into a circle while a huge, light parcel was produced. Crackly music blared from the stereo in the corner. As the parcel passed into his hands, he threw it on with great violence as if his fingers were burning, then sat back, bathed in relief, his arms crossed over his chest, resisting the next contact or the touching of anyone else. Then the parcel lurched into his lap again as the sound of the carol faded. He looked down in furious disbelief, kicked it on savagely, survived for five terrible minutes. He fixed a smile while the chocolate he gripped changed shape in his sticky fingers and he did not know where to put it down.

But hide and seek was a fate worse than death, a sort of slow torture recalled from previous horrors, unavoidable despite pretending to go to the lavatory, finding whispering girls in the path up the stairs, retreating, holding himself, his need frozen in the greater desire simply to pass the time before he escaped, remembering to smile when he came back. Sent first to hide, he hid obviously enough to be found in seconds, then was grabbed and hauled back, only to understand that this was a trial and he had to do the same again. 'Make it harder, Tom, there's a good boy,' yelled one voice, but he could not imagine anything harder than hiding away to be found, pushed, shoved, squashed with the enemy in a dark smelly corner where someone would pinch. He hid behind the melon boxes, gagging on the smell, but his nerve was gone. They were counting up to one hundred, going slowly to give him time, all of them with their hands over their eyes, and the chanting '. . . twenty-seven, twenty-eight, twenty-nine, thirty!' ending in a shout at the end of each ten, sounded like the barking of a malevolent pack of dogs set to tear him to pieces. Vomit was in his throat: shame at his heels.

Tombo stumbled through the back room, not really looking at all. There were two back rooms to this, the largest of all the shops: one where they had partaken of the tea which lay so heavily on his stomach, the other no more than an ante-room to the little yard which led out to the service road behind, a cold, draughty annexe. Tombo heard the counting grow louder, speeding out of control before someone would turn out the light for them to come creeping after him, less like dogs now than rats hissing in the dark. The terror of humiliation became uncontrollable, lending him strength. He pushed against the back door, knowing the pushing was loud enough to be heard, not caring, kicking it shut behind him, running through the yard before stopping, suddenly brave enough to turn back and yell, 'Yer, yer yer!' very loudly, frightening himself further by the echo into the silence. His fist was raised, shaking defiance.

The greengrocer's was at the far end of the Parade, once a house, and the first of all the shops which seemed to stream out like a series of additions to an original idea. At the back, everything was featureless. Tombo knew exactly where he was since he had explored this service road, poked into the little yards and delivery bays, but never in the dark which made this unlit backwater endless. Half-day closing today, the party starting straight after school and himself not expected home before seven, Mummy probably taking advantage to be out. Tombo breathed deeply, puffing out his chest as he looked round on the off chance for Daniel. Daniel often hung round here, no real fun, but big and company of sorts. At least you could sit with him. Tom looked hopefully at the building site. Empty. There was no sound in the wintery blackness apart from his breath on the cold air, a rasping noise which made clouds in front of his eyes. He remembered the coat left behind, hugged his arms to his chest, and then heard dim thumps coming from inside the shop. Like dogs and rats released, they would realise soon, follow him, hissing and barking, taunt him, put him inside one of the tall bins flanking the road. He began to trot bravely, going faster and faster past the back of the newsagent's, the off-licence, the butcher's, the takeaway, each with its own terrible smell, trying not to break into a run, pretending he was in control; not knowing what to do until he was level with the back of Carlton's Caring Chemist, no light shining out of his own upstairs home, and nowhere to go. Sometimes he had a key to let himself into the flat, a practice which made his mother so ashamed for all it signified, but not today. Any other day he could have waited inside the shop, but today they shut at five. Tombo stood, irresolute, becoming cold, then crept forward. Salvation. There was a light at the back of the shop where Mr Carlton's back room, his own, tiny dispensary, led on to a patch of ground below the stairs to the flats. Light shone from the window, so welcome he wanted to touch it. Better than nothing: he was cold.

Tombo had never quite brought himself to like Philip Carlton, whom he always addressed as plain Mister, nor could he rely on Mister to understand his predicament because Mister was clearly a person who liked parties, and because Mister always tried to be nice (call me Uncle Pip), but he did not believe he would be sent away. Formulating excuses and reasons, he crept to the window, which was, he had forgotten, the top half of the door. The light was the only sign of life. Thinking how sick he was of pushing unfamiliar doors either to get out or get in, he tried the door, which yielded suddenly to his touch, sending his light body into the chemist's back dispensary with all the grace of a jack-in-the-box.

'What the hell . . .'

Philip Carlton whirled round from the laboratory shelf which occupied half of the room, with the sink in the middle surrounded with what looked like medicine bottles, and a few very old and mouldy-looking books. It was the ante-room to the back room rather like the arrangement in Mrs Bum's but without stairs connecting with the upper landing. Philip's voice was thick with fury. He had seized a jemmy used for prising open cardboard crates and held it aloft in one hand, the arm lowering as he squinted, identifying his visitor.

'What on earth do you think you're doing in here, young Master Perry? I thought you might be one of those bad boys I know, come to steal drugs. You know bl . . .' he choked on a swear word, tried to stand up straighter, '. . . very well you're never supposed to come in here. Now what do you want?'

'Nothing, Mr Carlton, honest. I'm sort of locked out upstairs and I saw the light. I thought Mum would be back, but she isn't, you see not yet . . .' the fury in Philip's usually unctuous voice made Tombo gabble, come to a dead halt and stand there, hugging his chest. Then Mister smiled, very broadly, and Tombo felt another kind of doubt as he heard a complete change of tone, the voice becoming manically friendly, even a little dreamy.

'Oh, I see, I see, I see. Well that's fine then, absolutely fine. You'd better stay here until your lovely mummy gets back. Play with Uncle Pip, eh? Such a lot of fun we're having here, such a lot of fun.'

'What are you doing?'

'Me? You must mean me, ha, ha, no one else here, is there? Me? I'm making mixtures. For putting in bottles, keeping poisons safe and fit to use. Such fun, you see.'

He always repeats himself, Tombo thought, says the same things again and again and everything twice. Reassured, but unaccountably anxious, he couldn't help but notice there was something strange about Mister tonight: he was grinning so wide and his eyes were all sparkly, his movements expansive, so that when he waved an arm to usher Tom further forward into the room towards a chair, he knocked some books to the floor. Tombo was used to Mister being delicate and precise in all his movements, irritatingly, sometimes comically so: the big waves and big voice were more often the surprising hallmark of little Mrs Carlton. Remembering she who was dead, this one-time friend of his, made Tombo even more uncomfortable. Death was not something he understood, except to know it was discussed in low voices.

'Seen these books, eh, Tombo?' Mister was pointing at the old volumes on the shelf which appeared to have been the object of his study before the interruption, although the whole bench was littered. The books contrasted oddly with the modern, laminated manuals his mother used for reference, but Tom was not curious.

'No,' he said.

'Well, you can look at the pictures, but not if you don't want nightmares, ha, ha. Mares in the night, don't you know. Why call 'em mares? Why not nightfillies?'

'What's in the books?' Tom asked out of politeness. He was beginning to get used to the glittering eyes and the strange smell in there. Nothing like the faintly dirty smell in Mrs Bum's. This was at least clean. As his father had noted with disgust, Tom had become a fastidious little boy.

'Shows you how they used to do operations, Master Perry, in the olden days. I got all those books when I was a lad your age, wanted to be a doctor, but not to be, not to be. Not enough money. A humble chemist, never an anaesthetist. My mean old dad, no ambition. Dead, of course, my dad.'

That word, dead; a signal to change the subject.

'What sort of doctor is a neethtist?' Tombo enquired, looking dutifully at the books, which were dull indeed, containing pictures certainly, but nothing in colour and only of things which looked like masks, strange contraptions, old nurses' uniforms.

'An an-aes-thet-ist is the one who puts you to sleep before you have an operation, silly.'

'Oh,' said Tombo, turning the pages. The atmosphere was oppressive: between the cleanness of the smells, the party tea rebelled inside him and he was developing a headache.

'What time is it, Mr Carlton, please?'

A watch was consulted with elaborate care. Mister seemed to have some difficulty in reading it although the light was extremely bright.

'Six-forty-five. Or quarter to seven, whatever you prefer.' He was laughing again, seemed incredibly happy.

'I'd better go and see if Mummy's back, then. She might . . .'

'Oh might she? Yes I suppose she might . . . Your mother . . . your mother is a wonderful girl, you know.' The voice was now thick with emotion. 'Tell her . . . Tell her, oh never mind.' He was suddenly back to his more familiar self. 'Anyway, come back if she isn't there. Can't have you wandering round on your own, can we?'

Tombo was beginning to think this might be preferable. With all the uninhibited instincts of his age, he was aware, where Mummy was not, of Mister's funny, grown-up, silly regard for her, the way his eyes followed her in the shop when she was not looking and Tombo was in there, waiting on his seat by the counter where he had felt safest with Mrs Carlton, even when she was at her worst.

He did not analyse any of this but the defection of little Mrs Carlton through death made him angry with her: some form of safety went with her. Tom was also angry with Mummy who would, surely, if left alone, make friends with Daddy again. She had told him, categorically and often, that they were friends, really, Daddy and she, just not the kind of friends who should live under the same roof. 'You know how it is, pet; some people you like, but you can't be with them all the time. You've got friends like that in school.' Had he hell: the likening of his own situation to theirs brought resentment without a glimmer of understanding. Tombo was more used to yearning for friends: he could not imagine the luxury of turning them away; he could not even turn Daniel away, and if Mister here, with his great, wide, soppy smile and his glittering eyes . . . if this Mister thought he was going to step in where Daddy had stepped out, he had another think coming. Tombo slithered off his seat.

'Goodbye,' he said very formally. 'Thanks for letting me in.'

'Any time, old son.' Watching him for two steps, waving blearily.

Old son, new son, I am not your son, you, you stinker: you don't care about me at all. Tombo dawdled in the yard, hoping that the longer he took, the greater would be the chance of light in the upstairs flat. He paused by the wall, half-hiding, aping the game of hide and seek he had so recently escaped, peering round the broken fence although he did not expect discovery. Then, from just beyond the wall, he saw the tail lights of a parked car flutter into life, slightly ahead and parallel with the back of the baker's, two doors down, but close. An engine choked softly and began to purr: he recognised the familiar sound in one great bound of joy, ran from his sheltering place, shrieking after the lights and the puff of exhaust, 'Daddy, Daddy, Daddy! Dad, it's me, stop . . . Dad . . . stop . . .' But it was too late. He ran after the car up to the junction at the end, where it slowed, turned, too dark for the driver to see behind, leaving Tombo, standing still, shaking his fist and crying.

He wiped his hand across his nose. Traces of chocolate clung like mud, mingling with the tears.

CHAPTER FOUR

'You are old, you are old . . . And your bones are growing cold . . .'
Old. Nearing seventy, facing the vacuum of an evening in a
hospital room assigned for his use. Oh, Father William, you are
old, and you hide your depression in a cold. The softest pair of
hands, most catholic of knowledge, such talent in finding a vein,
but nothing to do with all those hours before sleep. Dr Hazel was
overly familiar with despair. His right hand stretched out for the
brandy bottle beside his bed: then the left hand followed the right
and slapped his own wrist. He squinted at the red mark he had
made, faintly visible below the age marks on white skin. No.
As long as he stayed overnight in the room, he might be
needed or entertained. Hospitals breathed by night: there were
generators and footsteps, life and crises instead of the sterile
death of empty rooms in an empty home. No one asked him to
stay and look in on his patients, but he stayed. On the desk at
home was paper, pen, the constant reproach of all he had meant
to write and could not write. The same reproach lingered here,
but not as pressing. No. Not the brandy. A lifetime's acquaintance with the unconscious patient left him prey to an inverted
view of human kind: cynical depression was the curse of his
existence. So much so, there was discomfort in the finding of an
occasional kindred spirit who whetted that appetite for life he
had been trying to kill, and awakened his talent to amuse and
inform. He was not grateful to Helen West.
'Dear God,' he muttered, folding his hands in mockery of
prayer. 'Will someone, somewhere, give me something useful to
do? Rancid, I am, with stale knowledge and old clothes.'
The jacket had thirty years, cavalry twills twenty, outmoded
like many of his drugs, only the fingers superbly useful.

Retirement, the blackest gift of his seventieth birthday, yawned like a black hole and suicide beckoned less as a sin against the Holy Ghost than as the exchange of one hell for another. He picked up his pen and felt it freeze in his fingers. No one would want to know. He eyed the medicine cabinet in the corner, which, being his own, was never checked. A few drops of this and that, oblivion so easy. Again, no. He had his pride, although he despised it. His wife and son stared out from the photograph fading by the sink. Dead, buried along with his own dignity and reputation.

A little of the brandy, perhaps. Only a little.

Helen knew she was better. Familiar energy was returning to her limbs; she had ticked her way through two days in the office and one very awkward interview with the Chief Inspector in the Carlton enquiry, but recovery was reliably signalled by preparations for an evening out with friends and the beginnings of an argument with Bailey. Understated arguments were frequent preludes to such occasions. Bailey only liked parties after they were finished, had fond memories of some, and actually loved conversation, but getting him out there was not always easy. What irritated Helen was the fact that the sociable part of their not very sociable lives was invariably initiated by her, never by him. He had no conscience about refusing invitations, nor did he aspire to the kind of acquaintance she seemed to attract without effort. Taking Bailey out to dinner with others was an activity she compared with leading out a dancing bear on a chain; he grumbled and snarled slightly, grizzled, but followed and once there, found himself baited.

'I like that. You look good.' Helen's dress always pleased him; he took a rare interest in her clothes, would have encouraged even greater flamboyance than she ever allowed herself in the plain lines and strong colours of her choice. He was proud of her, liked others to see her, but he never said so, of course.

'So do you. You always do. Handsome. If a little formal.' There was no sarcasm in the words, only a familiar teasing. Bailey could not master casual clothing. There were suits and other uniforms for work; then there were frayed jeans and shirts for carpentry, gardening or mending drains, but nothing in between. Helen liked to see his long, lean frame adorned by a suit, and it did not matter what others chose.

'By the way,' she continued from no beginning, 'do you know a Chief Inspector Davies? On your division, not your station.'

'Yes, vaguely. He doesn't report to me. Nice man. Not made for higher things and doesn't want them. Collects teapots.'

'Oh, does he? Might have liked him better if I'd known that. He came into the office yesterday: we had a bit of an argument about that Carlton death, you know the chemist near you. He thought I was telling him how to do his job.'

Bailey frowned, a look of real annoyance replacing the resignation which had been present a minute before. He picked the car keys from the top of the fridge, where a large dish contained every spare item, bills included, which lingered, sometimes for weeks, in Helen's home, waiting for a place to rest. 'Well . . . were you telling him how to do his job?'

'Not as I saw it,' said Helen, feeling round in the dish for the house keys which also lived there, assuming a life of their own whenever she needed them. 'But he just wasn't interested. I was telling him I thought we needed another post-mortem, household stuff analysed to see if there was any more chloroform around, and a lot more background detail into the drug as well as the family before we could say that this damn chemist's wife really had died without any explanation. A good look at the shop. Stuff like that. Re-interview the woman assistant . . .' Her voice had assumed that airy quality which meant she recognised some form of criticism from him was on the way. Helen wanted to circumvent that: it boded ill for an evening already fraught with pitfalls, but she knew she was too late. Bailey did not understand blind loyalty – he belonged to no tribe, policemen or otherwise – but something in him rebelled against hearing a colleague being criticised. Strangers could do so, newspapers did so all the time, but not, please, his nearest and dearest.

'Listen, he's a Chief Inspector doing his best. They have the worst of all worlds, poor bastards, all the administrative nightmares, almost everything routine to investigate, hit and run, unexplained death, with none of the facilities given to the CID. You have to let him do the best he can and accept the result. If you interfere, you'll make it worse. He has a healthy attitude to lawyers, anyway.'

'Meaning we're really congenital idiots who know nothing about the real world? Sit in judgement like gods on the universe and never get our hands dirty? Yes, that is what you mean.'

'No, not what *I* mean, but what he might mean, especially if you dictate to him. Neither party does a perfect job, but the one shouldn't interfere with the other.'

'I thought I'd ask Dr Hazel, you know, my anaesthetist, for some help on the subject. What am I supposed to do, let it ride?'

'In some cases, yes, unless you have excellent reasons to say you shouldn't. Which you haven't here. There's no real suggestion of murder or manslaughter, any more than there is in death by glue sniffing. Helen West's insatiable curiosity is about to request the invasion of some poor citizen's privacy. Nothing to do with evidence, of course. And enlisting the aid of a deeply suspicious old man in the process.'

She did not leap to the good doctor's defence: that way lay serious argument, but she was uncomfortable. There was no evidence of foul play, rather the reverse, plenty to indicate nothing of the kind. Only the smells, the shameful scent of a wild goose chase and the wonder how anyone could bear the perfume of drugs without overdose first. She felt slightly ashamed as her hands closed over the keys.

'You wouldn't be able to have a placatory word with Chief Inspector Davies, would you? Put him on the amenable track, since you know him, smooth the hackles?'

'Helen,' he said warningly. 'You know I won't.'

'OK, OK, leave it for now, sorry I spoke.' She deflected serious irritation by pulling at his sleeve, 'Come on, we're late.'

Late for an evening of good food, multicoloured salad and veal escalope which he enjoyed, conversational jousting with him as the target, which he did not. It only needed one liberal bounty hunter who believed the whole order of police officers was rife with corruption to lead a pack of interrogators, primed with the questions they had always wanted to ask. There was a dentist, three lawyers, a magazine journalist, not an abnormal throng for a dinner party. Helen, knowing he was far from defenceless and angry with him anyway, left him to the wolves at the other end of the table.

'No,' he was repeating wearily, 'no, I don't think London's policemen are particularly more wonderful than any other men: they do what other men do, think what other men think, are tempted in the same way by the same things.'

'Have you ever,' asked one intense woman, 'ever lost your temper, and you know, oh, I hope you don't mind being asked this, I mean, ever beaten someone, hit them? When you were arresting them, I mean,' she added hastily.

'I do mind being asked.' Bailey's voice was sharper, alerting Helen from her distance. 'But since you have, the answer's yes. Without much real excuse either. Not for some time, however. Hot temper goes hand in hand with youth, but also has an occasional association with courage. Difficult, in awkward situations, to have the one without the other.' He smiled at the woman like a piranha, making her duck back into her food, Bailey's most dreadful and terrifying smile, not deterring the man opposite. Oh, Christ, Helen thought; this was not one of the evenings worth leaving a fireside for, even to avoid cooking. She knew very well by the end of the second course that they would depart as soon as decency allowed, looked round at her own contemporaries. Better educated than Bailey, despite his law degree, painfully acquired through night school; better read for all his voracious reading; better mannered, certainly not. Bailey would not dream of harassing a fellow guest. In his case, disapproval bred silence, so did uncertainty, and no serious conversation was ever so public, so rudely monopolising. It was not his fault that despite his erudition he so often resembled a bull in a china shop. She was proud of him, loved him, but occasionally, they embarrassed each other.

Finding the safety of the car after they left the house and in the certain knowledge of being talked about, Helen wondered if it would ever end, this social awkwardness. Probably not.

'Your place or mine?' he asked, the ordinary smile which creased the face into a thousand lines showing relief at the end of captivity.

'Any home at all, James, and don't spare the horses.'

Philip Carlton's late wife Margaret had never actually disgraced him in public, but, as he saw it, she had never actually raised his stock either. I mean, he told himself, in the privacy of his spotless kitchen, allowing himself a little of her favourite tipple although it was slightly sour from the keeping, she wasn't an asset. Pip scarcely noticed the taste, bought wine automatically the same way he consumed one glass each evening alongside carefully prepared food. One pork chop, two vegetables, one small baked potato, efforts the women in the grocer's and the butcher's found commendably sad and brave. Almost as swift to commend and sympathise was that Chief Inspector who had phoned in the first place to say that Margaret was dead. Sympathy had diminished with the discovery of the chloroform angle, ebbed and flowed since, but he seemed to accept Pip's apologetic explanations. Besides, the chemist's drugs were all in order, not a single poison unaccounted for, the records immaculate, and although the telephone voice was clipped, it was still reassuring. Pip remembered how he had kept them out of the back dispensary.

'Sorry to bother you, Mr Carlton. I said I'd come back to you about the . . . funeral arrangements.' He had been going to say, about your wife's body, but changed the words instead. Chief Inspector Davies loved his own wife solidly; he imagined most respectable men did the same, despite the evidence to the contrary often shoved in front of his nose. Besides, any one of the few questioned in Herringbone Parade (a sketchy questioning, he had to admit) found Philip Carlton wonderful. That, with the Inspector's naive belief in the integrity of professional men, put him firmly on Pip's side. Women, on the other hand, were always difficult.

'But anyway, as I said, we can't release the . . . deceased, not yet. And another officer might see you tomorrow. Detective Inspector Collins. I'm off the case.'

'Why?' said Pip.

'Well,' said Davies uncomfortably, 'I had to report to the Crown Prosecution Service. We do, you see. It's them, not me: they want a few more enquiries. That chloroform, bloody nuisance. Silly of her to play round like that.'

People dying in bed were a burden for a desk already full of death and disaster mainly inflicted by motor cars. 'Nothing to worry about, the Coroner's doing his pieces, but there it is. Shouldn't take long. Only a matter of loose ends.'

'Can you bring back the things you took from the flat?'

There was a pause. 'No, not yet, sir, but please don't worry. He'll see you at twelve, OK?'

Pip was not worried, or not more than a jot. If they asked him more questions, he would only have to give them more answers since he had nothing to lose apart from the sympathy of another police officer. No one had yet asked for any elaboration, but he had never really supposed it was going to be as easy as that. What he and Margaret had done so often last thing at night might be considered odd, but hardly criminal. You would only have to look at a photograph of Margaret to see why. In any event, the entertainments of the evening had rendered him languid, full of confidence and bonhomie, and he was well on the way to believing that everything had been Margaret's fault anyhow. Bossy, officious, little Margaret with the lined monkey face and shattering voice, with her pathetic passion to be loved. Not quite as well off or as amenable as he had thought, this Margaret, owner of this freehold shop, all left by her dead husband. They had added this respectable wealth to the price of the house left by his mother when Pip entered into marriage for the first time. Margaret's fault too, if the glow had faded; she should not have been so bossy, so anxious to interfere with everything. He dwelt on this, working himself into righteous anger. It saved him from dwelling on the other. The shame, the hot, searing shame which pierced his groin as he sat in the kitchen, his hand moving automatically to guard his crotch. Small and perfectly formed, his mother had said, touching all the time and teasing. Alone and afraid, he could feel her fingers again, flicking and tickling his childish little stump, teasing him into life, that awful, disgraceful, involuntary life which Margaret had so craved.

He could feel the fingers. Pip suddenly screamed in agony. Sat back with his knees pressed close together, rocking to and fro until he was calmer, waited for the sweat to cool, still feeling hands along his spine and between his legs, creeping like insects. There was a knock on the door. His head shot up, the neat hair fell back into place and colour returned to his skin. Outside, Daniel was halfway down the steps. Daniel never waited.

'Oh. I was coming to see you. Heard you shout. Those boxes out the back . . .'

'No,' said Pip. 'Not now, tomorrow. It's late.'

'OK.' Daniel shrugged. A sly smile curved at his mouth, not a particularly pleasant smile. 'Don't want anyone going near your back room, do we?'

'Go home, Dan.' The voice was sharp.

Daniel went, his own pace never varying, carrying with him a cloud of discomfort. Ever watchful Daniel, that half-smile playing havoc. Pip was shaking, memory stirred uncomfortably, a different memory from all that panic which had preceded the knock. Another memory of a figure outside in the dim light of pre-dawn, but Daniel was not a man with memory. Pip shook his head again, concentrated instead on the image of Kimberley Perry's rounded bottom as she bent down, her legs when she climbed the step ladder to the top shelf in the dispensary, her comforting bosom under the overall. Give her time, give her time, stay still for now. And then he would really know. For now, he would clean his house and his best suit instead. Ready for a funeral.

Whistling tunefully, Pip set about his domestic tasks, a little apprehensive about tomorrow and what he would say. He swiped at the stainless steel sink, already shining from washing-up liquid, plucked the ironing board from a cupboard and fetched his suit. Went to hunt for the dry-cleaning fluid he used for spot cleaning wool flannel. Gone, missing from under the sink he had just made new, gone with all the other rubbish hidden along with it, Jif, Sparkle, environmentally friendly washing powder, all taken by the police. Now that gave him a moment's pause for thought, not a nice moment, but a minute or two in which he sweated freely and was forced to sit down. Repeating a few mantra-like phrases to himself, such as, it does not matter, this will pass, they won't connect, nothing wrong anyway. I've got an explanation, and the one thing they'll never do is find evidence, no one old enough. Policemen are not chemists. Then the lassitude of the evening won again, bringing in the wake of the sweat a repetition of the earlier optimism which was his own hallmark, along with a feeling of recklessness. Perhaps he would go and see Kimberley. He rummaged in the drawers of the dresser: sweets for children, children like any kind of sweet, even the fusty chocolate bars which Margaret had provided to make him fat; a sort of memoriam, never to be consumed. Armed with these, he made for the balcony, the thought of Kimberley sharpening his breath. He had to know: he had to find out: she was the only one who could show him, the only one he had ever desired . . . With his constant care for economy, he turned out the light before he opened the glazed back door. Stood by the rail, stung by the cold of the air, and heard, to his chagrin, his own name called from the road below.

'Never mind, Tombo, never mind. Honestly, it doesn't matter. Parties don't matter, only I wish you'd said how much you hated it last time and I'd have made an excuse for you not to go. What on earth made you think I'd be cross about something like that? You are a silly.' She ruffled his head. 'Anyway, you raced out of there, went to Uncle Philip while you were waiting for me to come back; you were lucky he let you in. No one's allowed in the back dispensary, not even me. Anyhow, then what did you do?'

'Sat on the step, in the dark. After . . .'

'After what?' She could sense he did not want to answer, but would answer if she was patient, stayed as she was, stroking his head which he always seemed to like. A worrying state to find him in, shivering without a coat, sick as soon as they came indoors. Put to bed with more ceremony than usual, attended by more than the customary guilt. 'After what?'

'After Daddy went,' he muttered, feeling the treachery reach to his stomach as well as to the eyes which still threatened tears. But he stopped when he saw that Mummy was calm and not even surprised.

'Just a minute, Tom, I'm getting a cigarette.' Out of the room to hide the shaking of the limbs, the feeling of shock. She lit the cigarette hurriedly and came back, disguising distress in the smoke and apologies. Tombo at his tender age was remarkably puritanical about smoking: so, at the best of times, was she.

'I didn't know Daddy was coming this evening,' she said conversationally. 'Though he does come quite often, I know. Just to check we're all right, you know. He doesn't have time to come in.' If only that were true, she thought: if only I had never let him have a key. If only he did not watch us, watch me, rather. He doesn't watch over Tombo enough. Nor does he steal Tombo's nightwear. Nor does he cross-examine him every time they meet, like he does me.

'What time was it roughly, tonight, when you saw Daddy, I mean, and did you get a word with him?' She slowed down the frantic puffing on the unfamiliar cigarette, pretending to try and blow smoke rings, pulling faces to make him laugh.

'Only ten minutes before you came back. I wasn't waiting long, honest. Bit cold though.' He was feeling comfortable now, warm and loved, sleep intruding into the corners of his busy brain.

'Bet it was, you poor old thing. You'll have to wear your anorak for school in the morning. I'll go back and get your coat from the grocer's, Mrs Beale. I know you call her Mrs Bum, but I can't call her that. Wouldn't I like to, though. Pretty good name, isn't it? Suits her.'

Tombo giggled, giddy with the relief of being part of a pair. Mummy was laughing: she rarely laughed but when she did, laughing with him, like now, he knew with great certainty how ready she was to fight for him, look after him, if only he asked.

Asking was the trouble. Pride was a barrier the size of a reef. Nor was this invisible support, this fervent love, so tangible now, always beyond doubt in a school playground which stretched for a hundred miles each side, to say nothing of the pavements of Herringbone Parade.

Mrs Beale was puffing on the customer's side of the counter at Carlton's Caring Chemist, enjoying a sense of her own importance and only faintly apologetic. Ever so sorry to bother him, she was, but she guessed he'd be in (he was never out and nor should he be, widowed so recent, wouldn't be right), and her need was greater. Mrs Beale did not believe in the local doctor, a gentle man admittedly but never a gentleman because of being as black as the ace of spades and called Dr Gupta. Not good enough for her mother-in-law's ulcer, oh no. Pip Carlton was the man for that, any damn chemist with a stock of pills was the man for that and bloody Mother playing up like a baby because of all the disruptions of that party. Pig. She had an ulcer from eating like a sow and complaining every alternate breath, serve her right. Truth to tell, she had been trotting up the back road simply to be out of her way as much as because she thought she needed medicine. Herringbone Parade might have been full of neighbours by day, but was certainly not particularly neighbourly by night, not like the old days. Not like it was in the days of the dim-remembered war. There was a proper spirit about the place then, Mother said; never stopped talking about the bombs which wrecked the landscape in the Blitz. Now, nothing stirred after seven o'clock, when the service road assumed the silence of a grave, the odd, snorting car, nothing else. So it was nice, very nice to have a word with Pip, who was never out of patience, never said no, was ever so caring. Yes of course, Mrs Beale, but how are you? Can't give you anything you could only get with a prescription, mind, but I think I've got something which is just the job; can you come round the corner to the shop? Never keep anything like that in the flat, you know: Margaret wouldn't have it. Mrs Beale was touched by the way he always spoke of Margaret as if she were still alive, maybe because they hadn't had a funeral yet. Sad, that, but not very. She was well aware that Margaret would have sent her packing, protected Pip from the inconvenience he actually liked and told her to call a doctor.

'I'm ever so sorry,' she repeated for the seventh time, although she hadn't meant it the first, 'but she does play up, you know. Wouldn't get a wink if I left her like that, would I?' 'No, you wouldn't,' said Pip with a twinkle in his eye. 'You could always, you know, distract her. How about one of these nice nighties here while you're at it?' She roared with laughter, always appreciative of his little bit of flirting. 'Oh get on, can you see me in one of them? I'd have a heart attack just looking in the mirror.' 'Sold one to your friend in the dress shop, you know. How was the party, by the way?' She ignored the question, but not the roguish glance, the raised eyebrows at the mention of the lady whom Tombo called Mrs Bosom, the chance of poking a little fun at that glamorous rival too good to resist. Not that Pip ever said anything nasty, but the look was enough. 'Did you now?' Mrs Beale murmured. 'Did you indeed? Just tell me what colour and I'll never mention it again.' His turn to laugh, handing her the medicine, putting both hands round hers as he pressed the bottle into her palm. Pip always touched first, before he was touched. 'More than my life's worth, Mrs B, you know that, more than my life's worth.' They beamed at each other in mutual approval.

'Come back for a cuppa,' Mrs Beale said. 'Not late, is it? Don't like to think of you on your own. Mum would love to see you. Talk about old times.'

Pip looked gratified, hiding the wariness. Ah, the love of the neighbours, the various kinds of love Margaret had denied him, but old Mrs Beale had known him as a boy, half a mile and a million years away. She had known the family, the aunts and his mother, the only person in the Parade who did, and Pip was not ready for reminiscence. 'Oh, you are kind, but not tonight. Work, I'm afraid.'

'Well, another time then. You look after yourself.'

Ten doors down, Mrs Beale senior sat by the fire, waiting. She wondered why, with her compendious knowledge, the police had never been to see her, sat as she had sat for weeks, in a state of silent offence.

Solitude was onerous. There were times when Hazel bore it as lightly as he carried his shambling fifteen stone; other occasions when these night hours were so oppressive he felt them suffocating his heart, remembered by logical association the anaesthetics he had used as a childish man. A believer in science and the power of healing, dear God, those were the days. Holding down a patient and making them breathe their escape from pain, even while they resisted. No, this was his imagination: he had never actually done so. That was what was done in the olden days, the earliest, mid-nineteenth century anaesthetics, when more patients were killed by the new discoveries than had been killed before, even when they screamed their way through hideous surgery, removed from the populous hospital wards so that other patients might not hear the yells. Well, as he reflected when looking at his collection of books, at least they gave the poor bastards a choice of death, these knock-out fumes applied at first by the surgeon himself or whoever happened to be around, magic formulae in unsteady, ignorant hands, administered with such liberality that the patient need not wait to die by the knife. There was no such animal as an anaesthetist then: there was simply a student or a nurse with the mask, looking like an executioner, often inadvertently fulfilling that same function. Sean Hazel knew all this and knew he would not have such nightmares if it was not his habit to read such history. There was in his brain the dream book, the papers he had never written, the story of these lives, as told by his own father, read in these dry volumes, known by himself, as one of the few doctors old enough to have used the same stuffs. The new breed did not want to know and did not need to know, what history was like. Or how they owed respect to their elders for their very existence, even if those elders, like Hazel himself, were burdened with useless knowledge.

He was talking to himself again, getting ready for bed in the

cabin-like room, gesturing to his books, the old Victorian manuals, to prove to himself his own point. 'You'd manage best in the
jungle, boy, surely. You'd know how to improvise.' The thought
was satisfying, pointless self-flattery, he knew, but still reassuring.
He looked towards the brandy bottle: only two fingers gone, good
lad. He had tried them all, alcohol last; none of them worked.
Oblivion was the hardest thing of all, fatigue the best he could ever
achieve to blur the pictures in his mind or rid his nostrils of the
smells.

He had used chloroform on his son.

There had been nothing else.

Helen had gone to work with Bailey's admonitions ringing in her
ears, not a lecture, only the same few words, very softly spoken.
'Don't interfere: let others do the work they are paid for . . .' She
had not told him how the self-same advice had already been given
by her own superiors, and since she was never immune to advice
or to criticism, she was beginning to think she should listen.
Arrogance was so foreign a sensation she did not really know
what it was: conviction was another matter entirely, but as she
strode up the corridor, armed with the second-best suit from the
dry cleaner's, conscious of feeling well, wanting a quiet life with
Redwood, Mika and everyone else, she was feeling blithely coop-
erative, ready to apologise to the world for causing it trouble,
anything to keep the peace.

Until Mika came into the room with a memo, on her face the
reproving glance given to the person who is late by the person
who has arrived early. 'Chief Inspector Davies has been phoning.
I wrote it down. He'll phone back, but he had to go out.'

'Oh, shit.' The in-tray was full again, the Carlton papers still on
the corner of the desk. 'Chloroform', said the memo, the one
word carefully dictated to ensure the spelling, never Mika's strong
point, was correct. 'Chloroform in dry cleaning fluid.'

'He was going on about something else,' Mika said. 'An . . .
afro, afrodissy . . . something to do with sex. Rude.'

'Aphrodisiac?' said Helen.

'That's it, that's it. You'd better ring him. He's ever so cross.'

'Shit,' said Helen again, and dropped the dry cleaning in her arms to the floor. It was the mere thought of the smell. Anti-aphrodisiac, and the world was not only bad, but mad.

CHAPTER FIVE

'THE truth, the whole truth and nothing but the truth, so help me God.'

Helen looked up from the document in front of her, met the eyes facing her own. The new officer, Detective Inspector Collins, was anxious to please without being deferential. So far, she liked what she saw. He caught Helen's expression, allowed a half smile.

'I didn't make him say that, Miss West; he insisted.'

'Well, that's quite enough to put me off.'

She had begun at the end, reached what she privately considered the greatest indecency in Philip Carlton's statement. Pleas to Jehovah, promises made on my mother's life, all that hypocritical hogwash in promises of truth, raised alarm bells as well as the slight tendency to be sick.

'I don't understand why he couldn't have said any of this before. It was the obvious thing to say.'

'Didn't want to shock, he said. Anyway, neither Mr Davies nor anyone else asked him. No one would have asked him, or looked at all the stuff under the sink if you hadn't, well, insisted.' Inspector Collins coughed in polite deference, a repeated cough. Helen considered offering one of the cough sweets in the desk drawer, decided he would be even less at ease if he had to sit there with a lozenge in his mouth. 'No one knew there was more chloroform until we got the dry cleaning fluid tested. Anyway, he explains that. Says he really did use it to clean clothes, much better than a normal solvent, he says. But really, none of this makes much difference, does it? Still an accident.'

'Accident. Only it turns out the poor, daft chemist's wife has been taught how to sniff this stuff by her bloody husband. She wasn't a pharmacist. She was only a shopkeeper's daughter. The bastard.'

'An accident,' said Inspector Collins firmly. 'Nasty accident, but not a crime. So far. Nobody made her sniff dry cleaning fluid. She was on her own.'

'I'd like to think about this,' said Helen firmly. 'For a day or two.'

'Is there anything else you want me to do? I could do some house to house, but it's not as if we're investigating a murder.'

'You'll check his alibi, of course?'

'I was going to do that again. He was definitely in his hotel, but we can check the details again. I should have said.'

Verbal rap on the knuckles, a reminder he knew his trade.

'And you've checked his shop?'

'Of course. Davies did that thoroughly: I don't think I need to repeat everything, yet. That chemist keeps immaculate records of all his prescribed drugs, very thorough, not that they have much choice, you know. He isn't exactly dangerous. They have to account for everything they prescribe. He has chloroform, for preparations, but that's legal. For him anyway.'

'Fine. Well I think that's all for the time being.' She smiled again reassuringly. Don't tell the man how to do his job, this one knows perfectly well and the sound of nagging was creeping into her voice. Anxiety put words in one's mouth. Helen's renowned patience was a sham half the time, a question of pretending to be the mild professional instead of someone who, once alone, strode up and down her own messy room, the pacing an attempt to subdue the energy of frustration and the futility of ignorance.

She looked at the statement again.

'. . . I once told her chloroform could be an aphrodisiac. We tried it, for fun. You pour some on to a clean duster, sniff it for about sixty seconds. Not me, of course, I told her about it from one of my older pharmaceutical books: I only kept some chloroform in the flat for spot cleaning a suit. Then I discovered she syphoned off some of her own. Used it to help her with sex and give herself a high. She knew I disapproved, but I couldn't really stop her . . .'

Chloroform? An aphrodisiac? How little one knew in this world. Helen had thought it put people to sleep.

'While ignorance is bliss,' Sean Hazel wrote, 'knowledge is dangerous. Especially pristine knowledge, untarnished by experiment. Or rather by experience which is the multi-plural of experiments. Experience also tells one not to trust, to use a small repertoire of drugs rather than a larger range, because the manner of use is as important as the quality of the substance itself, and the brain can only remember so much . . .'

Or very little, as the case may be. He wanted to write, in the form of a pamphlet, a history of futility. Something to show how doctors were prone to behave like dangerous sheep, getting others to chew what they had just been sold, but the written word, which he had hoped would be the solace of old age, turned any message from his pen into porridge. The analogy was distasteful: he had hated porridge as a child and he was very tired. 'Our little life is rounded by a sleep,' he said to himself, 'Only soon, I hope.' He could not wield a pen; cigarettes, whisky and wild women were also out, apart from the cigarettes and whisky. So what else? Nothing. And then, a voice on a telephone, needing knowledge which no one else ever even requested, let alone needed. A delicious voice, at that.

'It's Helen West. I'll say hallo properly in a minute, but listen. Chloroform, Doc. Tell me about chloroform. Everything you know.'

After a few hours, the day had turned foul. A grey, wet wind hinted at sleet, cut through clothes, lifted umbrellas, attacked faces. Inside offices, noses streamed; pub windows were thick with steam and the bare bent trees dripped dirty London rain. Even these ugly winter trees were in short supply on Bailey's route between Whitechapel and Bethnal Green through the concrete and redbrick jungle where the remnants of old squares, invisible to traffic, formed the only saving graces of the area in summer. In early December, there were no green compensations. Out of interest, he cut through Herringbone Parade, the address stuck in his mind from Helen's talk, less free on the subject than she might have been. He parked behind, leaving the car to be covered in dust, looked over hoardings in to the pit of a building site beyond. Further on was an elegant terrace, a pre-war remnant housing a mosque and a hundred families; the earth between was red. Bailey shivered. The London of his boyhood had been punctuated by wartime: nothing so different now even after two generations: he often wondered what lay beneath. Something had happened in the Carlton enquiry which had stimulated Helen's eclectic interest, but since he had warned her against interference, she had been silent on the subject. They were often thus, reserve descending on them like summer rain. Only a two-day silence, not one she would maintain, since Helen, unlike himself, was quite unable to hold still, always told him in the end. Perhaps she always tried to teach him by example a greater openness, or perhaps she was aware of the feeling of drabness and boredom which was now almost a fear in him. He did not like the idea of that. Turning the car into the lights of the Parade, all blazing in the premature dark of the afternoon, he realised that Helen paying silence for silence was actually quite justified. She had said nothing of new developments, which hurt a little, but on the other hand he had not mentioned his knowledge of the Parade and his knowledge of Mr and Mrs Duncan Perry. He would tell her, though: she would help. Had to do something to deal with Duncan, but not now. He could advise the wife, console the husband, but for this and all purposes, he felt quite unfit. Bailey felt fit for nothing.

Herringbone Parade was not a place anyone would choose to live and die in, he decided; more the sort of place in which a person fetched up, beached by fortune and left to make the best of it. But for all its older inhabitants, who had indeed been hostages to fortune, shipped here from older buildings, people who remembered his parents' war, it was a brave place for all that, lights blazing, a few Christmas decorations showing in misted windows, people huddling from one doorway to the next. Passing the Pharmacy, he saw two customers bundling out of the door, conversation frozen by the cold. Bailey laughed at himself. In other days, he would have come here for the market. Now he had come for the idle curiosity he professed to despise. To examine the geography for other purposes still quite unrelated to Helen's legal conundrums. He slowed down past the shop, blocked for a moment by a van offloading from a stall, then turned the car easily left into the service road. He manoeuvred past bags of rubbish and watched with distaste as his headlights caught a mongrel dog jumping away from a rubbish bag, dragging a chicken carcass. Winter cold brought out the predatory instincts even in a pet, but chicken bones were bad for a dog, Bailey remembered, too brittle for the throat: the silly brute might choke. He was slightly ashamed of his indifference. The animal slunk away, ready to watch him leave before returning for the best of human detritus. Dog eat dog. Let them.

As Bailey cruised the back of the street, Helen emerged from behind a shelf in Carlton's Caring Chemist. While her eyes had examined a dusty display of suntan creams in the shop window, her mind beset with the domestic detail of why they were there, she had sensed, in that flash of recognition reserved only for the acutely familiar, Bailey's car and Bailey's brief presence. Separated by a few feet and two sheets of glass, so far and yet so near to the sixth sense which made her duck as if to read the full particulars of factor sixteen creme, suitable for babies. Something akin to shame, but definitely unshameful, made her blush. She regretted this necessary secrecy, this subterfuge to hide a nature which was curious but cautious and still afraid of criticism. She suffered as well from that guilty fear which afflicts any reasonably conscientious person who has lied in order to leave work indecently early.

'Can I help? Gawd, what a mess.' There was, as she rose, a large, red-skirted behind, level with her face, with shapely legs gradually disappearing from view in a dim impression of red and black striped tights, an adventurous ensemble which owed more to experiment than taste, all dignified by a statuesque shape, large black belt on a small waist and the sensation of a very nubile body striving to get out. Half bent, Helen stood level with the kind of bosom she had craved at eighteen, and still admired; looked up at a face of intelligent, preoccupied friendliness. Big eyes, blue mascara, wide mouth, all the features of an artless Brigitte Bardot with none of the sophistication.

'No, I was just . . .'

'That's fine, then. Take your time. I hate people rushing me in shops, don't you? We got everything here. Watch out for the toothpaste stand won't you? Only it ladders your stockings.' The behind, as if drawn on its own momentum, moved out of sight with brisk undulation as Helen straightened. She felt small and inept.

There was nothing peculiar in what she was doing, Helen told herself, with the bag of files uncomfortable against one shoulder. She was simply looking because it was imperative to look, and she rarely disobeyed imperatives. Helen West knew what she was, and, as usual, never rebelled at the limitations. Her role was to act as a conduit: the shifter of knowledge, rarely vouchsafed the first-hand view, but at least allowed the second before the crown court stars got up and did their bit. Rather like being the dresser in a theatre as opposed to the lead player. Or an offstage producer, the peruser of post-mortem photographs rather than the pathologist or the sonorous barrister. A researcher, a broker of evidence, a gofor, a back-room person. No accolades anywhere, for what she did, and she never minded how limited was the view she was allowed, provided she could do what she did, well. What she could not stand was no view at all or any opinion either. She was damned if she would be denied a squint at the *locus in quo*. In any standard murder case, she would at least see the face of the body on the slab; be able to express a brief and unbusinesslike pity; or see a video of the house where the corpse was found, put colours into the scene, note the furnishings, the wear or tear which gave an impertinent clue to the pressures of that life and death, the very clothing a feature of the story. Part of her task would be, in photographic terms, to weed out the most obscene photographs from those showed to a jury, but here with dead Mrs Carlton carried away in a white wagon like any other routine death, without the benefit of a single flash bulb, Helen had nothing. No clue to follow except the smells, no perspective to what she had read in soulless, typewritten sheets. It was not prurience which dragged her here, but the need to feel the framework and the literal desire to be informed.

She had been patrolling the shelves, smelling the smell and blinking in the neon light, breathing deep and doing as she would always do at relative leisure in a shop, which was browsing. No one could deny that a pharmacy was bound to contain some item of necessity. Shampoo, corn plasters, Tampax, instant diets, new lipsticks, a lifetime supply of toilet rolls, dusters. Ye gods, dusters. It was a shop where you had to scan each shelf, from the very top to the depths. Stooped again, transfixed by the daffodil yellow of six artificial chamois cloths, her own slender rump in a full khaki skirt, and from above her own dark head, another voice, saying the same thing.

'Can I help? Was there anything in particular you wanted? We do like to help.'

Helen hated being hounded in shops; she resented the voice. They were identical heights when they stood, Helen West and the caring chemist, accidentally so close together as she rose, and Helen stepped back sharply. Her heel encountered a packet of cotton wool, an unpleasant yielding under her foot.

'Was there anything in particular?' he queried. She gazed at him, mesmerised, her face forming an apologetic smile while her eyes and ears were full of the scent of him. Lavender water, some subtle smell of baby powder mingling with other scents clinging to a white coat pressed to perfection. Helen thought of a spruce waiter when she looked at this man, so small, so neat, so deferential. His well-manicured hands were crossed below his waist: he stood as if a half bow were natural: his shoes were polished, his collar points faultless, his tie held with a pin. Not a hair on his head was out of line with the furrows of his comb. A sallow skin, and the palest eyes she had ever seen. Bleached blue as if the colour had drained from them, ostensibly smiling, but lifeless. A man well versed in pretence, powerfully vulnerable.

'Oh! These things.' She placed a small collection of wares into the hands which rose like a begging bowl to receive them.

'Anything else?'

Helen sensed a mutual frisson of dislike and the knowledge of being hustled to the counter.

'Not from round here, are you?' he was enquiring conversationally as his little fingers tapped the till.

'No,' she answered shortly. Somehow she had no desire to reveal any more, looked round hopefully for the red legs of the girl.

'Have a nice day,' he intoned, handing over the white polythene bag, the pale eyes unmoving, and suddenly, Helen was weak with conviction. I'm right! The internal voice was shouting so loud she felt he must hear. I'm right, I know I'm right. There would be nothing natural about a death in this man's house. He would never lose a wife by accident: he would never allow such loss of control. And the smell of him. So clean, a sniff of sanitised threat.

'Thanks.'

'See you,' he answered.

Not if I see you first. Helen trod the route back from the door, aware of him turning away towards the high voice of the girl speaking from the room behind the counter. A sweet sound of normality so ill suited to the strange artificiality of her well-groomed employer, Helen found the cheerfulness unnerving. I should not have come here, she told herself, while knowing she should. What was worse was the knowledge that she could never confess her reactions.

'Don't forget you said I could go early today, Pip. Sure that's all right?'

'Oh, sure, sure.'

She hesitated. 'Pip, what did the police want with you yesterday? You were gone for hours. Was it about Margaret?'

He cleared his throat. 'Yes, as it happens. Look, there's something I want to tell you. Do you mind?'

Kim did not know what she was supposed to say to that since she did not know what it was, but chats with the indiscreet Margaret did not make her relish the prospect of marital secrets now. She had been dreading this moment, but knew it was inevitable. All through the busy surgery hours that morning, she had been aware of Pip watching her, as if testing her sympathy in advance, his distraction so complete he could not even count pills into the pill-counting machine or handle the prescriptions in order. They were sitting in the dispensary now, Pip's back room beyond hidden by boxes as it often was by day, each with the cups of tea which were the punctuation marks in every single day. All sorts of tea; camomile tea, ordinary tea, peppermint tea; he insisted on experimenting. The shop outside was quiet. Rain stopped play, and apparently, pain.

'I'm afraid they discovered Margaret's little secret. The police, I mean. I hoped they wouldn't you see, but they did. Thank God you saw me leave the night before she must have died, you know. Otherwise I'd be in the frame. They'd think I gave it to her.'

'Gave her what? Sorry, Pip, love, I'm not following.'

He shifted on his stool, appeared to gulp at his tea when she mentioned the word love, shot her a look so full of sadness she could feel herself melt. Kim's harder edges dissolved when Pip looked so soulful, like a puppy with enormous eyes. He was so kind, no wonder Margaret had loved him. He was actually not bad looking either, although Kim was young enough to consider him a little old.

'Chloroform. I'm only telling you because you may well find out anyhow and I don't want to hide it from you, although I certainly don't want the rest of the street knowing. Listen, when I met Margaret, she was a junkie. Yes, I know it's a surprise and it never showed, but didn't you ever wonder how she got so thin? She'd been weaned off, then weaned on to tranquillisers and you know what they're like. So, from the hard stuff to the Valium she'd done them all and she was starting in on the alcohol. Then I once made the mistake of explaining to her . . . she was always asking questions, you remember, always wanting to get involved . . . anyway,

I told her how a person could get a high from sniffing ether, or even chloroform. I didn't have any ether, no need for me to stock it you know, but I do make my own chloroform water. For keeping morphine, if I have to stock it, which isn't often and never for long, of course. I showed her for fun . . .'

'For fun?' Kim echoed. Bloody hell, she thought, strange notion of fun. Wouldn't have thought she had it in her, never can tell. She could feel her jaw dropping, slightly.

'Yes, for fun. It can't do you any harm, and it kept her distracted from anything else she might have wanted to take. I put some on a clean duster, just a little. You hold it above your face, never on your face, breathe deeply, and hey presto, you feel fine. Happy. She liked it so much I hid it, said if she ever wanted to use it, she could only use it with me there.'

'What kind of duster?' Kim asked stupidly, for lack of anything else to say to prevent the shock showing on her face. She remembered Margaret Carlton's unnatural thinness, her silliness and her ebullience, but there had never been a hint of unpredictability. Margaret had always been the same, laughing, irritating, perhaps a little hyperactive. A great person for silly detail. Pip looked surprised at the irrelevancy.

'One of the dusters we sell. The yellow ones. We had dozens. Always the same sort. I told them that, too.' He looked more cautious, pathetically worried about her response, turning back to his tea to hide his face, trying to speak casually. 'Did Margaret never mention any of this to you? She did talk to you, liked you so much . . .'

Kim was ever more embarrassed, and muttered, 'She never told me she'd been an addict. I didn't know. But she did tell me she thought you needed . . . don't know what she meant, none of my business, but something. To improve your love lives.'

His loud and nervous laugh rang through the small room, so shrill she jumped.

'Our what? We didn't have a love life, she couldn't bear it, really could not bear it. I did hope, when she got better, but . . .'

'Couldn't you have locked the chloroform away?'

'Oh yes. But better the devil you know and it isn't addictive. Listen, Kim, I knew what my duty was with Maggie. I had to look after her as best I could. And it wasn't good enough. I go away, just once, God alone knows, I rarely get the chance, and when I come back, she's dead. And now they tell me she died of poison. She had twelve milligrammes of chloroform in her blood. Oh God, oh God, you can't imagine what it's been like . . .'

He rested his head in his fists on the counter used for bottling prescriptions, his shoulders heaving. Kim had seen him cry like this when he came back from the mortuary, the helpless sobbing of a young child, reminding her of Tombo in his furies of grief. And all this time, he had laughed and carried on as normal, bearing these dreadful burdens, poor, poor, Philip. Kim was easily moved by another person's tears, especially male tears, a weapon Duncan had never used, although with her they would have been the bluntest and most effective of all. Begging sickened her: tears worked.

Amid a genuine pity, came secret relief. She had had an absurd suspicion that violent, obsessive Duncan had somehow been involved in the untimely death of Margaret. Kim had never thought through how this could have been: maybe he scared her to death with his nocturnal lurking; maybe he crawled into the wrong flat and took the wrong underwear. No, no; he wouldn't do that; he would notice the size. But all the same, the dark thought had grown, and now she knew for certain he was innocent of something at least. There was also relief in the knowledge that there was nothing perverted about Pip, as his wife had once vaguely suggested. Among all those accounts of diarrhoea, dentistry, minor operations and such, what malicious ideas Margaret had sown, each conversation promising more than the last: the merest hint of something strange about her husband beginning to emerge. Kim felt a surge of dislike for the dead wife, moved to Pip's side and put her arms round his bent back, resting her head against his shoulders. 'There, there, oh, please don't be upset. I understand, honestly I do, oh, poor Pip, I wish I could have helped . . .'

He flinched at her touch, like a child shrinking away from the adult who patted or tickled, but then he held her hand briefly, fished in the pocket of his white overall for a handkerchief. Kim wondered how it was he both liked and hated to be touched.

'You did help. You always help. And it was awful for you, being there when they found her. I'm sorry, what a baby to cry like this, not very manly, is it?'

She hugged him again, harder, then let go abruptly. Standing on the far side of the shop counter, watching intently, was Daniel, his face split in that half smile which could just as easily have indicated contempt as curiosity. Kim realised in a split second why Daniel raised her hackles. He saw so much and was far from a fool. She patted Pip on the head, making him jump, flinch and turn. She watched, puzzled, then spoke without embarrassment, but still stiffly.

'Daniel's here, Mr Carlton.' Daniel beamed at her. Kim had always been gruffly kind, brisk, but with time for everyone, never asking questions. Even let him talk. He shuffled, deliberately slow.

'Delivery van outside, plus all that stuff from before, do you want it all moved now?' he asked, the face all innocence. Pip blew his nose noisily.

'Yes, if you've time. Yes, yes. You get off, Kim. You wanted to go early, go on, good girl.'

She went, the embarrassment of Daniel's cool regard lost in her haste to get upstairs, clean up a bit, put on her face and go shopping for Christmas. All that she had heard overtook her own unease. She was alive with the knowledge she had just acquired, full of pity, flattered to be the confidant. It made her feel wiser and stronger. She tidied the living-room, noticed the dust on the surfaces as she stuffed away magazines and Tom's toys. Stopped for a moment, puzzled before moving on, shaking her head. She had been there when Margaret Carlton was found. Calling Margaret's name to no response, entering the door of that pristine bedroom, full of stale air, unmoved by breath, she had known without further test that Margaret was dead, had not lingered to inspect that lined little face never yet seen without lipstick, but had raced instead for the other room. Minutes later, safe in early morning sunlight which made it all so harmless, she had ventured a brief, further look, but could not recall, not now, not then, anything resembling a yellow duster.

Enough: she was sorry and she was late. In view of other people's problems, tragedies rather than woes like her own, she felt surprisingly good. Anger and anxiety fizzled out of her. The thought of confiding or complaining, being weak all over again, drifted downhill like the breeze-blown rubbish in the street outside. Whatever there was, she would cope.

Kim put on her yellow coat, a bargain from the market and very short. Leg warmers, bright as the lipstick. Teetered past the shop on her way to the bus. She missed the hungry eyes following her through bright, misted windows, watching like a hawk.

Daniel found enough to do around the caring chemist's for at least half an hour a day. On a good morning, Kim made him tea and sometimes he acquired things to eat. He did a further half-hour down the road for Mrs Beale, but although she thanked him and gave him apples, she never paid, didn't believe in it, she said. Nor did Mrs Kennel in the dress shop, although Ahmed in the off-licence lent him videos and gave him the occasional free can of lager. They provided well for him, the whole Parade, with supplies or generosity, but only Mr Carlton and Kimberley Perry actually gave him money. Margaret, the all-time fixer, had fixed that. Money, she said, he needs money. Which was strange since there was no need. Whatever he said, whatever he did, he was bound to this dispensary as surely as if he had been tied, would have done whatever he was asked, but how mean of Pip to forget to pay. He had come to rely on it. Neither could Pip ever see how Daniel needed smiles, for instance, as well as cash occasionally for the sweat of his labours. Even recognition of their mutual manhood would not have come amiss. Pip would not talk about drugs the way Daniel liked to talk about drugs. Dan was fascinated: he learned from his own condition. He knew a lot about Pip and quite liked the idea of how little Pip knew of how much he watched.

'No, not in the back dispensary,' Pip said sharply.

'Why not? You've forgotten these.' He pointed to a pile of boxes, 'And there's no room for them out here.'

'The back room's not for storage,' Pip responded angrily, 'and I didn't forget.'

'Oh, yes, your favourite place. You like it in there. No records in there. It's like one of those priest holes. Do you know, I saw you in there the other night. And the night your missus popped her clogs. Oh, no, the night before. No, I'm wrong. You were looking out of the window. In the morning, early. Very early. I like getting up in the dark.'

Daniel meant nothing sinister by this: it was merely a thought which popped into his mind to dwell for a second, without any real association between one winter's night when someone had died and the next. Daniel was used to death: most of his peers were dead and the timing of any death soon became a blur. Margaret was someone he regretted without mourning, since he was incapable of mourning. He knew Pip ignored him the way he did not ignore other customers and for the moment he wanted to be seen. All these words were no more than a longwinded attempt to jog Pip's memory on the subject of money. Only a pound coin here and there, but every little helped.

'What's so precious about the back room anyway?' he grumbled. 'Not as if you have to make up any of your own stuff, not this day and age anyhow. You can get it all in packets. Kept you away from the missus, I s'pose, but not a problem now, is it? No need to stay out of Kim's way. Quite fun to bump into. Slowly.'

He stooped over a pile of boxes, laughing a little, straightening the sides, about to continue. Then he felt a blow to the back of his skull, a dull, heavy, stiffening blow, delivered by an iron fist. A bloodless shock, a hand pressing his neck into the dusty floor; words hissed into his ear.

'Shut up, shut up, shut up. Shut it, you piece of scum, you bastard . . .'

Tombo scuffled home from school with a large hole in his nylon satchel. There was also a large hole in his trousers and he was not sure which he should explain first, that or the graze on his forehead. He was numb with misery. Today had been one of those days when his own credibility in the playground had failed, not there, but on the way home, when they had seen his vulnerability. He should not have boasted about Dad's car coming to school, had them waiting as he waited, jeering, then fighting. Daddy was supposed to meet him, Mum had said, and he had promised. Failing which, she had said, come home with someone else if you can, try not to go alone, and if I'm not back go and wait with Uncle Pip in the shop. He had not believed there would be a 'failing which', but he was alone, skulking down the back service road like a thief. Dad was a bastard, a bum, a stinker, a sodding, sodding . . .

There was absolutely nothing he wanted to do, nothing at all, and no one he wanted to see. So profound was his misery that the odd cut and bruise did not matter and even the dark service road presented no threats. He was walking down the back of the Parade rather than the front purely in order to avoid any contact with Mrs Bosom or Mrs Bum, who might just enquire why he had run away from their party. Mum had explained, but he knew they would ask him direct. There were few enough children actually living in Herringbone Parade for him to stick out like a sore thumb, only enough of them to field one dreadful party, and he felt as if the graze on his forehead was the colour of scarlet. But slowly, the quiet worked some sort of calm. Even traffic was distant here, and the wind and rain had died away to a solid cold. Tombo, delaying the time he would have to go and wait in the chemist if Mum was not back, took three steps forward and two steps back, looking round at last for anything to absorb his rage.

The ground at the back of Herringbone Parade was good for nothing but storing the tall rubbish bins which frightened him a little because they were big enough to hide a man inside and he always imagined being placed in there, head first with his feet tied together. One way they might have dealt with him at the party. The bins were full, only half the garbage bags had been taken away carelessly that morning, leaving stray bits to dance in the wind. They often did that, the rubbish men: got fed up halfway through if it was cold and left their task for the next day so the service road was never swept clean. These were things he noticed, the high spots of the week. Nearing his own home again, Tombo found rubbish dropped in the street: they were often careless like that. A torn sack gnawed by a dog leaving a trail of bones. Something of interest at last, near his own back door; a bent-up wire coat hanger, maybe two, formed into a ring with wire crossing over the top, making it look rather like a skeleton hat. The contraption projected from a knotted bag which had once sealed it, and the careful covering somehow added to its value. Tom thought at first the thing was the framework for some sort of helmet, looked around and put it on his head. The wire sat comfortably: he regarded it as a find, slightly ashamed of himself to be so delighted, as well as curious to see what on earth he looked like. Really, he knew he was too old for make-believe, all those silly pretend games, but he liked the hat all the same and knew he would keep it. Things collected had a way of becoming more precious than anything given, because then you were burdened with the effort of saying thank you. He made a little feint towards a bin, growling; then looked around for somewhere to see himself transformed into a fierce space invader. Or a soldier, if he stuck in branches and made himself camouflage. The glazed window of his own back door was probably nearest and he trotted towards it, ready to examine his own blurred reflection in privacy, hide the hat in the torn satchel and only then go round to the front for a boring hour by the counter if she wasn't ready. Already he was reconciled to tellings off, excuses, tedium.

But not yet. His foot on the step contacted something hot and his heart flew into his mouth. Tombo almost stepped on the figure huddled there, leapt backwards in a jolt of fear and prepared to run, until he heard the figure moaning. But retreating more slowly to a safe distance, even in the dark, he was suddenly reassured by something familiar, a scent, a familiar slouch which told him not to be afraid, for himself at least.

'What do you want?' he hissed at the figure from the safe distance of six feet. The form on the steps groaned, moving slightly, the groaning turning into a singsong sound of despairing pain, 'Oh God, oh God, oh God.'

'Daniel!' Tombo said louder, moving closer. 'What's the matter? Don't be silly, what's the matter? Stop playing about, you scared me.'

'My head,' Daniel slurred. 'My head. Someone kicked my head. Hurts. Can't properly see. Hurts.'

'Who kicked your head? Where? Out here, just now?' Tombo had approached, touched Daniel's shoulder, looking over his own, conscious of danger. Daniel did not answer, resumed the keening moaning, his hands across his chest, rocking himself to and fro. As Tom touched, he shrugged him away. Tom withdrew his hand as if he had touched a live wire.

'Wait,' he said. 'Wait just here. I'll get help. Wait.' Daniel merely grunted: Tom thought he saw him shake his head. He ran to the end of the service road, round the corner, panting up to the door of Mum's shop, pushing between the shelves on his way to the counter where two people stood waiting. Shocked to find Mum not there, immediately visible, he stumbled behind the counter, forgetting his excuse-me's, and thrust his head into the dispensary, holding the doorframe with both hands. 'Mr Carlton, Mr Carlton, you gotta come quick. 'S Daniel, not well, very poorly.'

Pip turned briefly, then turned back. 'No children in here, Tom, you know that.'

'I know, I know, but you gotta come. Quick. You could go through the back. Daniel, I said. You know, Daniel.'

Pip smiled over his head, out to the two women waiting at the counter. He shrugged his shoulders in a what-can-you-do-with-them? gesture. They smiled back. 'Yes, I know Daniel,' he said gently, condescension lacing every syllable. 'And there's nothing wrong with him, nothing at all. He was in here a minute ago. One of his turns, Tom, old boy, nothing to worry about.'

'There is, there is . . . you gotta come and see.'

'No, Tom, can't you see I'm busy?'

Tom turned to the waiting women with a look of appeal. They smiled back. 'I should come out of there if I was you,' one of them said, irritated by being kept waiting. 'You heard what Mr Pip said.'

Tom had heard, clearly. And seen the ingratiating smile on Uncle Pip's face, which he returned with a look of hatred, a look which bounced back off the granite of that smile. He turned to go, pushing past the women again, so that one of them tutted in disapproval. Halfway to the door, slower this time, he heard Pip's voice hail him back.

'Tom, here, if you want to be useful, take Dan his prescription. Shouldn't let you have it, but I don't think you'll eat it. That's all he wants. Addict, you know; very sad,' he added in an undertone to the women. The hand was extended beyond the dispensary door, holding aloft a white carrier bag. Tom had seen this before, carried it once or twice. Daniel, he knew, collected this every day, but the bag he took was heavier than he remembered. He gripped the slippy plastic and ran.

Perhaps, he thought later, Mister was right and that was all Daniel had wanted. Back round the corner, into the dark, stunning dark after all the lights of the Parade. Daniel still there, himself full of breathless explanations. 'He won't come, Danny, he won't, got your prescription.' Daniel laughing, unbelievably laughing, a funny, sobbing sound. 'What should I do, Daniel, come upstairs with me, we'll just wait for Mum . . .' and then, both of them blinded by the flashing lights of Dad's car, slewing to a halt where they stood. Daddy, with whom he had been so angry, getting out, saying 'I'm sorry, son, I'm sorry, couldn't get to school . . .' and Tombo, standing his ground for a second or two, unable to prove his point by waiting, running towards him, awash with words. He stumbled over his lines, rushed them, pointing backwards and forwards, round the corner in a storm of explanation, then back to his friend. Father detached son and they both approached. Daniel watched them, boy with father in hand, a unit which excluded him completely and one of them a copper to boot, spoke his first articulate words. A poetry in lonely hatred.

'Piss off, why don't you? Just piss off. I'm fine.'

Then he had just got to his feet and stumbled away. Tombo remembered him, all in the black, in the dark, the only visible bit of him the white plastic bag. He knew he should have stopped him somehow; dragged him back to be with them, but there was Daddy, big Daddy, forgiven in a second for the whole hours of weeping distress he had caused by being late.

Bailey was home first. Helen's place, by prearrangement, himself armed with shopping since he liked to cook as much as she loathed it. Left to Helen, they would never eat. At least the East End was rich in markets, including Herringbone Parade, and Bailey found that cooking, mending clocks, keeping busy, was the best panacea for his current existence. Less taxing than people, who could all go hang, apart from Helen. Bailey's loyalties had always been few, but intense.

He could tell she was well by the way she came downstairs, crashing through the front door, across the corridor, down the steps to her basement, everything flying. Bailey could visualise her long, thick hair escaping, as it did by this point every evening, from the slide which held it on top of her head, her brilliant blue coat, bought as an antidote to boredom, left flapping open. And he knew, with absolute sureness, that she had been on some expedition before coming home. The pub, probably.

Not that he minded. Each had a life to be followed but he was sometimes aware of his own vulnerability, his social isolation as compared with hers. She was aware of it too, included him as much as possible in everything she did, as generous with friends as with money and time, but he was still an outsider. When Bailey thought of this, he was perplexed, although never for long. They had care of each other and no one else did; he as vital to her sanity as air to her breathing. To have this place in Helen's heart, that enormous love she reserved for him, was enough, but he was well aware she had room for others, too. Being jaundiced with humanity was only his affliction, his particular cancer. He hid it, since she did not seem to suffer and he had no wish to infect.

'What was it this time?' he asked mildly. 'Somebody leaving, somebody getting engaged, or just Monday evening?' She grinned, not about to say immediately. He brushed her cold, pink cheek with his own warm face, waited for her arms around him, Helen's affection, which so delighted him but which he could not initiate.

'I've got egg on my hands,' he said, wanting to return the hugging.

'And me on my face. Doesn't matter.' She shrugged off the coat.

'I've only been shopping.' There was something a little evasive about this, but Bailey did not mind. 'Oh, and I spoke to Dr Hazel today. I promised I'd keep in touch, I liked him, you see, and he liked me and he's lonely. And he's helping me with the Carlton case.'

'How?'

'Chloroform. He knows all about it. So does Mr Caring Carlton, I'll tell you. Only Dr Hazel is going to write me an essay on chloroform. Did you know it was an aphrodisiac?' She was prowling round the kitchen, sniffing, alert to the smells, excited.

'No, I didn't know. Why don't you bring some home?'

'Actually, no. And anyway,' she added demurely, 'I don't think we need it.'

'Oh, I don't know. I'm getting on, you know. Ten years older than you.'

'And wiser, most of the time. And a better cook. You often make me feel redundant, you know. You do every bloody thing better than me. I'm a cretin compared with you.' There was no anxiety in the tone, no teasing either, only a genuine humility. He looked to check on that, turned back to the food, smiling to himself. She had her ways of reassuring him after all.

CHAPTER SIX

Despite a pathological reluctance to listen, Redwood found himself almost fascinated.

'Yes, yes, yes,' he repeated, nodding energetically towards the tableau of faces six feet beyond. He had agreed to listen, but, as branch Crown Prosecutor, regarded Helen West as one of life's dirty tricks. Helen had been placed under his command in the more peaceful areas of village Essex, from whence she had departed to his enormous relief, only for him to find that the promotion stakes of the Crown Prosecution Service dictated he follow. Bit of city life, Redwood, do you good. You're bound for higher things and we have to see how you survive in the jungle. A far cry, this grubby office, from the civilisation of Branston, dull though it had been. Redwood struggled in these waters, and he knew, again with a clenching of the jaw in his pouchy face, that his survival owed much to this rebellious professional, who was never insolent, never crossed him, always deferred to him, but was never, ever entirely under his control. Never a particularly passionate man, he harboured a strong dislike for Helen that was mixed with resentment, and made worse by the fact that he needed her desperately for all the things he could not do. Such as keeping the office in harmony. A closet subversive was what she was; too clever by half and far too popular.

No one but Helen would haul into his office some ragtail of a wizened medical man with some time-wasting story. In semi-rural Essex, Redwood had been in the zealous habit of ordering the prosecution of everything which moved, but now the sheer volume of work in the inner city had wrought huge changes in his practice. If there was any excuse to turn away a case, he took it, in a desperate attempt to control the huge numbers of files which rolled through the office day in, day out, like volcanic lava, hot, inexorable and suffocating. Without the sort of evidence which would survive a legal firing squad he dumped that case in the waste bin. Reports not submitted in double-spaced typing were rejected and any case requiring the valuable and unavailable resource of man hours was likely to go the same way. So, despite the story-telling he was hearing, he regarded today's exercise as no more than an hour's entertainment. Something to tell his wife when he got home. He was beginning to consult his watch, listening to the medic, noting the pleasant Irish of his voice, distrusting him more than somewhat. Medical men, anaesthetists, surgeons, whatever, should not look like that.

Dr Hazel was in fine form. Work, a project of any kind, had lent wings to his mind and freed his tongue for an audience.

'Twelve milligrammes,' he was saying jovially. 'Not necessarily lethal, your pathologist said, and he was right. Just about the equivalent of light anaesthesia in a patient, but quite enough to polish off someone vulnerable. The difference is that the far higher doses on record, twice as much or near enough, were administered with oxygen. You can take far more that way. Chloroform used to be the darling of anaesthetists, but there were a few hazards. For one, the poor devil of a patient would fight it, never liked the smell, sick and heavy, like the fumes themselves. A very heavy vapour. Fight too hard with a weak heart, off you went. The other curse was taking too much, slowed down your respiration so much you were likely to give up the breathing business altogether. Then, once they got the dosages right, they discovered a dreadful effect on the liver, especially children's livers. Degenerated afterwards, so they died when they should have been cured. The whole thing improved when the heavy-handed gave oxygen with the vapour. The problem, you see, with any anaesthetic you inhale, is getting enough to put you under while getting sufficient oxygen to keep you alive at the same time. They managed that with a metal mask. Used masks, for chloroform and ether . . .'

'The *surgeons* used metal masks?' Redwood asked, clearly horrified at the vision of an operating theatre full of highwaymen.

'No, no,' said Dr Hazel kindly, 'but do you ever remember a mask on your face when you went to the dentist? No, perhaps not, you're not old enough.' For this flattery, Redwood was grateful. 'No,' Hazel went on, 'they would put a mask, more like a frame over the patient's face. A sort of wire structure, with a tube inside to give oxygen in the more sophisticated versions, but anyway, really no more than a metal circle with struts, on which you put gauze. On the gauze, you dripped the chloroform, or ether – both evaporate quickly – and the patient simply breathes in the fumes without the liquid touching the skin. It burns, you see, chloroform, leaves a white mark. All in all, ether was better. Pleasanter for the patient, so fewer heart attacks, didn't slow down the respiration either.'

'Why didn't they use that all the time then?' Redwood was beginning to be irritated. Time was short, his stomach was rumbling and medical details made him queasy.

'Fashion, for one. Combustion, for another. Ether is highly combustible. You could never have used it in the same room as a bunsen burner and a lot of primitive operating theatres would have had those. As well as a surgeon who smoked a cheroot during surgery.'

'How disgusting,' commented Redwood, a fervent anti-smoker at all times. Helen, who was longing for a cigarette, remained poker-faced, and Hazel, in similar state, merely continued. 'Besides, ether had a frivolous reputation. Ether frolics, not unknown, sniffing the stuff to make you high, a social pastime by the same sorts of people who might now snort cocaine. Chloroform too, clumsier, though. Made a fellow sexy. They once used chloroform as a truth drug too, you know. Gave it to a suspect in police custody, to make him talk. Couldn't see you people getting away with that now.' He chuckled, to Redwood's mind, obscenely. Redwood shuffled in his seat. His irritation was becoming obvious. 'We're not the police, you know,' he began, but the only effect was to make Hazel talk more.

'The stuff has a use in crime, too, of course. A woman was supposed to have murdered her doctor husband with chloroform and a few teams were up before the beak for using it in robbery. Not likely, I'd have thought. Takes too long to work, and the amount you could clap over someone's mouth would only work for a minute or two. Which is the point here, don't you see? Miss West and I agree on that.'

'Yes,' murmured Redwood, lost. What an unholy alliance, Helen West and some scruffy eccentric, making something out of nothing while he needed her to go to court or sit inside with a mammoth fraud case which had been lingering here in the corner far too long. Get on with it. If stupid chemist's wives wanted to ape dilettante Victorians, and sniff disused anaesthetics, killing themselves in the process, it might all be very interesting, but not the business of the Crown Prosecution Service. Of which, he was, he reminded himself, the local leader, with no time to spare. He was only interested in proof, and not as in whisky or drugs either.

'You see –' Hazel was leaning forward confidentially on the side of Redwood's desk '– you can only inhale chloroform, you can't drink it, or at least, never of your own free will, and anyway, there was none in her stomach. As far as I can see, you cannot, by yourself, get enough in your blood to anaesthetise you, let alone kill you, do you see? Somebody has to help you, do you see? To get that inside you, you need an anaesthetist. That's why we buggers were invented, you see? For the simple reason that you have to go on inhaling after you've gone to sleep. The point of this case is not whether twelve milligrammes is lethal or not. The point is you can't self-administer when you're unconscious.'

'Oh,' said Redwood, light dawning. 'Yes, I do see.'

'All right, Duncan?'

Bailey's question did not demand any real reply. Any kind of grunt would do to answer this expression of concern. Bailey had thought Duncan looked better over the last few days. Perhaps he and the wife had patched things up, or perhaps DC Perry had seen the futility of haunting the back of Herringbone Parade in the hope of finding her in need, finding her out, or simply seeing her, this wife of his. He knew this would be no use to the wife, but he was no stranger to the self-defeating nature of Duncan's kind of love. Nor was he unfamiliar with Duncan's kind of need. Less directly, and many years before Helen, he had discreetly haunted his own ex-wife, who had rejected him with more mad violence than Kimberley Perry could ever have summoned. Kimberley was at least sane, and unlike Bailey's one-time spouse, had a living child, not a dead one. Bailey understood far more about obsession than his bland expression could ever indicate and somehow Duncan recognised he would not be speaking into a void.

'No, sir, I'm not all right. Not really.'

Bailey got up and shut the door between his office and the next. The voices on telephones, the clack of a typewriter, another detective telling a joke, faded significantly. As soon as the door closed, the joke ended and there was a burst of raucous laughter. Duncan flinched.

'I crunched the car,' he said. 'Outside Kim's flat.'

'Were you drunk?' Bailey asked in neutral tones. Duncan snorted.

'No, but I was later on. I got a taxi home, don't worry. Sodding car was towed off. She came out and screamed at me, see? Because I was late picking up the kid and he came home from school by himself. After that, I'd picked him up from home, took him for a hamburger, and when she came in, been shopping or something, she didn't know where he was, only that he'd been round the corner into the chemist earlier and then disappeared. So she screamed, really tore me off a strip. Said I should sod off altogether, not come round the place any more, stop stealing her things and hanging about. Stealing her things? She got hysterical, I tell you. So I said, what the fuck did she think she was doing anyway, out at work all the time, and letting the boy play round with a junkie? He does, you know, he told me.' The memory of all this screaming was making Duncan agitated.

'Hold on, how old is the boy?' Bailey was always uncomfortable when the professional lives of Helen and himself were enmeshed, but for the moment, he was grateful that her conversation about Carlton's Chemist made him vaguely familiar with the lives of all who sailed with her. Otherwise Duncan would have been difficult to follow. People in distress, he had noticed, assumed you knew far more about them than you actually did.

'He's just ten,' Duncan said, as if Bailey should have known. 'And most mornings, this bloody junkie takes him to school. Oh, he's a tame junkie, not black either, stable, comes into the pharmacist every day for his prescription. But I ask you, still a junkie. Who does she think she is, to tell me off? Even I could do better than that . . .'

'But you were late for the boy, and you did take him off without telling her where you were going, or leaving a message. She must have been worried sick, you idiot. No wonder she shouted.' His voice disguised any hint of lecture or disapproval. Duncan looked at his hands.

'All right. But I got so mad when that poncey little chemist, her bloody boss, comes out from somewhere and tells me to piss off. He tells me, stuck up little fart, seems to think he's God's gift. I know Kim's always said there's nothing going on there, and I know his wife's just died, but I don't believe her nothing going on, what with him shaking his fist, putting his arm round her and taking her back indoors, my wife. *My bloody wife!*' The recitation ended in a shout. There was a sudden silence from next door.

'That's right,' said Bailey evenly. 'Let them all know, go on.' He looked at his watch. 'Come on, we'll go out for the rest of this. Leave your coat.'

Rather than running the gauntlet through the CID office where the laughter was now quiet, they both went out through the front office, raising the heavy flap on the counter to go through, Bailey nodding en route towards the custody officer behind the desk. In the small lobby which fronted the grey outside world, three people were waiting, one black, one white, one female, all dejected. Missing cars, missing friends, perhaps; they had not arrived to celebrate good news. 'Got a quorum there,' Duncan remarked. 'You know, one black, one white, one woman.' Bailey smiled at the signs of normality. The custody officer watched them go, as he listened to a man explaining why he was without a driving licence. Easy life for some, coming and going as they pleased. Form-filling with one laborious hand, he picked up the phone with the other, listened, breathing heavily. 'No, not here, mate. We can't send anyone from here, we don't cover Herringbone Parade. Yes, I know it's only down the road but we don't cover it here. I don't care if you've got Sophia Loren. Phone up Bethnal Green, good lad, OK?' Looking at the departing back of DC Perry, he scowled. Pull the other one sunshine, looking so miserable. He'd heard it all. One of these days, Bethnal Green would do them a favour. Catch Perry mooning around drunk, and good riddance.

'What exactly was it you wanted to achieve, Helen? I mean, Miss West?'

Oh, ho ho, no signs of a democratic set-up here. We are all Mr, Mrs, Miss. She never let show her constant amusement at Redwood's frightful pomposity.

'Well, at this stage, not a lot, beyond the fact that this death is most unlikely to be accidental. Which means it could be criminal. The purpose of introducing you to Dr Hazel was to show I'm not alone in my view. If this should ever come to trial, he could act as an expert witness, but, for the moment, I only want your blessing to pay him to do further tests.'

'For what?'

'To show how long it takes to inhale twelve milligrammes of chloroform vapour. To see if a person could do that by themselves. If so, no case.'

'Doesn't look like much of a case whichever way you turn it,' he grumbled.

'Granted. But we have to know, don't we? And Dr Hazel won't charge much. He came here this morning for free.' Helen cast a glance at the budget sheets hidden beneath other papers on Redwood's desk, sorry for him, relieved, not for the first time, that she had avoided promotion.

'Right,' he said, looking at her with resigned exasperation.

'Keep it cheap. Oh, and . . .' Helen was halfway to the door. 'Check the chap's credentials, will you?'

She nodded, avoiding his eyes, unwilling to confess a suspicion that these credentials might not be entirely immaculate. She had nothing to base this suspicion on other than the knowledge that she liked Hazel and knew full well how rarely she liked anyone with a blameless past. To Redwood, for one gratifying moment, she was merely five foot four slender inches of deferential servant. Until she smiled.

'Don't waste time on it, Helen,' he snapped. 'Plenty of real cases here.'

A dance, Helen thought. The law is a long, slow, dance. You learn the minuet in stages and you never hurry. No room for a sense of emergency anywhere: never frighten the decision-makers.

The whole day had gone on too long.

'You made him do it, Mummy. You did, you did. So why should he say he's sorry? You made Dad go right back into that wall, you did, by shouting at him.'

'Tom, I told you to stay indoors. And Dad lost his temper. He wasn't just reversing his car, he was trying to reverse it into Uncle Pip's car, which was naughty, to say the least. He deserved to go into the wall.'

'He didn't mean it. Why would he do that?'

Tom could guess why Dad should, and sympathised. On the way home from school with Mum, he was arguing for the sake of arguing, still angry from the night before, without tears, simply cold recrimination. She put a hand on his shoulder as they walked down the Parade, but he shrugged it away, deliberately hurtful. She pretended not to notice. At least there was conversation, unlike this morning when silence had governed breakfast. Kim felt very old.

'Daddy was cross with Uncle Pip for interfering,' she said mildly. 'And I was very, very cross with him for not meeting you from school, then taking you off like that. Can't I go out, once in a while . . . Oh, never mind. Anyway, I'm sorry: I shouldn't have screamed. Neither should he, so we'll both say sorry. All right?'

'All right.' He kicked a paving stone, felt his satchel thump on his back, the metal helmet inside digging into his spine. He wanted to show her the wire helmet, unsure whether she deserved such privilege. The sulk was receding, started only because he was sick of being asked to see Mum's point of view and he knew he deserved a better reward. For being good, fielding off all Dad's questions, saying Mum was fine and no, she didn't go out with the chemist, or anyone else, and then all Mum did was scream at Dad. And have Uncle Pip put his arm round her, so now Dad would think he, Tom, was a liar. You never resolved anything with grown-ups. They never listened.

Mrs Beale stood at the door of her shop as they passed and Tom cringed, too late. 'Evening, Kim. Oh, there's Tom. How's my little man, then? Don't like parties too much, do we?'

'No, I'm afraid not.' Kim stopped to answer for him, laughed. Asked, 'How's things going then? How's your mother?' Got Tom off the hook of questions. She was careful to be nice to the neighbours, natural in any event since she was full of defensive kindness, but Tom never guessed how much she passed the time of day for his sake. To cure their isolation, make them accepted. A vain hope while Mrs Beale gazed at Kim's voluptuous figure with envy. Thinking almost aloud how a girl like that, as edible as ice-cream, couldn't possibly be up to any good.

'Heard anything more about Mr Carlton's wife, then?' asked Mrs Beale, retrieving from the shop front an apple softened by the Christmas lights, thrusting it at the boy. He thanked her with a mumble and put it in his satchel. Tom hated apples. 'No, nothing,' Kim said. 'I mean, there's nothing wrong or anything, but they don't seem able to work out what kind of heart attack. More than a month now, dreadful, isn't it? Poor Mr Carlton, can't even have a funeral.'

'Well, you look after him, sweetheart.' Mrs Beale, hungry for scandal, delivered a grotesque wink, which Kim ignored. They moved on.

'Oh, isn't she awful?' Kim muttered to Tom, and the agreement united them. He felt too old to take her hand, someone might see, so he clutched the sleeve of her coat instead.

'What does she mean, look after him?' he hissed, running to keep pace.

'Just that, darling, look after him. Like he looks after us.'

At this point of accord, Tom did not risk going any further. Resentment had a habit of draining away long before he had said what he wanted to say, asked what he wanted to know. Or dared venture to Mum how he hated Uncle Pip, for everything, really. Such as putting his arms round his mother and even more particularly for that awful moment in the shop when he refused to come out for Daniel. Daniel was something else. He had been on Tom's mind all day.

'Did Dan come in the shop today?'

'I didn't see him, but Pip says he came in for his prescription this morning, so he must be OK.' She had heard a little of the saga of Tom's errand of mercy, but not how abruptly he had been forestalled.

'So Uncle Pip was right, wasn't he? Nothing to worry about.'

Nothing at all, but Kim was afflicted by the vaguest discomfort, marring yesterday's bullishness, and the odd kind of catharsis there had been in screaming at her husband. Although she entrusted Tombo to Daniel from time to time and only out of necessity, she did not even really know where Daniel lived. Around and about; one of the clutch of bedsits above the pub, a stone's throw, an address seen often on his record, but never quite visualised.

'You never go indoors with Dan, do you, Tom?'

'Nope. He never asks me. He lives down this end. Doesn't take me there.'

'Well, if he asks you in, don't go, will you?'

He looked up in surprise. 'Daniel's a bit dirty, Mummy. He's all right, but I wouldn't want to go.'

Don't want to go. Pip had not wanted to go the evening before. Kim thought of that as they climbed the steps up to the flat, she irritated as ever by the lack of light, still unsure after a day's thought whether Pip's not wanting to leave after another cup of tea gave her a feeling of warmth, or whether the memory of that proprietorial hand round her shoulder made her cold. Let's face it, Kim, she told herself later, when Tom had yawned peacefully to bed halfway through a video and well beyond another battle over homework, let's face the fact that you could do very well with Mr Carlton. You'll soon be a qualified pharmacist, only another month until you can register, but no hope in hell of ever getting a shop of your own. Play your cards right and good old Pip would help you. All you'd have to do is love him a bit. Carry on where the wife left off, be looked after, Tom too. Do a bit of looking after herself, and go to bed with him, of course. There she stopped and sighed, pulled her dressing gown around herself defensively, huddled back into the depths of the second-hand sofa and remembered how futile it was to dwell for a minute on what Pip could provide. No use whatever her thinking she could even begin to string along some man she did not fancy, and the merest touch of Pip was enough to show her that however much she admired him for all that industry and enthusiasm, sex, God forbid, was another matter. She'd rather Duncan. And come to think of it, she'd not liked Pip shouting at Duncan, telling him to shove off. She could say what she liked – she could scream like a fishwife; Duncan was still her husband – but if anyone else interfered, even on her behalf, she resented the insult. 'No, my girl,' she grumbled to the electric fire, a thing of such ineffective ugliness she despised it along with all her lousy furniture, 'there aren't any easy ways. Wouldn't mind a bloody good cuddle, but not Pip. Ugh.' The thought chilled her. She got up to go to bed, late. Bed had been her destination more than an hour ago; the lights were out apart from the artificial glow of the fire, invisible outside, but all decisions to move had postponed themselves. The parade, visible from the living-room window, was lit but silent apart from one passing car a minute: behind her, on to the service road downstairs from the kitchen door, a stillness she could feel through the walls, punctuated by that scrabbling sound, only now beginning to register on a mind blurred by fatigue. A scratching at the window, then at the door, nothing visible shadowed through the glass or the net curtain. Kim stood between kitchen and living-room, para-lysed, listening, gazing at the handle of the kitchen door fixedly, almost willing it to move, imagining it did. If Tom stared long enough at a clock, he could see the hands move. Now her own eyes took in no more than a fraction of play on the door handle, a soft, scraping sound outside, insistent, audible with straining effort, undetectable to a careless ear, a background to her thoughts, she now remembered, for five minutes or more. She was suddenly cold; then hot in a damp sweat of fear which cooled into a trembling. Each of her hands gripped the opposite forearm, fingers digging deep into her own skin to still herself, injecting pain enough to control the desire to shout.

'Duncan! Is that you? Well, fuck off.' The silence was omi-nous; into it crept the continued sound of the creeping scrape, no footsteps. The handle of the door was still.

'Duncan, don't be silly. I'm giving you ten seconds to go. One, two . . . or I'll call your boss . . . three, four . . .'

She spoke loudly enough for him to hear, softly enough not to waken the boy, spitting the numbers out of her mouth clearly and very slowly, as much as anything to calm herself, stop herself screaming her message. Then she walked towards the light switch, flicked it, opened the back door with a violent fling.

There was nothing, a big blank space of nothing. Silence, no car, no light other than her own streaming into the darkness. The pitted site beyond, a crane punctuating the horizon.

'Duncan?' she called again. Then, more doubtfully, 'Daniel?'

Still silence, but drifting around the concrete balcony, scraping against the rough surface, a white polythene bag, glowing in the light, fluttering in the breeze which had wafted it upwards from the rubbish in the dirty road, moving around like a live thing, frisking in the tunnel the balcony formed. No one hung washing here: the dirt defeated everything. Kim slumped against the door-way, dizzy with relief. A bag, a bloody bag, rustling. Moving the door handle, no, there had not really been any movement. Only a bag in a breeze. She closed the door, wanting to believe what she had cause to believe, put her hands over her ears, in case she might hear footsteps.

Bailey parked his car at one end of the grim service road, feeling a little sheepish and wondering what he would say if some police car, not from his own station, should ask what he was doing loitering in these parts. Looking for what, sir? A bit of nice Asian tart, sir? You're on the wrong side for the posh Chinese restaurant, sir. No, no, of course not, but what would he say? I'm out looking for a rogue copper, don't make me laugh. He did not doubt he would cope with such questions and also that he would be able to avoid them. The number of patrol cars was pathetically small, and the service road less threatening than it seemed. Unlike Tombo, large bins, nooks and crannies held few fears for Bailey. He seemed to have developed a sixth sense, like a heat-seeking missile, for the dangerous presence of human warmth; a sense which would send him, with apparent aimlessness to the other side of the street, avoiding the corner glowing with malevolence. Bailey had several scars, kneecaps, elbows, the back of the skull, the ribs and the psyche, knew very well how to fight and what it was like to lose control. Which was precisely why he preferred to avoid the conflict. The same knowledge influenced his dealings with Duncan, younger than himself by more than fifteen summers; at the age when he could not have been taught anything either, would always have known best. There had been no point then, in some wiser, older sergeant saying, wouldn't do that if I were you, or I should give up while the going's good, boy; or, when a woman's left, she's gone, old son, find another. He knew he would not have listened then any more than Duncan would listen now. They had spoken at length, the two of them, Duncan attentive to the warnings, the advice to woo and accept his wife if he wanted her back, taking it in like a balm on the skin, not really listening at all, the same obsessive jealousy as much in evidence at the end as it had been at the beginning, determined to go back. Two pints and more hypocrisy, Bailey well aware that he was saying, do as you should, but not as I did. Duncan was not murderous, Bailey decided; but as an officer capable of conspicuous bravery and equally conspicuous drinking, a man with a mission, little reflective sense and no other humanising influences than a one-time wife, he was possibly dangerous and certainly a nuisance. Duncan's problem was, in part, having nowhere else to go and nothing else to do but haunt his woman and embarrass everyone. Duncan came from the same streets as most of those he arrested; they did not read books. He needed the blunt approach of being found in the act and stopped like a criminal.

Which was why Bailey was walking down this road in his brothel-creeping shoes, soundless and almost invisible. The wind whipped rubbish in his face, the detritus of neglect and a neighbourhood of which few were proud. There was another cause for concern in his active mind, another cause for feeling ever so faintly hypocritical. All that stuff he said to Helen about never interfering, let be what will be, let people find out for themselves and don't sweat if you can't help. Load of rot, in view of what he was doing. He might have said, I am paid by the Commissioner to keep my men working, but he doubted the Commissioner expected this. Out at midnight, catching an obsessive husband who happened to be a policeman, in the hope of confronting him with his own stupidity, making him ashamed to be no better than a slightly ridiculous prowler.

    Bailey ducked behind one of the enormous bins, an instinct, nothing more, squinting towards the door and the stairs where he had never been, the exact location deduced from inspecting the front of Herringbone Parade. Kimberley Perry's flat, almost like all the other ugly flats. Next door to the chemist's flat, so close an agile man could cross from one cumbersome concrete balcony to the next. A car parked, without lights, next to the chemist, not Duncan's damaged car: a man walking away round the corner, an energetic walk, no skulking to it, no conscience either. Duncan, he thought, without being sure. Anyone really, but a windcheater like Duncan's, Duncan's brisk walk which Bailey had seen him maintain, drunk or sober. More silence. The figure rounded the corner, disappeared. Then Bailey heard the moaning.

'No, no, no. Too much . . . he did. Help me, uncle . . .'

The sound of it was borne to him on the wind, a hopeless sound of one human being not in agony but *in extremis*. He followed the pathetic half weeping from where he stood, into an alcove which formed an entrance to the yard behind a fruit and vegetable shop. Bailey could tell roughly which shop by the smell of vegetable, something reminiscent of a market stall after hours, or a school kitchen, a dead leaf smell, sweet rather than rotten. Mixed, as he bent over him, with the smell of this figure sitting with his head on his crossed arms, over one raised knee, the other leg lying as if he had already abandoned part of himself. The head, when Bailey placed one hand under the chin to raise it gently, was that of an old man, the indeterminate age only betrayed by the thick, lank hair. There was no protest against such summary handling: the breath snorting from the mouth was full of decay. Bailey squatted by his side.

'What's the matter, lad? Not well?'

'Oh God, oh God, oh God. Him, he hit me. Hit me. Gave me the wrong stuff, too much. Oh God. Don't know why. Him and his back room. Saw him come back.'

Bailey did not know what he was talking about in this gasping mumble of words, asked because it seemed what the man wanted.

'Who hit you? Who came back?' He could see eyes, glittering.

'Him. I saw him. Doesn't matter now. Help me.'

There were rules in a dozen police manuals about dealing with vagrants, drug addicts, filthy specimens in poor conditions. No artificial respiration without a tube, call for ambulance and only handle with rubber gloves, carefully. They scratch, they bite, they infect with Aids, hepatitis, they must never go inside a car which is not equipped. Bailey knew the rules: he had taught them. He embraced the man, warmed him for a minute, shocked to find thin cotton clothes with only a raggy sweater for warmth, spoke carefully into his ear.

'Wait here for a minute.' One claw-like hand clutched his coat.

He detached it gently, ran down to the end of the service road where his car was surreptitiously parked and drove back level with the man. He picked him up, and fed him gently into the back seat of the car, a manoeuvre that took minutes since the body was heavy. Saliva fell from the open mouth on to Bailey's coat: as he put one hand over the head to protect the man's skull from the lintel of the car, he felt on the back a swelling beneath the sticky hair. Bailey could have knocked on a door, run for a phone, taken a number of other options which would avoid the future embarrassment of explaining his own errand in this godforsaken service road, but none of them crossed his mind. For someone needing a hospital, this was simply the quickest way. But in shutting the door, and driving away by the swiftest route to the nearest casualty, Bailey sensed he was already too late. There was a rattle in the throat of the man behind, and he fell over in the back seat, covered by Bailey's coat, his face pallid, profoundly unconscious, the car's warmth scented with death.

Chapter Seven

'Tra la la, fiddly di dee, what a mess. The breath of life is the stuff of life, so it is. Without which one becomes a stiff who doesn't give a stuff. One forgets how much fun this was, a lifetime of drugs. Don't breathe now, there's a good boy. What a jolly time we're having here, Hazel, my dear. Tinkering, and being paid. Avoiding temptation, of course. Never did like the smell of this stuff, but ether, well ether was different.'

Sean Hazel turned away from the bench where he worked and took a deep breath, then fished in his pockets for a cigarette on the right side and the small hip flask of brandy on the left. Withdrawing both hands simultaneously, he regarded the contents with puzzlement, unsure which to broach first, weighing the pleasure of one against the other. He put both down, easily distracted, picked up instead a copy of *Playboy* from the opposite bench, a magazine absorbed with relentless enthusiasm by the lab technician who did not care who knew what he read. Flicking over the pages, Hazel was puzzled and alarmed by the dimensions of the women in the photos. 'Glory be to God,' he muttered to himself. 'They'd eat you alive.' And he wondered vaguely about the lab technician's preferences. Behind him, there was the steady sound of disembodied breathing, eerie in the emptiness.

He sat far away from the bench on which he had rigged an automatic ventilator, a device which mimicked human breathing, pulled paper and pen towards him, then wrote in his indecipherable hand, dictating to himself as he went, 'This is what I did last night. First I folded an ordinary, large, yellow duster in various ways and poured chloroform on it, just to see how much it would hold. About fifty milligrammes at best, if the duster was soaking not dripping, but difficult to handle. Holding the duster over my own face, I breathed it as long as I could, but within a few min-utes, while I was feeling dizzy and sick, the whole of the chloroform had evaporated. A heavyish concentration like this is rather unpleasant, and if the drug was being used for frivolous purposes, pleasure in other words, I doubt anyone would use that much. It might, however, have been sufficient to knock out a small woman, though not enough to keep her knocked out for more than a minute or two. Chloroform is many times heavier than air; much of it is wasted by falling around the face . . . Oh God,' he interrupted himself, 'even I find this complicated to explain. Now what the hell did I do next? Ah yes.' He walked three steps to the left, two to the right, counting.

'I took a sample of my own blood and had that lab technician test it today. Barely a hint of chloroform, a mere milligramme. And I certainly didn't feel randy, but I suppose that depends on the company.' He chuckled to himself. 'So you don't get anything like twelve milligrammes aboard even by the most determined sniffing, and since it evaporates so quick, you'd never get that much from one duster full, not ever.' He began to pace round the room, continuing his lecture. 'In fact, it occurs to me that it would take about twenty minutes' solid inhaling to get that much aboard, you just couldn't be faster. But looking at the books, old boy, and all the recorded levels, the average person would be out for the count, temporarily, that is, after five minutes inhaling a concen-tration like this, and five minutes was roughly how long the old anaesthetist would take to put them in the land of nod, holding them down too. Now, Miss West, and Mr Red Pig, how the hell did this woman take in the rest? Self-administered whilst already unconscious? Novel, but not possible. She could only take in twelve milligrammes if someone held the same duster over her face while she was unconscious, then poured on to it another fifty milligrammes, and then another . . . Whoever did this held the chloroform vehicle above the face and away from the skin, no burns, no contact with the mouth, you see . . .' He turned back to the lung machine, breathing with the sound of a regular heartbeat. He wished the sound of breathing had been as reliable in every

patient he had put to sleep, but this was simply a machine, pushing air in and out. 'No heart, my dear,' he said, patting it. 'No
anxieties, no lungs affected by a lifetime's fagends, etcetera,
etcetera. But in a little while, I shall measure, if I'm sober enough,
the levels of chloroform round this mouth which has been breathing in this stuff for a quarter of an hour . . . Then I'll think of a
way to put into words what that bugger did . . .'

He looked at his watch, turned off the ventilator. The whole
thing would be done again tomorrow. Over the mouth of the
machine he had placed the mask, a souvenir from former times,
the conventional anaesthetic mask. Covered in gauze, to be soaked
with chloroform or ether, different thicknesses of gauze for each.
He remembered; he remembered well. The Schimmelbusch mask
was the one he liked most. An oval of thick wire with crossed
struts and a rim to catch liquid. The one that looked like a helmet.
Hazel sighed. He had last used this in the war with bombs falling
around him. Buried bombs, memories and now disinterred ideas.

'Helen? Sorry to wake you, but . . .'

'What time is it?' Bailey always knew the time, as if a clock was
placed at the back of his eyes.

'Only two in the morning. Not very civilised, but . . .'

'Are you all right? You're not hurt, are you?'

There were times when he loved her particularly, for making
the obvious enquiry and failing to be annoyed. For sounding
asleep, like a person talking from the far end of a tunnel, but
responding without impatience.

'No, I'm fine. It could wait until morning.'

'No, it could not, or you wouldn't have rung now, would you?
What is it?'

'Oh, nothing.' Self-deprecation, an automatic downgrading of
emotion was a feeling they both shared, and one she understood
perfectly.

'Nothing . . . but I went to that street, you know, Herringbone
whatever. Where your chemist lives. To look for the sergeant
who's mentioned in your report, just to see if I might forestall his

arrest for loitering round after his wife, make a fool of him before a dozen others tried it. But I found a man instead. Dying, I think, drug overdose.'

'So you picked him up, I suppose?' Helen asked, knowing this was exactly what Bailey would have done. 'Blew your cover?'

'Yes, of course. Took him to Casualty, too late, I think. Can't have been very old, looked older. Left him there, comatose. Bit of a mess.'

She knew then the purpose of the call. In the face of meaningless, wasteful death, Bailey became angry, bewildered, moved for a while at least, in a fog of grief and fury.

'Want to come over? Or shall I come to you?'

'My car's warm. And I'm dressed.'

'Get a clean shirt then, see you in ten minutes. Drive carefully.'

The instruction was lightly given. Bailey drove with a racer's flair, but careless speed was a symptom of rage. She knew him, she thought, fairly well, when he was not a stranger. Began to guess how it took the cold breath of tragedy, the casual brutality of his own native streets, to bring Bailey back out of the doldrums and into life.

Kim enjoyed working alone in the shop. Pip chose lunchtimes to leave her in sole control, since it was only then that the morning trade from the doctors' surgeries dried. Between ten and twelve, there would be a steady stream of people, clutching their sheets of prescription paper which they handed over to the pharmacist together with a small fee in return for lotions, potions and pills. Pip stuck the prescription forms on a stake, like a short order cook in a kitchen, and they dealt with them in sequence. Kim could do everything but dispense direct to the public until her admission to the Pharmaceutical Society, which was imminent. Patients and customers did not understand when she said, 'Come back later, I can get it ready for you, but Mr Carlton has to check it, sorry.' 'Why?' they said. 'Well that's the way it is, I'm afraid,' for another month, and as far as she was concerned herself, the time would not be too soon. This morning she felt as if she had taken the soporific cough medicine which had such an exaggerated effect on her, but recognising that she was simply tired did nothing to help her cope with the effects, which were, irritation, an acute awareness of Pip's bossiness, and something she could only describe as a longing to escape, simply to something different. That mesmeric building site and all the rubbish in the streets, she told herself; rubbish creating ghosts which only died with the early-morning rumble of the cement mixer over the road, all these sights and sounds which made her feel imprisoned, while logic would tell her this was not imprisonment at all. Kim was not given to introspection: there was no time. This extra awareness of everything was unusual. Tom had been sweet this morning, making up for his previous sourness in that way of his, showing her some treasure picked up from the street. A wire helmet, someone's idea of fancy dress which she had not appreciated. And then Daniel, scheduled to appear for the school run, had failed to materialise.

All of this together created the disaffection, rising slowly after Pip went off to see some drug firm representative and left her alone. Facing her at the counter, a small old lady was shaking her prescription and trying to proffer gifts in a bag.

'For Mr Pip,' she kept saying. 'He'll want these, he will, he will.'

'Want what?' Kim asked, irritated by the customer's insistence and her own inability to help. 'What will he want?'

'These,' said the woman, her voice sinking as if about to impart a disgraceful secret, but still clutching the brown paper bag. 'This stuff. He said I had to bring it back if we had too much, and now, poor sod, he doesn't need it.' She leant forward, confidentially, beckoned Kimberley towards her with one crooked finger. 'And I found some other stuff too. From when Dad died.'

'What?' said Kim, desperately seeking clues, but already guessing. Pip had so many devoted, but harassed ladies, often old, not necessarily wise. He delivered to them in person, their medicines and their support stockings; they shared secrets and

jokes to which she could never be party, jealous with his influence and his popularity, never letting her near so many of his
own favourites, she suddenly realised with shock. Nor near those
who crept in like this specimen, armed with something rattling in
a bag. Leftover potions, the sort of poisons and medicines all
members of the public were encouraged to take back to their
pharmacist if any of them should prove surplus to requirement.
Especially those few, termagant carers of the terminally ill, who
were armed, for a short time at least, with the worst of the poisons. Heroin, perhaps, morphine sometimes, milder derivatives
more often. Old-fashioned remedies in new-fashioned capsules,
delivered as a last-ditch or very short-term remedy for those in
acute pain or near the end, those who would not or could not get
in the ambulance. The last brigade who thought of the hospital
as their grandfathers thought of the poor house. There were a
few round here. Survivors of a war, remembering desolation still,
persons to whom the welfare state meant nothing more than
access to a doctor who should never be bothered because doctors
were too important to be bothered. Or the Asians, to whom care
of their own in whatever state was a matter of intense pride along
with a fear of hospital. They did not leave each other, these
people, and though Kim did not understand them she had come
to admire them for their dogged, obdurate, sometimes stupid
courage. They waited, they obeyed, they gave heroin obediently
to their dying, took any advice which meant he or she would not
leave home, accepted the death. And then, like this scarf-swathed
woman, who trusted Pip as she would have trusted God, continued to obey local customs and brought back the remnants of the
medicine. Looking at the face, resigned, shrewd, trusting, all in
one, Kim felt humble. Despite her qualification in pharmacy,
she felt stupid and ignorant.

'Ah, I see,' she ventured, more kindly. 'I think I remember. You
looked after your uncle, cancer, wasn't it. You wouldn't let them
take him in . . . I'm sorry, I didn't know.'

'Can't be helped,' said the woman brusquely. 'But I don't want
this stuff in the house. The cat might get it. And I want some

medicine for myself. Night Nurse, it's called. Got a prescription from the doctor.'

'Do you want capsules, or the linctus?'

'Linctus, I said. The other doesn't work.'

It was on the tip of Kim's tongue to say, you don't actually need a prescription for any kind of cough linctus and the capsules are made of exactly the same thing, but, sensing that anything prescribed by the doctor would be preferable to something bought over the counter, she simply wrapped the bottle carefully and presented the parcel like a prize. In turn the woman handed over her own.

'Morphine, he said it was. Fat lot of good it did too.'

On her way out of the shop, the woman dislodged an arrangement of toothpaste with her bag on wheels. She carried on regardless, letting the tubes cascade to the floor behind her and Kim moved forward to tidy the mess, stopping as she realised she was still holding the paper bag. The possession of it made her feel guilty, as if she had just intruded on some secret, and when the door sounded to let in another customer, she started, stuffed the packets back and retreated behind the counter without looking to see who was coming in. With the bag still in her hand and cheeks slightly flushed, she faced the customer with an air of confidence. Smiled in relief.

'Dr Gupta. Nice to see you. Did you want Pip for something, only he's not here.'

He turned on her his bird-like, nut-brown face, then looked back towards the street, and jerked his head to where the woman could be seen standing on the pavement, uncertain where to go next. 'Poor soul,' he said. 'No one to look after now. Should have been a nurse. Now, what did I want?'

Kim laughed at him. Dr Gupta was sanguine, incessantly busy, frequently vague, and rarely came to see the pharmacy which served his patients and his practice. When he did, it was always for a purpose, such as giving a word of warning about one of the patients who was not above playing doctor and pharmacist off against one another in order to obtain the medicine he or she privately thought appropriate. 'Ah yes,' he said, 'I remember. Daniel. I'm a bit puzzled about Daniel.'

'Why? Isn't he well?' Dr Gupta looked surprised and consulted his watch as if the dial could give him important information.

'You could say unwell. Dead, actually. Didn't you know? But then there's no reason for you to know. Hospital phoned me this morning. Someone brought him in. Methadone overdose, they think. Or he might have taken tranquillisers along with his methadone, lethal sort of mixture. Obviously fell over, which didn't help. Large haematoma on the back of his head, but not fatal. Only the methadone. What bothered me was where he got the extra that pushed him over. I know it wouldn't be here, but it did occur to me that Pip might know if he was going somewhere else.'

'Oh.' She was shocked, felt close to tears. Daniel had flitted in and out of their lives like a wraith, but he was still Daniel and the abruptness of his departure was difficult to comprehend. Kim slipped into the dispensary and pulled out Daniel's record. A daily collection of oral methadone, without fail. Nothing untoward. She came back to the counter slowly.

'He can't have got it from here. We order his stuff exactly as we need it. You know how strict they are. Dan only had his regular amount this week, same as usual. We never have a surplus microgram of anything on the premises. Pip says it's too risky even if it wasn't illegal. That's the one thing he stresses. Keep the barest minimum of poisons.'

Even as she spoke, one eye on the paper bag beneath the counter, Kim knew she was not telling the truth. Somewhere on these premises, Pip could easily have a cache of poisons, little bits of heroin, physeptone otherwise known as methadone, morphine. Returns, they were called; all those little bits brought back after the funeral, like today's offering; tranquillisers no longer needed, a selection of drugs given to the chemist for safekeeping. Pip always handled all of that: she had been excluded, but what he did with the surplus, Kim never knew. They abided by the strictest of rules with everything ordered, but on the disposal of returns, there was no real control.

'What's more,' she said, putting conviction into her voice, 'we've been looked over by the police recently. Since Mrs Carlton died, you know.' She remembered that, too. The officers had teased her, never ventured into the sanctum of Pip's back dispensary. He had steered them away and she had helped.

Dr Gupta sighed. 'Oh dear, oh dear. I didn't think he could have got anything from here, that's not what I was asking. Pip's far too efficient. Did he go anywhere else, that's what I want to know? Could he have bought it from a friend, for Christ's sake? Makes no difference now, anyhow. Get Pip to ring me, will you? Not that I like to bother him. Poor fellow. Poor Margaret. He must miss her.'

She had been thinking ill of Pip this morning, but just then she felt the more familiar loyalty, remembered what he had told her. 'Oh, he keeps as cheerful as he can. But didn't he have a lot to put up with? I mean, I never knew she was an addict . . .'

Dr Gupta cocked his head at an angle in another, puzzled look at his watch. 'Addict? You must be thinking of someone else. Margaret Carlton? Treated her for ten years. Hypochondriac maybe, always hoping there was some magic drug to improve her life, fascinated by pharmacists on that account and willing to try anything, but addict never. The idea. Anyway, you won't need any more methadone for Daniel. Sorry about that.'

He was a little man, on little plump legs. As he raced for the door with characteristic speed, he dislodged the toothpaste stand she had just re-erected. She watched him go. Sat down to think, leaving the stock, with the promises of perfect dental whiteness, littering the floor. Teeth did not seem to matter. Daniel's teeth, cleaned intermittently, had been yellow, but Daniel's eyes inquisitively bright. Always seeking, always curious, knew his own dosage to the last detail. Not a careless man for all his other afflictions, only occasionally sly. Kim wanted to weep for him but found herself dry-eyed.

Bailey found the unfamiliar police station slightly intimidating. Not because he was walking down a yellow corridor of the kind

which was quite familiar to him, or knocking on a door and entering a room which was almost a carbon copy of his own, or finding
himself afflicted by awkwardness; all of that was par for the
course. What unnerved him was that tic in his left eye which told
him he was breaking one of his own rules, perhaps pulling rank a
little, something a good leader of men did not do. Never interfere
in another man's case without wishing on yourself a very cold
shoulder, and do not let curiosity rule the head. Instinct is a dirty
word. He knocked and entered Inspector Collins's office, feeling
every inch the interloper he was. Honesty was the only way out.

'Sorry, Jack. Got a minute?' Detective Inspector Collins looked
up from his telephone, replaced the receiver in its cradle and
stood up. There was no need for that. Between his own rank and
that of his visitor, the difference was less apparent and far less
abused than lower down the line. No one saluted any more and
good riddance.

'Listen, this case you have. Margaret Carlton. I've got two
interests to put on the table. One, my sergeant, Perry, is married
to the woman who works in Carlton's shop. I went to pick him up
from there last night and found a chap in the street, which you
might hear about, so I thought I'd tell you first. I want to know
about this man and I gather he was a customer of your Mr
Carlton. Secondly, you're dealing with Miss West in the CPS,
with whom I live, most of the time. Which means I have no right
to know anything about the whole bloody business, even what I do
know, but I want to know. You can tell me to fuck off if you like.
Or I might be able to help. If you like.'

The delivery was brusque, the patter swift. The timing, by
accident, was perfect. Collins felt he was swimming in treacle.
His face, almost as severe, but younger than Bailey's own, broke
into a smile.

'Sit down, Geoffrey, will you? I was just about to report to
your lady friend. About an alibi.'

For one absurd minute, Bailey thought the man was talking
about himself.

'Whose alibi? No one's accused of anything.'

'Carlton's alibi for the night his wife probably died. I've decided I don't like this sedulous little bastard. Too keen to please. Can't stand people with blameless lives. Forty years looking after his mother, then looking after a wife. No wonder he was staying in a hotel the night she copped it. Being wined and dined by some company making contraceptives. But if he'd wanted, he could have got home overnight with no one to see. Plenty of time. In theory.'

'In theory. Why do people who make contraceptives give dinners to chemists?'

'Why do you think? So next time I buy a rubber, which I don't have the luck to need, I'll know some shopkeeper has been given a perk to sell it to me. Funny line of business, pharmaceuticals. The clean end of dirty.'

Bailey grunted, grinned.

'As if we can talk,' he said, 'about dirty and clean. Tell me, this pharmacist, did he . . .?'

'What? Murder his wife? Naa. No chance. Something funny, though. I've been trying to find someone who knows anything about chloroform, but they're all dead. I don't understand any of this. Does your lady friend think he did it?'

'Seems so. From a long way off. And I think she's also found some bloke who knows about chloroform. You're right. Doctors in that category have to be pegging on a bit.'

'Shame. She did seem, your lady . . . Miss West . . . She's not a Ms, is she? I always get worried when they call themselves Ms. Sounds like a wasp. Anyway, she did seem to have got a bee in the bonnet.'

Bailey felt more than a little guilty. Talking about Helen felt like treachery, but needs must: he was loyal, but pragmatic.

'Well, yes, she has a bit. The bee in the bonnet I mean, but she has this uncanny knack of being right.'

'Bangs on about work a bit, does she, if you'll excuse the expression?' Collins was frankly curious about what it might be like to live at such close quarters with one of the legal breed, even an attractive one like that. Solicitors were funny animals, best lodged in a zoo, on display for purely educational purposes.

'Well, she likes work, you know. Very conscientious. And anyway, you know, women . . . All the same.' Again he felt more than a hint of treachery. Never mind: Helen would understand; she was a pragmatist too. Collins laughed.

'Yes. Women. Ever asked yourself why we say bee in a bonnet, never bee in a trilby? Or a titfer? Or a helmet? Because only women wear bonnets. Obvious isn't it? And go on like that. Anyway, thinking of proof, fancy a pint? I'll tell you all I know. You're welcome. Shouldn't take long. I could write it on the back of a postage stamp. And none of it secret. Women.'

Bailey thought of his own office and the longing for a pint grew steadily. The CID room in his station was taboo, struck with a fever peculiar to the time of year and quite equal in fervour to that of a newly formed murder squad. Fourteen detectives, including three women, were discussing, with all the intensity and argument of a parliamentary debate, the final details of the Christmas party to be held next day. Bailey was not supposed to know. He liked Collins.

'Fine. I tell you what, since it's so close, why don't we take in the pub on Herringbone Parade? Close enough, could be useful.'

'Bloody awful place, but OK, if you insist. The beer's not bad. Only the people.'

There were no signs of conventional Christmas weather as they left, lowered themselves into Collins's car in a back yard identical to the gloomy area behind Bailey's almost identical station, and drove the half-mile to Herringbone Parade. Collins left his Ford Granada parked on a yellow line, saying, 'Oh stuff it', as he hauled himself out of the driver's seat and led the way at a fast trot towards the Lion and Unicorn, last remnant of old architecture on one corner. He was obviously having a bad day, Bailey thought, whereas he himself was beginning to have a fairly good one. As days went, and up until now, this one had ranged from tedious to downright dull. Part of him envied Collins, a man still allowed to ask questions, still relatively free of the endless meetings which came with managerial rank.

'See what I mean?' Collins asked when they were safely ensconced. 'About the people?'

Bailey privately thought Collins was wrong about the pub, which was, frankly, nice, with its etched glass and brass rails around the bar, worn chairs badly covered in plastic disguised as leather, a flowered carpet faded by dirt and use into something his own eyes found entirely acceptable. The reason for the dirt was easily apparent. Outside, it was market day, and although a subdued market day, where the awnings on the stalls flapped in the wind and the cold bit through clothing, the road was dirty. And this was a pre-war pub, an unbombed island surviving rebuilding, made for a time when pubs weren't supposed to be clean. Hats and scarves carried indoors with the inevitable refrain, 'Brass monkey weather, this. Fucking cold . . .', but none as dirty as the navvies playing cards in the corner. Now they, Bailey thought, were really dirty, coated in mud from head to foot, yet indifferent to the fact as if what they wore on the front of their donkey jackets was no more than one extra layer of insulation. Mud and dust flaked round their feet where the working boots could not be distinguished from the trouser cuffs. He looked at them, drinking casually, beer with spirit chasers, three rounds each and back to the mud. Only an hour to work that off. Steady drinker though he was, Bailey knew he could not compete. He and Collins were both conspicuous because of their suits. He saw the latter adjusting his tie, caught his eye and grinned.

'Well we are on the edge of the City,' he said. 'We might be mistaken for gents. Or management consultants.'

'No way,' said Collins. 'Well you might. Not me. I look like a brick shithouse dressed in a suit. Feel a bit of a wally, too. No way,' he repeated. He took a long gargle from the pint, his throat working until the glass was half empty, then put it down, obviously relieved.

'Anyway,' he went on, 'the bloody City with one square mile of a thousand banks might be next bloody door, but Jesus, it's a hundred miles from here. The City gets rebuilt; this just gets patchwork. Bet these geezers don't come down here to do their shopping. Anyway, we haven't got the right kind of suits. Mine cost fifty quid. Probably fell off the back of a lorry. Fair bit of that sort of gear passes through this pub, as it happens. Got mine in a sale.'

'You must have canvassed this place before, by the sound of things?'

'Oh yes, course. Bit of local gossip never comes amiss. Like Coronation Street, down here. Only don't go repeating none of it to your DC Perry, might give him ideas. Had a word, we did, with a few of the shops round here. They got their ideas about Mr Carlton and Perry's missus. Quite a disappointment she is, as well. Not fulfilling local expectation if you see what I mean. Lady in the grocer's shop tells me she expected someone to catch them in bed long ago, even before his old woman snuffed it, but she never plays, Mrs Perry, I mean. Doesn't even seem to know that old man Carlton had the hots for her as soon as she stepped in the door. Too busy to notice, but she was the only one didn't. They like her round here. As much as they like anyone who hasn't lived here for ever.'

Bailey grunted. Collins took that as a benign hint, plucked from nowhere and told the story from the beginning.

'Anyway, like I said. Christ, that went quick . . .' The straight-sided pint glass was empty. Bailey did the honours and bought himself a whisky, to go with the half. He had never really liked beer beyond the first round and the habits of the navvies were catching.

'Ta. It's a bugger, this case, you know. Because it isn't even a case, and whatever there was got screwed up in the first place. Tried to explain to your brief, but there it is. Police get called to break down a door because some wife's gone AWOL, find her dead, but laid out so nice you'd think the undertaker'd already got there. So he radios in and gets the body shifted. Accidental death. Why not? No photos, no forensic, no nothing. No one's broke in, no injury, no struggles, right? Pathologist just out of school, doesn't give a fuck, does the necessary and gets a surprise. Some old-fashioned drug he's heard of but don't know nothing about.

Funny, he thinks, but not enough to kill her, I don't know why she was snorting it, do I? Which is what Davies thinks too, bit worried for his precious little chemist. Why? Because he's the best there is round here. Delivers to little old ladies, he does, not that anyone pays him for it, but he seems a good bloke. Time for all of them, can't get anyone here to say a bad word, know what I mean? Wife a bossy-boots, not unpopular, but not great either. Tries to stop our Mr Carlton from delivering to the old ladies, ordering in stock which don't make a profit, all that kind of stuff. Swept the floor when the builders came in looking for blister cream and rubber gloves, bit of a pain really, but not so bad anyone hated her, kind in her own way. Thinks her husband the best thing since sliced bread, absolutely worships the ground he treads on. There you go.' He took another, extraordinarily long draught at the beer in the glass. Bailey sat silent. He knew very well when not to interrupt a flow. Either beer or information, especially from a colleague having a bad day.

'So, as I said, we're fucking well scuppered. Because we never got the body, see? Because nobody looked in the first place and after that it's all over bar the shouting if they don't. We can't prove anything from the scene and by the time anyone's gone back for a second look, Carlton or whoever has had plenty of time to hoover the place, remove hairs, semen, anything like that. Not that there was any sign of sex on her, not a trace. Only he forgot to take the chloroform from under his kitchen sink, which was why he had to tell us about it. And his alibi's not watertight. Which is all we have.'

'What if someone can prove the chloroform couldn't be self-administered? I mean, if it could be shown someone must have given it to her?'

'So what? It means we really would be looking for a murderer, but who? She could have let in the local drug addict, that chap you found, and yes, I did know about it. She could have been knocking off one of the builders. Kimberley Perry could have slipped in and killed her, for that matter.'

'You don't think so?'

'No, as it happens, although she could have got in. There were spare keys to the Carltons' flat in the pharmacy, and she had keys for the shop because she had to open up for herself and a relief chemist while he was gallivanting away, but she says she didn't know about the flat keys. Anyway, I've given up thinking.'

The straight glass was empty apart from a tracing of froth. Collins eased himself from the rickety table and over to a gap in the bar with the skill born of long practice, returning with two identical orders. The beer did not appear to have touched him. That's what we've both learned, Bailey thought; how to drink. Pity DC Perry had missed out on such invaluable knowledge.

'What do I say to your Miss West, then?' Collins asked with mild belligerence. 'How do I calm her down? Sorry, mustn't make chauvinistic remarks. Maybe she doesn't need calming down. Men and women created equal and all that. I've been sent on a course so I know. Told me not to denigrate the fair sex or call them rude names. Wait a minute, that's not the same Helen West who got beaten up by some psychopath? Coupla years since? Your case, wasn't it?'

'Yes,' said Bailey uncomfortably.

'Stone me,' said Collins. 'The poor cow.'

They parted on good terms, Collins sympathetic, if slightly incredulous when Bailey said he would linger where he was and shop on the market.

'Apples and oranges, potatoes, that kind of thing,' he said.

'And a few pills from the chemist?' Collins asked, his whole face a question mark.

'Maybe. If you don't mind.'

'Nope. Not this time. Tread on my toes any time you like as long as you tell me before it hurts.'

'Thanks,' said Bailey.

Tom Perry, on strict instructions from his mother which applied, and were often ignored, on any of the rare days she could not arrange for him to be met, boarded the bus slightly ahead of the crowd leaving school, sat downstairs near the door and clutched the handrail until Herringbone Parade hove into sight. Then he ran down the road like a lamplighter, jumping over the rubbish which heralded the end of the market, closing down amid shouts and wind and darkness. His eyes darted left and right, looking for Daniel. Daniel, greeted with indifference, but somehow necessary to life, was always out here on market days, hoping for a tip, but it was difficult to see. Always so dark; you went out in darkness to be the first at school, you came back in the dark and you never, ever became used to being in the dark.

By contrast, the shop made him twitch, an effect he noticed in others all the time. They came in here, blinking like moles, all except Mummy, who never minded the light, only complained about headaches and drank more tea to forestall the next, never noticing anything. He sat on the high stool by the counter, wishing she would give him the key and let him go home out of sight, eating a sweet, bored as usual. Sometimes he tested her, like now, holding a book upside-down to see if she would notice while a short queue formed at the counter. Tom rummaged in his torn satchel for entertainment, looking for another of the sweets swopped for apples, noticing that the metal helmet, which he carried everywhere, had worn an extra hole in the fabric. He took the thing out, laid it on his knee, and continued to forage elbow deep in the mess in the bottom of his bag. Mummy did the same with hers. Pip came out to the counter, speaking across Tom's head.

'Here you are, Mrs Jones: three times a day, if you please . . .' His eyes fell on the helmet.

'Where'd you get that thing, Tom, old boy?' The tone was jovial, the expression fixed in a smile.

'Outside. At the back, I think. Maybe it was somewhere else. Don't know.' He wanted to say, what's it to you where I got it, but any words, even tame words like these, provided the chance to put a sneer in his voice and imply the insolence he felt.

'What a strange contraption. Thought you might have made it at school. Can I look?'

Tom's hands tightened on the metal hat he was going to give to Daddy.

'No,' he said, and pulled a face.

Pip smiled and shrugged. 'Suit yourself, old boy, suit your-self.' He leant forward, and pinched Tom's cheek playfully. Tom continued to smile, even when Pip's red fingerprints remained livid on his skin. He fingered the metal, slowly, to stop himself yelping. Pip still stood there; it seemed imperative to behave as normal.

'OK, then, at least tell me where you got it. Interesting.'

Tom thought wildly. His mother was in earshot and he remembered the slapping from the last time he'd collected rubbish.

'Daniel gave it me.'

'Are you sure?'

'Course I'm sure.' He was beginning to shout and the louder he spoke the more he believed himself. Daniel never cared what anyone thought: let Daniel take the blame. He was immune.

The eyes which held his own finally faltered, and turned away with a look of obscure satisfaction. 'That's right,' said Pip. 'I might have seen Daniel with something like that. Scavenger.'

Tombo did not know what a scavenger was, but it sounded rude, made him defensive enough to want to confess the truth.

'Have you seen Daniel today?' Tom asked. 'Only I thought he would be in, haven't seen him . . .'

There was a long pause. Tom was surprised to see Mister looking faintly uncomfortable.

'Ask your mother,' Uncle Pip said.

CHAPTER EIGHT

'How's your mother?' Helen asked the man at the door.

'Oh not so bad these days, Miss West. Better. She likes Christmas, see. Cheers her up.'

There was something about buildings which made them unwell, welcoming or not. The disease of Helen's office building was obvious. Stuck down a small side street, there was permanent twilight on account of the enormous block which stood opposite and stole what little light there was. The difference in the seasons was difficult to determine from inside, apart from the temperature fluctuating between two different kinds of heat, the dry and the cloying, hotter than average in winter. There were days when she could hardly bring herself to push open the door, shrugging off her coat as she did so. Full of petty economies elsewhere, this part of the Crown Prosecution Service was content to fry the staff alive with its central heating, rendering them zombie-like by mid-afternoon, while the most unfair thing about Redwood's superior room was the fact that he was the only one actually able to open his window. The psychology behind this had the accidental effect of keeping them all out of doors rather than in, which Redwood encouraged. Real work was done in court where success or failure was manifest. Preparation and consideration always came second since they tended not to show.

Helen saw the tinsel hung in the corridors, a coy reminder of goodwill. Mika had been busy and Helen's heart sank lower with the first unavoidable signal of Christmas. Even in robust health, Helen hated Christmas. Christmas made men and women mad. Redwood would be infected and tonight was the first of the parties. Bailey's party. Or at least, Bailey's CID party, where they entertained the whole district. Where she would stick out like a sore thumb, the way she had last year and the year before. Unable, quite, to charm herself into some sort of acceptance or dull the nerves by getting drunk.

Her carpet was like patchwork, and the office had once been a showroom. For some reason quite beyond the ken of any man, the original, cheerful blue and all pure wool carpet left by the previous incumbents had been torn up for replacement by inferior, all synthetic yellow. They had protested, stood on the carpet, yelled on the carpet, and in Helen's case, even laid down on the carpet, but Acrilan now dwelt where wool had been and the door frames tingled with static electricity. Why the hell do I do this? she was saying to herself: why do I work in this crap heap when I could earn twice as much somewhere else? With a secretary and fresh flowers daily and luncheon vouchers and a free car . . . Because you would be doing nothing but guarding other people's money, and you would be bored. That is, in general, what other, richer lawyers do.

Right. No moaning then. No whinging about how awful it was to be thus employed but how nice, how wonderful it would be if it were not quite such a struggle. According to Helen's calculations she spent half her life doing her job, with at least the other half devoted to the sheer mechanics of getting the simplest thing done. All that diplomacy, all that energy, like steam from a kettle, all spent creeping into the photocopying room, saying, would you mind terribly, come on, Dot, please . . . Or getting a letter typed, bended knees to a typist, blandishments and promises given like a tart. Prostitution was a useful analogy too when it came to getting major decisions made. Smile while you still got teeth. Convince the boss it was his idea, suggest, never dictate, wheedle, whinge, undermine with charm, talk as if talking were just invented, duck and dive, cajole, persuade, like a hockey player dribbling the ball up the long field to goal. That was the exhausting part, the time for losing judgement. Half a day, every day, coping with a hierarchy in order to do the simplest thing. In a place as hot as Hades.

The end results, of course, were not rewards. Such as this morning. She looked at the watch Bailey had given her. She had been thinking of Bailey, not always calmly, ever since she had met him, in an office like this. At least he was an honest ally, some of the time, even though his present job had threatened to turn him into a bureaucrat. Before he found dying persons in unfashionable streets. Enough. None of that was going to help her survive Bailey's party. She went into reception, where the man on the door was mopping his brow from the effort of greeting Dr Hazel.

'You'll know your way here by now, Sean. How've you been?'

'Better each time you phone. Do we have to go and see that little man again? Wee piglet?'

'Not yet. In theory, he takes all the decisions around here. We call him master.' She was mimicking his brogue. In the lift, rising towards the welcome ventilation of Redwood's room, Hazel grinned at her and frowned at his own reflection in the doors.

'What's that baggage you're carrying?' Helen demanded. Dr Hazel was armed with a small, bashed-about suitcase.

'Change of clothes,' he said. 'In case you ask me to stay.'

Redwood heard the sound of laughter going past his door, paused on his way towards his desk and sat down abruptly to polish his glasses. His once spacious office now contained three chipped desks, facing his own. Each one was covered with documents and the sight of them, as well as the sound of laughter, remained no more than a hollow suggestion of loneliness. Somewhere in all of this was the vain hope that the floor would sink into the basement and lose all this paper without trace. Bring him back to the camaraderie he had once enjoyed, and perhaps the blessed heat of the lower floors. His window was warped by winter, permanently open, and the back of his neck was frozen against the hackles he used to find rising occasionally round the hairline, all his instincts dulled by complaints and budget sheets, and Christmas too. He envied Helen West; he envied all the others. If she entered here, looking warm and flushed from the pleasures of meeting the public, he thought he would understand the meaning of the word murderous.

'Murder,' said Dr Hazel, 'is what it was.'

He had ended his peroration. They sat, Collins and Helen, facing him across a table in the messy basement room used for meetings and rudimentary library, both of them spellbound, Collins frankly shocked. His flushed skin told the tale of a celebration the night before, but he maintained the bearing of a soldier. Hazel looked like a tramp, but for that moment and the half-hour before, he had commanded their attention like a maestro, and thought he would never forget it. On the table lay a report, complete with diagrams, computer models, references and lucid articulate prose. He knew, as he finished, that he would actually write the book he had always planned to write. The thought filled him with grave exultation.

'I'd like to see you in the witness box, Doc. You'd slay 'em,' said Collins.

'Ah, now,' said Hazel, putting up his hands in a warning gesture, a look of alarm crossing his face, 'no one said anything about that. I doubt if . . .'

'Say it again,' Helen interrupted quickly. 'About this thing.' She pointed to the metal frame which sat atop the report.

'The mask? Imagine you're the patient. You are about to be anaesthetised with chloroform. Imagine an operating theatre, if you will, full of men in frock coats, all addressing each other as sir. You lie back, thus . . .' Helen grasped the metal object, an oval-shaped frame of wire with two crossed struts, and tilted back his seat to a dangerous angle, holding the mask across his face. 'The mask is a patent by Schimmelbusch, long since dead, and has a groove round the rim to catch surplus liquid. Sits over the face, wide enough in circumference not to touch. Gauze is placed on top, and chloroform is gently dripped on the cloth. The vapour sinks through, the patient breathes. Give him oxygen simultaneously and he can take more and last longer, as I explained.'

'Why a mask at all?' Helen demanded.

'Keeps the gauze and the liquid from the skin. Doubtless for the benefit of the doctor. These gentlemen in frock coats who started this did not have rubber gloves. You could, of course, manage without the mask – I have – but a fastidious man would use it.'

'And a chemist would know about this?'

'If he were interested in history, yes. Otherwise it might be a piece of forgotten undergraduate knowledge. Not all pharmacists are interested in the power of life over death but you might be surprised at the number who enter their profession because they have an unhealthy fascination with drugs. Drugs are power, you see.' He replaced the mask on the table where it made a satisfying clunk and reminded Helen of an empty crash helmet.

'If only,' said Collins, 'we'd had some chance to look at the room. We might have found something, I don't know. Like dents in the pillow. Wire sculptures. All Davies found, at Miss West's insistence, was chloroform.'

'Chloroform,' the doctor observed, 'would eradicate fingerprints too.'

'But it's all guesswork,' Collins complained. 'Apart from this.' He tapped the report. 'Apart from this reconstruction of how long it would have taken. Twenty minutes, you said.'

'At least. Longer without the mask.'

'And most of that time, she's unconscious? Christ, it's so coldblooded.' Collins stood upright, disgusted by the images. 'A man standing there over someone asleep, keeping a mask in place, quietly putting more on the cloth. It's worse than a slow strangulation.' He breathed heavily as if avoiding contamination. 'Shall I go and get a warrant?'

'He wouldn't have seen her face,' Hazel reminded. 'And the only sound would have been breathing.'

Helen tidied the papers on the table into a pile. 'No warrant without permission from above,' she said, jerking her head towards the ceiling. 'And only if I can put my hand on my heart and swear there was absolutely no possibility of suicide. No chloroform under the bed?'

'No one looked,' said Collins bitterly. 'And besides, what difference would it make? If he was there?'

*

Upstairs, Redwood heard the footsteps coming towards his door and quickly shoved his newspaper out of sight. There was no idleness in his reading the local rag since consumption of all relevant headlines was mandatory. 'CROWN PROSECUTION SERVICE COCKS IT UP AGAIN.' 'WRONG MAN ARRESTED: RIGHT ONE RELEASED.' Yet more horror stories and a few writs in the offing with the words on the page reaching out to grab him by the throat. His sensitivities were as raw as the back of his neck. Entering his room, report in hand, refreshed by the icy blast from the window, Helen looked at his face and knew perfectly well what the answer would be.

'And?' asked Bailey later.

'And nothing. Sweet nothing, apart from no, not yet if ever. A warrant for whom? Bring me proof, he said. Bring me some connection between this man and this so-called murder. Knowledge, I said: knowledge is the connection. Rare knowledge. Christ, why is everyone so slow? Opportunity. Motive.'

'There is no motive.'

'Yes there is. In marriage, you never need a motive.' She flashed a glance at him, one mixed with frustration and mischief; then resumed brushing her thick hair with quick, irritated strokes. Bailey looked casually, noticed her nerves. Not for this case, he knew, only for the CID party, and he could not for the life of him imagine why. Her fears and braveries seemed to have no sense of priority, ranging as they did from a peculiar recklessness about life or health to this telling, acute irritation before a simple celebration.

'He must have liked Hazel's report.' Bailey squinted in the mirror, knotting a tie.

'Loved it, very impressed after he'd read it. Reluctantly. Said without that, there'd be no case at all, and without Hazel, I'd be told to put the whole thing in the fire. Hazel is just about my only bloody witness. Hazel and his immaculate reconstruction of events, with mask.'

'Helen, I've something to tell you . . .'

'Oh, ho. Is it a story? Will I like it? I feel absolutely frustrated by the deliberately obstructive regime of things. Let's have a drink.'

'Yes, to the drink. On second thoughts, the story can wait.'

'Everything's got to wait, but I'm not finished yet.'

Bailey was uncomfortable, but she chose not to question. He knew more than he said and would only say in his own time. He went into the bright spartan spaces of his huge living-room, the room which was really the whole of his flat, looked for the wine, found only whisky, gin and a pile of tangerines brought from the market.

'The whole investigation may take time, Helen. You're so impatient, but once you've got Collins interested, you can leave it to him. No rush, is there? Even if the chemist killed his wife, it doesn't follow he's a danger to any other soul alive.' He thought of the man he had found in the back road to Herringbone Parade, then held his tongue, while Helen, not to be comforted, spoke his own words out loud.

'Bugger the stupidities and reservations of the law. I've been told I can't risk an assault on Mr Caring Carlton's civil liberties. So what if there's risk? Of course he's dangerous. Anyone who can mimic an anaesthetist is dangerous. Once you know what it's like, you don't relinquish the power over life and death.'

'Rubbish,' said Bailey. 'Sweetheart, you do talk rubbish.'

'Make us a tea now, there's a darling.'

'I'm just doing this, won't take a minute . . .'

'Well, now means now. Not later.'

He spoke very mildly, tapping the side of a plastic container of pills into the counting machine, his eyes fixed on the dial, muttering to himself, 'Four a day for fourteen days makes fifty-six. Tea, soon, please.'

The please was an afterthought, and Kimberley knew in that precise moment how none of the changes in him was the product of her imagination. Before Margaret's death, even before the last police visit, she might have answered back any peremptory order, teased his passion for tea, made light of his frustrations and bossiness, Uncle Pip, ruler of all he surveyed with the whole of this damn Parade in thrall and half the surrounding neighbourhood too. Make the tea, there's a love, sixteen times a day. In one month's time, she would be able to call herself a pharmacist, practise in her own right, and yet he ordered her to make tea, run errands. Kimberley remembered the back dispensary, its sacrosanct secrecy; remembered how Pip had always made the simplest things seem complex, adding mystique where common sense would do, all to make this career appear more difficult than it was. She did not think all of this at once: her mind was with Tom, bound to be awkward as always after an evening with Dad. She was yawning. Then Pip reversed the mood in one of his sudden moves, restored the balance.

'What am I talking about? Sound like some foreman, or school teacher. Stay where you are, I'll make tea. Sorry, Kim. I must have sounded short. Short! Ha! Like pastry. Just like I feel. Let's have some of that new herbal tea. Good for our nerves. It's all those Irish builders tramping in and out. They're behaving as if that site had a jinx. Wish they'd at least finish the foundations and go.'

It was on the tip of her tongue to say she did not want tea: she wanted sleep and an end of dreaming. Sleep without imagining things scuffling on her balcony. Sleep without this longing for Duncan, that brusque lover and husband who could still make her cry if only he waited to watch. Occasionally brutal Duncan, the treader of dreams, but oh, so certain in his certainty.

'It's OK, Pip, I'll make it.'

'Oh, no, no, no. Me. I mean I. Eye for an eye and tooth for tooth. I owe you plenty. Not just tea.' The last of this was muffled as he retreated into the alcove between the shop dispensary and his own little room. The alcove housed the kettle, and behind a door, the lavatory. 'Now look here,' he was saying, 'we seem to be able to do better than tea.' The hand in front of her face was flourishing a bottle of sherry. 'Nectar in a measuring glass,' he murmured, turning his back on her, rummaging on the shelves. Kimberley was so relieved not to have to drink tea simply because he had made it, the sherry seemed a good idea. One of these days, she would wake up and think of nothing. Maybe that was what Duncan sought on his binges. Waking up to the clear blue sky of nothing, with nothing to do, had to be a worthwhile state, however temporary. Kim had taught herself not to think: kept all observation to a minimum for the sake of her own peace of mind, and in one brief bout of recognition, she knew why Duncan drank.

'Yes, please, Pip. Sir. Lord and master. Just a large one.'

'And tea?'

'No. To tell the truth, I'm awash with tea.' He handed her one of the measuring cups, the sherry reaching up to the point of sixty millilitres. Rather a lot for a tired head. They sipped in a silence which was not quite companionable.

'Are we nearly finished, Pip? Only I've got to get back. Duncan's bringing Tom home, by seven o'clock, he said and it's nearly that now. Don't want him hanging about. He'll be off sharpish, though, Duncan I mean. Got a party, or something.' She remembered the Christmas parties she had enjoyed, thought of the lack of them this year and sighed, not listening.

'How about a Chinese takeaway, then? I'll come round later.' The invitation was slightly listless, as if he expected her to refuse, but she caught the same hint, that suggestion of an order which she was beginning to dislike.

'Sorry, Pip. I'm really tired. The wind last night: I kept hearing things and the blasted concrete mixer started before light. And I've got to tell Tom about Daniel.'

His silent offence only increased the feeling of helplessness. Carlton's Caring Chemist was becoming a place of isolation. Tombo rebellious, Daniel dead, Duncan obsessive and no one liking anyone else. Pip domineering and the wind howling.

'Another time, then,' he said mildly, back turned as he fetched more sherry. 'Do you want me to stay with you until they get back? In case Duncan's awkward?'

'No,' she said sharply. Every utterance she made seemed to be a refusal and she did not know how to soften any of them. 'Wow,' she muttered, rising from her stool and feeling giddy, steadying herself on the doorframe. 'Strong stuff, this.' Through her own efforts to stay upright, she could hear his smooth voice. 'Too much tea,' he was saying, 'and not enough food. I'll bring in some sandwiches for us tomorrow.' She was too tired now to recognise that same proprietorial tone, beyond resentment. Now which of them had been the bossy one of the two? Philip Carlton or his wife? The distinctions were becoming confused.

Kim plodded round the corner, slowly upstairs, searched for the key to her flat in the mess of her handbag. If Duncan was late, he need have no worries: she was too tired to shout, far too indifferent. The road was lighter than usual, a fact noticed by accident as she turned to prop the bag on her knee. Beyond the building site, she saw the huge crane which governed their view lit up with fairy lights across one magnificent, outflung arm, a red, blue, green salute, disembodied in the black sky, a sight so stunning in its savage but synthetic beauty that she could feel tears of sentiment and sheer surprise. She remembered tales of old paraders, memories of a sky lit by flames, night-time terrors, and suddenly felt their overwhelming fatigue. She left the door on the latch for Tom and stumbled inside.

Pip Carlton retreated to his back room, and closed the flimsy door behind him. The shaded light reminded him of a wartime he had never known and a secrecy which was second nature. Having drawn down a new blind on the back door window, which exaggerated the impression of a blackout and had the desired effect of making him invisible from the street, he began to feel safe. In contrast to the muddle outside, both in the real world and the ante-room to the shop, this place was now tidy: jars, boxes, pipettes, measuring jugs were all accessible: there was a large, locked cupboard which he patted vaguely. From outside, he heard the sound of a car, one door slamming and the hint of a childish voice, high with anxiety in its goodbyes. 'Go upstairs, you little runt,' Pip muttered, 'and tell me if she's asleep. If only you weren't coming home.'

There would be fantasies with these experiments. If not the real Kimberley in his arms, a dream instead. Pip reached for the yellow duster, soft and dry by the sink, sat in the armchair next to it.

What cocktail tonight, what treat in store. He could not be heard in the shop, where the lights still blazed as they would until morning. He was dimly conscious that the car he had heard was revving to depart, the driver infecting the engine with his own impotent anger. Pip lay back, duster in hand, a smile of benign joy on his face. He smoothed the crotch of his trousers beneath the white overall, watched the bulge forming. Oh, Kimberley Perry, oh my darling.

Helen saw the crane, lit with lights of many colours, prominent from Blackfriars Bridge, and wanted, for one uncontrolled second, to clap her hands at the first thing which made her rejoice in Christmas. One brilliant arm in the sky, standing solid; a spectrum of light seen for a few seconds like a firework display against black clouds. She could not even say, Look, look, for fear of spoiling this childish pleasure, and wished they were going home from this party instead of being en route. Earth hath not anything more fair, a poem on Blackfriars Bridge: the poet had imagined this crane twinkling against the water. No poet ever dreamt of attending a policeman's ball.

Number Two Area's CID party was the daddy of them all. An effort frantic with munificence, blinding with glitter, stiff with shoulder pads. Gone was any sign of epaulettes and caps, the jeans or worn suits which Helen privately preferred: the men were in mufti, some following instructions to wear silly hats. A joke, Len, a joke: I knew you'd believe it. You don't think we'd have a party and turn up in hats, do you? We only said hats, to see if some silly wankers would fall for it. This is plain clothes, Len, remember. Nothing plain in sight, except Helen's rather elegant dress, calf-length, red, without any adornment whatever, and in it, she felt like a misplaced grandmother waiting and hoping to be sat in a corner with tea and smelling salts. Helen did not know the meaning of snobbery: she would not, in general, have noticed who was black, senior or junior, but the prospect of a good old knees-up in company with five hundred others made her quail even more than the risk of being thought a snob. Which was saying something, since she knew of no greater social fear than that. Stupid, said Bailey; ridiculous. You are the last person in the world anyone would ever call that: you are, sometimes, too egalitarian, too indiscriminate in your likings for your own good, whatever that is, and besides, it really does not matter what people think. It does, she was thinking now: it matters because they are your colleagues, your peers, and I have helped to isolate you from them: it matters terribly what they think.

Not only they, but also their wives. Always find a nice woman at a party; female solidarity, the comfort of life. Helen was deeply suspicious of any woman without good women friends, but standing by that was sometimes an uphill struggle on occasions like this. The wives and girlfriends gathered to powder and puff, adjusting earrings which half covered profiles, teasing fresh hairdos, pulling down their short straight skirts which skimmed their shiny knees; excited and stinking of perfume, a breed of butterflies allowed to flutter three or four times a year. And as she crossed the floor of this old-fashioned dance hall in a converted cinema, housing three hundred people for bingo three times a week, Helen could see why the sparkle on the women's clothing, in their hair, round their necks and on their ears, was so necessary. If you had nothing about your person to catch the light from the revolving globe in the middle of the ceiling, you were lost for ever. She had joked with the ladies in the loo, yielded her place by the mirror as they all scrabbled for lipstick, but when they heard her accent, their jokes diminished into shyer smiles. Although she realised this was her own fault, Helen regretted it all the same.

She struggled through an anonymous crush with a dozen excuse-mes, gently pushing past the soft and solid suited bodies of all the men. Policemen one to one were fine – she knew how to deal with almost all – but weaving at sea in so great a volume of them, many the subject of awkward professional interviews, was a minefield of embarrassments. At first, she was the only woman at the bar. At this kind of party the men collected the drinks; the women hung back and awaited collection themselves. Helen was wrong again.

'Cor, look at that,' said a voice by her ear, the masculine appreciation sent straight over her head in the direction of the female huddle.

'Triffic. All right for them. Not enough to go round, is there? She'd have to be a right prune not to get lucky tonight. Ger in there, Dave. Oh, hallo, Miss West . . .' She grinned at a familiar face, aware that his guttural appreciation of the others was being swallowed in the knowledge of what she might think. Bailey was standing alone, the way he so often seemed most alone in a crowd, removed from these men by so many attitudes, rank and temperament, but pleased, like some paterfamilias, to see them relaxed. Helen took the proffered drink, gin and tonic, dispensed from barrels below the bar, free booze all evening and plenty of those present showing the signs already. She yelled in his ear above the din, 'Hey! Is this a party or a cattle market?'

'Both,' he yelled back. 'There's food over there.' He was itching to move, do his duties, meet what wives he could. He would abandon her to whatever she could find, confident she would manage with her usual panache. 'You all right?' he yelled, bending to impart the most commonly said words in the whole evening.

'Fine,' she bellowed back. Smiling encouragement, wondering quite what to do next and thinking, You bastard. I'd like to get revenge on you at our party where policeman guests stand around propping up the walls like a load of spare parts, but I suppose this is a fitting revenge for all those genteel dinner gatherings you've endured with me.

The generosity of policemen always amazed her: a party, by God, was a party. There was enough food for the feeding of the five thousand. Peanuts, crisps, curled sandwiches, scotch eggs, enough chicken drumsticks to have caused the death of a whole flock of hens, pies, cheeses, bread, a gesture towards salad. The whole groaning table, where the lightest thing was paper plates and plastic forks, was a reminder of the presence among the guests of almost every publican within a ten-mile radius.

More familiar faces approached: more conversations stilted by deference and the mistaken belief that solicitors could not laugh, however easy their manner. Helen found one lone woman in the gloom, and chatted with greater ease, but most of her own sex, determined not to be wallflowers, occupied the middle of the floor, some dancing dutifully round their handbags. They were kind and welcoming, and she liked them, but no conversation could be uninhibited as soon as she opened her mouth. And if life were about building bridges between yourself and others, there were times when it was better not to try too hard. She was the stranger here.

'Wanna dance?' a lanky young man with quite a few beers on board stood by her elbow, dared by a friend. Never refuse, thought Helen, so they danced in an uncoordinated but enthusiastic gyration from one foot to another.

'Hats!' he was shouting. 'Bloody hats, I ask you. Told us to come in hats, so the rest could have a go. Didn't half feel a berk.'

Smiling and nodding was the only possible response.

'Wass your name, then?'

'Helen.'

'Dave,' he shouted, pointing at his chest. 'Come on your own, did you?'

'No. With Superintendent Bailey.'

'Oh,' he said again, lower, in time with a lull in the music and an obvious lull in his mood. 'Well, hallo, Mrs Bailey. Nice to meet you.' It was neither the time nor the place, but she could rarely resist it. So pedantic you are, Helen, sometimes, said her own inner voice, too slow to prevent the words. 'I'm not Mrs Bailey. I'm his girlfriend.'

'Shit,' said Dave, slowing to a standstill. 'Where's his wife then?'

It was so easy to tread on toes, and she knew this floor was full of sensitive feet even though Christmas had already made men mad and driven them into the kind of drinking which might precede a year of drought. The music was louder, the voices correspondingly shriller: there was an argument raging on one side about someone being rude to a girl and quite soon there

would be some woman crying in the ladies' loo and the careful settling of a few animosities outside. She had seen it before, could
smell the sweet hilarity of a drinking crowd in danger of going
sour.

At least there was Bailey if anything came to a fight, as likely
here as at any gathering of the predominantly young and fit,
trained for conflict, never mind if they were paid to uphold the
law. There was something about Bailey, she thought, as she
perched on a stool beyond the edge of the dancing but in reach of
the drinking, chatting to another stranger. She knew that Bailey
would protect her, unlike the previous partners of her life, her
divorced husband, the other men of her own ilk. He would fight if
need be and she was aware that he would fight to excellent effect,
if not always to Queensberry rules. Not like a lawyer who would
worry about his image, his suit or the consequences, and the contrast was one which gave her enormous pleasure. Some
compensation for the vigorous display of good will and the sheer
hard work of parties like this.

These might be basic, their food and celebrations might be
primitive, but, thought Helen, she would really rather be around
them than any other men.

Helen stood on the top rung of her bar stool in time to see the
now swaying mass in the middle of the dance floor part to admit
a large man with his arms clasped round the waist of a woman.
His head was pressed into her back, whether for support or affection was difficult to tell at first sight, but in any event the total
effect was restraint of the woman, who obviously resented what
was more an arrest by force than an embrace. She was plucking at
the hands fastened round her middle, screeching in protest, looking round wildly for some protector, and she was patently
someone else's property. So much was obvious to the others,
hence the shouts. 'Here, Duncan, leave it out . . .' 'You daft
bugger, Duncan, bloody let go.' 'Sod off, Duncan . . . Piss off out
of it . . .' He seemed oblivious, swaying to his own beat, his hands
not loosening but splaying over the slippery fabric of the woman's
dress, dragging down the modest décolletage to dangerous levels.

There was panic in her expression. The man Duncan, his face obscured, was wearing a metal helmet slightly too small for his head, some makeshift wire object scarcely worth calling a hat. The others had abandoned their hats after initial teasing: the metal of his was digging into the woman's shoulder.

Somebody hit him. The one hand visible to Helen clawed at the bosom of the dress, and tore off a bright button reflected in the revolving light which distorted each movement and each expression as he slid to the floor and the hordes crowded in. Helen was afraid, paralysed afraid; and then she saw Bailey, pushing people this way and that, straight to the centre of the crowd where heads were bent and obscenities uttered. A man's arms were raised, a profile twisted as a foot was raised for a savage kick, bitterness caught in the light with a smell of sweat and an expression of surprise as he was pushed aside. The music went on: she could sense Bailey's voice below the pulse of sound, somehow being obeyed. Seconds later he emerged from the mass, dragging a man by the elbow. The metal hat rolled on the floor: Helen leapt off her stool, Bailey shoved the body on to her seat with the torso of it slumped fully over the bar and they sat down again in a trio. In one quick action, sign of an automatic tidiness in anyone else, Helen retrieved the metal hat. Duncan stirred, swore, looked at Helen with a leer and then looked straight ahead to all the bottles above the bar. Bailey coughed and straightened his tie. The gesture was so automatic that Helen wondered, not then, but later, how many times in his lifetime he had done exactly the same.

'Helen, meet Constable Perry. One of my best, at the best of times. Which this is not. Say hallo to the lady, Constable.'

''Aloo, Mrs B. Let me get you a drink.'

'He doesn't need a drink,' Helen murmured, fascinated despite herself. The truly drunk *were* fascinating, whenever there was someone to guard you from them.

'Yes, he does need a drink,' said Bailey. 'One more will make him malleable. With a bit of luck, even unconscious.'

'Fine, if you say so,' said Helen, signalling to the man behind the bar, rallying, even beginning to enjoy the situation. 'Who's going to take him home?'

'I am,' said Bailey. 'Will you wait for me? Shan't be long.'

'I'm coming with you.' Duncan was fixing Bailey with a baleful eye.

'No.'

'Why?'

'He might be sick.'

'And I have his hat. Nice parties you have. Come on.'

The car cruised onwards in silence. Stopped at traffic lights, started, behaved. 'How do people generally get home from police Christmas parties?' Helen asked. 'If they all turn out like that? I didn't see anyone sober for the last hour.' Bailey coughed. 'There are ways,' he began. In the back seat, Duncan snored.

'Always wondered,' Helen was saying, 'about what you do on the nights you don't get guarded by me. Ferry round unconscious people in cars. So it seems.'

'Not every night. Hang on. He's awake.' From behind the driver's seat, there was the sound of weeping. Copious, noisy, suddenly sober weeping, sounds of such desolation from so large a man, Helen was moved to pity. Turning round to the back seat, she put out her hand and found it grasped. A limp, hopeless grasp which made her curl her fingers round his while the smell of him hit her nostrils.

'Don't leave me,' said Duncan, 'Please don't leave me. Take me home. Please take me home to Kim.' Drunk. Lonely and desperate, clutching at hands.

'This is home,' said Bailey, brutally. The car stopped and he hauled himself out of the door and round to the back while Helen, less practised, jumped out of the front.

'Can we leave him like this? I'll come in with you . . . Poor bloke's in some kind of pain . . .' Detective Constable Perry was leaning out of the back seat, threatening to fall. Bailey dragged him upright, shoving one sagging arm round his own neck.

'No,' he said with one backward glance as he walked down the short path. 'For God's sake, stay put. You'll only embarrass him. I'll put him to bed. Stay in the car and lock the doors. Back soon.'

She sat, grateful to be obedient, conscious of her own naivete. She shuffled after a minute or two and wondered, selfishly, how long it took one man to put another to bed, only aware, from briefer experience than Bailey, that it took one woman quite a long time, so she settled to wait. Part and parcel of the life of a policeman's wifely half, waiting. Bugger Christmas. The half-hearted light of one street lamp shone directly into Bailey's big car: she could have read a book if there had been a book to read. Instead, she turned in her hands the metal hat, looked at it upside-down and inside-out, thinking, looking, coming round slowly and regretting the intake of gin and tonic.

Perry. As in Kimberley Perry. Husband of? Only connect. In any event possessor of some funny little item which could pass as the amateur double of that mask Hazel had shown them today. Oh Lord. An anaesthetic mask.

CHAPTER NINE

THE phone shrilling in the early morning was so rare for Kimberley Perry she could not believe the sound, woke with that frightful fear of not quite knowing where she was. Back in her mother's house or back with Duncan when calls at all hours were commonplace. In less than seconds, she saw where she was, loathed where she was, struggled a groggy route out of bed with a pounding heart and lifted the receiver. She had no strength to say hello.

'Mrs Perry?'

'Yes, who the . . .'

'Superintendent Bailey. We met, once or twice, I think. I'm sorry to bother you . . .'

Christ, by seven-thirty she should have been up a whole half-hour. What was the matter with her? She dimly remembered getting off the settee and into bed, finding Tom already there, herself so sleepy she had neglected to eat or even brush her teeth.

'You all right?' continued the voice. Such a question. She was asked every day, always replied as she did now.

'Fine.' Then a consciousness of the oddity of this crept in. 'Yes I do remember you. Duncan's boss. He's not here. What's the matter, what's he done now?'

'No, he's fine. Listen . . .'

So she had listened, promised to phone back, which was why Pip had caught her on his phone in the dispensary while his back was turned. She could have explained to Pip, asked permission first as she had done before when a phone call in working hours was vital, but she did not. She waited until he had gone down the road to buy fruit from Mrs Beale, because none of this was Pip's business. Thus he discovered her, explaining to a senior Superintendent of Police how her son had told her that the metal hat object they were discussing had been given to him by a drug addict in the street and left in his father's car. Describe the drug addict, Bailey said, and she had done that part. Name and pack drill, feeling as if she were giving something away. Kimberley was a jangle of nerves, assailed by emotion. Motherly instincts had told her that Tom, responding so defensively to questions that morning, had lied a little, and duller instincts, half formed and quickly rejected ideas, were making her withdraw from Pip; who had lied about his wife's so-called drug addiction; whose bloody sherry had made her sleep like someone hit on the head; whose eyes were drilling holes in her back as she tried to hurry the telephone conversation to a close.

'You all right?' Bailey was asking again.

'Fine, fine. Look, I've got to go. We get busy after nine.'

'Listen, Mrs Perry, phone me will you? Might help to talk. In confidence, of course. Will you meet your son from school? Yes, I know where. Could we speak then? Here, take my number.' She wrote the number carefully, feeling a flush spread over her shoulders as she scribbled on the back of a packet of paracetamol, crashed down the phone with relief. Yes, it would be nice to talk. About everything. And especially about the fact that Duncan last night must have taken advantage of her profound sleep, sidled indoors with Tom, and stolen half her underwear. Bras, knickers, gone. Kim rubbed the back of her own neck to postpone the business of turning round, thought of that half-empty drawer in her bedroom and wanted to vomit with a mixture of anxiety and rage. All her cheekiness, her ebullience and jokes in the face of hardship, were gone. She wanted to behave like the tortoise Tom craved and hibernate for the winter.

'Who was that?' Pip asked mildly. She wanted to say, no one, recognised that this would resemble the airy nonsense of Tombo telling a lie, and said, 'Oh nothing. Sorry I had to use the phone. About Tom. School. He was late today. Do you want some tea, before the rush?'

'Please,' said Pip. Kim went for the kettle, passing the door to the back room where Pip had half covered the entrance with piles of boxes. Quickly he looked at the writing on the paracetamol box. Detec Super Bailey, meet school, 471 66, the rest indecipherable. He thought he had seen enough.

'What none of you seems to understand here,' Redwood was shouting, 'is the b-balance of proof.'

Helen thought he might rise and strike the table, the pedagogue incarnate.

'Beyond reasonable doubt. Not beyond the immediate comprehension of the man on the Clapham omnibus: not scientific gobbledygook but straightforward proof. Without flaw.'

'Perhaps a man standing over a dead body with a knife in his hand,' Helen suggested lightly. Redwood glared at her.

'All right, something more like that. Juries are thick. So are magistrates. At least something we could get past the latter. Not a dead drug addict called Daniel Maley who apparently knew all there was to be known about drugs, apparent possessor of an anaesthetic mask which he gave to some child. This wretch has to be suspect number one, dead at the moment. Not some respectable chemist with at least half an alibi and no known motive to murder a perfectly good wife, even if she did like chloroform. You don't convince the Clapham omnibus man with a scientific reconstruction without identikit, provided by a crazy old doctor who should have retired years ago.'

'He's certainly not crazy.' Helen's voice was loudly defensive.

'No,' Redwood admitted, patting the report which was open on his desk. 'Not crazy. He writes like a dream: his thesis is elegant and convincing if only we had a culprit. But he cannot be called as a witness. I'm surprised at you, Helen. I told you to check his background.'

'What?'

Collins shuffled in his seat, coughed apologetically. Redwood leant forward.

'Doctor Hazel's previous convictions, Miss West. Your . . . I mean, I understand Superintendent Bailey did a check. Two for drug abuse, years ago. Suspended by the medical council, temporarily, for sniffing ether, likewise years ago and criticised heavily for anaesthetising, possibly killing his own son. Accident, of course, not deliberate. Do you want any more? The defence would tear that to pieces.'

'Oh.'

Shock fell like a dead weight on her shoulders. She should have guessed with Hazel: there had always been the sense of something hidden. A feeling of conspiracy was growing in this cold room, Bailey, Collins, Redwood, a united front. She rallied, raising her voice, knowing it was useless. 'Since when has there been a rule, house rule or otherwise, that we can't field a witness with previous convictions, especially spent convictions? We call people from prison, don't we? Hazel is the lynchpin. It strikes me we aren't in a position to choose.'

'We are actually. We only call witnesses like that when we don't have a choice. We have a choice here. And I'm exercising it. Anyway I think that's all . . .'

'I'll get someone else,' said Helen. 'Someone else can do Hazel's experiments.'

'As you please. But not in my time and not on my budget. I trust you're fully recovered from your operation having been so busy? I need you to go to court tomorrow and all next week. Mr Collins will continue to investigate.'

Though the sound of a slap did not actually reverberate in the room, she could nevertheless feel the imprint of one in the pink of her face. She knew her reaction bordered on the juvenile, and she was ashamed, but continued. Shrugging with insolent indifference as she walked past his desk to the door, contempt resonant in her footsteps even while she saw the sense in what he said. Like a frustrated child, determined not to agree, she told herself later. Murmuring as she went, 'Fine, absolutely fine, anything you say. By the way, how did Daniel Maley die? If he might have done for Mrs Chemist, they had nothing in common but her husband. See you. Happy Christmas.'

Helen remembered the all-singing, all-dancing bed in hospital. Wanted to lie there and be carried away to some place where wounded pride and the squirming of failure was not visible to any eye, especially her own. There was also the unworthy wish that Bailey had never been born.

Back in her own office, she grabbed the phone. Anger, frustration, a sense of guilt making her fingertips stab at the numbers. Speak to me, nice doctor, please. The one who put needles in my arm, let me sleep, so likeable, so trustworthy, such a good human being. Tell me my judgement of human nature is not as rotten as it seems. And the law which pays my labours not really such an ass.

'I'm sorry I woke you up so early, Duncan. You look as if you could have done with rather longer.'

The faces Bailey encountered at around two o'clock in the afternoon were universally haggard, variously flushed and disorientated, the figures sitting in the CID room slumped in degrees of lethargy depending on their party stamina. A few had been wise, gone home long before the end: they were the ones live enough to joke. There were a few red faces and one or two suspicious silences. Detective Constable Perry walked with a pronounced limp: his eyes were swollen, and he had no plans to speak until spoken to, until caught on the wing by bumping into Bailey in the corridor.

'Have a word, Duncan? In my office.'

'Look, I'm sorry, sir. About you having to take me home and all that. I gather I wasn't nice to know.'

'About time you gathered that, Duncan. So far you've confined the worst effects of your drinking to making an exhibition of yourself in front of your wife. Last night you excelled yourself in front of all your colleagues, well done. Might give you some idea of what a bloody fool you look when you hang around Herringbone Parade of an evening. *And* how many uniform coppers there are out there dying to arrest you. Still wondering why she doesn't want to come home?'

Duncan was in a state of fury, taking in each word, holding himself rigid, looking at the floor between Bailey's well-shone shoes and his own toneless ones. Then he pulled himself upright, gazed at a spot on the yellow wall past Bailey's head, and said again, 'Sir.' He was like a toy soldier, Bailey thought savagely, and himself like a sergeant major.

'Oh for God's sake, man, never mind, getting pissed and pawing a woman isn't the worst thing in the world. But you could have got your bloody head kicked in. Why are you limping? Did you fall over once I'd left you?' Silly question. Duncan would not remember, but Bailey could recall the two of them stumbling at least once on the way upstairs to Duncan's door, also dropping Duncan while he went through his pockets for the key.

'No, sir. I hurt myself yesterday when I was playing football with my boy.'

'And was that when he gave you that thing I was asking you about so unconscionably early this morning? That wire hat thing?'

'He didn't give it me, sir. He showed it me, then left it in the back of the car. I told him he shouldn't collect rubbish. He said it was OK, because it was all clean and wrapped up, but he knows his mother doesn't like it.' Duncan was recovering. 'Tom has a passion for rubbish, sir. He used to bring his mother flowers from the council tip.' A smile flitted across his face and vanished quickly, the grey cells not yet sufficiently alert to do more than wonder why some silly object, favoured by his eccentric child, was the subject of so many questions. Bailey judged that the instinct of the detective, if instinct was the right word for it, would be the last thing to surface in a still stupefied mind. For the moment he was grateful for that.

'I spoke to your wife. She said the boy told her some other lad had given it to him.'

Duncan clearly disliked the thought of such chatting. Bailey reflected he was the sort of man who would resent any man speaking to his wife, while reserving to himself the right to behave like a pig towards the wife of another. A common enough double standard, he supposed, not peculiar to policemen.

'No, sir. I'm sure he told me he'd picked it up from the road, outside where they live. I could be wrong. I'm sorry, sir, why do you need to know?'

'Nothing. Never mind. Nothing.'

Bailey did not know what Tom Perry looked like, but he knew he would be able to detect the mother. Not only from their rare meetings, but also from the photo with the cracked frame on Duncan's bedside table at home. Kimberley Perry had always been discussed: she had the open face of the streetwise girl next door and the figure of a siren, an effortless sexual draw which she did not seem to realise, a swagger which was not ostentatious but nevertheless drew wolf whistles from building sites. A homely body, not beautiful enough to intimidate or slim enough to model; the sort of woman a man might take home to mother and then to bed; likely to be good-humoured on either occasion and an irresistible combination to any officer on night shift. Bailey himself had noticed her, of course. Since Helen had arrived to save him from cynicism, as well as the succession of affairs which had distinguished his bachelor career after divorce, infidelity had never occurred to Bailey. Other men's needs were their own affair, but such betrayal of trust struck him as the height of bad manners. Nevertheless, he was not blind, still noticed, watched and admired.

The school gates were a mile and a half from Herringbone Parade, and the wind which had dogged the first two weeks of December was still blowing. A small clutch of winter-coated mothers stood gracelessly by the gate, as deferential but eager as those sulky fans outside a theatre waiting for a star who was bound to ignore them. It seemed to Bailey that it was only childless adults who wanted to proclaim their individuality; here, children and parents alike desired nothing more than to be one of the crowd, plead the same backgrounds, the same difficulties, wear the same uniforms to escape envy or scorn, seeking anonymity rather than be noticed. The school matched its scenery: an old-fashioned red-brick school isolated in concrete surroundings, the same vintage as Bailey's own police station, probably furnished with the same thick radiators and gloss paint, the fabric of it as solid as chipped granite. A school where he imagined he might smell cabbage although he did not doubt that meals catering more to contemporary taste were delivered by the carton. And children, he remembered, never did like cabbage. Cabbage was good when only shown the water, sliced with butter and coriander seed . . . Bailey was hungry and he had become adept at cooking.

Cabbage and the cabbage-like mothers, hidden under those coats, distracted him for a minute or more. There were no waiting men, which did not discomfort him, but he could see why it might have worried Duncan, a man too uneasy with women to stand alone with them.

Then school broke, and it was as if the building were coming apart at the seams with boys and girls shoving out of the main doors, swinging them back deliberately to hit the one behind. The crowd was heralded by one or two and then a great heaving, yelling mass, spilling forth with bravado, dragging coats and bags, and then, having celebrated their own escape, slowed down in the playground, reluctant to leave, shaping into small conspiratorial or sparring groups, full of unintelligible noise. Girls linked arms and walked in whispering pairs, boys circled, swooped, dived and shied away. Bailey could not help the sensation of wonder and jealousy which afflicted him. All that row, that blatant physical perfection not even hidden by the scruffy regularity of school clothes; skinny bodies, fat bodies, blessed with the energy of less than twelve years. His own child might have been thus: he was not contemptuous of the mothers. Found himself looking in that crowd for a girl who might have been his own, instead of looking for Tombo.

He could not imagine how teachers ever distinguished one child from the other, although each walked or gestured differently, pulled faces and wore their hair in different ways. But row on row, he could not have been sure to pick out his own, or anyone else's daughter. Bailey shook himself, concentrated on looking for Mrs Perry. He waited, looking shy by the railings like a man waiting for a date, remembering that too. Waited until every drab mother had disappeared with one or two young, the last posse of fighters fled from the playground, the last promise made before the weekend, and the pavement held nothing but echoes.

Slowly he went into the school building itself. She might have come in here to wait: so might the boy. He found one lone teacher, adjusting a coat in her headlong flight downstairs, comical in her hurry, less than pleased to be stopped.

'You might try the youth club at the back,' she said. 'Some of the kids wait there if their mothers are working.' She had never heard of one Thomas Perry. It was not that kind of school, despite the homely aspect. Watching so closely, he had missed them both.

'Tea?' he said. 'Tea, Kim? You must want a nice cup of charred char by now. Been at least an hour. I'll make it.'

So solicitous today, as if to compensate for yesterday's bossiness, the thin level of reserve covering all tensions like paper over a crack. Kim had recovered from the sleepiness, but not from the tiredness and a slight feeling of wanting to weep. She had been twice to her diary to look at the date and see if the monthly affliction of hormones could provide a reason if not an excuse, but the dates had blurred a little in front of her eyes after the mid-morning coffee which had been such a welcome respite from tea. Besides, when she had reached the handbag and found inside the paracetamol packet with the message, she forgot why she had broached the handbag in the first place. Always a dangerous thing to do: the market place leather contained lists of recriminations. Letters from Duncan, lurking there, the only proof she had he could write.

'Tea?' Pip was saying again. 'I haven't forgotten you're going to meet the little lad from school, plenty of time.'

'Thanks,' she muttered. The toothpaste stack was perfect: the cosmetics were at long last sorted back into place after two weeks' interference from teenagers thinking of Christmas parties and asking about special offers. As well they might, she had been thinking grimly as she kept herself deliberately busy and active in the lull spells outside the dispensary: half this stock is reduced. Wonder if he killed Margaret to get his share? The mere thought made her smile: Pip would not hurt a fly. He would wave a stick at it instead and call it names. Horrified, she had tried to check all such thoughts, stung by the fact that her previous admiration for him had grown to contempt in a matter of days, all without rhyme or reason. Ever since he had put his arm round her and shouted at Duncan. The tea arrived. Purple tea. 'Hibiscus,' said Pip proudly. 'To buck you up.'

'I thought it made you sleep.'

'No, no, only soothes the nerves.' Kim sipped doubtfully.

The door slammed open and shut, admitting one of the regulars from the building site, a recognisable hypochondriac who called in at least twice a week for a different patent remedy every time. He cantered from entrance to counter, looking worried, muttering, 'Jesus, it's cold.' Then stood indecisively, looking round as if expecting pursuit. 'Give us some of those yeller ones,' he croaked. Kim looked at the shelves behind the counter, tea mug in hand, could not quite see what he meant by yellow ones although she was usually quite astute in translating the odder requests.

'No yeller ones? Throat things, then, any kind.'

'You're in a hurry,' Kim remarked, pulling down a packet of pastilles, honey and lemon flavour.

'So will you be soon. All of youse. I'm off all right. Them buggers has found a bomb out there, and I'm not waiting to see how big.' He sped to the door, leaving his change. Kim watched with weary resignation as the toothpaste display toppled. They had their superstitions over there on the site: they were always talking rubbish in that pub. Pip watched her solicitously.

'Kim, you look all in. Why don't you go home and lie down for half an hour? Look, not a customer in sight.'

'Can't,' she mumbled, stifling a yawn. 'Can't. I've got to go and meet Tombo.'

'Don't worry, I'll phone you upstairs, wake you up in time. Go on, finish that tea and go.' He was gently insistent; so much so she forgot her resentment of his bossiness, thought only of his kindness and got out of the shop without succumbing to the tears which still threatened. The same feeling as yesterday, a not unpleasant drowsiness which turned her hands to sponge and her brain to water. She got as far as the bedroom, took off her overall, and fell on the bed she had not bothered to make. Even the sight of the open drawer, mute witness to last night's petty burglary, did not disturb her.

Tom always knew if there was someone to meet him from school or not. He sensed the presence or absence of either parent or dopey Daniel as soon as he crashed beyond the main door to emerge into the playground, jumping over the flattened flowerbeds which adjoined the building to be trampled daily. On the rare occasions Dad was there, he could be spotted immediately, hanging about with sheepish self-consciousness beyond the wire fence which separated school ground from street, Dad always moving like some kind of warden patrolling a compound. On those occasions, Tom would want to grab the nearest boy, or the largest, any of the casual tormentors who picked on him when there was no other unfair game, and shout, Look, there's my Dad! Point out Duncan's unshakeable six feet, stolid and official and unaware that he would act as a talisman for days to come. No Dad today. Simply some older geezer, a grandad in Tom's eyes standing close to the usual clutch of mothers. Such grandads were a joke: they hung round after the girls for reasons not yet fathomed but faintly disgusting.

Tom's eyes darted quickly. No Daniel, no Mum. You said you'd come today, Mum; you said, you said . . . When she was there, as most days, he approached her with diffidence, shuffling his feet and not indicating welcome, but his heart rising in the acute and hidden pleasure of seeing her, delight disguised in nonchalance. Today, obeying the alternative orders for such occasions, he ran past the throng to the bus stop, attached himself vaguely to some unknown woman and child, and embarked safely for Herringbone Parade.

He never got home. There was a strange sensation about the place, more bustle than usual although there was no market.

People gathering in the street, talking and gesturing; Mrs Beale in her shop doorway wearing a coat, smiling as she gripped Tom's arm. "'Lo there, Tom. Where's your shadow, then?' She meant Daniel, he supposed: Mrs Beale always exaggerated. Then she clamped her hand across her mouth. 'Oh, sorry, petal,' she said, looking up the road as she spoke, 'I forgot, he died, poor lad.'

'What?' said Tom, stupidly.

'Your Daniel. Yesterday, I heard. When I was at the doctor's. Oh look!'

Tom looked. There were four policemen moving slowly down the Parade, sweeping people before them with gentle insistence. A motley crowd of people, some of them carrying bags.

'We've all got to go, Tom,' Mrs Beale explained, her voice high with excitement. 'We've got to lock up and go. They've found a bomb left over from the war in those foundations they've been digging. All that time, fancy, lying there. Like being a kid again, this, being evacuated.'

'What did you say about Daniel?'

'Now don't you be worrying about him. Didn't your mum tell you? Come on, love, you'd best get a move on. You come along with us. I bet your mum's already gone, they started that end.' She put a possessive hand on his shoulder, then let go to adjust her coat, enjoying the situation.

Tom slid away and watched. The elderly of Herringbone Parade seemed to agree with Mrs Beale about the fun of the situation. There was cackling laughter, no sign of anxiety and a quite uncustomary obedience to the young constables led by an Inspector whom they addressed as 'Son', and who seemed to fulfil the role of Pied Piper, leading them away as they emerged and followed, clutching clothes, and, sometimes, cats. The Inspector was enjoying himself too. He raised his megaphone.

'This street to the church hall in Ash Grove, please. All to the church hall. Transport is arriving for non-walkers. There is an unexploded bomb on the building site: I repeat, an unexploded bomb on the site.'

Tom wanted his mother, trod delicately between those moving

in the opposite direction until his arm was grabbed yet again.
'Where you going, my lad?'

Born to respect this particular uniform, Tom answered defer-
entially. 'My mum, in the chemist up there . . .'

'No she won't be, sonny. She'll have gone to the hall. We started
down that end, you'll find her later, promise. Come along now.' So
Tom pretended to come along, the bile of fear combining with the
burn of panic and deliberate rebellion. At the end of the row of
shops, he slipped like a fish from a net and ran into the service
road. There were more people there, descending from flats into
cars, darkness adding to an orderly confusion. He was not going to
go anywhere, not he. Not with Mrs Beale and the kids from the
Parade, not without Mum or, at worst, Daniel. Not Daniel: he
had hardly comprehended what Mrs Beale had said, but knew it
was true, and added to the fear was a leaden weight of guilt, pictures in his mind of Daniel moaning in a huddle. His fault, all his
fault, a weight to carry with all this sense of betrayal, and where
was Mum? Ducking cleverly from one back yard to the next,
shying away from the dark bins, it became clear he would never
reach his flat before being collected again, but he found, in the end,
that fear of the herd subsumed the fears of these secret places and
it was not so difficult to hide. He slid down behind one of the containers he had always envisaged as a coffin, pressed his face against
the grubby cold plastic, and settled, heart thumping, to wait for the
street to empty.

It was later than normal closing time, but the shops still blazed.
Christmas. Decorations suitable for Regent Street's gracious
curve, where Helen sat on the top deck of a red bus, frozen by
words. She sat with thirty others, kings of the castle surveying
thronged pavements and top windows, contemptuous of crowds
and the unaffordable riches of Garrods windows. Hamleys for
toys, Aquascutum, Austin Reed for clothes, Liberty for luxuries.
A million pieces of china glowed in the crescent while feathered
angels twinkled above. I hate this consumer society, Hazel had
said. This bloody fixation with shops and goodies. Hate it,

although I concede it's an improvement on the war which formed me. And all my dead contemporaries. I was a boy at the end of it, with a son, lucky me. But himself and the wife met a runaway bus when they were out with the ration books, and they brought him home to me on a door. Chloroform, I used then to dull the pain because he was nearly dead and I had some there: ether I used after, for myself. Not for frolics, for oblivion: I've been seeking it ever since. One learns, of course, that there is no such thing. Not even after six years of ritualised conflict in a war and forty-five years' fighting ever since to make a society sick to death. So young you are, you don't know: despair's the real bit. You don't know: you only think you do, you seekers after truth. I'm sorry about your case. You'll find someone else.'

Write it down, she had told him fiercely. Write it down: you can write history, think, read, function. Take this as a start.

'Oh, I may, I may. This has been a shot in the arm, you see. There, Helen West, you've achieved something and people like you always have to be achieving things, do you not? You can never let life alone, can you? And I'll tell you something for free: that woman was murdered, probably deserved it. Not that it matters, you know, not really. Let the poor bastard be. And don't come to me with my raked up past, accusing me with questions. I don't care about your case.'

She looked down at the shops, up at the lights. Consumer society, the long after-effect of war, the antidote to peace. Do not strive so to achieve, he had said: nothing is worth so much. The woman is dead already. Only nurture what you have; learn to protect it.

A nihilist, for all his wit. She had not, after all, made a friend.

CHAPTER TEN

IT was only because of Hazel that the short bulletin overheard on the radio at home struck any chord. Unexploded wartime bomb: East End evacuation, reminiscent of wars. Army disposal experts on hand to defuse what may be largest amount of explosive yet discovered. Helen did not really register the area concerned; the East End was a widely ranging definition, loosely used, but in the middle of pondering the events of her day, she also considered the quirkiness of a bomb which did not do its business but remained underground for almost half a century. Maybe a lazy bomb, like a Friday afternoon car, made by the night shift, designed never to work. A soft sort of news item which she ignored until she realised the implications, and even then the news was still bizarre enough to be faintly funny. It was a change from other bombs, Semtex, the IRA, Palestinians and other hell raisers who were not funny at all. And no one was hurt, yet. Like everyone else whose curiosity was faintly aroused, she had blind faith in the experts, some vague admiration for such cold bravery and a belief that everything would be rectified quietly. Revenge from the Luftwaffe at this stage in history seemed absurd, an incident which lacked any element of justice. Even the kind which was purely poetic.

The reality of the thing only impinged further when Bailey rang. Helen had not forgotten his part in making her look an idiot in the little matter of the criminal record of one Dr Hazel. If she and Bailey had joined forces for the night, he was in for some sharp words, to which, of course, he would reply with sour reason, leaving her even more afflicted with futility. Of course he had not been malevolent: Bailey was well able to define the meaning of malice, but it had no part in his makeup, indeed, it was his mildness which sometimes infuriated her, but all the same, the timing was spiteful. As if he had chosen to say, there, I have always known more than you after all; we have our resources, we persons in authority, run away and do your homework. Sharpen the instinct and then try and pretend the law is not really your pet blunt instrument designed to miss the target. Tell me something new, Helen was thinking. Tell me the law is not such an unwieldy instrument that we cannot catch a murderer by legitimate means and we have to stage a trial like a strange musical, with everyone's face painted whiter than white to mirror the cleanliness of their souls. According to Redwood, she would never be able to invite to the witness box anyone who had ever lived hard enough for tragedy, long enough to make mistakes, or fallible enough to command affection. She would look for another dry and blameless doctor. Tomorrow.

When Bailey rang, there was no time for the bone picking, no more suggestion of it than her saying, Oh, it's you, is it?, instead of some more instantly friendly response. She would have thrown off the resentful feeling as being both idiotic and unattractive after a minute or two of this, but news prevailed over the need for such effort.

'Going to be around here, all night, I reckon . . .'

'What?' Helen had not been listening.

'Herringbone Parade, everybody out. They're being very good-natured about it. This bomb, you must have heard. Apparently big enough to devastate a large area. All police hands stand by, etc. I'll probably run a soup kitchen.'

'You don't cover Herringbone Parade. Oh, I see. They need you. Like a riot.'

'No, not like a riot. Peace prevails. But everyone available has to stay. See you tomorrow.'

'Oh, wait a minute. Look out for the chemist, will you?'

Helen still could not confess she had seen him. Remembered those bleached blue eyes.

'Women and children first,' Bailey replied, and that was the end of the conversation. Only later, chewing a sandwich, the sort of sloppy self-provision he detested, dissecting the duplicate papers she had purloined from the office, spreading them out over the living-room floor, statement by statement, in an effort to work out a whole new strategy, did she begin to wonder what Bailey was doing. Looking inside Bailey's mind was a rare privilege, a door opened to an occasional glimpse, like a view into a dim house caught in passing as someone came out or in. Never fully open, not even in summer. Beside him, she could feel garrulous, obvious, rather too talkative, as open as a book. Ah, he had said once. I know why you talk. A disguise, darling: in the end you keep as much secret as I do. Sitting by the fire, Helen could see an element of truth in the observation. She listed the cast of characters in and around the Carlton case, stung by the words of the doctor; conscious of a nagging sensation of danger which had dogged her ever since the first page of the report, wondered long and hard about the motives of men and the dearth of her own instinct.

Many of the refugees had gone to relatives, hence half the Asian population of the square next to the Parade was notably absent from the church halls. Others had been warned not to come home from work, stayed with aunts, uncles and occasionally resentful friends. All had blind faith in the experts, and muttered knowledgeably about steam and explosive, everything perfectly all right by tomorrow, old son. In the centres along with the Red Cross and the St John Ambulance, there were camp beds and blankets, tea and sympathy, laughter and card games with the elderly who never encountered such *esprit de corps* in daily life. Mrs Beale's mother, whom daughter had nurtured crossly for a dozen years, felt herself hugged for the first time in a decade, by a fireman who had lifted her out of her house and called her darling. The thought of that, and the sharp memories of war, made her weep. Amid the organising at which he excelled, Bailey's eyes were everywhere. Five streets and one square had been cleared, or so they'd been told. There was no telling where all of them were. Of Kimberley Perry, and the son he had failed to recognise, there was no sign. In that fact alone there was no cause for concern. She had relatives, she had, albeit reluctantly, Duncan: she need not have come to any of the centres, but her absence, as outside the school gates, worried him. Neither was there any sign of the chemist, which was merely strange without being sinister. On the basis of his reputation, Caring Carlton was unlikely to miss such opportunity for being seen to be charitable to a fault. He could have dispensed the aspirins and the soup, whipped up for himself a round of applause. Ash Grove church hall was stinking warm, fuggy with gas heaters borrowed from a warehouse. The scene inside was reminiscent of an airport lounge full of anxious people subdued into patient behaviour by their belief in authority. Some of them slept. Some of them were a nuisance, talking away anxiety, glad of the holiday. Bailey was a man who seemed to carry his own heat, never more than half wearing a coat, and the atmosphere oppressed him. Then he saw Duncan, huddled into an anorak which had seen better days, walking up and down the rows, checking. Looking for Kimberley. He felt a prickle of alarm, like an itch he could not quite reach.

Herringbone Parade was detached from the world by tapes across each end. From behind, the fairy light crane glowed obscenely, dimmer against the floodlights. A quiet noise, Tom thought: the kind of noise which you could almost touch but without any kind of form to it, like a muttered conversation indicating something important, events out of earshot, slightly languid. He wanted to go towards this mysterious noise of industry, but dared not. To do so would be trouble, yells, shouts, pursuit. He wanted to be on top of the crane, looking down and eating sweets, warm above the world, watching. At first, he visualised the bomb as something the size of a hand grenade, something thrown, and could not understand the fuss he had witnessed. Any understanding at all was diminished by the creeping cold and the leg cramp, the sucking of the strap of the satchel, biting his nails, nothing made sense, and the sheer emptiness of the street, the absence of all the familiar sounds, made for disorientation. Like a film on telly about what would happen after the other kind of bomb. A frightening film which he was not supposed to watch, showing a street which might have been desert, nothing in it, like this one, but buildings and drifting wind. The thought struck him that this was the kind of bomb they meant: it had already fallen and apart from the formless noise, he might be the only person alive, anywhere. That particular, whimpering fear made him move. He had to know the worst. Then there was a shout from far beyond him. His eyes, luminous and enormous in the dark of the service road, caught sight of a uniformed figure, adjusting the tape which isolated the road and fluttered in the breeze. The figure disappeared. Tom knew then he was not the only one alive, and therefore felt justified in postponing decisions to remain where he was. He resumed his chewing of the satchel strap, sticky and dirty, like a dog worrying a bone. In a minute, just a little minute, he would go home. In the bottom of his pocket, he found the key he had taken illicitly that morning.

At the far end of the service road, a door opened quietly. Philip Carlton stood outside in the tiny yard beyond the hidden entrance to his dark dispensary, looked at the glow of the sky with satisfaction. He was dressed in an overall which was a duplicate of the one he wore in the shop, apart from the colour. In the black cotton of the tunic, buttoned to the neck in the style of Nehru, he was insignificant in the dark, giggling slightly. While Tom crouched back out of sight, dismayed by the emptiness of the street, Pip revelled in it, Lord of all he surveyed. He was higher than the crane, brighter than the stars, glowed with more power than the light which oozed out of the building site. They were digging in there, excavating in the vicinity of a bomb and he did not care. Pip was too young for wars, a man of peaceful memory, bar the screaming of families, the confederacy of women who had brought him to adulthood and ruled him ever after. They spoke of a war he did not know, relived it for his benefit with tales of hardship and ration books, told him how lucky he was, but he knew them all, these aunts, as liars, cheats, persons of manifest ugliness who had held him down for his daily bath, fondling him into screaming, laughing with the laughter which still rang in his ears when he fingered what they had fingered, the echoes of that laughter coming back in his own small giggle of relief. They would tickle, too, oh you like that, don't you, look at him laughing, so comic, the agony of tickling, the hideous humiliation of the whole body squirming out of control. Rearing and arching like a frightened horse, oh please, please, please sto-o-o-p. And now what was he, a man who had only learnt what a man does with a woman with the help of the chloroform, the private ether frolics which made it all possible, but had never yet made him quite understand what he had to know. Such as why the pleasure was great enough to be the cause of wars, the pivot of life in peace. Margaret, poor wrinkled Margaret had not been able to explain the puzzle, but Kimberley Perry, pliant, luscious as fruit would be better than the honeydew melon purloined from Mrs Beale, who had offered other services too. Kimberley would be better than that, or the lonely masturbation of the back room, or the poking of Margaret which had led only to that out of control humiliation which was so similar to the tickling. Kimberley would give him release and she would not even have to participate (oh, if only Margaret had kept still). The girl upstairs had only to remain sleeping, as beautiful and passive as she was, fed with dreams, like a corn-reared chicken, loving without demands. That would do nicely.

Pip had made a new mask. Not new, but old, a replica of the one he had used with Margaret in the days when she had cavorted around the room wearing nothing but. She had raised goose bumps of disgust on him until he breathed the vapour from the duster and at last his penis rose like a flag hoisted at sunrise. Stayed fit for action only as long as it would have taken to whistle three bars of the Last Post, measure itself in supine Margaret, and explode into anticlimax leaving him nothing more than that same helpless sensation of fatigue which had followed the tickles. As for her, she seemed pleased, even if she wept after, unsatisfied, but less than she might have wept if he had never tried at all. She meant to be kind, kept insisting. Until he could bear it no longer.

Pip carried the mask, a duster hidden from sight up one sleeve, and a hip flask. He had plucked the key to Kimberley's flat from the hook where he kept all spare keys to every cupboard and door of his whole domain, enabling him to move from the back dispensary to his own flat, up to Kim's, into the shop; such short journeys, such ease. He staggered slightly. In the piercing cold which threatened frost before dawn, the only visible part of him was the still sweet-smelling vapour that surrounded his mouth, and the bared teeth of his uncontrollable smile.

Upstairs, Kimberley Perry slept the sleep of peace. Knocking on her door had failed to rouse her, as had the exodus of human life from every habitation. Drugging Kimberley Perry was easy, involving no poisons. Really, they had laughed, Pip, Margaret and she, at this small vulnerability of his assistant: one soporific cough drop and she would sleep. He had watched the reaction yesterday, the glazing of the eyes, the lack of co-ordination in the lovely limbs, the growing fatigue which had made her so muzzy today. Each cup of tea, another capsule of Night Nurse. Nothing lethal: she would wake tomorrow, fuzzy but unharmed, imagining herself ill with flu, perhaps. He did not want to harm her. What Pip had in mind for a winter afternoon, after she had left the shop to sleep and he had shut up the doors to follow, was something he had also had in mind to repeat. A very quiet impregnation, a coupling with one of them conscious, not too fast, but not slow either. But the bomb was a blessing: Pip had never imagined there would be a time quite as perfect as this, so free from prying eyes. That part was sheer fluke and when the warnings came, he had been thinking fast, pretending to obey, lock his doors and follow the crowd which departed in bus and car. Then he had stopped and smiled, retreated beyond his boxed-in door and stayed almost still; playing, thinking, smiling, putting against his face the smooth silky touch of Kim's stolen negligée, the brassières, knickers and slips as yet untouched.

Kim Perry had woken once. To be sick in one sleepy stagger to the lavatory, trailing back, confused by the sounds from outside but not caring, shrugging out of the nylon blouse which made her sweat in bed, not quite remembering where she was. She called for

Tom, thought she heard him reply. There had been a knock on the door which might have been someone bringing him home. Then she slept, half-dressed, her feet growing cold, her generous body half covered, one arm under her head, the other outflung in an attitude of open abandonment. Her hair was wild, spread on the pillow, and her half-open mouth suggested invitation. When Pip came into her room on his soft-shod feet, she looked like some picture he had seen, some Victorian depiction of a woman lost. He smiled, catching his breath, unable to stop smiling. Paused for a long moment, watching her.

Duncan Perry was following Bailey round the room, like a dog at a master's heels, three steps behind with a kind of urgent dignity, not quite plucking at his sleeve or tripping over his shoes, but almost. Bailey had noticed that Duncan smelled slightly of drink, not enough to cause offence or even be noticed by anyone less observant, and not enough to impair his performance. Only the residue of lunchtime or early evening when Duncan would seek the solace of a pub as soon as possible after darkness. Already they seemed to be swimming in the middle of the night, an impression extended by the dozing evacuees, but the hour was early, no more than seven in the evening, black as pitch. The winter solstice, mid December, drawing everyone away from the moon and into despair. Bailey no longer believed such thoughts were fanciful. His mouth was downturned, his spirits too: he wanted away from the irritation of Duncan's presence, a man with less to recommend him than many of the others who came looking, mildly worried, for their grannies.

'Sir,' Duncan was saying insistently, the way he did whenever Bailey paused. 'Sir, I can't find them anywhere. I thought she might come to me when they all had to get out: they had time to phone and make arrangements after all, why didn't she come to me?'

'Look, Duncan, she could have gone anywhere. Friends, relatives, anywhere. We don't know where half the people have gone.'

'She hasn't gone to her relatives. There's only her mother and she doesn't get on with her mother. She goes to her sister, but she didn't, I rang. I know. I want to go and see if she's still in the flat.'

'Don't be silly. We've moved all the uniform to the edge of the area. This bloody thing is for real. Why the hell would she stay?'

'I don't know,' Duncan mumbled.

'No, neither do I,' said Bailey briskly. 'I should go home. She may be trying to ring you. They won't let you anywhere near, so don't try. Go home, man, where you might actually be useful.'

Duncan gave him a look such as a man might give to one who had betrayed him, a look expressing plea and contempt.

'That's my woman you're talking about.'

'I wasn't talking about her, not as such.' Bailey's irritation took the form of pedantry. 'Listen, I'll go out there in a little while and look. Where's Tom?'

'That's what I've been saying. No Tom either. Tom would have been coming home from school . . .' The light of hope appeared in Duncan's eyes as he talked more to himself than his audience. 'Oh, I get it now. Kim would have gone to meet him, so they would never have got back into the flat, the timing . . . She must have gone off with someone else from the Parade. They would have been coming back just as everyone was leaving.' The anorak slipped further off one shoulder. 'I wish she'd phoned, though. Might've known I'd worry. Women. I phoned that bloody flat of hers, to make sure she'd gone, but there was no reply.' The smile which broke through on to his face illuminated his features into something human, even likeable. For one brief moment, seeing the mischief behind the smile, Bailey could understand why a woman might once have adored him.

'Well,' he said uncomfortably. 'Give her a chance. To get wherever she was going. She's probably been ringing you while you've been wasting your time here. Go on home. I'll check in with you later.'

There was a mocking, cheerful quality to Duncan's salute.

Bailey wondered as he often did about the true parameters of responsibility. Or, more precisely, whether he should have told his constable that Kimberley Perry had not met her son outside school: they had not gone home to be turned away from the street where they lived, herded to safety with the rest. The nagging unease which had afflicted him ever since he had waited outside the school gates, grew into alarm, and he wished he could trust Duncan enough to tell him he had made an assignation of sorts with his wife, without provoking hostility and suspicion. Duncan, if he thought at all, had long since concluded there was little enough reason to preserve his own safety; he was brave at the worst of times, and running into a street threatened by a bomb would not have troubled him in the slightest. Bravery. Duncan had always been content to act as the battering ram because he never foresaw that anything untoward might follow. Life was a joke to Duncan, the man who laughed until he cried, nothing between the extremes, but still he deserved to know something that might affect his family. There was no time for these considerations. Bailey knew he might regret what he said or did: he felt the prospect of regret like a breath on his face, and all the same, kept silent.

'Go home,' he repeated. 'I'm sure she's safe as houses.' And realised as he spoke what a bad analogy this was in the face of a ton of explosive poised to destroy whole streets. Duncan, who knew nothing of such subtleties, went, and in watching his progress out into the dark, Bailey's irritation was greater than his conscience. Duncan had nothing else to do with his evening. He could have stayed to help with the other volunteers: they needed people simply to talk, could have done with a troupe of entertainers. Thinking of one of Helen's opinions, Bailey smiled to himself. Not all policemen are born philanthropists, while those who are get it driven out of them.

'Scuse me, sir.' A voice at his elbow, literally from that level, the woman behind the voice tiny and bent, plucking his sleeve like a child, gentle but insistent. 'Scuse me, but where can I make a phone call? Got to tell my daughter . . .' He used his portable phone for her, watching the colour rise in the excitement of yet more novelty. Then, as an afterthought, he dialled Kimberley Perry's number. Bailey logged almost any phone number he had used in the last week into the bank of his memory, and pressed out the numbers without the slightest trouble. The line was engaged. He stood still, ignoring another plucking at the sleeve, his mind distracted but clinging to words. What did a man mean when he said there was no reply? Did he mean the phone rang without response, or did he mean the phone was engaged? What would a literal man like Duncan have meant? A man of Duncan's ilk would have meant what he said; no reply meant no reply, not any other sort of signal, however innocent. Bailey ran from the hall to see if Duncan might have delayed his departure, failed to start his damned car. The road outside was full, parked vans, well-meaning people, but no Duncan.

Kimberley Perry was not aware of having knocked the bedside phone to the floor in that last removal of her reluctant body back to bed, might not have cared if she had known. The shining eyes of Philip Carlton, so at ease with the interior of this place he could function in the semi-dark, raked the half-covered body from one exposed foot to the tip of the head, failing to notice the cream receiver on the old carpet below within touching distance of two outstretched fingers. There was sufficient light in the room from the window: Kimberley liked daylight: she was overlooked by nothing other than the crane and her curtains were rarely drawn. In some token gesture to her mother's principles, there were nets, saving nothing from anyone's gaze, but obscuring her own view very slightly, as if she cared. Kimberley kept her place clean and that was all she did. Tom kept his room cluttered to make his home there. Philip Carlton looked at his assistant's tidy room, sighed for no reason at all. Play your cards right, girl, and I'll see you do better. Don't wake, let me look at you.

He pulled back the duvet, dropped it as if the material were red hot as she stirred, then opened and closed her mouth, silent words forming in sleep. Her head moved restlessly from one side to the other and with one abrupt heave, she turned on to her back, one arm protectively across her breast, fingers splayed over the nipple, an ineffective covering. Then she lay as still as before, but although he knew how much any human being will move in sleep, he had not bargained for the shock. Pip's store of scientific knowledge intervened into his mesmerised mind, posing questions and answers. Does a woman partially anaesthetised turn or toss? Had she neglected any of the tea her politeness had obliged her to drink? Could she, in the meantime, have been sick, discharging with the vomit that which made her sleep deeper? He removed himself to the door of the room, came back inside noisily, walking with the businesslike step of an innocent man in case she should wake. Kimberley remained as she was. A slight snore escaped from her perfectly receptive throat. He considered that.

All the impedimenta were in the same kind of white polythene bag they used for heavier prescriptions. So prosaic, he had always thought, to sniff the stuff of dreams from a household duster kept in a polythene bag. He withdrew a bottle labelled dry cleaning fluid from the bag, unscrewed the top and poured a little on to the folded duster which glowed bright in the dim room. There was no other colour apart from the reflected glory of the Christmas crane. Pip did not notice the tiny buzzing sound from the phone, tempted as he was to raise the chloroform cloth to his own nostrils. Instead he bore the cloth towards her face, kept it there for her to breathe. Then paused again, lost in a kind of wonder, put the cloth on the coverlet, squatted by the side of the bed and began to stroke her. A tentative stroking at first, his hand hovering above the warmth of her belly, the palm skimming skin, his fingertips amazed by the texture. Then he inserted his whole hand between her thighs, shocked at the heat of her, stunned into the awareness of where he was and why. A little more on to the cloth, held above her face, not touching such a perfect face with the cheeks as flushed as if she had come in from the cold. Deep sleep, my lovely, and quiet breathing.

Something in the scent afflicted her; the young body warned her sleeping brain not to ignore it, waking her in time for a brief but terrifying protest. The hand which had lain on one breast joined the other to push away the smell, fluttering weakly while her back arched in a spasm of disgust, her knees bent to raise themselves so that her feet were inches from her torso and trembling. Futile protest. Pip adjusted himself on the bed, held her firmly by the hair and kept the duster over her mouth.

'Shhhh, darling, shhhhh. Sweet sleep, sleep tight.' Strange murmurings emerged from his own throat, reminding him of Margaret, their various stores of non-consequential words and revolting endearments. Kim's automatic protest faded as abruptly as it had begun. One hand fell on the pillow alongside her hair: the other jerked back towards the floor. Her legs flopped open with the heels still close. Pip sniffed the cloth. With automatic care, he placed it on top of the polythene bag, felt the rising of manhood in his trousers, touched himself briefly, looked down at Kimberley and at himself with enormous pride. He thanked God there was time to contemplate the wonder of both. Silence and time. Sweet sleep, my lovely. There is more of this.

Tombo's legs were numb. The gravel embedded in the one knee that was slightly less frozen than the other was a relic of an earlier playground struggle which had not hurt at the time. The silence was even more profound: he felt he could lean out and cut the darkness with a knife. The comforting mumble of traffic on the distant Whitechapel Road was so much a part of his breathing as to offer nothing. Quite suddenly, out of the emptiness came the bravery of desperation, because all the things which had seemed to matter in the halcyon late afternoon did not matter now. Such as being caught. Such as being the only person left alive. Such as Mum clutching the bomb or having gone somewhere else, or Dad never coming to look for him. Piglets, bums, bastards, shit shit shit: there did not seem anything to lose. Tom expressed his contempt for his own immobile cowardice by standing straight and directing the stream of his urine on to the bin which had sheltered him. Amazing how far the flow travelled: he could have won any competition with that and impressed many eyes, yes he surely could, and the sound was amazing too, like a steaming waterfall which fell to earth with a hiss. No one came near. No one could bear to come near a performance like that, but apart from manifold other needs, he needed to do the big stuff too. Nothing urgent, but his own fastidious habits forbade him to relieve himself here. Even in the privacy of a clean toilet equipped with copious quantities of paper, he could not bear the evidence of his own crude digestion.

Well, go home then, silly billy. You've got a key, all you have to do is wait. If anyone else is alive, they'll phone, but I hope Uncle Pip is dead. Why anyone as remote and disliked as Uncle Pip should swim into his mind was beyond him. There were a few others whose disappearance from the scene would not have disturbed a night's sleep either: Pip was simply the one whose demise was most devoutly wished. Even against large Larry of the playground, Mrs Beale and the Parade mob, and quite a gang otherwise, Pip was foremost as an object of hate. Tombo wished he had been pissing on Pip, dismissed that thought as more than faintly shameful, the joke better than the doing, stood even straighter and emerged from his hiding place. He tried to shout, but the shout refused to arrive. He looked up at the crane and dimly remembered some story about a star in the east, Christmas legends watered down at school because of his Pakistani contemporaries' lack of interest. He wondered if he should behave like the three kings and follow the crane on to the building site which he and Daniel had so admired. He would have company there. He went into the middle of the service road instead and tried to whistle in the dim hope that something, even a dog, would emerge and claim him. There was a cat, Mrs Kennel's mangy moggy, which emerged in a distinct black and white streak, howling in abandonment. For the first time in their few encounters, Tom knew what the cat meant and wanted to embrace it. She sat for a moment, distant from him, level with his own house, gesturing contempt from forty paces, and, using her as his guide, he walked towards home. The satchel with the frayed strap was carried across his chest, red satchel, plain as a pikestaff, but nobody saw. At both ends of the road, tapes flickered neon yellow. Not all of the windows were dark: some rooms had been left lit. Tom was grateful for the lights: he had not known they were there or he might have looked sooner for that stray comfort, but he knew the rooms behind those benign electric eyes were as empty as his pockets. The steps he took were solid and slow: he felt for the handrail announcing the stairs to the flat, paused to kick a stone under his foot. The flat was dark as pitch, but, from indoors, he imagined he could see the flickering light of a torch.

CHAPTER ELEVEN

HELEN was aware of becoming a nuisance, and did not care. The operation scar gave small stabs of recrimination for being ignored, nothing important. She had decided on the way across the city that being a nuisance, even being branded 'interfering cow', was better than the guilt which always attended indifference and felt like cowardice. Bailey's caution was another matter: he would often advocate doing nothing; if in doubt, do not buy, or move: impetuosity makes a good target for a sniper. You do not always achieve much by your addiction to movement. But in movement was comfort; in self-restraint, none.

It was not, of course, quite as unpremeditated as that. She had phoned the number given on the news, found out where some of the refugees from Herringbone Parade might possibly be and in another injudicious call where she had been content for once, to pose as Mrs Bailey, gained some clue from a sergeant as to Bailey's whereabouts. He was with the men, three St John Ambulance, two of his own, loading tins of soup from a van into the kitchen of a new community hall ugly enough for this patched part of the world. Helen slung her bag across her chest and joined the queue, so inconspicuous that Bailey had passed her a box before he noticed. He sighed in exasperation, relieved her of the burden, and walked into the hall without a word. She followed him.

'Anything I can do?' A careless invitation with a shrug of the shoulders. Take it or leave it.

'Probably. Quite a few things other than carrying heavy stuff three weeks after your operation. Why did you come?'

'I don't know. What a pointless question. Because it was Herringbone Parade. Because you were here. Coincidentally, because of that damn chemist and doctor talking about war. Is this the only shelter?' She was looking round, alert and interested. He usually responded better if she was very casual and she liked to pretend he could be fooled.

'Nope, just the largest. Most of them have gone to relatives. No sign of the chemist. Or his assistant or her son.'

'And the bomb?'

'Very dangerous indeed, possibly the biggest ever. Crazy, after forty-five years. Area isolated, no patrol cars, no uniform, no nothing at the moment. I'd like to go and look for Kimberley Perry. It doesn't make sense.' He was talking half to himself and Helen recognised the symptoms. Signs of unease, that reserve before action she so loathed but still admired. Fretful signs of involvement in a Bailey more familiar than the manager he had become.

'What doesn't make sense?'

'Kimberley Perry. She didn't answer her phone to Duncan soon after they'd all been herded out. When I tried half an hour ago, the phone was engaged.'

'What will you do?'

'Go and look, as soon as I'm allowed. Got to wait: I'm not in charge. In a minute or two.'

'No,' said Helen. 'You will not, do you hear me? You'll do no such thing.'

'Helen . . .'

'No. You'd make a lovely corpse, but no, not that kind of corpse. All smashed up. Don't go.'

'I'll think about it. I can't immediately. Listen, if you want to be useful, go on. The practical angles are all covered here, enough food, etcetera. Go and talk to some of these old ones. Tell them their cats and dogs are going to be all right. That's what we need, someone to chat, reassure. Lie as much as you like.'

'Don't go.'

'We'll see.'

There was a clear division of labour then. Men did the practical things, providing beds, blankets and food; women offered the succour. No one was dying. There was a sense in the hall of absolute safety while Helen, the easy talker, joined the women and did as she was told. Warmth seeped in and out of old bones and into the air. Once in a while, she stepped out into the cold in order to remember what cold was and to check, like an anxious hen, for Bailey. Heard with her sharp ears what the evacuees were not supposed to hear. About steam being used on a bomb, and no one, but no one being allowed to move.

Pip was aware of a faint hissing sound from outside. Half an ear registering some unfamiliar sound which was neither threatening nor any more alien then the kettle boiling in the dispensary for yet another cup of tea. His hands were still playing and he had no sense of time. Winter nights stretched from the middle of the afternoon until the morning beyond, a time of almost unbroachable darkness, making all thought of time irrelevant. Nothing moved but the bosom of his beloved, rising and falling, insensitive to his touch as he stroked her nipples and felt them harden, a sensation beneath his hands which made him laugh. So strange, so shaming: a woman would remain on heat even in the grave. This part of them never died, and something in this made him think of her as animal. So different from the wizened, black-dressed mother he had buried with such relief, hoping the interment was a route to freedom. Sweet dreams and quiet breathing, and then, dear God, she moved again. Pip was so shocked this time at Kimberley's violent stirring, he did not know for a moment whether what lay before him was indeed a sleeping beauty or a corpse. He leapt up from his knees where he had been praying by the bed, and swore softly and obscenely in a manner which would have made his mother faint. Then he seized the duster in a trembling hand, draped it over the wire mask, placed the whole ensemble over Kim's head, and held it there while he dripped more chloroform from the bottle. She had stopped moving before these manoeuvres were complete; the heave had been no more than an aberration, nothing real; no indication of intolerance. After a minute or two, Pip removed the mask and placed it on the floor. His trembling ceased and his smiling resumed. He began to stroke her hair, crooning to himself, stopped for a moment and raised the yellow duster to his face. He had come to love this perfume, breathed deep, fondled himself inside the unzipped trousers, gasped. A roaring in his ears, now, now, now. This is the time to discover. Now. Oh, my love.

Tom had intended to let himself into the flat with as much noise as possible, whistling, singing and banging to make himself heard, ensuring that he would be greeted if there was anyone there, detected if there was anyone nearby, and, in any event, make himself bold by striking back at the weird silence. But the stillness had defeated him: more complete a silence than he had ever known, even with the hissing; an awesome stillness which demanded a respect which he had found himself unable to defy with his clattering footsteps. Instead he had tiptoed up the steps, holding his breath, and stood on the balconette under the light of the crane. He paused to see what he could see in the building site and found there was nothing but the glow, a shh-ing sound, the generator which was always alive. There were no voices, no indication of human life, as if someone had left the machinery and run away. Tom turned from the light in disappointment, put the key in the lock and entered his own house like a careful thief. Put his satchel down on the kitchen floor, stood for a minute, feeling foolish. The flat was small: kitchen merged into living-room, their own rooms fanning away. Both bedroom doors were open. Mummy's white overall glowed on the sofa, visible in the light from the Parade which let him see since his eyes, used to the greater dark, adjusted easily.

He knew immediately there was someone there, someone alien and dangerous. The freezing of his movements was temporary: a great stirring of anger displaced fear as he stepped towards Mum's bedroom, following the sound, then stopped at the door, paralysed.

A tableau of two figures, one obscuring the other. Tom knew his mother lying on the bed: who else would lie on that bed? No one, except, hopefully his father. But the man leaning over the bed was not his father. Daddy was big, running to flab. These bare buttocks, with trousers obscenely lowered, were small and neat, the lights from the crane colouring them pink in the curves, unearthly blue in the hollows, and the black clothes glimpsed above the skin were never his father's clothes. A duster was on the floor and next to it was his metal hat, the one he had left in Dad's car. A little dirty man touching his mother, a sound of heavy, grunting breathing which filled him so full of disgust he wanted to retch. With a howl of rage, Tom launched himself forward in one massive leap into the room. He picked up the metal hat and struck blindly towards the back of the frightful head: he wanted to kick, bite and scratch at the same time, did not know he was yelling, 'You-you-you bastard, bastard, bastard . . .' struggling for the memory of every dirty word he had ever heard. The hat was heavier, infinitely more solid than he remembered: the metal was smoother, the rim sharper, so that in between blows he was aware of the unfamiliarity. Then the man turned, the eyes so intense, Tom could not meet them, sparkling eyes, hateful Pip, wafting the same smells he had known from the other cold night when he had trespassed downstairs. A smell of glue, deodorised sweat, and a sweet, sweet smell which was clamped over his mouth while his muffled shouting changed to desperation and his arms clawed the skin of the man's back. 'Daddy, Daddy, Mummy, Mummy . . .' His skin was burning, his face twisting and turning: he was on the bed, half off the bed, grasping at flesh and cotton, his heels drumming without sound.

'Daddy, Daddy, Dad . . .' And then, no shouting.

It was so easy.

Pip remained, holding the duster with liquid trickling between his fingers, pressing gently. C'mon, lad, c'mon, don't really want to hurt, don't want to hurt anyone. Please, please. The rage, the bitter disappointment, died quickly as he watched, silent and fascinated as one small fist clenched and unclenched against the dark carpet, finally remaining open with the fingers spread. Alongside that pale hand lay the cream receiver for the telephone. True to his meticulous self, begging time before making decisions, Pip replaced the receiver on to the cradle. Immediately, the phone rang and the eyes, Kim's eyes from the white pillow of the bed, opened wide. Pip ducked below the level of her sight, a gesture of sudden shame. The eyes widened further in puzzlement, then, slowly, closed.

Hot bath, warm bed, hot bath, warm bed, both of these dreams. The phone plucked in one hand, two rings, then silence. Duncan came to, looking at his watch, dismayed to find he had snoozed at all, but grumpy to see he had only snoozed for so short a time. Shouldn't have had the whisky. Not a tumblerful anyway, followed by another, without an ounce of grace to the whole proceeding. Get bottle out of pocket: open and pour straight into something which resembled a tooth mug, drink without aid of H_2O in the same way another might drink the water after a run, without any sensation of taste. Half awake now, he repeated the dose. A small dribble of whisky hit his chin: the slow drip on to his shirt made him feel ashamed. Trying to shake away the dream, he dialled Kim's number. Engaged. Duncan went into his bathroom, and saw with the acuteness of vision which was not a blessing, what a mess he was. It was salutary to see his own image in a glass so dirty. The spots on the glass horrified him more than the reflection; the surface was covered with what might have been smashed insect, white drops for toothpaste, grey bits for shaving foam, little speckles of something which may have been blood, the whole effect like a fly-blown windscreen. He had put out his hand, felt the surface of the mirror, felt through his fingertips how it was encrusted. No wonder, then, she did not want him, clean Kim.

Back in the living-room, suddenly aware of the musty smell, he dialled her number again. Remembered what he had dreamt; that hideous vision of his wife in the arms of another man. Forgot his coat, forgot being over the limit and fitter to walk than drive. Remembered the dream and the sound of the dialling tone. Ran.

Into the car with the still bent fender and the engine which roared. Not a single logical thought in his head, the man who was used by others to smash down doors, motivated by a delayed reaction to being stopped, a bad dream and a nascent rebellion. Someone had been lying to him, Bailey, Kimberley, something about that silly hat and a succession of days and nights like the party where he had existed only to be fooled and humiliated. Forbidden the touch of any woman. A certain cunning as well as the memory of bombs and officialdom made him slow down. At midnight, the tall buildings of the commercial city were empty, deep glass façades blank to everything but lamps and headlights, no sign of midnight oil, nothing stirring but hidden security guards drowsing behind doors, and in the distance, one, two, three cranes, lit for Christmas, bowing at the moon. Beyond the confines of the city, where the ambience of prosperity ended, he saw the first yellow tape across the road. Drove through, snapping the tape, heard a voice yell and saw a fist raised, drove further. Got out and ran again.

Only when he ran this time, blindly in the direction of the Parade and feeling his pockets as he went, did he see in his mind's eye the bedside table where all useful but never used items lingered for months. He stopped, cursed, ran on. He had forgotten to bring the vital key to Kim's flat.

There was a strange law of diminishing returns in talking to people this late at night. Like a priest giving a winter sermon in the church Helen remembered as a child, heated with a stove in the centre so that the congregation was ever thickest in the middle, his voice and message no competition for warmth; everyone wanting to be home, but quite content to postpone movement, complainers subdued into silence long since. There was that dormitory air, like a hospital ward. Helen was aware she had assisted just a little in the pacification process, and felt that for what it was, a dull task, helpful rather than vital. Like most of her daily tasks. She, too, wanted to go home. Not because her store of philanthropy was wearing thin, but because she was redundant. She turned to find Bailey. An old woman called Mrs Beale, who was telling her all about previous occupants of Herringbone Parade and its

environs, was enough to distract her attention. Somehow gossip
was better if you did not know any of the protagonists and there
was no guilt in the listening.

'There was the Carlton sisters of course. Lived next door to
me. He died in the war, and the three of 'em joined up under one
roof. Big mistake if you ask me. All them women and one little lad.
Didn't seem to do him no harm, though. A good boy that, very
good. Still is. Got the chemist's shop now, after his ma died . . .'

'The chemist's shop in the Parade? Must have been a clever
boy, then. Where else did he work?'

'Yes. Clever boy. His ma said she wasn't going to have him a
wastrel, brought him up nice, she did. He went to the Polytechnic,
then he worked in a big chemist's at Limehouse for years. Funny,
he married so late. Must be forty-five, still looks a lad. She put
paid to the girlfriends, though, his mother, she was like that. And
he couldn't go far: she'd have him back, what with her being so
poorly and everything. Mind, there was some said she was never
as ill as all that. And then when she's gone, he goes and marries,
just like that. Another one the same. Bossy, that Margaret, and
always at the doctor's. Sort of woman drives a man to it, if you see
what I mean.'

'Drives them to what?'

'Oh, I don't know. Things. Funny man, Pip Carlton. I could
have told them coppers a thing or two lately, only they didn't ask.
Like how he's always fiddling in his back room. Doesn't need to
do that. And what does he do with all that stuff he gets back?'

'Sorry, what stuff?'

'Stuff we return. People my age who look after other people.
Mr Ahmed, they're nice these darkies really, they look after their
own. Anything you've got left, always bring it back, Pip says.
Specially the worst stuff. He must have enough in there to poison
the whole district.' She laughed, looked round at her sleeping
neighbours, her eyes narrowing. Tiredness and spite. 'Mind some
of them would be better off . . .'

Helen crossed the arms of old Mrs Beale, so that she sat like a
pyramid, feet firmly planted, a blanket on her knees, the edifice

narrowing to a small and pointed head bedecked with regulation grey curls. The product of Sylvie's in the Parade, perhaps, half price to pensioners on Thursdays only. A fund of knowledge, Sylvie's, specially on Thursdays; the kind of knowledge which only the faintly malicious or the idle found time to accumulate. Helen was angry now. The curiosity, her conviction about the Carlton case was no longer dimmed by Hazel's defeatism, the criticisms of the day, the accusations of interference, restlessness, of being so bent on achievement she missed some vital point. Were common sense and energy really in such short supply she could afford to stay still and would it really have been absurd for someone in the local police to sit in the local hairdresser for a while? Women would make so much better detectives for local crime. Better chemists, better neighbours, better at just about everything. On such chauvinistic, irritated thoughts, she looked again for Bailey. Gone without word or whisper.

On second thoughts, she added to herself, men are better at subterfuge and avoiding embarrassment. Also regard themselves as better at the rough stuff. Little women don't interfere. She shut her eyes and tried to imagine Herringbone Parade in darkness. A comprehensive street, a good street, a tribute to life where everyone watched everyone else without watching for them, as secretive as any neighbourhood with the city on the doorstep. She had known the modern sham of real villages, liked that less. Crime, like blindness, was not a matter of diet or environment. Go on, then, Bailey, like a dog off a leash, Go on. Be a policeman, but I wish you could have let me go with you.

Bailey thought of nothing when he turned his back on the community hall, except a vague thought as he got in a car about how little community halls had to do with communities. They replaced churches, he supposed, and had little to do with those either. His mother, older than Mrs Beale to whom he had spoken at such length long before Helen arrived, had no truck with churches. She had pre-empted social workers in the East End, a woman of such conspicuous virtue she had driven her neighbours mad with kindness and earned their pity for having a husband who was always in the pub.

Mothers. Bailey could recall the power of mother, especially an East End mother. Mother and smother worked the same, post-war women with more than half their men lost to some sodding battle they did not understand, left with their infants, legitimate or otherwise. Mrs Carlton and her two sisters. He wondered about Pip Carlton, the caring chemist, such a lad, such a jolly lad, Mrs Beale had said, you should have seen him. Always the scientist, playing with stink bombs even as a boy, always collecting old muck and going on about history and being a doctor. Nothing alters, you know. People are like time. They are time. But he never got to be a doctor. Something happened, Mum was ill. He could have got a grant. Tell me, Mr Policeman Bailey, what did he do with all those drugs he kept?

I don't know, Bailey had said with his best humility, thinking as he drove how odd it was he was only let near the scene of this bomb because of reports of some lone lunatic racing the streets. A man who had missed a bus: such things drove people mad in central London, but this one had left a car and, what's more, he had known who it was. You will let me in there, he had wanted to say, to look for this lone man, whom I think I know, although I will not say so, but you would not allow me to when I wanted to check if everyone was out. Strange priorities, better say nothing. If only I could act on instinct and be furious at the imposition of other people's rules, other people's orders which I have been taught to respect even when they are ludicrous. I might have an ounce of Helen's anxiety, her fury with the formalities of law which get in the way of what is perfectly obvious. Something I seem to have lost, and I lecture her so she might lose it too. She knew she had a murderer: I did not. She knew what Mrs Beale knew; something odd about that boy. I have been in these streets for forty years, and I did not. If I have the instinct, I no longer trust it.

He had known when he held Daniel Maley in his arms that the man was not only dying, but dying murdered. It had awoken interest, but he had not moved mountains to pursue his belief.

Bailey was glad he wasn't a woman. No man in his right mind would ever wish to be a woman apart from a moment like this when he would have liked their instincts, their sheer, bloody-minded scent for blood.

But he was trusting to instinct now, looking for whoever it was who had abandoned his car and run through the lines. Maverick Duncan, inevitably going in the same direction as he was going himself which somehow lessened the need for speed. Say what one would about Duncan, he was good at beating down doors. And whatever else was inevitable about Duncan, if he got there first, he would not understand.

For the first time in a long time, Duncan was afraid. If he had been pursued in the last two hundred yards since he lost the car, he was not aware of it, nor did he care, but he cared about the silence which was terrifying. Streets were never silent like this; the dreadful stillness of desertion which allowed him to hear his own thumping breath. At the far end of the Parade he almost stopped, thought the hissing sound which filled his ears was a sound from inside his own head, his heart on the verge of explosion. Which end . . . where? He became confused: there was nothing, no one. He wanted no interference, but when Bailey's car caught him in the lights and he heard that despised voice of authority, cool where he was hot, the savagery of his expression softened. The phone, he began to say, the bloody phone . . .

'Yes, I know. Looks like someone at home.'

'You knew? Why didn't you do something, you cunt?'

He sprinted up the steps to Kim's door, rattled the handle, grunting with frustration. Glanced grimly at Bailey, their faces weird in the light, their voices raised against the hissing steam in the cavern beyond.

'Do you have a key?' Bailey shouted. Duncan patted his pockets, shook his head, sizing the door with his eyes. There was a plant, dead, by the side: Bailey picked up the pot and smashed the glass in the door neatly, put his hand inside for the latch, as couth as a burglar. A fragment of glass grazed the back of his hand, the brief pain a reminder. Duncan charged indoors, shouting, Kim, Kim, Kim. Bailey followed delicately.

Kimberley Perry lay in the bed, sleeping. Both men stood at the door of the room, looking at her half in awe, half exasperation. She lay curled, demurely covered, her breathing noisy, her head to one side and her hands beneath the pillow like a depiction of innocence. 'Kim, wake up,' Duncan shouted. Relief was turning to anger, concern curdling in the face of such peace. 'I'll bloody wake her . . . What the hell does she think she's doing?'

'No. Wait.' Something in the way she lay arrested Bailey: something in the smell of the room with the windows firmly closed. Something he had read or heard somewhere of how Margaret Carlton had been found without being photographed, with her head on one side, body curled like a foetus. Surely women did not copy each other in sleep as in other things: the peace was deceptive. 'Wait,' he said, 'don't touch.'

'Wake up, Kim,' Duncan shouted, obedient all the same. Bailey turned on the bedside light, saw the phone in the cradle, out of arm's reach from the bed; noticed a faint red mark on her forehead. The sickly smell, sweet and cloying, was denser nearer the floor and pillow.

'She's just asleep!' Duncan was fuming, relief still finding outlet in anger. 'She's bloody irresponsible, that's what she is. What's she done with Tom? And where's that fucking chemist who's supposed to be so good to them all the time? Kim, Kim . . .' He shook her shoulder, pulled down the cover, shielding his wife from Bailey's gaze.

'Get her up gently, Duncan,' Bailey said quietly. He was thinking fast. Such a deep sleep and unquiet breathing: she could not naturally have slept so long. They could not get a doctor in here with men steaming explosive from a bomb within a hundred yards: they must treat as they found. Rely on instinct. Phone Helen, get the number of that old doctor, ask what you should do with chloroform overdose. Quick quick. Slowly, slowly, Kimberley Perry responded to the shakings, surfaced into the light of the room, the sixty-watt bulb beneath the cheap shade, the colours from the window. Her eyes focused reluctantly, the pupils tiny: her mouth rounded to release a scream and she was suddenly, violently sick.

'Christ. Jesus H. Christ. Where's Tom, where's Tom?' The first words, noises rather, the sense slurred.

'All right, all right,' Duncan murmured, arms round her shoulders, immune to the coloured mess now on the pillow, the greenish skin, the wild eyes. 'He's safe somewhere, don't worry.'

'No,' she was mumbling. 'He was here. I saw. Asleep, on the floor. God, I feel sick.'

'You've been dreaming, sweetheart. Only dreaming. What the hell did you take?' Duncan's voice became harsh. 'You fucking whore.' On one of her rounded thighs, carelessly revealed as she struggled upright, he could see a fantail of fingerprints. 'What you been taking, you silly cow, and while you were at it, who took you?'

She looked at him, her eyes widening in horror, looked at the direction of his gaze, uttered a small cry subdued in a rising tide of fresh nausea, looked at Bailey in plea. 'Sir, Mr . . .' He was crouched, feeling the surface of the nylon carpet with delicate fingertips. Clinging to the tough surface were yellow threads, fluff, and, in spots, a stickiness he knew to be blood, that viscous texture horribly familiar. Far beneath the bed, in an otherwise tidy room, he could see a child's training shoe, adorned with dim red flashes on the side.

'Tom was here all right,' Bailey said slowly. 'His satchel's in the kitchen. He was here, with someone else. Duncan, you have to get her to hospital. Now.'

'It was that fucking chemist, wasn't it? Him, he did this, didn't he? He fucking did. You slope off to be with your fucking boyfriend. Where is he, where is the bastard?'

'Duncan, can it. You've got to get her to hospital . . .'

Kim began to cry, a retching cry, graceless in agony. Something terrible, a threat, a touch of clammy hands was crowding at her memory, making her whimper, wanting touch, but despising it.

'She can walk,' Duncan said brutally, relinquishing his hold on her like an abandoned toy. 'If she can go to bed with him, she can walk. I got things to do. I'll get that bastard.'

'There's the bomb. First things first. You're a sod, Duncan.'

Bailey was aware that his voice was high, his temper dangerous and all his diplomacy gone.

'Screw the bomb,' said Duncan. 'It's a con. Get out of my way.'

The rain had begun in earnest. An icy rain which fell in soft, cold sheets, straight lines of moisture unmoved by wind. Pip could not distinguish between what was rain on his face and what was tears, but the latter flowed with the same relentless ease, salty in his mouth, dribbling down his chin: tears flowing without sobbing or heaving, well behaved, very silent tears. Symptoms of despair, and more, the sadness of loss. Never to plant his seed without disgust, never know what it was like to be carried beyond himself on a tide of passion. Never, oh, my love; only the same feeling of rage when he struck Tom as the rage he had felt when Margaret had said, Shut the window please, it's cold in here.

'You all right, Tombo?'

There was silence. Oh Christ, such silence with the rain falling over them both. Tom and he were covered in a plastic sheet, the boy on his lap, sleeping trustfully, a sensation of warmth against Pip's chest he felt he almost enjoyed. Perhaps this would have been some substitute, a child of his own. Pip looked down at Tom's dark, wet head with something approaching affection. Something in him could never have liked any child, particularly this skinny little boy, a nervous, pansyish creature who reminded him of himself. A fretful boy who either asked too many questions or remained speechless, his whole attitude one of profound suspicion. The creation of such a large and brutish father, the kind of man women loved. Hateful, both of them, but for now, the boy was warm, and in his own arms, almost loving.

'I hope I didn't give you too much,' Pip murmured to no one. In his mind's eye was the bottle: impossible to say how much was too much: you could only tell when they stopped breathing and Tom had not stopped breathing. He presumed Daniel had stopped breathing on thrice the daily dose of physeptone, bullet pills of poison only to be swallowed by someone made unwary by a big, heavy blow. Mother had stopped breathing and Margaret; Tom did not. As if it mattered, but it did. The plan was clearly for Tom to stop breathing, but preferably not with some lethal overdose in his frenetic bloodstream.

'You all right, Tom, boy?' He said it louder. The silence was reassuring, but curiously dissatisfying. He shook the boy. Small feet, one without a shoe, looked sad as they protruded from beneath the blanket of clear plastic grabbed from the back dispensary as they left. Pip did a last mental check, wishing the tears were less blinding than the rain.

'Right. Kim never saw anything. Asleep. Will wake up feeling sick. Too much Night Nurse in her tea, doubt they'll test blood, you can always depend on ignorance. They'll only find alcohol. All signs, duster, white poly bag, removed into bin. Through dispensary, no muddy feet. Careful, careful. Not more than a few milligrammes of stuff in this boy either, not by the time they find him in the morning or whenever this stupid bomb business is over. Meanwhile, everyone, this is what happened. Little Tom ran away over the building site because he is frightened of crowds, never was a kid who could stand crowds, couldn't even take a Christmas party, Mrs Beale told me. Fell into one of the holes. An accident. Like all of this, really. Not my fault. Little bastard; you shouldn't have come home, you hear? You shouldn't . . .'

Pip felt in his pocket. On their way downstairs, gasping under Tom's weight, he had collected some of the worst stuff from his back room. Methadone, a little morphine. One vague plan was to give some to the boy, another half-formed plan to chuck it away in the same way he could hide the child. This plan was messier. Logical plans always avoided mess.

They were sitting below the hoardings at one end of the building site which both of them had explored, one with feet, the other with eyes, fascinated in different ways by the subterranean domain of mud which made for this strange series of vaults below the level of the earth. Pip remembered hating Tom most when Tom had begun excavating for Australia, from the yard. Not because of his proximity to the back dispensary, which Tom would find anyway, but for the similarity with something he had done himself. People like Tom and he were always excavating for a hiding place and it had always seemed as if the builders were doing no more than the same. Useful, said Pip to himself, trying to harden his own features, breathe hard, think hard. Concentrate, to survive. And this little one will go in one of those pits. Only a small fall into one of those dark graves called foundations. I'm sorry, boy.

The hissing of the steam persisted fifty yards away. Pip could not guess if the sound itself had increased or if they were simply closer to the awning erected against the rain. Arc lights and ve-hicles shrouded the sound like Quatermass and the Pit. Men busy in an island of light, leaving all the rest a pool of darkness, the noise fit to mask all footsteps over the mud. Move soon: put this boy down, he won't sleep for ever even with these cuts on the head, inflicted in revenge with the smooth rim of the anaesthetic mask. Soon. Any minute now. If only the child were not so warm: if only he could stop crying. Never, never, never. Oh, my love.

CHAPTER TWELVE

'Do not deliver an emetic if there is any chance of chloroform. She'll be nauseous anyway. If she's conscious, nothing but air; sit upright, keep airways open. Avoid excitement. If young and healthy, she's already past the risk of heart failure. Just let her gulp oxygen. Liquids, fruit juice if she can take it.' Hazel paused for breath, listened.

'Methadone? Narcan, intravenously. A lot. Not a stomach pump, for God's sake. Plenty of narcan, always brings them round.'

'Thank you,' said Helen hesitantly. Then, 'Are you all right?' Dr Hazel had poured acid on both their endeavours, but she never relinquished a friendship easily. She wondered as she spoke why she had mentioned methadone, as if the thought of Daniel Maley had provoked it.

'Am I all right? A greatly overused query, but yes. Phone any time you need. A bomb, you say? And not left by the Irish? We like a good bomb.'

'You need a new job.'

'Find me one, then.'

'I shall.'

Another phone call. Bailey's voice with a coughing in the background.

'Helen, can you come here, now? They'll let you through: I said you were a nurse. Only I can't really expect anyone else to volunteer. If you see what I mean, not fair, only . . .'

'Yes. Yes of course.'

'And you know the way.'

'Do I?'

'Yes of course you do. You left a bag full of things from that chemist's shop. In the kitchen, a few days since. I recognised the labels.'

She might have known her own inability to keep a secret and the thought of his quiet but unfailing observation made her smile. The distance was barely three-quarters of a mile, the sensation of movement and cold faintly enjoyable. The car made Helen feel slower, a person carried without volition with all her reflections as varied and vivid as the lights from the crane which no longer promised celebration. There were visions of dancing hospital beds, masks, small, fleeing boys and the inconsequential thought of how infrequent were the opportunities in life for someone like herself to be brave. Bravery was the stuff of dreams, the lot of police officers and soldiers. Her few acts of courage seemed to have been merely accidental and this was no exception. Someone removed a tape from across the road and waved her on like royalty, making her feel foolish as well as wishing that all driving were as easy as this. Queen of the road: the only thing moving in half a square mile.

Finding the right flat in Herringbone Parade posed no problem since the environs of the place were etched in her mind. She passed the chemist's and jolted to a halt. The window in Carlton's Caring Chemist was smashed, leaving a jagged hole, eloquently violent. She tried to ignore that, stopped in the road beyond where the dark hissing made her shiver, mounted the steps towards where the chemist's balcony fitted snugly against that of its neighbour. Such cosy passage from one to the other: no one had thought of that. There was suddenly no reason for speed: she paused again for a backward look at the building site; found the size and depth of the foundations faintly shocking. To live here must be like living next to a mine. Such large excavations, sites for future houses, looking like graves for giants. The rain glistened in the depths: the contours of the ground were uneven: all of it seemed to move with strange shadow and she believed she could see figures. Only here did this hidden and massive quantity of explosive become real, like a primeval monster about to rise. Helen shivered, and went through the door left open by Bailey.

He stood in a drab kitchen where every dish was clean, every
scuffed surface polished beneath the unsympathetic strip light of
the ceiling. On the lino floor there was a small, sinister patch of
blood. Bailey's skin looked yellow.

'Stay with her, will you? Tell her I've gone to find Tom.'

'I wish you'd explain. The son? Here?'

'Yes, I'm sure he was. Also the chemist. You were right about
him, I think, but this is no time for apologies. One of them's been
cut, don't know which. Worse still, Duncan's gone in pursuit.'

'Oh. Duncan the destroyer of evidence.'

Bailey looked towards the bedroom. 'If only that were all.' He
disappeared down the steps, soundless in the rubber-soled shoes.

'Bailey!' she shouted after him, her voice lost in the rain. 'The
building site . . . Careful. Look at the shop, window broken . . .'

He might not have heard. She sounded like a fishwife in the
silence: she felt absurdly like a woman leaning from a tenement
window and shouting at the kids to bring home fags.

Kimberley Perry looked at the new visitor with the sourness of
anxiety.

'Hallo.'

'Hallo.'

'He said you weren't a nurse, but you'd know what to do. Shoot
me, I would. I don't know what I've done or what the fuck's happened. I don't know why I feel like shit, and I'm a bloody
pharmacist. What the hell did I take? Tell me. Please. Nothing
much more than a dozen bloody cups of tea. Where's Tom? He's
all right, isn't he, and who are you anyway?'

'His friend. Bailey's, I mean. I don't suppose he told you
much.'

'Not exactly. Not much, not anything.'

'He's like that. Aren't they all? They think we're stupid.'

Slowly, reluctantly, they smiled at each other. Even in this state
of sick distress, Helen thought Kimberley Perry looked strangely
magnificent, like a vision of some *déshabillé* dancer from the Folies
Bergère in the days when it was fashion to be large. She had been
making a half-hearted attempt to dress, one stocking half up to the

knee, the blouse half on, thick hair all over, all sense of modesty gone, but, even in distress, embarrassed to be found thus. The smell in the room was putrifying.

'Out of here, I think,' said Helen. 'Shut the door on it, wash your face and nothing else. Windows open, all over . . .'

'I didn't shut it. I never have the window shut . . .'

'Never mind. Clean clothes, but don't touch anything. And then . . .'

'Not tea. Not bloody tea. That bastard put something in my tea.'

Light was beginning to dawn in Kim's dull eyes.

'Coffee then,' said Helen. Again, they smiled.

'Men,' said Kimberley Perry with a touch of her old asperity. 'What a load of arseholes. Where's my son? Where's my Tom?'

Duncan had never known how close his wife lived to her would-be lover. Even Tom, wary of Dad's temper, had never said how Uncle Pip lived right next door at the domestic level as well as working cheek by jowl, to say nothing of bum to bum, in that overcrowded shop. Duncan, ever woolly about details, never quite imagined the proximity, although if he had thought, he would have known it. Somehow he never visualised neat little Pip, so precise in answering the phone and the parking of his car, to be quite as near as that in those depressing little flats. On that account he did not leg it over the balcony in search of the man who had abused his wife: he ran downstairs, and round the corner to the shop front where he had peered surreptitiously on so many occasions, picked up a plastic bread crate abandoned by the baker, and hurled it through the window. The sound of smashing glass did not diminish his rage, a rage made worse by the knowledge of his own injustice, his inability to do anything else but react. Duncan followed the hole he had made into the shop itself. There was a stand of toothpaste en route to a night light at the back, illuminating the written wish that all customers would have a happy Xmas. Heavy breathing at the counter was enough to move the tinsel strands in yellow and gold which drifted down towards

Duncan's face. Pip's thumb tacks into the ceiling were inefficient and the tin foil drooped. Duncan seized it in one fist and tore it down.

'Come out, you randy little bastard, where are you . . .'

He did not expect a reply, nor was there one. Duncan stepped into the dispensary, marginally calmer. A slight breeze caught him from the jagged window and one large shard of glass fell with a delayed crash. He was legs, arms, underused muscle, sweeping away with one hand the contents of a shelf. Prepackaged goods, impossibly bound in cellophane and cardboard, fell to the floor. He squinted in the dim night light to read the label of a carton which fell against his head on the way down. Take three times a day. Towards the back of the room were more piled boxes, neat, obscuring a door under which shone a light. Duncan paused, smelt the familiar challenge of a door locked. He measured the length of the small corridor in which he stood, kicked the handle twice, winced as pain shot up into his knee, then cannoned against the wood. A flimsy door, easy Yale lock: the frame hung crooked as he went inside. A skill of his, to shoulder a door without propelling himself forward into the arms of enemy or dog, recovering soon enough to come to a breathy halt, with his hands over his groin, to protect what heavyweight denim could not. Silence. The place, empty, tiny, cramped and neat, enough to still all momentum, drown all sensation. The smell alone was one of aggressive innocence, the antiseptic smell of the hospital ward. Of righteousness and helplessness, persons in white coats saying they knew better, swallow this poison, and expecting obedience. Books ranged in neat lines, laboratory equipment, cupboards open. Duncan paused, awed by a sense of learning. Remembered instead the sense of revenge inflamed by a warmth and light in here. He caught sight of a small but uncongealed spot of blood on the floor.

Duncan cannoned through the second door, somehow expecting a succession of rooms, only to find beyond a deserted yard and the steps back upwards, the reverse of the route he had just followed in blind anger. In such anger, Duncan had only ever gone wherever he was led, directionless without guidance. He was essentially quite lawless: like a police dog which followed scents without landmarks, baying with excitement, protected later for its indiscretions. Part of him knew this, none of him cared. Get the bastard. The scent propelled him through a hole in the hoardings the other side of the road. Rapidly, hideously downhill in the rain, a sliding slippery slope like a sledge run, a trap. Stones and bricks fell against him: the bricks from some old cellar kept back by mud. He sat there, soaking and panting. Duncan had always needed a team.

Tom had never had a team, not even a quorum. He had been awake for a few seconds, which felt like minutes or hours, hugged as he was to this damp, muscular chest. Only when the man moved, rising with a sigh, did Tom's drugged mind begin to function, surfacing into fear with a swelling of nausea. But he was clasped tight in iron arms, large hands forming a cradle beneath his own buttocks, round his head polythene rustled with deafening sound. The chest was warm, but Tom had no sensation in his feet. His arms were folded against his chest and for a moment, he wanted to close his eyes again. He submitted to the temptation, but they refused to stay shut although he squeezed tight. Peering sideways, he began, in a series of blinks, to see where he might be and with whom. Then he opened his mouth to scream, but his throat, nose and ears were full of the sweaty scent of Pip's shirt and Pip's distinctive, lavender-flavoured, antiseptic smell. Tom's arms moved in compulsive disgust. Pip stopped abruptly.

'You awake, Tom, boy? Are you?'

Tom slumped. The voice was ominous, full of sedulous concern, the voice he knew and recalled hanging over him as his lungs filled with fumes: the same voice, now a loud whisper echoing against his head. There was silence all round them. Tom maintained it and Pip sighed again, adjusting the weight he carried by hoiking Tom further towards his shoulder as he walked. Footsteps squelched in the mud, slow, ponderous and purposeful, the rain easing down Tom's neck behind the cover. They were walking on a ridge between the foundations, Pip beginning to move slightly faster.

Urgency carried him forward to the destination he could see from the upstairs window. The foundations between which he trod had been mere scrapings of the earth when he had noticed them first on the night Margaret died, but now, below where the crane stood like a cross in the sky, and furthest away from the service road, was the largest excavation of all. Water below, only a few inches, but black water, ready to freeze before morning. He reached the edge. A mere sixteen feet of digging, plenty deep enough. Pip looked down, slightly giddy. If he threw Tom in here, he would hit the bottom via the side, revive perhaps for a minute or two, and perish quietly. In his mind's eye, Pip could hear the splash, the possible breaking of bone, the ensuing silence. No, not thrown: too brutal and the strength was draining from his numbing arms. The boy must merely be dropped, after a fashion. He walked carefully to the crumbling brink, leant right over carefully, Tom's foot swinging into view. Abruptly Pip heaved upright. The sight of that foot, a human piece of what he carried and held in this embrace, was unbearably pathetic, and the tears which had blinded him before were ceaseless still, blurring that spectacle of lethal black water. Feet without shoes. He hauled himself upright, panting.

'I can't, I can't, I can't . . .' Out loud, a voice he did not recognise as his own, a howl of despair. 'God help me, I can't do this . . .' Like the flash in the eyes of the drowning man he saw his orchestrated life, the love, the popularity, the carefully won respect, crumbling to nothing in the face of discovery. He could not move. The crane's lights shot daggers into his own, fragmenting tears. Tom's eyes, head lolling from sudden movement, caught the glimmer of water and the grave below their feet. He kicked, jerked, jackknifed his small body convulsively, and fell to earth. He curled where he fell, grasping the edge at Pip's feet, grovelling for the ankles to hold, an attitude of terrible, unconscious supplication. Then he heard, over and beyond another crescendo of sound bursting in his head, the banshee yell of his father, saw the mud-splattered legs of Uncle Pip vanish, heard a thin, fading scream.

Bailey saw them. Others, running from the workmen's shed, but not in pursuit, saw them. Boy and man, stumbling across the mud, Duncan in their clumsy footsteps, following. Watched the boy drop and Pip raise his hands in the air, gesturing to heaven. Duncan's renewed howling as he reached them both and dealt Pip a massive blow to the small of his back. Running, running, far too slowly through the weight of the mud, Bailey saw Pip catapult from sight, Duncan upright, and himself still seconds away. Bailey slipped, fell, ran again. Their growls carried on the air like the piercing shriek of a woman, Duncan again, a dark silhouette, standing mammoth as Bailey drew within feet of him, a gorilla of a man holding aloft a massive stone, raised above his head to fling on the recumbent form of Pip which lay below. Bailey cannoned into him, dragged both of them to earth in snarling, spitting fury, Duncan fighting him, fighting mad, pressing his face into mud. And then the heavens opened in one almighty crash, even the earth trembled and the world was full of the sound of smashing glass, rending metal. With his head jerked forward, Bailey could see the crane wobble before everything round them fell into complete and eerie silence. From a great distance, translated through his own, thunderous heartbeat, there came the sound of cheering.

In the early hours of dawn, the population of Herringbone Parade began to filter back. They came in staggered groups of cars, coach or ambulance, hollow-eyed, suspicious and relieved. As well as slightly disappointed by all this damp normality, the sad minimum of mess, some expecting to find a miraculous change. Such a fuss about nothing. Mrs Beale junior was enraged. The windows facing the service road and a mere few at the front were smashed, a crumbling of glass which left fragments inside as well as out, a sort of implosion. 'Bloody looters,' she howled. 'Where was those police boys then, shifting us all over the place. They should have bin here, watching.'

'They should've been keeping out of the bloody way,' Mrs Beale senior snorted with superior sense, clutching to the banister leading to her prison upstairs. 'What do you want? Young lads risking their balls to guard apples and rubbish?' She cackled. 'Besides, it's not looters, only the detonator. Same in the war, when they defused them. You don't know nothing.' Her daughter-in-law reflected how nimble she had become, as if the sudden change of scene had been a tonic: no talk of ulcers or heart attacks until she remembered the benefits of invalidity.

'Oh, dear, I need my prescription . . . Oh dear, oh dear . . . Having a turn . . .'

'Well you'll have to do without. Chemist's shut. Window boarded, police in there. See? Someone was robbed.'

Only Carlton's seemed to have been burgled, and the off-licence video, swift action perhaps by returning children, the one shop abruptly sealed by police, the video man left to seal his own. He was disgruntled by this unfair division of labour, ceased grumbling when told Mr Caring was in hospital. Poor Mr Pip, hope he's better soon. The bastards.

They seemed to like one another, Bailey sensed. Not, perhaps, destined to survive this particular emergency, but an easy attachment nevertheless, an exception to that strange and awkward shyness which seemed to afflict Helen amongst police officers' wives, the same defensiveness which crippled him with most of her peers of either sex. Two independent women, not surprising: they had probably spent half the anxious night talking. The fact that Helen liked Kimberley and Kimberley liked Helen enough for them to remain with each other was perfectly satisfactory for present purposes. Standing against the wall of the white hospital room, he wished he could summon half an ounce of affection for Duncan.

'I don't need to be in bed,' Kim said. 'For Christ's sake, they've taken samples of everything already. I don't even feel sick, specially now I know . . . well, he didn't quite get there, did he? I would have known that.' Flashes of the old bravado, desperately returning in search of itself. 'I've done a few things, but I've never been known to sleep through it. Have they finished with Tom?'

'Soon.'

All present fell silent. Tom, carried back to the flat, had been strangely withdrawn. My ears hurt, Mummy, they hurt, feeling sick. Nothing else, just that again and again like a litany. Sick as a dog. You and me both, said his mother, unable to prise away either her arms from his or his from hers, his face hidden in her chest like a suckling baby. Don't go, don't go, the same as he was ushered into the room in the light of mid-morning and placed himself immediately as close as he could get, only just becoming self-conscious about this need for touch. The skin was pinker, the eyes brighter, the attitude returning to some approximation of normal, enough for the enormous bandage round his head to be an obvious subject of pride. Half of him wished to show this dramatic badge to the world: the other half wanted to stay still and never, ever go back to Herringbone Parade.

'Do you want to tell us what happened?' Kim asked, her voice gentle but with an edge like sandpaper. His own version of roughly known or guessed facts was vital, but he shook his head. Helen held back any prompt, hating herself for thinking, I need this child as a witness: of course a ten-year-old boy can take an oath and doesn't even need corroboration. For seeing his mother prostrate, naked under the satyr-like figure of Uncle Pip, Tom had not quite forgiven her. For the rest, distortion was rife. He looked at them all. That woman, that man and Mummy. He was perfectly sure what he wanted to believe: there was a measure of hope in his voice.

'Daddy rescued me, Mum. He did, Mum, honestly. He rescued me, he was brave. It was Daddy brought me back. He was great.' The eyes held a challenge, a desperate dare, sliding away from Bailey's distant gaze, expecting, and prepared for, denial. Helen met Bailey's face across the tableau of the other two, noticed how no muscle moved, except to smile reassurance. 'Daddy's a big strong man,' Bailey murmured, and again Helen felt the treachery of other thoughts. If this boy lies here like this, will he lie elsewhere in a statement? If I know his evidence is tainted or embroidered to suit his own memory, could I ever present him as a witness of truth if the time comes? Thinking like Redwood. Kim was watching closely, feeling the silence through tired limbs. Continued simply to embrace her boy and, on the subject of Daddy's bravery, said nothing at all. Stretched instead. 'Where's you know who?' she asked after an interval. 'Getting better, is he? Only I am a pharmacist, and I'm worried about the shop. You know who can roast in hell, but I do care about the shop. Someone must watch it.'

Someone must watch, Pip thought. Someone is watching me now. Narcan, intravenously, dripping into his veins, the antidote for the methadone he had found in his muddy pockets and swallowed at the bottom of the pit, that damp hell where he had lain, weeping, listening to the world roar round him. In the moment of his own redemption, there had been that cataclysm of sound, like the thunderous voice of God, visiting revenge. He had lain there, staring upwards, his face half in water, proof against his own instinct to stand, watching the lights of the crane rock above him as if about to fall and crush his misery in one grand finale. He hauled himself to his knees in the pool, and his hands, not quite numb, fished in his pockets for some of the incrimination he carried. Returns from the shop, the same source of methadone he had given in that massive dose to Daniel the watcher, when Daniel was bemused by the blow. Raised and preserved in gentility, Pip the man had been almost proud of that blow. A step on the way to manhood, when no one was watching, a gesture disallowed in childhood when he was always watched. As he was watched now.

Someone watching him, someone always watching him, for ever and ever, amen. A life like this, no manhood, no privacy. When the nurse left him behind the screens, beyond which sat a man, Pip tried to pull the drip out of his arm. It was clumsily done, hurt with the dull insistence of toothache, but the plaster held it firm and he was weak. He did not want this antidote: he had not wanted to be alive. They knew more than he expected.

Narcan, intravenously, not a stomach pump which would have hastened the end, and he cursed them for their knowledge.

He turned in the hard bed. With the one detached hand, he drew the sheet round his chin and shut his eyes. So he would tell them. Everything, why not? About how she would not have the window open, dear, darling Margaret. How Mama had tickled him to death. He would tell them all about chloroform kicks, write it down for them, and he would be watched all the time, never ever knowing what it was to exorcise passion. They would understand: he hoped they would understand what was, to him, perfectly obvious. Prison. More and more watching. Until, with his knowledge of pills, he could find another route to oblivion.

Please, please, would someone open the window?

'It's stuffy in here. Smells. Is that dead dry cleaning in the back? Why do you always forget it? Shall I open the window?'

'If you like. Cold, though. You look terrible. Open it, I don't mind either way. Better than hospital air.'

'Sure you don't mind?'

Helen stopped pulling at the elusive seat belt of her car, a tangled piece of webbing which either spun enough belt to cover three fat persons at a time, or refused to budge without a series of savage pulls, and laughed in sudden, uproarious amusement.

'What's so funny?' Bailey was slightly injured to be the object of her infectious bark.

'You. You ask me three times if I mind about the window being open: you dither about something so small. I can see you looking at the handle, absolutely indecisive about whether to touch it or not, I'll watch you frown all the way home, wondering if you've done the right thing. Well, it is funny from a man who never thinks for a second about anything important. Leap into a pit of rattlesnakes, chase the devil barefoot over a minefield, juggle with bombs, no problem. Wind down the window, problem insoluble. Takes a good half hour to decide.'

He had the grace to smile, a full smile, reaching the eyes.

'Are you, by any chance, angry with me?' he asked.

'Nope. Never for long. Frequently puzzled. I'm well endowed with confusion, badly off for anger.' Her words, he noticed, always gathered speed and obscurity when she was tired. She started her car, which coughed into its own reluctant version of life. Bailey disliked being driven, hated the steam on the windows, wished she would consider a decent car for once. Then he opened the window.

'She's a great girl, Kimberley Perry. Will she go back to crazy Duncan?'

Bailey remembered the raging animal in the dark, ready to throw the stone which could murder, action without checks, strength without discrimination, love without analysis. 'I sincerely hope not,' he said.

'I was thinking,' Helen said, driving slowly, conscious of Bailey's discomfort and the ice on the road. 'I was thinking how it isn't all Duncan's fault. What he is, I mean. Somewhat abused. You told me he's always used because of the width of his shoulders, like a fearless animal. The person you send into the fray, the portable battering ram. Programmed, psyched up in advance. Then when he breaks down the door or brings another gorilla to earth, everyone fêtes him, buys him drinks, says, great lad, Dunc, yeah. Bit like being some sort of soft porn pin-up. Feed booze to the animal door breaker, don't encourage him to think, he's so useful as he is. As subtle with women as he is with doors. Until suddenly, it all goes wrong on him and he doesn't know how to change and being Mr Big Guy doesn't work. If he's got any finesse, he's been taught to suppress it. Sorry, if I'm not being very clear.'

Again, he noticed the speeding up of words. Remembered Duncan by the bedside, caring less for the wife than the despoiling of his property. Caring less for his son than he did for revenge.

'You're quite astute and very forgiving,' Bailey remarked, fishing for the cigarette which would shorten the journey, 'but I doubt if Kimberley will see it quite like that.'

'Oh I don't know. I really don't. He did come out, didn't he? Stopped Carlton. Got you there? Christ, the law's stupid. And slow. We mess round with statements and meetings and decisions and proof and personalities, while Hell freezes.' There was a hard edge of bitterness to her voice. 'And then it takes a drunken bum to do what we couldn't. It makes me ashamed to be what I am.' Angry tears were standing in her eyes, never to fall. They drove on in silence.

'Nice little boy,' Helen added, apropos of nothing, a very slight undertone of wistfulness in her voice.

'Yes he is. Wouldn't you like one?'

Helen was silent, thinking on another tangent. Changing from woman to lawyer.

'Will he tell the truth, though? I want him to forget it all for his own sake, remember it for a statement,' was all she said. Then, 'I want to see what the chemist has to say. Why? Why did he do all this? What festers with him? What's the background? He's talking to Collins. Collins says he won't stop. Good. We need confessions.'

The heater in Helen's car was always slow. She was right: it was cold, inside and out. Bailey wiped the side window with the back of his hand, feeling as he did so the cold of the moisture and an indefinable sensation of sadness.

She was better frail.

SHADOW PLAY

CHAPTER ONE

It was half-past six in the evening and felt like midnight. Everyone else had abandoned the ten-year-old court building, which was decaying at the edges in the effort to house cars on the roof, prisoners in the cellars and justice in between. Helen West had been discussing handcuff burns all day. Did they constitute assault? Was it only an insult to dignity when the handcuffs bit round your wrists? What was it Logo had said about them being the only legal means for a policeman to make you scream? He had volunteered this remark with his usual, ambiguous smile, harnessing all their sympathies to the scars on his wrists, and that was long before he began to sing. I might be small but I've got big wrists, Logo had said: look, they always put the cuffs on too tight. It was then, with this artless admission so late in the afternoon, that his trial had been aborted. Helen reached her car, quivering with cold. It was wet and dark upstairs, unlike the fuggy yellow warmth below.

The car stood on the only dry piece of concrete roof, next to the ugly spiral roadway which clutched the side of the building like a fat chimney. Children would love this, Helen thought, but children do not know it is here. Drivers began at the top of the spiral and drove down the curving funnel: skateboards would be better. Economy denied the provision of light. There had been no need for her to bring the car today, but since a space on the roof was a hard-won favour she tended not to abuse the privilege. She wanted to get out from under, out of the rain, into the cocoon of the car and not stop until she was home, for an evening with tomorrow's work and, in all probability, a row with Bailey. No, she had to avoid any such thing: he was going away, and although the boat in which they rowed was rocky, she did not want it overturned before he left. The car door clunked shut: she was suddenly in a hurry. It was even colder inside and she fumbled for the ignition. The lack of light was as suffocating as a blanket.

Oh Lord, would she ever be able to pretend she was not afraid of the dark?

There was a man caught in the headlights like a giant moth. A small man, slightly stooped but spry, standing in the rain with his hair plastered against his head and waving her out of the parking space with imperious gestures of exaggerated politeness, as if announcing a royal command performance. Waving her out as if it was necessary in all the empty bleakness of the roof, obstructing her at the same time. Retreating in front of her car, beckoning to it, moving back inch by inch, bending from the waist as if to coax. Nice Mr Logo, with his talent to amuse, the erstwhile defendant of her long afternoon, recently acquitted on a sympathy vote spiced with a pinch of legal technicality, the bastard. Helen felt the desperate urge to accelerate, a mad and joyous anticipation of seeing the smile leave his puckish face as he melted beneath the bonnet but the sudden rage which had displaced her great leap of fear on sight of him turned back on itself and became fear again. He was a strange spectre, Logo: a trespasser up here, waving his arms in his too short sleeves from which those large wrists grew into enormous hands. Helen wound down the window, kept her foot on the clutch and the car in gear, ready to move, frightened.

'Could you get out of the way, Mr Logo? You've no business up here. What do you think you're doing?' The voice was loud, the authority in it surprised her. Logo moved to the side of the car, stood a respectful distance, sedulous.

'Oh, taking the air, Mrs West, taking the air. I saw a door and walked through it.'

'Get out of the way, Mr Logo,' she repeated.

'I'm not in the way, now am I? It's all your imagination. I wanted to ask you something.' He moved closer. Suddenly his fingers were wrapped round the top of the half-open window, his smiling face close as he flattened his wrists against the glass. In the dark, Logo looked almost respectable, but the clothes were a parody of respectability which made her remember the frayed cuffs of his second-hand suit and the subtle odour of a body in dirty clothes.

'Tell me something, oh so fair Mrs West, just tell me. Can I sue for these burns? Can I, can I, can I?' The voice ascended to a singsong, mocking and pleading, the end of the interrogatory verse and the beginning of the chorus. 'I thought you were so fair, Mrs West. Fair in mind, fair of face . . .' The weals of his old hand-cuff marks were displayed to good advantage, his fingers relaxed.

'Why can't I sue? Can I? Can't I? None of it's my fault. Why did the police never find my wife? I can't help what I do,' he intoned sweetly.

'Listen you hymn-singing hypocrite, I'll get you next time. Now sod off,' said Helen.

Her car shot forward so fast she was momentarily out of control, dangerously close to the exit wall before she stopped. She reversed, grinding the gears, plunged towards the dark tunnel, sensing him behind her, laughing. Down the spiral she went, too fast for safety, the car careering like a toboggan shying from the walls. At the end, when the portcullis to the outside world opened, she came to an uncertain halt. She stopped to breathe, subject to a terrible desire to scream, and grateful for the light which graced the bottom floor. From a shabby shed of a room where a television cast extra light, the security man blinked at her, rose without ceremony but considerable resentment, and ambled across.

'What's with you then? You come down off there like a boy racer.'

'There's a man on the roof,' Helen said.

'Oh yeah?' The indifference was palpable. It was warm down here. 'Thought they'd all be home, the lunatics. It won't be someone escaped, I know that.' They were all gone by three-thirty, all those who were being taken back to prison for the first or fifteenth time. They went in vans with bars on the windows. 'Dare say he'll come down, whoever he is. I'm not bothered. Is he dangerous?'

Helen breathed out shakily.

'I don't know,' she said slowly. 'I just don't know.'

Logo? Dangerous? No. Only a poor lost soul probably, and it was unprofessional of her to swear at him. Solicitors acting for the Crown should not do that.

This time she moved away without speed. Oh Lord, I must pretend not to be afraid of the dark. The indifference of the security man to the presence of the trespasser on the roof of the magistrates' court was somehow soothing, an attitude which neutralised the sinister and made everything banal. Helen stared at the windscreen wipers, smearing across her vision with their worn rubbers, the rain spattering through the still open window on to her shoulder. She made herself slow down, think of something other than being made a fool of for the second time in a day. Geoffrey would not want to hear because his mind would be elsewhere, packing his mental and emotional equipment along with his clothes. Helen remembered where she was going, Geoffrey's place not hers and she felt the old, familiar resentment which was all the worse for being unreasonable.

Rose Darvey had waited a long time in the office to take the phone call from Helen West at the end of the case. She did this frequently. It was Rose's job to note down the result of the day's cases, to keep a running check in her notebooks of where all the papers were. They were City Branch North of the Crown Prosecution Service, big deal. Since she was not trusted or trained to operate the computer, the god of their existence, all she had to do thereafter was transfer the notes to someone else who logged them in and gave them back. Rose despised the computer, purely because she was not supposed to use it, although she could, it was easy, and because she knew it would be so much simpler if she took the phone calls, logged them on to the screen without an intermediary, and saved time all round. That was too simple for the captains of this ship. Rose was also supposed to know, and made it her business to know, where all the professional staff were at the end of the day and to ensure they collected or had delivered

to them what they needed for the next. She did this with a surreptitious disdain for the lot of them. Case clerks of her own stable
attracted her fierce loyalty; the lawyers were a joke. Dinsdale
Cotton was worth a laugh, Redwood was a pillock, but he was the
boss, John Riley was quite sweet, Amanda Lipton was a stuck-up
prune . . . Helen West talked to her at least, but they were all congenital idiots. Rose had long since surmised they were all failures
of a kind. When Helen West told Rose that she was wasting her
brain being a case clerk, and why didn't she try to qualify as a
lawyer herself, Rose had shaken her head in disbelief. 'Get stuffed,'
she'd said. 'What, be like you and work here for ever? You must be
joking.' Helen was all right, condescending old trout, and Rose
wasn't being truthful. She loved working here in this great big
castle of a building, didn't want to do anything else, but she would-
n't have said so at the point of a gun. Not to one of them anyway.

Today, Rose had waited, not just painting her nails and chewing that thin plait of soft, dyed hair which did not rise in spikes
above her head like the rest of it, but curled behind her neck
where she could always reach and tease it. Simply waiting without
fidgeting, tense, looking at her feet slung over the arms of an old
and rocky chair, regarding herself with the sort of half-admiring
disgust which was second nature. Admiration for her body
because of what so many men wanted to do with it, disgust since
she couldn't herself understand the appeal. She was worried about
the body, but other worries came first. Worry made many a
woman move: it rendered Helen West twitchy, rude, uncommunicative, occasionally funny and finally apologetic, but never
listless. It made Rose Darvey very still.

'I'm late, Rose,' Helen said on the phone. 'Mr Logo got off.
Why didn't you come and watch? It's good for you to see what it's
all about.' She sounded hurt, Miss West, in a bad mood. Lot of
those recently.

'Oh yeah?' said Rose with studied disrespect. 'Think I've got
sod all else to do? I mean, apart from watching you prancing
round some sodding courtroom making a tit of yourself for the
prosecution.'

'Well, I certainly did that.'

'How'd he manage to get off this time?' They all knew about Logo. Helen West's fury at the inglorious acquittals of him and others had rung round the office.

'He said he wasn't trespassing in the school yard. He'd gone in there by mistake. To sweep it, he said. Just to look, he said. Told us how he got so disorientated through being lonely. He's only a poor creature and this was only a misdemeanour, all that. So I had to throw in the towel. Look, forget what I said about being a prosecutor. Forget what I ever said to you about being a lawyer at all. You'd be better cleaning lavatories. See you tomorrow.'

'Right. Take care.'

Rose put down the phone, but it slipped off the cradle because her hand was shaking and she did not bother to put it back immediately. Would they ever get that man locked up? It was the last call for the evening and the worst. Well God bless you, Helen fucking West, letting that bastard get away with it again. But at least working here, I know where he is. Rose straightened the phone, pushed her fingers through her hair and replaced the single six-inch plait down the back of the neck of her red blouse. The collar felt damp and the front was creased. Well, what else would tonight's man expect after a day at work? The phone rang again. Rose was not particularly jubilant as she picked it up, the receiver still clammy from her previous touch.

'I'm down at the front door, Rose. Fancy a drink?'

'Oh yeah? And a hamburger? I'm hungry.'

'Are you now? Fancy that. So am I, as it happens.' There was a suggestive chuckle.

'Be there in a minute.'

She knew exactly how the rest of the evening would go. A couple of drinks, payment in kind for the company and a lift home and she didn't care. The main thing was always to leave the building with a man. Any man.

Passing through the office, hauling on her coat, teasing up her hair, pausing by a desk to straighten her tights, Rose thought

again. Why the fuck should I? Why? Her tights were thick, to go
with the weather and they had bagged at the knee. Distracted, she
pulled up her short skirt and adjusted them thoroughly, beginning
at the ankles and finally hauling them into place above her waist.
Tucking in the crumpled blouse, she slung her bag over her shoulder, patted herself down and looked up at the door. Dinsdale
Cotton, barrister-at-law, stood there, looking and laughing. Rose
was furious.

'Seen enough, have you? Want your eyes back, do you?'

'I'm sorry,' he said. 'So dreadfully sorry. Didn't mean to be a
voyeur . . . I really am sorry.'

'Thought you'd gone home.'

'I did. I left half my stuff, had to come back. Look, no offence.
Can I buy you a drink? No, not for the view, but because I embarrassed you. And to stop me feeling such an idiot. I really didn't
expect to find someone dressing, I'm so sorry.'

He stopped where he was, patently sincere, all his amusement
dismissed by the look of fury on her face. Poor idiot, she thought,
but not bad. No wonder he fancied Helen West and she him.
Apart from his silly name and his wonderful floppy gold hair and
the fact he was out of place in anything but a stately home, he was
nice, inquisitive but nice, and the best looking man in the office,
not that that was saying much. Rose relented.

'No problem,' she muttered. 'Don't worry about the drink
though. Another time.'

He bowed, he fucking bowed, he really did. Rose would tell that
to Paul later, by way of distraction, as if distraction would work.
To Rose's own surprise, she found herself bowing back, both of
them acting up, being silly. Dinsdale had this effect.

'Mind your tights,' he grinned. She smiled too this time, right
from the eyes. If he hadn't smiled and apologized, she'd have
bitten his balls.

They'd had a case like that in the office last week, a woman who
bit off a bloke's testicle during a row. Rose had been the only one
who wasn't surprised.

*

She stamped down the corridor, shoved two finished files in the old goods lift for carriage to the basement, adjusted her bag again. There were fifteen ways to the front door. Turn right and you came to the end of a wide corridor, so wide it could take a bus. Then you turned left down narrow stairs, but fifty feet away there were broader stairs which threw themselves against a narrow and futile door, blocked in to lead only to the floor beneath instead of towards the continuance of the sweep which had once been grand. The same, wide stairs continued to the front door, two floors down, with similar interruptions. So did the back entrance and the clattering stairs she trod to the floor beneath through swing doors which creaked. Down, down, down, in a clatter of deliberate noise, because she liked making a noise, enjoying the emptiness without ever being afraid, it was so big you could hide yourself. The room numbers made no sense. It had been a hospital once, a Victorian lunatic asylum. Helen West had told Rose that, in the interests of her education: Miss West was stuffed full of useless information. The conversion to an office had been minimal, hence the wide corridors and the super-wide doors, built for trolleys and straitjackets with escorts. She had listened to Helen's lecture, wide eyed, blinking, waiting her turn, which came finally. 'Naa, I don't believe you. This was never converted . . . It's just what it always was, still a loony-bin otherwise, isn't it?' Rose trod past the video room for obscene publications, past the library, all law reports incomplete, full of last week's newspapers, past the offices for fraud, tripped on the bulging carpet outside the passenger lift marked 'Out of Order'. Helen West had also said they should all travel up and down in the goods lift, it was more reliable, very funny, and could carry at least one pygmy at a time. Rose supposed this building was all they could afford. More fool the lunatics who worked here.

Suddenly she was unsure she could cope with the evening ahead, and then on the second turn of stairs, she knew she would. Reckless Rose: that was her reputation. Nineteen-year-old Rose, never leaving the office without a man.

*

Detective Sergeant Ryan and Detective Superintendent Bailey sat in the casualty department of Hackney hospital.

'Fucking lunatic asylum, this,' said Ryan. 'Run by a load of lunatic medics, far as I can see.'

'Don't speak ill of the doctors. We need them.'

'I wasn't speaking ill. Only as I find.'

'Will you watch your mouth then? How much longer, do you think?'

'Oh, ten minutes. Then they'll see you right in five and you can go home.'

Bailey looked at his damaged watch and groaned. His left eye was half closed by a huge purple swelling. A haematoma, the report would call it. To Ryan it was just another black eye, an occupational hazard not usually incurred by officers of Bailey's rank. Ryan was alarmed by the groan, the first yet. The rest had been a string of obscenities, not typical of Bailey either. Ryan wondered about sir's love life; he hadn't been too happy lately, but then he should have known better than to shack up with a solicitor.

'What's the matter, sir? Does it hurt?'

'Of course it doesn't bloody hurt,' said Bailey with heavy irony. 'But I've just remembered I was supposed to get some food in. And cook it, round about now. Damn. She'll have to make do with soup.'

Ryan was incredulous. He thought of his own marriage, far from unsatisfactory, despite its vicissitudes, a history of burned meals left in ovens, but at least they'd been put in the oven in the first place.

'Helen? Make do with soup. Why isn't she cooking the food? Doesn't she cook?' He might as well have said, does she wash?

Bailey turned the one good eye on Ryan. It looked a trifle sad, if not a little frightening, staring at him on its own like that.

'We take it in turns. Her place, she cooks, mine, I do. Only we seem to have lost the knack. Not much taking of turns these days.'

It was as close to a confidence as he would get and Ryan saw the signal to change the conversation. Besides in the aftermath of

Christmas and this raw January day, he did not want gloom on the brink of a holiday. He rubbed his hands together.

'Never mind. Bramshill. Day after next. Get away from all this. Don't we deserve it? Can't be bad.'

They were both going on extended courses at the police training college. Ryan said his was for reading and writing; Bailey's was for senior command. They'd get him talking to hostages next.

'Not bad today, either, was it?' Ryan continued, still rubbing his hands in a way Bailey found irritating. 'Last day's active duty, five arrests. You put a really good sprint on there, sir, you really did. Never knew you could run so fast.' He means pretty good for a man of my age, Bailey thought.

'No, you didn't know I could run, and you didn't know that the man was waiting round the corner, with his fist out either, did you? Why didn't you tell me? I could have just run into a wall and got it over with.'

They both shook with laughter. Ryan eyed the nurse who came towards them. There'd be women at Bramshill, surely. Time to get the old man out of himself.

'Listen,' he said to the nurse. 'When you've done with Mr Bailey here, would you mind putting a patch on that eye to make it look worse? Only he's got a woman waiting at home. He'll need sympathy.'

Waiting. Helen felt the emptiness of Bailey's flat as soon as she put the key in the door. Late again, always late, but she couldn't even criticise him for it because she had been so herself, often enough. For the grosser occasions of his lateness, she usually managed to pay him back by not turning up at all some other time. The games they played, so childish. The light on his answering machine winked at her. It might have contained a message of explanation since he was scrupulous about such courtesies, but, mindful of his privacy so that he would be mindful of hers, she did not stop to listen. They had a rule that although each possessed the key to the other's house, that was not quite the same thing as being entirely at home in it. Helen craved a sensation of righteous indignation and knew she did not deserve it. Geoffrey was a policeman: he did not have a timetable like other men. They had chosen to have a relationship that was both uncommitted and committed at the same time. It had been bound to bristle with difficulties and it was she who insisted on this awkward format. Living together had not worked particularly well either. Helen never quite knew whether Bailey's professed willingness to try again, or indeed to marry her, worked as a comforter to their impermanent arrangements, or an irritant. Perhaps they were just stale. Like the bread in his bread-bin. He would have forgotten food. There was rice, tinned shrimps, cartons of soup and more than sufficient wine to dull the day. Not a feast, perhaps. She could have gone out again from this warehouse top floor which was so much cooler than her own cluttered basement and found the late-night shop on the corner to improve on their provisions, but she didn't. Instead she waited for a quarter of an hour and then went home.

It was dark down the street where Logo lived and darker still in the alleyway between his house and Granny's. Neither owned their small houses, impossible on their incomes, even in a street like this where no-one in their right mind would want to buy a house. That's what Logo thought anyway. The estate agents may have disagreed as their signs festooned five dwellings over the road. Attempts had been made to gentrify Legard Street, but those who tried with the bravery and optimism of youth tended to move after a year or so. Artisans' dwellings, mostly privately owned now, a few left like his and Gran's with sitting tenants. The sitting tenants were old, an endangered and truculent species who did not band together, but jeered at the private owners with their new front doors. All were threatened by the proximity of the football ground. Every second week in season and plenty of other times besides, their street was blocked by cars, their gardens trodden by the thousands on foot who came to worship the team. As the team's fortunes prospered, so the fortunes of the street were endangered. Young Mrs Jones in number seventeen had left after her first baby because she could not stand the prospect of keeping a fixture list in the kitchen so she would know on which Saturday she would be able to get out to the hospital and produce the next. In comparison to the hazards of the football stadium, Logo's singing was a minor irritation.

He sang in a light tenor, his voice blending with the persistent rain, increasing the eeriness, but not diminishing the triumph of the sound.

'Come let us join the Church above
The martyr's praise to sing,
The soldier true who gave today
His life blood for his king . . .'

Tan ter ah! he finished, lost for the words of the next verse. A door slammed. There was the sound of scurrying footsteps in the wet, another door slamming, someone putting out rubbish. Logo did not look round. It wasn't a convivial street. He dived into the alley, feeling for his door key. As if there was any need. All anyone in the world had to do was kick it and they could come in if they wanted, but somehow, they didn't.

'Mother!' he yelled as he pushed the door. Beyond the broken fencing which flanked the alley as it grew into a mossy backyard, light poured from the glass door of the next-door kitchen. Logo stepped over and rapped on the glass. She might not have heard with the rain, but now she would and he wanted someone to talk at. Although she would resent it, just as she hated being addressed as his mother or gran when she was nothing of the kind, it usually took her less than three minutes to come across. Old Mrs Mellors was victim to her own desire for company. Logo was her lifeline. She was also the only one in the street who continued to like his singing long after the novelty had worn off.

'I may as well be your bloody mother,' she grumbled, heaving herself through the battered door he had left ajar. 'What do you want now?'

'Nothing,' he said indignantly. 'When did I ever want anything from you? But it's a wet night and I thought you might like a drink.'

She sighed. 'Well, don't you know me well, but you could have

saved me getting wet and brought it in to me. You're wet already.
I was doing my knitting.'

'Nobody calls me wet.' He adopted a boxer's stance and
squared up to her, the aggression diminished by the smile on his
face. Margaret sat down heavily.

'I know,' she said. 'Obviously, you got on all right today. No
wonder you're celebrating. Oh I do wish they'd stop picking on
you like that, all those police. It isn't fair. Not that prison would do
you harm. You'd get fed, put on a bit of fat.' She chuckled.

'Is that what you want for me, you ungrateful old cow? Is that
what you want?' From one misshapen jacket pocket he took a
half-bottle of whisky and from the other, a bottle of dry ginger.
Posh. Margaret Mellors found the sight of the whisky brought
saliva to her mouth. She looked down at her own legs stretched
across the rotten lino floor in front of her with her stick running
parallel. Margaret was waiting for a new hip, felt as if she had been
waiting for ever. She was pretty mobile with the old one, but by
this time of day, she ached.

'No,' she admitted. 'That's not what I want at all and well you
know it. I just wish you'd behave. But you're good to me, Logo. I'd
rather have you alive than dead. Are you going to be all night
pouring this drink, then?'

He tossed a pack of cigarettes from one of the bottomless pockets in her direction. She caught them nimbly in both palms.
Margaret's hands and her mind were unaffected by more than
seventy years' hard labour with no great expectations of life even
at the beginning. Blessed are they who expect nothing, she was
wont to say, for they will not be disappointed. Logo and Logo's
family had given her much of the joy she had ever had. He looked
at her with that smile which wooed magistrates and said softly,
'Good to you, Mother? Other way round, isn't it? I don't know
what I'd have done without you, but it's fat thanks we get, eh?' She
shook her head, not anxious to follow this line of conversation, but
he was determined.

'What would I have done with a wife like mine, eh? And a
daughter to raise with a wife like that? I don't know. You were

mother to us all, Mother, you and Jack, God rest him. And what happens after all that loving kindness, eh? Wife runs off with someone else, and the daughter can't give her father the time of day. Never mind you, Granny.'

Margaret shrugged, still hoping the conversation would die away. She had no real doubt she deserved the accolades but it did not follow she wanted to hear them, and the thought of the missing daughter, as well as that pretty wife, still filled her with anguish sharper than any physical pain. She was accustomed to it and told herself that since Logo was talking about his own blood she might not understand his obsession, having no kids of her own to throw into the balance. She had taken Logo's child instead but she knew she had no right to her now.

'You haven't seen them, I suppose?' he asked wistfully. For a moment she thought he might mean the neighbours who hated him most, the landlord of their identical houses and his wife, but that wasn't what he meant at all.

'Seen who? Oh, I know who you mean. No, you daft thing, of course I haven't. Not in four years. Don't be silly. Why do you always ask?'

The whisky, which she drank sparingly but greedily, was already in the system, dulling the pain, though not the regret and the guilt. 'I did what I could was all,' she said. 'I wish you wouldn't keep on asking. I've never seen your daughter or your wife since soon after Jack died, and you'd be the first to know if I had. Will you let up, you mad son of a bitch?'

Logo threw back his head and laughed with a sound as glorious as the best of his singing. The sombre mood, as quick and flimsy as the rest of him was light and spry, seemed to have fled. Oh, you had to love him: he was a character, rising like a cork over all his difficulties, holding down a job no-one else wanted: she admired him for that. Who else would be a road sweeper and trundle that big old trolley around all day, picking up rubbish? She felt as loyal to Logo as she had always felt, as protective as if he had been a son and just as worried. None of the other old souls in the street had a son half as attentive as this one.

'I've got some nice soup, if you want some,' Margaret said. 'But whether you do or you don't, I think I'll just have another of these,' and the pain in her chest, that premonition of tears, eased with the sound of liquid.

'No I won't have another, thanks. Two's plenty.'

'You're joking. We haven't even started. One more?'

'No, thanks. Look, do you mind if I leave you to it? I think I'll just go round to her place and see if she's in. It's not like her . . .'

'Sir, Geoff, it's just like all women.' Ryan was upset, more to the point, enraged. He'd seen sir home to find no-one there at all, not even a burnt meal or a cup of soup, just a scarf on a chair to show she'd visited and left sweet all else behind. Man could not live on a waft of perfume. The answerphone had been blinking and winking like some creature with a cast in its eye and no sign of a lit fire or a petticoat. Welcome home our conquering hero, amen. Ryan, who could stand anything but another man's discomfiture at the hands of a woman, placed the patched, black-eyed hero in his motor and shuffled him off elsewhere. In his own experience, if you were late, you might as well be very late and very pissed. The later you left it, the more relieved they were to see you and the anger was the same after two hours as it was after six.

'All right. Listen, I'll take you there. Then I have to go, OK?'

'Yes, of course. You've been very kind.' There was a strange chill in this return to formality. Bailey never lost control, whether punch drunk or plain drunk, he could be colder and more dangerous than black ice and all of a sudden, Ryan did not envy Helen West, whom he liked and admired, if only she'd learn to behave like a woman.

They pulled up outside the large old house which contained her flat. Ryan knew the route from the pub, the way he always did. Even though he lived outside London, he'd knocked around it like a cabbie. From the door of the pub, turn right, cut down Legard Street past the football stadium, left at the park, over the lights and into respectability. Not exactly Ryan's stamping ground, but Bailey was familiar with it, because the woman lived there, God help him.

Ryan waved and revved the car even while sir was stepping out. Then, two doors down, he cut the engine, got out and walked back. Helen West had a handsome front door to her basement and the lights were on. Ryan stood in the darkness and watched sir ring the bell. 'Where were you, Helen?' he was saying to her as the door opened. 'Where were you? Couldn't you wait?' He watched the older man push inside, heard her words. 'I'm sorry,' she was saying. 'I'm sorry. Oh, what have you done? Not again . . .'

That was more like it. Ryan was glad about Bailey wearing a patch. Made him look hurt but still like a pirate.

He cut back up through Legard Street on the way to the motorway. What did anyone mean by late? It wasn't late at all by his standards. He wondered about stopping off on his way home. Down, boy, down: he remembered. Bramshill the day after next, be good and get home by ten. His wife knew better than to call that late. Swinging right, enjoying the speed and the sensation of righteousness which came from being sober, Ryan dimly recognised a familiar face in a car he passed, weaving its way through the double-parking of those dubious streets round the stadium. Do you know, he was thinking to himself, I thought I could predict the way this evening might go. I thought I'd get him pissed and I shall yet. He'd taken bets on it.

Rose Darvey had known exactly the way the evening was going to go, but she was still disappointed to find it quite as predictable as it was. There was a price to be paid for any escort away from the office. Exacted now and all for a ride in a beaten-up Ford Cortina, the best a rookie police constable could afford. He'd taken her to a pub for three rounds of drinks and three of crisps, then, more reluctantly, to a McDonald's, where they had sat in silence, munching the best of the menu under the kind of light which transfixed her into silence, and all as the prepayment for dessert. Rose Darvey, with her knickers round one ankle and the tights which had bagged at the knee now hidden under the bed where she lay in a police section house. With Constable Williams working his way between her thighs before leaving for the night shift, and making a great deal of noise about it. Oh, Rose, Rose, Rose, as if the name mattered while he still had his shirt on, thrusting between her legs with his face all trembling. She watched him, uninterested, as he towered above her. Her hands were on his thin buttocks, kneading as she might have kneaded dough: men were dangerous when roused, you had to behave as if you enjoyed it. Rose was stretched and sore: he was taking his time to the tune of her artificial groans and the scluck, scluck of the sound, while her eyes gazed at the artex ceiling. Just when she thought he never would, he finished and collapsed. Oh, Rose, Rose, Rose. Shut up, she thought, but she remembered to keep on stroking. Ten minutes later they were back in the Cortina, he on his way to work and her to bed. They went down Northchurch Street, where Rose knew Ms West lived, because she knew all those things. Lights on down there: I expect she's drinking her cocoa. Her eyes at this point were fixed straight ahead, like they were most of the time. Paul began to doubt her silence, but he knew better than to question his luck.

'Which number is it again?' he said when they were two miles beyond the stadium.

'Wouldn't you like to know?' said Rose pertly, the tights now more or less in place, but a disturbing stickiness between her legs. 'Just drop us at the corner, it's easier. See you.'

He obeyed, his mind elsewhere, building up his concentration for the night shift, wishing he'd slept more by day. She walked down the street slowly for as long as he was in sight and then she began to run.

Oh Lord, save me from admitting I am frightened of the dark.

CHAPTER TWO

The offices of the Crown Prosecution Service did not look any more dignified in the early afternoon than they did after dark, but Brian Redwood, lord of all he surveyed, comforted himself with the thought that the visual irritations were at least unusual. He had always wanted a huge office if only to reflect status, though he now recognised it was a myth since he was a king without a crown. The room he occupied was large enough for a potentate to sit like a pea on a throne at one end, but the splendour was that of a ruined Russian palace and offered all the comforts of a cave. When forced into these premises the year before, in pursuit of the ever-cheaper lease, Redwood could not believe his eyes and although his incredulity had diminished, the disappointment had not. It was all part of the humbling process and he was never sure whether that process was deliberate. The only feature of the building he liked was the magnificent railings outside, which surrounded the place on three sides, standing tall and close-ranked with lethal tips at the end of each elegant fleur-de-lis, a barrier against the world. Redwood vaguely approved of these as a means of keeping his staff in, rather than keeping others out, defying the truant and the escapee, but he hated the rest of the building. He was an unmemorable man, one of the grey brigade, uncoloured by humour but far from stupid. He had never found problems with the letter of the law; which was why he had chosen it, but human beings were a different matter.

On this afternoon, he was conducting an exercise in better communication with his professional staff. An excruciating management course had informed him this was not only long overdue but imperative, since staff morale was his responsibility.

In vain he had tried to explain that no single chief marooned in a building like this could remove the dust of ages and make the Indians happy unless he increased their wages. The response to this from above was derisory: he was supposed to win their hearts and minds and make them tolerate the intolerable. The end result was monthly meetings for the lawyers only, held at teatime. They sat in his room on a medley of chairs, and ate the jam doughnuts he had paid for out of his own pocket. Redwood had a very old-fashioned idea of a treat and did not see why a waste of time should be expensive.

They were supposed to discuss, in mutual confessional, those cases which troubled them, which is what they did, more or less, among themselves, ignoring Redwood, whose gaze meanwhile travelled round the walls. High ceilings with broken mouldings, big, panelled doors so thick with a dozen layers of shiny paint the panels had all but disappeared. There was a large and ugly open fireplace from the 1890s obscured by an electric equivalent from the 1950s, now defunct. Gas pipes ran up the wall, again redundant since the newer radiators stood side by side with the old. It was a room of many additions with nothing taken away except what might have been beauty. He almost broke his fingers each time he tried to open one of the huge sash-windows which rose from near floor level to above his head. He was uncomfortably aware that below his feet and over his ceiling, there were rooms in this colossal warren of a building he had never even seen. On arrival, it had taken him three days to find the lavatories on this floor and even now, he took a different route each time.

Smoking was not allowed within his personal domain, and Redwood noticed with obscure satisfaction that Helen West was not only fidgeting but looked as if a strong gin would be preferable to weak tea. He regarded her with his customary mixture of grudging respect and awkwardness. She had changed, recently. Before, she had always seemed to campaign for them to be aware of the possible innocence of those charged with criminal offences, but now she seemed obsessed with their frequent inability to prove guilt. At the moment she was keeping them all entertained with the story of a man named Logo.

'Well, he came in, suit, tie, the lot, looking the soul of poverty-stricken respectability, and, oh yes, I forgot, clutching his Bible. "I brought my own," he said sweetly and bowed to the bench. He listened to all the evidence, asking only the most pertinent questions, as if he'd been representing himself all his life.'

'He probably has,' said Dinsdale, laughing. Helen was accompanying her saga with a number of gestures. He, too, had seen Logo before and he anticipated the perfection of Helen's mimicry.

'"Excuse me," he says to the mother of the first witness, "but your dear little daughter did not complain that I had touched her in any way, did she?" "No, she never," the witness concedes. "I only offered her sweets, as I offered them to others?" "Right on," says the witness. "I did not accompany my offer with any kind of lewd gesture?" Witness puzzled. "What's one of them?" "I don't know, madam. I cannot really define what I could not do, but I thought that was what I am accused of." Oh, he's so horribly articulate. "I'm afraid, madam," he says finally, "I only followed your daughter from the school gates because she was alone and crying, because I was concerned for her, and because she so resembles my own daughter, who I've lost." He had the witness in tears, feeling guilty. And the bench. He's sort of naïvely ingenious. Then he told us how rough the police were, showed us the hand-cuff burns and no-one dared point out they weren't recent at all. Everyone ended up turning somersaults to be nice to him and then when he was acquitted, you know what he did?'

'Yes,' said Dinsdale. 'He sang.'

'Exactly,' said Helen. '"Abide with me, fast falls the eventide. The darkness deepens; Lord with me abide . . ." He's got a beautiful voice, but he knew the limits, so he stopped after verse two.'

'I know,' said John Riley, the only churchgoer of them all.

'Swift to its close, ebbs out life's little day;
Earth's joys grow dim, its glories pass away;
Change and decay in all around I see;
Oh, thou who changest not, abide with me.'

His fine, bass voice finished on a cadence of embarrassment and he looked down, blushing. A pin would have dropped with a clatter in the silence which followed. Redwood stirred uneasily. This was really too much for a man who preferred others to remain inhibited.

'You see what I mean?' said Helen, breaking the spell. 'You can't cross-examine a man who sings hymns like that. Nor can you get across that it's the fifth time he's been caught prowling. You know his first speciality, years ago? Being found on enclosed premises. People would turn round in some office block he used to clean and suddenly, he'd be there. Now he's a road sweeper. These days he tries to lure dark-haired little girls to go with him for walks in graveyards. And he knows how impotent we are. He never actually does anything. Am I the only one who finds him so sinister?'

'He shouldn't have been prosecuted in the first place,' said Redwood angrily. 'Not if the evidence was as slim as you suggest. What were you thinking of, Helen? What's happened to your judgement? You're becoming a persecutor!'

It was an old joke, persecutor, prosecutor, the best he could do to make it seem as if he had listened to anything other than the singing, but Helen rounded on him without any humour at all.

'Of course there was evidence!' She stopped and blushed. 'There was at least half an indecent assault. I mean he was pretty persistent.' A smile began to emerge at the corner of her mouth. 'OK, point taken. He didn't actually touch her. He says he's driven mad by football. Like a werewolf by the moon.'

'What's half an indecent assault?' Dinsdale enquired.

'A decent one,' said Redwood, 'and now if you don't mind, I mean if that's all . . .' He had done his duty. They took the signal and rose simultaneously with relief. The meetings were a strain, the room was stifling.

'Helen, would you wait?'

Dinsdale paused at the door, ready to come back as Helen remained where she was. 'Oh, it's all right, man,' Redwood barked. 'I'm not going to tick her off, it's about something else

entirely. No need to be so protective, she doesn't need a witness.'
He wondered, not for the first time, how it was Helen acquired her
legion of allies. But once Dinsdale had gone, Redwood wished he
would return to save him from being alone with her. He coughed
with the hollow sound of a man looking for his place on a page,
unable to stand a silence, but wishing to postpone speech. He
waited for the door to close. At least the doors here closed with a
weighty quietness, unlike the windows which rattled like thunder.

'Helen, I could do with your help. Rather a delicate matter and
I don't know how to handle it.'

She looked at him sharply, waiting for irony, remembering that
Redwood didn't send people up, only brought them down when
they were not looking. Perhaps it was a genuine plea from a man
helpless when faced with the complexity of emotion, envious of
her own insouciance in the brash, prison corridors of life. She
decided to give him the benefit of the doubt. He coughed again
and searched for a handkerchief, abandoning the quest in the
desire to begin so he could finish. He often referred problems to
Helen and he was ashamed of it.

'Rose,' he said ponderously. 'Rose Darvey.'

Helen was instantly defensive. 'She's a great girl. Clever, should
have more responsibility, works like a Trojan, early morning, late
night—'

'It's the late nights I'm talking about,' he interrupted.

'Why? We should be pleased to have someone like her. I
thought you said she could go out, see more trials, take on more.
I know she isn't exactly polite, but who's complaining? She's rude
but she's keen . . .'

'How very apt, both rude and keen. I'm glad you see her as
that. So does the Chief Inspector at the local nick who has particular responsibility for the welfare of his youngest police constables
in the police section house up the road. He came in to see me.'
Another cough. This time he found the handkerchief, looked at it,
uncertain whether to blow his nose, but increasingly certain what
to say. 'Rose has been through the whole division like a dose of
salts. She's out with one or other of the bachelors every night. She

has favourites, but it all seems to depend which shift they're on and their consequent availability, otherwise one's as good as another. I asked the doorman downstairs and he confirmed there's a lad in half blues out there every evening when she leaves. What's more, I happen to know for a fact, she's changed her address in the year she's been here and we've only got an old one on the file. The Chief Inspector's worried: he says the section house is in a state of riot. Youthful jealousy, all that. Could we have a word with her? Oh Lord, what do we do?'

He spoke with the weariness of a man who has lost sight of youthful lust and jealousy; on that account alone, Helen sympathised. She was silent. Redwood went on.

'The CI is politely concerned because he says he's got six young bloods on one relief who are at one another's throats, though God knows why, they don't apparently have to compete for her favours, which are priced at roughly three drinks and a packet of crisps—'

'You mean that's all they offer,' said Helen angrily. 'Mean bastards. They aren't badly paid.'

'I mean that's all she seems to ask,' said Redwood. 'The Chief Inspector says of course there's nothing new about the situation, girls will be girls and boys will be boys, but they haven't had a man-eater from the Crown Prosecution Service before. Doesn't exactly engender respect from the constabulary for our service, does it?' he finished lamely.

'And what did you say to the Chief Inspector?'

'I said I wasn't responsible for the private lives of our case clerks, or lawyers for that matter.' He looked at her meaningfully. Helen's ongoing love affair with a police officer was still the subject of comment. 'I asked him if he had had a word with the lads themselves, since it takes two to tango.'

Helen, approving of this response, nodded.

'But he was insistent,' Redwood went on. 'Would someone have a word with our Rose? Well, it can't be me. She'd spit in my eye.'

'And in mine,' said Helen.

'But you seem to get on with her best.'

'Best doesn't mean well. How can I stop her, if this is really what she's doing? Perhaps I wouldn't want to, perhaps she's having fun . . .'

'I doubt it,' Redwood volunteered with surprising wisdom. 'I doubt it very much. I've always thought the height of sexual pleasure lay in monogamy.' Helen looked at him in one of those rare moments when they understood one another. He was not, after all, a man devoid of compassion and he did have daughters. 'I'll think about it,' she said. 'If you don't mind me taking her under my wing rather more than I do, perhaps we could offer her alternative stimulus? Like better quality work? prospects of promotion?' Redwood winced and smiled wanly. Helen always exacted a price.

He watched her get up to leave, recovering her shopping as she went. Only Helen West, always in a hurry, would be shameless enough to dash into a meeting late, armed with groceries, as if she was trying to make some kind of point. He forgot she had come in from outside and it was a long haul to her own room.

'You look as if you're about to feed the five thousand,' he grunted.

'No,' said Helen, suddenly embarrassed by the weight of what she carried. 'Only one. But I need a wife.'

The groceries bounced against her legs as she wandered down the endless corridor to Room 251. What on earth had possessed her to stop at a market stall and buy kilos of fruit and vegetables when she still had to do the supermarket on the way home? Oh yes, my turn to apologise for being so mean yesterday; my turn to cook and I hate cooking, why didn't I just say we'd go out? But, poor soul is a bit embarrassed about being seen in public with an enormous black eye which I wasn't qualified to kiss better.

Tapping down the corridor over the lumpy carpet, rustling as she walked, Helen forgot Rose Darvey. Rose could wait until tomorrow. Waiting, like everything else, until Geoffrey Bailey with his black eye (worse this morning than the night before) had gone.

The clerks' room was only three enormous doors down from

Redwood's office, but he visited it as rarely as possible. The red light for the ludicrous goods lift winked in the gloomy corridor. Helen passed the room where Dinsdale and John, the one as extrovert and charming as the other was shy, kept one another company. Three of the case clerks, Rose included, gathered by the door, drawn by John, who had carried on singing. Helen paused in passing, drawn as they were drawn, not only by the sound, but by the glamorous Dinsdale who was not like the rest of them at all. There was nothing of the misfit, for a start: he bore all the signs of privilege, private money, charm, humility and a way with words. Everybody loved him. Even Rose, which meant he had passed the acid test. To Helen Dinsdale was a divine problem: the thought of him made her go pink, remember her age (five years older than him), and also remember Redwood's remark about the joys of monogamy. As Helen watched, prepared to join the fan club, Rose detached herself from the group and sped off, running for the telephone, her spiked hair waving and that plait swinging against her neck. Helen plodded behind with her own prosaic shopping of which she was faintly ashamed. Bags of potatoes and fruit made her feel she had traversed the loop between youth and age: they diminished her into nothing and she quickened her step down this endless corridor in the shadow of the girl. Helen found herself standing outside the door, listening to Rose answering the call, looking for some sort of confirmation of what she had just been told about Rose and the police boys, uncomfortably aware that she had not really questioned anything Redwood had said, not shouted, Where's your evidence that our most promising non-professional is as promiscuous as a rabbit? Knowing she had not argued because she had not been surprised. Helen often worked late. She knew that Rose never left the office alone.

Rose's voice sang with irritation as she held the phone; it was an inflection carried on a draught from another huge window. Helen's belief in the imperviousness of youth fled. 'Listen,' Rose was saying, 'listen. You either fucking turn up or you don't. If you don't, well forget it. Sod you.' It was clearly milder than it might have been. Rose was speaking through gritted teeth, controlling herself. 'What do you mean later?' she was saying. 'What use is fucking later to me? Oh, I might be in a pub. Oh, Crown and Anchor, somewhere like that. You'll have to look, won't you? Bastard,' was what she hissed, putting the phone down. 'Bastard, bastard, bastard.'

It was already dark outside, darker than black velvet, darker than the charcoal with which Helen drew her odd but often accurate depictions of faces, and that was all Helen saw through the window as Rose looked up and spied her own reflection. Rose's face on the old glass bore wavy lines of a childish and unattractive fury, but the look as she spun round had changed to one of cunning.

'Oh, it's you. Well, I don't mind people hearing me mouthing off.'

'You're quite entitled,' said Helen. 'As long as you weren't talking to the Attorney General. Wouldn't do your career much good.'

Rose barked with laughter, her sharp little face alight with it and becoming animated into that of a different, more malleable creature until she stopped abruptly and looked at Helen assessingly. Helen could feel the scorn for the depressing bags of fruit and vegetables. Such luggage would never weigh down Rose Darvey or make her consider there was ever a time in Helen's life when she too might have lived on gin, tonic and crisps, a *modus vivendi* she still often craved.

'You look tired, Miss West. Why don't you come out for a drink with us after work?'

Helen was amazed, gratified in a way. Whatever the hidden motive, there must surely be in there some expression of approval which she needed in her present insecure frame of mind. But before she could think, she was stuttering the negative, raising the polythene bags in a helpless gesture which made her feel older still. Apples, oranges and potatoes, God help me.

'Rose, I'd love to, but I can't. Got to get home, food shopping, you know . . .' Rose did not know. Too late, Helen found herself making excuses for a refusal which could have been both warm and gracious but sounded merely lame. The moment in which she could have established some intimacy died in the speaking. Rose turned back to her desk, fiddled with the phone, showing no sign of disappointment, shrugging.

'No problem. Forget I asked.'

'Another time . . .'

'No, forget it. Only an idea. But listen, while you're here, can I ask you something?'

Perhaps the chance of mutuality had not fled after all, but Rose was businesslike. 'You know how I keep track of all the case papers in a notebook? And then who's-your-face puts them in the computer every day with all the dates for the remand hearings, so we know where everything is, and which dates someone's got to turn up to court the next time?' Helen was ashamed to say she did not really know, deliberately ignorant of the way the office worked. 'Well,' Rose continued, 'someone keeps nicking the notebook. You've got the untidiest room. My sodding notebooks haven't wandered in there lately, have they?'

It was spoken like an accusation, so unnecessarily aggressive that Helen had the fleeting suspicion Rose somehow sensed that she had been discussed in critical terms and was defending herself in advance. Or maybe it was her response to the mildest of rejections.

'I don't think so. Why should I have them? Does it matter, as long as it's all gone on the computer? That's the only record we need, isn't it.'

'Oh, you are stupid,' said Rose. The other five girls were clattering back, yawning, reaching for hats and coats, grinning at Helen. They were all so much nicer than Rose and so much less complicated, she thought with the rise of a familiar irritation. Rose's back view and her overbright hallos to her mates had the same effect as a dismissal and Helen took the hint. Rose had a shining charisma and energy in her which defied the brash rudeness; she would find someone else to go to the pub. 'Night!' she yelled, rudely, and then with a last, pitying look at the unglamorous bags, added, 'Have a good evening.' Suddenly her pretty face split into a grin. 'Listen, you can always wow a man with potatoes . . .'

I wish I was like that, Helen thought later, still wondering what strange and guilty fit of domestic conscientiousness had led her to purchase the vegetables. There were some days in which a weary stupidity seemed to take over and she was easily mesmerised by a shop or a stall. I wish I was nineteen and careless, energetic and about to fall in love, adopt a new career, go out giggling and screwing men every night, although not perhaps the rookie police-men from the section house with their fresh and pimply faces. Geoffrey Bailey had once been one of those, and the thought stopped her in her tracks as she struggled from the bus and into the supermarket. The thought of Bailey did not bring joy: it brought instead a dull weight of anxious dread and a feeling of guilt.

Geoffrey Bailey was not by any manner of means a vain man, but his own embarrassment at the public vision of his beaten-up face made him feel uncomfortable. He should have been too old to care, and as Ryan had said, 'You were scarcely an oil painting to begin with, were you, sir? Who do you think will notice?' Ryan did not quite do him justice. Bailey's appearance was never less than dignified. He was long and lean with a face of surprising asceticism for a man who knew how to handle himself in a fight, although the lines betrayed an age well beyond forty and a mal-nourished youth. Ryan had also been heard to say that Bailey got promoted because he looked so good in a suit, and that was not quite fair either. Ryan could not understand his master's obses-sion with fairness and conscience in a world which was supplied with neither. Bailey looked impeccable and unyielding in a suit, frightening to some, unless he was decorated with the comic effect of a black eye above. The eye throbbed with the foolishness of its own existence and Bailey had endured quite enough teasing for one day. The rest of him smarted for reasons quite uncon-nected. Helen West was his lover (he hated the word mistress, which implied an element of financial dependence and there was certainly none of that), and he had been gratuitously unkind to her the night before. It did not matter that the unkindness was mutual, but he had called her unreliable, selfish, self-absorbed. There were other epithets, far more extreme, from which he had refrained and the guilt was for things left unsaid, for the pathetic failure even to have a proper row with pots and pans flying. It had ended with mutual apologies and witch hazel placed on his eye by Helen, using all the kindly and remote consideration of a nurse. Today had begun with promises of killing some fatted calf to celebrate his departure which he suspected she viewed with as much relief as sorrow. The guilt had inhabited his day and led him to the supermarket which he knew, by instinct rather than information, she would visit on the way back to her place. Her turn to cook.

He yawned. Your place, my place, no place to go. He was never in the right place to find the shirt which went with the tie. He might as well shack up in the back of a caravan in the middle of a field, that was what he had wanted to say the night before. I do not mind any of this, Helen, but could you please relinquish just a little more of yourself than you do? I admit being born forty-five years ago with the expectation that a woman might cook my supper for life; I have shed that hope and did not particularly like it when it was offered, but I would indeed like it if you occasionally volunteered, although I cook far better than you. It becomes the yardstick of what we feel about things, this business of shopping and feeding. Nor can I rid myself of a notion which you have proved absurd, namely that a woman should be soft and have an interest in babies by the age of thirty-five. You accord with none of my expectations. I love you dearly, but there are times, especially latterly, when I have to say it in order to feel it, and you do not say it at all. You have become brittle, my dearest, the sugar spun hard, but I cannot speak too loud, because ten years ago, before I recovered my compassion, let alone my sanity, I was as hard as nails.

Guilt for things unsaid had him standing in the light outside the supermarket against the backdrop of a dozen brazen advertisements, 'Nescafé! 10p off! Jaffa oranges! 20p!' Absently, fond of oranges, fonder still of tangerines which reminded him of the Christmas they had just had, he went indoors and selected oranges, grapefruit, apples, potatoes. At least he would leave her with some supplies.

He saw her behind aisle one (soaps, detergents, bleaches, toilet rolls), already overburdened with a briefcase and three white bags of bulging plastic. Even in this cruel light, she was beautifully distinctive. He saw her first in the television monitor which hung above the door; his height allowed him to see above the corridors of produce, and he had thought, Darling, you could never rob a bank, you are so unmistakable. A big wide forehead, with that faded scar disguised by worry lines, the thick, dark hair pulled back into a slide which could not quite contain it, and the face which had always reminded him of some exotic dancer blessed with oddly imperfect beauty and enormous eyes. You could not even guess her nationality with those saturnine looks, and here and now, despite the casual elegance of her fine, swinging coat, you could not guess the authority she held. She looked lost. She stood at the counter labelled FISH! paralysed with uncertainty. Supermarkets did this to her. On a market stall it was different, but here, she failed to function. In an instant, he understood her better, loved her better, though the liking was still in doubt. He saw that she had bought vegetables and so had he.

People looked at her, without her ever seeing, he noticed, but they were not drawn to a man with a black eye as he went his aberrant way, tipping all he had chosen back on to the fruit and vegetable aisle. He looked like a thief who had abandoned the expedition, a reprobate who could not pay, and he felt a fool, for being ludicrously tidy in his replacement of what he knew she had already bought, putting back potatoes with potatoes, fruit with the same breed of fruit, plastic bags where they belonged. Bailey, who was willing to bet she had selected worse produce from her stall and paid more, replaced his goods with an element of regret. Then he walked up to where she stood, still immobile.

The red coat crumpled as he placed his hands around her waist and whispered in her ear.

'Fancy a night on the town, then? Take you away from all this? Man with a black eye, asking for you.'

She did not move, leant back against him.

'I never go out with strange men,' she said. 'I stay in. Do you want cod or plaice? I can't even spell the others.'

They might answer to their names, but he doubted they could spell them. At ten past ten, Sergeant Morgan examined the relief for night shift, E division, King's Cross. They paraded for duty in whatever shambolic order they chose and not for any other purpose than his counting them. You didn't brief them these days. Although the sergeant would have liked it to be different, half of this relief were probationers, rookies from the country with accents you could cut with a knife and as far as he could see, scarcely a good one among them. He was grateful he did not have to examine their consciences, but counting them was easy. Out of ten, three were missing. Those present, who had come via various routes to work, could not explain the absence of the contingent from the section house.

Sergeant Morgan sent the oldest constable, PC Michael, all of twenty-four, a handsome pugilist with a broken nose, and a temperament of surprising gentleness until he approached a fight and even then he seemed able to control his scarred fists. Michael was of a size which looked ridiculous in a panda car and the bulk of him made the door of the section house appear small by comparison.

Inside, PC Michael could smell the conflict although the place looked as empty as a closed shop. Late turn, the two-till-ten shift, were still on their way home, while early turn, who would work from eight till two tomorrow, were all still out on the town. Following a nose for blood, Michael broke into a run up a flight of stairs where the sounds of violence were now unmistakable. A hoarse yelling, grunting, the noise of falling furniture, a slow dancing of malice-filled steps, the vicious sounds of bone on bone and a cry of enraged pain led his progress. There was a bedroom door ajar through which the central light swung drunkenly from a low ceiling, casting a beam like a moving flame on the scene beneath. He could see a stereo system smashed, a cheap bedside lamp in fragments. In the far corner, illuminated as the light swung back, a wardrobe door hung on its hinges, supported from falling by the slumped figure of a slight youth with his left hand shielding his eyes, the other arm outflung to the edge of a rumpled bed on which sat a girl with spiky hair, balled into the furthest corner. Her knees were clasped to her chest and her hands were over her ears in an attitude which suggested both fear and indifference. Centre stage, two young men in half police uniform, with navy serge trousers beneath blue shirts, one ripped but both still buttoned, wrestled and punched with the savagery of fighting dogs. 'You cunt, you bastard.' Guttural, meaningless insults, as ineptly delivered as the blows which nevertheless made sounds of bruising flesh.

They were equal in weight, size and hatred, but neither had half of Michael's disciplined bulk. He stepped towards them, crunching over broken glass, and seized each rutting youth by the collar. He took a fistful of stiff cotton shirting in each hand, twisted it, yanking the material against each throat, and with this purchase, braced himself and flung them apart. One staggered backwards against the wall, his head striking with a sickening thud, the other reverberated against the wardrobe door, falling half across the crouching youth and the girl, who shrank further away. In the silence of panting breath, Michael noticed that she held her skirt over her naked loins and on the floor, in the brief moment when the light swung back, he saw a tracery of lace underwear. The room smelt strongly of sweat, fish, cooking meat; a stench of smells, with the last scent of blood carrying the taste of iron into his mouth. Gradually, the light slowed its wild arc and the faces became clear.

'Parkin? John! Williams! You clowns! Will you wash your faces now and report for duty? Or you'll catch it.' The radio on Michael's belt crackled: they all remembered who and what they were, moved in a dream of automatic response to orders. In stumbling from the room, all but the boy crouched on the floor, whose room it was, cast a look of venom in the direction of the girl on the bed. PC Michael glanced at her in sheer dislike and left her there. It was only on the way back he felt sorry for his behaviour. At half-past ten, Police Sergeant Morgan convened the nightshift parade again and shouted at them all, innocent or guilty, including PC Michael, for repeating the cock-and-bull story he had been told, designed to exonerate them all. Michael stared straight ahead with his mild eyes; the rest were silent and resentful. Third from the end, the smallest of the relief, PC Williams, displayed a swelling eye, now pink, soon to be purple. He kept his mouth closed to relieve the pain of a broken tooth, but he could not prevent himself crying like a baby, raising his fist to his swollen mouth to prevent the shameful sound of a boy whimpering.

'I knew you wanted steak really. You could have put it on your eye, then I could have cooked it.'

'Bit like getting a dog to bury it in the garden to tenderise it. You have the sort of ideas to encourage a vegetarian. Did you read that one in the book?'

'Fish is good for you. Isn't it? Protein without fat? But think of how they catch it, all that thrashing around—'

'You could do with a bit of fat. Slender's one thing, being thin, another . . .'

'Now look who's talking. You look as if you could snap in half.'

'Well, if you want to try,' Bailey said, 'I'm all yours. Be gentle with me, though. I'm not a well man.'

Helen laughed, like the old days, when she had first sat on the worn but brilliant colours of his junk-shop sofa and admired the barrenness of his walls. She didn't even think of the journey home, the cold outside, the balcony cat which had sat on her pristine blouse and made it grey without any comment from either of them. Even then, he had been haunted by the vision of keeping her thus, a fixture in his life instead of this ever-moving, ever-tantalising target. He supposed a woman as handsome as this, as kind but as definite as this, was bound to be this way. Bailey could no longer distinguish between the deficiencies and the necessities of their existence, could not see where they should go from here, only where they had been. He was humbled by the conclusion which had formed over the last twenty-four hours and found it difficult to articulate. Helen might have been relieved at the prospect of his enforced absence, but he did at least now know that she was not the only one. He was relieved too, even though she was in the crook of his arm, dressed in nothing but a shawl, her small athletic limbs bare beneath, enough to make a man forget his pain, the absence of dessert and the dry fish. Clinging to him, but with so light a clinging her finger's touch had all the weight of a feather.

'I forgot,' she said, deliberately drowsy. 'Do they let you out from Bramshill every weekend, or once a fortnight?'

'I don't know,' he replied, restive with the lie. 'I'll only know when I get there tomorrow.'

'I'll miss you,' she said, simply. Nothing more. He was not sure what he had hoped for. Remembered the hymn singing of his childhood. Oh, thou who changest not, abide with me.

Down the hill, far beyond the wilderness which was in turn far beyond the reaches of the football stadium, lit by arc lights still although the crowd was gone, Rose Darvey ran. She bore in her stride nothing but the encumbrance of her short skirt, her brutal shoes, a quantity of vodka and the dizzying effect of a light bulb swinging across her eyes. She knew she was pursued, knew she should not have stopped once to hide and howl quietly, should have known better than to give way to her fear of the dark. The car lights hit her full beam on the corner: the man who pursued her had gone round the back. She shrank into one of the hedges which skirted the tiny front gardens. Waited. A car door was shut carefully, with the deliberate movement of someone who was preoccupied. She breathed easier. Then footsteps came in her direction, hesitated, moved past with unerring pace, stopped, came back. If he had slammed the door, she would have maintained her hope: she was accustomed to such sounds, but the quiet precision made her want to scream. 'Come out, will you?' A voice equally careful, but harsh. 'I know where you are. Come on out. Don't be silly.'

When she moved, though, obeying him slowly, he caught his breath. He had expected a hard-bitten face and saw instead the beautiful eyes of a haunted child.

CHAPTER THREE

Mrs Mellors reached out her hand and stroked the head of the blond child who stood in front of her as they waited for the bus. She did so because she could not resist it. The child shook her head as if to dismiss a troublesome fly, then clapped her hand to her golden locks as the stroking continued, turned round, ready to be angry. When she saw who it was she grinned instead, the toothless smile of a six year old who had lost the top set of milk teeth early and was waiting for their replacements. She was an ugly little cuss, apart from the hair, a screamer and yeller, the kind Margaret Mellors particularly liked because there was something in Margaret which always applauded a talent for noisy hysteria. She didn't want to emulate it and besides, it was too late now to change the gentle habits of a lifetime, where the only vice was two drinks a night when she got the chance, but she still had an artless admiration for those born rowdy. Her own extraordinary patience with awkward children was one of many reasons to explain her popularity with the young parents in Legard Street. Yuppies did not live here. The newly partnered who started their dynasties in these tiny houses were not those who could employ nannies: they catered for their broods and their mortgages via more hazardous routes. There was the occasional father at the primary school gate, but mostly it was a question of babes in arms being ferried hither and thither by mothers grey with exhaustion.

Margaret Mellors had never advertised the fact that she would willingly look after any of the children with all the skill of the apple-cheeked grandmothers who featured in their books but not otherwise in their lives, but such news did not need to be shouted. In the last four years which had marked both a vacuum in her life as well as changing fortunes for the street, news of her willingness had spread into a kind of fame and her house had become inundated with children. Only now she was stroking that irresistible blond head with a tentative touch, because she had sensed a slight shift in attitude towards her from the mothers of children like this. There had been a perceptible if slow alteration in their willingness to leave children at her house. At first, Margaret thought it was all about the onset of winter and the deep suspicion held by all these young people for the old-fashioned decrepitude of her spotless abode, but she had come to recognise it as something more. The disparity of the lives somehow made the grapevine of unwelcome gossip appallingly slow, as well as inaccurate, but still Mrs Mellors was being sent to Coventry by those who needed her most.

'Hallo, Margaret! How are you? Say hallo, Sylvia, will you please. Nicely.' The warmth of the mother's greeting made Margaret relax and the acceptance of the child gave her a feeling of authority. Whatever it was that had blighted the reputation of her own home, it was not herself. No-one despised her bird-like body and her clean, talcum-powder smell. She hoped not, but in a way she would have preferred it if the opposite was true; if only they did not all dislike poor darling Logo as much, and if only they could realise that the lies which framed him were utterly and completely unfair. Talk about screamers and shouters, he was certainly one of them, but essentially a good boy, despite the Bible and the singing, if only they would see it. The problem around here was they were all so busy.

'Hallo to you too! Where are you going then? Shopping? God save us, you won't have much chance, will you?' Margaret's hand was still in the child's hair, touching the delicious warmth of the neck lightly. She knew when not to irritate and the child did not resist, squirming happily before she came to rest straddled over the old woman's leg, resting against her stomach and her stick, biding her time for attention.

'You haven't been round to see me lately, have you?' said Margaret, brightly. 'Are you going to nursery school now?'

'Yeth,' said the child.

The mother shifted her weight from one foot to another unhappily.

'Well the truth is, Margaret, she's supposed to go, but half the time they can't have her, so it only works out to two mornings a week, and the rest of the time she drives me round the bend. I take that much time off work and I'm only part time as it is—'

'Why don't you send her to me then?' Margaret asked mildly, looking away from the woman and peering down the street as if she had just seen something worth close examination. The child began to hum loudly, then set off round them both in close circles, making the dangerous noise of a wasp.

'Oh, do shush, sweetheart,' said Margaret. The child shushed and came back to rummage in Margaret's half-full shopping bag with noisy rudeness. Margaret did not protest, while the mother looked at her big, calm face, at odds with the little body, with something like hunger.

'Look, Margaret, I'd send her into you like a shot, but you must know I can't, not with that man next door to you. You know what I mean. Is he really your son? People says he's your son, you're both so . . . petite, but he doesn't look like you. Well anyway, if it's true, and someone told me it wasn't, I don't mean to be rude but I can't send Sylvie into you with him hanging around the place, can I?'

'Why ever not?' Margaret asked, stupidly.

'Don't you know? You must know, surely?'

But the look on Margaret's face confirmed an incredible level of ignorance of anything to Logo's detriment. She clearly did not understand that there was anything more than the merely indistinct vibrations of embarrassment which Logo attracted from his neighbours. For pinching the odd spade out of a garden, Margaret thought defensively; for looking through their rubbish bags like the scavenger he was. He was only a little bit crazy, poor Logo, and nobody likes anybody who carries a black Bible around with them, the reverse of a talisman. This wasn't a wicked neighbourhood, but it was godless. Margaret braced herself. If he looked like the son of hers who never was, Logo was her problem: she certainly didn't want him to be anyone else's.

'No, he isn't my kin, but I've lived next door to him and his family, when he had a family, for nigh on twenty years, so I know him better than anybody, you might say. It was when his wife and his daughter went off, you see, only a year or two since, that he went a bit barmy. You shouldn't take offence at him, he's all right really. Gentle, wouldn't hurt a fly, and he's been good to me, really. Ever so good.'

The younger woman's cross-examining glance was so sharp, Margaret thought for a second that the powder would be stripped off her own face. She always wore face powder, just a little, to correspond with the talcum on her body: she dressed and undressed in a shower of sweet-smelling dust and she tried to keep herself decent. It was her own compensation for age, infirmity, the bad hip for which treatment had never been successful, and as far as compensations went, it worked. Margaret Mellors, with her cake-like face, neat little frame and her almost edible gentleness, was never less than easy on the eye.

'Someone said,' the woman was saying, trying to keep the aggression from her voice, 'he's been arrested ever so many times. But he always gets off.'

Margaret rallied, she did not raise her voice because she never felt the need.

'Well, that'll be because he never actually does anything. He's always looking for some kid who looks like his daughter used to look, don't know what she looks like now, but that's what he does. Silly, but he does it . . .'

Her voice was fading softly into nothing. She knew as she spoke, with the child pulling on the shopping bags and dragging her sideways, that any attempt to explain or excuse the enigmas of Logo were useless. She had better try another route.

'Never mind what he does, it hardly matters,' she said. 'Anyway whatever gave you the idea he was ever in my house during the day? He does work, you know, after his fashion, but oh no, he's never in my place. Never. He's out with his trolley.'

It was almost the truth and she meant it to be the truth. She paused for dramatic effect. 'Never,' she added, with quiet emphasis, feeling disloyal as she spoke, but still determined. The child began to move again, re-creating the humming sound, but louder, until it became a kind of growling. The mother looked at her in alarm.

'I'm a dog, really,' the child announced.

'Of course you are,' Margaret murmured comfortably. 'Are you a big dog or a little dog? Only they make different noises. Wouldn't you be better as a cat?'

The mother's last defences were gone. Some persuasion had been necessary, but not much.

'Listen, if you could . . . Only I've got so much to get, and she's a nightmare round the shops—'

'Of course I'll have her if it helps. You just relax, you look a bit tired. Late-night shopping, isn't it? You'll be able to get a lot done. No need to hurry home.'

So Margaret Mellors had the company of hyperactive Sylvie for an hour or four in the dying afternoon. It hadn't strictly been a lie about Logo, she told herself. They did, after all, have an unwritten rule that they never went into one another's houses without invitation – never – but still the conversation left her uneasy, reminded her too much of things shoved under the carpet and best not brought out. His door would open with a kick, but something about the view from the window stopped anyone trying. And he was kept busy, she wasn't lying about that, cleansing officer he was called, she reflected with pride, that's what he was called. The Council wanted rid of him too: everyone picked on him, he said, but Logo remained on the equal opportunity pay roll, come what may, for a number of reasons. They liked an eccentric for a start and there weren't too many volunteers to brave the graveyard ghosts on his patch, even less to clear the rubbish after football, nor anyone else who came so much into his own for certain special tasks. They could raise him from the pubs where he was regarded as a singing-and-dancing mascot, though never quite a drunk. He would deal with burst water mains, drains in suppurating basements, the removal of a decade's worth of rotting rubbish: he would touch the untouchable with his bare hands; shovel up a dead dog or cat from a cellar, singing all the while. You didn't sack a wiry little man like that, whatever his timekeeping.

'Oh God our help in ages past . . .' Logo shouted, pushing the trolley. Big old thing, not the new-fangled plastic, double-binned variety, ergonomically, economically sound, he wouldn't have any, got the ole bin on wheels, hadn't he, suited him fine, but he'd fought for it. Despite the memory of that battle, the energy was low that afternoon and his feet in his training shoes were icy.

Logo took many of the opportunities his job presented for doing nothing, but he always noticed litter. Down in the gutters as he walked, some of last autumn's leaves were still half frozen from the morning frost, the slyest litter of all, unrecyclable, with nowhere to go, pretty at dawn but now becoming so much damp rubbish until the next night's frost would crisp them like toast, where the bugs and the slime slept easily until they melted and the smell came up. Logo liked that scent: he liked the earth when it was damp and stuck to his feet. He made his own timetable; lazy one day, industrious the next. Today he was finished with the grave-yard: he could go home, but he didn't want to, he would rather sit on a wall and read his dog-eared Bible. He liked the stories.

'Have we not power to lead about a sister, a wife, as well as other apostles as the brethren of the Lord? Or I only, have not we power to forbear working?' he intoned, his voice a high enquiry as he went towards his street.

It had been one of those days when light had never properly featured at all; there had been nothing to the dying of it. Turning the corner, Logo saw the figure of Margaret Mellors retreating from him with her narrow back, dressed in the same clean, dun-coloured coat which went on from year to year with no pretension to style. She was in the act of reaching inside her bag for an orange which she then bowled down the street like a ball towards a wicket. A small child whooped, yelled, barked in pursuit of the orange until she waylaid it in her little fist, catching it like some terrier while it was still rolling.

'There's no need to bite it,' Margaret was calling. Logo saw the blond head in the intermittent light of the lamps. Watching with quiet intensity as Margaret threw the orange again, he became slowly aware of disturbing sounds. People gathering for a footie match. Beyond their road he could sense the traffic bearing down on them, felt from a distance the arrival of the first hordes. It always reminded him of flies descending on a carcass but Margaret did not notice. He was trying to work out why she threw fruit for her charge; to tire her out, perhaps, you threw sticks for a dog and more edible things for a child, but his interest soon died. The creature did not resemble his own child, dark as a gypsy like him, run away a long time ago; she'd be a woman now.

Margaret called to the child and when she ran back, seized her firmly by the hand and led her up the street towards her house. Disconsolate, Logo remembered his icy feet and stamped them. He courted the cold, did not really mind it and the stamping was more ritual than necessity. He waited until Margaret was out of sight, then drew in a lungful of air and began to sing.

'Jesu, saviour ever mild, Born for us a little child, Of the virgin undefiled:

Hear us Holy Jesus.'

Keeping close to the walls, backing out of Legard Street, pushing the cumbersome trolley like a big old pram, he moved in the direction of the crowds which would throng the thoroughfares beyond. Looking for a small, dark child, with a headful of black curls cascading from the neck to her waist and streaming out behind her like the tangled mane of a thoroughbred filly as she ran away. From him.

Dinsdale Cotton thought Helen West was beautiful. He did not say as much, but the conclusion had been on his mind from the moment he had first met her. He could follow the present discussion with his brain all the more easily because it gave him a better opportunity to look at her eyes, hands, hair, legs in whatever order they happened to present themselves without quite seeming to devour her. He knew it was still far too soon to do anything else, that would be like spitting in public, but he planned it anyway, enjoying what he had for now. Besides the conversation was always worth while, even if they both chose to deny the undercurrent which flowed between them.

'Evidence,' she was saying. 'Come on, Dinsdale, why the hell aren't you doing this? Why me and not you, giving a lecture on evidence? How come I even got volunteered and not you, when you can talk the hind leg off a donkey and everyone knows I've never understood law at all? I only practise it. What do I say to them?'

He took a covert look at her slender crossed ankles, as she sat back in the beastly lounge of the Swan and Mitre, and decided he could look no further so he might as well entertain himself by intellectual effort.

'What you say always depends on the audience,' he said. 'And there's no audience, apart from a symposium of scientists, who do not want their information as simple as possible.'

'Just as well. I can't manage more than that. Come on, surprise me. Ten minutes is what I have to deliver, on the subject of, What is evidence? The audience being Justices of the Peace with nil legal training. Your starter for ten, please.'

Dinsdale sipped his drink, vodka in tomato juice, which did not look at all effete in his hands. He removed an imaginary pair of glasses and shuffled an imaginary sheaf of papers on the rather dirty table.

'Evidence, my dears, is fact. It comes in the form of brick or cement. There are basically three kinds of evidence. The first is the most direct, say from an eye or ear witness to an event, the horse's mouth evidence. Then it comes, less directly, from those who follow on behind, picking up the pieces of the smashed car, testing the blood samples and the semen stains and who can thus say, this event happened. This is circumstantial evidence, although they are recycled bricks, they are the most certain of all. Evidence also comes from a number of unrelated facts which surround the victim and the defendant but have nothing to do with them, and this is the cement. They are little facts, positive and negative, which point to one conclusion. Thus, one witness hears a door slam at three in the morning, another sees a man in a street soon after; a third person mentions someone he met in the local earlier that evening who looked the same; a fourth mentions, by chance, a possible motive. By the smallest and most innocent innuendos brother betrays brother. A network of facts, individually irrelevant. You need this cement if you do not have enough of the bricks alone. Like bloodstains and fingerprints.'

'Confessions?' Helen asked, vastly amused. 'Are they direct enough evidence to make into bricks?'

'Oh, certainly,' Dinsdale said airily. 'Finest kind of brick, but in this generation, it has a tendency to crumble. What you must tell this audience, of course, is that the only evidence which can be used in the construction of a case is evidence that has been properly obtained. Thus if you make the defendant shit the brick, you cannot use it to build the wall around him. Will that do?'

'Certainly. But your recitation has taken precisely two minutes. What shall I do for the other eight?'

'Tell them stories. The taller the better. Another drink?'

Helen was about to refuse, responding to the automatic pilot-light which ignited inside her head some time before eight in the evening to remind her it was time to go home. Then she remembered there was no Geoffrey Bailey at his home or her own, hadn't been for a week. There'd been no trailing around a supermarket in her inefficient pursuit of their needs. The thought of her own relief brought into her throat an indigestible lump of guilt which she decided to swallow. She might well love Geoffrey Bailey, she was usually well aware that she did, but freedom from the routines of the relationship, from the sheer time it took to be with another, felt like a prize she had worked towards for months. Especially if the privilege included sitting with a man of Dinsdale's distinguished ease, warmed by his admiration and his sheer ability to talk. It made a change from the barks and grunts of familiarity.

'Well yes, why not? Aren't you due home, or something?'

Dinsdale shrugged noncommittally. Helen could not imagine his life to be unaccompanied by less than a select harem, but his domestic loyalties were his own concern and she did not have to consider them. She did not, at this moment, have to consider anyone or anything at all apart from the state of her digestion.

'Speaking of evidence,' said Dinsdale, returning from the bar with a napkin which he used to wipe the table clean in small, fastidious movements, 'is what I see over there evidence of anything at all? Or is it a figment of my over-fertile imagination?' Helen looked and whistled softly.

The Swan and Mitre was a pub with little to recommend it apart from proximity to a thousand offices and a heavy sense of age created by sherry casks hung above the bar. The grime was unfeigned and the crowds stumbled their way through raucous gossip in the artificial gloom. Smoking was mandatory: scores of men and women had been released from work to indulge a number of bad habits before retiring to the rigours of their homes. The wooden booths lining the walls gave some scope for intimacy: for the rest, the assignations were as public as a meeting in a telephone kiosk. In one booth, selfishly occupying space enough for four, prohibiting invasion by the cunning placement of coats which made it look as if someone else was expected, sat Rose, flanked by a young man. The size of him, the uniform shirt and the short haircut betrayed him as a policeman or a security man or suchlike, but there was no need for guesswork.

'Don't look so obviously, Helen, you do stare so. Is that PC Michael? He of boxing fame?'

'I think so. Why shouldn't I look? My God, they're actually talking to one another . . .'

'Well, so were we, it's a natural consequence of human proximity.'

'Among others,' Helen said lightly, 'in which Rose is supposed to be something of a specialist. She's been looking very pretty over the last couple of days, have you noticed? More subdued, less spiky.'

'I thought that might have been your influence. You know,

having a little chat with her, woman to woman, like Redwood asked you to do.'

'Asked once, then again and again, after more complaints and a fight in the section house. Yes I did try and talk to her, you know, Rose-is-there-anything-worrying-you? kind of thing, anything-where-I-could-help-you? But I didn't do much good. Quite the reverse, I must be losing my touch. I've never heard such a stream of insults in my life. No, that isn't true, I have, but not usually so fluent. The message was, Fuck off, leave me alone, you old cow, how can you understand at your age? And if Redwood wants to sack me, let him try. I made a tactical withdrawal.'

'Bloodied, but unbowed?' Dinsdale asked, smiling to show teeth which were admirably white.

'No, both bowed and bloodied. I wish there weren't such a thing as the age gap. I like her, I can't bear to see this brooding anger of hers, but she finds it impossible to like me. You can't convince her you might know what she means.'

'The effort was commendable,' said Dinsdale gravely, sensing a real humiliation. His hand on the now clean table hovered close to hers. The sight of it, pale, with its neatly pared nails, made her feel unaccountably lonely. The fingers tapped a neat rhythm, as if listening to some hidden music which was not hers to hear. Like the music which vibrated between Rose and her man, hidden but harmonic, cutting across the smog of the room to where they sat, the two adults. Helen thought she remembered what it was like, the music of romance, and felt older than Noah. Older than the sherry casks and just as deaf.

The pub on the corner of Legard Street and the main avenue which led to the football stadium also served sherry, but only if asked, with the request repeated several times. Their speciality was the kind of pie which, even when microwaved within an inch of its life, still challenged the digestion of a steam engine. The pie was held by the edge of the cellophane wrapper and it was not wise to examine the contents. Logo was indifferent to food and the pub was empty.

He ate his pie. It was burnt on the outside and chilly in the centre and did nothing to cure his hunger, but it made him feel bigger as he swallowed it. The concave stomach, knitted together in the middle by a scar which made him look as if he had been bitten by a shark, relaxed beneath the belted trousers. He belched, softly, looking round for an audience. The barman regarded him with marginal interest, less tolerant than usual. He was restocking the shelves for when the crowds came out of the stadium. On a night like this, during the silence in the middle of the two storms, he could do without Mr Logo, and if the bastard sang, he would pack him out of doors among the phalanx of parked cars, into the roar of sound which would reverberate as soon as someone scored a goal.

'All right, are you?' he said pleasantly and threateningly enough.

'All right,' said Logo. 'And you?'

'All right. Time you went home, isn't it?' He leant over the table, wiping the surface with a busy fussiness which betrayed watchful idleness and anxiety. Logo always leant over things without ever actually sitting down, the better to clear his chest for the next hymn, the barman thought, although Logo knew different. He found it uncomfortable to sit. The old scar was a wound known only to himself and some doctor who had long since moved on without his notes. The stitches were cumbersome, but they had been inserted in the middle of the night in a casualty ward without thought of future vanity, and they were old now, twitching in their wisdom to remind him not to sit with his small store of belly flesh curled into him, but always to stand proud, like a tin soldier who cannot bend. The barman made a mock punch in the direction of the old wound. No injury was meant – it was a playful gesture to underline a point and occupy the idleness – it was supposed to be friendly. But the reaction was absurd: Logo doubled up as if to pretend the punch was real, cried out in pain and lurched against the wall behind the now clean table. His arms were crossed over his abdomen and he wailed like a child. 'Aagh, aah, aah, please, please, don't. *Aagh!*'

The barman was unmoved. He did not care for the ulcerous pains of anyone who ate his pies; nor did he have to take hysterics from a little Bible-pushing creep like this.

'Oh go home, fuck off. I never touched you. Get out! Go on, get out, get out, get out!'

Logo, clutching his stomach, went out into the gloom without a backward glance. It had been warm in there, the pie inside him was warm enough and he had enough cash for another drink, but he went anyway. He took his litter trolley and its brushes inside from where he had parked it outside the door: it gave him stability as well as music as they went down the silent streets. Rumble rumble, wheels of worn rubber going round and round as if, in their bad design, they were as bewildered as he was himself, though he wouldn't have changed them for the world. The big trolley was good for a scavenger.

Home, don't spare the horses.

"'His roots shall be dried up from beneath, and above shall his branch be cut off,'" murmured Logo to himself, thinking of the barman, and then, self-pityingly of himself. "'His remembrance shall perish from the earth and he shall have no name in the street.'"

There was a great, sore-throated roar from the stadium as he passed; the streets were full of cars without people. Logo clutched the handle of his barrow and moved on, listening to the sound of thousands singing, 'Walk On! Walk On! You'll never walk alone!' feeling his Bible thump against his pocket, his feet warm now, as long as he kept moving. Which he did faster and faster, as far as the distant doors of his own house, no singing, no carrying on, nothing of the kind. He'd been a good boy, a very, very good boy; it was still early, so he wouldn't go in and see dear old Mother in case she was still trying to tire out that little blond brat playing hide and seek. Then he stopped, suddenly sober and cold.

Hide and seek inside his house as well as Granny Mellors', that's what it looked like. The lights were lit on his own ground floor, pouring from the frosted pane of his kitchen into the alley.

He could not believe that Margaret had sent the child, that blond, naughty little thing, to play in his house, but that was the only explanation that sprang to mind. Unless the child had gone there alone, pushed the door open, entered to plunder and explore. He knew he was not expected home before eight: he rarely was, but for Margaret, for both of them, especially the child, to assume his absence, felt like a violation. He quietly laid down the trolley and tiptoed to his door.

Little Sylvie's mother was further up the road, trying to fight her way through a barrier of parked cars, three deep, no room for a leg in between. She was late to begin with, stopped at the Tube because of a football fight, then the bus stopped for the same reason. All transport became coy on football nights. She was panicking a bit but not greatly until now. She knew Margaret would take care of Sylvie but everything seemed to take longer and longer, and the child was in Margaret's house. She had tried to phone, but there had been a queue, so she hadn't done and now it was half-past eight. Never mind. She click-clacked down the road, on the long walk from the Underground, wondering when her husband would be home, looking forward to that, and then halfway home, at the back of her head, she heard the child screaming in the way only her own child could scream. She felt it in her bloodstream: the pain in her chest like swallowed razor blades as she began to run, stumbling with shopping. She ran and she fell down in the dark alleyway between Margaret Mellors' and the house alongside. She was sure, from the distance, she had heard the child scream: she could feel it. Crashing through the broom handles which struck out from a rubbish cart in the alley, knocking her hip and all the shopping against the brickwork, she pushed into Margaret's house without ceremony, still hearing screams. *Where are you? Where are you, my love?* She was panting with the effort, but there she was, Sylvie the tyrant, in Margaret's arms, in front of the television.

She was lying there, the next best thing to unconscious, with her arms around Margaret's neck and one of her feet twitching.

There was ravelled knitting at their feet, a jumper sleeve poking from a bag, the child clutching rather than resting, and the mother was jealous. Then she saw the merest suggestion of tears at the corner of the old dear's eyes. Oh, she must be tired, the inevitable price of rendering Sylvie so quiet. But for all the reassurance of the scene, despite the comforting smell of powder, oranges, cocoa and the bright light, the mother could still feel something pulsing in her veins. She threw a couple of pound coins on the sink, made effusive thanks and removed her child with speed. Sylvie was sullen, almost catatonic, her little feet making leaden sounds on the lino of the kitchen floor and the passage outside.

Only when she was inside her own door, did the mother recall that the trolley against which she had collided on her way in had not been any sort of obstruction on the way out. It had been a bit like a pram. The memory flitted through her mind in a brief and inconsequential passage.

'Come in, Margaret, why don't you? Every other bugger does. All your friends.'

There was his whisky on the table, dusty from passage in the trolley, now out of sight in the yard behind. Logo's skin was as ashen as the dust on his shoes. He had taken off his jacket, revealing the drab, worn, black clothes he bought from second-hand shops, and Margaret had time to wonder how it was he always managed to keep up the appearance of being clean when his clothes were so ingrained with dirt.

'Listen, Logo, I'm sorry, I'm really sorry. Oh, she's a trial that child, she really is, but I thought she was tired out, and then I gave her something to eat, and then, I sat down, dropped off, I suppose, and she was gone. I was calling to her, thought she was upstairs in my place, and soon as I knew, she was upstairs in yours. Come on, you know you only have to push the door. So I'm sorry, but you shouldn't have done that. Wasn't her fault.'

He turned his big eyes on her.

'Done what?' he questioned. 'Done what, exactly? She done nothing. *You* did plenty.'

She sat heavily, exuding her clean dust, making a whoomphing sound, which was part chair, part a sigh of exhaustion. She settled herself into the chair and curled her fingers over the ends of the greasy, cloth-covered arms. She showed no signs of tension, but looked as an old woman might look after a doze, adjusting herself into the realms of dignity as if she hadn't been caught napping. Or been frightened.

'Oh don't be silly,' she said comfortably. 'All the poor thing did was wander out of my place when I dozed off and wander into yours, she can push the door as well as anyone. She turns on the lights, 'cos she's just about high enough, and has a look around. Then I came and found her, but by that time, you'd frightened her to death, you daft bastard. Why did you have to do it? Flapping your hands at her like that, was it a game?' She spoke as she always did, never raising her voice or changing tone. She could have calmed a herd of wild horses, and out of the corner of her eye she watched him relax and hand her a grubby glass, half-full of his precious nectar.

'I don't know,' she continued, in her grumbling, placating tone. 'All the years I've known you and I've never been upstairs in your house. Wouldn't want to either, looking at the rest of it. Never did have cause to go further than the kitchen. All the best parties are in kitchens. Where everything happens. Kitchens. About the only important room in a house. Yours could do with a bit of a clean.'

She stretched out her legs to prove her point. 'Ooh, this is nice,' she said, raising her glass to him with a well-rehearsed wink. 'Very nice.' She was choosing not to notice how dirty the glass really was, but whisky would save her from the germs, and she wasn't frightened of them anyway. You swallowed them as an infant and you were therefore preserved for six generations. Bleach and disinfectant featured in her own home, but she never really expected it to have the same dominion in another's.

If she was frightened, and she was, severely frightened, she did not show it. Margaret had kept from her husband the knowledge of his own terminal illness for two years; and she had always played games with children, so she knew how to pretend. She did not tell Logo that she had followed Sylvie into the house, not once but twice, had gone upstairs the first time and into all the rooms until she had found her hiding. Sitting in apparent ease now, it seemed better to say nothing; it was cold, so she drank. Two glasses a day, and she loved him as ever, but now, she was beginning to see what the neighbours meant. The child had been terrified: it wasn't fair to do that to a child; she felt ashamed of him.

Geoffrey Bailey found his room on the third floor. Inside his locker was his own bottle of Scotch, from which he poured a large measure into the tooth mug. Nothing else was his own, of course, it was provided by the Establishment, which left him the freedom of the guest to abuse it. He rubbed his thinning hair as he looked in the mirror. He could colour it purple in here and no-one would notice. The smile faded: he had been surprisingly well fed for a canteen service, as he had been the night before. He might nip out to a pub with Ryan later to watch his black eye fade. The swelling seemed to diminish whenever he smiled, which was often.

It wasn't even late, half-nine of a Thursday evening, and he was pleasantly tired, stimulated by learning.

He could be going home on weekend leave tomorrow, he had that option. On balance, he thought he wouldn't.

It wasn't a Rest Home, but it was a rest. And it was Ryan's turn to buy a round.

CHAPTER FOUR

The panda car cruised down Legard Street rather faster than usual. It turned right at the end and began a dizzying circumlocution of the streets, left, left, right, right, a progress which seemed to owe nothing at all to the military precision of a prescribed route. It sped down Seven Sisters, looking neither left nor right, in search of the nearest exit which would take it round the back. There was no point pausing here in a car with a stripe down the side: observing the ladies of the night had to be covert or not at all. The punters might not notice a train bearing down on them, but the girls doubled up and disappeared into the black of the road itself, leaving male faces staring out of car windows on the third, desperate time round.

The policemen in the panda car looked straight ahead. It was an unacknowledged fact that neither was interested in finding anyone whose behaviour would necessitate arrest. Even after an hour and a half, they needed another five minutes with one another to formulate a conversation which was as necessary as it was difficult. Both of them hoped it would be brief. Past Seven Sisters, where the unsuitably shod women had run like athletes, sharp right, to the back of the still-lit stadium, all gone safely home, the car radio silent to their mutual amazement, the moment now riper for a talk, although neither could be described as a talker.

'Shit, I don't believe it, nothing's happening, nothing at all. Football out, all gone, nothing. Is it always like this?'

'No.' Police Constable Michael was less reticent than most, which still made him, on matters emotional, very reticent indeed with his fellow man. 'It's usually different, but it's early yet. We don't break till twelve, pubs aren't shut yet, there's no telling.'

Suddenly he pulled the car into the side of the road, wound down the window and fished in his pocket for a packet of fags. The car rocked as he explored.

'Whoops,' he muttered, checking the brake, still fishing as his huge body arched against the wheel, the better to dig into his back uniform pocket. 'In here somewhere, everything is, everything's always the wrong end of your bloody trousers.'

The youth beside him rocked with mirth and the ice of awkwardness melted into something like slush. The cigarettes, when finally produced, came in the form of a battered pack of ten, all squashed and so pathetic in appearance, it was difficult to fathom what they might achieve. Probationer Williams, a lad from Wales, did not really smoke at all, once a year, Mum, but this would be an exception. His mouth hurt still, especially when he laughed.

'Looks like my cock on a good day, this does,' said Michael, staring at his cigarette, bent in the middle, a poor, pathetic thing, held between his fingers by the filter, smoke drifting drearily from the other end. 'Needs rewiring. And what's the matter with you then?'

The youth to his left took a drag on his fag and trembled. He was a good-looking lad, Michael thought, but he'd be useless in the ring where you couldn't let nerves show, awful. Might be just as bad if they had to get out of this car and show muscle to a group of youths on the other side of the stadium, fresh out of the football match and the front door of the pub, all crazy shouting and wanting to slap.

'Look,' said the youth, breathing in the fag smoke which clearly made him as sick as an over-rich cigar. 'Look, about the other night . . .'

'What night?'

'The other night, you know, whenever it was. God, ages ago, at least a week. Well, I thought you were all right. You know.'

'Oh, that. Never mind about that. I wasn't going to tell, was I? Why should I?' Michael became almost belligerent, chewing on the cigarette rather than smoking it. 'Might have been different if you'd hit her, but you'd none of you done that, and no, I don't want the story.' Williams was puzzled. He'd expected Michael to want to know how it started, and there he was, only thinking about the girl. Michael threw the half-done cigarette out of his window. It hit frozen leaves and remained lit. He turned his head and watched in wonder. Fire and ice, ice and fire, neither capable of extinguishing the other. Informed by strangely exquisite and painful moments of the last few days, he noticed everything with peculiar anguish. Trees, leaves, rubbish, the detritus of life and nature had all assumed some poetic status, but he was still what he was before. A kindly and loyal man with a better brain and greater heart than most of his colleagues, but still a policeman, whose greatest loyalties were his fellows. Only now he had other loyalties too.

'Bit daft, wasn't it?' he said softly. 'You lot, fighting. You took quite a thumping. How did it start?'

'You can guess, can't you? That bloody girl. I heard, through the wall of my room. Brian screwing her, God he makes such a noise, like a pig. I'd heard her voice first, then the sounds of it, and well, I saw red, because she'd been doing the same with me the night before. And with the others, but I didn't know that then. Cow.'

'All using your rubbers, I hope?' said Michael paternalistically, wincing all the same despite the calmness of his voice and wishing he still had the cigarette for his fingers to fondle. It was quite true he had not needed to ask about the origins of the section house brawl to find out what had happened, but he had needed this verbal endorsement. Suddenly he relaxed.

'So, I gather you'll have taken her home once or twice?'

'Once or twice,' the other muttered.

'Right, you can show us where she lives then.'

'Pardon?'

'Where she lives. Which street, which number.'

'I can't,' said the youth, surprised. 'I can't because she never let you take her to the door, did she? She'd say, "Drop me off on the corner," and I was late and Oh . . .! I see.'

The respect and the gratitude which had illuminated his face earlier, disappeared and he looked at his companion shrewdly, attempted a laugh which emerged as a yelp. 'Oh, I see. You're on to her now, are you. Picking up the pieces. God, you—'

'Bastard,' Michael finished for him helpfully, starting the engine. 'And yes, maybe I am, but not in the way you might think. There's a difference, see? I'm not screwing her. Now, show me the corner where you dropped her. So I know if it's the same place as mine.'

His mind changed smoothly with the gears. The man beside him sat silent and defeated, waiting for the radio to give them work and dispel the gloom of jealousy.

Rose sat in the window of the second-floor flat she occupied with two other girls. She had been waiting all evening to watch the car go by. Not any car, but this particular car, with the white paint and the crowded wall of bodies on the inside. *Watch the wall, my darling, while the gentlemen ride by.* She'd learned that poem in school, taught by some silly old fart who was trying to get across to them that all speech had its own rhythm, but no-one she knew talked like that. She was idle in her badly lit bedroom, watching her face in the mirror, over which there was the only light she was willing to use. Even a presence behind half-closed curtains was not something she wished to advertise. The street outside was peculiarly silent: the cold had driven all revellers and would-be visitors indoors. From the window opposite came the eerie neon light of a television.

Rose moved across the room whenever she heard the sound of an engine, then she moved back to her mirror, where she watched her own face, without vanity, and let her thoughts meander. At times, she made play with shadows, using her fingers, creating on the opposite wall through the unattractive spotlight, the shape of a rabbit waving huge ears with an obscenely large tail, the edges furred, the thing making gestures all by itself. It was almost compulsive, this nervous habit she had, creating, when the light was right, these not unfriendly little images. But all of a sudden she was irritated by the twitching of the clownish shadows, frightened by the life they assumed for her own distraction. Slowly she uncurled her hand and used it, coupled with the other in a voluntary handcuff, to wave itself goodbye on the opposite wall. Her spread fingers now resembled the wing of a huge bird flying away across the sun: she made the wings move until the thing, half sinister and half exotic, blocked the light completely and made her afraid.

Then she heard the sound of another engine, familiar without being tantalising. The shadow play had calmed her: she moved to the window without haste, knelt and put her chin on the window sill with the thin curtain behind her head. She was rewarded by the sight of a panda car, not speeding but cruising, a face on the passenger side looking out and looking up at the windows like some mother looking for a lost child in a department store. Dimly she recognised the face, withdrew her chin until her nose was level with the window, and giggled a little. Then she raised her whole head and turned it obliquely as the car stopped two doors down, the opposite door opened and he got out. She stole one lingering glance at his size, standing in the street with his breath on the air like mist, looking back towards his car door before looking up to her. She watched, with palpable pleasure, the straightening of his clean, pressed uniform, and then she was gone, scrambling across the floor with the curtains concealing her, towards the light-switch.

There was silence for a minute, then the doorbell sounded into the vacuum of the empty first floor, without response from the second. The two girls with whom Rose shared the upper storey were out: otherwise, they would have asked anyone in, especially uniformed men. Rose waited until the buzzer echoed away, then heard the sound of footsteps crunching on frost, a large body colliding with the dustbin and the general shuffle which heralded departure.

Back at the window with the light out now, she saw him adjust his jacket again before he climbed into the driver's seat. She tried to make herself laugh. Bet you always do that, you silly big twit, she said to make her lips move, but when the car edged away, she could only feel the pain of grief, so sharp she was tempted to bust the window with her fist and yell, Here I am! But the impulse passed without the grief passing too. She had come home from the office in a taxi and made up her face in case he found her: weeping would disturb her looks, so instead she turned on the light, and, crouching in the corner, began the shadow play again.

'Does he love me?' she asked the rabbit. 'Could he ever possibly love me? Can it happen so quick, just like that? Oh, please . . .'

Her bedroom was festooned with soft toys; they sat in vigilant rows along the wall-side of her single bed, allowing little space for herself. She had a frilled pillowcase, frilled bedspread and a clutter of other possessions. The whole effect was somewhere between a boudoir and a toy shop.

There was a crash from downstairs, a clattering of steps and voices which led to their cramped quarters. Cheryl had the largest room since she had found the place first and, with great self-importance, furnished a deposit through the bank where she worked. The others had smaller rooms, all off a tiny lobby which led to a smaller kitchen. They had chosen to relinquish communal living space and not double up on bedrooms for reasons which were obvious but understated. In case they got lucky, as Cheryl put it; with a man, she meant, but in fact the other two had never got lucky on the premises or anywhere else yet: they were hard working, young, full of ambitions and romantic dreams, and not inclined to promiscuity. As flatmates, they had embraced one another through mutual need and the columns of the *Evening Standard*, but this was not the same as friendship although it passed for that between Mary and Cheryl. They went out together in the general direction of pubs and discos and presented a politely united front against Rose, because Rose was odd, secretive, not quite like themselves, and although she cleaned up the mess they made in the kitchen without complaint, the habit was not exactly endearing. There was nothing as keen as dislike. The regime worked, after its fashion, better than most.

Rose heard them lumber into the kitchen, then one to the

bathroom on the landing, where they always locked the door quite unnecessarily since none would have invaded the naked privacy of the others, unless desperate. In which case, Cheryl kicked the door, Mary knocked and whined, and Rose simply waited. She liked this aspect of their forced intimacy least of all, and kept her cosmetics, her washbag and her towel along with her life in her own room, but now she remembered she had not quite honoured that self-imposed rule this evening in their absence, and she groaned. She should have done that test in the morning, like it said on the packet. The groan and the realization coincided with a kick on her door. Cheryl, friendly, concerned and voraciously curious.

'We're phoning out for a pizza. Do you want some? And what's this doing here by the lav, then?' She was holding aloft the self-testing pregnancy kit, clearly labelled on the cardboard frame which enclosed a small tube.

'You got something to tell us?'

Rose shrugged. It was too late now.

'I dunno. There's three versions. One says I am, another says I'm not and the third says it isn't sure to make you buy another test. This one isn't sure, but I think I am anyway. Yeah, I'd love some pizza. Tuna.'

They sat in the kitchen which could scarcely hold the three of them and a telephone at a small table. Mary phoned for pizza, looking at Rose out of the corner of her eye with the same expression as Cheryl. The discovery of the pregnancy kit precluded any talk about work or the weather; they were looking at her as if examining a strange animal in the zoo, with a mixture of reverence, curiosity and only slight distaste. As near-miss virgins, they'd sort of assumed she was too, and they wanted to know what actually happened to get you otherwise, blow by blow, thrust by thrust, what it felt like. They wanted to ask all that before the pizza arrived and made everything all right again, but Mary and Cheryl were beginning to understand it was not quite possible. Cheryl, more streetwise, opted for making light of it. She hauled a can of beer from the fridge and offered it round. Rose shook her head.

'Trouble is with sex,' said Cheryl, mournfully, 'nobody will ever actually tell you. What to do.' They both looked at Rose, half challenging, half beseeching. She grinned.

'You just don't do what I did,' she answered, making it sound rueful, as if the act in question was entirely isolated. All right, so she would tell them, make them laugh by lying all the way, anything to harness enough tolerance to help her deal with the molten anxiety which seemed to have taken the place of her blood. Anything to postpone the evil hour of wondering what to do.

'Are you in love, then?' said Mary, with her staggering naïvety.

Rose sniggered uneasily. Going downstairs for the pizza, she wiped her eyes and her nose on her sweater sleeve and hoped they would think she was only laughing herself to death.

'Don't tell me you're in love, then.'

The younger constable was recovered enough in the canteen after midnight to inject into his own voice an element of jeering. He winced as the scalding tea hit the tender spot inside his mouth and he thought briefly of an impending visit to the dentist. PC Michael was making notes with assiduous attention to detail on the subject of the juvenile they had just arrested at the back of an off-licence, more hopeful than wicked, he thought, a very quiet night.

'With her. That Rose, I mean,' the young one persisted, gratified to see the beginnings of a dull red blush colouring the skin of Michael's placid forehead as the other bent back to his writing. The same blush might have been present, but unnoticed, in the car. It gave Williams the upper hand.

'Oh, I shouldn't think so,' Michael said. 'I don't know about love, do I? But after you lot were kicked into touch last week, I thought about how nobody was looking out for what happened to her, she was just chucked out. So I kept an eye open and then I saw her, a bit later, running down a road she was, I mean really running as if she was in dead trouble. She saw the car and she hid, in a garden. So I fished her out, and took her to where I showed you I dropped her, got her number at work. I was just sorry for her that's all. She might be a scrubber, but she's only a scrap.'

The young one sniggered again and straightened his face. The tea was more comfortable and the cold outside was uninviting. He wanted to prolong the story and his own advantage. Michael's qualities often had the effect of making other men feel mean.

'Sorry enough to see her every night last week?' Jeering again.

'Yes.'

'I reckon that's love then. You must be mad. You've broken all the records.'

It was here somewhere, among all the other records of her life and that was why it was so hard to find. By foraging among old chocolate boxes kept in the big dresser in her living room, Mrs Mellors gave herself ample opportunity for distraction, since each box out of the five was like Aladdin's cave. There were her wedding photos, dashing wartime economy, a borrowed hat she recalled as if it were yesterday and a corsage the size of a bush. Penny-pinching then, pound-pinching now, nothing altering. No photographs of children followed: they wouldn't have bought a camera for years after and there was little enough to record. Mr Mellors being Mr Mellors, herself working in a school as a dinner-lady, moving into this house and him getting another job with the council, a foreman dustbin man in the days when a foreman was something powerful, and yes, yes she had been proud of him, but not of the constant struggle against dirt and smell and men who cared about neither, and about him sometimes reproving her for her inability to have babies though he tried every night, and about her never knowing until much later, when they were past it, that the failure was not hers but his, and never saying anything.

All that took more than an hour, the second box, almost as long, the third, longer.

In here were letters, not just invitation cards, birthday cards, Christmas cards, old keys (she could never throw away a key, you never knew with keys), photos, bills, pieces of ribbon, brooches from Woolworth's, pieces of lace, hatpins (ouch, her finger caught a point, but the wound was bloodless, memoryless), ornate buttons waiting for a rainy day, but only letters. There were postcards, from the children she had looked after, and a bound volume, of messages, cards, childish and adult scrawls from the Logos. Because life had begun afresh with the Logos next door, a whole new, fifteen-year chapter which covered the last years of Mrs Mellors' working life, the illness of her spouse, his death and the decline of the family next door into this one weird little eccentric. The Logos had marked the most productive era of all, when, in her fifties, she had felt, at last, as if she had acquired some family who would honour her, and did, oh they did. Logo the road sweeper (Mr Mellors had got him that job when the office cleaning failed), then his wife, then the child, all babes, all incompetent, waiting for a granny like her. But you never quite knew your neighbour, even when you thought you did, even when it sat in your kitchen eating your grub and weeping its heart out over some tale you knew even then was half truth and it wasn't your business to question. There are no truer contacts than blood, thought Mrs Mellors, putting on the kettle to unseal the envelope which years had resealed. Blood's thicker than water, thicker than glue, but between husband and wife, what is there? Some sort of flour-paste only made permanent by kids. So, among all the postcards, there it was, amongst all those childish letters from that little girl whom she and she alone had taught to write and read like a true grandmother because no-one else was going to do it, there was the final missive from next door's wife, that hapless, silly woman with the sweet smile who could not cook or clean and had let her daughter become Margaret's own. Mrs Logo wrote a lot of notes, always asking for favours; wrote this one as if it was not a sin to break a person's heart.

Dear Mags,
   I'm ever so sorry, but I'm going now. I know I said to you things weren't right, but I didn't know how wrong.

The writing was bad, even though Margaret had read this script a thousand times, in scrappier missives which asked, Will you do this? Will you do that? Always in a feather-brained rush.

I'm leaving him, I've got to, I can't say why.

Why not? Margaret had howled at the time and was still howling now.

I'm taking Enid with me, we're going to my cousin in Scotland where I can get a job and everything.

A job? Feather-brain could no more earn a living for herself and a dependent daughter than fly over the moon.

I'll write when we get where we're going. Please don't tell Logo when he gets back, he'll go mad. Or should I say madder. And don't ask and don't interfere, I do know what I'm doing, honest. Will write, promise, so will Eenie.

Margaret had abided by her instructions not to interfere and not to speak, as discussed with her invalid husband, both sticking to the habits of a lifetime, he the one-time soldier, herself the soldier's missus, non-complainers both. She obeyed and watched as shortly after the delivery of the note, she saw Mrs Logo exit the house carrying a fibre suitcase and pulling the door closed behind her. There had been something jaunty in the carriage of the little woman on her escape, so that Mrs Mellors had assumed not ill-treatment, but the existence of another man, and she had never doubted that assumption. The daughter was behind her, carrying a school-bag, and it was only she, whom they called Eenie, who looked back, waved to nothing but waved in a sad desperation and hesitation which had made Margaret want to run after her and shout from where she stood. The fibre suitcase carried by the mother was old; it expanded on one side but failed to expand on the other: the weight of it was less cumbersome than the bulk. And so they had gone, the two of them.

More weeping in the kitchen, and the yelling of, Why, why, why? from Logo over weeks, while Margaret had listened, not said much while she kept looking at her own stairs and wondering if this were the night her husband might die. After some days, Logo reported his wife and child missing. The police came and searched their house; enquiries were instituted, but she never wrote, that silly bitch of a wife, and Margaret never said how she had seen them going down the back alley in the middle of the afternoon with the fibre suitcase which did not expand properly, because it was so etched in her memory she could not have given it words, and because she had been trusted and that meant she was bound by a promise.

'Why?' she muttered to herself. 'Why? How could they just go?'

You never know your neighbour. So her man had died, she had lost her substitute child and grandchild, and Logo had gone about howling, searching the hills and dales of North London, convinced he would find, if not the wife, the darling daughter. Poor, poor soul, with the police picking on him ever since. Her heart had gone out to him, she respected his privacy, believed and pitied him, never intruded, same as always. If it hadn't been for Sylvie, she might never have gone upstairs in his house, not unless he had fallen ill and he never did that.

But this evening, following Blondie, tut-tutting and still playing games up Logo's stairs, feeling cross with the naughty child, she had stopped in her tracks on the top landing. Facing her from the corner of his bedroom, spartan, bare of the superfluous, not a frill or a flounce like the rest of this house, was that fibre suitcase. As it had been, still crooked. The suitcase of a wife who had left with it and who, according to him and everyone else, had never come back.

Margaret separated Mrs Logo's letter from the rest and put it in the drawer where she kept knives.

Helen West was rummaging in the kitchen. From time to time she eyed the telephone, not quite wishing it to ring, but somehow resenting its silence. She had willed the fridge to yield exciting secrets but after her own time-honoured fashion there was nothing inside but a jar of pickle, one of dead mayonnaise, butter, rock solid, a lettuce which was brown to the point of liquefaction and six suspect eggs. I have no rules, she said to herself, no rules at all. I feed like a soldier on the retreat in some frozen waste and I have grown as thin. I like being a renegade: I forage in shops rather than buy. Is this the life for me? It took ten days without Geoffrey (two phone calls, one too many), for all the old regimes to be reestablished. Through the very thin veneer of her domestication, acquired only through contact with men, the way they were supposed to acquire similar habits from women, she was emerging as an alley cat.

Though truth to tell, the scrappy eating and total lack of cooking which had featured in the last ten days, during which time she had passed the supermarket with two fingers raised and no potatoes to rub her shins as they strained at polythene bags, owed only as much to retrograde eating behaviour as it did to a strange feeling of nausea. The eggs eaten late were committed to the sewerage system so quickly it was as if they only lived in her digestion on borrowed time. They were unable to pay rent, these eggs, like most other foods except crisps, sharp, artificial, savoury tastes, or items of sickening sweetness. And she was thinner, definitely thinner: the waistband of her skirt that morning had hung loose: halfway through a court case, she had risen to shout some reply and found the skirt had swivelled round, back to front, crumpled and out of shape. That small incident vexed her.

She stood in her kitchen, admired for its warmth and flair like all her other rooms, the product of a hundred junk shops encouraged into interesting life and a little out of control. 'I love this old dresser,' Geoffrey had said. 'I love your old, cracked, unhealthy enamel sink, your mugs from the wedding of Charles and Di, and I love the ancient carving knives which came from car-boot sales, but, my dear, they do not cut.'

She was hungry and sick, sick and hungry. Three, four drinks with Dinsdale and the mastication of nibbles with all the nutriment of air, and she ran for the bathroom with its old and beautiful tiles, pictures on the walls even in there, only to be sick.

What is this? she thought, raising from the basin to the mirror a face which was horribly pale. What the hell is this?

Helen West, arrogantly accustomed to health, an avoider of doctors when possible, rummaged in the cupboard beneath the mirror for something to settle this intestinal riot. Bisodol, Rennies, Nurofen, aspirin, every hangover cure under her sun. A pregnancy kit about a thousand years old which her hand nudged and knocked to one side in search of something efficacious enough to allow eating without retribution later, but the fingers stopped of their own accord and dragged out the unopened box as she squatted back on her haunches, rocking with the shock of her own conclusions. When was the last time she'd had the curse? And when last had she and Bailey celebrated the one thing they always seemed to get a hundred per cent right? His house, her house, something usually missing. You weren't fertility plus at thirty-five, but age was irrelevant to an egg.

Helen got her coat and made for the street. Dammit: she craved the produce of the Chinese takeaway; she would have it in any event, and she could not stay here with her own thoughts.

Outside, the night was peculiarly still and stiff with an icy cold which formed her breath into puffs of vapour, so cold, she immediately wanted to turn back inside, but driven by her own hunger, she did not. The frost which had formed in the darkness of dawn and melted in the afternoon, now drew exquisite patterns on car windscreens like some exotic artist. From the great distance of a mile or more, she heard in the stillness the great roar of an enormous crowd. There was no sound the same: the sound of the mountain moving to Jehovah. Helen stopped, chilled to the marrow by that distant roar of the jungle lion waiting to get out. Then the cars started again: the lights of the main road hit her eyes. The sickness had passed.

Oh Lord, do not let me be afraid of the dark.

Chapter Five

Redwood was often asked to give lectures – to new recruits, to clubs, to Justices of the Peace. They were good for his profile, so he did them when he could not farm them out.

'The mandate of the Crown Prosecution Service,' he was fond of beginning in a good, loud voice, 'is to prosecute without fear or favour, according to the evidence, those who break the criminal law. Evidence is supplied to us by the police. It is we who decide what to do with it.'

He made the process sound civilised and eminently stream-lined. What he did not say was that his own office was drowning in paper. They were more vulnerable to paper than they were to heart attacks. The paper would kill them first.

'Our office is computerised, of course,' he would say, remember-ing not to cringe. So it was, in a manner of speaking. The computer received information and dictated the next move for every case: they all had pathetic faith in it without any under-standing, but it did not obviate the necessity for portable paper to go to and from courtrooms and barristers' chambers, fraying in a dozen sets of hands, often without a duplicate, until finally it was filed in the vast areas of the basement where Redwood never trod.

'Because of the confidential, incriminating nature of the ma-terial we keep, we do, of course, take great care with security . . .'

Even he had to wince at that. By security, Redwood meant the high railings with their lethal spikes, the assiduous security men they had by day and the lazy character they had between seven in the evening and the same hour next morning, and also at the weekends. He came from an agency, it was cheaper. Redwood hated the building so much, he couldn't imagine anyone wanting to get in. Only a fearless child could climb the railings. It didn't occur to him there was any need for better security.

'Rose, any chance I can have tomorrow's paperwork by one'clock? Like I asked earlier? Only I'd rather not come back this afternoon.'

Rose raised a harassed face from the files she was marshalling into piles, in date order, each like a rocky monument on the floor round her desk.

'I dunno. Doubt it,' she said rudely. Helen felt her temper rise. The link between her worries and her sense of humour was proving tenuous, the thread of it not only thin but frayed. She made a last effort.

'Please can you find me tomorrow's files? Surely it isn't too much to ask?'

Rose was embracing a bundle of six to her bosom, and she dropped them abruptly, turning as she did so. She was shaking with tension, but it looked like a gesture of petty defiance.

'Rose,' said Helen with warning in her voice, 'I really do have to go at one, and I might not be able to get back. Can you sort tomorrow's stuff for me now? Please?'

Rose turned to face her, livid with anger. The spikes of her hair, subdued of late, seemed to rise round her head like the defensive spine of a hedgehog.

'And supposing other people have to leave early too? Supposing there's no-one else to do their fucking work and the computer's screwed and silly cows like you are asking for the moon? You can fuck off. Your bloody files are in here somewhere. Either find them your bloody self or come back later.' She kicked one of the heaps with a booted foot and the files lurched sideways, but Rose had not finished. There was an impulse to malice she could not resist.

'And while I'm at it, don't you come this holier-than-thou bit with me ever again. You and Mr Cotton, both with an afternoon off each? Good, isn't it? What's it to be then, your place or his?'

Helen wanted to slap her: Rose was waiting to be slapped, but something in the insinuation raised an inhibiting twinge of guilt. The files toppled in slow motion as Rose strode from the room. The other clerks watched from their tables and desks in a deathly silence. Helen breathed in and out slowly. She stared at the window where she had seen Rose's reflection two weeks before and saw only her own, paler and older face. With the others as an audience, she knelt on the floor and began to go through the papers, looking for those which bore her name, seething but still using her eyes. For the moment she hated Rose to the same degree the girl seemed to despise her in return. Perhaps that was why none of the clerks helped her, but let her grub around on the floor, humiliated. If they'd offered, she would have refused.

Redwood came into the room, as uncertainly as he always did for fear the clerks might bite him or reveal his failure to remember most of their names.

'Who was shouting in here? I won't have it . . . Oh! Helen, what are you doing?' She looked up from the floor with a fiendish grin.

'Looking for a contact lens, sir.' Sir was inconsistent in his observations, but there were some details he never forgot.

'I didn't think you wore lenses.'

'I do now. Was there anything in particular you wanted?'

'That shouting . . .'

'It was me.' He beckoned her out of the room with evident disgust, poised for a reprimand. From beyond the door, Helen heard the buzz of voices no longer suppressed, cutting through her back like an icy wind.

In the lavatory, Rose Darvey sat and gulped. Trained as she was in several aspects of self-control, she had long since mastered the technique of crying while remaining silent. You held your nose, so that the effort of breathing through the mouth somehow suspended the rising of the noisier sobs. Putting her hands over her ears also encouraged the silence which had always seemed so imperative when she cried. She sat with the door locked, trying one method after the next, while large tears ran down her face and made a mess of the make-up so carefully applied in the spot-light over her bedroom mirror. She couldn't make shadows in here: it required a light without a shade. She had bitten her fingernails down to sore stumps, another reason for habitually playing with her hands. Granny had placed some bitter solution over them once to make her stop it: it had worked temporarily. Granny, Granny, help me now, please help me now, where are you? The vision of Granny somehow increased the size of the hairball in her chest: the effort to make no sound felt like a thistle lodged in her throat. Granny, she thought. Got to try and see Granny. Granny could help. See Granny and do something about this bloody baby, before I go mad. Can't tell Michael, just can't. He'll never love me.

'Rose?' A timid voice. 'Rose. You all right Rose?' A plaintive whine from one of the others sent to enquire. Rose was her colleagues' heroine; she made them laugh, she knew more than any of them and was afraid of no-one. 'Rose, come out of there, will you? Only we're worried about you. Come out, please.'

The plea in the voice made her freeze for a moment. Come on out, darling, and no harm will ever befall you again. Rose dropped her handbag on the floor, rummaged inside for her make-up bag, the old protector. She made a loud noise with the toilet roll, tearing it, blowing her nose with unnecessary violence, scrubbing at the ruin of the mascara. The same voice again, though not so wheedling, assumed less reminiscent proportions. It might be all right if she just carried on without too many cracks in her armour.

'Rose, are you all right? Talk to me, what's the matter?'

How she despised the tragedies of the ladies' lavatory; why did she come here when she could have hidden in the nice, warm womb of the basement? She gave an exaggerated sigh.

'Of course I'm bloody all right. Just get me a vet. I need putting down.'

The voice beyond the door giggled in relief. Same old Rose, their leader. And which one of you, Rose thought, as she ran her fingers through her hair to encourage the spikes she had been subduing because Michael did not care for them much although he never said so, which one of you is fiddling the computer then and stealing the files? Which one?

Margaret Mellors sat in the doctor's waiting-room at twelve-thirty, wondering who would go in next. She knew her own turn in this never-ending queue had been delayed for an emergency: she had been asked if she minded, which was an unusual courtesy, and out of habit, she had said, 'Of course I don't,' but she did. She had lost her faith in medical expertise when Jack had been dying, but she had never ceased to regard doctors as God. Even if they did not know what made a sick man sick, they surely had the last word over many things, police, fire engines and madness. They told you what to do and they gave orders to multitudes, and that was why she was here. Margaret never thought of her own long-delayed treatment, six weeks' wait for every appointment, the wilful continuation of her own disability while she waited one year, two years for a new hip; she still saw a doctor and smiled as if he or she could alter the world, and she still gave up her place in the queue, composing in her mind a series of apologies for being there at all.

'I'm sorry to bother you, but . . .'

'Yes, that's what I'm paid for. How can I help?' A strained smile from a young woman who had listened to her fill of winter casualties. Carmen something, her name was. Margaret preferred doctors to be middle-aged men, they were better fitted for their deity, but why oh why did she never ask, and why did she feel so wretchedly tongue-tied? As if her pension was charity and this white-coated waif a grand inquisitor.

'Well, I wondered . . .'

'Let's have a look.' She had a look, tutted, wrote on a pad.

'It's been a long time, hasn't it? You'd better go back and see the consultant . . .'

'Actually,' said Margaret, gathering courage in the panic-stricken knowledge that she would be out of the door in thirty seconds if she didn't, 'I can live with the stick. It was something else.' The doctor smiled encouragingly, sat back, unoffended by this oblique approach.

'It's my neighbour.' Having got this far, Margaret could only continue to blurt it out. 'I'm worried about him. He hears voices. He sings a lot and he told me yesterday his favourite place was the graveyard. He's mad you know, well, he's always been a bit mad, but now he's madder. He frightens the children.' The patient smile of the doctor was fading and Margaret's message was fading too: she could not bring herself to say Logo was dangerous, correction, might be dangerous.

'How does he frighten the children?' The doctor's voice was sharper.

'I don't know. He chases them I think, he's always looking for his daughter . . . They keep taking him to court, but nobody ever asks me.'

'Well, the police know all about it, then. Does he have a job?'

Margaret nodded. The white coat relaxed visibly. 'They must know about it too, I suppose. Have you spoken to the police?'

Margaret leapt, as if the doctor had spoken an obscenity. 'Oh, I couldn't do that. I wondered . . . I wondered if you could send someone round to him.'

'Well, Mrs . . .' she looked hurriedly at the notes, 'Mellors . . . I just don't think I can do that. He wouldn't come in and see me, would he? No? I didn't think so. Are you sure he's registered with this practice? Well, you try and persuade him to come in, will you? Only it has to be voluntary, or not at all. Look, I'll put you in touch with Social Services, see if they have any ideas.'

No, they did not, and yes, he was getting madder. Banging about in his own home these last three nights, weeping and wailing in his kitchen. For the first time, Margaret had hopes that he would get arrested again, and attract some attention. She met patience without comprehension whenever she complained, but then she was not quite telling the truth, and when invited to exaggerate the eccentricities she described, she could only minimise them. One thing she understood clearly was that there was no provision for those in the limbo land he occupied of the half mad, half dreadfully sane, and there she was, a second-class citizen, an elderly woman, part disabled but smelling sweet. They looked at her as if madness was contagious; until she began to think it was.

She did not, could not, tell anyone about the suitcase.

Margaret Mellors trudged the dim route home on a grey afternoon, promising herself she would light a fire. Down the alleyway, the last light already fading, she wondered how anyone could endure the cold without a fire. The landlord had blocked up her own years ago: with Logo's help, she had unblocked it and the thought of that and all the firewood he brought her, made her feel guilty. When she opened the door, there was a letter on the mat. First-class post, such extravagance. The writing had a vague familiarity. She turned the envelope over in her hand, postponing the excitement until her hands began to tremble and she put it to one side while she lit the fire. When the kindling wood began to crackle, she tore open the letter and read the single sheet within, flushed with pleasure and the light of the flames. 'Oh my dear,' she kept murmuring to herself, 'oh my darling dear.' Four years without even a note, and her darling writing now, oh, my dear. She found it difficult to let go of the letter: it simply could not be consigned to the hidden boxes of other letters, it had to remain visible as a constant reminder of its tidings. With great reluctance, Margaret finally placed the letter along with the other in the drawer where she kept her kitchen knives.

That way she could look at it again and again.

At six o'clock on Friday morning, someone rang and rapped on the grim doors of the old hospital. The bell sounded in the night watchman's room where he locked himself in with his TV and the phone every evening and all day Saturday and Sunday, neglecting to patrol since he found the confusion of stairs, corridors and ludicrously insecure exits peculiarly eerie: there were rumours of a ghost. Nothing here but paper anyway. Nor did he obey the stricture to note in a book the names of members of staff who sought entry outside office hours. Sometimes they came late at night, especially the fraud teams on the first floor, forewarning him by telephone so he knew to be by the door as they sped in and out with armfuls of forgotten files required for the next day, but it was rare for anyone to arrive so early in the morning.

The person on the other side of the door, stamping feet in the cold, smiled, waved an office pass and disappeared upstairs with all the swift ease of total familiarity. The watchman shrugged and fell back to dreaming of breakfast.

Three floors up, a feminine, well-manicured hand turned on the computer. There was no code for entry into its realms of information introduced by the surge of power. The hand tapped out in quick succession the serial number of a file already retrieved. The fingers shifted the burden of paper, deleted the last line from the screen which described a date of trial and the necessity to warn witnesses, and added instead, 'No Further Action: Withdraw summons . . . Defendant now deceased.' For the next file, the hands simply deleted the whole text. For the next, the finger paused and the hands massaged one another, still cold. A fastidious piece of destruction. Redwood was right: software made life easier. Then with equally neat footsteps, the person concerned went down the innumerable stairs to the basement to take an alternative exit, shoved up a sash-window down there, next to the boiler room, humming. There was less chance of being remembered if one did not pass the doorman twice.

Helen West, trying to think of other things than the constant queasiness, dredged her memory for nicer times. Thinking of cases at 3 a.m. was reminiscent of counting sheep and often worked, but at the moment it hardly sufficed to blot out the other thoughts which had surfaced from nowhere with alarming speed. Such as where, among the clutter of her colourful possessions, she would house a baby, let alone a child? These reflections, passing through with dramatic speed, induced sensations of panic which nothing could cure, so she rose, showered and encased her hot body in cool clothes. Normality, the continuance of life as it was before, danced before her eyes like a tantalising vision.

Helen caught sight of her face in the newsagent's window as she waited for a bus, and that was normal, with the eyes and nose still in the same place. But she found herself standing back from the crowd, avoiding contact as if there really was something, for once, worth preserving from crush or contagion. She did not like herself much. Then she thought of Bailey as a father.

Squashing into the seat next to her was a young woman, pale and enormous, balancing her workday bag on the rock of her pregnant abdomen against which her coat strained. Helen made more room and stared ahead. Like a person counting sheep.

The graveyard was never closed. There was no need, despite the disturbing tendency in recent years to steal the stone angels. The late-Victorian church stood like a monument to disbelief, the small congregation rattling inside, but the graveyard took the corpses of faithful and faithless alike into soft earth which turned easily on the spade in summer. In the absence of a creed, interment in consecrated ground often appealed more than the queue at the distant crematorium. Logo could see benefits in both and did not much mind. He could clear the leaves as easily anywhere, but he found the graveyard rewarding and he liked the fact he knew so many of the recent names. There were dead flowers, souvenirs of the children from the junior school beyond the gates: and among the earliest, forgotten tombs, were Coca-Cola cans and empty cider bottles. He liked that. It added a little something to the place and confirmed his own usefulness.

Fifty-five years old, still young in comparison to these dead with their lead-etched names on stone. Logo felt healthy. He had loved this site as long as he had known it. By eleven that morning, there was a misty sun, glowing rather than shining behind the blanket of grey sky, giving a diffuse light which created no shadows but warmed the ground. Logo always marvelled at the gravediggers, stopped to watch them now. They dug in sequence along preordained lines with little space allowed in between each grave. Raw January, post Christmas, was the busiest time of year and their method was always the same. No measurements, rulers or spirit-levels, they dug out their troughs with automatic precision and no more modern conveniences than huge, sharp shovels, but they grumbled about the frost. The earth here had been turned, freed of rubble and thus softened, but the task was still hard.

The regular shovellers were unused to an audience: people tended to stay away, but there was the occasional macabre eccentric, Logo the least favourite. His interest bordered on the unhealthy, his jokes were vile and his habit of beginning the funeral service even while they dug was unnerving.

'Asses to ashes, dust to dust. If the Lord won't save you the devil must,' he quipped, squatting on his haunches beside them.

'Oh shut it, will you, Logo,' said the younger man.

'All right,' said Logo. 'I'll sing if you insist.' His voice passed over their heads, defeating the sound of distant traffic.

'Spare oh God, thy suppliant groaning!

Through the sinful woman shriven

Through the dying thief forgiven,

Thou to me a hope has given . . .'

The older man turned round, raised a hand. Logo stopped his singing.

'If you don't shut it, Logo, I shan't be able to give you a cigarette.' He was more diplomatic than his companion.

'Who's dead this time?' Logo asked cheerfully, accepting the bribe.

'I don't know. Why should I?' said the gravedigger. 'I just get the message, dig one. A new one, I mean. Which means, don't dig up an old one to put someone in on top. Might be anyone. But I tell you, there're bound to be two or three more in the next fortnight.'

They never seemed to know for whom they dug, or care for whom the bell had tolled. They were as immutable as the graveyard itself where the gravestones were practically identical from one decade to the next, no innovations, no plastic, only stones the same shape as always with the same words and sentiments. The richer or the guiltier of the mourners had marble, but it all went grey in time.

'Why do you say that?' Logo asked with his bird-like curiosity.

'Say what?' The gravedigger had forgotten his prognostications about local death. 'Oh, I just know. It's Christmas kills them. Their families, probably. Bugger off, will you!'

Logo obeyed, not in deference to commands, but because he so wished. His boots scuffed the edge of the soft earth the diggers had displaced and he left his footprints with satisfaction. Look where I've been, he told himself. Look where I've been.

He set off on the day's perambulations with his trolley, the cumbersome old brute, obscurely satisfied, pausing by another grave several rows back and saluting a headstone which commemorated the death of an Angela Jones four years ago. He had known Angela, nice woman from Legard Street, died of cancer you know, a shame, and her only ninety-four, the bane of her relatives who had moved to another city to get away. Logo chuckled, oh, he felt youthful today. From beyond the road at the left gate, he heard children going to school, the end of the Christmas holidays signalled by their shrieks and yells. Logo sat on the grave nearest the gate. He felt for the Bible in his pocket, but did not take it out, determined to stay still until they had all gone indoors. He quoted, out of context, the way he always did, those chunks of the Bible which stuck in his head without rhyme or reason. Logo took no lessons from the Bible, only told himself he did, but isolated verses were merged and burned into his mind.

'"I will send wild beasts among you,"' he droned quietly, '"which will rob you of your children, and your highways shall be desolate. And the flesh of your daughters shall you eat. And the sound of a shaken leaf shall chase you, and you shall flee as fleeing from a sword, and you shall fall where none pursueth."'

As the sun rose further, an effortful sun only waiting to retire without grace by midday, and the clock in the magistrates' court showed ten-thirty, John Riley, Junior Crown Prosecutor and new

to the game, rose to his feet, his small height almost obscured by
the pile of paper in front of him. He had command of the daily list
of the drunks and disorderlies, those soliciting on Seven Sisters,
those burgling the night before, and all those remands postponed
from previous dates for the preparation of papers and defences
before a full hearing in either the magistrates' or the Crown Court.
John waded through, bobbing up and down as the occasion
demanded, gathering confidence as he went. The magistrate was
fierce: speed by advocates was the only attribute rewarded by a
grim nod and the sort of smile imposed on a corpse by a mor-
tician. Finally, they had dispensed with all the two-minute
appearances. 'Drunk, Your Honour, shouting and screaming,
fourth offence in six months.' 'Anything to say?' 'Nothing, Your
Honour.' 'Ten pounds or a day, take him down. Next? Get on with
it, Mr Riley, get on with it.' The Clerk of the Court, second only
to God, shuffled to signify a pause.

'Mr Balchin next,' she said sweetly. John felt for the next
volume. Balchin, the name rang no bells even on the inner ear. His
hands dug through the remaining four files, no Balchin. 'Where's
Balchin?' yelled the magistrate to whom delay was a mortal sin.
Balchin stood in the dock, a smart businessman in a shirt which
gleamed through a sober suit below a face of fleshy success. 'Trial
adjourned until today from December, plea not guilty to driving
with excess alcohol?' said the clerk, questioningly. Balchin nodded,
anxious, but presentable. All eyes fell on the prosecutor, waiting
for him to begin as he rose to his feet with all the steadiness of the
drunks earlier in the list.

'I don't seem to have any papers,' he said lamely. 'May I seek an
adjournment? We don't have the witnesses—'

'I object to that,' said the defendant mildly.

'So do I,' said the magistrate. 'Mr Balchin's third appearance in
this court and the Crown Prosecution Service still not ready?
How often do you want him to come back, Mr Riley, hmmmm?
Case dismissed. Next.'

John sat, flaming red, scrambling for the next file and the
chance to redeem himself. It was twelve o'clock and the day was

suddenly long. Mr Balchin, businessman, left the court house and raised his eyes to the sun in quiet thanksgiving. Then he walked round the corner to his parked BMW, patted the shining roof in reverence and climbed in, to return to his business which so depended on his ability to drive. God had been good today. It was worth the thirty pieces of silver which had changed hands.

CHAPTER SIX

'Pregnant and happy? Fine . . .'

The advertisement Helen and a million others saw daily on the Underground, showed a late-teenage girl with a curtain of perfect hair falling across a pensive face of model proportions. Her elegant neck was dressed with a single line of pearls. A well-manicured finger rested on her white teeth in a gesture of coy indecision, as if trying to decide which chocolate to pick next, like a princess merely troubled by too much choice and a heavy night sleeping on a pea. 'Pregnant and happy?' said the advert. 'If not . . .' Beneath this there was the telephone number and address of a clinic. The urine sample burning a hole in Helen's handbag had been decanted into a miniature whisky bottle for lack of any other receptacle. She did not know which embarrassed her most.

Standing in line on the escalator first thing on a crowded morning, she passed the serene face on the poster and felt a strong desire to rip it, but she was borne onwards and upwards to the air of Oxford Circus. She did not trust the pharmacist's pregnancy kit and did not like doctors. This was also the first time in her life she could recall responding so directly to an advertisement and that was irritating, too. Although the nausea had faded after thirty-six hours, it had been replaced by a kind of grim elation.

The cold was muffled by the crowd who swayed away from the fetid warmth of the Underground, filtering through cars and the buses which disgorged even more people into the shops. On a day like this, Helen hated to leave the claustrophobic but volcanic warmth of the Tube.

The women she noticed most were those with the smoothest faces, en route to the make-up counters to sell promises through the medium of their flawlessly counterfeit cheeks. Her own face was comparatively bleak, but she was jauntily dressed in a scarlet jacket, tight black trousers, red shoes and a scarf of vivid stripes. Helen West, supporting her own team.

The family non-planning clinic was above other premises in the wide backwaters where the huge department stores gave way to the environs of Harley Street, with its shops full of medical supplies, private dentists and wholesale pharmacists scattered among esoteric restaurants and the head offices of the rag trade. The plate-glass windows of one of these flanked the nondescript door at the side, which led in turn up four flights of ever narrowing stairs past small, locked offices on each floor. The air grew cooler, more rarefied and, as she turned the last bend, developed into an antiseptic smell of cleaning fluid rather than medicine. Worn carpet, an electric heater and mismatched chairs in the waiting-room said the rest. None of the other three women, perched on these uncomfortable chairs and staring at the surrounding walls, resembled the princess on the poster who had drawn them there. Least of all Rose Darvey, sitting apart, in a state of defiant misery, chewing her pigtail.

They were the last people each could have borne to see on the opposite side of the road, let alone a place like this. The hostile nature of their surprise was felt even by the other two girls who waited, booted, spurred and disguised for some verdict on their lives. Helen had the feeling she was old enough to be everyone's mother. Rose looked away in disgust while Helen presented her fee and the whisky bottle to a receptionist whose drabness belied a personality ecstatic with *bonhomie* and a whispering voice of solicitude. Rose spied the label on Helen's bottle; stress, worry, the million reflections which were steaming through her head at a hundred miles an hour, all emerged through her mouth in a great, barking laugh which turned abruptly into a cough, then a series of violent coughs which almost brought her to her feet in her effort to breathe, before she slumped back in the chair and slid further down on the polished seat, still gasping. Helen took the empty chair next to her. There was no need for explanations: all that was obvious.

'Sorry,' said Rose. She looked as if the giggles of tension would consume her. 'Something I ate. Swallowed the wrong way.'

'Swallowed? I bet you wish you had,' Helen murmured.

Rose's coughing resumed a new note of yelping. This time she put her hand over her mouth and leant forward as the coughs slowly came under control. Helen patted her back, with a balled fist to take out of this stray solicitude any hint of intimacy. She stopped as soon as Rose sat upright.

'Keep that up, will you, and you won't need anything else. You'll give birth on the floor. Twins,' said Helen helpfully. Suddenly the whole situation was ludicrously funny. It couldn't have been worse if she'd sat in line with the wife of a lover.

Rose was off again. 'What a game,' she gasped between breaths. 'What a game. A whisky bottle, I ask you. I bloody ask you. Miss bloody West.'

Helen's expression became severe. 'Well I didn't drink it, he did. Present from Malaga, that little bottle. What do you think I am? Cheap?'

They were suddenly doubled up in their scarves, snorting and laughing like schoolgirls in church.

'Ms Darvey!' The receptionist called Rose's name, suddenly officious.

'Christ,' muttered Rose. 'Oh God, this is it. What shall I do?' She looked desolate, childlike as she began to stand wrapping her coat around her, wanting to delay, drawing a deep and painful breath.

'Listen . . .' she said, and paused.

'Listen,' said Helen, 'when you've finished, will you wait for me? Please?' Rose nodded, her eyes turning towards the glazed-glass door of the other room, to the received wisdom, the result of the test, the possible kindness and advice. It looked, she said later, like the entrance to an old-fashioned lavatory. She went like a prisoner to the gallows, turned at the door, pulled a face and waved.

Helen wanted to weep, on both their accounts.

★

Sitting inside a small cubicle with a counsellor, listening to the murmur of other voices, Helen found the need to weep became an actuality positively encouraged by the woman who told her with a no-nonsense sweetness that she was not pregnant, not this time and what was her reaction to that? Time marched on, did it not, and if she had not wanted this crisis, had she considered more effective means of birth control? She found herself accused some-how, of a lack of self-respect, an indigence about her own life, a laxity of purpose, a constant ambivalence. Or so she took it to be, having levelled these same accusations at herself over the last two days with all the sure-firing action of a rifle. Mixed in with that was relief (life could now, after all, go on as before), and a grief of such proportion it made her speechless, nodding and smiling and saying, thank you, thank you, you've been very kind, but let me out to smash things and scream and speak to someone else. For the five terrible minutes of the interview and the passing over of leaflets and wishes of good luck, Helen forgot Rose Darvey, but that was only temporary, because what she most wanted was to think of someone else, anyone else.

Waiting in the foyer with ill-concealed impatience and a smile on her face which could have lit a coastline, Rose gripped Helen by the arm and propelled her to the door.

'Come on, let's get out of this place. It smells.' Rose led a race downstairs, making in her progress the maximum noise, saying nothing until they reached the pavement, where she leapt across the threshold, flung her arms in the air and yelled, 'Yeah! Yeah, yeah, yeah!'

'Does that mean you are?' asked Helen, her own responses dulling her perception of this display. Rose stopped and laughed out loud.

'Pregnant? Course it doesn't. It means I got it wrong and I'm not, I'm not, I'm *not*! God, I feel better. Christ, you've no idea what it's been like, awful, thought I'd die . . . you've no idea . . .' Then she stopped, looked at Helen apologetically, still unable to suppress her own smile, and her expression of dawning compre-hension. 'What am I talking about?' she said. 'Of course you know.

I mean, you wouldn't be here if you didn't know. Sorry. Only I never imagined . . .'

'That someone my age had a sex life?' Helen suddenly found herself able to laugh. Rose's state of joyous liberation was infectious: there was something oddly comforting about her present embarrassment and an overpowering desire to talk.

'No, no, I didn't mean that, not really—'

'Yes you did. Are you going back to work, or are we both playing hookey?' Helen asked. 'Only I want a pint of coffee, and then I'll tell you the story of my life if you aren't careful. Come on.'

'I'll buy you a coffee,' said Rose magnanimously, hugging herself.

'Too right you will. You owe me an apology, but if we can find a bottle of wine, I'd rather have one of those.'

'I know where,' said Rose, tapping the side of her nose in mock wisdom. 'Follow Rose. God!' she shouted again. 'God, I feel great!'

They didn't drink. Despite her much-vaunted knowledge of West End drinking parlours, gleaned from young policemen (and Helen heard more of them anon), Rose's wisdom proved deficient on the availability of booze outside regular hours and there was no need for a drink while each felt strangely high. Helen made a phone call to the office, on behalf of them both, announcing their absence rather than deigning to explain it. Then they went shopping. The mood of confidential euphoria lasted for several hours and left in the wake of all its conversations the sweet scent of friendship and a large bill.

They looked like mother and daughter, small, neat and dark, chattering like sparrows.

'Have you got any kids, Geoff?'

For once, the diminution of Bailey's Christian name which had been standard procedure for the length of his long career, failed to irritate him. He sat not in the college bar, but in a pub not far from the precincts. To his left was Valerie, the detective from West End

Central, on his right was a local woman who happened to be a friend of hers, and opposite them both was Ryan, grinning like a fox who had managed to marshal a flock of hens into a pen. It was early Friday afternoon and lectures had finished for the day. 'Playtime,' said Ryan, ushering sir towards his car. At first Bailey had assumed he was being offered a lift back to London, but the detour was scheduled and he found he did not mind in the least. It was Valerie's divorced lady friend who was asking him about kids, a gentle probing into his background. He normally resented personal questions of almost any kind, but mellowed by the ambience of an oak-beamed pub, a succession of pleasant faces and the sensation of being liked, he did not mind at all.

'No. None. My wife and I had a child, but it died when it was a baby. We never knew why and we didn't survive it either.' As soon as he had spoken, he wished he had not. Such a statement contained an invitation to pity which he neither courted nor felt he deserved. Bailey's failure with his young spouse so many years ago, his ignorance in the face of that misery of hers which had turned into madness, his failure to keep or cure her, still haunted him. It had haunted him through the several liaisons which had prefaced his fragmented existence with Helen, whom he loved profoundly, although he did not mention her name in this company.

On his first pint, he remembered the optimistic phases of his life as a truly single man, after the second, he remembered his age and ordered a whisky; but the euphoric sense of freedom did not pass, it intensified. Oh yes, he was bound for home this weekend, but there was no harm in the delay. And there was always next weekend. The woman on his left laid a light hand on his arm.

'I'm so sorry,' she said with the same quickness of touch. 'It must have been terrible. Mine spend most of their time with their dad, but I'm glad they're alive.' She removed her hand as imperceptibly as she had placed it, a nice woman, called Grace. Ryan rose to get another round. They all laughed and offered him money, a sensible confederacy of classless, adult friends, who all knew about life and spoke a common language. Ryan was delighted by the passivity of his master. They might convert him yet.

The afternoon faded again, with its usual lack of glory, until school came out. Logo had parked his trolley in the graveyard, so ungainly no-one would steal it or even play with it; full of bits and pieces lifted from skips, an old chair to be cut into kindling for Margaret, his whisky, his Bible and a couple of other things he didn't want shown the dim light of day. It was some distance from the school gates but, despite himself, he went to watch. Then, again despite himself, he chatted to a girl he had watched before, dark as himself, with old-fashioned plaits fraying at the edges, her thick curly hair not quite tortured into submission. She might have been a foreigner, most of them were, but she still looked like his daughter. It made him over-react.

Despite the anxiety, Logo usually found he got a buzz from being arrested. Ignorant of drugs, but not of the whisky he carried round in little bottles with all the silent glee of a successful smuggler, he knew that the sharp excitement of a chase was better than booze tingling in his veins. He was incredibly strong for his size without being swift, he could scarcely run at all, but he loved the brevity of his futile sprints for freedom, that fierce joy in the initial confrontation with the policeman, his neck bent like a penitent until they were off guard enough for him to pull away, giving himself just a small headstart because he always meant to be caught in a few yards. Logo's long, untidy hair would flap round his eyes as he ran, sometimes whooping and screaming enough to frighten the pursuer to a standstill before they pounded in his wake, and all to feel that last, delirious moment of surrender.

Thus it had always been, five or fifteen times, each time of the many he had been arrested, some gentle old hand with the fingers on his arm or, just as comfortably, some lone novice sent out in a miniature car on a call like this to a mere local nuisance, stepping out of his toy vehicle with grave self-importance, straightening his new uniform before they all ran a few steps of their ritual dance in front of their spectators who all but clapped. Both of them des-

tined to get a little hot in the chase before Logo could compose his
face into an expression of terror so pale he looked like a man in
front of a firing-squad and they all went peacefully home to the
nick where he would recover and protest his innocence, and then
ask, sneering, Why did you never find my wife and daughter?
That's how good you are, what have you ever done for me?

He should not have asked the child to step into the graveyard
with him, nor told her he had something for her in his trolley, nor
promised her a ride, but she was delicious. The cunning little
brute smelt him downwind and said she wanted to go to the sweet
shop first, so they did that instead and on the way, met her
mother. The child screamed as if he had in fact touched her,
although she had not been remotely anxious before, and the
mother, screaming too, blocked him into the door of the shop,
while someone called the police. Now Logo was at the end of the
ritual, and there had been no gentleness in it, not this time, none
of the usual contemptuous patience which had dignified the other
occasions.

The rookie cop had grabbed Logo by the jacket after he ran,
holding a fistful of shirt as he yanked him backwards. The frayed
collar bit into his throat and he gasped for breath as an arm jerked
his chin into the air. It was more than enough to subdue a man
who wanted to be subdued, but the boy officer thought otherwise.
The pressure on Logo's neck increased until he thought he saw
stars, and it was then he began to struggle in earnest, kicking,
hearing the satisfying crack of his foot against a shin, digging back
with his sharp elbows, twisting like an eel, almost free, screaming
as soon as he found the breath. He turned in surrender, but the
sight of the other face frightened him more than the touch. Logo
felt his elbows pinioned from behind, his still flailing legs kicked
away and his body crashing to the ground, landing painfully half
on one side. He screamed again as his arms were twisted up his
back, the blades of his shoulders standing out like chicken wings,
he felt something tear. The handcuffs locked around his crossed
wrists. His fingers splayed in a futile agony of resistance. A radio

crackled. Logo whimpered. 'Shut up, you bastard.' Logo's whimpering rose a pitch: he must have an audience. 'Help me,' he muttered, but all he felt was his hair held, his half-turned face raised and then let drop against the sharp gravel of the road, pressing into the surface.

The shock of that deliberate cruelty made him close his mouth against the punching, saving his teeth but not the kick to his throat. There was a numbness which was the forerunner of real pain, and when he opened one eye he saw his spittle in the dirt of the gutter and, inches from his face, the remnants of damp cigarette packets from a spilt bin. He felt he was on the level of a large dog turd and all his own litter, while the half-frozen wetness of the road seeped into his bones and his own blood and urine seeped back.

They were not saintly, the boys in blue, they always put on the handcuffs too tight, but they were not unkind either. They did not usually yank him into the back of a van and lie him face down as if he was a true man of violence. He knew later he had not imagined either the kicks to his ribs and one which seemed to connect with his face by accident, or the foot on his neck and the taunting from the officer who had arrested him. 'Bastard,' said the voice. Kick. 'Leave my balls alone, you pervert.' Kick. 'Going after girls, are we?' Kick. There were two others in the back of the van where he lay between the seats. He could sense their youthful disapproval in their silence; he reckoned they would save him if the kicking got worse, but not until it did.

The custody sergeant had time to stop and stare at a small, prematurely old man, wet and filthy, with one eye shut, blood seeping from his nose and forehead to mingle with the dirt and the snot on his torn shirt; a man breathing with an alarming, rumbling sound, a tiny, dilapidated creature.

'Take the cuffs off him for Christ sake.'

'He's very violent, sir.'

The sergeant looked at the oddly triumphant face of young

PC Williams with a weary loathing, noting the absence of filth or even damp on the barely ruffled uniform.

'I bet he was,' he said heavily. 'Take them off. You!' he barked towards Logo. 'Sit down over there.'

The other two officers hung back, afraid to touch and anxious to be gone. Logo shambled slowly across to the bench against the wall and sat heavily. There was an argument, raised voices, which he heard without registering the words and then he was placed, with strange solicitude, in the cell he occupied now.

'My trolley,' he croaked. 'Look after my trolley. You'll get me sacked.'

'Yes. Anything to complain about?'

Logo looked at the sergeant levelly. 'No.'

For that he was brought a blanket and hot, sweet tea, but he sat on the bench, weeping and seething, waiting for the doctor who would cure nothing.

It was all her fault. Everything. She had been his nemesis from the start, the black-eyed angel he had loved so much. Find her, bring her back, kill her. She had organised this; she stopped his very attempts to find her. The whole world blocked his attempt to find her. The cell smelled of urine which was not his own.

By teatime on Friday, Margaret Mellors began to believe that life had taken a definite turn for the better. Yesterday, she had written a reply to her treasured letter. If she found it peculiar to send it to the address on the back of the envelope, an office called CPS something, which made her think of the gas bill, she did not dwell on it, and in the thrill of arranging a meeting, the mechanics did not seem to matter. The writing of the letter had been laborious: the posting of it had been a special expedition to the main post office, because she needed to believe the service for this missive would be first rate. That done, at vast expense, with a special-delivery sticker, Margaret breathed easier. It was also easier, she now felt free to confess, if several hours or even days could pass between her sightings of Logo. She had heard him go this morning with his dreadful rumbling trolley, and although visits home mid-afternoon were rarities, the absence was a relief. He might have caught her writing her letter and she did not want that at all. In her mind's eye, there was still the strong image of that suitcase upstairs; when she was braver, she knew she would have to go and look again, but not yet, please God, not yet.

Then there was the second surprise. A letter from the hospital, inspired by her visit to the doctor. Yes, she was still on the waiting list, shouldn't be long, it said, might be short notice, it said. The impact of this news made her head swim: it meant that within weeks she might be able to walk as other people walked, behave as others of her spry age behaved, go further afield. Go to see Mabel in Croydon on the bus, go to visit Mary Cruft in Enfield, go to the house of George's brother, recently widowed, in Brighton. 'Help me,' said Margaret, fluffing her hair in front of the kitchen mirror. 'Help me get through this, there's a life out there, I always knew there was.'

There was also life indoors. The fire was lit. All the excitement had made her feel extravagant enough to coax her hearth to life in the middle of the afternoon, before dark, even. She settled herself with her box, to work out who she would visit in a month or two from now, who to tell the good news, and also to work out if the cure of her hip was going to cost her money if she lost the disability allowance which was currently helpful. Never mind, there were always children to look after and houses to clean if you were fit. She was knitting a sweater: she was always knitting something, making her hands work. There was a moment of doubt when she wondered if the operation was worth it, but the faith in doctors as gods and carpenters reasserted itself. The only worry was that Logo and child-minding didn't go together.

Then came the third delightful surprise to mitigate her money worries for the future. As surprises went, it did not rank with those of the last twenty-four hours, but it wasn't bad, in the scale of things.

Sylvie the hyperactive stood at the door, snivelling and clutching the hand of her father, who looked for all the world like a man leading a savage dog, while she in turn looked as if she had already bitten the hand which fed her many, many times. Sylvie did not smile until Margaret smiled, but she did not snarl either. When Margaret said, 'Hallo! How lovely to see you!' the child looked at her inturned feet and raised her father's wrist to wipe her wet nose, while the corners of her mouth turned up in some semblance of pleasure. The father let go of her hand hurriedly.

'I think I may just have some Smarties back here,' said Margaret without fuss. 'If your dad says you can, that is. My, you are a sight, you little rascal. What have you been doing then? Playing in a pond?' By some strange sleight of movement, the child's hand had become transferred to Margaret's apron pocket. Sylvie did not want to be here, but she liked it at home even less. The father let out a great, juddering sigh.

'Mrs M, it's very rude of me to disturb you, but . . .' He wiped a hand across his brow and tried to grin. The worry lines seemed impossible to erase and she felt suddenly sorry for his youthful cares. He was a handsome man, and you were never too old to notice that.

'It's my mother-in-law, you see. She came to stay last week, and now she's been taken ill. Very ill. She had cancer last year, we thought she was all better, but anyway, we had to take her to hospital today, and we've just been called in now. Got to go, there's a football match tonight . . .'

'She's going to die,' said the child matter-of-factly, and with a shade of satisfaction.

'Hush, you,' said Margaret without shock or rancour. 'Or no Smarties.' She turned her large, reassuring face to the father, put her hand on the child's neck, reaching for that small cranny underneath the messy hair where her touch could control the child. Margaret was suddenly firm. In the last twenty-four hours, she had become a person of greater consequence.

'Of course she can stay here while you go to the hospital. I hope your mother-in-law's going to get better.' They both knew it was a formal wish, but the words helped. 'Try and get back by eight, if you can. It's my neighbour, you know, he can be a nuisance.' There, she had said it, but she added the rider because she had no choice. 'If you can't don't worry. We've got plenty to eat. Would you like a cup of tea, or something?'

The man shook his head. Instead of words he made a vague salute and disappeared up the alleyway which he had told his wife he despised, but did not notice now. Behind him, he left his daughter, who went straight for the drawer which held the knives. Margaret stopped her. She took out the drawer and put it out of reach on top of the cooker. 'Silly,' Margaret said, with a note of authority the child had not heard before. 'Very, very, silly.'

It was the same syndrome as strangers on a train, a silly desire to confess which somehow did not diminish the third stop for coffee. There weren't many shoppers in Oxford Street, post holidays and post sales. They could move freely from one mammoth department store to another. They smelt of the perfume counters where both had sampled in plenty, buying nothing but aftershave as a preliminary to the second coffee, but they were warming up to it. Helen joked to herself and to Rose that they were like two negatives making a positive. Rose didn't get the joke.

'OK. Who's the aftershave for? Your dad?'

Rose flinched, buoyant enough to recover quickly because it was only a send-up. She was getting used to the fact that Miss West teased a lot, she rather liked it. It was better than being serious.

'My mum and dad split up when I was little,' she said quickly. 'Mum lives up north, Dad died. No, the smelly stuff's for my . . . boyfriend.'

Helen stirred her coffee. 'Ohh, is that the one I spied you with the other day? The tall good-looking one with the nice face? Great big chap?'

Rose flushed with pleasure. 'Sounds like Michael,' she said. 'Yeah, that'll be him. Anyway, there hasn't been anyone else for two weeks and there won't be neither.'

'Is he as nice as he looks?'

Rose blushed pinker. 'To tell the truth, Miss West—'

'Oh for God's sake, my name's Helen.'

'Well I can't get my mouth round that, Mum. I shall have to call you Aunty after today, but you don't meet your aunty in the pregnancy clinic, do you? Nor one of your bosses.' She giggled. They had both been finding anything and everything immoderately funny.

'My Michael?' She stressed the possessive with enormous pride, speaking as if she could burst. 'He's brilliant, just brilliant, that's what he is. I can't get over him. I can't get over my luck. When he touches me, I go all funny, but he doesn't try anything, honest. He treats me special. He says we've got to be friends before anything else and he wants to take me to places, show me things. Meet his mum!' Rose pealed with the laughter of delighted incredulity. 'But he knows what I've been like,' Rose continued, somehow assuming Helen knew too. 'He found me in the section house after all, he says he don't care who I've been to bed with before, as long as there's no-one after. But I haven't yet.' She looked at Helen challengingly. 'Only you know what? I know he holds back. I know when he touches me, just holding my hand or giving me a hug, he goes all funny too. I can feel him trembling, you know. When he looks at me sometimes, I think I could die.'

Said in this fashion, Helen believed her. She ached for the intensity of the other's feeling. All the world loves a lover and she was no exception. She felt a fierce hope that all the optimism would be justified. No wonder the result of the test had been so important.

'It sounds like a bit of old-fashioned true love, if you ask me,' she said gravely. 'Anyway, it has all the symptoms. But who was the one who might have put you in the club? One of the other boys?' Her desire for information was compulsive.

'Yeah, one or the other.' Rose was not quite beyond embarrassment: there was still a trace of it and more than a hint of reserve. She would only talk about what she wanted to talk about. 'I don't know why I did all that. I didn't even like it. Why did I do it, Aunty? You can tell me. All those blokes.'

'I don't know why any more than you do. We all do strange things and the daftest thing you did was not to take precautions.'

'Listen,' said Rose with all the old aggression, 'you can bloody well talk. What about you?'

'Yes, OK, but I'm an old lady and I did know where my bloke had been. I don't know why you were giving it away when you could have been making your fortune. Could be something like being afraid of the dark. Not wanting to go home alone. Something like that.' Rose looked at her in consternation.

'How did you know? How did you know that?'

'Been there,' said Helen promptly. 'And you don't have to pay for protection. Not that way, anyhow.'

Rose shifted uncomfortably. 'Yeah, I know now. Oh, I do love Michael. I really do. Nothing else matters. I can't see anything the same way. Nothing at all,' she added, fervently. 'Strange, isn't it?'

And I loved Geoffrey once in that delirious kind of way, Helen thought, and there are times when I still do. I hope he's home this evening. Rose sensed her preoccupation.

'Here, Aunty . . . you wanted a baby, didn't you? And here's me rabbiting on, but you weren't like me at all. Michael see, he knows quite a lot about me, what I've been like, but he couldn't have stomached a baby any more than me . . . Different for you, though, isn't it?'

Helen hesitated. 'I'd got a bit used to the idea, and when someone told me, No, you aren't, I felt as if I'd been robbed. Sad, furious, deprived, confused. Does that make sense?'

Rose nodded, but it didn't really. 'Listen, I'm sorry I made that crack yesterday about you carrying on with Dinsdale. I knew you weren't.'

'No, but I am tempted,' said Helen lightly. 'Who wouldn't be? You weren't so far off the mark.'

Each of them was lost in her own thoughts. Rose was looking forward to seeing Michael with a level of anticipation that gave her pain, but she was not going to tell him any of this. She wanted to shout. She was feeling hope for the first time that she could remember. Michael today, Gran tomorrow; she was fighting her way through all her shadows. Helen was pensive.

It must be age, she thought, where optimism was failing to triumph over experience and mistrust triumphed over everything.

'More coffee?' she asked.

'More shopping?' said Rose, shyly. 'If you've got time. Only I'd like a jacket the same colour as yours, only decent thing I've ever seen you wear, Michael would like that.'

'Did you know,' said Helen, 'that shopping for clothes for me or anyone else, is one of the greatest pleasures of my existence?' Rose grinned, cheekier than ever.

'Better than sex?' she queried. Helen paused, grinning just as widely.

'Not all the time.'

CHAPTER SEVEN

Redwood waited in the office until everybody had gone. No-one lingered on a Friday night and although he resented their defection, his own staying behind was a self-imposed obligation for which their absence was crucial. On a Friday evening Redwood acquired nerves of steel and turned himself into a spy. He forced himself to come out of his room to join the ghosts in which he believed as much as the idle doorman, although Redwood, as a man of logic, could not let himself acknowledge the belief and so could not allow the fear to deter him. Like a ghost, he was licensed to go wherever he wished at any time, but if he did so in office hours, all those over whom he lorded it would know how often he got lost. More to the point of his present subterfuge, they would resent what he did in their absence – sneak around their desks, look in the cupboards and cabinets, read letters, check schedules, investigate all those aspects of his domain which he should have known about but was too ashamed to ask. He alone checked how many times per annum each person cited a visit to the doctor or dentist as the reason for an afternoon off. He checked by desk diaries what people had done on those days when court finished at twelve and they had failed to return before five. During the weekend ahead, he would analyse all the information and work out how to use it without revealing his source, thus preserving his reputation with his superiors for effective, if unpopular, management. He called it keeping one step ahead. Helen called it something else.

The contents of Helen's room (all drawers open to the touch, had she never heard of thieves?) revolted him. It was hygienic but a complete mess. Helen West was the only one who had ever caught him at this game. With her own version of the thumbscrew, she extracted from him his promise never to repeat the exercise if she promised never to reveal it. One of them had been honourable about this deal: it was not himself.

There was an Anglepoise lamp on her desk he rather fancied, if it would only go with the odd decor of his own room. There were three comic cards from Dinsdale Cotton, signed affectionately, plus cryptic notes in her diary about meetings. Oh, ho, ho . . . Redwood found himself chuckling like a malevolent Santa Claus. Then he had stayed even longer, still rejoicing, to read a set of notes headed, 'Evidence', ah yes, that lecture. Bricks and mortar, she was talking about, then she sidetracked on to the duty of the prosecutor. To sift and evaluate evidence, it said; to make sure no inconsistently sized stone was left unturned; to render the bricks and mortar with compassion; never to create the facts or deny them either; always to give the benefit of the doubt without allowing sabotage. All so much specious rubbish, he thought, fine-sounding crap, but could be useful next time he had to stand up and spout. Worth copying and she had such a legible hand.

He turned off the lamp, then found himself fumbling round the room, tripping over files, cracking his shin, stumbling, banging his wrist on the sharp edge of the filing cupboard she never used, preferring the floor. Why, oh why did they still have such savage furniture, full of lethal angles and poisonous metal? Pain made him incautious. Hobbling down the endless corridors, lit only by the red light of the goods lift which always reminded him of a dumb waiter in an old café, he was level with the photocopying room before realising it was occupied, full of light and the clack-clack of the machine. Too late to go back now. He coughed and strode into the room, looking businesslike. At the last minute, as darkness turned into blinding light, he remembered to shove the notes inside his jacket, from which they lurched, too heavy for the pocket, as bulky as a gun. Redwood was not built for stealth.

'Ah! Dinsdale! Late, isn't it?'

Dinsdale Cotton smiled his enigmatic, patrician smile, the lazy smile of the winner, which seemed to say, I love you, even when it didn't. He worked efficiently, like a man well used to a graceful economy of movement, retrieving documents from the feed tray with a flourish while the machine still clack-clacked out the copies then fell silent.

'Is it so late?' he said genially. 'Really, I'd forgotten the time. Actually, I'm glad to catch you. I was trying to help out Riley. Bit of a débâcle at court yesterday. Can't really work out how it happened. Just running off a copy of the computer printout for next week, to make sure the thing isn't fooling us. It seems to write things off of its own accord. Or one of the case clerks does it. For what purpose, I don't know.'

'What happened yesterday?' Redwood asked for want of anything better to say. The lump of paper inside his jacket felt most uncomfortable.

'Well, the computer record on one of Riley's cases was altered by mistake to say no evidence offered last time, or the case was finished, don't know which. File put away, so poor Riley has no file, but defendant live and well, expecting to be tried, magistrate lets him go and we have egg all over face. No-one could possibly mind,' he hastened to add with the same charming smile, 'except the defendant, who is not complaining, and the police who do not know since none of them was warned to attend court.'

Redwood slumped. Another crisis. Another example of how the office managed without reference to him. His shin hurt, but he could not say why, so he said nothing at all.

'No complaints?' he asked, hopefully.

'Oh no. Except from Riley.'

'Is that all? No publicity?'

'None.'

'Good man,' said Redwood fervently. 'Good man. Sort it out. Tell me next week.' Dinsdale nodded, still smiling as if Redwood had his approval in everything he chose to do. Unable to meet his eyes because of his own sense of having been found out, Redwood focused on Dinsdale's hands. They were rather like his own, small, feminine, unscarred as women's hands were, awkward, soft little things, no good for holding a golf club. Redwood crept back down the corridor, into Helen's room and replaced the notes where he had found them.

The sergeant told Logo that he would be charged with assaulting a police officer, unless he would like to admit it and accept a police caution for breaching the peace. Predictably, Logo said no to the latter. He had recovered enough of his wits to remember that he'd liked the drama of the courtrooms as much as he had enjoyed his arrests up until now. The sergeant had looked at the collator's records on Logo with some anxiety: there it was, all the handwritten, locally known facts for police eyes only; a dozen arrests recorded, no convictions, mostly enclosed premises. The man had a talent for getting in, always said he was looking for his daughter or someone, otherwise he kept harassing children, harming none, a recent record too, nothing much before the last five years, never violent. Nothing to justify these livid bruises and that much blood. No broken bones, but injuries consistent with a beating, the divisional surgeon had said. Two paracetamol; fit to be detained, just. Whether the surgeon was drunk or sober, there was no fooling him. He cleaned Logo up and advised him to see his own doctor in the morning.

Then the sergeant told Logo that his trolley would be safely parked down his own backyard, if that was all right. Better than taking it back to the council depot and letting everyone there know he'd been arrested, wasn't it? Logo agreed. Telling this brought the sergeant the only real pleasure of his whole evening as he envisaged brave, young PC Williams wheeling the trolley through the streets as instructed. Most likely it was the only piece of retribution the rookie would get – and there was more than one way to skin a cat.

Logo was offered a lift home, by different officers the sergeant hinted delicately, but the prisoner declined. The half-mile walk would be good for his soul and he went down the steps clutching the piece of paper which ordered him to report on bail to court the next week. Watching him go, the sergeant wondered if the bruises would have faded by then, considered it unlikely and was not displeased by the thought that he had done what he could within the parameters of well-established tradition. He hoped some lawyer would notice the gaps, but doubted they would. That was all he felt he could do.

Down the damp streets, coldly, Logo went, his clothes not quite dry and his body weak, sick and aching. Halfway home, he noticed something which made him laugh – the lit football stadium and the blocked streets. Friday night, special match, was it? So some bastard copper had been wheeling his trolley back, clanking with brushes, in the teeth of the descending crowds. Logo hoped they had leered plenty. A modest attendance tonight: not the same density of cars or sound that signified a real gathering of the first-division tribes with all their war cries. There would not be the same level of chanting and he would scarcely hear them at home, unlike the other days when their communal breathing and gasping hit the windows of his house like a gale and drowned the sound of the television in a hundred living rooms. Logo tried to sing.

'Eternal Father, strong to save,
Whose arm doth bind the restless wave . . .'

The foot on his neck and the pressure on his throat made his voice sound cracked and the same mood of bitter self-pity which had sat on his head while he waited in the cell descended on him again. He needed to talk, he needed Margaret's soft, scented bosom in which to confide; he had to make a plan in which she would assist him to find her, his missing child. His daughter, find her and bring her home before the cancer of her loss affected all the extremities of his life and limbs. Love or revenge, either would do.

Lurching down the alley, he saw first the light of Margaret's door, then his trolley, upturned in the back yard with the contents spilled. He picked up the broken chair and threw it feebly, and when he bent over to examine the rest, smelt the whisky from the broken bottle and thought his head would burst. He knocked at Margaret's door, heard a scuffle inside, followed by a suspicious silence. The second knock was a good deal more aggressive. After another long pause, he saw her silhouette through the reeded glass of her half-glazed door, standing back.

'Who is it?' She sounded muffled, unwelcoming. In the near distance, he heard a ragged cheer from the football crowd.

'Me,' he said impatiently. 'Who else? Come on over, will you?'

'I can't,' she said. 'I've got a child here, asleep, Logo, I can't.'

'Well, let me in then. Open the door when you're talking to me, can't you?'

'No I can't do that either.' Her voice was firmer. 'Not tonight, another night. Or maybe later.'

'Let me in, you old cow!' he shouted suddenly. 'Just let me in! I need you, I need you . . .' He kicked the door hard with one foot, winced as pain jarred through his ankle. Her voice rose in reply.

'You aren't the only one who needs me. Stop it, Logo, don't be silly. I'll see you later.'

He kicked the door again, with the other foot, sulkily.

'Go away!' she shouted. 'Go away!'

The surprise of this unprecedented rejection made him obey. He lurched across to his own door, pushed it open and turned on the light to his dirtyish, cold kitchen. An acidic bitterness burned through his bruises. He had helped that woman rebuild her fire while he had none, he had brought home the kindling and some-times stolen fuel even when he needed none for himself, the old cow. Logo switched on the electric fire with its two sparking bars and waited for the warmth to fill his bones with that cheerless heat. He huddled over it, tempted to weep and watch his tears sizzle themselves to death. Oh, they were all such turncoats, women, beyond redemption. Tempted a man with their bodies and their creature comforts and kind words and in the end gave nothing, took back all you had given with the talent of usurers, extracting the last drop of interest.

'Man that is born of woman is of a few days, and full of trouble. He cometh forth like a flower, and is cut down; he fleeth also as shadow and continueth not . . . Who can bring a clean thing out of unclean? Not one.' He was moaning, words came out by themselves.

Shivering still, he dipped back out into the backyard and in the light from his own doorway, found his Bible on the ground. It, too, smelt of the spilt whisky, another desecration, but the damp solidity of the paper still gave comfort. He had never really needed to read his Bible, only to hold it and quote his disjointed quotes from it which memory jumbled into meaningless mantra phrases.

He went upstairs and found his daughter's school exercise books. Saw the handwriting of old essays and spelling tests, school projects all stored with the dismembered torso of a teddy bear in a drawer in his room. She had left so little behind. The central light in the room had no shade; neither did the lamp by his bed which shone on the immovable suitcase. Logo lay down, still cold, raised his hands in front of his eyes to examine the red weals left by the handcuffs, felt his grazed and grossly bruised face, wondering at its whole new set of swollen contours. God help me, even with these afflictions, Margaret would not let me in. A deep and dark suspicion began to haunt him. Then he looked at his hands again, more carefully, balled them into fists and punched them. Then hooked them together by the thumbs and began against the far wall, his game of shadow play.

What should she do next? What did a person ever do when they were waiting, especially if they were not used to waiting? Helen had found it thus when waiting for a jury to come back with a verdict, waiting for a case to come on for trial, the waiting time was useless, captive to expectation, a vacuum where logic and concentration were displaced by rage or anxiety. Waiting time was the only time in which she could ever acknowledge boredom. People waiting together grew close; people waiting for one another grew distant with every passing minute.

Helen was waiting for Bailey. The tersest of messages on her answerphone announced his presence which was more than half expected this Friday evening anyway. He could get away with a week, not with a fortnight. She had been turning somersaults in the last eight days and she had been shopping.

Shopping was always that mixture of excitement and guilt, but better than yoga in terms of total distraction. She and Rose had parted with genuine regret. Rose's boy would not keep her waiting, he would be straining at the leash. If ever Helen had flung a leash round Bailey's neck, now would be the time to pull it. Instead she was doing housework because he was very late indeed and she was storing up trouble like gas in a balloon.

The sound of his steps fell into her basement, with the loud tread of uncertainty. A car roared off into the distance with a joyous burst of power, not his car, Helen knew the sound, and not a taxi. Someone had given him a lift home. Maybe that little troublemaker, Ryan, who always found her lacking in female duties and judged her accordingly, Helen knew, although their mutual liking was as strong as the disapproval. Bailey hit the French windows at the front of her flat with a stern and well-controlled rap of his knuckles, which she ignored. Sober persons came in through the front door, having rung the bell. To hell with his short cuts. He rapped again. This time she relented and let him in.

'Sorry I'm late,' he beamed. 'Or did you get the message? Only we finished mid-afternoon, then we stopped off, you know how it is.'

She did know how it was, she had done it herself all too often. It was a hazard of both their lives, but she still remained stiff and unyielding in his large embrace. Bailey, who was normally so immaculate without the fastidiousness of perfume smells or perfect creases to his trousers, now smelt a little stale and beery. His hair was messy, his tie crooked from being loosened and hurriedly straightened, then loosened again and she did not want to investigate the source of the other scents he carried about himself, like nicotine, perfume, dog. He looked like a man who had spent a week camping and returned via a brothel, still pleased to see her.

'Did you forget your key?' she asked by way of a purely neutral greeting.

'Yup. Forgot everything. Shouldn't have let Ryan drive home

either. Back to college! Must go on more courses! Lessons in irre-
sponsibility! I can't tell you how nice it is, on one level anyway.
Everything structured, even get woken up in the morning, good
food. No decisions about where to go next, even after lessons,
then Ryan makes them. How are you? Oh good, you've been
shopping, something new. Lovely, I like it.'

Helen was washed and changed, two glasses of wine away from
total sobriety. Part of the spoils of shopping were the tiny earrings
which sparkled in her ears, very understated, she resented him
noticing. Rose had not approved. 'You want great big earrings,
Aunty, not them mingy little things,' but Rose had approved the
steak and packeted salad, bought on the run with extravagant ease
for the West-Bailey supper. 'More time for real shopping,' she
had added, a distinction which Helen heartily approved.

Helen returned the pressure of Bailey's embrace without much
of the feeling, deciding he was not really drunk, merely a little
under the influence, which was the most he ever got since the stuff
seemed to lodge in his bones rather than his brain. It explained the
geniality.

'A drink?' she asked, over brightly. 'There's food too, of
course.'

'Oh yes, oh yes. A drink first. Then let's go out to eat. I don't
take you out enough. Oh my God.' He sat down suddenly, still in
his winter coat, laughing.

'What?'

'I've left my car in Bramshill. Well, that limits any movements,
doesn't it?'

'I'm not driving,' she added, flourishing the wine bottle and
pouring him a glass, thinking of drunk drivers.

'Oh,' he said without rancour or comprehension. 'Never mind.
Actually, come to think of it, I'm not very hungry.'

Helen thought of the mountain of food standing by and suppressed the desire to shout at him. 'I'll do something anyway,' she
said, keeping her voice level.

'Great,' he grinned.

She couldn't bear to be in the same room so she made herself busy, action being the antidote to irritation, but when she came back to where he was, only minutes later, still ready to shout, Bailey's wine was drunk and he was fast asleep.

His coat was on the floor, lying at his feet like a dog. His suit was rumpled. Helen undid the loosened tie, tucked a blanket round him, neatly under his chin so he looked like a baby with an extra-large bib. With that image in mind she finished the bottle of wine and went to bed alone.

Rose Darvey's hand inside Michael's was warm. He was silent which she did not mind, since it was a warm silence and her hand was being held inside his pocket and she was more than glad to chatter. They were walking away from her flat. For the first time ever she was being collected from home by a man she adored to go for a meal out in formal fashion. The relief from the morning's anxiety and the day which had followed, had both been times of unholy joy, but this was the cream. They were late because they had lingered on this the first time she had ever allowed a friend across the portals of the upstairs rooms. The two other girls had been agog, they had preened before him, and in return he had been his usual, easy, friendly self, crowding in the kitchen with his big male presence, while behind his back they had made exaggerated signs of approval to Rose, thumbs-up gestures accompanied by great rolling of the eyes.

'Did you go for that test?' one of them hissed as she crossed with Rose coming out of the bathroom door.

'Yeah,' Rose whispered back. 'Don't say nothing. It was negative, false alarm. What d'you think of him, then?'

The other put her finger on her lips, to promise silence. There was no envy in the gesture, only a gleeful solidarity. 'He's OK,' said Rose's friend, diffidently.

That had been the understatement of the year, Rose thought as she walked along with Michael. She was acting like a chattering celebrity, regal and voluble.

'Well,' she was saying. 'You'd never guess what happened to me today . . .' It was on the tip of her tongue to tell him how the day had started, but then caution prevailed. 'Well, I had to go up Oxford Street, on a message, and guess what? While I was there, I met that Miss W., you know Helen West, the lawyer in our office I told you about, the one I said was a stuck-up cow, but she isn't really, not at all. So she buys me a coffee, well six coffees and a sandwich to tell the truth, and the two of us go shopping, just like that! Six hours' shopping, I ask you! It was easy.'

'Six hours!' was all he could echo. 'Six hours! Don't ask me to go up the West End with you, will you? Six hours! You must be barmy, but then I always knew you were a bit cracked.' It was said with light teasing and increased pressure on her warm hand, as they reached the car.

In fact there was little he could say or wanted to say; he felt like someone in an extract from *My Fair Lady* or *Singin' in the Rain*. There should have been a big band playing at the end of the street while he danced down it, singing and swinging on the lamp-posts, throwing his helmet in the air, that kind of thing. A copper in love. The thought was laughable. He felt more disposed to laugh than to sing, and although he had never had difficulty expressing himself to Rose, he was short of words now. Michael was silent because he was entranced by her. She had greeted him at the door (the address, God knows, had taken a fortnight to prise from her), blushing through her make-up, dressed in black leggings and a longline jacket of red wool with a black collar. Her hair was slicked back against her head, and apart from that absurd plait the whole effect was just amazing. He had said so immediately and she had blushed further. There was about her a certain joy, a rich chuckling and the proud embarrassment with which she introduced him to her flat-mates. To know that he was responsible for that gaiety, that swift but steady metamorphosis from the sad and spiky waif he had picked from the damp garden of a damp street, made him giddy. All day he'd been counting the minutes, couldn't stop thinking of her any more than he could stop looking at her now.

There was one thing which niggled him, though only for a

minute, as he ushered her into his car like a princess. Her bedroom, spring-cleaned, shown with shy pride, was full of traditional chintz, dolls, teddy bears, lace, toys, in so much contrast to the stark provocation of her usual clothes. Michael had seen and noticed the room of a child.

'I'm starving,' she said with enthusiasm. 'Where are we going?'

'Oh, not far, round about Finsbury Park. I should think you are starved, six hours' shopping—'

'Not too close to the stadium?' she asked sharply.

'Well no, pretty close, but supporters never go there, if that's what you mean. They only eat hamburgers. Why?'

'Oh I hate football, that's all. And there's a match, I know there is. I always read in the papers to see when there's a match. Anywhere. So I know to stay miles away.'

'Clever you,' he said admiringly. 'You should be on duty when they start.' He could not resist a little boasting. 'Go mad they do. The noise! We need earplugs, but then we wouldn't hear them thumping one another. Actually,' he added, honesty prevailing, 'it's not usually that bad. I don't really mind football duty.' She was silent: it was his turn to chatter. And the Greek place was dark and cheerful, half full, swagged with rich and tired velour which did not bear close examination, but half covered the windows from prying eyes and gave it a look of expense even before the waiters prostrated themselves for each visitor. Rose was nicely flustered. They sat after the table was adjusted three times, the candle and the flowers slammed back with the efficiency which gave the lie to the humility of the service. Michael held her hand over the darned, pink cloth.

'It's one of my locals,' he said simply, not quite explaining the explosion of attention. 'And I usually come in here by myself or with one of the lads. I just wanted to show you off.'

Her cup ran over. The waiter cantered across with another flower and a complimentary drink, but all she could do was look at the man who held her small hand in his big, warm one. If this was love, no wonder she had never known. It was almost too much to bear.

I don't know what's happened to me, Michael wanted to say. I just don't know, but I want it to last.

'Here, this is expensive,' Rose muttered, looking at the menu. 'Well quite expensive. You've got to let me pay some.' The challenge was back in her voice.

'No,' he laughed. 'When I take you out, I take you out, right?' She opened her mouth to protest. Years of fighting for survival had not bred a person of graceful acceptance.

'No, love,' he warned. 'Another time. When you haven't been out buying new gear for six hours at a time. Come on, I know you get paid fuck all.'

'Do you call everyone love?' she asked pertly.

'No,' he said. 'Only little old ladies. And you. 'Cos I mean it.'

'Why?' she said seriously, looking down and playing with her flower. 'Why ever would you mean it?'

'I don't know why,' he said simply. 'I don't know if anyone ever does know why. I dunno why my mum loves my dad, but she does. You can't pick and choose. Leastways, I can't. I feel stuck with it, but it's a nice way of being stuck.'

Was it his imagination, or did her eyes fill with tears, either of petulance or sadness? Then she blew her nose, having fumbled in her handbag to look for an over-used scrap of tissue. Sophistication did not spread as far as her handbag. She was not a person to tease, he decided; she was as raw as a peeled onion and not like anyone else. Not at all like anyone else.

'So,' he said, returning to the topics which had been the staple and ever-effective subjects of their conversations. 'Tell me about work. When did I see you last? Day before yesterday? Seems ages. Let's have the *meze*, shall we, a bit of everything?'

Rose liked talking about work. He liked a girl who took work seriously and also knew a little about his own, that was a bonus.

'Well, there's something worrying me there. Can I tell you? Promise you won't tell anyone else? I wanted to tell Miss W. today, but it sort of never came up. Everything else did though.'

'Go on then,' he made a face at her. 'I'm all ears.'

'We've got someone fiddling the books, is what. Only I don't know who. Oh, not fiddling books for money or anything, just playing around with the computer, wiping off cases. So people don't know to go to court, and the magistrate chucks it out. We've had about ten, only no-one's said anything yet and no-one listens to me, I'm the only one who seems to have noticed—'

Michael snorted. 'You know what?' he said. 'Like I told you before, we got jokes on our relief about why bother going to court at all any more. Just wait for the CPS to lose the papers.'

'All right, all right,' she said defensively, her hand still in his. The waiter hovered but Michael dealt with him quickly, the boss without arrogance, smiles exchanged all round. How easy it was to unburden when your hand was held. Perhaps all burdens could be shed this way; she felt the beckoning of freedom. 'That's the whole point, don't you see? You just have to make a mess up with the papers and everyone thinks it *is* just careless, short staff, what-ever . . .'

'While someone's taking advantage, and doing it deliberately?'

'Oh, I wouldn't like to think that,' she said hurriedly. 'I don't like to think that anyone in our office would do that. It's only cases about driving—'

'Why not?' he interrupted. 'Look, what's a licence worth? Hundreds? Thousands if you could get prison. Thousands? And the rest. Depends who you are.'

'I wasn't thinking it was for money,' she repeated stubbornly. 'I was thinking it was maybe for spite. But what I was really thinking, was that when they notice, they're going to think it's me.'

'Why?' he asked, surprised, although he half knew the answer.

'Because I keep the back-up records and they've gone too. And because I'm awkward, can't help it.' He nodded. Food arrived in quantity, dish after little dish, some of the plates cracked, but the contents delectable. They abandoned any other dilemma except which dish to attack first, but not before Michael had the last word.

'Well, if they blame you, they'll find out otherwise. Now you've got me, we'll sort it out. Listen,' handing her the hot pitta bread, 'I'm boxing next week. Want to come and see me?'

She had a mouthful, shook her head. 'Only if you win. I don't want to see you being punched.'

'Promise,' he said. 'I don't want to be punched, either.'

It was then that the face pressed itself against the window. A bloated red face with one eye half closed and the colours of tropical sunset beneath nasty, dirty, thinning hair. The figure beneath wore indecipherable clothes, brown, black, damp, funeral clothes and a grubby shirt collar, streaked with blood. A hand sheltered the eyes the better to peer inwards at the diners and their food. The face adjusted itself further to avoid the curtains, then flattened one cheek against the pane, making the expression of it lugubrious and exaggerating the swelling of the skin. Rose and Michael were in the corner window-seat, she had her back to the wall. Michael looked up, his eyes suddenly level with the eyes outside, inches from that terrible face, ghostly in the light from the framed menu outside. The eyes moved sideways, gazed at Rose, and Michael was uncomfortably alarmed, then violently angry. His first reaction was to stand up and bang on the windows, but it was tempered by the desire for peace.

'Here, Rose, love,' he said equably. 'You seem to have got a fan out there. Friend of yours?'

She looked up, he waited for the laugh, watched as the colour of her skin drained to a dull white. Michael had seen the same in people about to faint, but all she did was drop her fork and choke on what she ate. He leapt from his seat, round to her side, patted her back and waited for the coughing to subside. The man outside did not move. For a moment, the two inside stared at him and then, most hideous of all, the face broke into a great, flattened grin, a hand appeared clawing at the glass beside the smile, then sketched a wave as the glass was misted by breath. Michael went outside.

He pulled the man by the shoulder, feeling the loose fabric slip over a knob of fleshless bone. A ghost. The man was still grinning.

'What's your game, mister? What's your bloody game?' Michael shouted. 'Fuck off out of it! Go home!'

Logo appeared to consider. In height, he reached somewhere about the middle of Michael's chest and he would have known a policeman at fifty yards, even in the fog. Restlessness had driven him back outdoors, but he was in no condition to run, fight, beg or face another arrest. Michael, too, remembered to conciliate.

'You should be at home, old man, not out on a night like this, frightening people. Go on, go home.' But he could not resist a rough push which sent the other reeling back a few steps, wiping away that smile for three seconds until it reappeared with his balance.

'All right, all right,' in a wheedling tone which irritated more than any sign of aggression. 'I was going anyway.' He turned with dignity and his voice came floating back. 'Tell her I'll find her. Tell her I'll go on looking.'

'Fuck off,' Michael muttered, watching until the man was out of sight. Logo, that's who it was, seen him before, poor old loony. That was all right: anyone recognised was all right. He shook himself like a dog, tried to get rid of the anger and returned inside.

The corner-seat where Rose had sat was empty. The waiter hovered, anxiously, with the next course on a large dish.

'Keep it warm a minute, will you? Where'd she go?'

The waiter shrugged and pointed to the back. He was used to alarms and squabbles and ladies hiding in the lav after too much retsina. Michael forced his way to the back behind the bar. She was standing against the lavatory door, holding the same piece of tissue she had produced before to press against her mouth, as if that talisman alone could stop the trembling.

'Come on, love. It's all right. Don't be upset. It's all right. He's only an old no-good, lives the other side of the stadium, harmless old fart.'

She shook her head. He put his arms round her, began to lead her back to their table. She resisted.

'Come on, no damage. Come on, love, we've hardly started.' She mumbled something into the disgusting rag of tissue.

'What? Didn't hear you. Tell me what's up. Look, he only likes scaring people, that's all. I can tell you a tale or two about Logo.'

She took the tissue away from her face, heaved a large sigh to control the shaking.

'Don't bother, will you.'

Michael felt the huge wave of irritation for the wreck of a well-planned evening.

Bailey woke with a crick in his neck. The fire was out and for a long half minute he wondered where he was. In the house of the woman where he had spent part of his afternoon, not innocently, but no actual disloyalty either? In his own home? He looked down at his own long length covered by blanket, tucked firmly if ineffectively round his stiff shoulders, bunched round his middle and kicked away by his feet. A covered corpse which had managed to move.

Now he was in the present he liked the conclusions less than the confusion. He was hot and cold by turns, his hands sweaty, head chilly, and surely, she knew him well enough after three years to rouse him from a stupor and put him to bed. Wincing, he threw off the blanket and surveyed his crumpled suit in the soft light she had left on for his benefit. No doubt to stop him stumbling and waking her up. Then he looked at his watch, although he knew as he always did, roughly what time it was, just this side of midnight. There was no sound anywhere until he heard the faint rumble of the North London Line, vibrating to remind him.

Well he needed a bed and he needed more sleep, so he rose stiffly, took off his clothes and slung them over the chair, padded naked to the bathroom and stood beneath the shower. A warm body is always more easily forgiven than a cold one, he reflected, making as much noise about his scouring as possible. Deliberately noisy, clumsy in any event from fatigue and headache, knocking things over. She had dishes and jars in her bathroom where he had merely closed cupboards and soap, it was easy to make his presence audible. During the teeth-brushing stage, which he did with great vigour, splashing the mirror, he noticed a new brush by the side of the basin, wondered briefly, decided he was too tired to wonder about the significance of anything. Then padded next door. He slipped in beside her and hauled her close without any resistance.

'We aren't doing very well, are we?' he said. 'I've missed you. And I'm sorry I didn't say so.'

'So am I. So did I. Miss you.'

Silence. 'Tell me,' she said more distinctly, 'if we split up, do you think we could just be good friends?'

Silence.

'No,' he said. 'Couldn't we just be lovers?'

CHAPTER EIGHT

Margaret deliberately recited to herself the events of the last evening as a way of passing time and speeding the progress of the bus which went from the end of the road all the way to Oxford Street. Perhaps Eenie remembered the route, Margaret thought.

The night before, Sylvie's mother and father had come to collect her long after Logo had knocked, it was closer to midnight by the time Margaret offloaded one sleeping child. The mother was tear-stained: Granny in hospital was dying, she said, and Margaret remembered how nothing was ever quite as bad as the death of a parent. Not even a husband. Perhaps the defection or disappearance of a child was something worse than a death. Even with a clear conscience as far as Sylvie's safety was concerned, Margaret could not triumph in her contribution to it. Her sense of guilt was becoming permanent and she worried about shouting at Logo. It did not do to shout: it was not her style. Neither was the habit of hiding things from anyone, although to do so was one of life's clearest duties. So she had lumbered over to call on him after Sylvie went.

His house showed no lights and no sign of life. Margaret knew she could open the door, but ever since she had seen the suitcase, she had not felt the same. It was not Logo who made her frightened, it was the ghosts, so she went home, wondering how she would ever manage to rediscover that love for him which seemed to have fled. She would just have to wait for it to come back.

It wasn't even lonely without him: the day had been too busy, replete with the promise of what she was doing now. Debenhams, Oxford Street. Coffee shop, half-past four, Saturday, just as the crowds were clearing. She had got up last night, one more time, to look at the letter in the knife drawer to make sure she had the time right. If only she had never seen the suitcase, if only there was some way to talk without breaking any promises.

Debenhams had changed since Margaret had gone there first for knitting wools and sensible shoes. The present format of crowded escalators moving up past vast but cramped floors made her dizzy although she was glad they were not stairs. Holding on to the rail with one hand, juggling with stick and handbag, she felt she was being propelled into the sky by catapult and there would be no way down. She panicked. After four years, how would she recognise the runaway? Four years was enough for any young woman to change out of all recognition, but then she calmed herself as she managed to step off the last escalator with greater dignity than the first two. All she had to do was sit herself down and wait to be recognised; she knew she hadn't changed at all.

'Hallo, Gran.'

There she was, a beautiful young creature. Oh, what would she be now? Margaret, of course, knew to the day, one whole month beyond nineteen years. Still with that lovely skin under too much make-up, why do girls do that when they need nothing at all? Funny hair, not the long dark curls which had bounced in abundance on her shoulders, such a waste. Thin as a reed, skirt too short: a mixture of beauty and a ferocious little beast, standing by Margaret, towering over her, half anxious, half defiant.

'I can't get up so easy,' Margaret said. 'But give me a kiss. Oh, Eenie, sweetheart!'

With one bending awkwardly and the other raising thin arms restricted by the too hot winter coat, they clutched each other. 'Oh, Gran, oh Gran, where have you been?' said Rose with her face in the old woman's neck, breathing in that scent of sweet powder which brought to mind a range of comforts, closeness and discipline. She was not going to cry: there was no time to cry, and although her need was great, Gran's helplessness still made her obscurely angry.

'Listen, I'll get us some tea.'

'I'm paying,' said Margaret. 'You fetch it, I'll pay.'

'I could get used to this,' said Rose darkly, with a ghost of a smile, flouncing away while Margaret admired her ankles, dismayed by the short hair and the plait. Oh dear, oh dear, why couldn't the young be themselves, and why was she thinking of that now? Don't nag, Margaret, don't nag just because she looks like all the others, a stranger. But she was, a stranger.

'Shop tea's never the same.' To her horror, Margaret found herself grumbling when Rose came back having brazened her way to the front of the short queue. 'But lovely, dear. Here, take the money.' Rose opened her mouth to protest, shrugged, took the money. Now Margaret was peeved. Four years without a word and the child shrugged. Never mind. She was overcome with emotion, dazed with a delight which she had wanted to be uncritical, but wasn't.

'Eenie, you look marvellous, really you do. I've been all bothered since you wrote, been bothered and worried sick for four years, come to think of it. Why? I asked myself. Why? Did that little girl never love me at all? Was I so bad to you? What did I do wrong, Eenie, what did I do? Not a word from you, or your mother—'

'Oh, you neither?' said Rose with more than a trace of bitterness. 'You and me both then. I hate her. She dumped me. And I did write to you. At least twice.'

Margaret was only following slowly. 'Where did she dump you, pet?'

'I told you. With a cousin up north. One Dad wasn't supposed to know about. We were both going to go, but we went from Legard Street to a hostel and then she put me on a train. She said Dad would find her, but might not find me, so it was better that way. She just couldn't face going up north and getting a job, was all. I knew she'd either go back to him or off with some bloke she was seeing. That's what she did do, anyway, wasn't it? Went off? Her cousin said she never went home. I suppose that's why you didn't write either.' Oh Christ, what was happening? Why was this so snappy? In her confusion, her mind buzzing with letters and more letters, Margaret remembered the suitcase with sickening clarity. Oh, yes, Mum had come home, and yes, Logo sometimes brought in her post.

'Didn't Mum write to you then, after that? Not at all?'

'Not ever, but she never was a writer and she said she might not. Then I ran away from the cousin, who was weird and demented. I got a live-in job at a school, but then I always liked school, would you believe. Got two O levels and got paid! They were good to me, a convent school too, they saved me.'

Yes, Eenie had always liked learning. Margaret remembered a funny little girl, often withdrawn, accepting all those extra-curricular lessons she had given to a child whose parents had no idea how anxious she was to learn. She'd needed a firm hand, mind.

'Oh why didn't you come back, pet? The police came looking for you both. Your dad left it a little while, but he did report you missing.'

Rose looked at her with complete incredulity, eyes darkening with anger at the other's innocent partiality, forgetting all the anticipation of this meeting in its sudden sourness. All this time, and Gran still nagged.

'You don't know, do you?' she taunted. 'You just don't know anything. Of course he knew where Mum was! She'd always joked about where she'd go if she ever left him, to that hostel where you didn't have to pay . . . of course he'd find her if he wanted, only I don't suppose he was in a fit state, oh never mind. Anyway, it doesn't look as if he did want. It was me he was after. And I thought I'd killed him.'

Again Margaret did not follow.

'You nearly killed him,' she said sternly. 'He drives everyone insane, talking about you, asking about you. It's made him strange. You've got to help him, Eenie, put him out of his misery before it drives him mad. Come home for a bit. He's your dad, after all.'

'Oh Jesus, God! You haven't the faintest idea.' Rose gulped tea, shook her head and went on talking more to herself, so Margaret strained to hear, deafened by puzzlement. 'I've moved address twenty times. I don't know why I moved back so close to home; I don't know what it is, I hate it anywhere, but there's something about . . . something draws you back to what you know.' She looked at Margaret challengingly. 'I wanted my mum. I thought I might run into my mum. I want my mum every day. I wanted my mum.'

'Is that why you wrote to me after all this time?' Margaret asked humbly. 'Because you wanted someone? Your mum? Not me?'

She was irritated by the selfishness of the girl, loved her at any price, was hurt, confused, unloved. You never talked about yourself to the young: you only listened since that was what they expected of you, as if you had nothing to say. The meeting bore no relation to the cloudy script she had played over in her mind a dozen times, tears and copious huggings and reminiscences. All she wanted to do was stroke this strange, prickly adult and be held; remind her of her childish loveliness and the chasm of loss and memory in between. Instead, remembering the schoolgirl Eenie had been, she let a scolding note creep into her voice.

'You've broken his heart, Eenie. Your mother did and now you. And both of you broke mine. You haven't got anyone else but your dad. He loves you and so do I.'

The word 'love' seemed to sting Rose into a fury.

'I'm not called Eenie any more. And did Dad tell you what I did to him? I bet he did. You were always on his side. I bet he told you and cried all over you: he was good at that too. Why do you think Mum and I went that day? Why? You silly old cow!'

'Shh,' said Margaret, red with embarrassment at the noise. 'Keep your voice down. People can hear.'

'I don't care if people fucking hear. They can fuck themselves. Oh shit.'

Margaret was crying. Great gobs of soupy tears running rivulets down her powdered cheeks, dropping on to the formica table top. Heads turned. Rose glared back, stuck up two fingers in the air, then leant across the table.

'Oh, listen, Gran, I didn't mean that, I'm sorry, got a short fuse, you know that, I'm sorry. Christ, you've got me going too.' She scrabbled for a handkerchief, but the piece of tissue had finally died, so she used the stiff, unyielding paper napkin instead.

It reminded her of something. 'Listen, Gran, don't cry, I'll make it up to you. Look, I bought you a present.

'Four years,' Margaret was murmuring. 'Four years, and you shout at me.' With shaking hands, she accepted a carrier bag, opened it uneasily. Talcum powder in a presentation box, the finest kind, her favourite, relatively expensive and saved for high days and holidays. A treat she had always demanded for birthdays and used sparingly for two decades.

'You remembered,' she said tremulously.

'I remember everything, don't think I don't. Are you all right to get home?'

They sat staring at one another hungrily. Other tables had resumed talking. The row had been dismissed as a squabble about a birthday present.

'Home? Why? You aren't going now! You can't, there's so much I've got to tell you, please, pet, please . . . I'm worried, Eenie, I'm getting frightened—'

'Not now, Gran, eh? I've had all I can take. We've got to do this in stages, you know, and I've got to go.' The powdered face was crumbling again.

'Gran, *please*. Listen, I tell you what. Same place, next Thursday, six o'clock. OK?'

'Why don't you come and see me?' Margaret wailed softly. 'Only I'm waiting for this hip, it's not so easy for me to get about—'

'I'm not going anywhere near Dad, Gran, I'm just not. Don't ask me why, you won't want to know the answer. And you mustn't tell him or I'll never speak to you again. Promise? You never broke a promise.'

'Promise.'

'Right, come on then, I'll take you to the bus.'

Margaret Mellors was paralysed by the briskness of it all. They were floating down the catapult and out into the street without another word. She clutched her handbag, the carrier bag with the talcum, her stick and Rose's arm in alternate grasping movements as people pressed by them on the way out. Margaret kept saying sorry. The bus appeared obligingly and uncharacteristically as soon as they were outside in the breathtaking cold. She staggered, found herself assisted aboard, holding on to the rail, unable to wave with her hands fully occupied and that was what she remembered later. Watching Rose waving and smiling until the crowd closed around her and her not waving or smiling back. And not understanding anything at all.

PC Michael Michael, No. 711749, turned up for late-turn duty as clean as a new pin. This did not reflect the fact that his Friday night out had gone according to plan, or that he was luxuriating in any kind of wellbeing. It simply meant he had had more time at his disposal than he might otherwise have had if all yesterday's expectations had been fulfilled. He had taken his girlfriend home to her flat instead of his own, at 1 a.m., which meant he had gone training at the gym the morning after, with time for his domestic chores as well. His mother would be proud of what he'd achieved in an hour on Friday, but perhaps not of what he had had in his mind. Wait till you find a good one, Michael boy, before you let her indoors. Wait till you find love, then go for it, his mother had said. Well, he hadn't waited, in the virginal sense, but he hadn't exactly gone mad on wild women and whisky either. Saving and boxing had preserved him from much, and he thought he'd found love in Rose, an utterly gorgeous, bad-record, mixed-up kid, thrust at him by fate. Only he was just now realising how fragile and complicated a plant love could be. No wonder Ma had said, Wait. She was only trying to ensure his survival.

His mum had been wild, so his policeman dad had confided in closet admiration, ever so wild. It hadn't stopped her being marvellous, the envy of other men, as well as other sons, and that was how Michael thought he knew the difference between what was real in a girl and what was shadow, but it didn't stop him wondering why it was all so difficult.

The late-turn relief was idle on Saturday afternoon, idle and fretful. No football, no major events to police, no major traffic breakdowns, in fact nothing to laugh about at all. Even shoplifters were kept indoors by the cold, although someone was bound to steal or have a fight at home after Saturday lunchtime drinking and the enforced proximity necessitated by the cold. Just now, there was plenty of room for friendly chat in the panda car, manned by three of them, for a change. Scope for that or malice, whichever came first. Even since yesterday, word had got around about Williams and Logo. For a man who had been seen almost crying on parade, Williams had a lot of image to build. He was trying as best he could.

'See that fight last night?' Williams was saying in the locker room. 'See that bloke get it in the third round? Whoom!' He was feinting blows at his locker door. 'Whoom! Down he goes! But he hasn't been done proper, see? Up he gets, and then the other bloke hits him between the eyes, then he really goes down . . .' Williams was dancing round the open door, pulling out a creased jacket. There was silence in the place, the silence of men resenting a lost weekend, towards a boy with something to prove. Michael sauntered by Williams' locker. 'Mind if I borrow a spare pair of gloves, Paul? Only I left mine at home.'

It was an excuse to look inside. Williams was too naïve to respond until he noticed the intensity of Michael's brief inspection. Then he slammed the door. 'Sorry, mate, gloves are off.' He walked away, humming loudly, but not before Michael had seen a vicious-looking pair of handcuffs, a bowie knife and two truncheons, one more than regulation and both more than he carried. Plus a lot of mess. Michael shook his head and passed on. He had a sudden, disgusted sympathy with a frightened man like Williams. Last night, Logo had scared him half to death. He wished he had been more sympathetic, less sharp on the subject, with Rose. Love was as fragile as smoke, but at least his uniform was durable.

As Williams strutted on to the parade, twitching his shoulders and standing to attention ostentatiously, grinning left to right as if a grin assured acceptance, the sergeant thought he was a right nasty little toad, who fancied himself as well. Williams looked at

Michael for consolidation of that view, but Michael refused to catch his eye.

'Something to say, Michael?'

'No, sir.'

'Will you lot stand still?' The irritation with one was expressed against them all. Michael felt a brief draught of bitterness for all the mores that surrounded him. He would have to give Williams a chance to get rid of his contraband before he suggested a locker inspection. All this, although he had no respect for the fool.

Patience waned as the car skidded from corner to corner. It could have been an afternoon rich with jokes as the grey sky winked through the windows and they were free of any of the gut-wrenching, silence-inducing panics. There was PC Singh, a steady constable of two years' experience who joked; Michael, with more than five years on the clock, capable of uproarious laughter, and Williams who somehow deadened the atmosphere and began the teasing.

'Still going out with that girl, Mick?'

Michael hated being called Mick. A Mick was an Irish hooligan on the terraces.

'Which girl was that, Will?'

'Ohhhh, now he tells me! Who was there first then, apart from half the Army? Who did you take with you to see if we could find out where she lived?' Michael had often regretted that. 'Has she let you in yet, know what I mean? Not saying nothing, are you? Suit yourself.'

They turned a corner at high speed, Michael driving as if the car was stolen so that Williams toppled over in the back seat. He recovered, sat forward and tapped stolid Singh in the front.

'Here, you know what? Our Mick here is going out with the biggest scrubber of all time. Only he likes his birds to have practice, see? To make way for the big one!'

The radio crackled with some meaningless message, a brief interruption. Michael's back was broader than most, but he was seething. It touched a raw nerve as he'd been thinking that maybe he should have known sooner in his brief, intense and so far celibate relationship with Rose that she would be as loaded with grief as an anonymous parcel left on a station concourse during a bomb scare. All that fear last night, all that talk about being followed. All those difficulties ahead, rocks sensed but unseen, feeling ashamed for wondering if it was worth it and if he had the bottle to cope with a girl who was half angel, half mess.

'Come on, Mick, you can tell us. What's she like?'

'You should know,' he said evenly. Then slammed on the brakes on the car. 'But I bet you don't. That'll be my privilege.' In the same moment as spying the open door to an empty, half-derelict house in a street consisting of many of the same, Michael had made up his mind and felt a keen exhilaration, the way he did before a fight. Of course he had the bottle. Of course he'd go back and see Rose tonight. Of course he'd wait however long it took to get through to her and make things better. Like his dad with his mum. If it didn't work, it didn't work, but it wouldn't be for lack of trying.

'Here, Will, get out of this motor and see what's wrong with that building. It wasn't like that yesterday. Looks like someone's broken in. Go on, get out and take a look.'

'What about you two?'

'Just get out. I'll turn the car.' Williams got out, whistling, and sauntered over to the broken door. Michael sped up the street.

'Are we ditching him, then?' said Singh hopefully. Michael grinned. The exhilaration of his own resolve was catching.

'Like I told him, I'm just turning the car. Slowly.'

When they got back, Williams was standing outside the house, businesslike.

'Contact the key holder, do we? No-one about.'

Michael peered into the dark hallway of a small, old, terraced house. Council owned, awaiting renovation and waiting a long time. 'Looked inside, have you?' he asked. 'Squatters? Anyone in there been pinching pipes and fireplaces?' He knew as he asked it the question was futile because Williams would not have been further inside than a few steps out of fear of the dark stairs and any lurking presence, and because, despite the arsenal in his locker, the silly fool didn't carry a torch. Michael took his own from his belt and strode into the house without waiting for an answer. Singh followed. Williams came last.

'There's no-one there,' he was saying lamely. 'I'm sure there isn't.'

The intruders were long gone. Dust danced in front of Michael's eyes in the dim light from a dirty window at the top of the stairs. The banisters had been removed, leaving drunken treads with traces of carpet. He shone the torch into the empty living room on the right where the ugly, twenty-year-old fire surround was still intact. In the back kitchen, there might have been a stone sink, he thought, knowing as he did the geography of the houses in these particular back streets better than the lines on his own hand. No stone sink, no copper piping either, but a smell of cat and mouse. Everything recyclable was gone. Michael retreated and went upstairs gingerly with each tread creaking under his weight. There was a pole of sorts which obstructed his entrance to the bathroom door and he pushed that aside, imagining he could almost hear the ticking of dry rot in a place like this, wait till he told Rose about it. Rose, he'd say, I've found our dream house . . . and they'd laugh. He shone his torch into the room where daylight was obscured by curtains drawn over a small window, bath gone, basin left. Yeah, love, he'd say, a real *bijou* residence. Michael squatted studiously to see if he could see if the removal was recent, looking for signs in the dust like footsteps in the desert, and then, the room came crashing in on him.

Something the size of a railway sleeper hit the side of Michael's head, felling him to the floor for the plaster to rain down on his back in sharp and blunt lumps while he registered nothing more than a vague surprise and no pain. Then stunned, but conscious, he was aware of footsteps on the stairs, shouting, thundering, and the light of his own torch, free of his hand, shining a futile beam into a corner. More noise, louder; then a silence full of images and a red glow behind his eyes.

He thought with great clarity, I'm going to miss boxing next week, the championship, now is that a relief or not? And I'm going to miss Rose tonight.

'I wish I knew where Rose Darvey lived, ' Helen said to Geoffrey Bailey, standing at his kitchen door and briefly admiring the functional nature of all she saw, himself included. Hostilities had not been resumed, but the morning's sleep had been interrupted, admittedly late in the morning, by a phone call for Helen. Bailey had taken it, a man called some silly name like Dinsdale. 'Sounds keen,' he'd said wryly, handing her the receiver and watching her blush, very slightly, but still a blush on the pale, unmade-up face that Dinsdale never saw. 'His toothbrush, is it?' Bailey mouthed as she turned her back on him and cradled the receiver against her shoulder. She ignored him. 'No,' she was saying. 'Sorry, I'm fully occupied this weekend,' without specifying how she was occupied. 'Would have been nice,' she said to the voice on the phone, which Bailey found himself mimicking. Could I possibly speak to . . .? Naice, very naice. No-one at Bramshill talked like that. He also wondered how much of the conversation was for his benefit or the benefit of the man on the line who was obviously wanting her undivided attention. She had never mentioned a Dinsdale, which was suspicious in itself, since she could talk until the cows came home about everyone else they knew, especially if they had problems. Maybe this Dinsdale was the problem. Bailey told himself to remember that Helen did not play games, but then he was a policeman and knew there was no such thing as truly predictable behaviour. The phone call was not mentioned again. One of Bailey's duties, both public and private, was to keep the peace and treasure it.

There'd been some corny stuff, about come on over to my place, the vintage of a song he remembered and she did not, but she was easy to please today. The ceasefire, which had looked like remaining stable, almost broke when she slung his baggage to one side of her car and put some of her files in; had looked more fragile when he insisted on the supermarket and the dry-cleaners, and nearly cracked into ominous silence as he watched the way she drove. Still he was a man of iron reserve; he'd been driven by worse and at least she knew she was bad. In the afternoon, they went back to bed. Housewarming, he said. In the evening he embarked on cooking. She read some of her damn files, to make Sunday less depressing, she said, and after a while came to stand at the kitchen door.

'Rose Darvey? Oh, the case clerk you told me about.' He never forgot a name or an anecdote. 'Why do you want her address? She won't thank you for calling on a Saturday night.'

'Just a feeling. For one, I know she'll be lonely. Unless she's got the beloved Michael, of course, and that one's invested with so much great white hope he might not turn out to be Saint Christopher. I can't explain her. She's woman and child, all wrapped up. Streetwise and childlike. No parents. I was thinking of her.'

'You said "one". What was two?'

She looked blank, mesmerised by his activity.

'The second reason for wanting to speak to her?'

'Oh, that. I haven't got the right files. Or something's gone wrong. I noted in my diary a remand case for Monday, same court, asked for it to come back to me because I want to get the little bastard.' She launched forward and picked up an olive from the work surface of the clean kitchen.

'Tut, tut,' he said, sweeping her away with an evil-looking knife.

'But it isn't here. Now, I told you, both of us were playing hookey on Friday, but I went back for my papers. That file isn't on the list and it isn't with me.'

'Forget it. Tomorrow will do. We can go into the damned office and check. Open that wine, will you? Maybe the defendant's died.'

'Ha ha,' she said. 'Fat chance. Drunk drivers never die, if only more of them would. What the hell are you doing?'

There was the satisfying sound of emerging wine cork. 'Ooh,' said Helen, casting her eye over the open page of his cook book. The page was already stained with his preparations. Bailey was a good cook; something you learned from following the recipes and being bothered to buy all the ingredients without substituting something else to save yourself another hundred yards.

'One chicken, roughly four pounds, two large peppers, chorizo sausage, four ounces basmati rice, sun-dried tomatoes in oil, white wine, garlic, three ounces pitted black olives, sorry there's only one ounce now,' she added with her mouth full, '. . . cayenne pepper, three thousand other ingredients. I mean is that all, is that really all? What about the kitchen sink? And ear of bat and eye of toad? What do you have to do, apart from brown and chop and sauté and slop it all around and wait for Christmas?'

'Eat it,' he said, 'in about an hour. And don't be so morally superior about all things domestic. Especially cooking.'

She paused with a bottle of wine in one hand and an olive stone in another and nodded.

'Yes, I suppose I am, a bit. I don't mean to be, but I am and it must be irritating. And while I know I like it better cooked, left to my own devices, I'd probably eat the olives first and the chicken in a sandwich.'

'You always admit your errors of judgement,' he said, opening the oven door, 'to exonerate them and have an excuse for going on exactly as before. A bit like a Catholic going to confession. How long does that recipe say for cooking? If you can bring yourself to read it.'

'Geoffrey,' she said, still leaning on the kitchen door. All conversations were fine until one sat down, they were somehow better on the run. 'You know I told you about my day's shopping with Rose Darvey? Well, we met up by mistake yesterday morning. In a pregnancy clinic.' The oven door slammed shut on poultry magnifique. 'And?' said Bailey, even toned, busy.

'And nothing.' He wiped his hands carefully on a tea cloth, with his back to her, before turning round. He seemed to speak from the middle of the kitchen sink, and she heard him from the distance created by her well-controlled, dim ache of misery and disappointment and the struggle to stop crying which had been the hallmark of the week.

'I have to go back to my course tomorrow evening. I think we have twenty-four hours.'

'So long?' said Helen, wanting to cry, hoping he noticed. 'Really that long?'

Walking was more difficult than usual for Margaret. It was as if the pain of her emotions had transferred itself to her legs and made her slower. On the way back down the street, having been spat out by the bus, it was only the ingrained force of polite concern which made her stop at Sylvie's home to enquire after the granny. Her sense of failure was intensified by the presence of a young stranger, attempting to feed Sylvie in the kitchen. Sylvie was screaming and kicking. 'I want to go with Mags!' she yelled, but it was not gratifying: it was all for show. The parents were out. The old lady had died, said the stranger in a murmur, there was a lot to do. Leaving offers of help and messages of condolence, Margaret withdrew.

No sign of Logo, but she knew he was there. She wished he would come and knock at her door, but she also wished he wouldn't. She couldn't contrive the expression of a lie, but she ached for the company, to talk about anything. Meeting Eenie had carried all her hopes for redeeming loneliness, but all it had done was confirm it. Margaret locked her door firmly. Later, she thought she heard the rumbling of his cart down the alleyway, but going in or coming out, she couldn't be sure. By that time, Margaret was cocooned in her warmest nightdress and the luxury talcum had been used with great abandon. It was the best she could do for comfort.

Logo sat in his bedroom and played with shadows. His reflection in the mirror, showing a puffed-up purple face, told him he was ill; his wiry constitution told him he was not. He was not sure which to believe. He still could not sing, but he could croak and howl in a kind of triumph.

So. He had seen her and been driven off like a fox from the hens. Seen his Eenie child, fancifully named to remind his wife of the Ena Harkness rose she had once tried, in her usual, unsuccessful fashion, to grow in the backyard. They should have stuck to calling her plain Rose. 'Eenie' had soon been coined out of Enid at school. It was an ugly name, but it stuck somehow, as she grew ever more beautiful. A lithe, lissom, little thing with a bottom like a peach and long legs like a colt and all that glorious hair. When her mother had combed out that hair while the child stood still, temporarily mesmerised by the touch, Logo had watched, equally spellbound until the spell was broken by her energy and she twitched to move again. He would watch while the little body wriggled away with sinuous grace: enough, Mummy, enough of this being still. And then when Mummy began to go out, more often, as she grew bored with the child and the child with her, Logo and daughter would play together. Shadow play, she squealing and screaming with delight.

At first, only shadow play. And then less and less of the delighted screaming until she was silent.

CHAPTER NINE

Sunday afternoon saw the doorman at Helen's office let Bailey past the door on the merest flash of a warrant card, nodding Helen through on sight of a small plastic permit because it looked the right colour. 'You could have shown him your bus pass,' Bailey said, admiring but aghast. 'This place is about as secure as a football pitch.'

'Or a lunatic asylum.'

'No, far worse than that.'

'Don't tell,' said Helen. 'Everyone thinks it's safe. The railings, you know.'

No file, and no computer record of a file when Bailey found his way into the screen. No sign of back-up records in Rose's neat hand. Helen looked in the open book which contained each person's home address and phone number. Rose's was crossed out. Secretive, isn't she?' Bailey commented mildly. Helen was defensive.

'So? She may have reason, poor child. They may not have a phone.'

'All teenagers have phones. They live on the phone.'

Helen wasn't listening. 'I'll have to ask for yet another adjournment. Unless the court's changed the date, but it still doesn't explain why everything's gone from here. I could try the basement, but I don't know where to start, all that paper—'

'You said this would take one hour out of our twenty-four,' Bailey pointed out reasonably. 'So far it's taken two and a half. Come on, cases are lost all the time. You must be used to it by now.'

'No.'

There was that hard edge in her voice which he hated. 'Losing them fairly in court is one thing. Losing them through negligence is another. Let's go home. Your place or mine?'

'Mine. Ryan's collecting me later.' She grinned an apology.

'Good, we can have a drink then. With the steak. Just for something completely different.'

Not perfect, but functioning as a team. This time she didn't want him to go. Nor did he. Neither of them said so.

And by Monday, the briskness and the fury were back in business. Because Miss Helen West was a dozen times more persuasive than her junior colleague, John Riley, she managed to secure a two-week postponement of the drink-drive case without papers. The expression of anger on the face of the defendant as he left the dock was one to which she was well accustomed, might even have sympathised with, if only he had not looked so sublimely smug before. Something was wrong; something stank with a lingering smell, sniffed but not forgotten, tucked away in the hurly-burly which followed. Two thieves, four burglars, one rapist committed for trial, a posse of football hooligans up for affray, five neighbourhood fights to be bound over, three arguments between prosecutor and the clerk of the court, one with the magistrate, but none with the defence, and Helen was out of there, back to the office at a canter. Racing up the stairs with a bright coat flying over funeral black, unselfconsciously elegant and consciously impatient with the world. On a good day, Miss West could move mountains. On a bad day, she blew up tunnels with herself inside.

There was no sign of Rose. Off sick, someone said, she'd phoned in with a cough. Helen paused only to hope that Rose was not really sick but having a lovely time with Michael. Her own work ethic had taken a battering recently, she wasn't going to impose it on someone with such a meagre salary. There was also a big distraction. Notices on desks. All professional staff to go to Redwood's office at four o'clock. Helen went out to find Dinsdale, merely for the effect of his smile.

'Panic attacks,' he said languidly, waving his own, photocopied notice. 'He gets them on Mondays.'

'What's it all about? He hates meetings.'

'Don't we all? It's all about missing cases. Something of the kind, anyway. You know that débâcle with poor Riley last week? No, you wouldn't, you weren't in on Friday.' It was said neutrally, but still made her feel like a defector who had left the family behind. 'Anyway, I told him about it on Friday evening, which he was quite content to ignore, but there's been a bit of a stink. Not from public authorities or the police, I hasten to add. Only from the solicitor who was hired to represent Riley's drink-driver, but was sacked by the client before the last hearing, on the basis of the client saying, I quote "it was all fixed". The solicitor's furious at the loss of a private fee. He wants to know if it was "fixed". He goes to the same golf club as Redwood. That's what it's all about.'

'Drink-driving?'

'No, suburban golf.'

'So what's this meeting for? Increased handicaps?'

'Something like that,' murmured Dinsdale as they dawdled towards Redwood's throne room. 'Sorry about the weekend by the way. I gather your man was back.'

Dinsdale could always make her blush. So did the mention of Bailey.

'Pity,' she said lightly. 'Another time, if your harem lets you go.'

The door to Redwood's room was open: the meeting was already called to order. This is my life, thought Helen, should I ever want to progress in it. It will owe all the success in terms of status to being good at meetings, attending courses, bullshitting selection boards. It will have nothing to do, as Redwood's elevation does not, with being a good advocate and a creature of passionate common sense. Nothing to do with falling over in the course of justice, spending days on your knees looking for paper. She looked round the room at the others, seeking a mirror to her frequent frustration. The set of gargoyles looked meek and expectant. Optimism shone on their little faces, all but Dinsdale, who had the serene look of the respectful, ever-amused, ever-removed cynic. Redwood looked as if he were about to embark on a witch hunt. Normal.

'It has come to my attention,' he began, portentously, 'that we may be losing files from the office.'

This opening was greeted with hoots of laughter, some loud, some smothered. Lost files, lost cases and causes and egg all over advocates' faces was not exactly news. It might have been ironic if he had not looked so thunderous. The laughter died away. Aren't you a little worm, thought Helen, who had laughed loudest of all. Redwood raised a hand like a vicar stressing a point in a sermon, a gesture both of blessing and cursing.

'Be quiet. Is this the way you behave in court?'

A long time since you've been to court, sir, we laugh all the time.

'Someone has been interfering with the computer . . .' again, more smothered laughter. It sounded indecent.

'. . . and emptying it of vital information,' he continued. 'About ten cases appear to have been syphoned away, quite deliberately.'

'The evidence?' Dinsdale's voice, calm and interested. 'Does the evidence point to a culprit?'

Redwood looked at him meaningfully, man to man.

'Yes, Mr Cotton, we have a very good idea, from purely preliminary investigations, I hasten to add. We have one absentee from the whole staff, one only today. Of course, the nonprofessionals are not at this meeting, they will have their own, and I think we may know who . . . The whys, apart from some kind of vendetta, have yet to be established. Obviously we cannot ask the persons who have managed to get themselves acquitted, and we don't want to involve the police who have no powers in these circumstances to do more than ask for voluntary responses . . .'

'You've got to try. Even if it's entirely off the record, you've got to try. I'll try, if you like.' Helen's voice. Riley was nodding. He was remembering his own drunk driver of last week, the smugness of the man. Helen was remembering hers of this morning. Bribery and corruption? Mistake? Redwood thinks he knows who. She knew in a flash which way his meeting was going.

'I needed you here to discuss,' Redwood was saying, 'alternative methods of record keeping. New forms are being prepared. To be submitted to me, each week. With your diaries.'

Helen remembered him looking at desks late on a Friday night. She found herself on her feet.

'You think it's Rose, don't you?'

'. . . She's off today, was off Friday, has refused to leave an address . . . knows how to work the machine, spends a lot of time in the basement . . .' Redwood was saying it like a litany.

'And is down with the lowest paid and the easiest to sack, so that's convenient, isn't it?' Helen was shouting. The others shifted in their seats with embarrassment. Redwood was shouting back.

'She's the only one who stays late. The only one—'

'With an attitude problem? OK.' Her voice had gone down an octave: Redwood was momentarily relieved. Then it rose again, not quite as high but still rising. 'What about her notebooks?'

'What notebooks?'

'You don't know? Well, they're the sort of thing you might collect on a Friday night, if you happened to be tidying up,' she hinted broadly. Redwood had the grace to pause. 'Anyway,' Helen continued, 'anyone can get in here. My friend got in here, yesterday; so did I, just by flashing plastic, all of us here know how easy that is, apart from you. And it isn't Rose. If it's anyone at all.'

Helen sat down to refuel. She wasn't finished yet. Dinsdale looked discomfited. 'Steady on,' he murmured in her ear. The proximity of his shoulder to hers was disturbingly public. 'Steady what?' she hissed, recoiling from his reservation. Now all she noticed was the perfection of his hands which she did not want to restrain her.

The room, with its draughts and floor-length windows, was alive with little sights and sounds. The wind outside, rattling those inside, the muted buzz of shocked conversation, Helen's red cheeks, Redwood's sudden, public paleness. So that was what they were, those notebooks, bottom drawer left, next to one of his feet. He could not move. He had amassed them on Friday-night perambulations without any notion of their significance.

'OK,' said Helen, conciliatory but ominous. 'No meeting with the clerks, no stones thrown without evidence, OK? And if there's a real suggestion of malpractice, the police can investigate us just as they would anyone else. And no more forms to make up for lousy security, all right? We're already sinking in paper.'

'Thank you,' said Redwood frostily. 'Now, unless there are other comments, I suggest we postpone this meeting for a day or two . . .'

There were other suggestions. There was a chorus of complaints, a comparing of notes, a vote of confidence for prickly Rose Darvey, who treated them all with equal rudeness and served them well.

Dinsdale was silent, apparently vastly amused. Helen found herself irritated; all he could do was sit with one elegant hand fingering his silk tie. True to form, nothing emerged from the meeting; no master plan, no conclusions, nothing except an adjournment for a week and their silence requested. And Redwood's agreement that Helen West could keep Rose Darvey strictly at her own side, until the next meeting.

'That man,' she said, striding away with Dinsdale, 'needs a sign on the door asking you to knock so he has time to jump into a cupboard in case you ask him to make a decision.'

'Could you do better?' said Dinsdale lightly.

'No, probably not,' said Helen cheerfully. 'But it would be different.'

Cheerfulness to this degree often followed the catharsis of anger. It always made Bailey deeply suspicious.

Helen went to the clerks' room, casually. They were ill at ease, full of speculation and her grinning presence was reassuring.

'Anyone know Rose's address? Thought I'd send her some flowers.'

One of them gasped in astonishment; flowers for Rose, after what she'd said, but no, they didn't know. They all knew vaguely where one another lived, but names and street numbers, no. Helen phoned PC Michael's station from the privacy of her room, he would surely know where Rose lived, but Michael, she was told, was also off sick. The reserve officer was cagey, but a little verbal bullying and stressing of urgency revealed more. An accident, Whittington Hospital. Too bad if Michael didn't want visitors: if he couldn't worry about Rose, she must.

On Ward C, Michael Michael was sweating. My, haven't you been lucky, they said, if you'd been less fit, that beam would have killed you. But you've only got a hairline crack in your great big head, ha, ha, plus a face which would not look good in a mug shot at the moment, and a broken arm. No, you can't go home, not yet. The manic cheerfulness of doctors depressed him. He didn't feel lucky, he felt indescribably foolish. Flowers from Mum and Dad in Catford, fruit, food and forbidden alcohol from his relief, a trickling of cards so far, all with rude messages, winks and conspicuous attention from the rare nurses, a headache fit to blind and a heartache of worse intensity. What would Rose think? What had she been thinking? He could no more have told the wretched Williams, or Singh, or any of the others he knew well enough, to go round to Rose's place, knock on the door and give her a message. Faced with such a caller, she would think she had been placed back in the section house pot.

Michael persuaded a nursing auxiliary to try at work. Not there, said the auxiliary, apologetic for not being able to aid the course of romance. When told there was someone to see him, his heart had leapt against his ribs, then descended.

The woman was slim, dark and smart, a professional-looking stranger with a nice face, but she was not Rose Darvey.

'Don't worry,' said Helen, presenting a dozen white daffodils. 'This isn't a social call.'

When she left, he felt better.

Rose Darvey's mind had crawled up and down walls for thirty-six hours. Late on Saturday night when the disappointment was becoming terminal and she was sick with the cigarettes that her body loathed but her misery craved, she was stationed by her bedroom window when she heard a panda car cruising down the street. By that time the bitter hurt was belly side up and beyond logic. Oh, go on, she'd told herself earlier, he only half promised, no more than that, and was not comforted, then the sound of an engine sent her rushing to the light switch to turn her bedroom into darkness. If it was him, she would be out, teach him a lesson, make him worried; who did he think he was, that Michael? Half of her knew, even as she resumed the watching by the window, that she would never keep it up. That if he got out of the car and rang the bell, she would fling open the window and yell at him, or run down to the door, whichever movement occurred first, but she could not have let him go. The other girls, with their new friendliness, told her what a find Michael was. 'Yeah?' she shrugged.

They went out, she stayed in, couldn't bear to step out of doors in case she missed him, waited in silence with her mounting anger and misery. Gran was forgotten, except for a furious guilt about how she had made a mess of that longed-for reunion, but then what did she expect? She always screwed up everything, every bloody thing. Rushing Gran home, so she could be back here to wait for nothing but this agonising pain, making her feel as if she were some live specimen, with a spike through her head and a chain to the wall, confined to the circuit of her room, tethered, pacing, wincing.

On Sunday she rallied, after furious dialogues with herself had somehow induced a sort of sleep. She thought briefly of all the reasons why he might not have arrived the night before. None of them bore close inspection.

'Did he turn up? Mr Gorgeous, I mean?'

'Naa. He phoned though,' she lied. 'Extra duties, he said. Probably a football match.'

'What, at the stadium? But they didn't play last night. At least I don't think—'

'What do you know?'

She cleaned her room again, singing to pretend she hadn't been found out and that within this little, expedient household she was becoming ever more the freak. Out to an off-licence with her much abused credit card to buy beer for the girls and enough booze for herself to induce a total anaesthetic. On Sundays, they went home to see mothers: complicated journeys to Crystal Palace and Neasden which made a trip to the Gulag sound easy, the way they described it. They would come back grumbling about nagging and trains while she died of envy.

Sunday, early evening, the phone rang. She launched herself towards it.

'Hallo, is that Rose baby? How ya doing?'

'Who's that?'

'Paul. Paul Williams. You remember me, surely? Police *Constable* Paul Williams. Thought you might like a drink.'

'Who was it you said you wanted?' She put on her haughtiest mimic, trying to sound like Dinsdale Cotton. The odious voice on the other end paused, briefly.

'Aw, come on, Rose, I know it's you.' He knew it from the diary taken from Michael's pocket as they looked for the address of his next of kin. 'What about that drink, then? Aren't Sundays boring?'

'Not that boring,' said Rose.

The room swam as she crashed the receiver back on the kitchen wall. Little shit. Cheap jack little shit with a cock like a thin banana. Shit on Michael too. They all did that. Passed you along. Left you wide open for your big daddy to find you, with your legs spread open on a slab. Get your knickers off, Rose.

Sunday night, bad coughing. Glazed over a TV film, beer, martini. Monday morning, decided she couldn't show this face to the world, wouldn't be able to keep up the façade and crack jokes all day. Lay down, got up, walked around, afflicted less by Michael than all the dirty laundry of her grubby little life and the self-disgust which went with it. Shadow play, distraction as the light fell and the condensation formed at the window, and she had nothing to do, the phone was silent and she felt dead. Shadow play, lying alone with the second tumbler of stuff, her back uncomfortable against all her teddy bears and dolls, her fingers making eagles on the far wall. Then a bunny rabbit with waggling ears. Then a house with a roof you could turn inside out by inverting your hands against the light. Here's the church, here's the steeple: open it up and you see the people.

'No, I liked the bunny rabbit,' she heard herself saying, nervously. 'Give me the bunny rabbit. Or the kangaroo, jumping, I don't mind.'

'You don't mind?' Daddy's voice. 'You don't mind? Here, feel this.'

'Don't, Daddy, please don't, don't, don't, I don't like it, please don't, Granny wouldn't like it.'

'Granny says it's fine, it's good for little girls, to look after their daddy . . .'

'Don't, Daddy, please don't. I'll scream, Daddy.'

'You wouldn't do that, now would you? What's the matter? It's only my little lollipop.'

'I don't want it, Daddy, I'll scream.'

'No you won't. Who'll hear? Just put it in your mouth. No harm . . .'

'I can't.'

'Yes you can. No, put it in the other place. You want Daddy to love you, don't you? Then I'll make you a bunny rabbit.' That sound of desperate breathing he made as they lay on his bed, she sticky, weeping.

And on, and on. The shadow play for two years: pain and soreness and itching and crying and never telling, in case she should lose him. Only her and Dad against the world. Then a pause for two whole years in which she could not quite stop looking round all the time. Then again, with a different violence when she was nearly fourteen, still a child, but old enough to know and to fight. Hit him with the kitchen knife. Trying to cut at Daddy's lollipop because she could not bear it any more, didn't care if she lived or died, carving a loop in his stomach instead. Blood all over the lino on the kitchen, that look of hatred on his face, Mum coming home.

Daddy said she tempted him, she was the devil. No wonder no-one could love her. They would want to stone her, he had shouted, like they did in the Bible. Outside the city walls. Stone her to death and leave her there.

Rose came round, sweating. You could always relive being fucked by Daddy.

A shower of gravel hit the bedroom window. Small stones stinging the glass. Rose had been transfixed by her hands twisting themselves into shadows against the far wall which she watched like one waiting for an omen. She swung her feet off her bed as another shower followed the first. An alarming sound, one which should have had her hiding, but so novel in its peremptory summons for attention that hope sprang, then faded as she heard someone shouting her name. It came from the great distance of the street below. The voice sounded like something from the penumbra of the same dream, Gran's voice, scolding to make her achieve.

Down in the street, Helen waited for a response. She had aimed for the only window showing light and now she leant against the front door. When it opened fast, she stumbled and both of them swore.

'What the hell . . .? What the fuck do you think you're doing, chucking things at people's windows? Oh, for Christ's sake, come in. You doing welfare as well as law, now? Come in.'

Once the foundations of defence showed cracks, it was easy to let them crumble further as long as a bedrock was left. Rose took Helen indoors because they had found each other in a pregnancy clinic and they both liked shopping. Tea was made. The kitchen was immaculate; somewhere in two days' meandering, Rose's small amount of surplus energy had taken a domestic direction. Helen opened the fridge to find milk to go with tea and found four cans of lager, diet coke, jam, low-calorie margarine, all the typical foods for three girls slimming or slumming.

'Now, Rose. What's up?'

The child shrugged, desperately relieved to see another face but trying not to let it show.

'If you're ill . . . you don't look too hot, can I contact anyone for you? Or will I do?'

'I'm not that ill. It's just this cough. No, like I told you, no-one to tell. No mum and dad, no thanks.'

'Fine, but you might like to put your coat on and go and see your beloved if you aren't at death's door. He's champing at the bit, but leave it for half an hour, then I'll give you a lift. His mum and dad were arriving as I left, and he's a bit rocky. Are we talking about the same bloke? Michael.'

'What? Oh, him.'

'In hospital, you dope. Accident on duty, Saturday; something fell on his head, but part of the headache seems to be worrying about you.'

'Worried!' Rose burst. 'He only gives away my phone number and tells all his mates where to find me! Fat lot he cares!'

Helen considered this. There was something pathological about Rose's secrecy; Michael had hinted as much and it was obvious anyway. Takes one to know one, Helen thought. She knew about secrecy, but not quite to this degree.

'He didn't give anything away, at least as far as he knows. Maybe he rambled in his sleep, he was knocked out, see? Men never do have control over anything important. On the other hand, the lads might well have gone through his pockets. Anyway, he told me he couldn't send anyone round with a message, because you'd think he was "throwing you back in the pond". Does that make sense?'

It did. Rose's face was undergoing a gradual transformation, from pale to pink, from pinched old woman to glorious juvenile, until finally, she smiled. There is nothing in the whole wide world, Helen thought, quite as powerful as a beautiful girl, so powerful, it was as well so few of them understood it. As suddenly as she smiled, Rose slumped again. Not back to where she had been, but halfway up.

'I bet he doesn't really want to see me. He thinks I'm a mess.'

She pulled out a cigarette and lit it, grimacing with the coughing. 'And he's right, I am a mess. A right, fucking mess.'

Helen took this literally, quite deliberately.

'If I looked as gorgeous as you on a day's sick and a broken heart, I'd be out there dancing a tango.'

'Not that kind of mess. The other kind.'

'Look, do you think you could give me a clue? Just a small one, no need to go mad. Such as why you're so cagey about your address?'

Rose twisted her hands together, turned her fingers inside out. Here's the church, here's the steeple . . . She looked at them, funny-looking mitts, and sat on them, fixing her eyes on the smoke from the abandoned cigarette.

'It's my dad. It's all his fault, no, all mine, in a way. He keeps looking for me.' The rest emerged in so sudden a rush it was as if she had recently swallowed an emetic. 'You see, what happened before I left home, with my mum, well I had a go at him. With a knife, as it happens. A big kitchen knife. We borrowed it from Gran . . .' Rose added inconsequentially, the voice trailing away, hidden in a lunge towards an uncomfortable drag on her cigarette.

'Oh yes?' Helen said conversationally. 'What had he done to deserve that? He must have done something.'

Rose was silent.

'I once bit a bloke,' Helen volunteered. 'On the arm, not the balls or anything, but it wasn't a nibble either. I was like a Rottweiler. I think it bled a lot, but then he was trying to kill me. I often wonder if he would have done it. Probably not.'

Rose's eyes widened.

'That's how I got this,' Helen continued idly, gesturing to the thin line of scar which graced the width of her forehead. 'So I reckon he did me more damage than I did him. I hate that boy. I wouldn't have bitten him for nothing, but it was the best thing I could have done.'

'Why?' Rose was incredulous.

'It made me realise afterwards that I wasn't a total victim. I wasn't exactly brave, but I wasn't helpless either. It's the sort of thing that stops you losing your mind.'

The tannin in the tea was as sour as the memory. Silence fell at the kitchen table.

'I thought you led such sheltered lives, you lawyers,' Rose said finally, a shade mocking.

'Sheltered? Oh yes. By and large I have, we do. Anyway, what had your father done?'

The barriers came down on Rose's confiding. Enough was enough.

'All right, as long as you know I'm on your side.' Helen put down her mug and grinned the grin which went from ear to ear. 'I mean, we'd better be friends, hadn't we? We're probably the only women we both know who go round knifing and biting people.'

Rose snorted with laughter and stubbed out her cigarette with an angry passion. She spoke only after she had ground it into a saucer and watched its demise with apparent fascination.

'My dad's looking for me 'cos he wants to pay me back. He writes to me. He writes when he finds out where I am. So far he's always found where I am, someone says or whatever. I thought it was safer in a way to come back closer, London's so big. Anyway, so far, it works. Go to work for a big office. I love that place: it's safe, you can get lost in it. Only I can't stand the dark anywhere else, and my dad wants to have me back and pay me back. I can't fight him any more. I can't.'

With the last, shivery smoke from the cigarette, the confidences had now ended along with the tea. Helen sensed a mere scratching of the surface but there could be no more talking without both of them having something to hold; tea, food, anything. No acting without a cue, no speech without props, something to do with the hands.

One more try as she got up and put the mugs in the pristine sink.

'Have you told Michael anything about this?'

Another mug crashing against the first, both of them standing, which made it easier.

'No. I sort of tried, last Friday, when I thought I saw my dad – I'm always seeing my dad, but then I thought, I've only just started with Michael, I can't, can I? Not about knives and all. Couldn't blame him, could you? Him being a copper and all.'

'Oh, I don't know. I'd say, just take a deep breath, you know, before you jump in the deep end. Got my car outside.'

Beyond the door, Rose thought, what an ugly, battered, old car with a twisted bumper, a few dents and winter filth an inch thick from the frost turned mud. Someone had written on the boot, 'Also available in red'. Rose saw this and another of her perceptions about the lifestyles of lawyers hit the pavement.

'Oh, something I ought to mention,' said Helen airily, fumbling with her car keys, using them on the door like a knuckle duster. 'There's a rumour about someone stealing files from the office. Probably nothing, but some people are having their jobs rejigged in a Redwood efficiency drive until they find out a bit more about it. So you're on court duties, with me, like it or not. OK?' The door yanked open as if it was yawning.

'Do you know,' said Rose, looking at the litter on the inside of the car with fascination, 'I didn't know Michael was working on Saturday. I thought he had a day off.'

'Listen,' said Helen, lurching them down the road, 'let me tell you something important. If you're going to hang round with a copper, get a copy of his duty roster. You've got to know when they're working. Otherwise, there's no controlling them at all.'

Rose thought, Miss W. looks like a funny monkey with a grin like that.

Oh Lord, make us not afraid of the dark.

CHAPTER TEN

The rain came down on Monday, Tuesday and Wednesday morning, driven by a buffeting wind, obliterating any view. The two days went by in a fight with the elements. There was a train strike.

Logo lay in bed halfway through the week, thinking idly about which of his half-clean clothes he should wear today. The texture of the sheets on which he lay reminded him of his own neglect since his feet lay in gritty socks on a gritty patch of sheet. He had never been so lazy in the days of Mrs Logo's sloppy dominance, but the abandonment by women had come to equal dirt and somehow, in the last three weeks, he was even dirtier. The Bible, through which he flipped for something bo do with his cold hands as well as to search for passages to soothe his soul, was symptomatic of the change. The pages were as rippled as the surface of a pond and still smelt of stale whisky.

Deuteronomy, chapter twenty-two, verse twenty-three. 'If a damsel that is a virgin be betrothed . . . and a man find her in the city and lie with her; Then ye shall bring them both out into the gate of the city, and ye shall stone them with stones that they die . . . the damsel because she *cried* not . . .'

He flipped back through the wavy pages, some of them stuck, so that he could read one side but not the verses which followed, which suited him fine. It was the words he wanted, not the sense. Leviticus, chapter eighteen. 'The nakedness of thy father's wife thou shalt not uncover: she is thy mother . . . The nakedness of thy sister, the daughter of thy father or daughter of thy mother, or of thy daughter's daughter, even their nakedness thou shalt not uncover, for their nakedness is thine own . . .'

No mention of a man's daughter, or not as such. Maybe that was over the page. Logo laughed and twiddled his toes inside his socks. Then back again to Deuteronomy. 'If a man find a damsel that is a virgin, which is not betrothed, and lay hold on her, and lie with her, and they be found: Then the man that lay with her shall give unto the damsel's father fifty shekels of silver.'

He sniggered. *If* they be found . . . that was what it was worth. Logo swung out of bed and attempted to sing. The damage to his vocal cords did not prevent sound but there was still a temporary dearth of music from that source. While shaving, he looked at his face in the mirror with grim satisfaction and smiled at it. The left profile was the best to present to the magistrates this morning; it was every colour of the rainbow, ranging from a sick yellow to a violent indigo, one malevolent-looking eye half open.

"'And I will set my face against you, they that hate you shall reign over you: and you shall flee when none pursueth you,'" he murmured to his mirror where the specks of toothpaste, soap, and hair all but obscured his own image and hid the grubbiness of a once white shirt collar. He shaved in part, leaving patches of beard to add to the effect.

A grave had been dug in the graveyard yesterday. Ask not for whom the bell tolls. The diggers had waved Logo away but he lingered, looking at the fog while they ignored him but allowed him to eavesdrop. One of them was saying how the dead woman was from Legard Street. The detail lodged in Logo's mind as he waved to their broad backs and passed that other grave which he saluted in acknowledgement. The knowledge remained with him now as he picked up his bail notice, left the house quietly and took the bus to court. He didn't want Margaret ever since she'd shouted: she had joined the enemy.

The court foyer was full, but then it always was. Dense with smoke under the no smoking signs, floor pitted, plastic chairs full of draped backs in attitudes of nonchalance or anxiety. Many sat with their families, drooping under the pressure of the nearest and dearest before whom it was so hard to tell the truth because of what they would think. Logo was an old hand, absorbed in one amused glance the nagging and the embarrassment, the loneliness

and the boasting. He always stood himself; no other position
enabled him to watch the human tide of misery, fear, jubilation,
bravado and sick jokes, twisting to observe each innuendo from
his slouched superiority. People were uncomfortable with those
who would not sit.

Out of the corner of his eye, he saw Helen West, hidden behind
paper, nursing an armful of files which she held against one hip
curved to meet the load, swaying along like an elegant but listing
ship and reminding him of a mother with a child which had grown
too large to carry. As he saw her he remembered to avoid the
challenge of the eyes, ducked his head right down to waist level
and began a close examination of the fingers on one hand while
the other covered his face. Looking up through his spread fingers,
he continued to watch as she stopped at the door of court three,
readjusting her burden, and although he knew he would not be
facing a trial today, only a remand on further bail for a trial time
to be fixed, and although he knew for once he was innocent of his
trumped-up charge, he was unaccountably afraid. Last time he
had seen her, she had been running scared, driving her car like a
dodgem at a fairground, now she had eyes like melting ice. He
kept his own skulking against the wall for cover, waiting for the
bellow of his name.

After an hour of waiting, in which he recited in whispers the
Bible passages which came to memory, plus the hymns he knew
he could not sing, the fat usher, in a gown which reached the
ground, called for him. He smiled at her, but she flounced away
and let the swing-door flap back against him and his bruises even
as he followed her bottom into the fray.

Somehow the lights in court were loud; stepping into the dock
was like going on a stage where the footlights dazzled. All those
present, clerk, magistrates, lawyers, shuffled paper for what
seemed an eternity, only a few seconds, he realised later, seconds
that seemed to last for an hour each. He could not assume an act,
for once; he could not even look around and assess the weak-
nesses in his audience, gauge when to burst into song. Behind him
was the public gallery, full of idlers looking for a thrill, curious

witnesses, people sheltering from the cold, families. None of them was looking out for him: they never were until he entertained them, but all of a sudden, he had no energy for that, no inclination to play the holy fool. Then he saw Helen West's melting eyes upon him, saw the shock, the passing sensation of fear, and then the terrible pity. She was staring at his colours, this woman whom he had loathed through three trials: looking at him without fear or alarm, but with that dreadful, debilitating concern which was worst of all. The clerk yawned, spoke.

'Charged, assaulting a police officer, 31 Jan.' A mumbled formula of words followed. 'Do you plead guilty or not guilty?'

'Not guilty,' he croaked.

The clerk leafed through her diary, a large volume, held so close the pages crept up against her face. 'Remanded to 14 Feb,' she uttered. 'On bail? Valentine's Day,' she sighed with a highly audible breath.

Logo's eyes, shielded for the last hour, began to function again. Saw first but not last, Helen West. 'Wait a minute,' she was saying. 'Can we put this one back? He's charged with assaulting the police what, four days ago? No, five. I'd quite like some information on his injuries,' she turned, apparently panicking in her concern, to the girl who sat behind her. Logo could hear: the magistrates could not.

'This isn't right,' she said, pushing one piece of paper in the direction of the girl. 'This statement of facts doesn't mention injuries. Can you get me his custody record? I need to know how he came by that face.' Helen turned back to the clerk. 'Could we make a few further enquiries, please? Maybe Mr Logo could see the duty solicitor.'

'Sit at the back, would you, Mr Logo?'

He moved as the girl behind Helen West moved. An angular child with slicked-back hair he had noticed from his vantage point, before she ran from the court with the speed of a frightened cat. Logo knew her at once. He reached a hand towards her as she passed: they almost brushed each other, as close as a shadow, breathing in each other's faces. He sat silently behind the dock,

looked at the scuff marks in the wood, filled with incredible jubilation. God was good to him: what was lost was now found.
Found on Friday night; seen through a window, a dazzling vision
of beauty viewed by the beast pawing at the glass. Seen now,
sensed, smelt, dragged within inches by the hand of God. Logo
did not resent his bruises, no longer minded that searing look of
pity from Helen West, the look which deprived him of any power
he would ever have to make her afraid again. Logo had just seen
his daughter, heard her gasp and watched her run. Enid, named
after the rose, making his thin blood race and his heart pound, the
same ache of desire gnawing in his groin, the same fury, the same
hatred. His daughter. He sat unsteadily, weak with joy.

The court scene broke into fragments. Ten minutes, please.
Footsteps went by him in the direction of both doors; one downstairs to the cells, the other to the foyer, led by the big-bottomed
usher, a crowd in search of coffee, cigarettes, clients. Logo stayed
as he was, dreaming. Gradually, sounds of a muted conversation
from behind the cell door, penetrated into his dreaming.
  'What's the point of putting it off? You say the arresting officer
had no injuries . . . I *know* this man hasn't got the habit of violence, never has . . . and he looks like a punching bag, so who
assaulted who? No-one's even saying he fell over. No, I'm not
going to run a case we can't win. OK, fine.'
  Footsteps back inside. A slight smell of perfume. Helen West's
cool voice.
  'Mr Logo?'
  As if she didn't know who he was.
  'We'll be offering no evidence, this time.'
  'That's good of you,' he mumbled, the emphasis of his irony
lost in the croak. 'I came off worst, I can tell you.'
  'Yes,' she said quietly. 'I think you did. Do you want to see a
solicitor?'
  'No.' Humbly. 'Will you tell me something, though?'
  She paused, for once anxious to please.
  'Does that girl, the one behind you in court, work with you?'

'Yes,' said Helen, surprised. 'In our office. Why?'

'Nothing.'

She did not stand close, he noticed. Either the unwashed hair on his head or the livid face deterred her, but he could smell the pity in the same way he could smell her cleanliness, and only the pity stank. He kept his head down: the footsteps went away and he heard the shuffling of paper, the hum of the air-conditioning and the people coming back. All of them but Eenie. His case dismissed, Logo did not linger in the foyer with the dead coffee cups and the overflowing fag ends. There was no point. He would never find her there.

Out in the fog he would find her. Vengeance is mine, says the Lord. Are you guilty or not, my child? Yes, you are the guilty one.

'Rose! What happened to you? Why didn't you come back for the rest of the list? How do you think you're going to learn anything?'

Helen West was extremely angry, but since she was also irritated with the nerves which arrived as soon as she doubted her own impetuous wisdom, the anger lacked force. In particular, fury against individuals could not be sustained for long, any more than she could sustain sulking. So what? Rose had been sent on an errand, had looked at her as if she had been mad to issue that particular order, had gone from the court, done the necessary in fetching the policeman responsible in double-quick time, and then disappeared. Did it matter? No, not really. Before that, she had been a perfect mother's little helper, interested and industrious, a luxury, if a mite hyperactive this morning. What infuriated Helen at the moment was not so much Rose's disappearance from half-past eleven in the morning until one, but her own reactions and abreactions to Logo. How could she ever have found him sinister? Seeing that messed-up face, and succumbing against all the odds, to that little cancer of pity she thought had died. All these times, knowing he was bad and dying to get him, only to throw in the towel at the first sign of blood. He'd be grinning and singing all the way home and she would be in trouble. Rose was shifty, staring at the wall, her skin whiter than the scuffed paint.

'Why didn't you come back?' Helen asked again, far less icily. 'Did you by any chance spot a friend on the premises?' She and Rose had been getting on well; a little teasing was allowed.

'I was sick,' Rose murmured, still whiter than paper. 'Very sick.' Helen was immediately full of concern.

'Oh, Rose, you idiot, what am I to do with you? Why didn't you say?'

'It's all right,' said Rose, shrugging, but without the more familiar insolence. She looked small, weak and defeated, a persona Helen neither liked nor approved. Her own anger was finally converted into puzzlement.

'Why sick? It can't be . . . You never did look after that cough, you've still got it, you make yourself sick trying to keep it down and you don't eat. For Christ's sake, do you want to go home?'

It was brisk enough to help. Rose shook herself. No, it did not do to hide in the lavatory, any more than it would have done now to go home, or anywhere else alone; better stay with the pack.

'I'm much better now. Sorry. Next time I'll send you in a message by fucking pigeon.' That was more like the usual Rose. Helen grinned.

Rose continued. 'What happened then with, with . . .' She waved a languid hand as if unable to remember the name, 'Him? Logo?'

'My *bête noire*? Oh, I don't know. Think I did the wrong thing as usual, offered no evidence. After all this time. But there's something so fishy about a statement of facts which doesn't mention injuries, not with a bloke who isn't violent.' Rose began to cough, violently.

'Are you all right?' There was a nod and the colour had turned from white to pink, a spreading blush of relief. Helen regarded that as a sign of health and a licence to continue in a self-indulgent vein.

'I mean, what do you think? Do you know, I've hated that little hymn-singing man every time I've come across him, but today? Well today, I just knew it was all wrong. He didn't assault anyone, he wouldn't, couldn't. He's just pathetic. And do you know what?

He wanted to know where you worked. Another fan. I don't know how you cope.'

Rose looked up, between coughs, the pink complexion verging on a sickly purple. 'And you told him, I suppose?'

Helen had no reason for the lie, but it came forth unaided anyway.

'Course I didn't. You could have been the usher's cousin for all he knew.' Rose relaxed and Helen felt a sense of shame as acute as it was undiagnosed.

'What you need,' she said, leading the way, 'is some food.'

Bailey's palliative, she thought. He may know something I don't.

Margaret fussed. First she bothered and after that she fussed, a process which meant everything took longer, slowing down into a crawl of non-achievement. She would walk into a room, in search of something such as a pen or a piece of knitting, forget on the threshold what it was she had come for, see something in need of a dust, go back to fetch the duster and forget halfway back why it was she was aiming for the cupboard. Concentration on anything was limited to thirty seconds: she would end up with something in her hands, looking at it, puzzled, her sense of priorities shot to pieces. The condition repeated itself into a hundred meaningless errands, and endless dithering from room to room until the whole place became an ice rink of silly exhaustion. Should she seek out Logo? Her ally, friend, adopted son, whom she was betraying? Should she, on the other hand, deliver the flowers she had bought for Sylvie's grandmother, or do that later? Should she press her clothes for meeting Eenie tomorrow? Would that help? All day she dawdled, until the tiredness finally made for clarity. Take flowers to Sylvie's house. *Then* press clothes. On the way out or back, put a note on Logo's door, saying would he please come in for tea or something. Confine her shopping to the expensive corner shop today, simply because it was the nearest, even though each time she bought whisky in there, she blushed for shame. And oh yes, stoke the fire. Make the man welcome, mend fences. Hadn't seen him for days.

Once established in their right order, the tasks became simpler. One hour all told. The flowers were accepted on the doorstep with murmered thanks but without, thank God, an invitation indoors, even though Sylvie was screaming. Margaret was served her half-bottle of whisky by a woman who smiled as if she was dispensing lemonade, and at home, the fire burned briskly against the fog which had followed the rain outside. The note still pinned on Logo's door looked friendly. Five in the evening and the day still hers. Margaret felt suddenly at ease. What would be would be, with Eenie, with Logo, with all the world, now smoothed by the fog which took her back to a safer childhood. Fog and yellow smog in London, that sense of safety when you reached your own front door and banged it shut and waited for tea and argument. Far worse fog than this gentle mist which deterred no-one from movement, but gave a gentle glow to the street lights and made her imagine that each lit window hid a happy, laughing family behind itself. She was suddenly at peace, a great, grand peace.

I am resigned, Margaret thought, to the occasional sweetness of life. I *love* this room, but how I managed to clean it today, I shall never know. What a fuss, what a fret to be in, because of what? Because of telling lies to Logo, as if that mattered, lies are as necessary as breathing: they exist to keep us sane. Because of a funny kind of grief about Sylvie's grandmother, although I never knew her, because she is mourned and I shall not be. Margaret sat by her fire and chuckled. No, but I'm not dead yet. Give me my new hip and I shall move, and no, don't be fooling yourself now, that isn't what has stopped you, Margaret, it's your own silly willpower and being a coward and not wanting to look a fool as you sway along, but if you smell nice and look clean as well as cheerful, nothing else matters.

On that reflection, Margaret went for a wash and change of clothes. She could never change her clothes without washing first. She used Eenie's expensive powder, all over. Life was for living. The speed of her knitting was electric as she sat back in front of her fire; calm carried energy into her fingers which knitted with ineffective speed the sort of sweaters she realised she would hate to wear. The thought made her judder with laughter, but she still went on knitting. Still a fool, Margaret, after all these years. Tomorrow, Eenie and she would really talk, or perhaps they would. Everything took time. She would cope with Logo if he deigned to arrive, oh, for heaven's sake, she still loved them both and love conquered all provided you didn't look for reward. When he did knock at the door, she wasn't even surprised, let alone alarmed, and that was before the whisky.

'Oh, it's you, is it?' was all she said, opening the door and turning back to her chair. The one opposite, old and worn with a brash new cushion, welcomed him as if he had not been absent from her company for more days than had ever passed between them before for many a year. He looked terrible: the sight of him shocked her, but she wasn't going to remark on that, not yet anyway.

'Where've you been?' she said, in her familiar tone of scolding and grumbling. 'Thought you were dead.'

He looked at the whisky bottle and the two shining glasses all standing to attention on a lace cloth.

'Dead?' he queried. 'I may as well have been dead, for all you cared.'

'Now, now,' she said placatingly. 'Don't go on. You know you don't really want me banging at your door all hours of the day and night any more than I want you banging at mine when I've got company. But if you needed help, you only had to ask. Get us a drink of that, will you? Stop standing about looking like a lemon.'

He grinned. Like herself, she noticed, he had made a bit of an effort. The shirt was cleaner, the shoes had been rubbed up and down the back of his trousers where streaks of dust showed disarmingly. His face looked frightening, like a hand put through a mangle, but he still had eyes and he still had teeth. Living with the dying as she had done, Margaret had seen worse and she knew Logo's reaction to any kind of pity he had not personally solicited.

'Walk under a bus, did you?' she asked as they sat, facing the fire, each with a huge glass in hand.

'No, it was a train. What do you think?'

They both chuckled silently. 'Hope the other fella looks worse,' said Margaret nonchalantly.

'Oh, she does, *she* does,' said Logo, lingering on the 'she' with deliberate crudeness, then gulping, while Margaret failed to flinch. Instead, she took the proffered cigarette. She thought about lotion for bruises, wondered what she had and calculated at what point she would produce it. They were worrying, those bruises, but not fatal. She could tell the doctors about those bruises and then they might listen. She could tell them he beat his head against walls. They understood real injuries like that, nothing else.

'Has that horrible little girl been round again?'

'She's not horrible. She's just got parents who are trying to do too much. Anyway, you should feel sorry for her. Her granny came on a visit, but she was sick and she died. Awful for them, isn't it?'

'No, not really. People have to die. No work for the gravediggers, else, is there?' He laughed uproariously. Margaret felt uncomfortable, continued with her knitting, sipped the whisky which he gulped. Half a bottle was not going to go far with him in this mood, but at least he was laughing.

'Guess who I saw today?' Logo's voice was oddly croaky, she noticed, but still loud. 'Just you guess who I saw!'

'God,' she said, knitting faster.

'Oh better than God, much better. More of a goddess. Maybe it was the devil. Sometimes it's difficult to tell. Sometimes the things which look innocent are the opposite, you know? Sometimes something very beautiful has to be wiped out for all the damage it can do. Killed, burned in the fire. Stoned outside the city walls, then burned.' He was murmuring, Margaret growing more and more uncomfortable, but keeping her veneer of placidity with admirable calm, gazing at her knitting for inspiration.

'What are you talking about? Who did you see?'

'Eenie.' He looked at her cunningly. 'You know, Eenie.'

This time she reached for her whisky tumbler and took a gulp as large as his. 'You never did,' she said.

'No,' he answered. 'I never really did. I just thought I did. I just

felt her close to me, that's all. I don't suppose you've got anything
to eat, have you?'

Margaret relaxed. 'You and your dreaming,' she said equably.
'There's some bread and cheese hanging around. Get it yourself.
I'm knitting this sweater for you, you know. When you've got
your snack, you can help me make this wool into a ball.'

A wave of noise hit the house, the roar of the football crowd
she had seen foregathering as she came home. Not even an irritation any more, nothing to remark upon after all these years, less
of an event than thunder and less frightening than a storm. Eenie
used to complain, but then Eenie had been a difficult child.
Margaret remembered Eenie holding a skein of wool between
her hands while she wound it into a ball until the child was bored
and then they swapped. She could have bought wool in neat,
ready-wound packets now, but the cheaper wool on the market
still came like this, pieces which had to be joined. Her bag was full
of wool from decades ago, unpicked jumpers washed and saved:
she remembered old economies. All those tasks were soothing,
imposing continuity. Maybe the winding of wool would soothe
Logo as well. She sighed, foraged in her deep bag for the next,
comforting lump of royal blue, while Logo foraged quietly for
cheese. There was a rattle of sound as he looked for a knife. Oh
let him be: she was tired, so tired, she closed her eyes for a minute
and let another roar from the crowd wash over them. If you listened, the fire made more sound than the rest of the world: it
could speak to you, it was company. Maybe all she needed was a
cat.

'I think I'll get one,' she said out loud.

'So,' he said, sitting in the chair opposite, picking up the new
skein of wool which had fallen into her lap, holding it in one hand
while the other held a lump of cheese, cut into a neat square.

'I think I'll get a cat.'

He looked at her with an expression of sad disgust, the look she
might have given to a damaged city pigeon, some poor earth-
bound piece of vermin.

'Help me wind the wool, will you?'

'I can't. It'll stick to me, my wrists, they're all sore. Look.' He held them up.

'What's wrong with them? I can only see dirty tidemarks.'

With a lightning movement, he sprang towards her and stuffed the square of cheese into the mouth which was opening to speak. Two ounces of solid, sticky, soap-like cheddar lodged with violence between her gums. Margaret spluttered, tried to spit it out, but he held her hair and put his palm over her mouth. She tried to chew and swallow, thrashed with her arms, dug her nails into his wrist, her eyes bulging and her face changing colour, until he relented and stood back. Margaret coughed, disgorged the cheese, continued coughing, supporting herself on the arms of the chair, staring wildly, trying to rise. Logo patted her on the back, firmly but kindly. Then he squatted at her feet, picked up the skein of wool he had dropped, fingered it.

'A pullover for me, Granny? Now whoever asked you to do that? I didn't. I wouldn't ask you for anything, not now. You knew where she was all the time, didn't you? All the time.'

'Who?' she whispered, massaging her throat, trying to sound calm, croaking as he croaked. 'Logo, stop messing about. Get out of here. I'm too old for horrible games, don't.' Her eyes travelled beyond him to the back of the kitchen and the knife drawer, standing open. Two pieces of paper were on the floor. The remainder of the cheese stood on top of the unit, the piece she had disgorged was on the floor at her feet. Oh dear God, why had she invited him to feed himself and look in the knife drawer? Letters for her eyes only and he had seen them. Logo stood up and ground the cheese into the carpet with his heel.

'You treacherous old cow. You knew when the pair of them were going, you probably helped them plan it, and you didn't tell me. How many letters has Eenie written you then? Keeping you up to date with the news, laughing behind my back, while all the time you pretend to sympathise . . . laughing at me.'

'One letter, Logo, I promise. Only one. One in four years, I promise.'

'You what? Promise! Don't make me laugh. You, knowing

where she is, all this time. I bet it was her in here last Friday when you shouted at me to go away. Come on then, Granny, where does she live? Tell me, tell me, tell me,' he was wheedling, kneading her ankle in an attitude of comic begging. Margaret had a brief belief that she might get the situation back under control, then she knew she could not. Ah, the treachery of it: now she had betrayed them all, Logo, his wife, Eenie. She had kept secrets for none of them. The royal-blue wool draped over her feet.

'I suppose I should have known. Ever since you got into the house with that child the other week. And went upstairs.' He spoke wistfully, still draping the wool round her puffy ankles.

'Why does it matter so much? Oh dear, stopit, stopit, you idiot, that black eye's gone to your head. Get us another drink, go on. Stop messing.'

It seemed best to treat him as a child, sound like the good-natured scold which had been her second nature, but somewhere in the depth of her fast-beating heart, Margaret knew it was too late. 'I've had one letter from Eenie, ever,' she said querulously. 'And why should it matter if I've been inside your house? Oh, I see.'

The vision of that suitcase at the top of the stairs floated back to her with a memory of her nervousness towards him ever since she had seen it, her lack of friendliness in these last days, all that to fuel their mutual suspicions. 'Tell me,' she said as evenly as she could, 'did she ever come back? Eenie's mum? Did she really just disappear off the face of the earth, just like that? It isn't right, is it?'

The wool was now wound round her ankles, fashioned into a clumsy knot. He had always been clever with pieces of string, clever with his hands, but lazy, preferring games to achievements, not like his daughter. She knew that if she got up now she would fall over and she felt weak at the very thought. Logo sighed.

'Oh yes, she came back. I brought her back, coupla days after, you were out, I know you were, but then she wouldn't tell me where Eenie had gone. I got angry, you see, very angry.'

'Why wouldn't she tell you where Eenie was?'

'To save me from her. Save me from that little temptress who'd eaten up all my goodness, made me lie with her. She gave me the apple and made me eat. She made me fuck her. She made me go to the devil, all on her own. Where does she live, Margaret?'

'No, no, poor child, poor child. Oh no, poor child.' Margaret was weeping, little corners of tears creeping round her bulging eyes.

'Where does she live?' he insisted.

'I don't know, I don't know,' she was shrinking from him.

'What does she look like? Black hair, all smoothed down, with a little plait at the back!'

Margaret screamed. 'What did you do with her, Logo? What did you do with her mother?'

He shook his head sadly. 'Only this. No blood at all. Only this.'

A great roar of victory from the football ground reverberated down the street. He could hear and feel the stamping of feet, the beginning of that swaying singing. It drowned the beginnings of her scream. His hands were round her throat, the thumbs gouging under her chin. Margaret was already weak and panting. She struggled again, vainly, one hand holding a knitting needle jabbing at him, catching him in the stomach, so that he yelped, but held. Her skin was purple, there were strange animal noises emerging from her throat as she went on and on struggling. It seemed endless, ebbing and diminishing. She acquired more vigour to resist after each successive wave of weakness. Then she slumped. He loosened his hands slowly, sensing a trick. Then dived quickly into her knitting bag, pulled out another hank of wool, put it round her neck almost reverently, twisted it in his fist behind and turned it. His hands slipped on the wool, felt hot and greasy: he realised he was trembling violently. Logo reached for the poker in the fireplace, inserted it into the wool and continued to turn it like a tourniquet. To stop the flow of blood, he thought irrelevantly. Finally there was no sound from her at all.

Logo stood up and drank some more of the whisky. Gradually the trembling ceased. He picked up the letters from the floor, read them again and threw them on the fire. He sized up the body of Margaret in his mind's eye, chuckled briefly and tapped his nose. When you were weak and ill with stitches in your stomach, it was so much harder, but he wouldn't make the same mistakes as last time, waiting until the limbs were stiff. He might have to wait to travel, surely the match was almost ended, half an hour to clear the ground, they were so good at it these days, then he could travel with his burden.

He pulled her from the chair by the ankles, then dragged her by the armpits to the kitchen door. She was the size of a bird, her blouse riding up to show smooth, white skin grazing on the floor. Outside was her chariot, lying on one side. First he took the blunt end of his axe and hit her elbows and knees scientifically: he had thought long and hard about this. Then he pushed her into the trolley, still warm, still malleable, but it was difficult. Finally, with a great heave, he managed to turn the trolley upright on the third attempt. All this took a while. In the meantime, crowds passed the bottom of the alleyway, whooping and yelling. He regarded that as encouragement.

Logo covered her head with a piece of black polythene, stuck a shovel down among her ribs. He trundled the trolley down into the street and out, past the little shops on the corner, on to the main road. It was not the route he normally took to work, but he had always found before that the more obvious he was, the less he was noticed. One whole hundred yards of the main road, before he detoured, left then right, into the graveyard, whistling. The ability to whistle always came back after a trauma long before the ability to sing.

Logo found the grave they were digging for the woman in Legard Street this morning. He took the shovel from the trolley, leaving Margaret as dead as she was, and leapt down into the trench. The gravediggers' footsteps were all over. He had brought a torch but did not need it: they were so close to the edge, the street lights would do, and anyway, he did not need to be particular. He had watched enough funerals to know the carelessness of city incarcerations on grey days like tomorrow; no-one would notice the faintest signs of his presence tonight. They were buried here without a sense of place: Margaret would like it here. Inside the trench he dug like a demon. Soft, north-London clay, cold but free of frost, turning easily. No-one looked at the sight or the sound in a graveyard late at night. Even the vagrants and the human residue from pubs, the teenage lovers went home at the merest signal of other life in here, drunk or drugged, they were easily spooked. Digging in a cemetery was only a sign of death, consistently ignored. I do not want to die, Logo thought, but the thought was not unappealing after he had dug down a foot, neat but frantic, sweating in his black clothes. He smelt of powder, not earth, a sickly scent of talc clung to him like a mist; his lapels were white with the sheer moving of her. More powder billowed out of her in a thin mist to complement the fog as he hauled her, all lumpy and bumpy and huge, out of the trolley and into the hole, where she landed with a sound like thunder.

Then she moved: she moaned and moved and lay still. Logo had carried the whisky, took a swig, looked again. Margaret was so obliging. Freed from her polythene, she lay spread-eagled. He jumped on to her spine and with his hands, filled in the shallow covering of earth over her. She was still warm: not even the soil was cold; her presence rendered it tepid. So it was not without regret he covered her and tidied up. There was a certain economy in burying two at a time; they should try it more often. For himself there would be no family vault. They would all lie outside the city walls.

He packed up the trolley with his shovel and wheeled it towards the far gate. On his way, he saluted the same grave he had acknowledged earlier that day. After all, it was not the first time he had made this journey with a similar burden. First his wife, then Margaret, both treacherous. The wife had been heavier, he seemed to remember. Or maybe she was just stiffer and clumsier and he weaker with his stitches and fury. Logo touched his nose. He stank of talcum powder; he would never get it off; it was not fitting for a grave.

Chapter Eleven

There was something about a hospital ward. Perhaps it was the casualness, as if those who lay in bed had nothing to worry about at all. It reminded Rose of the foyer of the magistrates' court where people sat around as though nothing was going to happen and nothing ever would again. Hospital was all pervading: on Wednesday night Rose suddenly wished she belonged to this small community of souls who knew the manners of the place and revelled in its comparative security. Patients had to work for their visitors, please them in a way which would not have been mandatory at home, but Michael was delighted to see Rose. She looked at him anew, feeling a little jealous. He was like a man holding court in the kingdom of his safety, surrounded by gifts. These tributes to a man much loved by friends and family made her feel small and inconspicuous, a person who did not count.

'Mum and Dad,' he explained sheepishly. 'They keep sending things. I wish they wouldn't. I'm out of here tomorrow and I couldn't have eaten this lot in a month.'

'You'll have to leave them here, then. For the others.' Rose could hear her granny saying that.

She was holding his hand, loosely. With the other arm immobilised in a sling, she merely touched his fingers in a way which would leave him free should he want to scratch, gesture or simply abandon contact. They were both a little awkward; she was tense, full of her own anxiety, but determined not to undermine his optimistic mood. There was so much she wanted to tell him, but none of it was for the ears of a hospital case, the most handsome man in the ward, who looked so solidly secure that she wanted to crawl into his lap and stay with him there for ever, even though no-one would believe that he was hers.

'How's the office, then? Still standing?' He was determined not to talk entirely about himself.

'Well, I've scarcely been in there. I expect so. You know what it's like. Another bit falls off every day. They've got notices up about IRA bombs.'

'Not again? I don't know why they bother with the notices. Any old tramp could get into your building.'

'Oh, I don't think so,' Rose said, shocked. She was defensive about the mausoleum she had always considered as solid as a rock. It was one of many reasons that she liked it, regarding it as the only impenetrable place she knew, because no-one would ever try to get inside. Besides, Michael did not really want to talk about her work, let alone the place where she did it.

'Sergeant Jones came in today. And Smithy and that bastard Williams, getting in from the cold. I told him to fuck off.'

She didn't want to pursue this line either.

'They only come for the chocolates,' she said.

'Do you know, that's what I thought.' He shrugged it off, but she could tell he was flattered by the number of his visitors, slightly regretful that this period of being spoiled was coming to an end. Rose could see his point. His position in this bed made him quite invulnerable.

'What time tomorrow?'

'Oh, the morning, I think.' Now he was less comfortable, conscious of deserting her. 'Mum and Dad want me back for a day or two. It's probably as well. I won't be much use with the scrambled eggs just now. Gives Mum a chance to fuss.'

He was very proud of having loving parents, but also vaguely ashamed of them, with their chorus of soup-making and well-wishing relatives singing love from the sidelines. But Rose would have none of his guilt.

'Just what you need. Save me coming round to you with dishes of cold spaghetti bolognese so I can cut it into pieces for you.' They both giggled.

'Only for a day or so, and only in Catford. You could come and see me, meet them all. Saturday? I've written the address and phone number for you. Come on, Rose, say you will.' She shook her head, secretly delighted but terrified by the prospect.

'Yeah you will. And after that,' he was holding her hand very firmly with no sign of wanting to escape, gazing at her with eyes which felt capable of melting her bones, 'after that, you are coming round to my place. With your suitcase if you want. I love you, Rose. I want to bloody shout it.'

'Shhh,' she said. 'Shush, someone will hear you.'

'I bloody won't shush,' he said. 'I won't.'

On her way out via three sets of antiseptic, polythene doors, she was weak with a transient happiness, before the dark world beyond flapping exits intervened. Inside the ward next to him, she could see a future twinkling away, somewhere beyond the ever-persistent fog, but the trouble was how to survive the time before the future could begin. Somehow, inside that greenhouse warmth, Rose had managed to suppress the cough which now returned for revenge. With the sound of her hacking went the pleasure of illusion. Michael could not help. She would have to find a safe place all on her own. Logo was everywhere: no-one could lock him up. Rose looked left and right before crossing the road. There was a taxi rank on the other side. Taxis were a luxury she could not afford, but there was no question of going home alone. Both girls would be in, Wednesday night was for complaining and hair washing. She would be fine until the morning, unless the doorbell rang.

Daddy looked round every corner. He had seen her.

Thursday dawned with a milky sweetness. The fog sank against Helen's basement windows as daylight pushed itself into her dreams. Nothing but the fog peered through the bars which covered the panes, and although she loathed the necessity for this iron security, she could not have slept alone without it. It was a slow January light, with fog making her think of the sea and of being far away.

Thursday. For the untroubled it was a day of promise when the back of the week was broken, but Helen rarely came into that category. The morning's work would be easy enough, but all played to the tune of Wednesday's emotional hangover. Helen did not think of Logo as she dressed. Pondering cases in lieu of counting sheep was proving a distraction which no longer worked. An obscure guilt was nibbling at her bones; guilt for things done badly or not at all; guilt for somehow missing the point and for not making sufficient progress with that girl, Rose, and for discussing her with Dinsdale the night before. Guilt for drinking white wine with Mr Handsome, as much as anything else, while knowing there was something wrong in this intimacy, however much she defended it by saying it was Wednesday and no phone call from Bailey this week, he deserved whatever he got.

Come now, there are no real, concrete commitments between Bailey and me. Oh yes there are, for all there is nothing on paper: the unspoken promises are the most important you have ever made.

'I don't know what ails that child,' Helen had been saying to Dinsdale about Rose, while they sat in a wine bar which was, by mutual consent, a long way from the office and prying eyes. Perhaps it was that which made her less comfortable, this definite movement towards the clandestine. 'One minute she's open, next, closed for the day. One minute an ordinary giggly girl, next sulky and unpredictable.'

'*Cherchez l'homme*,' said Dinsdale. 'Moaning hormones. How's the new man?'

'In hospital.'

'Not the best place for love to bloom, might have something to do with her moods.'

'I don't think so. Monday and Tuesday, she's brilliant, then this morning she didn't want to come to court at all, I practically had to force her. Then she kept her head down in her hands, did everything grudgingly, as if she was hiding . . . Don't know why.'

'Do you suppose,' Dinsdale ventured, 'there could be any truth in the Redwood theory? That Rose could be the one who's been sandbagging the system?'

'No. I'd literally stake my life on it. What a silly, dramatic thing to say.'

'Yes, it is. Anyway, you should know better than that.'

Helen watched his fingers round the stem of the goblet, holding it with the casual delicacy of a discriminating drinker. The bowl of his glass never became dirty, greasy or marked as hers did with fingerprints and lipstick long before the bottle was empty. She wondered how it was he managed to keep himself so clean, and also why it was she was struggling to keep the conversation on neutral, fixed to the main highways of law and objective gossip, away from anything to do with themselves. They had been playing with each other for several weeks, an element of teasing in all this chat. It amounted to nothing less than a prolonged flirtation, admittedly of an obscure kind, consisting as it did of two people listening to one another with the intentness only given to a potential lover. Now as the tenuous nature of the relationship began to slip, as it began to slide in the direction of an affair, and she knew he was teetering on the brink of either proposition or declaration, Helen, who had been as enthusiastic as Dinsdale for the flattery each gave and received, was thinking twice.

She had left the wine bar in full flight with an excuse which sounded as false as it was and now she felt furious with herself. She was a grown woman, she should have talked to him, she shouldn't have let things go so far. What she had wanted was the attention, she admitted bitterly. She had required fresh armaments in her war with Bailey, needed the uncritical, unreserved admiration which her younger colleague gave with such generosity along with Dinsdale's support while he laughed at her pathetic jokes. She had not really wanted to give anything back. Cock tease. And what is so wrong in that? She asked the mirror. Am I not supposed to *talk* to men and enjoy their company? You have every right, her conscience answered back; but you knew this was different. Did she really like Dinsdale, with his patrician manners, splendid articulacy and shining cleanliness? Yes, apart from the last. Yes, yes. So that was all right then. An honest cock tease.

The fog helped. It always helped but it would clear before noon. Helen West loved the cold anonymity of winter. It was as if the void left by the non-existent pregnancy had been filled with a strange kind of longing to be different, to acquit herself well by someone in the world, instead of failing everyone in a subtle fashion, all the time.

Sylvie's parents had debated long and hard the several issues raised by Granny's funeral. The first was, should Sylvie attend? Was this part of the necessary education of a child of such tender years, and would it make things easier to explain? Opinions had been canvassed, but they had come back in contradictory forms and it was pragmatism which won. An early morning call to Margaret Mellors had elicited no response; the child could have been shuffled off elsewhere, but there had been so much upheaval lately, it did not seem entirely right and there was no time to consider the alternatives. The second subject of debate was should they wear black, but there was no black garment in the house and no time to borrow. Mr and Mrs went to church in blue and grey and Sylvie, spoiling for a fight, in red.

It was the coffin itself which made Sylvie's mother weep, such a helpless weeping it had no self-consciousness and she clutched the child for comfort. Too late she remembered why children were left behind; not to spare them the sight of the coffin but the sight of the parent out of control. Letting go of the smaller hand, the mother clutched her solid husband instead. Sylvie forgot to fight in this alienating atmosphere. She picked up the hymn book her mother had abandoned and looked at it, before beginning to gnaw the cover with silent concentration.

'I am the resurrection and the life, saith the Lord; he that believeth in me, though he were dead, yet shall he live: and whosoever liveth and believeth in me shall never die . . .'

Sylvie twisted round with the book still in her mouth. She saw the last member of the congregation come in and sit at the back. Her jaw worked faster. It was the man with the fingers. Sylvie searched for her mother's sleeve, saw her huddled away against Daddy, both of them smaller, ignoring her.

'. . . We brought nothing into this world and it is certain we can carry nothing out. The Lord gave and the Lord hath taken away, blessed be the name of the Lord.'

It all went on too long. When the priest led his tiny flock from church to graveyard, the daylight hurt their eyes, but the movement was welcome, although as soon as the coffin shifted on the shoulders of the dull, professional pallbearers who had been outside for a cigarette during the ragged singing of a single hymn, the bereaved daughter wept afresh. The coffin was so tiny: she could not imagine it actually held the remnants of a life. She imagined her mother in there, sitting cramped like a small animal in hiding, squashed into that box the way she herself had once carried a pet mouse to school. There was a fine drizzle outside; the hair of the priest rose in a frizz, but he did not seem to mind. He enjoyed traditional funerals for the opportunity they gave him to raise his voice in prayer, the only chance in his current existence to remind the agnostics of the power of God and the futility of these little lives without Him. So he warned them in sonorous tones of our traditions of the graveside, warned them how the coffin must be lowered to the tune of his prayers and then they must each throw earth. Denied contact with her mother, Sylvie followed him closely, fascinated by the flowing surplice and the dash of colour in his sash. Boldly, she stepped up to the grave and peered down. The priest shielded her: this was no time for sharp words.

'In the midst of life we are in death: of whom may we seek succour, but of thee, O Lord?' He cast a meaningful glance at the twenty still gathered. Sylvie was gazing down into the trench, looking for worms, her eyes held by a bright skein of royal-blue wool which seemed to shine artificially against the grey-brown of the crumbled earth. She knew without being able to say that there was a hand holding the wool. In the middle of the space left for the coffin, she could see a footprint and on the other side, half submerged, a shoe. No-one else looked into the grave: all eyes turned elsewhere, even those indifferent to the deceased did not wish to examine the depth to which she would descend. Sylvie's gaze ranged the length and depth, looking for the other shoe, saw instead more threads of the same, blue wool, and then her whole, small, punchy little body arched itself into a piercing scream. Sylvie had no real idea of why she screamed as she was hoisted away, kicking as the prayer continued and the coffin descended effortfully, held by straps, everyone ignoring the extraneous sounds.

'. . . We therefore commit her body to the ground, earth to earth, ashes to ashes, dust to dust . . .'

'No!' Sylvie screamed. 'No! No! No!'

With a soul full of anguish and guilt and one hand strained with the dirt of the earth she had just thrown, Sylvie's mother turned back from the side of the grave and slapped her daughter on the face. The blow was automatic and the sound of it as loud as the silence which followed.

The current of the shrieking was abruptly stopped: the child's face was white with one dirty imprint to the left of her nose. Scooped into her father's arms, she did not turn the other cheek, but remained speechless for a minute more and silent until he had walked her back towards the entrance with his hand steadying her head against his shoulder. Then she muttered, 'No, Daddy, no, someone down there, Daddy. There is. Don't put the box on top, Daddy.' He cooed at her and patted her back, out of his depth and blushing for shame at the behaviour of his family in front of others. His anger embraced the whole world except his child, but it did not mean he listened to what she said. Out of the corner of his eye, he saw one mourner backing away from the edge of the crowd, a faintly familiar figure, looking towards him. He felt Sylvie stiffen in his arms and hold tighter.

'It's that man,' whined Sylvie. 'That one, the sing-songing man with the funny hands.'

'There, there,' he said. 'We'll all go home now, shall we? Nice cup of tea?'

In the early evening of Thursday, Rose sat in Debenhams' coffee shop, chewing her nails and letting her tea grow cold. She had raced down into the bowels of the Central Line to get here in time, and Margaret was late. Rose remembered the old lady

teaching her how rude it was to waste all those particles of someone else's life, by being late. Then she thought, with a greater
panic, how Margaret did practise what she preached, unfailingly,
and this was nothing to do with tardiness, accidents or bombs. She
simply wasn't coming. After that, Rose ceased to think in any
consistent way at all. What she felt among the plastic ferns and
wooden seats was merely a numbing hurt, followed by loneliness
and finally fear. Margaret hated her, had decided she did not want
to know her, had defected finally, did not care, had told her father
about this meeting. On this thought, Rose was unable to move,
even to pick up the cup. Shop tea, Margaret had said, not like I
make in front of my oh so cosy little fire. Telling Daddy all about
it. Oh no, surely she would never do that, could always, always
keep a secret. And she isn't a bitch.

Daddy. In court yesterday with his malevolent, pale blue eyes
and his tiny, destructive little self, his face like a coloured balloon,
but still his face, passing her, reaching out to touch her, surrounding her with the smell of his dirt and his curses. That was fear
incarnate, and yet she had pitied him too. As if she had not tried,
tried to extract his papers and put them in the shredder, as she
would the next time, so that their paths might never cross. But she
could not do it, could not leave Helen West to face the music, had
done her errands on Daddy's case like a good girl, and then hidden,
wrenchingly sick, among the graffiti of the public loo, where the
walls bore last week's legends. Level with her eyes as she sat staring,
there had been a fading felt-pen scrawl which said, poignantly, 'Is
there anybody out there?' and Rose knew there wasn't. Now that
Margaret had failed to arrive, she knew it even better.

Rose looked round, surreptitiously, beset with a brand-new
fear. Would Margaret have told her old friend Logo? Was he lurking round here now, waiting to follow her home to an address he'd
already found from a postmark? Was that why Granny had not
come, displacing one loyalty with another? It was dreadfully possible.

Rose felt safe in company, in shops and in large buildings. Dad
used to take her with him office cleaning: it somehow dictated her

present choice of destination. She picked up her bag with a degree of decorum she did not feel, catapulted down to the ground floor and bought a toothbrush and a shawl, waiting with bated breath to see if they were daft enough to take her overstretched credit card. Then she dived back on to the Central Line, still full of shoppers. At the other end she ran from the train, stopped at the hamburger shop on the corner and the off-licence next door just before it shut, spending her last pence. Then she bounded up the steps, past the comforting railings, to the office entrance where the night doorman sat blearily.

'I bought you something,' she said, handing him the bottle in blue paper. 'Oh, and I'm going to be working ever so late, don't mind me, will you?' He smiled, bemused. Rose tramped upstairs. There was something corrupt about earning a man's goodwill with a half-bottle of whisky, particularly a horrible, leery man like that, but it had worked between her mother and her father.

A chill began to descend on the place. Rose did not mind. The office was eccentric, but it was big and above all, it was safe.

Helen met Redwood in the corridor at about five. He was looking aimless and defeated and she found room to feel sorry for him. He did not see her until she was upon him and it was too late to turn back.

'What's new about the office thief?' she demanded. All of them had been ready to confer, then they got the message, Don't bother and don't ask why. It was her best-natured sharp tone, but he still shrank.

'Oh, nothing to report, I suppose, that's why,' he mumbled. 'No point in having you all sit down to tell you that. Besides, I'm busy, I've—'

'So you'll let the office saboteur ride his bike, will you?'

'What else can I do? No-one else has complained. I can't disrupt the whole ship with an official inquiry, we're sinking as it is.'

But you were ready to blame Rose to make it look as if you'd done your duty, Helen thought furiously. Sack someone to make it look as if you've tried.

'Won't do,' was all she said, firmly. Redwood scowled. Challenges only frightened him initially; after that he remembered to become aggressive.

'What do you mean, it won't do? It's got to do. But security's being tightened up, dramatically overhauled, electric locks, that sort of thing.'

'When?' she asked stolidly.

'When? Over the next month or so.' He was getting angrier the more defensive she made him feel. 'Look, if you don't like it, you don't have to work here. Or you can find out who or what is playing with the system. I give you my blessing. We've decided it might be some kind of computer virus—'

'Which also removes the paper? Clever little bug.'

'It fits the bill. But as I say, if you want to find out more, feel free.'

'All right, I shall. As long as you aren't busy blaming the clerks. I'll report back if I find the virus lurking in a cupboard, shall I?'

'Oh, very funny.'

They parted on almost friendly terms. Avoiding Dinsdale's room with a feeling of discomfort, Helen set off to find Rose. Their conversations in and out of court today had been all too brief, perfunctory almost, but Helen did at least know about darling Michael going to his parents' home that evening, and she had it in mind to grab Rose before she left, suggest a drink, a shop, or something to prevent their recently broken ice from forming all over again. Her own passionate curiosity for Rose was far from satisfied; it defied logic and had been there for a long time. It was Helen's unerring instinct for vulnerability in people who hid it by shouting. She stopped at the door of the clerks' room. Too late. The bird had flown, unaccustomedly early.

A note on the desk, defiant. 'Gone shopping.'

It didn't seem a bad idea at that. Helen was ludicrously calmed by crowds, warmed by lights, seduced by displays, could sit in a shop for hours. The tawdry splendours of Oxford Street beckoned and she moved towards them like a pilgrim.

She went down the escalator to the Central Line. It was late already, half six. The office was empty, her flat at home was empty, and she longed for that populated vacuum in between. It was an old escalator which protested at the weight of feet as she descended with a thinning stream of people at Holborn. Passing on the other side, ascending to the air and looking like a person distracted, was Rose, clutching a bag and staring straight ahead. Helen shouted and waved to no response. Other people looked, then kept their eyes fixed on the posters. 'Pregnant and happy? Fine', or other pictures describing the magic effects of alcohol, pizza, books and clothes, trundling by as they sniggered at Helen's gestures as if they were the sudden, funny aberration of a mad-woman.

Helen lost her taste for the shops.

Geoffrey Bailey realised that he missed things like shopping in this structured existence where all was found, but he did not miss it to any great degree. Shops had become so alien that when he and Ryan sat in the local hostelry which had become their regular haunt, with the same two, attractive women, he did not immediately realise that the older one was wearing something so obviously brand spanking new he fancied he could almost smell the tissue paper and see the marks of the hanger. The woman, called Grace, had a house near by: they'd been there before, why not again now? Plenty of drink in. The invitation had been sidestepped for a while until, with an operation which was so smooth as to be painless, they had seemed to transfer themselves from the snug of the pub to the splendours of her living room via the mechanism of Ryan's scented car which had acted rather like a time capsule. It was only when they sat on a moquette sofa, which Bailey both noticed and hated without quite knowing why, perhaps because it was so deep it immobilised him completely, that he realised what it was all about. He craved beer and skittles. Or the prospect of Helen, guiltily and noisily home from the Thursday shops to sit with her nose in papers on a worn, chintz settee while he sat reading a book in her armchair with its springs straining against his behind, not minding the habits of her furniture. Helen had a cat, so did he, both of them the independent, alley cat, beaten-up variety which could never have house room here. The impressions passed like quicksilver, leaving no visible mark on his face. Where he was now, there were three bedrooms upstairs, one each and one for their consciences, should any of these considerations apply. Bailey thought of the homework he should do before the rigours of tomorrow, remembered the opportunism of his relative youth and decided Grace wasn't such a bad alternative, conscience was soluble, she reeked of perfume and sympathy. He might not like her furniture, but she was from the same stable as himself with the same humour; she smelt of uncomplicated generosity.

At what point Ryan and his lady disappeared upstairs, Bailey did not quite gauge, midnight or thereabouts. 'I'm going to bed,' said Grace, with a yawn like a cat. 'I think you may have lost your lift back to school. You'd better stay. The bathroom's on the right at the top of the stairs. You can either come in with me or sleep on this thing.'

'Oh,' he said sheepishly. 'I'm sorry. I'm not—'

'Used to doing this?' She hesitated and he knew it was not feigned. 'Nor me. Which is why I'm wearing a new dress and being so brisk.'

He could not bear the risk of humiliating her and yes, he liked her. He liked a woman with an accent who spoke her mind and talked his own language.

'Yes, it's all right,' he said.

There was silence on the upstairs landing of this new house in a new estate full of picture windows mirroring closed lives. One of the rooms full of teddy bears gave witness to an absent child. The door to Mother's room was open, she was in there, taking off her new clothes. Bailey went into the bathroom. He was depressingly sober, depressingly helpless and he wanted to stay in there as long as possible.

The crash from downstairs hit him like a blow. His face, with all its multiple lines, stood solid as a map as he stared into the mirror with the fixity of a ghost. A door slammed. It took him several seconds to move and feel grateful he was still dressed. Out on the landing, Ryan's plump torso with the bottom half clad only in a fluffy towel, cannoned into his own thin and steely rib cage. It was bone meeting flesh; he knew Ryan's fist yearned to punch him for the stranger he was.

'Shit,' said Ryan. 'I think we got burglars.'

'Put some bloody clothes on, said Bailey. 'For Christ's sake.'

The stage-whispers alone could have won them an Oscar. Grace appeared at her door, the stage-left entrance in négligé somewhat impaired by her white face.

'Stay put, I would,' said Bailey, mildly. It was years since he had seen a woman deliberately *déshabillé* to please, an uncommonly pretty sight. She did as she was bid and shut the door. Ryan re-emerged, with an unbuttoned shirt, a jacket on top, trousers zipped as he moved, shoes, no socks and, as Bailey rightly sensed, no underpants.

Talk to me, Chief,' Ryan said in the same hoarse whisper. 'But make it loud.'

'What?'

'Make a noise. Sing or something.'

'We've got burglars.'

'Naa. This house might have burglars,' Ryan hissed, grabbing his arms. 'But we mustn't catch them. What do you want? A headline in the paper? Sing, will you? Give them time to get away.'

Bailey coughed, loudly. Coughing seemed to be infectious. Ryan coughed, but only as a preliminary to yelling, 'Is there any-body there?' in a voice so loudly artificial it made Bailey wince and then want to laugh. Then they went downstairs.

It was an awful room, Bailey thought sadly in the absence of its owner. A room which tried and failed to be all things at once, a comfort, a luxury, potted both inside and out. The glass doors led to a version of the tropics beyond. One of the palms had fallen through the window in nothing more than a fit of pique. Two huge plants lay embracing one another among broken glass.

'Thank Christ,' Ryan muttered fervently. 'It's only the wind. Time we were going. Sir.'

'In a minute,' said Bailey. 'In a minute.'

The women appeared as he was Sellotaping cardboard to the glass while Ryan swept up the broken fragments. They all did what they could whilst making the noises that go with the end of a party, laughing with a cup of coffee in one hand before, all desire spent, Ryan and Bailey left in a silent, cowardly posse.

'Sleep well,' said Bailey, something he said automatically to Helen if he should leave her late at night.

'I shall,' said the woman, smiling without a trace of bitterness. 'See you soon.'

Bailey blushed.

Sleep well, my sweet, be good tomorrow, awake refreshed, the aim of every man. Logo sat back on the cold kerb, gazing at the lights which still blazed in the windows of the building he surveyed. Didn't they ever turn off lights? Yes, they did. They turned off most lights on each floor, but forgot to extinguish them all. In the narrow street which flanked the back entrance to the vastness which he watched, Logo could see the silhouettes of clumsy furniture behind the net curtains of the huge ground-floor windows. There was a doorman dozing in there, but Logo knew how to get in; one or two sash-windows had already welcomed him, but he had doubted the point of the exercise. The offices of the Crown Prosecution Service whose address was so easy to elicit from the big-bottomed usher, or even from an old alibi notice, guarded itself against terrorists only. He was not one of those. Logo was only a man who wanted his daughter and had come to collect her from kidnappers. And, had he doubted her presence here, his doubts were soon destroyed. There were symmetrical windows in the basement below his eyes, all lined in a row, all dark save one, where the light flickered against dirty net curtains, and someone, against the back wall, was conducting a little concert.

She might have had head phones plugged into her ears: she was acting out a rhythm, but she knew about shadow play. There were long thin fingers in that room making an eagle against a yellow wall and Logo could see it, clearly.

He moved towards the railings, looking into the well of the basement, easy, with time, but a huge post office van rumbled by with radio blaring and stopped at the door. Logo retreated.

Tonight, tomorrow night, another night; rest up first, what did it matter when he was so close? He liked the expectation. The shadow play went on.

Now there was a rabbit: now, a church with a steeple.

She was still his own child.

CHAPTER TWELVE

The office building was the only place where Rose had never been afraid of the dark, but nothing could prevent her from missing the comfort of all her frills and teddy bears. Down in the bowels of the basement, she had been able to select from a number of rooms, each more private than the next. The cabin she chose out of this luxurious suite was the size of a cupboard with a smeared sash-window below the railings which flanked the front door of the building. The top of her head was well below the outside wall, the glass so dirty and the view of the street so restricted, the feeling of safety was complete. The yellow-painted walls were lumpy with layers; the stone floors had been painted with red tile paint, the whole brutal effect subdued by age. Outside and down the hall, the central-heating boiler for the whole vast palace hummed with harmonic fury behind a locked door, clicking disapproval from time to time. In the subterranean space, Rose felt she might have been in the bowels of a ship, with all the reassurance of noise and the vicarious life of the engine to chase away ghosts. Lighting in the cabin took the form of a single bulb hanging dolefully, augmented by the anglepoise lamp Rose had borrowed from Helen's room to illuminate her bed. Here, the mattress consisted of piles of old papers taken from store and formed into an oblong, covered with an abandoned curtain shaken free of spiders and on this makeshift arrangement Rose lay and aspired to sleep after playing games with shadows on the wall. Fully clothed except for shoes, covered with a winter coat and the shawl, she turned off the lamp into a darkness which was suddenly complete and then, before terror struck, her eyes adjusted to the oblong of light from the window and her ears to the roar of the boiler, and she was able to close her eyes.

But at 5 a.m., uncomfortable and cold, the stupidity of it all sank in. Sleeping in a dungeon on a mattress of paper with sweat gathering in her armpits and ice round her feet, Rose thought, So this is what I have become. A vagrant, a dosser, moving my shell each day with no good reason, always looking for a new corner because some little old man is chasing me. Down in the basement in the bleakest reaches of the night, Rose could not begin to congratulate herself for what she had done with her life to date, nor perceive even one of her extraordinary achievements. She was literate, presentable, employable; she was a mass of scars but she was not a cripple, and all she could see of herself was a snivelling thing, hiding in a cellar like a rat, the way she had hidden out with men. In the last analysis it was the terrible vision of what Michael would think if he saw her thus which drove her to groan. She thought of Helen waiting all week for her to talk without prompting. She thought of Dad in court and cringed.

She could sense the wind outside, smell the rain. From the well between the railings and the wall there came the steady sound of dripping water from the distant eaves above. The boiler burst into a new phase of life, then reduced its volume to a sinister muttering. Rose felt dirty. At six, she ascended the back stairs, feeling her way, dying for daylight, found the washroom on her floor where all the clerks ran to hide. Ever fastidious, she stripped, lingered over her ablutions with the powerful office soap and the harsh paper towelling. Upstairs, the silence was astounding apart from the minute sounds of her own effort, until she heard footsteps. Footsteps and a cough, which made her suppress her own. A pair of feet, walking along the corridor outside, unhurried but purposeful, receding shoes with steel caps sounding on the worn bits of carpet. Rose put her damp hand on the door of the washroom, opened it a crack, just in time to see a slim figure disappearing through a set of old swing-doors at the end. The doors were heavy: he was forced to pause long enough for her to recognise the set of his shoulders and the colour of his hair. Mr Dinsdale Cotton, carrying a couple of files, a sight which sent her mind snapping into sharp connections. Rose knew in that moment the identity of the office thief. She was unable to move, looking out into the empty space with the door still juddering at the end, paralysed with anger. Of course Rose knew about someone purloining the files, fouling the system, getting cases deliberately lost, she was equally well aware that the inefficiency of her own team had been casually blamed, none of them told anything, all under suspicion, herself in particular. She did not need Helen West to hint by way of warning: she wasn't a fool; she had tried to tell Redwood about it long before, but had been told to make an appointment and she wasn't going to do that, let them rot if they wouldn't listen. So what had she done? Told Dinsdale, once, weeks before. She trusted Dinsdale, presumed he would act, tell his buddy Helen all about it at least, but even when she knew he had done no such thing, she had still trusted him.

What time was it? Half-past six, still the middle of the night and she had grit under her eyeballs. Rose carefully made up her face in the mirror, to offset the effect of her crumpled clothes. It wouldn't be the first time she turned up to work looking like this. She shivered as she thought of nights in the section house, surprised herself by thinking, You've come a long way, Rose, in a short time; don't go back, will you? Thinking of favours, she also reckoned she owed Helen West one: she'd better blow the gaff on her bloody boyfriend before anything went further between them. It was strange how one problem displaced another; in Rose's life that had been the history of her sanity.

Outside the loo, she coughed loudly to warn anyone else of her presence. She also whistled. The cough was still painfully real while the whistle was tuneless with nervous artificiality.

Even with this complication, it was still safer in here. Her gran had always wanted her to work in a place like this.

Three hours until Helen came in? Rose had the feeling that once she started to talk, she might not be able to stop.

It was a rain-soaked, blustery, purple-sky kind of day where the sun would never rise and the winter was interminable. The same kind of savage day in which Helen had encountered Mr Logo on the rooftop. She remembered him as she woke on Friday, for no reason except for the rain slapping against the window and her own, foul temper. No phone call from Bailey. All right, she'd unplugged the answerphone, but it was still his fault. She guessed by now he wasn't returning today, wondered if he ever would, didn't much mind; she wanted time to slouch, think and be a slut. Far fewer of us, Helen thought, swinging herself out of bed with the usual violence, need a constant man than any of them ever imagine. Three days a month would do nicely.

It was only when she crashed into the bathroom wall while reaching for a toothbrush that she realised that the symptoms of this depressive malaise were not merely mental. Her tonsils rose to close her throat like a portcullis; toothpaste tasted fiery; she felt as if her neck had been held to a flame and yet her face was unnaturally pale with deep red rings under the eyes. Rose's cough had been passed like a gift. Put make-up over that lot and she'd look like a corpse dolled up for a funeral. Take the day off *again*? Who cares? Who'll miss you? Point taken, they won't even notice, apart from Dinsdale, lovely dangerous man with the silly name. That fixed it. She wasn't going anywhere: she could make up the work before Monday. Helen sat instead in her basement living room with the dirty winter windows sluiced by the snarling rain, watching other workday feet go briskly by while she considered all her duties and personal obligations, finding them too numerous to contemplate without screaming. By reflex action, she phoned Rose on the number she'd noted down from the phone inside the girl's house (like the sneak she really was), simply to ask Rose to present her excuses at work (like the lazy coward she also really was). Only to find a girl who said hallo, nicely, but Rose hadn't been home last night and wasn't there now, and Helen found herself saying, 'Fine, it doesn't matter,' while feeling that little jolt of alarm which was akin to electric shock, then sitting back in the chair, to watch more feet.

Her cat came in from the great outdoors via the flap, wet and disgusted, sniffed at her feet in pure cupboard love and disdained to come closer. All right then, one phone call like a prisoner in

custody allowed to say where he is, and then she would wait since
she was in no position to do anything but fall over. Story of her
life. Nobody loved her and she deserved nothing better.

'Then came the woman in the dawning of the day, and fell down
at the door of the man's house, and her hands were upon the
door of the threshold.

'And when he came into his house, he took a knife and laid
hold on his concubine, and divided her together with her bones,
into twelve pieces, and sent her into all the coasts of Israel.'

Logo was well acquainted with those biblical passages which
smelt of blood, while he chose to ignore all those which favoured
forgiveness over hideous retribution. His present serenity owed
much to his loving contemplation of blood as well as to the
lethargy of his limbs following all the dreadful exertions of the last
thirty hours. Lifting heavy weights, lugging, lying, spying, mourning at a graveside, and suddenly some kind of end was in sight,
only he was not sure what the end was. The reverie was broken by
someone knocking at the door. He stood behind it and shouted,
'Who's there?'

'Mr Logo?' Assuming it was, the voice went on, young, brisk
and efficient. 'Dr Smith, Mr Logo. Only your neighbour,
Margaret Mellors, had an appointment to see me yesterday
evening. I sent her a letter about the date for her hip operation,
only she didn't turn up. She gave you as her next of kin; you
wouldn't happen to know where she is, would you?'

'I am not my neighbour's keeper,' yelled Logo.

'I didn't expect you were. But do you know where she is? I
don't want her to miss this chance—'

'Margaret who?'

The voice went away. He was suddenly afraid. People would
come looking for Margaret, of course they would, a popular
woman with friends, which in the case of someone over seventy,
meant a visitor a day. He'd left the kitchen tidy, locked the door,
thrown away the key. No, no, he would say, he hadn't seen her for
a day or two, and it wouldn't be the shadow of a lie. And where

did you see her last? Knitting, sir, only knitting. Oh yes, he could imagine the question and it made him put his fist to his face and giggle out loud.

Today he'd make amends to the old dear, put flowers on her grave if he could find something suitable left on another and no-one was watching. Something to do on the way to work; he supposed he had better turn out, knowing as he did how far to push the line of absenteeism and today was a day for scoring points, what with the weather like this and everyone else playing truant. Then he'd rest, maybe take a long walk later . . . Logo rumbled the old trolley through the nine-o'clock streets, glaring straight ahead, his substitute for singing, frightening people another way. A man needed a tribe. To be disenfranchised by blood or sin was a terrible fate. Eenie had done that to him. She had made him the man who always walked alone, with others making their signs against the devil in a dozen different languages as they passed him. She had consigned him to hell. He paused by the graveyard gate. There was a man by the distant grave with a little girl, a smart-looking man with a suit, holding a bright show of daffodils in the one hand and the child's gloved paw in another. Then the man stooped and put his arm round the child's waist, intimately. See? Logo crooned to himself. Look at her flirting. Look at him! We all do it.

Daffodils, Rose thought, just daffodils. They were suddenly in tight-budded profusion on barrows near the office, bursting from buckets by the Underground, lining the street. They had all laughed today, must be the promise of spring, Rose their cheer-leader, cracking jokes, mimicking the bosses, flying round, sharp and brittle as a thorn, hooting and yelling, hoovering work like a machine, flirting on the phone and making eyes at men. Everyone loved it. Rose on insolent form made the day go quicker, and as she led the gang out for sandwiches, the daffodils stood to attention along with the man on the stall, mesmerised by four noisy girls. Rose stopped and stared back.

'What you looking at?' she demanded.

'You, darling,' he answered.

'Cost you a free bunch of them.'

He gave them a flower apiece. Rose pretended to eat it. 'Lovely,' she said. They all snorted.

Anyone would think I was normal, she thought. Thinking, If I went round to Aunty West's flat with a bunch of daffs, would she let me in? Why's the silly cow off sick, when I need her? Promise me she won't mind. Can I please, please trust her? I'm not going back and I've got to tell her about that little fucker anyway. The bank machine ate her cashcard, a punishment for overspending. She winked at the girls and cashed a cheque at the counter without anyone being shot or yelling stop thief, and they huddled out like conspirators. In the middle of the afternoon, because of something else decided in the nether regions of the night, about how she couldn't face his parents, not as she was, she phoned Michael. Her heart thumped like a bass drum when she heard his voice, but she'd already made it into a public joke, about parents and everything, what a bore it would be, so she was brisk, said she couldn't do Saturday, she had to work. The lie was apparent; he was hurt and offended, but she was on a course of action she couldn't change, not even to avoid the corners. She threw a file across the room, let the papers spill out like confetti, teased her hair into spikes, chewed her pigtail, shouted some more. Put more files in the goods lift beyond the door, pressed the red button and shouted down, 'Egg and chips twice, please!' Dreading the ending of the working day, wanting it too, and it was still raining.

Enough stolen from the bank for the taxi fare and three bunches of daffs. Dark at five forty-five when she rang the bell to Helen's flat, and when there was no immediate reply and she was shivering on the doorstep, the old terror struck again. Until Helen appeared, looking like an alien without her make-up, letting her in, coughing like a car with a flat battery, but welcoming, oh yes. No fuss. Put your coat on the radiator and shove that cat off the chair, let's have a drink, excuse the way I look, all in one sentence. After that it was all right. It really was all right. More than all right, after all this time, to dump some of the shit on another pair of shoulders. She never could have done it if Helen hadn't told her about biting that bloke.

There was an interruption around seven when Bailey phoned. They'd covered quite a lot of ground by then, one bottle empty, a bit dry for Rose's taste, but not bad, and then it was Helen's turn to play the fool. Making faces at Rose while holding the phone. No, he wouldn't be coming home this weekend. As if I didn't know, Helen whispered with her hand over the mouthpiece. Neither mentioned the other's neglect. Bailey was always tense on the phone, sounding like someone in a call box with a queue outside.

'Other fish to fry?' Helen was asking lightly, while Rose took lessons. Truth to tell, Helen was feeling a whole lot better since Rose had arrived, deeply troubled but a damn sight more useful and therefore better. At least she and Rose coughed in unison.

'No,' he said, equally lightly. 'Work. They work us like slaves.'

'Can I ask you something?' He half hoped it would be something personal, but it wasn't.

'If a chap has paid someone to get his drink-driving charge dropped, by say stealing the papers or bribing the copper, what do you reckon it would be worth?'

He thought for all of a second. 'Oh, two, three thousand, if his car was vital. It would depend on the alcohol reading, who he was and how greedy the person was he was paying. Helen, are you all right? Why are you asking?'

'Oh, a little academic problem.' More faces at Rose.

'Helen, if you go around asking questions, you get what I get, black eyes. What are you up to?'

'Nothing. See you when I do. Have fun.' The alarm in his voice was revenge enough.

Bailey remained as he was, furious. He was angry for her being nice about his absence when he wanted her to shout, I still need you, come home. For leaving him free when he needed chains. For not screaming at him, as if last weekend's sweetness and closeness had counted for nothing. He needed to be told, for God's sake, he needed that all the time. She acted as if reassurance was her sole prerogative. Ah well. Then he phoned Grace.

It was the room which soothed Rose as much as Helen's languorous stillness when she was listening, but then it hadn't been dramatic reactions she had wanted. A room with warm red walls lined with pictures, all differently framed, and books standing crooked, nothing new, no furniture without wear and tear, the gleam of mahogany, a worn carpet but densely coloured and comfortable, an ash-littered grate below guttering flames, litter and learning, something to look at all the time when you didn't want to meet eyes. What was it Helen was saying? Rose felt her lids twitching, watching the fire after talking for two hours.

'People care for you, you know,' Helen said, bowling coke at the grate and making a mess. 'An awful lot more than you think, so phone the flatmates, will you, stop them getting alarmed.'

'OK.' Rose was enough at home to take orders.

'And it goes without saying you can stay here as long as you like, you'd be doing me a great favour,' Helen added in a cunning throwaway line. 'Only there's nothing to eat until I go out to the corner shop. There's never anything to eat here. It's you ribbing me about carting home all those potatoes. I've never been the same since.'

'I'll go,' Rose struggling to find energy, thinking of the dark.

'No you won't. I've got a cough, but it isn't terminal. Open this bottle will you, we don't have to get up in the morning. Back in a minute.'

She wanted time to digest some of Rose's revelations. She had taken them calmly. Rose didn't want outrage; she wanted belief. Abuse, betrayal, the deep, murky waters of systematic cruelty, all described, but no names, no pack drill, simply facts, no weeping please, no cries of horror. Rose needed empathy, she needed love, therapy, she couldn't do it all on her own, no-one could. She wanted to be normal, so Helen acted normally, a lawyer listening with quiet credulity. Out in the street she wanted to scream with pity and rage.

The wind had lessened, so the trees now swayed elegantly rather than furiously, whispering not hissing without their leaves. It was a street of handsome houses where people walked day and night, confidently, and despite her history here, Helen had forged a sense of safe belonging. She wondered as she walked down her own road to her own parade of shops, what it was like for Rose to live without that blanket. Everyone needs a tribe.

Redwood had thought twice about staying late in the office on this particular Friday, since it did not do, in the current climate, to act in any way out of the ordinary. Whatever was going on here, he was sure he did not want to know, but his habits of insecurity could only die hard and he needed this sneaking about as much as he needed the evening drink when he got home. And there was something he had to do, could only do with the place empty, and that was somehow secrete or destroy all those case records which had got inside his desk as the result of expeditions like these. All he had achieved this week was procrastination, shuffling jobs around and the invention of another form which they would all accept in the end provided he never had a meeting to discuss it. In the meantime, he had this worthless cargo to unload which, if found, would brand him as a sneak or worse.

His idea of upstairs, downstairs was sound as far as people were concerned, but he was less good at geography. He aspired to the discovery of a sort of incinerator device such as he had in his garden, and might otherwise belong in the cellar of a place like this. The building had a basement, didn't it? Files came up and down from somewhere like prisoners being shown daylight from the hold of a ship. Somehow Redwood imagined the paper moving itself into the ancient goods lift on their floor without human guidance; he also imagined that everyone here hated the place equally and that none of them ever ventured to explore if they could avoid it. Armed with cunning and nervousness he kept on descending stairs and wondered if he would ever find his way back.

It was dark down here, oh yes, extremely, but there were also lights and it was warm. By the time he rounded the corner to where the boiler was locked away, humming loudly, he already felt he was about to meet a ferocious animal and was glad there was no incinerator to be found. This building has *too much heat*, he decided, lights left on everywhere, disgraceful, and too much hot water, with the noise that thing made, a fiver a breath; he could do something about that, surely. Now, where could he hide these notebooks since they were not for burning. If he took them home his wife would notice them.

Blundering about he found a small room, just off a large empty space, and stopped in surprise. He could have sworn he heard someone throwing something towards the window. There on the floor was an anglepoise lamp plugged into the single point, recognisable anywhere. Helen West's lamp, old but coveted, and what was it doing down here? Redwood took the lamp, meaning to return it. On his way to search for the stairs he found a suitably old and disused radiator behind which he stuffed Rose's notebooks. Nobody who counted came down here; it wasn't even very clean.

Puffing up the stairs, confused by the alien regions of the first floor and the constant choice of exit, he thought about the lamp. Wait a minute, he wouldn't put it back, a dead giveaway of Friday-night sneaking. Some might call it evidence. Redwood was confused. He left the lamp in his own room: somehow that seemed better and less incriminating, although he didn't know why.

The doorman was not at his post, but there was nothing unusual in that and the overhaul of security didn't begin for a week. Redwood let himself out of the front door, feeling like the keeper of a castle but not the king, never too keen on signing out and signing in anyway, especially on Fridays. Clutching to himself the important-looking briefcase containing very little, he strutted down the steps. Straight into a little man standing in the street, rubbing his wrists, appearing out of the dark, bowing.

'Excuse me, sir . . .'

'Oh, sorry,' said Redwood, sidestepping and striding on,

momentarily afraid until he reflected that muggers weren't usually middle aged and knee high to grasshoppers, even he could work that out, it said so in the files; all of which occurred to him in the first two seconds of his flight down the street before he realised that the little man was following, running to keep up.

'Excuse me, sir, excuse me . . .' Redwood wished people never said that. It created an instant obligation.

'What?' he barked, turning, holding the briefcase in both arms like a shield. 'What do you want, man? I haven't any money and I've got a train to catch.' Both were true. The face, on a level with his briefcase, looked harmless and smiling, but showed signs of having been in a fight. He relaxed a little.

'I don't want nothing, if you'll excuse me, sir, but I was waiting out here for my daughter. She works alongside you, sir, said she'd meet me here . . . I didn't like to ring the bell, she must be working late.'

'Name of?' Redwood barked.

'Enid . . .' the man hesitated, but Redwood was already barking back. He knew all the names off by heart, but could never quite connect them with the right faces.

'No-one left in there at all. Even the doorman's asleep, at eight o'clock, I ask you,' he added for good measure. 'And no-one named Enid at any time of day. Wrong building.'

He marched off. Logo watched. My, weren't they all such dreadful liars.

'Her granny called her Rose!' he shouted after the retreating figure. 'Rose!'

Redwood looked back at the little figure standing by the railings, but did not stop.

CHAPTER THIRTEEN

Margaret Mellors' doctor was in the area and tried to call on her patient for a second time late on Saturday morning. Monday was the deadline for the old dear to claim both her bed and her new life, otherwise she went back to the bottom of the queue. Looking through the kitchen window, the doctor could see a clean and tidy room, the fire not cleared and a knitting basket beside it. There was nothing in any of it to raise the slightest suspicion. Walking back out of the alley to her car, she met Sylvie and mother bound for the house she had just left, her attention drawn by the screaming child being tugged along like a reluctant bulldog, feet skidding, snarling between barks. It was a quiet sort of street, apart from that, the doctor reflected; a pity it was so close to the football stadium.

'Excuse me, do you happen to know Mrs Mellors?'

'Yes.' The reply was tired, but affirmative. The child stopped making a noise and began to pick her nose.

'Only I've been trying to get hold of her. Looks like she's gone away, perhaps.'

'She never goes away,' said the mother in a voice flat with disappointment. 'Never.'

'Any idea where she might be then?'

'Around here somewhere. She always is. Have you tried next door?'

They looked at one another meaningfully.

'She's dead,' the child piped up. 'Dead and buried.'

'That's enough from you, thank you very much.' The mother was apologetic, recognising a doctor, and suddenly chatty. 'Sorry, she's very morbid. We took her to a funeral, a big mistake.'

'Oh, maybe not. Look, when did you see Mrs Mellors last?'

'Yesterday,' the child said. The mother turned to her.

'Are you sure?'

'No.' Sylvie giggled.

'I don't know,' said the mother despairingly, in reference to what the doctor was not entirely sure. 'Two days? Three days?' Her brow cleared. 'Before Mum's funeral, she was fine then.'

The doctor went back to her surgery after four more visits. Winter was a terrible time for death. From there she called the police.

When Logo came home at about two, they were all over him like a rash, doubling up, he supposed, on him and football duty. There was that lippy little bastard with the hammer fists and the weak mouth, another callow youth and a big darkie. My, my, Margaret would have loved it, always had liked men, liked everyone, come to that. She would have adored a whole houseful to make tea for and feed home-made biscuits, might even have offered them one of her everlasting, ever-shapeless sweaters. He told them as much.

PC Williams was twitching and eyeing him sideways, waiting for him to say something provocative and refer to the yellow tide-marks of his bruises, but the other two were as civil as the kind he usually encountered and Logo held his tongue. Acted as Mr Meek and Mild: no he didn't know where she was, he wasn't his neighbour's keeper (the phrase was becoming tired), but he'd like to know, of course, if they should find out. She was a good old soul and they often called on one another, but no, not in the last day or so, he had to confess.

'So your fingerprints would be in her kitchen, if we looked, would they?' said Williams, tauntingly. Logo looked at him, all wide-eyed innocence.

'Of course,' he said. 'I often brought in her coal.'

They'd have a job finding cause for a search warrant. Old ladies were allowed to go on walkabout, just like young ones. The boys were only there with their bristling radios and razzamatazz to make sure she hadn't fallen over in the bath. Once they'd heard how able-bodied she was, they didn't seem to have much else to do now they'd shouldered down her door. There was very little damage, a skill they had. Logo helped them refix the lock and showed them where Margaret kept her spare key, like the fool she was, hanging on a piece of string inside the letter box. It made them feel idiots for all that wasted effort and not thinking first. I thought you learned things in training school, he told them, only you don't know anything about the habits of the old. To compound his subtle insults, he waved them goodbye like passing royalty, hoping someone in the street would see he was on such friendly terms, like the actions of someone who really did help a neighbour with her knitting.

But they would be back; it was obvious they would be back. They'd come back last time, like some recurrent disease, saying, Sorry to bother you, acting as if they were too, but that time he'd been crying all over the place, weeping his cotton socks off, crazy with agitation for the loss of his wife and daughter, and they really had been sorry for him then. Now he reckoned he had two lines of defence to stop them coming into his house, the first being that they wouldn't like the smell of it (it was beginning to get that ammonia-tinged, fusty scent), any more than he liked theirs and the second was he could prevaricate as long as he wanted because there was nothing to hide. But he didn't want that PC Williams and he didn't want attention, and besides, he was really tired. The football crowd would imprison him indoors if he stayed with all their racket. The best thing to do would be to go away, just for the weekend. He knew where; like father, like daughter, he knew exactly where.

I brought her up to be cunning, he said to himself sorrowfully, standing in the backyard; made her sly and fond of the dark and good at getting into things, clever with her hands. He sniggered loudly at that, still revelling in his triumph with the officers. Only once before had he encountered so many and not even been arrested. *Oh Lord, forgive them for they know not what they do.*

Without the trolley, as he had discovered on recent perambulations, he was first without an alibi, second without ballast. He found himself swaying from side to side and not quite sure what to do with his hands. Today, he was restless after three steps, turned round, went back indoors and for some obscure reason, changed his clothes from one very dirty set to one less dirty. The black funeral jacket he had worn when he went to see Margaret last, a little grimy, not bad, but the lapels covered in white dust which seemed to have penetrated the lining with a sweet smell. Logo punched his chest and the powder billowed. He only tried that trick once. The trousers were cleanish jeans, the shirt he left as was, only worn three days in the last week, maybe it went with the jacket, he couldn't remember. He liked both for the wafts of scent they sent over his head. Walking down the road in his training shoes, he buried his nose in his armpit and kept it there, nice. As well as the smell he carried a scarf and one of Margaret's home-knit sweaters hung round his neck. The combined effect, along with his open donkey jacket, made him look and feel substantially fat, a man who ate well. That reminded him about bread being the staff of life, so he bought some and gnawed it out of a paper bag. Stopping at another shop for three bars of chocolate, he worked out that the lack of a good pie might explain why he was so twitchy. He'd given up going to the pubs since acquiring his bruises and even drink had lost its appeal.

When he got there, though, after the long walk, he wished he'd bought some booze. He looked up and down and decided he liked the railings in particular. Shining black, a row of spears, including the gate he had discovered before, still to the touch, but movable, with an impressive padlock holding a chain so loosely his thin self could sidle through the gap. The well of the moat was slimy with water. In the shallow pools created by three days' gusty rain, a pigeon bathed, cooing. 'Shoo,' he said, 'fuck off, or I'll sing to you,' and as it struggled into flight with the grace of a slow torpedo, Logo felt beset, as he had all day, by the endless desire to laugh. He paddled through puddles underneath the steps to what looked like a grand entrance for trade, down the side. A delivery door, secure as the crown jewels, a window into the basement which was not. He knew all about offices, from having cleaned them. Inside, it was warm as toast.

Rose was sorry in the morning, for having said so much. She woke up with a feeling of emotional indigestion, worse than any hangover she had ever known. A pint of wine hadn't done this to Rose; she had coped with a pint of spirit before now, and last night's ration had gone down like water, but it wasn't right to talk so much and eat another person's food. Not that she hadn't talked to people before about her life; to do so was another clue to sanity, she'd found. But it had always been in dribs and drabs and mainly to strangers, because that was like talking to a wall; they wished you luck and you knew you'd never see them again. Anyway she'd never opened her big mouth as wide as this. Helen and she slept late; Rose had got up in the middle of the night to find all the lights still on, which was comforting, and had gone back to bed in Helen's small and barred spare room, thinking, I could stay here for ever; it even beats the office for safety, but with daylight, it seemed less secure and her own position untenable. She might have gone before Helen was up if she had known how to unlock the door and her sense of shame had not frozen her will, and the boiler hadn't twinked into life and made the place even cosier, so she stayed put.

Helen had woken, coughing like a dead engine, wondering what Rose might think. She didn't know what it was like to be sexually abused, but she did know what it was like to feel violent and she certainly knew the deep dark shame of telling.

'Christ,' she said, slumping at the kitchen table in a dressing gown which cheered Rose for its sheer age. Will you look at that thing, she was thinking; even her own was better, and she was up and dressed, far too wide awake for comfort, with that guarded look over her face like a visor. 'Christ,' Helen repeated, 'I do feel ashamed of myself. Will you promise me, Rose, you'll never repeat to anyone what I told you last night, all that stuff about fancying Dinsdale and my sex life before, during and after Bailey, and about being frightened of the dark? Promise?

Blackmail me until the money runs out, could be soon, but don't tell.'

It was a bit of a comic turn with exaggerated gestures; Rose saw through it but smiled, the guarded look retreating. She has an extraordinary face, thought Helen; a face which turns from hunted to haunted to hard and insolent and then into the softest and most vulnerable beauty you ever saw. I wish I had a daughter. Looking at what had happened in the life of this mother's child she thought again, perhaps not. Helen had often felt maternal, but it was mostly applied towards adults.

'Instant coffee or the real knee-jerk variety? Got both, usually have the latter. We've got things to sort out.'

Rose liked the briskness. It made her meek all over again.

'We've got to go and get some clothes for you. I meant it about staying here, by the way, don't think I was just being polite, so you need stuff, though you're welcome to mine.'

Rose looked at the dressing gown, like some sort of old carpet. 'No thanks.'

'And after that,' Helen went on, 'I thought we might go and see your adopted gran—'

'No,' said Rose, panicking. 'He might be in. He'll see us.'

'So? I'm big and ugly. I bite people and—'

'You don't know how he hates me,' Rose said. 'You really don't.' She was aware now how ridiculous it seemed in the cold light of day to harbour such fantasies of persecution, for which she could produce so little evidence. It was ludicrous to expect anyone else to accept that one small man could loom so large and be every- where at the same time.

'All right,' said Helen, 'we'll drive. Cruise by.' Nobody cruises by in your car, Rose thought, specially not the way you drive it. 'You can duck down and tell me what to look for.'

That was better. 'Do you think,' Helen continued, 'you could speak his name? I mean his surname? You haven't told me that.'

'Darvey,' Rose muttered.

'It isn't Darvey. I know Darvey isn't your real name. Don't ask me why I know, but I know. You just don't answer to Darvey easily enough. I bet you've got a really silly name, as silly as Dinsdale's. You just want to keep it secret.' She was making toast in that horrible dressing gown, busying herself.

Oh why couldn't she guess? She'd had enough clues.

'My mother's name,' Rose snapped. 'She used to call me Rose and her name was Darvey.'

'Which brings us,' said Helen, pouring coffee, 'to the vital point. We want to find your mum. We want your father rendered harmless.'

Oh, help me, Rose thought. Could no-one ever understand how her own father could never be rendered thus? And would Helen never see, without actually being told, how it was that the idea of her father being punished or imprisoned was not pleasant either? So what if the talk last night had all been about hatred and fear and hunting, it had still failed to include all the sneaking parts, the dreadful bond of blood which even while fearing him did not want him tortured either and could not abide him covered in bruises. That was what she was afraid to admit.

'So,' Helen was continuing with the same briskness, 'I think that means we should go to the police and get the whole thing looked at again. To find out what went on, where your mum went. And report your father.'

'That means Michael would have to know.' Rose was faltering, looking for the excuse which Helen might find easiest to understand.

'Not necessarily, and besides, if you're going anywhere with Michael, he'll have to know.'

Rose took one of Helen's cigarettes. They coughed in concert. It didn't do to be too sensible. The nicotine made Rose dizzy, yet cleared her head. 'I think I want to wait a day or two for that,' she said in her firmest voice so far. 'Can we clear up the Dinsdale thing first? If I help sort that out, I'll feel I've done something. Feel better. Stronger.'

'Fine,' said Helen, thinking, Don't push the girl, let her do things her own way. 'I've been thinking about that too. Dinsdale. We could go to the office, pull every file he's had in the last year, cross index it to drunk drivers, see if we can find a pattern.' The Dinsdale side of things was sad, distressing and guilt creating: she wanted it over and done with. 'Only I can't work that bloody computer.'

'I can,' said Rose.

Nothing happened quickly. The car would not start without an hour's persuasion. Another hour was spent collecting two of Rose's teddy bears, a ton of cosmetic equipment and, as an after-thought, more clothes. Then Rose changed her mind, said she did want to drive by the house which had once been her home, feeling suddenly braver. They were silent as they covered the two miles in the unhealthy-sounding car; Rose terrified it would stop and leave them marooned on Dad's territory, but she dared not say, nor even state to herself the reasons for sitting like a stiff wooden sol-dier. In case she saw Gran hobbling down the street, alive and well. Or saw Mum, as usual with a shopping basket. She wanted Helen to guess, from the address she must have noted half a dozen times, who her father was without her having to say it out loud, and so save Rose feeling so resentful that Helen hadn't worked it out already. But it was a Saturday afternoon, football season. The road was blocked off, the surrounding streets triple parked, noth-ing moving until the end of the game. Rose heaved a sigh of relief. Now they could go to the office, postpone the issue, and the office was safe.

Logo squatted down on his haunches in the basement, winded by the warmth, disorientated and aware of the discomfort of the knife which lay inside his torn trouser pocket against his thigh, hooked on to his belt. Margaret's best kitchen knife, useful for cheese. There were footsteps upstairs. He scuttled to a window facing the railings, craned upwards to see if someone was leaving, but no door slammed. The footsteps were so muffled they were almost infinitesimal and as they stopped he thought he could hear the dis-tant murmurings of a television. Football, he guessed: the bastard doorman hypnotised for a couple of hours. He thought of those big arc lights for the winter games, thought how gloomy it was down here with the feeble supply of daylight fading and the railings gleaming wetly above. Logo began to explore. Empty rooms and rooms full of paper, dull little alcoves and meaningless passageways, a distant humming; he liked it a lot. There was a fire-detecting device winking and whirring after twenty steps in one direction and after that he encountered the boiler-room door and wondered how the place seemed to be full of such strange, heavy-breathing animals, but apart from these, quieter than a graveyard. He found a set of narrow stairs and next to that, a lift in the wall for goods, with the shutter doors open. This piece of equipment delighted him in particular. There were a couple of dozen files on the floor of the thing: he threw these to one side and squeezed himself in. Cosy, like the size of his trolley, an excellent hiding place for a little man, if a little cramped. The thought of Margaret fluttered into his mind and then out. He uncurled himself and continued to wander round. Paper, miles of paper, it would make a good fire. He liked the idea of that, but on reflection, decided it was the wrong kind of paper, and he was an expert on rubbish, it wouldn't burn easily.

Now he was here, he realised he had nothing to do and although it was late afternoon, night-time was a long way off. He sat on the edge of the lift, surveyed the stairs to the upper floors, listened to the boiler, ate one bar of chocolate with loud smacking noises, finished it with a sigh and took off his coat. He wanted to sing for this sense of safety and completeness, tinged with excitement: my, my, so Eenie came to work here on Monday, sometimes stayed over, hadn't she done well. But the chocolate made him thirsty, he needed a source of water, some cover in case the present warmth did not persist, and he needed a place to pee. None of that was available on this level as far as he could see, just paper. The stairwell beckoned; the wooden banister felt warm to the touch. He ascended in his best training shoes, silent, still wanting to laugh. There was a game he had in mind. That woman, the one he'd scared on the court rooftop, the one who had let him off the other day, who had the nerve to pity him, she worked in here too, she said. He could find her room if he wanted, use that as a toilet, show her: wipe his bottom on her chair. The stairs went on up to the ground floor, led into a corridor which fanned from the foyer. Behind a closed door facing him, the sound of the television was louder. Full of impudence Logo knocked, ready to run, although it had been a quiet tap; he felt like playing games, but there was no response. He danced a jig where he stood, remembered the desire to urinate, found a door marked 'Women' and inside there he rationed his own relief, saving it gleefully, and flushed the chain without thinking. Still no response from the TV room. Onwards and upwards, having crossed the foyer and found a grander sweep of stairs, he progressed, walking down each corridor on each floor in turn until finally he was lost. That distressed him, but only a little. Those that are lost shall be found, he told himself, and there, like a message from the New Testament, was another version of the same goods lift, staring him in the face, like home. Logo realised he had gone full circle. He suddenly fancied a ride in that thing, not the big conventional lift which he had also seen, marked 'Out of order'; all he had to do, surely, was go straight back down, if he wanted, and he'd be back where he had started, and whatever his boldness, he knew he wanted a way out, as well as a warm and quiet place to sleep. He pressed the red button; the lift whined up to join him. Here it was even warmer.

Logo looked into a large room with a grand chair, big desk, very tidy, organised and controlled. Ah yes, looked like hers, the room of a bossy-boots with pretty clothes, full of severe authority and better carpet than outside in the corridor, but it smelt of man, and whatever else Mizz West was, she was certainly not male, better be sure. He giggled, coughed back the ever-present laughter, still wanted to sing. Until, like an echo of his own mild noise which he carried with him as he moved back into the corridor, he heard more laughter, more coughing, a chorus line of sound coming closer. In a moment of panic, he was incapable of discerning the direction of the sound; in one second he thought it came from behind him in the grand room, then from his right, then from his left, but it came towards him up the stairs and he had no notion of where these people might go. He looked wildly for the smallest space to hide, wanted to curl up rather than stay still, spied the goods lift with open jaws, thrust himself inside with his knees to his chin. He pressed the metal shutter half together with the palms of his hands. Neat.

'That doorman ought to be sacked, never mind anyone else,' Helen was raging on the way upstairs, coughing. 'You have to phone from a call box to get him to open the door, and even then, we might have been anyone. No wonder Dinsdale—'

'And me,' Rose cut in sharply. 'And me. He let me stay here on Thursday night, like I said, so don't knock him. Or shop him. I'll have a word if you want. He needs a job like everyone else.' She was somewhat sick of the diatribe which had lasted two flights. The lift was broken. Helen was being a nag. Sometimes she understood, other times she knew sweet nothing about anything and she looked sick. Keep reminding yourself you like her, Rose was thinking as they puffed to the door of the clerks' room, you do really.

The room was always a mess, less so when Rose ruled it, but discipline had slipped on Friday. Helen found herself resenting the way they were all cramped in here, while others, like Redwood, had rooms as big but all on their own. Rose went to where the computer sat, behind a screen on a kind of pedestal as befitted its status, pressed buttons and inserted disks with the ease of a pilot.

'How do you know how to do that?' Helen asked, feeling inept.

'I watched,' said Rose. 'I'm a quick learner.'

'Quicker than me. Give me something useful to do.'

'You can sit and knit. You aren't well, you know.' She was mimicking Helen's solicitude. They both laughed.

'I think we'll start,' said Rose thoughtfully, 'with the finished cases from last month, beginning with his, Dinsdale's, I mean. If he was deliberately losing papers, there'd be files he was given either to look at or take to court first time, that's how he'd know which ones he wanted to lose. He'd often get bloody cross if he was sent to a different court at the last minute. I reckon the ones you and John got, you got by mistake. He was supposed to go out there and lose gracefully. Right, let's have his list.' Helen watched the screen in amazement. 'It says the first twelve have gone to store,' said Rose, proud to act as interpreter. 'That means they're in the basement somewhere. We just shove 'em down there, and then file them every now and then, we're supposed to keep them for five years . . .'

'I wouldn't know where to start down there. Are there rats?'

'Course not,' said Rose scornfully. 'I wouldn't have slept down there otherwise, would I? All the rats are upstairs. I'll go down. You have a look in Redwood's room. He keeps the main diary in there, showing where everyone is. Make a list of the courts old D goes to most regularly. There might be a clue in that.' Rose was showing off a little; Helen, humbled by her lack of knowledge of the office machinery, demurred slightly, but it seemed best to let Rose control.

'Why don't I come down to the basement with you? Aren't you a bit nervous going down there?'

'I'm never nervous here. It's the only place I'm not. Save your breath.'

Her footsteps pattered away down the stairs with light speed. Oh, for youth, Helen thought, wandering out into the corridor, down a few doors and into Redwood's room. Hot in here, close, with an odd smell, like old air freshener. She noticed her anglepoise lamp on the desk, you're welcome Mr R, I'm sure, turned it on, fished in her bag for a cigarette, enjoying the sensation of doing what was normally forbidden in the throne room, went across to the huge window behind Redwood's desk and flung it open. She looked out briefly into the street where a single mean lamp reflected a fine drizzle now descending into an area which was never light. They had been chilled and coughing on the way here; now she wanted cold air to clear her head, so she approached the other window, guilty for being a trespasser, thinking, I can quite see why Redwood likes sneaking around, fun really. Then stopped. Coming from behind, reflected in the old and wavy glass, a creature tiptoeing like a child sent out to hide and seek. Even before she turned, she could smell him. His was the scent of the room, artificially sweet, menacing, not immediately recognisable, and there he was, creeping towards her with a silly smile on his face. Helen spun round before he reached her. He was still five paces away over the dun-coloured carpet when she spoke, the voice not reflecting her panic as she measured the length between herself and the telephone.

'Hallo, Mr Logo,' she said neutrally. 'Who let you in? Perhaps you better tell me before I call the doorman for the police.'

He giggled, followed her eyes to the phone, shook his head. Helen got the message.

'I want my daughter,' he announced. 'I want Eenie. You've got her here. All of you, you keep her locked up, away from me.'

'Your daughter? There's no-one called Eenie here. What's her real name?'

'That's what the man said, no-one here called that, what a stinking load of liars you are, and you gave me these, people like you. You like my handcuff burns? Her granny used to call her Rose. Never liked calling her Enid.'

He was dancing in front of her, little swaying movements from foot to foot, pushing back the sleeves of his powder-stained jacket, releasing more of the same sickly smell and showing her his thin wrists, ringed with brown marks she'd seen before.

'See these?' he said. 'Gives me strong wrists. You give me handcuff burns. People like you.'

He stopped thoughtfully, inches away, Helen pressed against the glass of the window which seemed to creak against her weight. Truth was emerging with alarming confusion. Logo, the father of Rose, of course, of course, and in that split second she could at last understand the reason for the child's terror.

'Her mother used to call her Rosie Lee. After tea,' he added inconsequentially. Helen gazed at his wrists, hypnotised. Saw the knife hanging from his belt, thought, Oh, God no, I cannot be brave, I cannot bite back, not this time, not again, I have used it all up, whatever little courage I used to have.

'I don't think those are handcuff burns, Mr Logo,' she said contemptuously. 'I think it's just dirt. Show me.'

He stopped, open mouthed, distracted, held his hands, palm upwards. 'Come towards the light,' she ordered. He did as he was bid, never once taking his eyes off her face, shuffling to the desk, moving his hands to the light; he smiled suddenly, angled the lamp neatly, and began to twist his hands into shapes. Shadows sprang against the far wall, moving monsters, a pig with a snout and a tail, full of strange energy. Helen turned to look, her heart thundering in her ears, her eyes rounded, her left hand feeling for the telephone and her voice forming a scream.

'It isn't you I want,' he said suddenly. 'You're in the way. Where is she? I heard her.'

'I sent her home,' said Helen. 'There was nothing for her to do until Monday. She's gone. Come back and find her on Monday. She'll be here then. There's only me here now.'

The shadow play stopped abruptly. 'I don't believe you,' he said. 'And it isn't just dirt. There's no such thing as just dirt.' The anger was sudden and malevolent. The brown wrists were level with her eyes, his hands grabbing great chunkfuls of her tied back hair, shaking her head about like a rag doll, his spittle landing on her face to add spite to his words. Then he twisted her round, so one arm was across her throat, bending her neck back, the wrist of the other hand was in front of her eyes. 'Dirt,' he said. 'Dirt, is it? That's what she is, dirt, but you, you're the real filth.' The pressure grew stronger. Helen bent and jerked her elbows back into his abdomen, flung herself free and ran for the corridor. She ran blindly, glancing wildly into the darkened rooms as she passed, looking for salvation, somewhere with a lock on the door, a weapon, enough time to be with a telephone, open a window, scream, but her legs were leaden, her mind in the paralysis of futile fear, unable to stop running. There was a sense of *déjà vu* about personal attack; as she ran, she was in the throes of the last, remembering it, full of the images of her bedroom and Peter's brother, stinking with his own bitterness. She knew she would not bite this time and kept running. Too late, she realised, even as she sensed how his pounding footsteps behind her had faded, that she had run the full square of the floor and was back where she had begun, with him behind or in front, it made no odds, but the smell was with her, in her hair and her eyes. She paused, uncertain, by the goods lift where the scent was strongest. It was darker, someone had turned off the corridor light. Helen turned and shouted, 'Rose, Rose! Get out, get out!' hoping against hope the sound would travel. Silence and dark; for a moment she breathed easier.

He leapt from the lift, a black sprite with his kitchen knife, lunging. 'There!' he hissed. 'There! You were lying, you were lying . . .' Oh not my face, she remembered thinking, please not my face, let me die pretty, please. Putting up her arms to shield her eyes she kicked wildly, connected with thin knees, heard him grunt in pain, shift his balance. There was a thud as the knife dropped, whether because of the impatience of his violence, or clumsiness, she did not know, but his hands were in her hair again; she was pinned against the frame of the lift, nerveless, his braced legs prising her own apart as he banged the back of her head repeatedly against the metal surround, until she slid down, leaving him holding her half upright by the hair alone. Logo let her slump, bent over and hissed, 'Where is she? Where is she? I don't want you, no-one would want you.' There was no response.

He let go of her hair. She rolled over on to the floor. 'Filth,' Logo muttered with a quick kick to her ribs. 'I don't need you.'

As if he could not have guessed if he used his wits. Rose would be hiding where she could play with shadows. He stood and waited to see if Mizz West would move. She didn't. That was all right then. He hoped she was dead.

Oh why had she not run downstairs, instead of in this hopeless circle? Helen wanted to be dead, wanted never to have to fight back against anything ever again. Her eyes were closed, but she knew she had rolled on to the knife, the wooden haft of it digging into her waistline, the scenery inside her eyes a mass of purple, exploding clouds. Stay still: let him do what he wants, it doesn't matter, just finish it. She heard him giggle, then footsteps going away, unhurried, purposeful. She could sleep then, simply sleep, wait for someone to come, Monday would do, nothing mattered, she wanted to let go of everything. Rose, though: somewhere down there without the rats, was Rose. It was only Rose Logo wanted and the doorman was useless, wouldn't hear a bomb. Move, Helen, you've got to move, there's nobody else, there never is, but it was difficult. So she rolled, tried to sit up, half successful, but hurting. The light was still on in Redwood's room, insinuating itself into the darkness. The red light button for the goods lift shone in reflection, the only way of issuing a warning, give Rose a weapon. As she picked up the knife with a shaking hand, Helen could feel herself fading. There was blood on the knife. Oh please, not my face; it doesn't matter about your face, you should be ashamed, come on. She struggled to her knees, let the knife drop into the open mouth of the lift, pressed the red button, listened to it whirr away, and then sank back. In a minute I'll move, in a minute: not now. Find a telephone. Slowly she crawled in the direction of the light from Redwood's domain, wanting to keep her face near the floor, then raising herself half upright, began a different and shuffling progress on her knees. She debated briefly in the middle of the crawl: go forwards to the light, or back to the clerks' room? She made the decision to go forward, called by the light, thinking, I don't think this makes sense. Oh Rose, please run, I know what you mean, just run, out the way he came in, any way, but run. And halfway there, still gathering speed, she heard the sound of a phone. From the direction she had abandoned, the clerks' room, the logical place to go, but dark in there. Rose, phoning from the basement before Logo reached her? The doorman at the end of the football game, sensing drama? She crawled back, her knees rubbed raw against the harshness of the worn carpet, reached the door on the twelfth ring, managed to get to her feet on the leverage of the first desk and then it stopped as she reached and fell, down into another kind of darkness, lay quiet and winded, praying it would ring again.

Oh let me not be afraid of the dark.

Michael put the phone down in his parents' house, vaguely angry.

So she'd said she could not come and see him today because of working, but he didn't think that was the way Civil Servants ever worked, even her kind, and if she was at work, why not answer the phone? So she wasn't at work, she was somewhere else, with someone else, doing God knows what, he didn't want to know. A girl like that wasn't for changing, he could hear it said, chanted by a thousand voices sounding as loud as the Red Army chorus or a first-division football crowd. Easily bored, was what she was, playing with someone else, off and away as soon as the new boyfriend was immobilised, that was what it was, it had to be something like that. Couldn't-wait Rose, that's what she was, and he had been taken for a sucker, played it all wrong.

'She doesn't answer, Mum,' he said savagely. A woman sat in the corner of a comfortable living room a few feet away from him, sewing. They had just turned off the football. She became a travesty of her normal, tranquil self when she watched her team, even though she still continued to sew, with big, stabbing movements.

'And I suppose that means that you think the very worst. You don't think of an innocent explanation, do you? She's been let off early, something's happened, she's out, that kind of thing. Even after she came to see you in hospital how many times? You men. You policemen.'

Michael sat back, absurdly comforted but irritated as well.

'I think about her all the time. I don't seem to be able to stop it.'

She put down her sewing, eyed the arm in a sling, sighed.

'Well, think nicely then. If you've got to go up west, your dad'll give you a lift. And back, if need be.'

'Thanks, Mum.'

She took up her sewing again. 'We were robbed,' she was muttering under her breath, 'robbed blind.'

It took him a while to realise she was talking about the football.

CHAPTER FOURTEEN

Rose was looking at the files thrown out to lie on the floor, when the lift thudded down beside her, level with her waist. Ha, ha, ha, Helen upstairs joking, asking what the hell she was doing all this time. Rose smiled, pushed up the shutter and thrust her head inside, grinning and muttering, 'Silly cow.' Her mouth, still creased open in a smile, was suddenly full of a familiar smell laced with an undertone of nausea. Someone's favourite powder, passed from body to body, sickening and cloying, mixed with dirt and sweat. That was her first impression, forming quickly, the second glance, from a distance, showed a kitchen knife, its blade swinging towards her like a wavering compass, faintly smeared, unmistakably a tool for cutting meat, suffering from use. Her whole body became rigid with shock; she put a hand towards the knife, withdrew quickly, extended again and forced her fingers to close round the handle which had the warmth of a reptile. Rose did not understand the message; it crossed her mind that Helen was playing with her. For a minute she thought the woman was mad, and stood winded by the cruelty of the joke, then some kind of logic prevailed. There was no sound but the ticking of the basement machinery as Rose stood gripping the knife, seeing its present purpose in a rush of images which came with the traces of scented powder and body-dirtied clothes, saw herself lying on a bed, and Daddy with his shadow play and his clothes not changed from work and herself stealing Gran's favourite powder as she would a talisman. Daddy in the kitchen as she sliced at him with another knife, warding him off, hurting by accident.

Rose did not think she would be able to do that again.

Flight was the course she had always adopted and that was what she was going to do now. She wasn't going to think of anyone else, she was going to run, leaving behind any loyalties and hopes in that headlong rush as she had before. Go home, don't bother saying why because there is no point, pack a bag, never come back, find another job, it was silly to have come so close; there was nowhere safe, not in the whole wide world, if it wasn't safe here. She had believed in this place. In one hand she had a sheaf of notebooks she had found behind the radiator. Rose dropped them on the floor, ran towards the back of the building, still holding the knife, but loosely, looking for the delivery doors. She took only a few steps, then turned back to stare at the open mouth of the service lift, big enough for a body. She ran left for the stairs, fool-ish and indecisive, feinting towards ideas like a fencer with a blade. Somewhere over her head, there were small sounds; the door-man, the enemy, both of them the same since the doorman must have let Daddy in; must have told him, pointed, go upstairs, that's where she went. It might even have been the doorman who pro-vided Daddy with the knife. She held it to the light. Smears without colour, perhaps used to cut a sandwich, even Daddy had friends. Suddenly Rose stopped. He wasn't the only one with friends. Helen was upstairs.

Rose bent down and eased off her shoes. Instead of the wider, main stairs which led off from the right of the lift, she sprinted left down the stone corridors, turning off the lights as she went. Past the fire-detection unit, the noisy monitor of water supply, the tick-ing boiler, she sped up the narrow iron steps two at a time, pushing through a stiff swing-door at the top. If there was ever a fire here, no-one would know how to get out. On the ground floor, there was a distant sound of a television towards which she was drawn and then she pulled back, inexplicably disgusted by the excited sounds of sports commentary, flew round the corner and up the next narrow set of stairs. She had lost the desire to sit and sob: by the time she reached the second floor, breathless, aching to cough but afraid of the sound, she was consumed with a terrible, attacking rage, the rat in the corner which would die rather than not fight. It was a familiar sensation, she had felt it sometimes during her loveless sex, biting back the desire to snap and snarl which moved her now, something remembered from the time she had lashed out at Daddy, not knowing or caring who or what she hit, hating them all, anything within the sweep of her arm would do.

Someone had turned off the lights. Someone running in that wild way she herself had been running downstairs, she could feel the panic. In the corridor, the only light came from Redwood's room. With her mouth clamped shut against the desire to shout and cough, Rose tiptoed towards the door and went in. The anglepoise was turned at a drunken angle to illuminate the far wall, the desk was as rumpled as a newly abandoned bed, there were papers on the floor and one of the windows was open wide to the floor sending a fresh draught of air. She was drawn to it, leant out, coughing, then caught the sides of the window frame in the midst of a spasm, suddenly dizzy. Careful, Rose, she said; it would be high enough if you fell into the basement well, but that's no way out. The rain had begun again, spiky cold against her face, head clearing. The impulse to scream for help, on and on, into the silence of the side street, died in her chest, it was easily stifled; she might have been yelling into an Arctic waste for all the help it would bring, and she was still ashamed to scream. Helen: where is she? Where is the cow?

There was a sound, a mirror of her own, spasmodic cough. Rose leapt away from the draught, poised for more flight. Helen was in the doorway, leaning against it, slipping slightly, the pose at first looking nonchalant, like someone lounging at the entrance of a party, ready to make a scene, languorous in the pose of a model but playfully pissed. So contrived was it that Rose was furious all over again, yelled at her with all the pent-up fury, 'What's your game, then? What's your fucking game?' The words out of her mouth as the resting position of Helen's slender figure became less natural, sinister, the head supported on the arm, but lolling, the knees buckling, legs straightening in a sudden staggering lurch towards the desk, moving like an uncertain toddler aiming for the nearest knee, missing, ending up kneeling with a thump, her torso over a chair and her head bowed in contrition. There was a stickiness on the back of her neck, one sweater sleeve hung by a thread, and as she raised her head she stared fixedly at Rose, trying to summon the last powers of concentration.

'Did he cut my face?' she asked almost conversationally. 'Only I need to know. I can't tell.'

'No,' said Rose. 'He didn't.' She stuck her fist in her mouth. Blood was running down the fingers of Helen's left hand, which she stretched upwards with a strange elegance, focusing, bringing the fingers towards her face to rest gently on the bridge of her nose. Slight though it was, the movement cast a huge, brief shadow as the hand flickered down out of range of the light.

'Are you sure?' Rose wasn't.

'Yes, I'm sure.'

'Oh, good. Listen,' said Helen. 'Did you get the knife?'

'Yes.' A whisper.

'Good. I can't get the phones to work. They're switched through to the doorman on weekends, incoming only. He should be up on his rounds soon. Every hour, he does, Redwood says.'

'The security bloke doesn't do his rounds,' Rose said, tersely. 'He shirks. And he let my dad in, didn't he?'

'Oh,' said Helen. 'I didn't think of that. Have you seen him?'

'Who, the doorman?' Rose asked stupidly.

'No. I mean have you seen Logo? Your dad?'

'You mean you knew who it was all the time?'

Helen sighed without exasperation, as if everything she said was very, very difficult. It still looked as if she was playing a game of being drunk. Rose wanted to believe it.

Under the sigh, Helen's words came faster.

'No, I didn't know all the time, but I do now. He went downstairs, to find you. Did you see him?'

'No.'

'And now he's coming back up,' said Helen dreamily, shaking her head slowly from side to side. 'Like a plate of spaghetti. Go and jam the lift, quick.'

Rose was slow, traumatised, mesmerised by that fluttering, bloodied hand, watching for more shadows on the wall.

'Which lift?'

'No, don't: it's too late. Listen, will you?'

From below, came the grumbling of machinery.

'Run,' said Helen, her voice suddenly clear. 'Will you bloody well run? It isn't me he wants. Just run. Go on downstairs, I'll keep him happy for a while. I'll nag him.' The face found the means to grin. 'Keep moving till you find a way out, take the knife, threaten the doorman, but will you please run?'

The lift was whining now, groaning beyond the first floor, coming closer. 'Oh for God's sake,' Helen yelled, the languidness entirely gone. 'Will you just, for once, do as you're told?'

'No.'

But Rose ran, into the corridor. She was still holding the knife. The red light for the lift glowed. Rose dropped the knife, seized the steel handles of the pull-down doors, picked up the knife and shoved it down between them, jamming the wooden haft flat. Got you. The silence was deafening: the lift seemed to have stopped without any of the usual bump, stuck somewhere, below her feet. There was a dampness on the frame of the lift against which she leant, listening. Rose lifted her hand away in disgust, wiped it down the side of her skirt, not wanting to look at what was on it. She backed away in sudden exhilaration. Stuck, that's what he was, let him rot. The smell of powder and body odour lingered. She shouted, barking like a dog at a safe distance, her voice full of gleeful venom.

'You just stay in there, Dad. You stink, Daddy, you know that. You stink.'

The use of her voice brought relief, then guilt. She stepped forward, less venomous. Was he all right? She tried not to care if he should smother, but did care a bit. Then she thought of Helen, bleeding all over Redwood's floor. He'd done that. Rose could feel the onset of sobbing, confusion, doubt, tried to retrieve that brilliant feeling of rage which was such comfort, stood irresolute. Should she go forward or back, down to the washroom for towels? What did one ever do with blood but stare, fascinated and helpless, smothering the same old instinct to run? Then, like Helen before, the decision was made by the phone. Pealing from the clerks' room. The response was automatic. Rose was in the room, banging the receiver against her ear in haste, wincing, no time to wonder why it was that the telephone's sound was always first imperative, anywhere, anytime, even if it promised nothing.

'Is Mr Cotton there?'

'No, listen—'

'He told me to ring him, this number, this time.' The man's voice was smooth, ragged at the edges with nervous irritation, not a man to be kept waiting. 'Give him a message from me. Tell him it didn't work. I've got a letter saying I've got to go again tomorrow, it didn't work. Tell him I don't like paying for something I haven't got, and why hasn't he done something. You tell him—' The voice grew angrier, words a little slurred, fear lurking behind.

'Shut up and listen,' said Rose, the fury beginning to return. 'Listen. I am locked in this building with a woman who's hurt, a maniac and a phone which won't dial out. Help me, please, phone the police. Now.'

'. . . to stop mucking about,' the voice went on. 'You tell him what I said—'

'Listen,' said Rose again. 'I'm stuck in this building with a maniac and someone hurt bad, will you please do something and call the police . . .' This time the man registered. After an incredulous pause, he burst into a splutter of outraged laughter.

'Call the police? What me? After what they've done? You must be joking.' The line went dead. Rose continued to hold the receiver, looked at it in disbelief, began to punch numbers, any numbers, 999 numbers, the number of her flat, listened to the buzz of uselessness. She could not bring herself to fetch the doorman, didn't know why, but she sensed the enemy, remembered him the other night, taking the whisky, leering a bit. Run, Helen had said, run. The doorman would let her out if she showed him the knife, though, wouldn't he? But then she couldn't take the knife out of the handles of the lift, could she, in case it decided to work again and . . . So she ran back to Redwood's room and closed the door, dragging another chair across it, useless, the desk so old and heavy, it was unshiftable, but any kind of barrier was better than none.

Helen was lying on the floor, her head against her wounded arm, the pose uncomfortable. Rose angled the lamp to see better, winced and looked away, then stripped off her jersey, took off the T-shirt underneath, looked around. A vase of flowers on a filing cabinet at the side, Christ there were enough silly chairs in here to seat an army, she thought impatiently, tossing the flowers to one side, sloshing water on the T-shirt. She dared not go out into the dark corridor again. The water from the flowers, early spring daffs, was none too clean, but it was cool. Rose cradled Helen's head on her own lap, folded the arm with the tattered sleeve over the chest, thinking inconsequentially what a nice sweater it was, classy, she'd admired it this morning, hadn't said so, of course. She dabbed at the clotted blood which had transferred itself to the cheeks, embarrassed somehow by the intimacy of this strange physical closeness.

'Will someone please come?' she said loudly. Then she looked down, adjusted the profile on her knees, more frightened of the sound of its breathing now than anything else, terrified it would stop. Hesitantly, she traced the line of the old scar with one finger.

'He didn't get your face, this time,' she murmured. 'Honest.'

There was no reply. They would have to wait.

It was quiet and warm, even with the window open wide. Rose began to feel unreasonably calm.

Dinsdale Cotton was more than an hour late. He had missed his meeting in the pub, caught in the football crowds, and now he had missed the phone call. He bumped his car on to the pavement round the corner from the office, with scant regard for its ridiculously inflated value and sharp, metallic paint, not a car he could ever trust to a magistrates' car park or want placed anywhere in sight of a colleague, even though he could pass it off as part of an inheritance. They would believe that, of course, in the same way his contemporaries at the Bar had believed his patrician background at first, the fabled public school (never quite specified, only suggested by the uniform, the speech, the tie, the well-worn-in quality clothes which looked as if they were part of an inheritance too), the patrician thinness, like a lean-boned race-horse. All of which belied the foundling survivor of endless scholarships obtained by cheating. There was nothing wrong with his intellect, but Dinsdale never could resist a short cut. Nor the materialistic ambition which did not equate with his instinctive imitation of a duke.

The Bar rumbled him after a year or three; it was the women who sniffed him downwind with their nose for a thoroughbred, but the Civil Service, blindly egalitarian, had been easier to fool. And then he'd met Helen. Just at the point when she had begun to change her mind about him, the way women always did in the end, he had begun to think how nice it could be not to act all the time. She wouldn't give a damn about his lineage. She had seemed to like him, might even forgive what he was with those big blue eyes, but really she didn't want him, and he didn't like the discovery of how much it mattered, just a game, but coinciding with everything beginning to go wrong.

The car door shut with a satisfying clunk. There was an old wreck next to it which he didn't recognise.

Dinsdale understood the world of the *nouveau riche*, had been adopted into it, pushed up like a piece of forced growth under the greenhouse roof, fatally flawed and prone to insect life. He knew how to choose from his own corruptible kind. Nothing wrong, surely? He wasn't taking bribes from murderers, merely those who wanted to keep their cars and he hadn't even been greedy. Only two more, the ones he had already approached, maybe do something to square the one which was going wrong, one more drunk driver with a small business and a large car. Then he would think again.

He rang the bell, a big, brass brute lacking polish; the kind of thing he would have liked on the front of his little house, with a butler to respond, instead of this shuffling, ever indolent but still suspicious slob of a night doorman whom it was best to confuse rather than persuade. The man took his time, the second ring reverberating into silence before he was on the other saying 'Who's there?' but unlocking the door at the same time like a Shylock unlocking his own vault, grumbling. The doorman was flushed red, cross from afternoon sleep. Drunk, Dinsdale thought, amused for the first time in hours.

'You should have phoned,' the man said.

'Should I?' asked Dinsdale, drawling, eyebrows raised, flicking the fine mist of rain from his coat. 'I wonder why?'

'So you might. Them others did. Like Paddington Station, it is.'

Halfway across the foyer towards the lift, Dinsdale could feel his hackles rise.

'Oh yes? Which others?'

'Coupla gels.' The doorman was mimicking Dinsdale's accent, revenge for the provocation. 'They been sending that goods lift whizzing up and down like there was no tomorrow. Oh, by the way, don't bother waiting for the other one, I mean, it ain't working. Sir.' The 'sir' was loaded.

'Nothing changes in this hole,' said Dinsdale, making for the stairs with elegant speed, but stopping round the first turn. On the landing, he saw a belt curled like a snake lying on the carpet. There was a slight smell which could have been urine. Two girls, looking for a warm space on a Saturday evening? He doubted that, but not his sense of unease, sat where he was and lit a cigarette.

Everything was coming unstuck; he was never going to get what he wanted, whatever that was, though he thought that in some obscure way, it had included Helen West, if only on the periphery. He remembered them talking about evidence. She had never given him evidence of anything more than liking. Silence. He did not want to move. Sit here for a minute to make it look as if he'd come to collect something, then go home.

The swing-doors at the top of the stair well moved. Slightly. A light appeared through the glass panels. From his vantage point in the semi-darkness, Dinsdale saw a face passing, not looking down. It wasn't a girl.

★

Helen's breathing came quieter, even and peaceful.

'We aren't well, are we, Aunty?' Rose murmured, coughing. 'Neither of us. But at least we haven't got to cope with Daddy.'

She had moved the lamp on to the floor next to them, played with the shade, angled it against the wall so she could send out shadow signals to herself with her fingers. Beyond Redwood's desk an enormous V-sign appeared on the yellow paint, cheering her. Rose smiled, looked down at Helen with her head pillowed on Rose's sweater, twitching and frowning this last half-hour. With sweater and T-shirt deployed to Helen's use, Rose was beginning to get cold. She hadn't noticed at first.

'I know you've got the flu and all,' said Rose reasonably, 'but don't you think this has gone on long enough? If you don't bloody well wake up soon, I'll brain you.' Saying that made Rose laugh. She was talking out loud, better than crying and hiding the fact that she was beginning to feel kind of guilty for being passive for so long, even though she felt as if something was being resolved in her head without her having to do anything. Querulously, she started to sing, the tune and the words coming from nowhere.

'The day is done, its hours have run,
And thou hast taken count of all;
The scanty triumphs grace has won,
The broken vow, the frequent fall . . .'

Logo had found himself disorientated again. It came from being distracted, stumbling down all those stairs, knocking against something sharp, his belt snapping. All the way back down to the basement, slowly, all round it even more slowly, admiring those pipes in the ceiling which looked like links of giant white sausages, turning on the lights again and somehow knowing she wasn't there. Thinking that maybe the woman he'd hit had been right after all, maybe Eenie had been sent home, but then, why shout for her? Then he'd found a pair of shoes which hadn't been there before. They didn't look like Eenie's shoes, more like bovver boots, Eenie would never have worn those as a kid, but it was enough to make him set off again. His voice echoed round the stone passages, more confident now, loudly plaintive, then getting shaky. 'Come out, Eenie. Come on out, my lovely. I loves you, Eenie. I always loved you, that was all.'

He could not understand why he had begun to cry. Level with the goods lift again, he leant against the wall and sobbed. Couldn't she see that he only wanted to love her? He punched the wall, punched the red button in frustration, startled when the lift juddered and disappeared, jumped back, thinking something was going to leap out at him just as he had done upstairs. Then he peered at the thing shrewdly, getting angry again, wiping his nose on his sleeve. They were playing games with him, and where was his knife? He began the weary march back upstairs, this time going into every single room on the ground floor, except the doorman's where the telly was still on, making music now, above the sound of snoring. Up one more flight, beginning to move a little faster after he had stopped for a bite of chocolate. All those rooms, losing his sense of which side the street was on, looking out of windows into brick quadrangles, panicking a little until he found the goods lift on that floor and got his bearings. Up one more set of stairs, looking for it again, and there it was with doors jammed shut and his knife acting as the bolt. He stared in disbelief, working it out slowly.

That's what Eenie'd done, was it? Thought he was in there; tried to put him in a box and leave him there to rot, stab him with the knife again if he tried to get out. The anger rolled back like a clap of thunder, burst inside his head and descended to a low growling.

He prowled towards the clerks' room, hesitating to touch the knife, turning back towards the other direction as he heard the sound beyond the door of that posh room. His trousers were slipping without the belt. They felt as if they were held in place by the tightness of his stomach when he heard that sound, the sweet hesitant sound of someone singing for courage.

'. . . Through life's long day, and death's dark night,
Oh Gentle Jesus, be our light.'

He turned the handle quietly, but it would not be quiet. Turned it once, tried again, pushing gently. The voice faltered into silence.

Helen stirred and moved with grumpy abruptness. Rose eased her into a sitting position, head between knees, patted her back, watching the door as she did so. She did not for a minute consider it might be the doorman; she knew exactly who it was, never really doubted that Daddy could play Houdini. Stood up now, holding the lamp, backed towards the window, stopped by the desk, not thinking much, simply reacting, put it down there with the hot shade facing the door, so the light shone on that useless barrier of the flimsy chair, waiting. If the unconscious desire to blind him was the motive, the effect was lost as he crashed through the door, a bent little man, carried far into the room by his own momentum. Rose stood, thin shoulders bare, nothing covering her bare torso but a skimpy bra, short skirt and thick tights below, no shoes, her legs apart, braced against the window frame, paralysed. The little plait lay sweetly against her neck. Logo looked at her in wonder.

'I only wanted to love you,' he said. 'I've never loved anyone else and you wouldn't understand, would you?'

She was stony faced. That look of mulish insolence which said, You stinking little worm, put it away and yourself with it. Her eyes flicked from his face to his waist. Disgust, pity.

'Come home, Eenie.'

Silence. His anger had not died. Logo went up to his silent daughter, took hold of both sides of her head and kissed her fully on the mouth. She stood as still as before, her lips sealed hard, each muscle of her body rigid.

'Open your eyes,' he commanded. Rose would not, could not. He tore at the lace of her bra, put one hand round a nipple as hard as a nut: she remained a resistant, sullen child. Then erupted into movement, her knee crunching into his groin like a hammer, making him stagger back, wild eyed.

'Like that?' he said. 'You liked that, did you?' He came back towards her, eyes full of tears and murder, hands stretched for her throat. Pressed himself against her so she could not kick. Her bravery was gone.

'Your mother's in the graveyard,' he said softly. 'Underneath someone else, the way she liked to be. So's Margaret. Buried with her neighbour. I'll take you too, if you like. Why can't you love your father? I only ever wanted to love you.' Then his hands began to tighten and she could not fight, not this time.

They formed a strange tableau when Dinsdale reached the door. He came through the band of light, blinded for a full second, until he saw someone on the floor, clutching at the leg of a man who was braced by the window, grunting. Helen was on her hands and knees, pulling at the ankle, looking as if she was about to bite. There was a sickening glimpse of white buttock where the man's trousers had slipped, a sound of choking, a rich, full smell, a mixture of vomit and parma violet; it made him want to retch until he saw a hand, clawing at the back of this double-headed beast, a helpless little hand. Dinsdale could not bear to see a woman abused. He simply measured the length between himself and that bent back like a football player eyeing the ball, ran forward and kicked with all his strength. Kicked again at the ankles, sensing Helen rolling out of the way, kicked again as Rose fell from the grasp of the hands at her neck and Logo twisted round. Again as the little man turned to catch the full force in the abdomen, roaring with pain. Logo seemed to trip over the trousers, scrabble for the window frame against which he fell as Dinsdale kicked him one last time, a vicious thud against the knee, he could hear the sound of bone. Logo howled this time, let go of the frame to clutch the area of pain, and then toppled backwards without a sound. For a moment, Dinsdale could not understand where he had gone, what he had done himself and why, until from far enough below, after what seemed an interval of minutes, not seconds, there rose through the rain a thin, watery scream.

Michael had tried to talk himself out of this. So had his father. You don't chase women, especially if you don't know where they are, you let them chase you. That's not what you did, Dad, grinning, feeling a bit silly. Is this the street where the office is? Do you want me to wait? Well yes, just until I see if she's there, if she isn't I'll buy you a beer. It's OK to park here, Saturdays, place is like a grave.

They turned into the side street, Michael looking up. He knew the window of the room where Rose worked because she'd leaned out and waved at him when he'd come to collect her one night last week, no, the week before, so nice and reassuring at the time he would always want to see it again, couldn't fail to look. Three weeks, was all, of coming here and it felt like he'd done it a million times. But all he saw was a sack of clothes hanging over the magnificent railings, probably blown there by the wind, he thought. Until, as the car stopped, he saw it flutter, jerking like a scarecrow on its back, moving all the time, the hands waving and the mouth on the upturned face open in what looked like a smile.

CHAPTER FIFTEEN

They were moving offices. That was today's news. Nothing to do with the incident two weekends before, but because the boiler had broken and, somewhere in the basement, there had been a small fire. No-one knew if the two had been connected, but speculation was rife, hidden beneath a deluge of groaning. When were they moving? Soon. In Crown Prosecution terms, that could mean months. They worked to the indifferent heat of a hundred electric fires, mostly provided by themselves, cheerful in adversity. Redwood had a meeting, but not in his own room, conceding that the recent security survey had shown that proper precautions against the IRA would take seventeen guards, six Alsatians and a bank of electronics, none of which was in the budget and, besides, the lease was up.

His other news was that yes, rumour was true; a tramp had got in and for reasons best known to himself, jumped from a window, and yes, it was his room the intruder had chosen, yes it was fatal, no he was not going to give details, only that death was not immediate . . . Oh, yes, and just by the way before we finish, Helen West, Rose Darvey and Dinsdale Cotton were still suffering from a particularly virulent form of influenza and in these hard-pressed times, he would take it amiss if anyone else followed suit. Especially now, as they were expecting a surge of cases from the last big football match in North London, which seemed to have ended in a riot.

When they had all gone back to their desks, forgetting to ask questions because it was so cold, Redwood went across to the window and looked down at the railings. It was just as well Miss West was off sick, convenient really, since hers wasn't a bad room, and his own room was thick with tape, powder, dried blood, and locked. Dinsdale's seat was also vacant, but in view of the shock waves which would rock the office when the golden boy was charged, it didn't seem tasteful. They were still gathering evidence to build the wall round him.

The day was bright and dry. Helen's anglepoise lamp stood on her own desk. Redwood did not admire the railings as much as he had. He was full of resentment for the inconvenience, using that as a device to quell the nightmare. It was all down to Helen. She should never have provoked a defendant so much that he came in to their citadel to take revenge. And put Redwood's job on the line. What about me? he thought to himself. What about me? Everyone who matters thinks all this is my fault and I don't know the half of it yet. I'm having to take Counsel's opinion on the law on exhumation. He wondered if there was such a thing as a lawyer who knew every inch of the law. A bit like someone with every volume of the *Encyclopaedia Britannica* sticking out of his ears. Friday. He would never stay late again.

In the corridor, waiting for the lift, he could hear a chorus of goodbyes.

'What I can't understand,' said Geoffrey Bailey, corkscrew in hand, pretending to be calm, 'is why you never told me. You told me about missing files, the way you sometimes tell me about work. You had me harnessed to that damn computer because you were too scared to go into the basement, you tell me nothing—'

'That isn't quite fair. I might have told you all about Rose if I'd known, but I didn't, I didn't bang on about Logo, because you get sick of me talking about my cases and so do I. Not hearing about yours, talking about mine,' she added. 'I want to hear about yours much more than I want to talk about mine; what I can't stand is you thinking all the time that you're boring me. You leave out all the best bits, as if I was a real lawyer who only wanted to hear what you should have noticed instead of what you did. And anyway, I don't own you. You've made that patently clear. One weekend's whole-hearted devotion is supposed to go a long way with you—'

'You're sidetracking, Helen.'

He had got the cork out of the bottle, setting about it like an amateur, she noticed, crashing the bottle on the table. Good red wine, she also noticed. Good job she didn't much mind about the polished surface, easy come, easy go: things were meant to be used and surfaces scarred but it was a shame to waste the stuff by spilling it, even if there was plenty more. He'd arrived at the flat, at the end of his course, with a load of supermarket bags, most of them clanking with bottles, possibly the remnants of their end-of-term midnight feast, she thought maliciously. Not enough to allay her fears, but then all the crises of the last two weeks seemed to iron one another out, leaving her lightheaded.

'What did I do wrong?' Bailey shouted. 'Tell me what I did wrong!'

'Typical male, turns everything into a personal accusation. You didn't do anything wrong.'

'Well why were you so brisk with me when I phoned last Friday, before all this happened? Why not ask me to come home and help you with Rose Darvey et al, instead of just telling me afterwards about being hurt and then saying airily, "Doesn't matter, I'm managing fine . . ." How do you think that makes me feel?'

'I didn't ask you to come back because it was perfectly obvious you'd rather not. I wanted a volunteer or nothing, but you were all hooked up with your course and whatever you and Ryan were up to – don't tell me, I don't want to know. After the weekend before, when you got here half drunk, not exactly eager—'

'When you had us spending half Sunday in your office!'

'What's that got to do with it? After a week, I wanted you to be all over me, dying to see me and you weren't, that's all.'

He didn't venture to say he might have wanted the same, was silent, poured some wine with an unsteady hand. Helen had all the answers and his conscience was – how could he put it? – cloudy, like this wine.

'Anyway,' he said without a trace of bitterness, 'you seem to have recovered from everything very well.' Oh no, don't do that, she thought. Don't go back into your professional detachment. I know I haven't been fair, I'd want to shoot you if you did to me what I've done to you this last fortnight, but I had to see if I could cope alone, or I never shall, and please don't retreat like that, I want you to come out and fight.

'You know the worst thing that has happened to me since you went away?' she asked. 'The very worst thing? It's the reason why I'm so calm about everything else.'

'What?'

'Not being pregnant when I thought I was. Even though it scared the hell out of me, that was the worst. Puts all the rest of it in the shade. Even all the cowardice, the running scared round the office, the being absolutely useless, as well as blind, everything. I didn't care too much if I survived anyway. I thought it was far better if Rose did, because she can have lots of babies. And you didn't seem to see how much it mattered.'

He put down his glass.

'I know it mattered. But you never wanted a baby anyway. What about you comforting me for what might have been and wasn't? It didn't cross your mind. The more I sympathised, the more you'd think I was putting on pressure . . . Oh, what's the point?'

'Whatever it is, that isn't it.'

He was silent again, drinking rather quickly, a bit defensive, quiet, even by his own standards. He looked at his watch, needn't have bothered since he always seemed to know almost exactly what time it was. He was just filling the silence with a gesture. Typical male, she thought again, if they ever had any idea how closely they are observed, they'd resort to permanent blindfolds.

'You wanted me to remind you to phone someone before eight,' he said. 'In case you forgot, it's now seven forty-five. By the time you've done that, I might be halfway through some cooking.'

'We could go out, spare you the trouble.'

'No.'

'Why didn't you tell me?' Michael asked Rose. 'Why couldn't you tell me, when we first met, even after a week, what you told my mother and she told me?'

Rose and Michael's mother had been a case of love at first sight. Rose had been unnaturally calm like some creature caught in the headlights before death, poor little bird, you could feel her heart beating and her bones about to break when she was thrust into the bosom of the Michael family in the early hours of a Sunday morning with only enough warning to call a doctor and make a bed. Days of grieving and talking, poultices placed on wounds, ripped off again, replaced, an intermittent healing. Making statements from the living room to endless supplies of tea, with Michael holding her hand until by fits and starts the whole thing emerged with the ease of a Caesarean birth. Now they were in his flat. He wondered if it was too soon, he wondered what he'd got, but it was better, just by themselves. Like children playing house, she seemed to enjoy that. And she couldn't get over the fact that he was still there, not bossing her around or anything, but still there, knowing exactly when to shoo the people away and when to let them in, even his mother.

They were lying with their backs to his sofa. There was a fair bit of dust around, but he kept everything presentable. Helen West had sent over her two teddy bears, which was a nice thought, but she didn't want to think of Helen West. Chinese takeaway was a relief after relentless home cooking, but Mrs Michael wanted them back for Sunday lunch. Rose thought she could get used to it. She twisted her plait. Time to cut it off, it was beginning to annoy her.

'I couldn't tell you. You wouldn't have wanted to know. I didn't want to know either.'

'Look,' he said, 'I didn't think you were a virgin, did I? I couldn't have thought that. But I always knew you were still a kid at heart, innocent. Didn't make any odds, either way.'

She considered it, nodding. 'Nope. But it makes a difference, doesn't it? Going with blokes because you're frightened of the dark, and going with your dad—'

'Stop that,' he said, suddenly authoritative. 'Just stop that. You didn't go with your dad. Your dad got his dick out and hit you with it, that's what. And nobody is ever going to do that to you again.'

She was silent again.

'I think Dinsdale's all right,' she said suddenly. 'I hope they don't fix him.'

'Why "all right"?'

'He wouldn't let me look out of the window.'

Yes, that did make him all right, whatever else he'd done. Michael shuddered. Rose began to cry. 'Shh,' he said. 'Shh. It'll get better. I promise it'll get better.'

'I wish he wasn't dead. Not like that, not like that. I wish they weren't going to find Gran in that graveyard . . . I wish . . .'

'It's getting cold,' he said. 'Here, cuddle up.'

He moved closer, nuzzling her bird bones into the warmth of his chest, the clean smell of him, the comfort of beginning to believe him and oh, this terrible wanting which should not have been the birthchild of grief for Gran and Mum and everyone else, but was.

'You won't leave me, will you, Mikey?' she mumbled finally, her voice low and childish.

'No. Not until you're fed up with me, don't want me there.' He wondered how long, pulled her closer.

She extended her hand over the lamp next to them on the floor, let a huge shadow fall across the wall. Then snuggled back against him.

Steak, salad, ridiculously expensive new potatoes at the wrong time of year, followed by cheese. She could cope with this. Second bottle, nearly gone. Any invitations cancelled. Helen knew that what she had to say might have to bear the brunt of several repetitions. Bailey put down his knife suddenly, smiled at her, on the brink of laughter.

'You look as if you've just been exhumed,' he said with grim relish. 'Steristrips in your head, eight stitches in your arm and skin the colour of a lemon. You're an awkward, unreasonable woman and I still fancy you rotten. You're a walking nightmare, for me, do you know that? What am I going to do with you?'

She wondered. Had been wondering for a long time, but never as much as when she was helped out of the office into an ambulance last week, insisting she could walk and knowing she was going to have to fight for ever to quell her fear of the dark. Dinsdale being kind, but still a thief, Rose with her champion, everyone with someone, and she as she always was, alone, slugging it out with the whole universe.

'I thought we might get married,' she said. His knife clattered to the floor.

'I'm a pain in the neck, I know I am. It just struck me that the way to cure going backwards was to take a leap forwards.'

'Quite a leap.'

'You always said you would.'

He took a deep breath. 'Perhaps I meant at any time when you weren't speaking out of fear and a reaction to being attacked.'

She did not know whether to be disappointed, angry, humiliated or relieved. Dear Bailey had had his taste of freedom. Better to make light of it. She got up to clear the table, make the thick black coffee which he liked and which never kept either of them awake. It was nice to know a man's habits, even if they did irritate.

'I suppose that means you've gone off the whole idea? Marriage I mean.'

'Yes, for the time being. Doesn't mean I don't love you. Means it's my turn to be ambivalent.'

'That's all right then.'

She stood by the kitchen window with a tray full of dishes which would wait, looking into the dark winter garden, aching. There was a line from a hymn running through her head . . . Oh thou who changest not, abide with me.

Dear God, if you exist, don't let me be afraid of the dark.

A CLEAR
CONSCIENCE

PROLOGUE

Life was dull, monochrome. Live dangerously. It was her own perception of herself which made her take the risks. Such as not looking left or right when she crossed the road, staring straight ahead and moving slowly. She did not walk deliberately into the path of the bus, simply did not seem to notice the squeal of horn and fart of brakes. The same sloppy attitude, fed by exhaustion, made her take short cuts, although all she really wanted on the way home was to postpone getting there. It was hot inside her second-hand coat. The pub which she would have passed on the main road would have crowds against the windows, a few pretty girls drooping like half-dead flowers around the pool tables, waiting on busy youths with pectorals like carvings and small muscular bums; the girls so bored, they were looking for something to scorn. Someone ugly. One of them would notice her, point, sneer, and although she seemed to have mislaid the habit of thinking, she knew she did not want to be the subject of comment. In any event, concentration was limited to ten seconds a time.

So she went through the back of the leisure centre instead, into the park. There was a running track round the edge: she liked the feeling of the cinders beneath her feet, the shoddy barrenness of it all, and the sense of importance she got unlatching the gate at the opposite end and walking through as if she was the only person who knew it was there. The park avoided the street. Once, she would have chosen the route rationally. That point in time was a long while ago.

The leisure centre was run like a gospel church and looked like a warehouse from the outside. Local children, disbarred from the place for less than total devotion to either the architecture or the mystical purposes of the building, seemed to haunt it, inspired by a kind of envy for the mysteries within. The leisure centre was not really for the untouchables. She knew the reputation of this particular part of the neighbourhood – she lived here, could read the local paper as well as anyone else – it simply did not make any difference because it did not apply to her and she did not care. This was the way she was going to go.

Muggers on a warm, spring night were unlikely to be fussy animals, she had to concede that. They cared as little as dogs round dustbins They would knock her down for the contents of her small and bulging shopping bag, but if all they wanted was two bottles of bleach, assorted cheap groceries, a packet of washing powder and her front-door key, good luck to them. And if the motive was rape, they would obviously turn back as soon as they saw her, look around for a better target. They would have to be blind to persist; youth could be wicked, but, surely, never so desperate. Not even a male on heat would do more than sniff at this small woman, twenty-five going on sixty, plodding down the alley which cut alongside Smith Street, led her round the edge of the kiddies' playground, wired in like a prison compound, whether to keep them in or keep them out she did not know, flanked by the tennis courts, also wired in, and skirted by the path which led to the gate, and then up a terraced road to her door.

She could have looked at the tower blocks looming to the left and felt gratitude for not having to live there, never again having to trudge all the way to the top of such spartan splendour. They were like the stars in the darkness – oddly glamorous unless you knew better, which, after a fashion, she did. Bevan was the most ominous, sticking up into the sky; but she was not in the mood for counting large mercies, let alone the small. The hurt, with grief and bruises, was all she knew as she trudged, feeling the slack skin of her arms rub against the worn cotton of her blouse. Her skirt rode up between her legs, bunching in the front under the coat, emphasising the slight prominence of her stomach, however slowly she walked in her training shoes. She had the beginning of a double chin, pasty cheeks, hair pulled into an elastic band and eyes already laced with fine lines.

She walked with a slight stoop. Rape? Don't make me laugh, she told herself, to hide the first *frisson* of fear. They'd pay me to go away. You want good looks, find someone like my brother. He got them all. The niggle of fear persisted, despite her coughing to clear it. It grew like a bubble of air in her chest, felt like indigestion, at first merely uncomfortable, then becoming sharp, sticking in the throat like heartburn.

It was the sudden sound of the wind in the trees which began the alien sensation. Whispering branches, full of budding leaves set too high for vandals, added sibilant volume to the sound of bare limbs. Maybe there was nothing new in the sound, simply a novel ability in herself to notice the symptoms of the seasons. She registered summer because it was hot, winter because it was cold, that was all, but now the sound of the trees made a noise like a whispered command. Don't, don't. The fear grew larger, enraged her.

'Don't do what?' she shouted back, stopping to draw breath. The trees seemed to obey, falling silent for a minute, then began again, moaning. Trees were alien here, belonged in another place. They shed dirty leaves in autumn: they made a mess. She had never rejoiced in their triumph of survival. Now she did not look up or down, only straight ahead and did not allow herself any distraction: she would be fine if she kept going at the same pace with her eyes ahead and, all the same, she found herself walking faster.

There was always a point where she had to decide which way to take round the perimeter fence, left or right, to complete the circle, reach the other end and emerge through the gate. One way was longer than the other and she had chosen it by mistake, flustered by the trees. Walking faster with her ungainly stride, she tripped over the lace on her shoe, an accident, because of trying to hurry and the laces being too long, that brought her heart into her mouth, the shock of nearly falling, lurching instead like her brother did when he was drunk, bouncing off the wire fence, the almost falling always worse than the fall itself. She steadied herself, adjusted the bag which bit into a calloused palm suddenly slippery with sweat. Her skin, as dry as the washing she ironed most mornings, felt the texture of rough parchment. She could imagine a knife going through her plump, papery cheek: it would not bleed, not now. What was the matter with her? Come on, come on! No-one could possibly want her for anything, no-one knew her enough to think she deserved malice; there was nothing to fear, but the fear still grew from somewhere. The short route ahead seemed endless, lengthening in porportion to her silly attempts at speed, with the bag heavier all the time and the bathroom bleach slurping about in its bottle. And then when she reached the gate out of the park, it was shut. Not simply shut, six feet high and locked. Keep them out, keep them in.

Turning round with a deliberate, deep breath, she saw him then, slinking away behind a tree. Just someone, some youth who would climb the fence with ease. Probably a black boy: they could climb like monkeys, robbed anything which moved, so she'd been told and so she believed, although she would not know. She only knew that without making any conscious decision, she was beginning to run in the other direction, round the link fence back towards the trees. As soon as she started she knew this was a mistake: there were no lights this side, and it had been the lights which had drawn her to the longer route in the first place. Here there were only dusty bushes by the side of the track, the cinder laid thickly, which made her slip. He was after her now; she did not have to turn to know he was there, jogging along behind her, his feet crunching, his wide, white eyes watching her graceless progress, waiting in the knowledge that she would never manage a real turn of speed. The shoelace snapped; she tripped again, righted herself and stumbled on. The sound of the trees grew louder as she reached them. Only the alley to go, leading out by the off-licence, round the corner from the very pub she had come this way to avoid. Don't, said the trees, don't.

Before the dark alley entrance, she turned, teetered in a staggering circle, letting the PVC bag carry her so she became a whirling cudgel, with her eyes shut against whatever she might see or hit. Nothing. The bag stuck to her hand making her overbalance, carrying her into the mouth of the alley, before it hit the wall with a crunch and the air was full of the caustic smell of bleach. A large hand, smelling of booze, grabbed at her hair, took a hold, hauled her back.

She came to a trembling halt, dizzy, her arms by her side, the right still holding the dripping bag she could not detach, her mind wondering irrelevantly what had happened to the safety cap, her head yanked backwards, exposing her throat. The skirt was fully bunched round her waist by now, the coat heavy, the sweat pouring from her armpits, she would smell; and he was not even breathing faster, perfectly calm. She could feel the light of a lamp, made skittish by the moving branches of the trees, flickering across her face. Do it now. I shall not scream and I do not bleed: my cunt is so dry, you'll have to push. Put the bleach down my throat, only do not use a knife: please do not use a knife, and make it quick.

The hand released the hold on her hair. The elbow round her neck drew her closer. She could feel a rough jaw graze painfully against her own soft skin.

'I want,' a whisper in a honeyed voice, 'I want . . .'

Slowly, she twisted towards him. 'Oh,' she said. 'It's you. Is it really you?'

'Me? Oh yes, it's me.'

The sound of his laughter rose into a shriek of hilarity. She knew that sound: he must have laughed in that same, uninhibited way since childhood. It went on and on and on, cutting across the sound of the trees and a distant yell of celebration from the pub. The diesel engine of a bus grunted in the near distance, and still the laughter went on.

The bleach from the bag dropped onto her shoes. She considered the waste of them and then, slowly, with all the repetitious obedience of passion and terror, she raised her mouth for the kiss.

PART I

CHAPTER ONE

If it ain't broke, don't fix it. Don't mess with the system. Leave well alone. Etcetera.

When I am old, Helen told herself, I shall cease even trying to be good. I shall have no conscience, wear lavender, lace and false bosoms, and, in the meantime, I shall never learn to wield an electric drill.

She continued muttering and shaking her head as a substitute for obscenities while she stood in her kitchen and watched the dust settle. An old friend was dead on the floor after all these years, lying among a shower of mordant flies and the remnants of breakfast. Deceased, still twitching in the extremities, filthy in parts with her own sweaty fingerprints. Murderess.

She watched the butter dish teeter on the edge of the table before a delayed landing, greasy side up on the floor among the other detritus. Someone from a laboratory could examine the life cycle of the dead flies to give an estimate of how many summers it had been since the roller blind had refused to roll further than half mast and only then after gentle treatment. Helen had simply forgotten the habit of teasing rather than pulling. Carelessness so often led to death, but, with the fickleness which so horrified her, the wavering thoughts moved on to rejection. Why had the blind been there? Why mourn it? Because it hid three panes of glass, one cracked, two dirty, in a window where the sash-cord was uncertain; a state of affairs reminiscent of everything else in the place: the chest of drawers which demanded pushing and pulling, the toilet roll on one fragile nail, the wonky chairs on uneven floors, the windows which did not shut. Everything in her domain required concentrated co-ordination of hand and eye to make it work, but there was nothing so broke it needed fixing; the whole place was merely a kind of assault course requiring extensive training. Strangers would need to know how to pull the lavatory chain only with a certain force, kick the hall cupboard before trying to open it, ease the living-room door over the rug and not touch the kitchen blind without further instruction. If it ain't broke, don't.

Helen West, hot and sticky after a long day's work, sat and waited for the resentment to die. The only debate remaining was between the merits of gin against white wine, but even such decisions were academic in this house. There was no ice for gin; the fridge, panting like a dog in a desert, was capable of cooling, but not of making ice after all these years, so she held the wine while wandering from room to room, only four in all, excluding bathroom, suffering as she went the kind of discontent which felt like the rising damp she could detect in the bedroom. There were also a few summer beetles escaping garden predators in favour of a hostess who hoovered her basement floors as rarely as Miss West did. Helen thought, If I took down the wall between the dark hall and the living room, the place would be lighter, especially without a blind at the kitchen window. The legal mind which was her curse and her profession turned on complications such as planning permission, building regulations and other bureaucratic interference, before moving on to simpler ideas, such as new colour schemes, which required less fuss. Major alteration would only spawn a thousand minor problems; the hell with it.

The second glass of wine began to wane, and the mess from the kitchen floor was inside the rubbish bin when Bailey arrived. Her turn to cook. After three years of evasion she was finally learning how to overcome reluctance by buying only the best and simplest ingredients she could prepare inside ten minutes, but despite that, he usually came prepared for the eventuality of hunger, armed with a polythene bag, this time containing cheese, bread and a punnet of leaking strawberries. Usually she was grateful; sometimes irritated; today, simply neutral. The hug was perfunctory.

'What happened to that blind, then? Finally gave up?'

He was careful not to jeer. Most things in his place worked. He had one efficient floor on top of a warehouse, acquired before fashion knocked the prices out of sight and then knocked them down again. A distinguished flat, clean, clear and easy to keep. She liked it, never envied.

'Drink in the garden?'

'Fine.'

She hated him for knowing when to hold his tongue. Also for dusting an iron chair before sitting down, so that he would rise with the trousers of his dark grey summer suit clean enough for a man who did not like anyone to detect where he had been, while her cotton skirt would be striped with the dusty pattern of the seat. The garden always soothed her spirits, resembling, as it did, a warm, wet jungle in need of the kind of ferocious attention she could not apply indoors, but even while she was admiring the fresh sprung weeds, the controlled shambles of the kitchen remained disturbing.

'I was thinking of knocking down the living-room wall,' she volunteered. 'Or painting everything yellow. New curtains, new everything.'

He nodded wisely, sipped his lager. Two of these and he would feel the difference, but Bailey's diplomacy survived any amount of alcohol, while Helen simply became more talkative, more expansive with the wide-armed gestures which knocked things over.

'Expensive plans,' he murmured. 'You been taking bribes again?' She laughed, the bad mood lifting like a driven cloud.

'Oh yes, of course. Chance would be a fine thing, wouldn't it? Imagine anyone paying a prosecutor to lose a case. They'd have to be mad to think there was any need. They lose themselves. Anyway, I was thinking, yellow all over. Let the light in.'

Ah, my generous girl, he thought, with the dark hair, and the dark flat and a liking for light. Bailey thought of his own current work, more darkness than light, plenty of jokes. A solicitor for the Crown and a senior police officer should never meet like this to discuss the decor of their lives. They had tried to keep their professional roles apart since their personal fortunes were inextricably mixed, half the week at her place, days off in between, half the week at his, in a muddled relationship, full of affection and argument, waiting for a better formula to occur to both of them at the same time. Bailey looked at Helen. If it ain't broke, don't fix.

'Hmm,' he said. 'Yellow's a nice colour. Some yellows, anyway.' The woman he had interviewed this morning had worn a yellow blouse, blood from her broken nose mottling the front. The whole effect had resembled rhubarb and custard. He could not remember the colour of her skirt, only that it was held in her fists as she spoke and her bare arms were patterned with bruises. She loved the man, she said. She did not know why he did this to her. Bailey did not understand why. Even less did he want Helen to understand why.

Bailey loved Helen. Helen loved Bailey. It was as complicated as that. The thought of either of them raising a hand against the other was as alien as the planet Mars. Making a simple suggestion was dangerous enough. The cat, fresh from a roll in damp grass, rubbed against his calves, leaving a green stain which Helen noticed with satisfaction.

'But,' he continued cautiously, 'whether you paint it yellow or not, you'll always have a downstairs flat, therefore dark. Won't you? Why don't you just get in an odd job man and a spring cleaner? Then you'll be able to judge what else you really need.'

She pulled a face and stroked the cat with a bare foot. Bailey had often offered his services as Mr Fixit, carpenter, and, latterly, been rebuffed. He had been hurt by this, sensing in retrospect some tribute to the doctrine of the self-sufficient, liberated woman Helen would never quite be.

'Are you suggesting my home is dirty?'

'No, of course not. Only that you don't have time to clean it. Not clean isn't the same as dirty. The place gets a lick and a promise at least once a month. Why should you clean it anyway? Liberated women get help.'

'From other, unliberated women, you mean?'

'There's nothing wrong with domestic labour. You never mind

helping someone else scrub their house, you just don't like doing your own. And if you were otherwise unemployed, you'd be glad of the going rate.'

'A pittance.'

'Regular employment, a mutually beneficial arrangement and clean windows.'

She went inside for more wine and another lager for him. The cat followed, licked up the traces of butter on the kitchen floor with noisy enthusiasm. Bailey's nonchalant figure in the garden was slightly blurred by the dust.

He was not ornamental. He was infuriating but consistent. He was still slightly more defensive than she was. There had never been a courtship, there had just been an event. If it ain't broke, celebrate.

The wine gleamed light golden through a slightly smeared glass; the lager was deep amber. In the evening light after summer rain, the red walls of the living room resembled a fresh bruise. Like the inside of a velvet cave in winter, with the firelight covering all the cracks, it was dull and garish now.

She could make it corn coloured, all over. Get some good old-fashioned, middle-class chintz. Clean up the cat; forget the blind. Start all over again. Make herself and her home both elegant and safe.

Cath's lampshade was yellow. A colour once parchment, a nice shade from a second-hand shop, faded even then, the fringes dark brown. A pig of a light for sewing, but Cath liked it. Not that she could sew here, anyway; she hadn't done such a thing for months. Perhaps it was years. She just sat by the lamp and waited.

The room around her bore traces of effort, now sustained on a less frequent basis. The walls were smudged from frequent cleaning and the patchy renewal of paint. She shuddered to think what was under there. Some of her blood, she supposed, a lot of her sweat and a bucket of tears.

Joe had offered to cook. Ready-made, frozen pancakes with something called chicken 'n' cheese in the middle, about as good for a man as they were for a small woman, accompanied by frozen peas, boiled to death, and the bread and butter which was better than the rest put together, her contribution. She sat listless although aware, ready to spring into an attitude of appreciation, her eyes tracking his progress in the kitchen, stage left, while her head was turned towards the TV screen. When the meal arrived, she knew she was supposed to murmur appreciation, ooh and ahh as if the man was a genius to find a plate; she was already rehearsing the lines, dreading what he might burn, unable to suggest a better method. So far, the mood augured well. Cath did not quite know the meaning of relaxation, but as far as she could, she allowed herself lethargy, listening to his movements and his voice as she slumped, forever guilty in the slumping.

'Anyway, this bloke says to me, Jack, you're a very fine chap. Know an ex-army chappie when I see one. Got discipline, knows how to mix a cocktail even better than I know how to get'em down, hah bloody hah. That's fine, I said, but the name is Joe, sir, not that it matters, much. And then, Cath, do you know what he did? Right in front of the bar at the Spoon, the bastard downs his drink in one and falls off his chair. Could not rouse the silly old sod. He was a picture, I tell you. Gets this look of surprise on his face, grinning all the time, trying to focus, just before he slides away. Laugh? I could have died.'

She tried to match the pitch of her own laughter to his shrill giggle, managed fairly well, encouraging him to continue. Surely, oh surely, there was a formula for managing her own tongue.

'What did you give him, Joe, to make him fall down like that?' Joe worked in the kind of pub which catered to what he called the gentry. And their ladies, haw, haw, haw. And their bloody sons, baying at one another and sticking crisps in the ear of the next person, all good clean fun with Daddy picking up the bills when they were sick or went outside to kick cars on their well-heeled way to somewhere else. Joe had a love-hate view of the officer class, mostly love, an adulation which also got a thrill from seeing them in the dust.

Cath, tired beyond even her own belief, which marvelled

constantly at how exhausted and how hurt a person could be while still remaining conscious, sometimes pretended to share his prejudice. People's problems, she reckoned privately, were all the same, provided you liked them enough to listen.

'I said, what did you give the bloke to make him fall over, Joe?' There was a smell of burning from the kitchenette: the transformation from frozen to carbon, all too easy.

'Vermouth, gin, mostly gin. Oh, a touch of Campari to give it colour; a smidgeon of fruit juice. Mostly gin and French. He downed it in one. For the third time, would you believe?'

The smell of burning increased, a waft of smoke drifted in from the oven, bringing with it an end to relaxation.

'Can I help you, Joe?'

'No.'

Anger stirred. Because he would not let her salvage the food. Because of the vision of some poor, lonely old man, buoyed up to spend his money until he fell off his stool, poisoned by a barman he trusted.

'Joe, you shouldn't have done that . . .'

'Done what?'

He was struggling in the kitchen, couldn't find the thing to strain the peas: it made him mad. Cath could see the end result of all this; she should not carp at his cruel jokes on drunken customers, could not stop, either.

'Done that. What you did. Encouraged that bloke to drink that poison. He relied on you, didn't he? Poor old sod. Poor old Colonel Fogey. Shame.'

There was silence. She turned her head away towards the inanities on the TV screen, wondering too late if there was time to move. Then the food arrived in her lap. Without plate or tray. A heap of hot, burnt pancake and soft peas which burned through the fabric of her skirt into her thighs. She braced herself, with her hair hiding her face while he hit her in the ribs and bosom, finished his flurry with a punch towards the abdomen exposed by the futile defence of her arms across her chest. They were hard blows, repeated for emphasis, making the peas bounce and flutter among the folds of her skirt. The sound from her mouth was simply a grunt as he stopped.

'Pig,' he said, dismissively. 'That's what you are. You even sound like one.'

He retrieved his plate, sat back and ate with his eyes fixed on the screen. For a while she was quite still, then she got up and carried her skirt in front of her, like an apron, her movements silent and unsteady. He did not take his eyes off the television and she did not speak. On her return, five minutes later, she was carrying a plate of bread and butter. Cath ate more bread and butter than anything else.

'What did you do,' he demanded, 'with that food I cooked for you?'

'I ate it, of course. What did you think I would do?' she whispered.

'You might have thrown it away, or something.'

'No, it was lovely. Thanks.' She began to cough, stopped herself because it hurt and would annoy him. Coughing lead to vomiting and that annoyed him more. She had learned to control nausea, to use it as a last resort, since there was an element of fastidiousness about the man. He would not go on hitting while she was being sick, but the downside of that was the knowledge that the presence of regurgitated food always stopped him feeling sorry afterwards.

'They don't feed you,' he grumbled, still not taking his eyes off the screen.

'No they don't, Joe, you're right.'

She nibbled at the bread and margarine spread. Not the stuff of genteel sandwiches, nor the stuff of doorsteps. The sight of it sickened her: pallid dough, golden fat. At work she had another kind of sustenance: bread with nuts, rich brown stuff with real butter layered on with a trowel.

She could have eaten anything out of their fridge if she wanted. She could have told them she was in trouble, but then she was not really in trouble. As long as she was clever and he did not hit too hard or scar her face, and she was able to pretend that the cleaning job was as hateful as the gentry who employed her.

'Joe?' she asked, pleadingly. 'Joe, would you get me a drink? Tea, I mean?'

Joe only drank tea at home. He drank alcohol behind the bar where he worked, noon and evening, not that it showed until he came home, unless anyone could call the odd snarling a symptom. She could imagine what he was like, wondered why they put up with him, hoped that they always would since the thought of Joe without work was tantamount to a nightmare. If he did not work, he would stop her working, but as long as he stayed where he was and she pretended her job never involved any conversation, that was all right. Drinking alcohol at home was not. Together, they preserved the pretence that he never touched a drop; she acted now as if she believed he could not bear the stuff, which, in his way, he could not. His body could not. On a bad day, which meant a day when he had trouble crossing the road, an argument with a customer, or suffered any kind of assault on his pride, the alcohol combined with disillusion to make a poisonous cocktail. It was only the booze which turned him from saint to sinner. He was staring at the screen, his plate empty, his belly unsatisfied.

'Joe? Please? I hurt all over, Joe?'

He wavered, then hooked his right thumb inside his ear and used his whole large hand to cover his face. She watched him, hardening her heart without great success, even while her own fingers moved cautiously across her aching ribs. He always covered his face when he was ashamed.

She went to make tea, bending in the middle to ease the pain, wanting nothing more than her bed. He spoke in a small voice, at odds with his well-muscled frame, in keeping with his height.

'I love you, Cath. I'm sorry.'

She felt his left hand clutch at her skirt as she passed, feigned anger. Inside the kitchen, she tidied with long, slow, regretful movements, coughing, spewing into the sink. Carefully, she chose his favourite mug, put a tea bag inside, poured on the boiling water from the new kettle without a cord. The kitchen gleamed. After a deep breath, which caused as much pain as effort, she took the tea in to him.

He was asleep in the chair, his face wet with tears. She brought the duvet from the bedroom, covered him and left him.

Their own bed was new, with drawers in the base, from which she withdrew a spare duvet, as pristine as the one over his knees. There were other rooms, all of them bursting with goods.

Cath worked hard to achieve this daily promise of oblivion. In the bathroom, postponing the real bath until morning the way they both did unless there was blood, she forced herself to slosh cold water over her warm body and face, recognising the nature and degree of this kind of pain and doing her best to ignore it. She averted her eyes from the puckered scar on her abdomen, washed carefully and estimated the size of tomorrow's bruises. He never hit her face. Never.

Nothing broken: nothing which quite needed fixing.

'Can anyone remember Cath's phone number? Oh, Christ, where have I put it?'

'Darling, why do you want to know? You don't need to phone her, surely? She'll be here in the morning; besides, she doesn't like being phoned at home, certainly not this late.'

'Late? Time for bed, then,' said Emily Eliot, roguishly, ruffling his hair, winking in the mirror which hung over his desk. He looked up from the papers across the surface in orderly confusion, caught her eye and smiled.

'Not tonight, Josephine. I need another hour on this. What on earth were you doing downstairs? Bit of a row.'

'Oh, sorry, playing Scrabble. Mark was winning, he crows when he's winning, frightful child. Have you really got to work?' By this time, her arms were draped round his neck, smiles meeting in the mirror.

'Yup. You know how it is.'

'Dreadful,' she said mockingly, the kiss placed on his cheek denying even the slightest hint of resentment. 'A wife refused her connubial rights in the interests of paying the mortgage. OK, I know my place, I'll simply warm the bed. Now, where's that number?'

'For the second time of asking, why?'

'Oh, Helen rang. Can you believe, she said she was asking me because we're such an organised household, little she knows.' Emily's laugh was loud, clear and genuine. 'Only she was looking for a cleaning lady. Our Cath was saying she wouldn't mind a bit extra, and knowing Helen, she'll pay the earth, so I wanted Cath's number.'

'At this time of night?'

'Oh, yes, it is, isn't it? Bedtime.'

She stood slightly perplexed, as if she had totally forgotten the urgency. Emily's hectic sense of priorities, her need to fulfil each task as soon as it was suggested, fuelled this house and made it work, with the effect of a huge and elegant boiler. The occasional irritation this caused a hard-working barrister on the up was more than compensated for by the very sight of her and every single one of their children. Emily shared their high energy and that sand-washed look which was pale, interesting, and fiery; a big-boned woman, dressed in an old dressing-gown patterned with dragons cavorting on a purple background. Her hair stood on end: her face was scrubbed and shiny. Alistair pulled her into his lap:

'Give me a hug. You smell gorgeous.'

She plumped herself down while he pretended to groan at the weight and, with her arms round his neck, she squeezed the breath out of him. Then she looked at the papers on the desk. There were bundles of them, loosely undone, with the red tape which had bound them pushed to one side.

'What have you got here, my love? Murder and mayhem?'

'Bit of both. I told you about it.' He did; he told her all about his cases, including the most tedious ones, and, even in the middle of the night, she listened. 'Murder, of course. What else can you call it when you have a fight in a pub, one side loses, goes away, arm themselves and come back? One youth stabbed, but only one man caught. Someone else is getting off scot free.'

'Won't he say who?'

'Nope.'

'Is this one of Helen's briefs?'

'No, Bailey's. These are Helen's.' He waved his hand towards the white-taped bundles. 'Even worse. Domestic violence. Wife-bashers. She seems stuck on wife-bashers at the moment. I wonder if that's connected to wanting a cleaner?'

Emily rose and kissed the top of his head.

'You wouldn't ever bash me, would you? However aggravating I am?' He slapped her large behind gently as she moved away. His hand made a clapping sound against the fabric of the dressing-gown; she felt the caress without irritation. It had the sound of shy applause.

'Bash you? I couldn't, even if you begged. Perhaps, if it was strictly consensual. A long, slow collision. No-one's injured by a meeting of true minds.'

'Certainly they are, if the meeting of minds also involves skulls. And I think,' she added demurely, holding out her calloused hand, 'you could finish that work in the morning.'

They got as far as the door, leaning against each other lightly, the old familiar relief flooding through him. What did men do, if they did not have a partner like this who bullied, cajoled, seduced and led them to bed with the stealth of a courtesan? A chameleon she was, a sometime tigress, tolerant, fierce; she kept them safe.

It was an impractical house, full of nooks, crannies and the assem-bled possessions of five individuals of varying ages. On the first-floor landing stood Jane, the youngest child, with snot con-gealed on her nightdress. A plump nine-year-old, moist with sweat and tears, her face framed against her brother's surfboard which rested against the wall, her skin pale and pink in patches. Older brother Mark was dark and handsome at fifteen, her twelve-year-old sister, serenely fair and sophisticated, but Jane's carroty hair grew in twisted, uneven curls about her face, the longest locks sticky with saliva from being sucked into her mouth. Jane was not lovely, although in the eyes of her parents and in the words of their constant praise, she was beauty incarnate.

'It's that thing in my room, again,' she said, trembling. 'That thing, Mummy. He's been there again.'

She flung herself into Emily's arms. Father had his arms round mother's waist; they stretched from there to tickle Jane's damp and curly head.

'Well, what a nerve he's got, coming back after all this while. You'd have thought once was enough,' Emily said indignantly. 'Some people have no consideration. Come on, we'd better go and fumigate the beast. You know he loves warm weather. Funny how he never visited when it was really cold.'

Jane snuffled, mollified.

'Cath cleaned my room today. I thought if it was clean, he wouldn't come back.'

'But Cath doesn't know about the perfume, and anyway, he's gone now. We'll just make sure, shall we? And then leave all the lights on, so you know to run upstairs to find Mark or us, OK?'

Emily's voice denied the right to winge. The child nodded, made a sound like a hiccup and then turned away from their tableau of hugging and set off downstairs, confident they would follow. Alistair marvelled, and occasionally worried, how it was that Jane had acquired her mother's authority and graceful, plodding tread. They pounded downstairs with maximum thumping of feet. One of these days they could get the kind of carpet which softened sound: school fees came first. Jane had detoured, with a swiftness which belied her weight, into their own bathroom, where children were forbidden most of the time. She was after her mother's cologne. There was plenty of perfume in this house. Alistair brought it from duty-free shops on those visits abroad which left him sick with longing for home. Then he would buy more whenever he saw it. Nothing extravagant, but always the largest size, a habit of his. The end result was a wife who always smelled sweet, even when knee deep in household dirt, and a daughter with such a passion for *eau-de-parfum* sprays, she used them to control her own childish demons.

The ghost who Jane insisted haunted her room on an intermittent basis – usually as the aftermath of either bad behaviour or greed on her part, her father noted wryly – only did so when the room was a mess. Tidiness and cleanliness deterred him. Perfume killed him off completely. Emily sprayed the room, liberally. It had the same effect as a charmed circle. Alistair laughed and supposed it was cheap at the price.

Helen West fell asleep with the grilles left undrawn across the basement windows, the way she did when Bailey slept alongside her but never dared otherwise, and never told him what he already knew, about her being tough and also constantly scared. The presence of the grilles induced a distinct sense of bitterness and a slighter sense of panic when they were closed. Supposing the threat was fire or flood, something from within rather than without, how would she escape when panic made her fumble? Why was it always assumed that the danger came from outside?

Because that was usually so. Certainly so for her. The memory of that violent intruder, faded by the passage of time, came back not only when she saw someone in a street who resembled him, but also at night, making her sweat. Sometimes she could smell his presence in this room, simply by brushing away her hair, from where it fell over the scar on her forehead.

She could taste the blood in her mouth, squirm at the memory of her own violent reaction and all the helplessness which followed. She turned restlessly, distracting herself with visions of daylight streaming in to a clean and sanitised room, washed bare of all reminders. Yellow. The colour of corn and cowardice; bright enough to exorcise the devil.

Bailey felt for her hand.

'You all right, love?'

'No.'

He drew her close. 'All right. Come in here then. I'll tell you a nice, long story. A good one. Happy endings.'

She wanted to stick her thumb in her mouth, wishing she could give up thinking about present, past or future. You do not need me as I need you, Helen thought, taking the hand gratefully, listening to the voice talking through some silly tale until she would fall asleep.

If it ain't broke, don't fix it.

Chapter Two

Mary Secura stepped out of her car, in the clean light of a summer morning, pretending to look as nonchalant as a local authority official come to check on a broken window pane or the defective lift in Bevan House. She realised as she saw her own reflection, distorted in the driver's door, that she had slightly overdone the disguise. Officials from the council's repair department might have been in proud possession of identity cards pinned to the lapel, but they did not generally look quite as tidy. Mary had a weakness for handbags, too; and suspected that the average council official might not possess the same good, worn leather. It was big enough to hide a radio, the only weapon in her armoury which did not depend on common sense.

The radio was heavy, not intended as a weapon although sometimes used as such when it was quicker than calling for help. Bevan House stretched above like a sheer cliff; her mission would take her no further than the third floor.

She ran her fingers (bitten nails, indicative of something, she was not quite sure what) through her short hair to make it appear less groomed, and walked briskly along the walkway to flat fifteen, steeling herself to be both brisk and reassuring against the possible hysteria of the inmate. Shirley Rix might be as brave and resolute this morning as she had sounded on the phone yesterday, but she might not. The two of them had spoken almost every day for the last six weeks and if it was not quite friendship, it passed as such. All Mary had to do was get Shirley to the door, and she'd be fine. Once she had introduced her to Miss West, who was good at her job, then, hey presto, the bastard husband would be committed for trial.

The one thing which bothered her, less obscurely than the

nagging doubt which made her nervous, was the hope she carried like a torch for women like Shirley Rix. Plus the fact that when she, a police constable specialising in domestic violence, was finished with the case, Shirley Rix would realise that despite all the support, she was still on her own after all. Having a husband who tried to murder you with the regularity of Mr Rix did not exactly enhance your prospects, either, even if he remained, as Constable Secura hoped he would, in prison on his wife's evidence for a long time. Poor Shirley: she did not have much of a curriculum vitae.

Mary knocked at the door, amazed, as she always was, at how Shirley managed to keep this little flat as free from squalor as it was, not exactly clean but far from filthy. Once upon a time, using the standards of her own parents, Mary would have regarded the semi-cleanliness of the Rix household as intolerable. Now she saw it as the triumph of motherhood, which also saved the lives of half her witnesses since it was usually the kids who made the mothers either leave or give evidence, in the end. The day this violent daddy forced his three-year-old son to drink beer, made him sick, shoved him into bed and then beat his wife for remonstrating, was the day Shirley Rix decided to give evidence. Good girl, Shirl.

Mary knocked again, this time louder, the feeling of dread beginning to take hold. She checked the time: nine twenty, forty minutes before they were expected at court. Miss West would be early, she always was; there were still minutes to spare. The third knock was louder still; she had the absurd desire to use the radio in her bag to shatter the wired glass which took up a quarter of the door. Through the glass an electric light glowed in the hall. Mary had been cheered by the sight of that, now she knew it was ominous.

When the door to flat sixteen opened Mary supposed she was halfway to acceptance, as close as cool Helen West always seemed to be with her bloody good manners. On the doorstep was a woman of indeterminate years, somewhere between thirty and fifty, short on speech and square against the kind of ill wind which blew no good.

'If you want Shirl, she's gone. Kid and all. 'Bout an hour ago. Not coming back.'

The door slammed. There was the sound of two bolts sliding into place.

Mary Secura looked at her watch again, then knocked on Shirley's door one more time, knowing it was useless. Inside, the light winked at her while the place reeked of emptiness. When she got back to the car, she found herself trembling with rage. Six weeks' work, hours of building trust; such was the nature of friendship.

The foyer outside court number five, North London Magistrates' Court, was almost deserted. There was none of the stink, smoke and grumblings of the waiting area outside courts one to four, which Helen could see as she leant over the balcony watching the human traffic ebb and flow. Court number one was remands; she was glad she was not down there with a hundred cases to shoot from the hip: the overnight arrests, the bind overs to keep the peace, the guilty pleas, the postponements for preparation or non-appearance; the whole thing an exercise in concentration. Better to be up here, with a single case listed for the whole morning, if it lasted that long. The prisoner was in the cells, the two police witnesses had booked in, everything was set to go. She looked downstairs again, in time to see Constable Secura coming through the main entrance and barging, rudely, through the crowds. Alone. Even as Mary made for the steps towards the comparative calm of court five, Helen could feel her own bile rising, the vomit of frustration.

Mary Secura reached her side, slightly out of breath, said nothing, simply shrugged her shoulders. The defection of a crucial witness was not a phenomenon requiring an announcement. Even one still recovering from her split lip, missing teeth, fractured skull and broken arm, all suffered in the name of obedience to the man in the cell downstairs. Helen felt a brief white rage against the victim who remained a victim.

'The stupid, stupid bitch,' Helen said. 'The silly cow. What does she think she's doing? Are you sure she knew the date?'

Something snapped in Mary Secura's brain. She leaned

forward with her hands on her hips and her face inches from Miss West.

'Of course she knew the bloody date! We've been through it enough times. She knew the date, the place and the fact I was coming to pick her up. And don't you dare call her a bitch. You've seen the photographs, you know what she's like. I can call her what I fucking like, it's me who's got her this far, but you can't, you stupid ignorant cow. You've got no bloody idea . . .' And then to her own consternation, she was in tears, turning to one side to fumble in the good leather handbag for the sheaf of paper hand-kerchiefs she always carried, dropping the radio with a clatter on the stone-tiled floor.

'I think those things cost hundreds, don't they?' said Helen. She bent to retrieve it while Mary, blowing her nose, made the same movement. Their heads almost clashed. Helen held the radio to her ear, shook it, pulled a face.

'Receiving Radio One, I think. It'll do.'

Both started to talk at once, breaking off with a touch of awkward laughter. Helen breathed deeply, pulled another face and sat down. Mary Secura did the same.

'OK, so what do we do? This committal has been on the cards for four weeks, he's been in custody for six and we've given every reassurance it will go ahead. We've got outside evidence of a row, shrieks and screams, injuries found after the police were called. His admissions vary from saying she fell over a pushchair to saying she went ape shit and hit him first and he had to calm her down. We can put him there, but not tie him down. Whichever way you look at it, there just isn't enough evidence without her.'

'Nope.'

'So I don't have much choice about going in there and discontinuing the whole thing, do I?'

'Please,' said Mary Secura. 'Please. Just try for one more adjournment. Give me one more chance to find her. She'll have to come home sooner rather than later.'

'Why should she?'

'Because she hasn't got anywhere else to go.'

'And then she'll only skip again, next time. After another few hundred pounds of public money?'

'Please,' said Constable Secura. 'Please, Miss West. Next time he might kill her.'

The usher stood by the door, smug with sympathy and the prospect of a short morning.

The tea was cold, the service indifferent.

'Look, I apologise for calling you a stupid ignorant cow,' Mary Secura said with a touch of stiff formality an hour later as they sat in the canteen. They had bypassed the rows of cheese rolls, weary even this early in the day, ignored the bacon smell from the steamers, the rack of sad toast which no-one would eat now, the baskets with packets of biscuits and the plates holding forlorn scones. Court canteens always purveyed food to the lowest common denominator of taste, bland in the extreme. Helen imagined the custard for the lunchtime apple pie was made once a month and carved into slabs.

'Don't wrap it up, say what you really think,' she said cheerfully. 'I wouldn't be here if the occasional insult made me curl up and die, but I don't like them much from someone I respect. Which is why I should apologise too. Of course I knew you'd have done everything you possibly could to get that woman to court. I implied you hadn't, because I was irritated.'

'Irritated?' said Mary. 'I was furious. I like Shirley. And the child's just beautiful.'

They were silent for a moment.

'Anyway, you're halfway right,' said Helen. 'I am ignorant. I mean, after all this time and all these cases, I don't understand the pressures. Not really. I still don't quite know how a woman stays with a man who hits her.'

Constable Secura stirred her filthy coffee.

'Oh, I think I do, a bit. Which is why I'd like a change. Something simple. Like catching criminals and getting convictions.'

'You been reading fairy stories again?' Helen asked. 'Or do you want to join the robbery squad?'

Secura shrugged and smiled. 'You know what I mean. From where I sit, a stint on robbery or murder looks like a holiday. You don't get too many results with battered wives.'

'If I were you,' Helen said cautiously, aware of her own frustration rather too freely expressed earlier, 'I'd sometimes want to hit them myself.'

'Well I don't, because you get to the point where you can't get angry, any more than you would with a child. I only get angry with the man. It's like treading on eggshells. The neighbours call us out more often than the victim, and off we go. Usually the drunken bastard gets arrested on a late-night domestic and we come in to collect the evidence next morning. By which time the victim with her limited knowledge – and I can't tell you how limited it often is – looks at us like a dog turd. And screams. So you get her to climb down and maybe make a statement. Then she sits at home with a couple of screaming kids, works out that the devil she knows isn't half as bad as the one she doesn't, especially if the feckless sod helps keep the roof up. Oh yes, and then there's this little complicating factor of love.'

'For someone who breaks your ribs?'

'Yes, ma'am,' said Mary, saluting Helen mockingly. 'C'mon. You've got Bailey, I've got mine, we know all about Love.'

'Not that way, we don't.'

Helen sensed that Mary did not want to go on in such a serious vein. She cared too much, Mary did, took all professional failures personally. They had got their temporary reprieve, Helen implying that Shirl's absence could well be the result of illness or kidnap rather than reluctance. She could lay on the guilt with a trowel, Mary thought: she could make the buggers think they had no choice in the matter at all; and I do wish she'd talk about something else.

'Tell me something,' said Helen, leaning forward in so confidential a manner, Mary recoiled as if this normally calm prosecutor were about to confess to a bizarre sexual deviancy, 'do you and your bloke agree about colour schemes? I know Bailey and I don't actually live together, but he does spend a lot of time at my place, and I suddenly want everything yellow, and he seems to think yellow is nothing more or less than the colour of, well, pee.'

Mary bridled. 'What the hell does his opinion matter? Yellow? Paint or wallpaper?' she went on, eyes alight with a fervour. It was an illumination Helen recognised, the single-minded devotion of a fellow shopping-addict. 'I've got a yellow bathroom. Big roses. Love it.' She was fumbling in that big bag with the radio and the mass of tissues. For the sixteenth time that day she looked at her watch. Helen had a fleeting image of Bailey who never looked at a watch, even in the middle of the night, he always knew the time. Strange that he should also be a man who was passionate about clocks, when he was the last person to need them.

'Well, I have to phone in again,' said Mary. 'In case anyone's seen Shirl. Otherwise, I've got an hour. There's an amazing do-it-yourself paint and wallpaper shop down the road. Why else do you think I like this court?'

Eyes met in mutual recognition. Despite the photograph of Shirley Rix, shown to the magistrates, despite the memory of serious common purpose, there was also that peculiar elation which followed the demise of adrenalin, the slow ebbing of tension which brought about a certain euphoria. Then they were out there, heels clacking on stone steps, moving with the guilty speed of children playing truant.

Superintendent Bailey could feel Detective Constable Ryan's reluctance to get out of the car.

'I dunno, sir. Can't we just look from here? This thing might be short a set of wheels by the time we get back.'

'It's got an alarm, hasn't it?'

'Sure, but I don't quite know who it would frighten. Nobody under fourteen anyway. School holidays, guv, nothing's safe.'

'I can see cars with wheels. Let's go. Your tyres wouldn't pass an MOT, anyhow. Just don't want to look, do you? You've lost the honourable art of walking, that's your problem.'

They set off across the road towards Bevan House, which

towered above them. It was fronted by a scrubby green, once landscaped by non-surviving trees, now littered with cars, which dipped down into a concrete approach that led in turn to a central portico, also concrete, before deviating left and right to side entrances and stairwells. Three stairwells, three lifts, most defunct at any given time. There were open walkways along the first twelve floors; after that the remaining twelve rose like a monument, too high for the windows to be smashed by anything but a passing rocket.

'Would you believe', Ryan volunteered, interested despite his truculence and his resentment at being there at all, 'that they put families with children on the lower floors, well, as far as possible they do, the council, I mean. Unmarried mums and dads go further up, singles at the top, but no bugger wants to live at the top. Least, that's the plan; it all gets muddled, except for nobody wanting to live at the top. I mean, is that where you'd want to live on a pension? Half empty, the top. Little flats, cubbyholes, really. Council can't get rid.'

Bailey looked with indifference at the frontage. He felt a distant rage that anyone could ever design a building so alien to human beings, then repressed that familiar old-hat opinion and wondered instead how much it would cost to persuade the children who played around them, dusty as the concrete on which they moved, to get organised and burn the thing down. Heartless architecture did not cause a riot all by itself, but it certainly helped.

'Show me,' he commanded.

Ryan shrugged. 'Damien Flood lived on the top. Would you believe he could run up all those stairs, even when he was pissed, which was often? He had another place, too, always running away from women, but this was his main gaff.' Ryan turned abruptly, almost full circle, so that instead of pointing upwards towards the height which made him giddy, he pointed away.

'Over there, see it? Just poking out, that's the leisure centre, right? Kept that nice, they have, video cameras and bouncers all over the place. Got a park round the side. The park was there first, if you see what I mean. Got proper trees and stuff. Damien used to go to the centre to work out: a lot of boxers did, though really they've got their own places. He wasn't so regular since he went to seed a bit, but he was still a fit bloke.' Ryan turned back, looked upwards again and shielded his eyes.

'I mean, anyone who could run up all them stairs, he must have been fit.'

Bailey squatted down. He was wearing a jacket over slacks, had had the sense to take off his tie. His thin knees stuck out: Ryan hoped his trousers would bag and knew they wouldn't. Nor would his voice stop.

'It was your job, Ryan. I gave it to you and said get on with it.'

'I did, too. We got a result, didn't we? Committed for trial. And if you've been too fucking busy to worry until we have to go and see some fucking barrister about it, why the hell are you on my back now?'

A child came up to them, dirty faced and full of cunning, trailing a skateboard. He stood with his powerful ten-year-old body full of challenge.

'See that car?' Bailey said, pressing two pound coins into a grubby palm. The child nodded. 'Go and look after it, will you? Got a man here worried about his wheels.' As the boy rushed away, Ryan felt the old, familiar humiliation spreading through him like his mother's hot flushes.

'I done what I could. We got a body, like I said. All right, they were all of them in that pub over there.' He gestured again. 'Near the leisure centre. Well-run pub. Damien Flood was in there with his mates. He won too much money at pool. The losing team came back for a fight. Damien got separated from his mates and then got stabbed. All right, I didn't get the three lads on that team, but I did get one. And you know I didn't force him to talk; I done every rule in the book to stop him talking, but he sang like a budgie. Lot of budgies, in these flats. They aren't supposed to keep pets.'

Bailey sat back on the grass. His silence was never a relief, even when he lay, squinting at the sun with his face red from the heat.

'What you got was a skinny little boy. You didn't look any further. You made no enquiries in the pub itself.'

'So what?' said Ryan, trying to hide his own irritation and all the guilt Bailey's nonchalance induced. It was all compounded by the man's ability to rise to his feet without a helping hand, like a dog bounding up to play. There was a sound of breaking glass. Ryan supposed it came from the prominent rubbish bins which flanked the main entrance, and marked the only attempt at architectural grandeur. Bailey heard it only as a normal sound.

'I hope that little sod isn't doing in the windows of your car.'

'Not yet. Why can't you get stuffed, sir?'

'Because I like to needle you, that's why. And you didn't try with this one, did you?' Ryan could have sworn that one of them spat, but Bailey, when next he looked, was as impervious as ever, kicking the dry ground with the toe of his shoe.

'Only I've seen the photos,' Bailey was saying as they walked back to Ryan's car. 'Seen better, seen worse, but Damien Flood wasn't killed by any nineteen-year-old kid who lost at pool. Or his friends. Come on, Ryan, come on.'

'All I could find,' Ryan said.

Bailey did not sigh any more than he ever looked at his watch or opened his mouth without purpose.

'Shame,' was all he said as they pulled away from the cliff face of Bevan House. 'Bloody shame.' Ryan knew at least the half of what he meant.

His footsteps padded down the corridor, tripped on the curled edges of carpet tile and moved on with less assurance. He opened the door, sidled his way inside, closed it behind him and breathed deeply. Now he had her. Half-past lunch and not back at work. Bull's-eye. Brian Redwood, Branch Crown Prosecutor, Helen West's boss, among other problems, a man of ferocious timidity, lowered his large behind into her chair, puffed out his chest, shook his head, drummed his fingers on the table and still looked like a man who bore the imprint of the last person who had sat on him. Then he began to prowl.

Mess was what he found. No evidence whatever of the clear-desk policy he advocated, less evidence still of respect for rules. A towering in-tray, nothing in the out, two dead plants and a packet of sticky mints in the top desk drawer. Redwood huffed, ate one absent-mindedly while continuing his researches. Old birthday cards, a shopping list, a pair of shoes requiring mending, nothing more personal than that. Perhaps she hid things, these days. His eyes fell on the paper sack in the corner of the room. Confidential waste, the place to put litter with no destination other than the shredder, cleared once a fortnight. Hmm. The brown paper crackled at his touch accusingly, and the contents were revealing. Policy manuals, vital memos from himself, delivered daily, part of his own attempt to rule by written words. It was faintly shocking to find that in Helen's case, his efforts represented nothing but the shortest route between the in-tray and the bin.

Redwood gazed out of the window and found, to his horror, someone gazing back. The office was separated by the mere width of a narrow street from other offices over the road, where a comely woman stared, and then waved. Redwood, a guilty thing surprised, felt as if he had just lost his trousers, and ducked out of sight still clutching a bunch of paper. He was on his hands and knees with his bottom pointing towards the door when Helen opened it. Just as she always did, he reflected later, she turned the tables on him.

'Something you wanted, sir?'

She dropped the file she carried under one arm. The paper spilled out and the photo of Shirley Rix's injured features lay uppermost on the floor. While Redwood looked at it without interest, Helen neatly hid her shopping bag behind the desk.

'You're late,' he barked, scrambling to his feet. 'Where have you been?'

'You should know. North London Court. Battered wives society. You've had me doing nothing but battered women for six months. Another no-show this morning.'

She was thinking of the contents of her bag. Of how she had substituted the vexed question of whether it had been right to ask for a witness summons for the woman in the photo with the search for yellow paint. Thinking of the various hues of silk emulsion paint, so delicious looking in little sample pots, she could have grasped them out of the hidden bag, peeled off the plastic lid and eaten one like a fruit yoghurt.

'We need a policy,' Redwood barked, 'about what to do when these women don't turn up. When to give up and when to carry on. Write it.'

'Write what? What's wrong with deciding what to do in each case as it comes? Each one's different. Sometimes you should give up, sometimes not.'

'You might get it wrong.'

'Yes,' she said patiently. 'I might, you might, we might. And so might an inflexible set of rules. We don't have a policy written in stone for other kinds of reluctant witnesses; why have one for victimised women? We just have to listen to the police.'

'Helen, we're supposed to be independent of police opinion.' Redwood regarded her warily, waiting to see if she would take such remarks personally. He had a deep suspicion of all policemen and supposed her own view was jaundiced as a result of her misguided, miraculously long-running affair with one of them. Redwood was waiting for Miss West to recover from her strange infatuation with Superintendent Bailey with the same weary patience he had experienced when his daughter was recovering from measles. Partnerships like that were not against the rules, but they were not comfortably within them either.

'We can't be independent of their judgement when they've met the victim and we haven't,' she was saying calmly. 'Besides, there's hardly much scope for bribery and corruption in a Domestic Violence Unit.'

He was silent, then shrugged. 'I don't know,' he said. 'I really don't know how it happens. I thought this was the age of equality. If I hit my wife, it would be the very last thing I'd do.'

Visualising the bulk of Mrs Redwood, Helen privately agreed.

'Think about the policy,' Redwood urged as he found himself, without knowing quite how, being shown out like a visiting window-cleaner.

'Sir,' she said sweetly, 'I think of nothing else.'

★

The sun had flattened itself behind their own building. New offices, nasty furnishings which would not outlive the lease. Men like Redwood promulgated bureaucratic nonsense in the hope of saving their seats from the encroachment of younger, even greyer men. Helen felt a quiet despair, suppressed by the dancing visions of yellow paint now hidden in the bottom drawer along with a supply of make-up, biscuits past their sell-by date, books loaned or borrowed and the ashtray Redwood had failed to discover. Sunshine reflected off the glass frontage of the offices across the way, obscuring her daily surreptitious examination of their lives. She buried her head in work.

The light faded, gracefully. The out-tray grew. Shouts of laughter echoed in the corridor outside. Someone ran past her door, yelling, 'Wait for me!' in a long and eerie wail. Someone else tripped on the carpet, and then there was only the disturbing descent of silence, penetrating slowly until, with a stab of disappointment, she looked up through the window to find that all the workers in the opposite block had gone. Alas, no chance this evening to see who had lingered and finally left with whom; no chance of an update on the fate of the opposite office Lothario.

The phone bleeped. A new phone, anchored to the revolving desk.

'Go home, Helen West. Go home now. Stop whatever you are doing and go.'

Her heart stopped for a moment: the silence of the building was suddenly oppressive, until the distant sound of traffic restored sanity.

'Emily, you scared me. What time is it?'

'Half six, you ninny. Don't you have a watch, for Gawd's sake?'

Somehow those strident patrician tones never struck a discord: hers was a voice inspiring pleasure and confidence; artlessly kind Emily, enviably efficient and, in truth, a bit of a bully.

'Two things. First, I left the number of the cleaning lady on your answerphone, but I doubted you'd ever get around to organising a meeting, so I did. You're halfway down the fifty-nine bus route between where she lives and here, and she says it's no bother. OK? Be with you in an hour, so get your skates on.' Skates, bikes, Emily drew metaphors from all the impedimenta of her children. 'And the other thing is, she's here so late, helping me, because I've got people coming to supper. They don't include you and Bailey by any chance, do they?'

'Nope. Soon, I hope.'

'Christ. I wish I could remember who's coming. Isn't that awful? They could be a posse of vegetarian judges. Oh, by the way, she smells of carbolic soap or disinfectant, or something. And she does tend to eat with her mouth open, but that's nothing. Really. Helen? Don't forget to go home, will you?'

Home. With the dusty windows and the wild garden and the floors in need of a clean and the bees at the window. The thought made her shiver with pleasure. Halfway down the corridor, she remembered the little snack pots of paint in her desk drawer. She would not have trudged back for anything less, but these had the innate value of contraband. She was the only person she knew who had left a chicken defrosting on the office floor for a weekend. She boasted about that one, but not about the fish left under the top deck seat of the number 59.

She avoided the bus in the interests of speed. Below the hot streets, the Underground was tolerable with the mad work exodus an hour old. The street where Helen lived seemed fresh, dignified, safe, adorned by large Victorian houses with white stucco frontages, elegant in whatever state of repair, built for affluent families, currently subdivided, the basement flats like hers, euphemistically known as garden apartments, were sunny at the back, darker at the front. Helen walked down her own road with familiar pleasure, noting the age of the trees, the clematis on the black railings, the emergence of blood-red geraniums and startling blue lobelia in window-boxes. Then she did as she did with shameful frequency: stopped, looked in windows to see what people did with their rooms.

On the doorstep was a woman, waiting with preternatural

patience, as if she never needed to move, would wait for ever, like a piece of garden sculpture.

'Yes?' Helen queried abruptly. 'Are you selling something?'

The sculpture stood up from the step and smiled. 'I'm Cath,' she said. 'I've come to clean. If you want me.'

'Cath?' Helen echoed. 'Cath? Oh, yes!'

She unlocked the door, turned back, smiling apologies for her own gross delay, muttering how she was usually early; forgive me, she was murmuring. She wanted to apologise for her own house, suddenly spotlit as they went into the kitchen, which caught the full blaze of the sinking sun from the south-facing garden; and it was then, catching in the absent smile of the other woman a signal of nothing, that the cat came in and Cath lifted her off the floor in a crow of delight. For one split second, hers were the same hurt, brown eyes which had stared from the photographs of Shirley Rix, defying the world to say that her own fate was her own fault. Helen shook herself.

No-one had identical eyes, any more than the same voices or fingerprints.

Aside from that, Cath had the face of a madonna.

CHAPTER THREE

If it ain't broke, don't fix it. Which raised in his mind the strict definition of 'broke'. For 'broke' read broken, not penniless. Bailey could hear some pedantic judge translating the phrase for the benefit of a jury. 'Ladies and gentlemen, this means, if an object is not broken, it should on no account be repaired.'

Somehow that did not sound quite the same. Lacked a certain *je ne sais quoi*. Bailey looked at the clock in his hands which had sent him off on this tangent. Not broken as such, M'lud, but working overtime, with the hour hand racing round at the same speed as the one counting seconds. He set the clock down on the work surface. 'Just let me know which hour of the day I'm in,' he murmured, 'and I'll phone up the speaking clock to check the week.'

The repair of this old timepiece could wait until Helen had seen it. 'Look,' he would say. 'That's what happens when you see your life passing in front of your eyes. At the last glance, you are now fifty-six.' Maybe it wasn't so funny after all.

Bailey, long and thin, with his slightly cadaverous features, did not look like a man who smiled easily, although he could and did, frequently, if sometimes shyly, like a man amazed by his own amusement. Helen made him smile: he could catch himself watching her from a distance and grinning. He supposed he was lucky. Not many men could have these ups and downs, these swings of mood, these black days and this unfair ambivalence in the face of commitment to a rather beautiful woman, and still find themselves loved and tolerated, albeit with a degree of exasperation. As an old-fashioned man, raised to regard marriage as the desirable norm, Bailey was ashamed of his lack of formal commitment; sometimes, he realised that Helen had reached the point in their relationship when that was what she wanted. If you don't want to make a lifetime of it, he told himself sternly, you should let go and make space for some other bugger to do better, but he did not want that either. Nor did he want anyone else, not even the freedom to search for a relationship less complex, although he had flirted with the idea, as had she, both retreating from the brink. And he had proposed marriage, repeatedly, in the early days, to be met by her uncertainty, hurtful at the time, like someone refusing a gift he had taken the trouble to wrap. The tables had turned in the last few months: he supposed he was getting some small revenge.

According to the clock, one hour had passed in one minute. Helen was late. They were currently in one of their tranquil phases, a celebration of the hazy days of summer, but despite his silent insistence that their relationship remain as it was, the uncommitted, nevertheless exclusive kind, he had to admit that all this talk about tearing down walls in her flat disturbed him a little. He wanted her independent, of course, but not so independent that she built a life without reference to him at all. You're getting your cake and eating it, said Ryan, ever jealous of the bachelor state. Bailey supposed he was. He hadn't said to Ryan that even eating cake took effort.

Nor did he confide in Ryan that Helen and he had hardly made a good job of living together the one time they had tried, although the choice of place, which both of them loathed, had been less than fortunate. And their tastes did not coincide. She was all for deep colours, dozens of pictures, warm fires, dark old curtains, so that her red-walled living room resembled a gentleman's club. Bailey's huge single floor, with not one curtain, contained less colour than her bathroom. There was wood and more wood. Shelves rather than cupboards, the pastel work surfaces of the integral kitchen where he placed the clock all cleaned with a spray and wipe. The only dirty thing around here was the cat which came and went and remained missing for days at a time. Cats are like women, Bailey told himself with the cynicism of a policeman; they stay if they want to.

Eight thirty, supper simmering and no-one to share it. If all else

failed, he would read a book. He had been thinking of going further than his LLB, acquired at night school; he might even read a
law book. Pity, though: it was one of those evenings when he
really needed to talk. There were not many couples, he reflected,
who could discuss murder while eating lamb chops. Nor those
who study post-mortem photographs for dessert. He wanted to
share his current moral dilemma: a trial in which he knew they
had not arrested the right man. If not exactly the wrong man, not
the right one either.

The flat was clean: he was clean. Only his conscience was like
a dirty windscreen.

Helen did not know what to do with a cleaning lady. The confrontation made her awkward. It struck her as a rather lonely and
boring job; and, for that reason, she hated to ask anyone to do it,
even though as a Crown Prosecutor, not rich like her City and
commercial cousins, there was enough for a good standard of
living. Including someone to clean the house, if only she could
suppress the guilt which came with asking.

'And this is the living room. And this is the bathroom,' she
heard herself saying, sounding to her own ears like a condescending estate agent to an idiot client. Cath nodded. Of course she
would see what they were, she wasn't blind, Helen told herself
furiously, her own embarrassment made worse by Cath's passivity. She was a strong-looking young woman, but she walked with
a slight stoop, as if she carried something heavy round her waist,
and instead of speaking, she inclined her head. But she showed no
sign of recoiling from the scattered clothes in the bedroom, or the
gritty feel to the kitchen floor.

'I'm sorry about the mess,' Helen was saying, 'only I don't have
much time . . .'

'I wouldn't call this mess,' Cath said neutrally. 'It isn't even
really dirty. You've got a nice place.'

Helen was instantly charmed.

'And of course,' Cath continued, 'I could help you with the
garden.' That made Helen defensive again. The garden was hers.

'I like doing the garden,' she said. 'It's the housework I can't stand.'

'That's all right then,' said the woman mildly, in a quiet, almost whispering voice. 'I was only suggesting it because Mrs Eliot said I should.' She was suddenly disconcertingly chatty, as if she now knew the worst and could cope with anything else. 'Now, when it comes to dirt, you should see what Mrs Eliot's lot can do. Amazing. Bathroom and kitchen look like bomb sites most mornings. And what those kids take to bed is anyone's guess.' She spoke of them with a kind of urgent fondness and reverence, shaking her head. Helen felt a guilty treachery to find herself so avidly curious about the true state of Emily's house. It was like looking in windows: she could not suppress it.

'Tell me more,' she demanded.

Mark sometimes went to bed in his wellington boots, could she believe that? Yes, she could. Jane had learned to make pastry recently, then thrown a lump of it at the old-fashioned extractor fan in Emily's kitchen, there were still clods of it stuck to the ceiling and probably getting mouldy in corners. Along with the fragments of boiled egg which Mrs Eliot had left on the stove while she got embroiled in one of her incessant phone conversations. Boiled eggs go off like bombs, Cath remarked. And then there was the grill pan with fat in the bottom, set alight when Mr Eliot had forgotten his bacon; the marks of that joined all the others. Helen was secretly delighted. It was a relief to know that Emily's fine house also carried scars.

'Well, do you want me to come or not?' Cath asked.

Helen did, very much.

'I can do Tuesdays and Thursdays, say two hours in the afternoon. You're a long way from Mrs Eliot, but it's halfway home for me, same bus route. Number fifty-nine.'

Her voice was peculiarly flat when she stopped talking about the Eliots. She seemed in no hurry to leave, but stood looking round the walls of Helen's living room with slow pleasure. 'I do like it here,' she said.

*

On her way to Bailey's, driving with careless abandon, Helen felt as if she had passed some kind of test. And, as far as the Eliots were concerned, achieved some kind of equality. The Eliots were a couple of very few friends she and Bailey could call mutual to them both. Usually, it was difficult to share friends with Bailey. He was not a sociable animal, despite his great and diffident charm, and there were hazards in taking him out and about among friends who thought policemen were dangerous freaks. He would find himself attacked for a parking fine, sneered at for the release of a terrorist, forced to defend himself for the latest police scandal, cross-examined for ancient miscarriages of justice; and although he ignored it all, she could not. Many a supper party had ended in awkward silence, with the pair of them relieved to depart. He was too proud a creature to be baited like a bear. But with Alistair Eliot there was the firm foundation of professional experience and mutual respect. They had all shared the same cases and similar concerns, while Emily shared gossip. The charismatic Eliots had no preconceptions about whom they should and should not know. Alistair's father was a bishop: Bailey had suggested there was something loosely Christian in their ever-open door.

When we next go there, Helen was thinking, I must remember to look at the kitchen ceiling. And ask Em why she thinks Cath smells of soap.

The number 59 bus route rose like a sluggish wave in the depths of north-east London, where Cath lived, and moved with the speed of a canal boat right through the centre; it dawdled around the glories of South Kensington, where the Eliots lived, and then over to the depressed south. The depot, into which she had often ridden on the top deck, remaining where she was until the bus turned back again, always saying, if asked, how she had gone to sleep or there was something she had forgotten to buy, was a place she loved for the serried rows of buses, coaches and double-deckers standing under the high roof like so many Thomas the Tank Engines. The fumes filled her nostrils, but the place was cool in summer. There was something immutable about the number

59. They were all such old buses with conductors and drivers, never the newer, one-man-operated type which she hated for their impersonality and the rude noise of their brakes audible from her bedroom on a quiet night. When the number 59 had gone in for a cream and maroon livery, she had simply sat up straighter in her seat, as proud as any shareholder. If anyone got on the bus and refused to pay, Cath was incensed, even if their inability was accidental or their condition clearly wretched. Cath despised people who did not pay their way. She did not think she was poorly paid, abhorring those who were poorer still.

Joe was well paid, he had not wanted her to get a job. Between you and me girl, they would show 'them', a thing or two, the bastards. She thought of 'them' whenever the bus took her into Kensington where Joe worked. Not really a public house, more of a hybrid between that and a wine-and-cocktail bar, standing in a mews and, at this time of year, obscured by blooming window-boxes, flowering tubs and trailing plants which covered the white walls in a blaze of pink, blue, white and green. Busy Lizzie and ivy added an air of discreet and tasteful attraction, underlining the promise of privacy.

By this point in its journey, the number 59 had lumbered into the undisputed territory of 'them', Joe's adopted territory and that of his enemies. Part of her was infected by his formless class hatred as the bus turned through Sloane Square and shot up Sloane Street to Knightsbridge. It was as though it traversed foreign territory, littered with women shaped like horses or greyhounds, wearing a uniform of smart cotton shirts embellished with pearls. They got on the bus for jolly short hops, braying at children called Justin or Hugo. The children were all rather like Emily's, Cath had reflected with a shock as the bus had lurched round the corner, taking her to Islington and Helen West. Cath had never thought of Emily as one of this alien breed. She was just Mrs Eliot with a face full of freckles, husband and family, the epitome of everything Cath admired.

Thinking of Emily and her brood made Cath wince with longing. It was the hot love for the children she would never have, the love for a family who asked her to belong, poured praise and gifts upon her head, said, come in, come in! and seemed to mean it, whereas she knew she couldn't come in. Not ever. Not even close.

Twenty minutes north from Helen's, forty minutes from Emily's, accelerating as if scenting home territory, the 59 bus lurched level with the leisure centre. It could have been a million miles from Harrods. This was where she lived, in the maisonette with attics which Joe had wangled from some army connection, next to the park where Damien had died. She was now in the land of the 'us', where never a 'them' was seen, but the local community had forged a similar version. 'Them' was those with houses worth burglary; 'us' was those who did it. She felt light hearted, almost light headed, as she took the longer route to the late-night super-market, avoiding the leisure centre grounds. She had found another place to love, if not a person. Another set of keys, belong-ing to a voice which did not have the same high, light tone of enquiry that Emily's did. And a place to clean which was, to Cath's mind, safer than houses.

Dark and secret and safe, with a cat and a garden. Down there, without a view, where she could make everything shine, and Joe would never know where she was.

When Emily phoned Alistair in a slight state of panic at seven to say, darling, could you possibly remember exactly who the hell is coming to supper, he consulted his diary and said he did not know.

'Where did they come from?' Emily asked, wildly.

'I really don't know. Are they friends of mine, or friends of yours?'

'I don't know. Listen, darling, are you ready to come home?'

'Not quite. Need to talk to the other junior in Monday's thing. Matter of fact, I'd arranged to meet him for a drink. Is that all right with you?' he added, anxiously.

Emily was glad to have a husband as uxorious as this, but there were times when his delays irritated, even though she did not really want him home yet. She did not care whether he met a colleague in a pub or a playground. It was a different sense of anger, fuelled by the fact that although Cath had been there, labouring all day, the house remained doggedly out of control, with Emily, as usual, inexplicably relieved to be rid of her. Emily stood on the first-floor landing and yelled, her voice drowning the racket of a fight below.

'Quiet, you downstairs, just bloody shut it, will you?' Then on a lower scale, no less authoritative, in a voice sounding more like a growl she abandoned the subtle approach.

'Help required here, you bunch of little sods! All hands to the mast! Those who do as they're told get to stay up watching this perfectly wonderful video I've got. Loads of sex and violence. Those who don't, go to bed. And that means you, Jane. Mark, your surfboard is going out of the window, now. Jane, do you hear me?'

It was a long, skinny house where voices echoed. Three children, fifteen, twelve and nine, stood in the hall looking up as their mother came down.

'Ah, there you all are,' she said in mock surprise. 'Dad's in the pub,' she announced, casually. They looked at her, wide-eyed, expectant, suspicious, trusting.

'So will someone lay the tables, please. For eight. I want the knives and forks, one big knife, one little one, not from the kitchen drawer, all in straight lines. Two wine glasses each. And I want both bathrooms tidy. If you please. Oh, and while we're at it, can anyone remember if I wrote down the names of the people who are coming?' There was the sound of a small stampede as they disappeared. She had, after all, taught them everything they knew about bribes. She had not really needed the help; simply needed to look at them, check they were still there.

The oh-so-busy Lizzies and the vivid, purple lobelia, balm to the spirit, bloomed on a preternaturally hot July evening, when the light seemed endless. Outside the Spoon and Fiddle, a title hidden by greenery, Alistair Eliot sat and regretted the lie he had told his wife. He was not meeting anyone: he had simply wanted to stop and nurse half a pint of lager the way he did once in a while in summer, and even then he agonised about deceit. Last summer, during the reign of a super-efficient, albeit slightly sluttish nanny, alas, now departed, Emily and he escaped their progeny to sit for an hour as he sat now when the house seemed fit to burst and Em had to admit she was going mad. They needed to be somewhere else to discuss their domestic concerns and the show of flowers here was better than any left remaining in their own little garden after the stamp of juvenile feet and the constant cry of 'Catch this!'

Emily had brief but intense flirtations with places outside home, and for this one in particular, they had cause to be grateful. It was the barman here who had listened to them talking a year ago about what Em described as the rising tide of scum in their house. He introduced them to Cath. Excuse me, he had said with a careful swipe of the table, I couldn't help listening. I happen to know of someone who's rated highly. You hear things in here, you see? Shall I tell her to call? Cath had been a godsend, but it did not follow that the Eliots both went back to the Spoon. Emily alone had surmised Mr Fixit the barman was married to Cath, but, apart from that, they did not know quite from whence she came, and cared even less. She was Cath, the Treasure, with no surname and a telephone number only for emergencies.

Alistair sat, early in the evening, fiddling with his half pint and his good fortune. Raising his right fist level with his mouth in order to sip the drink, he noticed his cuff smelt of perfume, a lingering smell, which had been with him all day, competing with the window-box flowers, irritating and refreshing by turns. It had been pleasant to smell the blossom among the disinfectant fumes of the cells where he had been first thing this morning, but not so pleasant now. The scent of it seemed to have grown stronger as the day wore on. Alistair smiled. He need have no conscience about his wife. He carried her with him, wherever he went. Or it might have been Jane, with her arms round his neck this morning, her nightie soaked with *eau de parfum*.

Quite aside from the need to have an interval, however short, between the circus of court and the more stimulating circus of home, Alistair stopped at the Spoon and Fiddle to nod to the barman. There were refinements to Alistair's conscience which Emily did not share. She did not see that once you were bored with a place, you did anything other than simply stop going there, even if the service had been excellent and the memories delightful, and in this wide, pragmatic sweep of temporary patronage she included hairdressers, butchers, bakers and restaurants in the constant search for something new if not necessarily better. Alistair, on the other hand, would have gone to the same small rat-run of entertainments and services, year in year out if left to his own devices. To do otherwise made him feel slightly guilty. Objectively, he was well aware that he owed nothing to the Spoon, with its strange decor of flowers outside and an odd assortment of military memorabilia above the bar inside, either for good times had or for the respite it had given during the difficulties of last summer, nor was there any real debt to a barman because he was so pleasant and married to the cleaning lady. He simply felt a kind of duty to call in from time to time, just in case Joe felt unfairly abandoned. There was another feature, too, in this strange refinement of manners. For all that he was born of patrician stock with a lineage in Debrett, Alistair was secretly more at home with the little people of his world than he was with the great, the rich and the good.

In any event, the motives did not matter, since Joe the barman (known as nothing but) seemed to appreciate the effort. When Alistair had walked into the miniature saloon during the slack hour between the end of post-working-hour sippers and the start of serious evening drinkers, the smile on the barman's face lit the dim interior. Joe knew everyone by name and with minimal supervision from the owner, he ruled this little roost with all the efficiency of a quartermaster. The cocktails, along with the military memorabilia, were only an optional extra to attract those seeking either novelty or the quickest road to oblivion. Alistair wished they would take down all those regimental badges on the wall, as well as the ceremonial sword and the crossed bayonets which did not go with the immaculate chintz. He drank like someone who has never really learned the habit, ordered the usual half.

'Ah, Mr Eliot! What a pleasure. No need to come into the dark. Sit outside, I'll bring you the usual. I feel like one myself. Get into the sun, will you. Tomorrow it'll rain . . .'

The man never showed sign of drink. He looked like the ex-soldier he was (ex-barman, officers' mess, sir, he had told Alistair once), so the latter supposed he had long since overcome the alcoholic hazards of his profession. Alistair did not mind the chattiness, he liked it, in fact. It was a change from the taciturnity of many of his clients, and once he got home he was in for a long evening of holding several conversations at once.

'Family well, Mr Eliot?'

Alistair was a literally minded and humble man. If anyone asked him a question, he answered it fully. Joe Boyce thus knew quite a lot about his family.

'Well, Jane and her brother have been fighting like cat and dog. Funny that, they used to play like puppies and in between bouts of scrapping and when they aren't leaving marks all over one another, they still do. Strange, isn't it? I don't understand these relationships, really, do you? I was a one and only. I would have loved a brother.'

'Well, you say that, Mr Eliot, but they can be a mixed blessing, you know.' It was one of Joe's virtues, Alistair decided, that he not only spoke softly, but also expansively. Alistair loved to listen. Part of him did not want to be a barrister at all: he was sick of talking.

'Me, I'm like yourself, the only one. They got rid of me into the army as soon as they could, don't blame them. But my wife, now, she had a brother and he was a real trial to her. Needed looking after every day of his life. Always on the scrounge for money, always in trouble with the law, drunk as a skunk. I tell you, Mr Eliot, he nearly had us divorced. Because you can't turn away your brother, can you? You have to let him into your house, come what may, even if he is a disgrace.'

'Yes, I suppose you do,' Alistair agreed, genuinely curious. 'And then how do you get rid of him?' He had a sudden vision of how Emily might deal with a recalcitrant relative of his own. The thought was not comforting.

'Well, this one, Mr Eliot, he got rid of himself. After I'd tried to befriend him and everything. Got him a job, even, but no, he wasn't having anything, that one. You can't stop a man if he wants to kill himself, can you?'

'Is that what he did?'

'Yes, you could put it like that, in a manner of speaking. Got himself killed in a fight.'

'Sad,' Alistair murmured, the lager suddenly sour on his tongue, even though Joe spoke airily, as if the incident were many moons ago and a hundred miles from here. Pub brawls, affray, the spontaneous formation of little gangs to exact petty revenges were all part of his stock in trade. He had dabbled in more cases of manslaughter than he could count, and suddenly did not want to talk about it. As usual, Joe Boyce sensed the need to move the conversation aside, in the same way he knew how to move a chair for a customer who was only on the brink of deciding they needed to sit.

'Now, Mr Eliot, here's a joke for your daughter. We're down at the bottom of the sea, sharks swimming about all over the place. One shark is a moneylender shark, and another one in debt, so the second one he goes off and catches a poorly old octopus, brings it back to the other one, for breakfast. So what does the money-lending shark say?'

'I don't know.'

'He says, Hallo there. Have you got that sick squid you owe me?' Alistair, who loved such childish and ghoulish wit even more than his youngest daughter, laughed immoderately.

There were times when even Joe Boyce forgot the distinctions between them and us.

'So how was your day really?' Bailey asked, rolling the clichéd question on his tongue, turning it into a drawl.

He did not think of himself as a detective, nor had he ever

invested his own job with a scintilla of romance. He was simply a functionary who had to mop up trouble and sometimes go searching for it, but there were times when he could resemble a machiavellian private eye with the looks of a seedy lounge lizard. He even had a silk dressing-gown, provided by Helen, which had seen not only better days, but better years.

'Which day are we talking about?' she asked, looking at the clock with the speeding hands. 'Oh, today. Well, I told you about Cath, the cleaning lady who is going to revolutionise my life. She might even oversee the revolutionising of my flat. The nicest thing about today is the comforting discovery that Emily Eliot is not quite the domestic paragon I thought she was.'

'Are you being bitchy?'

'No. It doesn't count as bitchiness when you're talking about someone you like.'

'First I heard. I'll never understand women.'

He was teasing. Helen thought of the vacant eyes in the photograph of Shirley Rix, and the tragedies of wilfully wasted lives. Of Mary Secura's passion for her job and of Cath with her apparent passion for cleaning.

'You don't understand women? I'm not sure anyone does, even other women.'

She had not mentioned Shirley Rix to Bailey. It made her too sombre, and her lingering guilt would have to fade before she could speak of it. Instead, they had talked long and late about Bailey's case, never thinking it was wrong to talk shop, since neither of them did so with anyone else. It re-established sanity in his mind to tell her why he was worried, although he was often economical with the harsher facts, wanting to protect her; she did not exhort him to get on with it and forget moral self-indulgence in the interests of results. So Helen knew all about the pub murder, nicely far away from her patch, so that she would never have a professional hand in it, to Bailey's relief. She knew about a group of men going out drinking, an argument with others in a pub. Three of the visiting team went away, see, coming back armed to the teeth, ready for the fight which ensued, leaving one of the home team injured, the other two in pursuit of the assailants, who had run soon after the first exchange of blows. The home team thought their injured friend was merely winded or scratched; when they came back to find him, he was dead. Brutal, foolish, wasteful and bloody. It was the drink which did it, said the one assailant who had been caught soon after, knife in back pocket. He had gone to the scene deliberately armed, ready to do serious injury. He would not name his companions. Death had been the result of his part in this loose conspiracy and since he had contributed, he was charged with murder. Although he had not intended to kill, struck once, he said, and ran as soon as blood was let.

'And who'll care?' Bailey had said over supper. 'The three who were armed were all yobs. They couldn't have won against three men. Only the one we've got is less of a yob and stupidly loyal.' They had wandered from that theme to others, to weekend plans, to the speeding clock which told them a month of their lives had passed in one evening, until Helen's thoughts returned to Bailey's laconic narrative of pavement death.

'What was his name, the dead man?'

'Damien Flood. Ex-boxer. Pool player. Handsome man.'

'I don't understand men,' she said. 'Why do they always want to fight?'

'Hormones, I'm told. I wouldn't know. I don't want to fight any more.'

'No, you don't.'

Not for me or against me, she added to herself. Not for anything. You sidestep, like a dancer. You would fight for your own version of justice, but you will not fight to keep me.

CHAPTER FOUR

She could hear the thump, imagine the silence which would follow; then the chorus of voices. Then the screaming. Mary Secura played it like a video in her mind, first fast, then slower, until the frames were frozen. A slow wash of blood came down over the scene, like the crimson curtain in a theatre. End of Act Three. Time to go home. Act One: Shirley Rix, pretty child, bruised by her dad. Act Two: pretty woman, battered by her husband; devoted mother. Act Three: on the run, for reasons she wouldn't begin to define for herself. She tries to cross the road on the way to her sister's at nine thirty in the morning. She has an old suitcase in one hand, the child is being dragged along by the other. Shirley has to adjust the suitcase: it is heavy. She loses hold of the child who wants to go home. He runs into the road; she runs too, screaming at him, unable to see where he has gone before someone grabs him as the bus grunts to a halt. And as all the passengers lurch forward in their seats, Shirley gets a sidelong blow from the lumbering beast, enough to send her spinning into the path of the car which is late for work, impatiently overtaking the number 59. Shirley Rix, crashing against the windscreen, teeth bared, arms and legs waving like the obedient puppet she was, sliding out of sight, her fingers clawing the bonnet, leaving marks. The driver, numb, the whole scenario falling into silence apart from the boom of sound from his stereo, until, with the actions of an automaton, he turns it off. Other sounds, then. The wailing of a car horn, a woman's scream which turns into a chorus, the drumming of heels on the road as the body with the broken neck jerks without control. Someone at the side is hugging a child to an ample stomach, pushing his head into her skirt while he protests at the embrace of a stranger, but the stranger will not let him go.

They all watch, paralysed. Someone else moves forward, treading carefully.

Mary Secura waited in the Unit in case someone rang. However pointless and aimless it seemed, she needed to remain where she was, to play with paperwork, and compensate her own nagging sense of failure. She had often suggested, to blank stares of amazement, that if they wanted to be more effective than they were, there should be someone on duty at night. It was the drink, so most of the victims said, which meant someone should be sitting in this office beyond the witching hour when public houses closed and men went home to beat their wives. Poor Shirley Rix had denied her husband the chance to kill her. Mary had no business being here. No-one was paid overtime to wait for a call when the answerphone worked and victims of any kind had universal recourse to dialling 999. The sergeant at the front desk had asked, didn't she have a home to go to? Mary resolved to use the back way out.

She had what her employers described as a stable existence, particulars of which had been added discreetly to her annual reports for the last two years. Officer resides with PC Dave Inglewood (nice lad: should go far), attached to traffic, 'A' division; joint mortgage on maisonette. There was no mention of her hunger for achievement which he did not share, or the relief she felt when the patterns of his duty rosters meant they scarcely saw each other for weeks on end. Her parents, regretting the absence so far of a wedding ring, looked with pride at the photos, dusted daily, of their daughter in a starched white shirt and blue uniform. Hadn't the girl done well?

The office nested in the nether regions of the police station: second floor, through two fire-proof doors, turn left, right and straight ahead. No-one rang while Mary fixed a photo of Shirley Rix to the wall. It showed Shirley's bruised profile hidden behind the smiling face of her fair-haired baby. The picture had been taken merely to make her relax, c'mon Shirl, let's have one of Jason, oh, isn't he gorgeous. Pride made Shirley turn to the

camera. This mother-and-child picture was not part of the case
which, like all good prosecutions for domestic warfare, lumbered
off the ground with all the speed and efficiency of a crippled
jumbo jet. They had given Shirley a copy of the picture: Mary
supposed Mr Rix would find it amongst her things on his release,
flourish it in indignation while he sued for false imprisonment.

Finishing the careful pinning of the photo to the notice board,
Mary realised she was being stupid. Each additional minute here
achieved nothing more than compounding a reputation for eccentricity, hardly a virtue in police circles, especially for a woman.

She had reached the first set of heavy fire doors when she
heard the phone behind her. She turned back in a hurry, but there
was always the wrong decision to make with these double doors,
whether to pull or push, which one to shove first, what to drop in
order to use both hands, and by the time she was back inside the
tidy office, with the files ranged against the wall and the empty
computer screen staring at her, the ghostly, cheerful message on
the answerphone was halfway through its reassuring recitation,
ending abruptly with a click and purr as she grabbed the receiver
and listened to nothing else.

That was the point when Mary Secura sat down and wept for
Shirley Rix, who had died while her one protector had gone hunting wallpaper with a solicitor. She would never be able to forgive
Helen West for distracting her. She hit the double doors with her
fist on the way back out, stopped, winced, then used her palm to
push the door in the right direction. Outside in the car park,
someone whistled, slow but loud.

Mary was thinking, there must be another way. She was still
thinking it when she slammed through her own front door to a
clean house with a yellow bathroom.

Is this all? she was asking herself. Is this really all?

Home, sweet home. Cath put down the phone and giggled. Joe
had an answerphone; they had everything. They had the top two
floors and the attics of this creaking house for next to nothing.
Home, sweet home. There was a landing at the top of the stairs,

living room and kitchenette on one small floor, bedroom and bathroom on the next, then three attic rooms above, each with a brown stained ceiling, and in one a hole in the plaster through which she could see the stars. Someone owned the place, Cath supposed. Some poor old fart who had forgotten about the rent and the legal action long after Joe had ceased to pay and said it was now their own, since no-one had bothered them for a year, and let's face it, Cath, it was cheap at the price even before then. Yes, even though she felt they lived here through some kind of theft. Spacious, yes, but it leaked, was cold, and probably condemned.

'Oh, Joe.' She had been hot with pleasure. Now she blushed at the memory of her first sight of those bare dark walls, the stains, the lino floors, the dripping kitchen tap, everything else taken except for the stains and the stairs.

'I said I'd look after you, didn't I?'

He could not have a wife of his in a council house, even if they could have got one, and he hadn't tried. Got to be black or lesbian, he had said, and oddly, she had believed him. Council houses were for poor people, he had added, and we're gonna be rich. Cath had risen to the challenge like air bubbling out of water. She was already an expert at what could be lifted from skips and second-hand shops, the dirtier the better; a keen bargainer at the kind of auction where no-one looking for valuables would bother, fought over pennies for things worth their weight in gold. Cath knew to walk down a street the night before a weekly rubbish collection, finding treasures; she could knock on doors where someone had left a square of carpet, a three-legged chair, a kitchen cupboard. She could make shelves using good wood and breeze blocks, and find the posters with the daisies on and the tea towels to match. She was built for work: she had no embarrassment in her quest for a home.

Needs must as the devil drives, she had said cheerfully, although Joe was not the devil then. Cath had been homeless once, and that was the memory which drove her. But Joe's pride was a different animal, one which could not feed on leftovers.

The more she did, the quieter he grew. When the walls were painted, and the floors more or less covered with something or other to hide the scratched and broken boards, and the kitchenette had recycled taps which did not drip and a cooker which was free along with a fridge, he was so pleased he beat her black and blue. All round the body, leaving buttocks and thighs a patchwork of bruises. Had she possessed the ability to speak to anyone at all, she might have confessed that the beating took the edge off her decor, since she never quite lost her sense of irony, but the voice had gone the way of two broken ribs, and she did not have any friends. In his insidious fashion, he had seen to that.

No friends between them, either, except her brother, Damien.

The light on the answerphone maintained a steady glare, which Cath liked when she came home to a dark room; it had the same effect as a night-light, although to all other intents and purposes, it was redundant. The light indicating a message never meant more than a wrong number, an occasional call from Joe's employer, big Mickey Gat, or someone selling double glazing. The latter struck in the early evening (Hallo, my name's Lucy, have you got a minute?), and Cath always found she had enough minutes to make them run through the gamut of their wares before putting down the receiver. There, she would say to the wall, that's stopped YOU bothering anyone else, although she had liked being bothered. When Damien was alive, there had been more phone calls, of course, and even if his voice had been so slurred that he sounded as if he was on the other side of the world, he was always an improvement on a salesman. These days, without the occasional illumination of his voice, Cath used the phone to gain access to other answer machines, listening to the messages, sometimes leaving one of her own, slamming back the receiver as if it was hot should anyone real happen to speak. There were all kinds of company to be had this way; all kinds of dreams. For instance, the girl on the Domestic Violence Unit message had a nice voice. Friendly. It could have belonged to the girl the neighbours sent round one morning after a worse than usual row. The one who had not believed Cath when she had said, no, nothing's wrong, will you please go away? The old couple downstairs who had done the reporting did not live here any more. Instead, there were new people: kids, who made enough row themselves to cover Joe at his worst.

It was nine in the evening. The day was beginning to die, and through the sparsely covered floorboards of Cath's living room, the steady thump of the bass rhythm entered her feet without a tune, and echoed in her ears.

She took a plate of bread and butter and a cup of tea one floor up and ate it, perched on the side of the bed, careful of the crumbs. Sometimes, if it was not too cold, she took her snacks in the attics, unbearable though they were. She loathed these rooms not for the temperature, or the dampness which dried out over each successive summer, but for the objects the rooms contained. Boxes from mail-order firms. Joe's dreams of a better life, drawn from the imagination of his which was as fat and one dimensional as the catalogues he regarded with such reverence. Joe's storage dump, the warehouse of his dreams, lovingly acquired against the day when they would move into their palace. She had said to him once, in the days when she still teased him, that if he ever went near a court of law and they offered him a bible to take the oath, he would ask for a mail-order catalogue rather than scripture, on the basis that there was not a word or promise in there which he could bring himself to disbelieve. Better than all that military stuff he'd had once, though, even though Damien had liked it. At least she'd made Joe get rid of that, once he realised that it too was second hand.

Cath ate the bread and butter, still hungry. He would not want her going out for chips. Once she was indoors, she remained there. It was an aspect of him she had loved, the big man guarding the small woman. Lovable Joe. Even if she shrank from the man in his living room; even if she despaired and ran away again; even if their mutual entertainments outside these walls consisted of no more than yet another visit to yet another pub, she was proud when it happened. At least she had her man, and her home was spotless, which was more than that poor Helen West. If it ain't broke, don't fix it.

The attics seemed to sway with the sound of traffic. She hated the height, thought lovingly of living below stairs, hurried down again to the same pulsating noise from below. The phone rang when her mouth was still full. Cath looked at it in amazement, her jaw drooping before she clamped it shut with her fist and winced. He never rang, not Joe. Cath remained paralysed and then started to chew furiously as the phone spewed out Joe's cheerful message – 'Hallo! We aren't here at the minute . . .' – a message which made it sound as if he and his spouse were constantly out at parties. If he was not behind a bar working, he would be in front of one drinking, and still Cath found herself looking over her shoulder, chewing even faster in case he was in the doorway, commenting on her manners for not acknowledging his presence and eating like an animal. As she stood, head turned, limbs immobile, all she could hear was the warm and hesitant voice of Helen West, beginning as if she too was thrown by the sound of Joe's pretty speech. The voice grew more confident and assured as it went on. Without putting her conclusions into words (a pastime Cath found dangerous and deeply suspicious), Cath sensed someone who was not entirely at home with a machine and not nearly as confident as she looked.

'Oh, er, hallo, message for Cath. Christ, I've just realised it's a bit late to be phoning, but did I actually give you the keys? Anyway, tell Mrs Eliot if I didn't, I'm so stupid. Look forward to seeing you next time. Take care, Helen.'

The voice hurried towards the end, as if the very sound of it made the speaker nervous. I'm so stupid, it said. Cath rocked on her heels, surprised into a sudden snort of laughter and a sudden, delirious sense of pity. Fancy, this other woman was really a bit pathetic, looking the way she did and being the age she was, ten years or so older than Cath, and not having a man who looked after her.

Cath washed up her plate and knife, used them again to make sandwiches for Joe, then went round the kitchen with a damp cloth and a weary touch. She thought of Helen West, weaving a romance to explain the inexplicable phenomenon of a pretty woman without a man. And there was something else. Helen West verged on the beautiful, but she had a great big scar in the middle of her forehead which showed when she swiped away the long, almost black hair which was held back in a slide that could not quite contain the mass of it. Cath knew about scars. The scar alone was sufficient reason to tolerate the woman.

Cath found herself standing over the machine, looking for a way to play back the message so she could hear it again. She had liked the sound of insecurity and her own luxurious feeling of pity, and she had not thought of Damien for at least an hour.

Joe Boyce walked towards the number 59. He had a satchel in which he carried some of the tools of his trade. He did not want them stolen, such as they were. A small knife with a comfortable handle, a shiny Thermos flask for mixing and shaking, a chamois leather, soft as silk, for polishing glasses to a high shine. Last month, someone had broken and entered the Spoon and removed all the spirits from behind the bar. Joe had only shrugged. He had told Mickey Gat more times than he could count that the back of the place was insecure and, besides, the loss of the spirits was not the end of the world. Cocktails were out of fashion; the buggers only wanted beer and wine in summer, apart from the strange old school from the jungles of Chelsea, living on pensions and borrowed time, who bundled themselves into a corner to drink one whisky sour after another. It was the younger varieties, throwing money around while they yawed in those dreadful voices, who got so far up Joe's nose and down his throat he wanted to hit them, but they were the kind big Mickey wanted in the pub. Big Mickey knew nothing about fine wines, but was not a fool. Don't encourage these slow, steady drinkers, Joe was told; nor the ones who come in for half a pint and stay for ever. Joe was respectful to the boss. Mickey Gat was an outstanding and unusual member of the British working class and Joe had plenty of time for those, even those coasting round the edges. Mickey may have been a wolf in sheep's clothing, but still a wolf. If Mickey, born Michaela, had been a mere male, instead of a creature of male mannerisms and attitudes, that male would have been intimidating. As it was, Mickey the woman, with all the strengths of a man plus all the subtleties of her own sex, presented a combination fit to terrify.

''Ere's a little something for your lady wife,' patting Joe on the shoulder with a power which made him wince, one broad-built person to another. 'She'll like this. You could put yourself in luck, old son.'

Mickey was all East End charm, laid on with a trowel, half of it genuine, half of it borrowed from a childhood fascination with the Kray brothers. She had little enough in common with Joe. Mickey's sporting career had been successful for a start: she had been women's weightlifting champion, and had dabbled with wrestling until it ruined her make-up. The muscles still showed. Joe's inglorious boxing career had been monitored by Mr Gat, Mickey's old man, once famous in the ring himself, wily enough to turn triumph into promotion and management, a good gambler, clever enough to diversify the business in all directions, make a pile and a retinue of friends; while Joe's small stature and lack of discipline both inside and outside the army boxing ring had cost him a disgrace. Mr Gat (Harry to his friends) was now 'him indoors', wreathed in the cigarette smoke which had curtailed his career, and, without spite, Mickey liked it best that way. She wore the mantle of his local fame, the business of boxing and pool, the pubs, the merchandise, with the ease of a cloak. It was not anything she told anyone, Harry least of all, but it had always been she who had the brains.

Takes one good bloke to know another. Mickey winked like some amateur comic performer about to tell a lewd joke, adding to the most innocuous exchanges an air of harmless conspiracy. What else Mickey did for a living, except own this pub and two more in Clapton to augment the market stalls, Joe did not know and made it his business not to ask. Mickey rarely came near the place at opening times, unless early or late when the bulk of customers were gone. The morning uniform of shiny shell suit was replaced in the evening by more glamorous gear. Even without the colours, the sheer size of Mickey would have terrified the regulars with their elbow patches. Despite the soft voice, her body seemed to have been poured into the mould of a muscle-bound character from a comic. Superwoman expanded into a mountain range without too many valleys. In comparison, Joe was only a minia-ture, just as he had been with his brother-in-law, Damien, Mickey's best friend. When the takings were particularly good, Mickey would slip a paw into a capacious pocket and hand Joe perfume. From the outset of their acquaintance, Joe had been left in no doubt, without a word on the subject being spoken, that if his own hands extracted anything from the till of the Spoon, he would find his knuckles mashed to a pulp.

Mickey had manicured nails, a curious affectation for such a masculine female.

'Here, take it,' thrusting the perfume again. 'She'll love it, I promise.' A shiny fingernail with a half-sovereign ring tapped a sharp nose, knowingly.

There was a small living area behind the bar, a bathroom and kitchen, full of boxes left by Mickey, all preserved in exactly the same state in which they had arrived. If you were loyal to Mickey, loyalty was returned, but what Mickey did not know was that the only occasion when Joe was ever tempted to laugh, was when that paw with the bright nails extended itself with a boxed bottle of perfume held in the palm.

'Go on, Joe. You'd think I was giving you an f'ing bribe. Take it!'

'Thanks.'

Joe half adored Mickey, except for the sweet smell which accompanied all her gestures, and the scent in the back room, from the boxes.

Present for Cath, just like Damien had done.

Eleven thirty and all quiet tonight. He locked up, heady from the smell of the window-boxes, satisfied with a day's work, soberly conducted, untroubled by the perfume in his satchel. The pretty mews, all low houses, solid doors and cheerful lights, was softly silent as he walked towards the main road for the bus. He had encountered nothing all day but open politeness and sweet-mannered customers, no drunks, no wrecks, no-one drowning sorrows and no aggression. Until that motley crew who had arrived just on closing: kids, already drunk and wanting to make it worse. He shut the door in their faces, listened to them banging on the windows for a while, took no notice, apart from sticking up two fingers in between wiping the bar. They had barked and sworn in upper-class voices, summer holiday kids. Leave them. That's what Mickey said. No after-hours stuff, Joe, not ever. I'm the licensee, right? It just ain't fucking worth it.

He hit Sloane Avenue, walking with a lilt to his step, and it was there they began to follow him. It was not as if he ever aped Mickey's appearance, not consciously at least, but he was a small, well-groomed man with fashionable baggy trousers, the short back and sides of his haircut artfully trendy; he was thirty-three and a man has to look to his youth. Even if he never could have looked a patch on Damien.

'Wanker,' someone said out of the darkness, three feet behind.

'Fucking queer,' said another.

'Naa, just can't get it up,' said a third, and that last remark, intended to do no more than insult, but loaded with a horrible element of truth, made him turn. He saw there were five of them: one fat, bare chested, belly hanging down like a sumo wrestler; one thin as a rake, so the hand holding something in his pocket stood out from his skinny thigh like a growth; two others, middle sized, shifting and sniggering; one more little one, hanging back, as if in need of his mother. He eyed them for a minute, weighed the chances, his mind clear. One fat slob, three others more drunk than sober and a little frightened fairy. Enough, in terms of weight, but his legs could not move. He had a terrifying sense of *déjà vu*, as if he had been in the same place, same time, again and again. The whole scenario assumed a sickening familiarity: he should have braced himself to find that old aggression, the adrenalin sending heat waves to beat against his temples and make him mad, but instead he looked at their faces and heard the music of a siren in the distance. The faces were implacable. They all looked like Cath's brother, features masked in a kind of genial malevolence, all of them twitching. He shut his eyes for a minute, blinking to blot out the presence of that dead man. When he opened his eyes again, the predators were that much closer, only a few feet away, circling with the inhuman technique of animals surrounding prey.

Joe acted instinctively. He screamed at the top of his voice, a shrill shriek, like the high-pitched wailing of a baby. Then he fell to the ground, clutching his satchel to his chest. 'Oh! My heart, my heart! Help me please, help me please!' The words stuck in his throat with their own indigestible hypocrisy, rising like bile along with the peanuts he had consumed behind the bar, with water, in lieu of drink. The effect was the one he desired. With his head turned south, he could look towards Knightsbridge, the bus stop and the presence of taxis. To the left, and a hundred yards away, there was Mr Eliot's house, where he had once peered through the window and frightened a child; he could not stumble towards that source. He writhed in the dust of the pavement, moaning and twisting, not all of it feigned.

They ran. He looked like he was dying, so they ran. Except the last, the little fairy who had hung back in the first place. He paused, then he stopped and then he kicked with remarkable precision. One to the head, his training shoe connecting with the swell of bone just below the left eye. Joe tried to shield his ears, crossing his arms across his face. The little fucker was not out of breath as his boot connected with Joe's ribs, casual kicks which carried the whole weight of the body behind them. An agile body, bending to whisper in his ear. 'Get you next time, sonny. Here's one for luck.'

One final kick which made him scream. He could not meet the eyes.

Damien's eyes, to the life. It was all so bloodless, so shameful.

The conductor on the number 59 had an ebony face, stretched

across beautiful bones, and soulful brown eyes which refused to connect. It was the distant expression of a man who has learned to see no evil. Joe stared at him, challenging him to say something as he got aboard, the only passenger clambering upstairs as the bus moved away, using his hands so that he practically climbed on all fours, clinging to the satchel like a lifeline. When he began to fumble inside it with trembling hands for his travel card, he started to feel the first sensations of sheer relief and the enormity of what he had missed. Christ, they might have got the keys to the pub, and what would Mickey have done about that? He dreaded to think: he would have had to go back and stay there all night, waiting for them to come back. There would have been no question of calling the police, that much was understood. The relief made him tremble more, so that when he held his card up for the conductor, it danced in front of his eyes. He was aware of the black man standing there, swaying slightly instead of moving away.

'Hey, man, where have you been?'

Joe thought the conductor must have noticed the mark on his cheek, the dirt on his clothes. He looked at him but the man was not looking back. He was simply standing there, wrinkling his nose.

'You smelling real sweet, man,' was all he said with a twisted smile, lumbering away to the only other passengers on the top deck, three girls, huddled together giggling at the front.

Joe delved back into the bag. The smell was overpowering. Perfume, the box mashed where he had rolled on it, the liquid sending out fumes which seared his nostrils, made him close the bag and push it away from him.

The shame of it. To lie down and scream like a baby, and come up smelling of roses.

Joe hated perfume. He walked down the road to the place he called home. Perfume made him feel as though he should be followed by cats; it assailed his senses like the smell of manure; it reminded him of being clutched to the bosom of his mother, his grandmother, his aunts, and all those who had left him somewhere along the line. He never gave Mickey's perfume to Cath. He could buy his own gifts for his own wife.

He could not bear to fumble in the bag again, to contaminate his hands by looking for the key. He rang the bell and waited, imagined its throaty and croaking sound upstairs, another thing to be fixed. There was no answer. He rang again, started shouting, Cath, Cath! Let me in. He knew where she would be, up in the attic rooms, staring at photos of Damien, lighting a candle to his memory. The hands around the keys were unsteady: he thundered upstairs.

She was there at the top, holding the door open, anticipating him with her timid brown eyes, dressed in nothing but a towel which she clutched to herself. He could see the faint shadow of bruises on her arms, and another wave of sickening shame swept over him. She saw his face, the bruise grown swollen and livid on the journey home.

'I bought you some perfume, Cath,' was all he said as he stepped inside.

'Joke from Joe,' he added. She looked at the bruise, without touching him, still holding the towel across her chest. Then she wrinkled her nose, slightly, smiled with the smile of a sphinx.

He had no idea from where the blow came, only that it was he who had administered it. She went reeling back, into the living room, hitting the wall. He followed, feeling for his belt, panting. And then he was pinning her to the floor, pushing himself inside her, oblivious to the dryness, pumping his seed in there, quickly shouting as he came. Then he lay across her on the rough carpet, sobbing.

'I love you, Cath. I love you.' She stroked his head.

'I know you do.'

One hand stroked his hair against her chest. The other fingered the scar on her abdomen which made her so impossible to love. There had been the promise of a child, long, long since. She had not wanted it then, not while she was a child herself, and now, in her arms, she cradled this other.

CHAPTER FIVE

'Why is it, Bailey, we offer you administrative jobs, suited to the rank you've somehow managed to achieve, God knows how, and you sidestep the issue? We send you for management training and you go straight back to the street. Like some bloody homing pigeon.'

The blank face before him showed no glimmer of emotion, less of humour, a face carved from granite. It reminded Bailey of a gargoyle, weathered by centuries into something almost beyond further decay: not the face the divisional commander showed to his grandchildren.

'I suppose I like nicking people, sir.'

'You've got a degree, haven't you? We need brains like yours in think-tanks, Bailey. We need you at the top.'

'I don't think so, sir. With respect,' he added thoughtfully, to make it look as if serious thought was a habit, 'I think you need me at the bottom.'

'Of which heap, Bailey?'

'The dung heap,' said Bailey. 'The septic tank, not the think-tank.' The commander's smile did not alter the gargoyle effect. They would speak again soon, he said, and to Bailey's ears, the words contained more threat than promise.

He walked down the corridors of New Scotland Yard towards the lift. Each floor was the same, built round the central shaft, with minor alterations to the layout. The gents lavatory was always in the same place, the senior command offices had similar styles, and on one floor, the number of which he could never remember by some Freudian convenience, there was a foyer of portraits of old commissioners and a dining room reserved for those *en route* to becoming the next. Bailey had indeed managed to skip his way up the ranks without ever resorting to politics or policy. All he had done was remain industrious and effective, but inconspicuous, making no complaints and telling no tales. For useful loose cannons like Ryan he had simply rearranged their duties; in the case of men with a propensity to violence or light fingers, he sidestepped the whole paraphernalia of discipline proceedings by telling them exactly what he was prepared to do to them should they fail to reconsider their careers. Turnover could be high under Bailey's command. He could exert more quiet terror than a hanging judge and inspire the kind of loyalty reserved for the Queen. Ryan said he was a secretive bastard, who never caused embarrassment: that was all there was to it.

Which meant those on high should let him alone to perform where he excelled: troubleshooting, organising an investigation wherever he was asked, a humble, only ostensibly obedient maverick, rolling with the punch of being landed with teams of inadequates. Some learned to take responsibility; others, like Ryan, would always be the second lieutenant in need of a leader. Most police officers were eminently adaptable. Except himself. He could no more live and breathe in this ivory tower than he could have flown above it. Senior officers' mess, waitress dining in cosy style, a corridor of portraits and committees, advancement beyond the stratosphere; speak now, the commander said with his forked tongue, and all this could be yours.

Outside, there was another bomb scare. Bailey had to wait to get out from the underground car park while someone stuck a mirror beneath his car. Girls in skirts were asked to consent to the same examination on their way in to work, and he wanted to suggest to the man on duty that if he had brought in a bomb, it would have been gift wrapped.

The sun shone, melting the irritation and sense of impending doom. Bailey might have lost that capacity for fury which had made him want to hit walls, but he could not shed his contempt for ambition, any more than he could rid himself of the far more corrupting force of pity; he looked to his own demise without a sense of tragedy. At forty-seven he was old, for a policeman. The equivalent of an honourable discharge would not leave him penniless. He just wished he had reached the age when he was really pragmatic enough to leave alone a delegated quick-result case like the murder of Damien Flood.

He chuckled with a sense of freedom as he rounded Parliament Square, saw the traffic jam, stopped and ran his tongue behind his top teeth, executed a U-turn with the satisfying ease of a taxi driver diving towards the prospect of a fare and then found that the change of direction left him, suddenly, directionless. He was pointing towards Victoria when he wanted to go northeast to his own happy hunting grounds. There was no other immediate reason for Bailey to go for a drink at the Spoon and Fiddle. Owned by Mickey Gat from Whitechapel. Run by the brother-in-law of a four-month-dead, one-time athlete, pool player turned drunk, killed in the aftermath of a pub fight. Bailey could recall, word for word, the statement made by this brother-in-law, Joe Boyce, background material only.

'I get one day off a week from being a barman,' the statement said, 'and when I do, I go to a different kind of place to drink. If Damien was around, I would go with him. To tell the truth, he wasn't the best companion, since he could not hold his drink, always picked a fight, while me, I get quiet and sleepy. Anyway, he did pick an argument with someone in the pub, the Lamb it's called, only round the corner from where I live, as a matter of fact, and it all ended up in threats, you come outside with me, all that stuff. Damien loved it of course, Damien would. He had three friends with him, big blokes, like himself, all ex-boxers, they could handle anything. I dunno why it is when blokes are big, they seem to attract trouble. One of them wanted to go home, so Damien said go then, but he didn't, and then Damien says to me, stay, will you? And I said, the hell I will, if this lot are coming back for a fight, I've your sister to look after and I'm not getting hurt for anyone. Fine, he says, fine, and we get another drink. I don't drink much myself; you can't when you run a bar, but when I'm not at work, I take anything offered. They're a good laugh, that crew of Damien's, when they get together. That other team were long gone, I forgot about them.'

Ryan had taken this statement. He had an ear for the vernacular and an ability to make people talk, something to do with his deceptively friendly face.

'Anyway, I hardly noticed that the crowd had left and I forgot the fact they threatened to come back. I can't, for the life of me, remember what the argument was about. Damien was good at pool; the pub has five tables; he'd won some money off a bloke who thought he was better; Damien had fleeced the poor kid on a bet, that was it, I think. Oh, maybe three or four games. What was lost? I've no idea. Maybe fifty, more like a hundred, but Damien was so shambling and so clever, they couldn't see him coming. He was more than good at pool: he was brilliant.'

There would have been a pause in the statement, for tea, Bailey guessed, rehearsing it all in his mind. The man was not a defendant, merely a witness. He would have been afforded all the luxury the police station could allow. Which was tea or coffee in a smoke-filled interview room, not quite far enough away from the sobbing and grunting in the cells.

'Anyway, the place closed and out we went. Damien wanted to go to some other place, I said, no, not me, I must get home, your sister has an early start. He nodded, he never thought much of me, to tell the truth, and you were either with Damien or against him. So I didn't wait to see if there was anyone there in the shadows, if you see what I mean. He had more than enough going for him with his friends around him. I was only ever asked along for the ride because my wife wanted Damien and me to be friends; he's a bit flash for me. If he wanted a fight he had one. Boys will be boys and there never was any stopping my brother-in-law. I never dreamt it would go so far.'

Not a bad bloke, that Joe Boyce, Ryan had said to Bailey. Bailey had never seen the man whose evidence had been agreed as part of the setting; it would provide nothing of great interest to either prosecution or defence at the forthcoming trial. Pleasant Mr Joseph Boyce had helped with descriptions, that was all, leaving before the action, as Damien's friends had confirmed in their own, sorrowful evidence. Since they too had failed to prevent the death, they could not afford contempt, although one of them suggested it. Joe was nothing but a hanger-on, adopted by Damien and Mickey Gat because he was wed to Damien's sister, Mary Catherine Boyce: there was a statement from her too.

Bailey could not have said why he wanted to cast his eyes over Mr Boyce, some little trace element of bitterness in the statement, perhaps, but with his car accidentally pointing west instead of east, the time was as good as any. Ryan was a fine investigator. He got on the wavelength and spoke as he was spoken to, but his judgement, well, that varied.

Bailey always knew the exact time of day, and as long as it was greater London, exactly where he was without reference to any-thing or anybody. The map and the minutes past the hour always seemed to tally with his preconceptions. The talent was one he dismissed as no more than accident; you walk round streets, he said, you get to know which way is south and how long it is since last you slept.

The Spoon and Fiddle surprised him, first for its diminutive size, then for the luxuriance of the flowers, third for its signs of taste and privacy, and lastly, as an afterthought, its proximity to the Eliots.

'Mr Boyce?'

The man turned from an assiduous polishing of glasses at the bar, responded with an almost stagy deference, clicking his heels.

'At your service, sir!' A small man, Bailey noted, muscular; soft round the chin.

He produced his warrant card. 'About the Donovan trial. Can I have a word?' It sounded such a clichéd way to begin but Bailey knew life was full of clichés; most people understood little else and expected a policeman to talk like his TV equivalent. What he had not expected was for Joseph Boyce to respond in the same clichéd terms, by looking visibly shocked, turning white, so that the livid bruise on his cheekbone and round the left eye burned in a pale skin like the mark of a branding iron. The reaction was quickly controlled. Boyce shook himself, looked resigned, then smiled with a sigh and extended his hand.

Bailey did not want to take it, did so reluctantly. The pressure was dry and firm.

'My, but you gave me a shock. I thought all that was over, bar the shouting. I hope they hang the bastard, but you can't these days, can you?'

'You seem to have been in a fight, Mr Boyce.' Bailey pointed at the bruise, somewhat rudely.

'Kids. Followed me home last evening after I wouldn't serve them a drink. It's nothing. I got away lightly.'

'Did you report it?'

'C'mon, sir, you know better than that. When I couldn't begin to tell you what they looked like? I just wanted to get home. How else can I help you?'

There was a hidden truculence behind the easy manner. The man was clean, but Bailey could sense fear.

'I just wanted to check a few points on your statement. About your brother-in-law and the evening he died. I'm sorry if it upsets you, but if I dot the Ts and cross the Is, there's less chance you'll be needed at the trial.'

The light of hope sprang into Joe's eyes. 'That would be great,' he said firmly. 'I don't want to go anywhere near a court if I can help it. Upsets the wife, see? What do you want to know? Thought I said it all.'

Bailey hoiked his long frame onto a bar stool. He had not quite thought what to ask, an investigator without portfolio and a car pointed in the wrong direction, but he was rarely at a total loss for words.

'Were you fond of your brother-in-law, Mr Boyce?'

'Oh yes, of course, even though he could be a problem. Anyone who knew Damien loved him. You should have seen the turnout for his funeral. I've never seen flowers like it. Never.'

Bailey nodded, without adding that he had been present himself on the edges of the same funeral, taking in the appearance of Damien's friends and looking out for signs of his family. There had been one woman sobbing, only one. The flowers had been repellent; Bailey's experience showed that the amount of floral tributes at funerals was often in inverse proportion to the grief, indeed they were sometimes a last revenge.

'Is your wife the only relative?'

'There's a cousin or two somewhere, but otherwise, yes. The parents died when they were kids; Damien and she grew up together. Like peas in a pod. Very close.'

'What does your wife do, Mr Boyce?'

Boyce turned from friendly to angry.

'Leave her out of it, will you? She's had quite enough, what with having to identify her only kith and kin and then being asked to confirm what time I came home that night, as if it was me who needed the alibi! What does it matter what she does for a living?'

Bailey could picture the statement of Mary Catherine Boyce. Short and to the point. Identifying her brother. Saying what time her husband had gone out and come in. Cleaning lady, he remembered suddenly, as if that mattered.

He got up. 'I'd only want to ask her a few questions about Damien's background. I know there was a fight, but we're still, well, how can I put it, short on the motive.'

'Anyone can get killed in a fight,' said Boyce, pointing to the bruise. 'Happens every day in this God-forsaken place. You could work hard all your life without ever putting a foot wrong and still go that way. What difference does your background make?' He was becoming increasingly agitated.

'Where could I find her, Mr Boyce? I'll do my best not to cause any upset.'

'I believe you. Others wouldn't. Why don't you send that other bloke? I liked him.'

Because Ryan is so often blind, Bailey thought, watching the other man struggling for control. Boyce was working out how to minimise the inevitable, a primitive, Bailey concluded: a body responsive to orders and not so stupid as to imagine he could hide his wife for ever. Nothing unusual in that: there were not many men who wanted police officers calling on their wives, especially a spouse unlikely to declare her meagre income or pay tax on it. But it was not this aspect of the black economy which worried Boyce. He was weighing up the pros and cons of where such an interview with Cath should take place. Should he invite this interference home some afternoon when he could insist on being present, or could he ensure Bailey saw Cath somewhere where she would be equally awkward, embarrassed and taciturn? He smiled. There was no malice in the smile, Bailey noticed, merely satisfaction.

'All right, if you must. No time like the present. She's working round the corner here. Chantry Street. You might know it. Big houses. Number seven.'

Then it was Bailey's turn to mask surprise. Declining the now effusive offer of a drink, something Ryan rarely did, he left with a nod of acknowledgement.

As he reached his own car, Bailey saw a large, silver-coloured Jaguar, old but perfectly preserved, moving with all the grace of an ageing ballerina as it rolled over the cobblestones of the mews. It stopped outside the flowers of the Spoon with scarcely a sound, while Bailey looked on, enviously. There were few materialistic ambitions which moved him much, outside the clocks he collected, but the sight of this elegant vehicle inspired an acquisitive admiration. The very best vintage, he thought, I would love one of those, a car which was more than a car. He was thinking, as an antidote, how such a motor would not last five minutes in his neck of the woods without a garage built like a fortress, when a figure rose out of the driving seat, yawned, stretched and executed three karate kicks, before ambling into the Spoon. A huge creature, dressed in a vivid shell suit, with a walk both languid and energetic, the sun catching pale hair and a face tanned by sunbeds. Bailey smiled to himself, envy of the car dispelled. Awesomely gorgeous Mickey Gat. A legend in her own time, except for lazy investigators like Ryan who never listened to important gossip and never kept their eyes open wide enough. Feminism incarnate, in one sense, that was Mickey Gat; big enough to make jelly of a man. One of a dying breed, lawless, but law-enforcing. Like the Jag, Bailey reflected: they were both in their way the very best of British. The sight of Mickey, looking like a bull in a china shop amid the discreet wealth of the mews, somehow made Bailey feel at home. He smiled after the retreating figure with affection, almost with desire, which was only in part for the car.

Mickey had attended the Damien funeral, probably contributed some of the flowers of which Joe had boasted, but it had never been part of Ryan's narrow mandate to explore any closer link. It made no odds, surely, who the murdered man knew; he was killed in a pub brawl and no single witness had suggested it was more complicated than that. Bailey shrugged. Neither had the ripples of the investigation turned up the fact that the sister of the deceased worked for a family Bailey knew. Why should it? Mary Catherine Boyce working for the Eliots; the fact did indeed stretch the long arm of coincidence. Bailey had learned never to be surprised by the elastic length of that particular limb. He decided, all the same, not to go to the Eliots' number seven Chantry Street. Something told him that was a move which could embarrass Emily Eliot, and her Treasure. Let well alone. If the woman the Eliots called Cath, and her statement called Mary, had not told them anything about her family, least of all the death of a brother, it was not for Bailey to invade her privacy; after all, he had no real purpose, even less official blessing for these formless, further enquiries. He was only here because he had turned his car in the wrong direction. Mary Catherine, known as Cath. The woman who had also turned Helen's flat into a different version of itself over the last week or two. If Bailey vowed to keep diplomatic silence with the Eliots, should he then use Helen in pursuit of his own curiosity? She would not like that.

Emily Eliot sang as she worked. Occasionally, when her usual reserve deserted her, Cath would croon a little too, stopping if she thought she was heard. For some reason Emily could not discern, Cath rarely seemed to get further than 'Onward Christian Soldiers', and only the first verse of that. 'With the blood of Jesus, going on before!' The words would emerge in the midst of a barely recognisable tune, half grunted, half sung. She and Emily rarely sang in unison, although that was often the way they worked. There was never a shortage of tasks in the long mornings Cath spent in the house. One day a week, they would tackle something specific. Today it was a large dressing room attached to the main bedroom. Emily was sure it had moths in it. One of Alistair's suits had been eaten to death. She did not enjoy these joint tasks: they made her loud.

'Little sods,' Emily yelled. 'Look at that! Why the hell can't they go for cheap old sweaters? Why concentrate on the one thing which costs money? Mohair and something, this was once. Nice and soft for them to get their little teeth into, they can't even make an effort. Look at it.'

'He didn't wear it once, last winter,' Cath pointed out. Emily beamed, her rage subsiding. Put Cath in here, with her awful disinfectant smell, the moths would die anyway.

'He never really liked it, that's why.' She emerged from the depths with an armful of clothes on hangers.

'In fact, most of the things in the back of here no-one really likes. I just hate the thought of the bloody moths chomping away without asking permission first. Most of this belongs on the rubbish heap. Unless there's anything you want, of course.'

'I'll think about it, can I?'

Emily nodded, suppressing the irritation which so often beset her when she and Cath worked in close proximity. It was a reluctance to touch her, no more than that, which Emily translated into a slight aversion to one who was at once so passive and deferential, and at other times as stubborn as a mule. She knew Cath would take the clothes as soon as her back was turned. She just could not do it while she was being watched, and that was irritating too. If Cath felt the slightest insult at the idea that she was a fitting recipient for old garments otherwise unfit to wear, she did not show it and knew no such insult was intended. There were features of the upper middle class which made Cath marvel. The money they had never seemed to go on new things: people like

Emily could bargain like a trader in an Eastern market, she was always making do. The children wore hand-me-downs without complaint since they had long since realised there was no choice; the cars were far from streamlined and the furniture was old. Cath could see the value of the furniture she treated with such care, but although she admired the taste, she wondered why Emily would not give her the second-hand rug with the faded colours and get herself a new one. If their positions were reversed, she was quite sure that Emily herself would take home the contents of her employer's wardrobe without turning a hair.

'Coffee,' said Emily firmly. Cleaning ladies were supposed to have a reputation for time-wasting gossip, talking when they should be working, or so she heard, but here, the situation was reversed. Emily talked, at length, about nothing and everything, and it was usually Cath who rose and said, time to get on. Emily sometimes talked to avoid the challenge of silence and a sense of intimacy she resented, but she did not admit that, even to herself. It seemed ungrateful. Instead, she loathed, without comment, the way Cath ate wholemeal bread with open-mouthed hunger, never closing her mouth until it was finished. They went downstairs, Cath last, Emily singing and shouting for Jane. Cath watched her.

On the first landing, Jane appeared, with one finger over her lips in a request for Cath to say nothing, then took her hand. She was an affectionate child; they all were, even Mark, the surly teenage son home from school. He would greet Cath with a bear hug; she would pretend to protest, giddy with the sensation of outrageous affection. She bent towards Jane. 'What is it? A game? Are you hiding?'

'No. I got something for you. Quick.' She darted away into her father's study. Cath shook her head. Mr Eliot's study was strictly taboo: no child was allowed inside; even Cath herself was forbidden to enter Alistair's domain which remained more or less orderly, the way he was himself. Cath made a warning tut, tut.

'Lovey, you know you shouldn't be in here. What if Mum catches you?'

'I know,' Jane whispered. 'But I wanted to draw you a picture and I didn't have any paper. Not the right kind.'

The child loved the perforated listing paper which spilled out of the old and faithful printer in the study. Her own supplies were never as good as those she stole, and Cath could see the point. Jane held up a banner of three pages, waving it like a flimsy flag. The multicoloured drawing began with a large head, wearing a hat with flowers. A stalk-like neck led on to the next sheet, containing a thin torso with the suggestion of a bosom, dressed in a black dress with straps over the shoulders. The waist led on to curvy hips and the final sheet depicted a pair of inordinately slender legs ending in high heels, and the name CATH.

'It's a picture of you,' Jane said, urgently, impatient at the lack of comprehension. 'You. Going to a party. In Mummy's clothes. Can't you tell? Here.' She thrust the fluttering paper, already creased, towards Cath's calloused hands and Cath wanted to weep. Emily's voice came from the kitchen, faint but definite from this level.

'Thank you,' said Cath gravely. 'Thank you very much indeed. I shall keep it for ever.'

They grinned. Cath pointed towards the desk.

'Is that how it looked when you came in?'

Jane nodded.

'Are you sure?'

The nod became more definite. Cath shut the door very quietly behind them and, rolling her extraordinary portrait with great care, led the way downstairs, the first line of 'Onward Christian Soldiers' bubbling in her throat. She put the gift in her bag which lay on the hall floor, felt a moment of happiness. They love me, she thought, they really do. They think I'm lovely. Like Damien thought I was lovely. She caught hold of Jane's hair as they approached the kitchen at the back, pretended to drag her in.

'Look who I found, playing all by herself in her room like a good girl,' she said.

'Hmmm,' said Emily, tearing at the cellophane covering of a packet of biscuits with her teeth. 'Not the last time I looked.' And then with the sudden change of subject which often took Cath's breath away, she asked, 'Cath, what's that bruise on your arm? You didn't have that yesterday, did you? It looks jolly sore.'

Cath glanced quickly to the point of her right arm where she had pushed up the sleeve of her blouse well beyond the elbow. Casually, without showing the hot flush of guilt which crept across her, she pulled the sleeve down.

'Oh, that? Oh, I'm not too sure.'

'You must know,' said Emily, equally casual.

Cath pretended to think, taking the proffered cup of coffee, sitting down slowly. The kitchen table still held remnants of breakfast, a movable feast in this house. Her brow cleared.

'Now I have it, I do remember, yes I do. You know I go to your friend, Helen, on Tuesdays? Well, I was doing out her bathroom, yesterday afternoon, leaning in to do that big bath of hers, you know, and I sort of fell in. Bang, with my arm right against the taps. Stupid, wasn't it? Doesn't hurt,' she finished, addressing her remarks to Jane who sat pressed so close to her, the warmth of her skin passed into her own.

'You fell in a bath?' Jane chortled. 'Silly!'

Emily laughed too. 'Really, Cath! Listen, you must tell Helen. She'll have to pay you danger money. Are you sure it doesn't hurt? Only I've got all sorts of liniment, stuff like that . . .'

'No,' said Cath, firmly. 'No, it really doesn't hurt at all.' Not here, it didn't. Not in this house, in this sun-filled kitchen where a child drew a picture showing the cleaning lady as a glamour queen; where people really cared for her. At that moment, nothing hurt. Nothing needed fixing.

'Tell me,' said Emily, still casual but consumed with curiosity, 'is Helen's flat really as dirty as she claims?'

Sometimes Joe went home in the afternoon. If the lunchtime trade had been rich and the afternoon trade promised nothing, Mickey told him to use his sense and shut up shop for a while. It took almost an hour with the number 59 crawling through daytime traffic, so that he never had time to stop for long before turning back in time to open again at half-past five. He never quite knew why he bothered, unless to see if Cath was in; he hated the sight of his own front door with the peeling paint in the bright and unforgiving light of a fine summer's afternoon. Walking away from it in the morning, he did not look back; coming home after dark, he did not notice the outside either, but in the afternoon he did. He looked at it with disgust, and considered what a raw deal his life had given him. Nothing was fair; nothing ever had been, not since he had been a little kid with parents who gave him everything and promised him the earth.

His bedroom had been full of toys, anything he wanted, and their new house full of new things, until Dad disappeared and Mother found a grateful widower who had no room for a spoiled son. Joe had left them as soon as he could, and never gone back. He did not think of his parents with gratitude, he remembered only the bitterness of their defection.

A new house in the place where he grew up was what he knew he deserved in life, if only he could fight his way through the conspirators who combined to keep it from him. It was never his own fault that he had failed to become a First Division football player or a champion boxer, that he managed to leave the Army after seven years without the beginnings of a trade, that he could not concentrate, had a problem with drink, relationships and, unless motivated by the fear he had for Mickey Gat, laziness. Nothing to do with him: it was them; they were gunning for him.

Afternoon journeys on the bus could render him incoherent with self-pity, especially if he was forced into a seat next to someone who smelt. Bus people hardly entered the conspiracy against him, but he hated them anyway. Not as much as he had hated his brother-in-law Damien; a different kind of hate, a fearful, envious loathing of someone who, drunk or sober, remained the epitome of everything he was not. Joe unlocked the door and trod upstairs. The heat was stuffy, stuffier still when he went up to the attics. It was not true that he had secured this substandard flat through an army friend as he had told Cath; Damien had got it for them. Just as Damien had got him the job with Mickey Gat. Damien had been a fixer. Everyone loved Damien, including his sister. His sister loved the sod 100 per cent, he could not do wrong in her eyes.

It took a person who hid things in his own house to know when someone else did the same. When he had come home last night, he had heard her hurried footsteps descending from the attics as he opened the door and met her bright, guilt-tinged smile of welcome. Cath did not much like the attic rooms; he knew she did not. She would watch him receive yet another parcel from the mail-order firm with tight-lipped disapproval, murmuring nice, very nice, then buttoning her lip, as the package was all wrapped up again and consigned to one of the rooms. She would not willingly go upstairs, he thought, as he often did, to gloat over the colour TV, the camcorder, the three-piece luggage set, the patio furniture, the barbecue, the tool boxes and the wealth of smart kitchen equipment they somehow never used. Knives in a block, a fish kettle when they never ate fish, the blender, the coffee maker, the gadget for scooping ice cream; she just could not think the same way about these things. She simply did not see that they were the way to a better life.

Joe forgot how these goods made him feel rich, as well as safe. The first room was gloomy, with three boxes obscuring the light from the window, and yes, he was right, something had been moved: they had not been there before. He moved to one side a telephone, a twenty-four-piece dinner service, a set of casserole dishes, all encased in packing. There, beneath the window, was the shrine in all its obscenity. He almost expected to see a lighted candle, but found only three photographs of Damien, covered in clear polythene bags, sitting on a tray among three small vases of dying flowers.

For a moment, he wanted to tear at the flowers with his teeth. He plucked them from their containers and crushed them underfoot, for fear of contamination. He picked up the first photograph, gazed at it briefly and tore it in half, put the two pieces together neatly and tore it again. Then he took a lighter from his pocket and holding the other photographs together, held the flame to the corners. They were slow to ignite, the polythene melting rather than burning, the photos inside curling grey then brown. It took a matter of minutes to create a pile of slightly sticky ash, and in that time the trembling of his own limbs did not improve. The lighter flame scorched his thumb, but he ignored the pain until it was done.

Oh Cath, with all she owed him, would she ever learn how to love him best?

CHAPTER SIX

Thou shalt be cured, brother. The course of justice ran as smooth as a saloon car over boulders. More like an engine heated beyond endurance in a summer's-day traffic jam. The courtroom faced south at the back of an old building with a view of railway lines, there were blinds across the windows, diffusing a sulky light as the heat poured in. Air-conditioning had been abandoned: it was louder than the trains.

Helen's allotted place was uncomfortably close to the witness-box, so that when the woman inside it made her nervous gestures, Helen could feel the drops of perspiration, gathered from the armpits into the palms, flick across her own face, like a kind of spittle she could not avoid. The pages she turned were damp.

'Fifteenth of March, this year. Can you recall that date?'

'Yes.' Voice no more than a whisper, fingers moving uncertainly, looking for something to hold.

'Speak up a little, if you would. Questions come from me, answers to the magistrates. You don't have to look at the defendant. Please.'

Her voice barked the series of orders, plaintive to her own ears, brisk to others, merely compelling to the witness. The defendant looked harmless.

'We've established you live with the defendant. What time did he come home that evening?'

'About eleven thirty.'

'Normal time?'

'More or less.'

'Did you have any conversation?'

'Yes. He said he wanted something to eat and I said there

wasn't anything. He got angry.' She was gaining confidence now, going faster.

'What happened next?' (Oh for a pound sterling in the bank to mark every occasion she had prompted a witness with such a neutral question.)

'He hit me.'

'Can you give us a bit more detail?'

'He . . . he head-butted me. You know, bashed his head into my face. I felt my nose go, there was blood everywhere, I started screaming and the baby woke up and . . .'

'Could we take this just a little bit slower? You see that lady writing down what you're saying. If you could just watch her pen.'

Phrase by phrase. The words, the blows, the crying of the baby, the decisions, should she go first to the child or to the bathroom for fear the blood would touch him. Helen's hair was piled neatly over a crawling scalp.

She leant towards her opponent. 'No argument about calling the police, is there? Can I lead on that?' She turned over another damp page, as if she did not know it by heart. Behind her, she could feel Mary Secura relaxing slightly.

'You called the police. What time was that?'

'A bit later. About half an hour.'

'Why delay? Why not do that at once?'

The skin on the girl's face was flushed a dull red, swollen with the first signs of anger.

'I only called them when I saw what he'd done.'

'Do you mean your injury?' There was an impatient gesture of denial; another flicker of moisture landed on Helen's hair.

'No. He'd only gone into the kitchen and eaten the baby's food. Two jars of baby food, and he'd drunk all the milk. I didn't have any left for the morning. That's when I phoned.'

The cut-off point varies every time, Mary Secura said. No telling what will make them crack, the smell of another woman; the drinking of the baby's milk. Presto.

Summer had grown into a stultifying incubus of grey skies and humid life. Later, cooler, Helen was attempting to explain to Emily Eliot not only the wonder she was feeling two weeks after the arrival of Cath to clean the house, but also the mixture of emotions she felt at the end of a case she had managed to win. How it should have been a sense of triumph, justice done: a man waiting sentence of imprisonment, Mary Secura grimly pleased, witness weeping. There was no sense of triumph at all. Nothing but the sensation that all her manoeuvring, posturing, bullying and flirting in cross-examination could ever reveal was simply a pale and inaccurate version of the truth. Emily did not really want to listen; no-one wanted to listen to this, not if they came from the foreign realms of normal family life. No-one wanted to hear her expound on the frustration of playing justice by the rules, not for the sake of actually doing any good, but simply because that was the only way of doing the best possible. Emily did not want philosophical conversation.

'I think your lifestyle is perfect, you know,' Emily was saying, mournfully. 'A virile man visiting a couple of days a week, no kids, double income, all that,' she added in the wine-and-coffee bar next to Peter Jones, late-night shopping, Wednesdays. For the first time ever, Helen was irritated with Emily, which was why it was important to put the record straight. A friend was a friend. A friend with kids was one you always had to cross London to see, since your convenience was always subject to theirs, your time infinitely less important, your own commitments to keeping yourself alive, apparently, nil.

'You make it sound as if I do nothing for the rest of the time,' she said. 'And I don't have access to Bailey's income, don't want it either. Pity, he earns far more than me.'

Emily looked crestfallen. 'Oh, I'm sorry,' she said, defusing any misunderstanding before it grew into discomfort. 'I'm not being very sensitive or realistic, am I? Only there are times when I envy you.'

'You joke,' said Helen. 'All I'm saying is you wouldn't have envied me this morning in court. And, as it happens, I often envy you.'

Her own words came back at her like little arrows. Envy for another was anathema. Even if they did have healthy children, faithful husband, wonderful house and a vision of life Helen found increasingly appealing. Castle walls, she told herself. Just build them.

'No, I don't joke,' said Emily pulling a face. 'I know you work hard, and it isn't easy, but keeping a family like mine often makes me feel like the clothes in the tumble dryer, all mashed up, even if they come out all right in the end. I don't know how long it is since I read a book.'

'Well, tough,' said Helen, crossly. 'I read them to stop having nightmares.'

They had only come out to make the final choice on the blues and yellows which had haunted Helen for a fortnight and now made her see double. Helen loved to shop; Emily Eliot knew how. Emily turned shopping into a mission with measurable targets; Helen treated it as an excuse for glorious indecision.

'You wouldn't like a conventional family life, Helen, you really wouldn't.'

Funny how people go on protesting that their own fortune is not as good as it looks, Helen thought. Samples of the chosen curtain material lay on the table in front of them; Helen had a dozen others at home. She slightly regretted the finality of choice, still agonised, reeling at the shock and the cost, wondering if there was still time to change her mind before Emily's needlewoman did her worst.

'How could you say I wouldn't like married life with 2.2 kids? I could just about do it if I got a move on, even though I'd be an elderly primagravida and I could save precious time by having twins.'

'Yes, well, you'd better decide before you redecorate the house. Don't think you know it all just because you've got a cat.'

Helen said nothing, feeling the stirring of a depression which often arose, like the beginnings of a headache, when she subjected her life to scrutiny. Emily watched her closely, then picked up a small piece of golden coloured cloth with blue woven into the fabric in thin stripes.

'You were right about this one,' she said. 'Listen, H, am I right in thinking you've got to the stage of wishing dear old Bailey would make an honest woman of you? Do I detect faint yearnings towards the joint mortgage and the patter of tiny feet?'

'Put like that, I don't know.'

'Well, just in case you were, let me suggest the primitive approach. You know how they dislike upheaval, poor darlings, and adore their creature comforts? Well, once your three or four rooms are revamped, beckon him in to an oasis of domestic bliss, nice food smells and all that. Works a charm.'

Helen laughed out loud. 'Is that what you did with Alistair?'

'You'd better believe it. Even the nicest men are ambivalent, you know. You have to lead them to it.'

'And now,' Helen said, 'even if it crossed his mind to want to go, which it wouldn't, of course, your darling Alistair couldn't possibly leave, could he?'

'Over my dead body,' Emily said, with a grim determination Helen found slightly disconcerting. 'I'd fleece him,' she added, 'then kill him. Another glass?'

'You only have to go round the corner. I have to get the 59.'

'Oh Gawd, never mind.' A hand was waved. Emily shuffled forward on the small table, arms across bosom, confidential. 'Now, never mind men. How are you getting on with Cath?'

'What?' Helen was thinking of nest-building, a spider making a web to catch a big, ungainly fly. Emily drummed her fingers on the table, then snapped them in front of Helen's eyes.

'Look, I need gossip. Cath, our cleaning lady. Listen, I never mentioned it, because she is such a treasure, and I trust her absolutely round the kids, but she can irritate. A bit clumsy here and there. Sometimes she's so careful I want to scream. Then she goes off into a different world. Must be why she's got the most frightful bruise from falling into your bath.' She bit her tongue, in memory of Cath's habit of open-mouthed eating.

Cath never cleaned the bathroom. Helen had been specific in saying leave the bathroom, that is the only bit I never mind doing and besides, I just can't ask anyone to clean my lavatory. The bathroom was the only thing pristine in the first place: Helen felt defensive and evasive.

'I've scarcely seen Cath since the first time,' she said, carefully. 'I don't have to. She's usually going out as I'm coming in. Otherwise, I've only seen what she can do. Oh, by the way, who came to dinner the other week?'

Emily put her head in her hands.

'Vegetarian judges. Three. With their wives. I'd cooked a leg of lamb.'

The sultry day had transformed itself into an evening of treacherous splendour after a shower. The light was perfect, and the stillness made the trees flanking Helen's street and Helen's garden droop with graceful relief, the leaves green and luscious from the earlier rain. There was the pretence of a fickle greeting in the languid movement of the branches, like a hapless crowd of tired school-children hired to greet a late-arriving celebrity.

Curtain material bought, paint purchased. Renew the house; there was nothing more important.

No Bailey tonight, no hand and body held in the dark. Helen let herself in through the basement door, noticing as she did so how clean the windows were, reflecting her pale face and long dark hair, distorted into greater untidiness. And then when the door swung inwards, she noticed the smell, the first, now familiar and pleasant scent of Cath's ministrations. Lavender polish, a whiff of bleach, an absence of dust and the removal of any other odour. Helen revelled in this smell, liked it enough to mitigate her own reluctance to give away keys, an aspect of the arrangement she detested. She was not like Emily Eliot: she did not really like an open house.

But there was more than a smell; there was someone else there. She could sense the breeze which wafted down the long corridor and threatened to slam shut the front door when the French windows were left open in the bedroom. As her hands fell to her sides, nerveless with a sudden fear, the door slammed behind her. There was a momentary return to throat-constricting panic, but as her eyes adjusted to the light, the fear refused to emerge. In the gloom of the hall, she saw the Hoover crouching like a sleeping animal, a duster on the floor, and from the bedroom, the strange grunting sound of someone humming 'Onward Christian Soldiers'. Burglars did not clean; Cath did that. The slow development of relief turned to anger.

'What the hell do you think you're doing here?'

It was a stupid question, and even in the phrasing of it her anger ebbed away. Cath was cleaning the French windows, standing with her mouth open in mid-verse, the cat curled at her feet, the woman herself smelling of work, blouse abandoned and wearing nothing but a T-shirt, modestly ill fitting. They gazed at one another in mutual shock.

'I'm cleaning the windows, aren't I?' Cath mumbled defensively. The light was bright, the way it was at the back of the house. Helen squinted, eyes adjusting yet again, still taking in what they had to see: the upper part of Cath's arms covered in bruises which extended across her chest. Cath followed her glance, then deliberately turned away.

'You frightened the life out of me,' Helen said, moving towards the bed which was central to the room. She took off her jacket and laid it down over Cath's white blouse. The other woman did not speak, did not resume the singing either.

'Working late?'

'Yes.'

'I'll make us some tea, then.'

It was cruel, she supposed, to make a woman sit in the light of the south-facing room where clean windows spared neither her exposure nor the aggression which suffused her face, as she sat with her arms hugged across her chest, a picture of defiance and misery combined. Sweating, just like the witness. Wary eyes, like Shirley Rix.

'I thought you cleaned for me between three and five.' She looked at her watch. 'Seven thirty now.'

There was a mumbled response and a violent shaking of the head. She has lovely hair, Helen thought. Rich and curly.

Instinctively she felt for her own head, the hair lank from the effect of the courtroom.

'What did you say, Cath? Didn't hear you, sorry.'

'I said, it was so hot, I couldn't stand the thought of that bus.'

'Did you sit in the garden, then? Fall asleep or something?'

Helen wanted to relinquish the simple art of cross-examination, to rid herself of the habit of incessant questions, and make herself turn a blind eye when the woman's eyes pleaded with her to do just that. She put the tea on the table. It seemed quite inappropriate to offer wine, especially since she remembered her own embarrassment at the thought of Cath finding so many empty bottles in the bin. Helen leant towards her, biting the bullet reluctantly.

'Listen, Cath, you don't know me and I don't know you. Perhaps that makes it easier. Only you aren't going anywhere until you tell me about those bruises. Is that understood?'

'Is that understood?' said Bailey to Ryan. 'No wisecracks with this lot. We've got to be sober and reasonable.'

'I'm always reasonable,' Ryan objected.

'So said the fox in the chicken run. We want to look like two coppers out having a drink and a chat.'

'They won't expect us to be sober, then.' Ryan was slightly mutinous, he hated drinking halves, almost as much as he detested combining work with pleasure.

'What was it you said we were here for?' he asked. 'I thought you just said we'd go out for a drink. I haven't been out for a proper drink since—'

'Last week,' Bailey interrupted drily. 'I saw the state you were in Friday morning. You think I'm blind? Your eyes were like candy floss.'

'Never touch the stuff. Tell me again. That Damien Flood murder is all wrapped up. So what the fuck are we doing here?'

'Oh, nothing much. Mickey Gat, maybe. Having a word with anyone who might like to come over and chat with us.'

'Who is this Mickey Gat? Not much chance of anyone chatting in here, is there?'

Bailey sighed. Ryan's ignorance of Mickey Gat summed up exactly how much effort he had made with this case.

'Oh, I don't know. That's Dave Jones' cousin over there, giving us the glad eye. Surprised they let him in.'

It was not such a bad pub. There was none of the sensation of danger Ryan secretly enjoyed in half the East End pubs, where a policeman was as obvious as a flag and as much loved as a black beetle; where you could feel the boots aching to crush, smell the mood and taste the hatred on the tongue. Not here, it was a well-run place, a drinking parlour sure, catering for old lags and young blood, of all races, but its real *raison d'être* was the pool tables. Most of the custom played pool, which made for an atmosphere in which any other kind of contest was irrelevant. Equally *de trop*, most of the time, were wives, girlfriends and anyone who did not play.

'They must earn a fortune off them tables,' Ryan remarked. 'Fancy a game?' Bailey shook his head.

The bar was a stark contrast to a place like the Spoon and Fiddle. This was the kind of place where Mickey Gat would be at home, full of highly domesticated drinkers. Mickey would not risk a fight. Risks for money were a different matter, because in Mickey's book dishonesty was not even antisocial. Which was why it was so odd that the place where they sat should be the scene of a violent argument leading to death. Not here. There was never any blood on Mickey Gat's floors, only in the little park round the corner, next to the leisure centre.

'I still don't understand why.' Ryan had a complaint in his voice, which, however irritating, still acted on Bailey's conscience. God alone knew why: Ryan owed Bailey more favours than either could count. The two men never acted in accordance with the irrational affection between them. They did little but joke. Ryan was sulking because the atmosphere made it impossible even to do that. He looked down at his feet, moodily examining a new pair of shoes which were too hot and too heavy for summer. He wriggled his toes inside the unyielding leather. Nothing doing. No more new shoes either, what with the kids going to school and his wife talking about feeding him on sand-wiches. A bit like Bailey's bird, although the occasional remark from sir seemed to indicate that she had improved. He bent to adjust the laces, froze.

Mickey had changed into evening gear. The feet were squashed into white high heels. There was a gold chain round one ankle. Black leggings extended over huge calves and gargantuan thighs, disappearing beneath a brilliant white shirt, on which the legend 'Michaela' was stitched in lurid gold thread over the straining bosom which merged into the stomach to form a massive trunk. A series of chins ascended into a wide face. Pale blond hair danced in fat, salon-disciplined curls. The lips were coral coloured, the eye-shadow piercing blue, and the age of the vision indeterminate. Ryan's eyes landed back at the level of an enormous pair of hands, manicured nails held delicately at waist level, cradling an orange juice.

'Can I get you boys anything?' asked Mickey Gat. Ryan was petrified. So that was why Bailey had brought him here on the pretext of a treat. He had needed a minder, or, perhaps, bait to throw to the lions.

'Only I don't seem to have seen you recently, Mr Bailey,' Mickey's voice continued in a good natured rumble. 'And I need to know to what I owe the pleasure. What are you drinking?'

She was the largest woman Ryan had ever seen, six foot all round. He would rather have tried to stop an oil-tanker. Ryan could feel the earth move with each breath. He raised his eyes fur-ther towards Mickey Gat's vast, squashed face and found it was wreathed in smiles, and even Ryan could tell a grin which was not quite a preface to a threat. It meant either she would play with them first or she was pleased to see them. The slap to Bailey's shoulder would have knocked a lesser man to the floor. As it was, only the table shifted position by an inch. The legs of a chair creaked ominously as Mickey sat, heavily.

'How you doing, Michaela? No, haven't seen you in a while.'

'More's the pity, Mr Bailey, because I haven't been doing so good. Oh, I mean the kids are fine, so's the old man, and business isn't bad. I take it you aren't here to check up on the licence or anything like that, 'cos if so, hop it. Otherwise . . .'

'No, Mickey, nothing like that. You know me better.'

She sighed. 'Well I thought I did, but you never can tell.' She let out a roar of laughter which shook the hanging light above her head. At the bar, where drinkers had paused to listen, heads turned back and normal conversation was resumed. Ryan began to breathe normally.

'I'm always pleased to see you, Mickey. Better luck than I expected. I'd have stopped to chat outside the Spoon, nice pub that, but it didn't seem right, you were busy. About Damien.'

'They got him, didn't they? That poxy kid who did it? Little bastard.'

'We got one of them, Mickey. Only one.'

Mickey shook her head slowly. It reminded Ryan of a bull shaking away the irritation of flies.

'That was a bad business, Mr Bailey. A bad business. They were strangers in here. We shouldn't have let 'em in.'

Same could apply to us, Ryan thought, vowing to keep his own mouth firmly shut, unless to drink.

'Anything I ought to know, Mickey? I mean, we'd like to mop it up a bit better than we have. The boy came back armed, sure, but he says he didn't use his knife for more than a scratch.'

Mickey snorted. 'He would say that, wouldn't he?'

'And this Damien,' Bailey continued, sliding his cigarettes off the table and into his pocket, 'he was a bit special, wasn't he? I mean no enemies you'd know about?'

Mickey nodded approval at the disappearance of the cigarettes. She could drink the tank dry, but never had much tolerance for smoking; bad for sport. She shook her head, smiling sadly. The fags reminded her of little Harry at home, coughing his guts up.

'No, Mr Bailey, no enemies and I wouldn't tell you a lie. He was magic at pool; let's face it, Damien was magic, full stop. Full of laughs, could have been a great boxer if he hadn't liked life better. Oh, there was some people got ratty when he took their money at the end of a game, but that never lasted. He'd give it back if they asked nicely. Everyone loved Damien. Naa, it was a bunch of kids from another pub, what a bloody waste.'

Sentiment was Mickey's second nature; Ryan noticed she was near to tears. The spectre of that was terrifying. The arm of an average man would only go halfway round those shoulders.

'Family?' Bailey asked, tentatively.

'Only his sister. He used to take her everywhere when he first started, till she met Joe Boyce. Think they was orphans or something, close, anyway. Nice, innit? Family sticking together. Well, they were all they had, that's why. I owed Damien a few favours, Mr Bailey. That's why I gave Joe the job at the Spoon. He's another one drinks too much, but not so's you'd notice.' There was a slight element of caution. Two pints appeared on the table. Ryan restrained himself from seizing the glass, stared at it hungrily, nodded thanks.

'Well, this Joe Boyce, he wasn't much help, was he?' Bailey suggested. He was boxing in the dark, Ryan could tell by the voice. He couldn't understand the man, really he couldn't. They'd got a result on a two-bit murder, hadn't they? Or they would, after the trial. Why this time-wasting when it was time to move on? Plenty more bodies out there. Mickey spread her hands, and rumbled with laughter again.

'C'mon, Mr Bailey. Wee Joe Boyce is just a hanger-on. Trails after heroes, thinks he's hard, but couldn't hurt a fly. I mean, I can't hold it against him. Damien was good to him, sure, but he would never have expected Joe to act as his minder. Joe had his wife to look after, and besides, he'd be fucking useless. They'd often go for a drink together, then Damien would give Joe a present, perfume or something to take home to Cath, and off he would go like a good boy. That's Joe Boyce all over. He does what he's told.'

'He's like this one, then,' said Bailey, nodding in Ryan's direction. 'Ever-obedient and full of respect, aren't you, Ryan?' Ryan nodded back, dumbly, followed Bailey's lead and got to his feet.

'Which is why I've got to get him home to his wife,' Bailey continued. 'You know what you married women are like.'

'I do, too, Mr Bailey,' said Mickey, moving a manicured paw in and out of the side pocket of her shirt, extending it towards Ryan. 'We're like cats, us women, you know. We only stay if we're fed.'

'Why do you stay?' Helen felt she should have known, but she could not keep the incomprehension out of her voice.

Cath succeeded in keeping the amazement out of hers. 'Oh, I wouldn't want to go. He's good to me, really. I dunno why he is the way he is, but he is. It's only the drink, without the drink he's not so bad. He can be lovely, my Joe.' Cath could not keep a note of pride out of her voice.

'Have you ever told Emily about this?'

'Course not. Why should I? She's a respectable married woman.' Meaning of course, that Helen was not. There were enough signs of Bailey's presence about the place, second-best shirts in wardrobes, the odd pair of shoes which would only be worn by a male, items of underwear, which indicated an alien presence. Cath's obvious discovery of these, and the sentiments it evoked – either pity or disapproval – affected Helen, just a little. She had lived her own life far too long to sink beneath the weight of other opinion, but how she lived remained private territory. She shook herself. It had been a good idea to offer wine, after all. It loosened Cath's tongue.

'What brings it on, though, the violence? Not just drink?'

'Mixture of things, I s'pose,' Cath muttered. 'Like I've bought something second hand. He only likes new stuff. He can't stand the idea of someone else having used it first. Unless it's army stuff. Me, I'm the opposite. There doesn't seem any point in get- ting new things if you can get old ones with wear in them. Except a bed, of course. I couldn't stand a second-hand bed.'

Suddenly Cath was weeping, a guttural series of sobs, more like a fit of sneezing, ugly. Helen did not move. The air in the garden into which they had moved, grew colder; the perfect evening had waned away into a red sunset. She did not know, or, for that matter, like Cath Boyce enough to offer comfort, and somehow sympathising with Emily's irritation with Cath, did not quite want to touch her. Or maybe it was Mary Secura, teaching her, by adverse example, how to keep her distance. Cath did not try to control her tears, as if she knew it would be a vain attempt. She let them flow without the slightest effort to dab her eyes, blow her nose or control her face, before the storm passed as abruptly as it began.

'I like your house and Mrs Eliot's. I couldn't tell Mrs E because I need my job.'

'She wouldn't sack you because . . . because you were having a rough time at home.'

Cath raised one eyebrow, shrugged, and then spoke carefully.

'No, she wouldn't. Anyway, Joe gets the hump, sometimes. He's never quite worked out what he ought to do, you know? Apart from marrying me. I'd been working in one of them big hotels, chambermaid, he'd been in the Army. I think he met my brother through boxing or it might have been pool but anyway one night I go to meet Damien, and there he was. My man Joe.' She suddenly leaned forward and clutched her stomach. 'Got anything to eat?' she demanded.

Helen found the three packets of peanuts she had earmarked for a typical supper in Bailey's absence. Cath launched herself towards them with sufficient hunger to scatter the contents far and wide as she tore the packet. She did not seem to notice, chewed loudly and swiftly. Helen turned her head away.

'Well, I just loved him. Damien always said he'd find someone for me. He's my brother. We were always together since we ran away. Almost always, anyway. Joe was living in a hostel. Wasn't no good, nowhere for us to go, see? We got married anyway, Damien had a lot of money then. Joe loved Damien, everyone did. He knew Mickey Gat, Harry, and all the boys. I don't suppose I could have one of your cigarettes?'

'Of course.'

'Joe got us our flat, Damien got Joe his job with Mickey Gat. I think it was round about then he started.' She took a drag of an extra-mild Silk Cut, looked at it, puzzled. It was quite clear to

Helen that it made her feel nauseous. Lunch was a forgotten memory, half a sandwich somewhere. She felt equally, vicariously, sick.

'What's he going to be like tonight?'

Cath waved a hand in an airy gesture. 'Oh, he'll be fine. He's usually fine on Thursdays. He's OK as long as I don't criticise.' And then with an abruptness which belied the fey gesture of the sweaty hand a moment before, she was on her feet, her face suffused with embarrassment.

'Got to go,' she announced. 'Where'd I put my shirt?'

'On the bed.'

'Got to go,' Cath repeated. 'Got to go.'

'Sit down,' Helen commanded. 'I can drive you there or get you a cab. Which would you rather?'

'The bus,' Cath said.

'You told me you stayed late today because you couldn't stand the number 59.'

'I live on that route. Damien and me had a place on that route. I met Joe in a pub on that route. I go to work on that route, so does Joe. I'm sick of the sight of that route. Not all the time. Now.' She had grown. She seemed to expand before Helen's eyes into something she had never seen, then shrink again, back into the folds of Cath.

'Your brother? Can't he help?'

Cath looked at her with hatred. 'Of course not. He's dead.'

There was a silence which defied words.

'I'm sorry,' Helen mumbled. 'Should have kept my mouth shut. Will you do something about it? About Joe?'

'No, and you can't make me.'

'No, I can't.' Helen remembered Mary Secura. You can't make them; they have to volunteer.

'You won't tell Mrs Eliot, either?'

'Why? You haven't done anything wrong.'

'No,' said Cath, uncertainly. 'I haven't, have I?'

When the front door closed, Helen felt only relief, tinged with guilt. She knew what they all meant now, the Mary Securas and the judges and the great British public. In her heart of hearts, she did not want to know either.

She did not want to know: she had too much knowledge of guilt and misery already. She did not want to be sensitive, compassionate or an ally. If she could not have a dull life, she could have a secure one, behind walls, where all problems could be postponed unless they were her own. A life without a cleaning lady who brought in garbage instead of taking it out, in a place where there was no-one to pity or ask her to treat what could not be cured. She did that all day, already.

While Bailey and Ryan, in their sobriety, drove away from Mickey Gat's bar to venues more convivial, Helen West began, first half-heartedly, then with increasing energy, to wash the surfaces of the red-painted room. She removed all the pictures first, then scrubbed. Ready to paint. Revamp, renew, building walls.

PART II

CHAPTER SEVEN

It was raining outside. Too warm for central heating, too chill for the window to be open, they huddled in a fug, windows misted, adding to the sense of claustrophobia in an office already too small. The photo of Shirley Rix was no longer on the wall. Instead, there was a series of postcards, bright blue seas, golden sands, legends of absent colleagues having a good time. Only the childless remained at work in August. If you can't take a joke, Sylvia had been saying to Mary Secura for the fifteenth time that week, you shouldn't have joined.

'All right, Mike Ryan, if you want to be useful, get a mop and bucket and clean up here. We've got rain coming in these brand-new windows. If you don't shift your bum from off my desk, I'll scream harassment.'

'You're so lovely when you're roused,' he murmured. 'I shan't fight, I'll take the compensation. You reading dirty magazines again, Mary?'

Ryan shifted his weight from the edge of Mary's desk, picked up her copy of *Good Housekeeping* and flicked through it. He was a frequent visitor to the Domestic Violence Unit of his neighbouring station, which had the added attraction of an all-female staff. Besides, he had a soft spot for Mary. Ryan liked females between sixteen and fifty, full stop, but Mary could see beyond the winking, sledgehammer humour, into his odd dependability, while all the time, there was that little *frisson* of mutual attraction, heavily disguised.

'You don't want to talk to her. She's in the doghouse, she is,' said Sylvia, shoving her bag over her shoulder, preparing to leave.

Ryan took no notice. 'The things you girls read,' he was

murmuring, looking at an illustration of the perfect bathroom, offset by a bath full of foam with toes pointing coyly out of the water. 'And are you?' he continued, without looking up as the door closed. 'In the dog-house?'

'Yup,' said Mary.

'What did you do, then?'

Mary leant back in her chair, eyed the no smoking sign on the wall and lit up a cigarette with an air of nervy abandon.

'Well, you know that Shirley Rix case? No, you don't, but I told you about it. We'd got this bastard husband dead centre, in custody, court date fixed, perfect. Only the wife skipped on the day of the case and the CPS got it put off for a month. Clever, yes? But on the same day Shirley gets run over. Won't be giving evidence, except in heaven. And I don't tell anyone, right? I'm so frigging mad because this bastard's going to get away with it, I reckon he may as well stop where he is for another couple of weeks.'

'Didn't tell anyone? No-one at all?'

Mary shrugged. 'Oh, I told his solicitor, who informed the ever-loving spouse he was a widower, before going on holiday himself. But I should have told the CPS, shouldn't I? So they could go to court and discontinue and get the little rat out. But I didn't. I left him to run up the walls and now I'm in deep shit. So's the woman from the CPS, though God alone knows what she was supposed to do. She's been quite good about it really. Phoned me this morning as if nothing has happened, but then she wanted a favour. Do you think I'll get the sack?'

'Naa,' said Ryan. 'They should give you a medal.' He reached for one of her cigarettes. 'Poor innocent languishing in jail, is it?'

'Innocent, my eye. He's going to get his kid back and turn him into a drunken little yob.'

'Look,' said Ryan, not quite the expert since Bailey had saved him from all but three disciplinary proceedings. 'What you've got to do is plead mistake and overwork. Blame the solicitor. Say you put the memo in the out tray. Just don't let on it was deliberate, right? You'll be fine, honest. Wear a short skirt and loads of perfume.'

She looked at him, a shade wearily. 'Right,' she said. 'Right. That'll make all the difference.'

The silence was heavy; the rain dripped, making a mockery of summer.

'How's home, anyway?' he asked casually, eyeing the magazine. 'You decorating, or what? Preparing for the patter of tiny feet?'

Mary gave a strangled laugh. 'Preparing to split up, more like.' Then she sat up, dragged her bitten nails through her hair in a gesture he always found endearing. 'No,' she added, 'forget I said that, I didn't mean it. He wants the patter of tiny feet. I can't stand the idea. Working here doesn't just put you off men, it puts you off the whole idea.'

'If you two split up,' Ryan said with his melting smile, 'there might be a chance for me.'

She laughed this time, stood up and shoved him off the desk. 'C'mon, Mike, what do you really want?'

He sighed, theatrically. 'Your body. And a favour. Not necessarily in that order.'

It took less than a minute to turn up the name in the card-index. Mary Catherine Boyce. One negative visit, nine months before. Police called by neighbours, Mary taken to hospital, discharged herself the same evening, follow-up visit next morning by domestic violence personnel. Further assistance refused.

'We keep all these,' Mary explained slowly to Ryan, 'for future reference. In case they come up again, which they usually do. And we leave them a number to call us direct. Some of them do, months later.'

'Not her, though,' said Ryan. 'Just a one-off. Not even a breach of the bloody peace.'

'Funny thing with her, though,' Mary mused, 'she was half stripped when they took her to hospital. That's what made everyone panic, made the lads think it was a whole lot worse than it was, a few bruises, not nice, not too nasty. She had this massive scar, see, puckering her stomach, a real corker. Looked as if the old man really tried to kill her once. But when we went round, she explained it was a scar from a caesarian operation. In her teens, she said, nothing to do with her husband. Doctor must have been a butcher in training. Yeah, I remember. She wasn't like the others, I mean not frightened. You going to tell me the connection?'

'Nope. My guvnor's idea, not mine. Not enough to do.'

'I'd like to work for Bailey,' said Mary, 'if and when they push me out of this.'

'Play your cards right, why not?' Ryan squinted at the card, waiting for inspiration, shrugged. 'Bailey wanted to know if he had any violent tendencies, God alone knows why. Personally, I don't think a single fight with the nearest and dearest counts.'

'Speak for yourself. Anyway, what makes you think it's like that?'

Ryan tapped the card with his finger. ''Cos it says here, file dormant, stupid.'

Mary leant forward.

'You know I told you about the CPS solicitor asking for a favour this morning? All a bit vague, hypothetical. Well, it was about her cleaning lady. Cath, no surname known, but telephone number same as on this card. Covered with bruises, and what should she do? Nothing, I said, there's nothing she can do. But it looks like your Mr Boyce is still at it.'

Ryan sat down heavily, knocking *Good Housekeeping* off the desk.

'Oh, my lovely Mary,' he said. 'In the interests of your career, do you think you could see your way to another favour?'

'What do I have to do?'

This time his leer was more pronounced. He leant forward and kissed her on the lips, so briefly it was a peck. Then sat back.

'No,' he sighed. 'Not that. Just go and make a follow-up visit, will you?'

The rain stuttered against Helen's windows in the afternoon. She pressed her nose to the glass, transfixed. Those in the offices opposite, full of personnel so much better dressed, weaving their way through banks of office machinery the CPS did not have, achieving goals of which no government agency would dream, also had cleaner windows.

There was one middle-aged supervisor who held her attention. He had receding hair and glasses, was slim, trim and busy, and equipped with his own room and secretary, while his opposite number occupied another room at the far end of the floor, which Helen could see if she craned her neck. The two men were almost identical, so were their secretaries. Man number two (without specs), never stirred from his little sanctuary, but man number one (with the specs) was certainly flirting heavily not only with his own typist but also with her equivalent, six rooms away, while nobody in the open-plan area in the middle seemed to realise. From the distance of a narrow street, Helen could see it all clearly and toyed with several ideas. The first was to stick a notice in her own window; then there was another, more complicated scenario of blackmail. She would collar Mr number one, tell him how she had rumbled his little game and offer silence provided he kept his eyes peeled and returned the compliment by delivering her a weekly video record of Redwood. Redwood poking around offices and writing policy was not an exciting prospect, but catching him doing his exercises or changing his trousers, that would be fine.

I could show it at this afternoon's meeting, she thought, wake us all up.

She was pretending not to be shocked by Mary Secura's omissions, acting as if she did not believe they were deliberate, murmuring about communication problems, while all the time she knew it was utterly wrong to leave a man inside any kind of prison, even a remand prison, when there was no longer evidence to present of his crime. Rough justice surely, but too many lies had been excused on such a basis. Justice, about which she was quietly passionate, hence her constant frustration, was not a deity ever served by pathetic revenge. Justice was only achieved by laborious attention to the long-winded method and process of the Law, however deficient that was, since nothing, in the end, worked

better. Truth and rules were the only workable formula. She knew
that. Creating justice was putting yourself above it, a wilful and
destructive arrogance.

Look at him now, over there. Man with specs is on the patrol.
He dips into offices, saying hello, bowing himself out, making
sure he knows where they all are, having a word, passing by, leaving them all frightened to move. Then he makes sure, when he
reaches the other end, that man number two is hopelessly en-
tangled in a long phone call which necessitates his waving his
hands about, obviously stuck on the line for at least ten minutes.
Seen through the clarifying blur of two sets of windows, the little
Romeo embraces number two's secretary passionately, having just
kissed his own. He was sitting on her knee, and she, heaven help
her, looked grateful.

The phone rang. 'Convene now, you're late,' Redwood barked.
Helen sighed into the receiver. Trust a man like that to spoil the
film.

'We need to know,' he was saying to the assembled group as she
entered his room and took a seat at the back, 'why we have these
failures.' He held his hands in front of his face, looking at them as
if they were his only inspiration, and Helen thought of a very old
lady, following a knitting pattern.

'We need a system,' he added, looking in Helen's direction, 'to
monitor at least those most conspicuous failures in our communication with the police. That means, of course, building up
relationships whereby we trust them and they trust us.'

A few silent heads nodded wisely, no-one noticing such public
inconsistency from a man who found any kind of trust anathema
and thrived in an atmosphere of mutual uncertainty. Helen drew
sketches on her pad and did not raise her eyes. Once the walls in
her flat were painted, supposing the paint would cover all the
lumps and bumps, then the windows would be ready for new
curtains, and would Cath come this week, and what would she
think of the mess?

'We must impress upon police personnel the need to tell us

everything. Everything,' Redwood repeated for effect. 'Such as when a witness is never actually going to turn up.'

'Like when they die,' Helen said, audible without being loud.

'Did you say something, Miss West?'

'Nothing.'

'Good.'

Pardon me for being alive. Insolence would be her downfall. All this was about poor Shirley Rix, with those great big eyes, staring out of a photo, a nameless, numberless person she had seen depicted but never met, to be remembered as another notch on the bedpost of guilt, one more tick in the record of personal failures. Mourned by Redwood like any other source of embarrassment. Helen sat at the back of the room, mulish. Even from that distance, he could feel her bitter impatience.

'We've had a bit of a débâcle,' Redwood went on. 'In a case which should have been dropped at a far earlier stage. Ladies and gentlemen, please, if it is clear that a witness is not going to give evidence, make the clean decision sooner rather than later. Don't seek adjournments simply for the sake of saving face. And then don't just put it back on the pile for someone else.'

Helen cringed. She watched the others, nodding, puzzled, sensing that someone in their midst was in disgrace for disgracing Redwood's service, wondering which of them it was.

She drew on the pad a rough sketch of rearranged furniture in her living room, slapped her own hand as if receiving a reprimand, and tried to suppress tears. Regret less for her own humiliation than for Shirley Rix and the failure to survive. Also for her own reserve, which would prevent her from tapping on the window of her office and waving at someone in the building across the street. It was that same reserve which had made her hesitate this morning before phoning Mary Secura for advice, suddenly suffused with shame both for doing nothing and for not knowing Cath's surname. What a fool was conscience, so effective in restraint, so weak in the spur to positive action.

She was grateful for the protection of home.

★

To call this place a mess, Bailey thought later as he squeezed himself in, is the understatement of the year. He recognised Helen's present mood although he had rarely seen it in such an extreme. There was nowhere to sit. Furniture from the living room was in the hall and in the kitchen; he was forced to insert himself round the door with indrawn breath and clamber over a chest of drawers until the dying wheeze of the Hoover stopped him in his tracks. From the small room she used as study and dining room, he could hear a theatrical sigh, before she appeared, dishevelled.

'Who was it you were trying to keep out?' he asked, pointing to the chest. 'Or is there someone you were trying to keep in?'

'I'm cleaning cupboards,' she said, with dignity. 'And yes, I know that may seem strange, but I've got a man, painting ceilings only, tomorrow. Decorator had a cancellation. Isn't that lucky?' Bailey did not look as if this counted as luck. In fact, he looked acutely disturbed. It had been a long, wet day. He had brought no provisions with him and it did not look as if the kitchen was fit for use in any event. The floor had become a dumping ground for plants and ornaments; the surfaces were littered with books. She followed the direction of his eyes, and looked a little crestfallen.

'How about a drink?' she suggested brightly. He smiled at her.

'Don't worry, I'll get it. Don't look so guilty. You're not a wee wifey who has to warm my slippers, you know.'

She could sense the irritation behind the light words, and countered it with a rising irritation of her own. No, she was no wee wifey, or even a *grande dame* with a gin and tonic waiting for her hero and provider to come home. She was a working woman, gritty with the residue of the day's guilt.

'I thought the wonderful Cath would do all this kind of thing,' he said.

'You've seen what she does. She cleans everything which moves. She doesn't wash walls and make the place fit for painting. I do that.'

Helen followed him into the kitchen and adjusted herself into a leaning position next to the fridge, where a dusty bowl held a selection of meaningless keys, none of which she could identify but she preserved them all the same.

'Listen, Bailey, I want to ask you something about Cath . . .'

Bailey shifted in immediate discomfort and kept his back to her. He had deliberated whether to reveal Cath's connection to the dead Damien Flood, and, after a day or so, found the decision to remain silent easier than the alternative. This was always Bailey's way when in doubt, although when Helen copied his secrecy he could quite see how infuriating it was. There was no reason why his professional knowledge should impinge on Helen's life, or the Eliots' for that matter. What would it achieve apart from unease, if either of them knew that the woman wielding their dusters had a brother who had died by the knife and a barman husband with a dubious boss? He shrugged. Silence was not always golden.

'What about Cath?'

'Only that she's being beaten up by her husband.'

'Yes, I know.'

'You what?' She was furious. 'You knew, and didn't tell me?' She handed him a glass of beer with an expression which made it clear she would rather have thrown it.

'Whoah, now, climb off that high horse. I only knew recently and because of something else entirely. Background material. Remember me talking about that murder a week or so ago? The brawl? The victim was Cath's brother.'

'Well sod you, Bailey. Aren't you good with a secret? I suppose you would have told me if I'd given my keys to a homicidal maniac?'

'Look, don't be stupid. If you or I handle confidential information because of what we do for a living, that's what it's supposed to remain: confidential. Of course I would have told you if I'd known before you hired her, but she hasn't done anything wrong, has she? She didn't confide her family history to you or Emily Eliot, why should I? What difference does it make?'

'The whole bloody difference between knowing something and

not knowing. And the fact that you seem to assume I'd broadcast the information on a loudspeaker, along with details of where I'd heard it.'

'I never said that. I didn't even think it, either.'

'Christ, Bailey, I sometimes wonder if you're hiding a clandestine wife and a tribe of kids. Anything else you'd like to tell me, such as you're leaving for Timbuctoo in the morning and it slipped your mind?'

'OK, OK. I'm sorry.'

He was not sorry: he was angry; and the fact that it was an anger without rhyme or reason only made it worse.

'What should I do to help her?' Helen demanded.

'Nothing. There's nothing you can do. Besides, your friend and Ryan's friend, PC Mary Secura, might call on her. I just want someone to get inside that house. Don't ask me why either, because I don't really know. Do you think we could drop this conversation?'

He had finished a glass of the amber liquid, still in the jacket he had worn against the rain. In the shambles of the flat, he had no desire to take it off. The cleanliness and order of his own home was suddenly appealing.

'Do you want some help?' he asked diffidently.

'No, thanks,' she replied with equal diffidence.

'What shall I do, then?'

'Sit and read the paper, but since you're itching to go home, perhaps that's an option you'd like to consider. I was going to get cleaned up and take you out for supper.'

'But you're not quite ready yet, and you'd really rather clean your house?'

They stood glaring at one another for a minute. Then he nodded and turned to leave, the dignity of his exit marred by the chest of drawers and the need to breathe in to get by. That small idiocy made her smile for a minute, but only until his footsteps died.

Oh, shit. The understated disagreement was worse than any row. She wandered into the red-walled living room, still fuelled by anger, and stood there listening for his car, while a small voice told her, You know him by now, you might also know he keeps things from you, and in all fairness you do the same to him. But she had looked forward to seeing him, she always did, and there had been a particular desire to talk to him this evening: he was a fair, kind and honourable man and he would have made suggestions to soothe her sense of inadequacy even if the advice in the last resort was simply to live with it. And if she was honest, the bit about not being a wee wifey had gone home like a well-aimed arrow. What was she supposed to do for the pleasure of his company? Comb her hair, paint her face, recline in négligé with Vivaldi in the background and a kitchen smelling of coffee?

The steam had gone out of the cleaning. She looked at the emptiness of the living room, the marks on the walls where the pictures had been, the gouging of the nails making it resemble a gangsters' hideaway where the walls were peppered with shot. When Bailey finally went, which surely he would in the absence of either the commitment or the support which were the vital plant food to any kind of relationship, would he leave his mark? Would there be rectangles of faded patches in her life, imprints all over her body, like a rash, to indicate where he had been? Would she just carry on? Should she fight the inevitable, become an Emily? For the moment, she could only follow instinct. Clean the walls. Offer practical help to Cath. In that order.

Blue and yellow curtains, this time next week. Ceilings, tomorrow.

Joe was not the only one good at hiding things. He had been quiet last night, home late, hunched over the TV, refusing the sandwich she had made, so silent she hadn't dared speak. It was often thus after conflict, a complete withdrawal by them both until finally one reached toward the other in shy desperation. A cold reaching out; a brush on the arm, a cup of tea accepted with mumbled thanks, a comment ventured on the weather. And then a few halcyon days of sweet normality until the whole cycle began again. It was only the drink, plus the terrible fact that he seemed to require a level of fury to complete the act of love with her. She supposed it was the scar, it put him off; he liked to touch it but then he was repelled. On that one time the policewoman in the plain skirt came round, the one whose voice she occasionally ordered by phone when she played with the answer machine, well that girl had not made a lot of sense, but on the other hand, Cath could still remember everything she said. Don't say he only hits you because of drink, she had announced. It's him *and* the drink, don't you see? Other people drink and simply go to sleep, or buy their wives perfume, or cuddle the cat. Against her better judgement Cath had laughed, explaining irrelevantly that the man could not stand cats and as for perfume, he was allergic to that and, really, he was a good man most of the time. Your choice, the woman had said. Yes, it is, Cath had replied. My choice. Everyone has a cut-off point, the woman had said, let us know when you get to yours.

Cath would never have cut off from Joe. Unless Damien had asked. Until now.

They both hid things from each other: the small objects which would cause trouble. It began with his army memorabilia, pre-served against the call to arms he would always crave, since, despite the disappointments, he had loved military life and dreamed of it still. Like everything he did, the memorabilia col-lection was half-hearted: uniforms, caps, badges, in the main, bayonets, all cheap to buy, cheap to sharpen into usefulness, until, of course, Joe's horror of the second-hand and the discovery of how many thousands of others did it, made him desist and hide the small collection with a suggestion of shame, since she had always loathed it. Most of it had long since gone over to the Spoon. There had been days when he did as she asked. She did not know whence that syndrome had fled, only that it was long gone. Gone even before Damien died.

Cath never said 'killed'. She only said 'died'.

She breathed deeply. In the attics sound was muted: reduced to a steady thump from downstairs and the steadier drip from the residue of the rain through a point in the ceiling. Boxes had been moved from the floor beneath. Nothing could be allowed to happen to Joe's hammock until they had two trees, or the grass strimmer until they had a hedge, and Oh, the waste of it all. She had placed the shrine by the window, on a dry space on the floor surrounded by Joe's goods, in the hope it would lie undisturbed. Now the flowers, admittedly dying when last she had tended them, bore the imprint of a foot; there were stains on the wooden floor indicating the colour of the pansies taken from Helen West's garden. The photos had gone. The candle she had lit in the hope of bringing Damien back, like a moth to a bright flame, lay on the window ledge. Cath touched a fresh set of livid bruises on her thigh. They were not important. It was the desecration of memory which was the cut-off point.

From far down below came the cracked sound of the doorbell. Cath did not panic. She moved downstairs out of the attics, slowly and demurely. It no longer mattered who it was.

I'm mad, said Mary Secura to herself. And I wish that meant I was bad and dangerous to know. She had the good leather handbag slung across her chest, and was oddly grateful for the raucous beat emanating from the ground floor. The door sprang open; a voice shouted from upstairs. Mary followed the sound, away from the life below, fishing in her bag for a card, a leaflet and the radio which would signal help into a well-deserved silence.

The door at the top was open. 'Hello?' she called with a false gaiety, looking into a hall and the room beyond, both impeccably clean. The woman appeared, long curly hair round her shoulders, surprisingly smiling. She was dressed in a dull skirt and long-sleeved white blouse; no sign of neglect, perfectly normal, but stooping.

'Don't mind me if you're busy,' Mary said, extending her warrant card. 'Only I'm from the Domestic Violence Unit. For a chat, if that's all right. Any chance of a cup of coffee?'

This neat little person showed no symptom of alarm. Cath thought she had guessed the reason for this call. It was all down to that Miss West, and while yesterday she would have resented this breach of promise not to tell, this manifest interference in her life, today she did not mind such an act of fate. Her smile grew. Mary was confused, taken aback by such docility.

'I don't have any coffee,' Cath said, 'only tea. What time is it?'

'Nine thirty.'

'Well, I suppose we've got time. Only he comes back around midnight, and I've still got to pack.'

'Fine,' said Mary, 'I mean fine. What do you want me to do?'

'Put the kettle on, I suppose, since you wanted a drink. Then give me a lift to my brother's place. I've always kept the key, you see.'

'You're leaving?' said Mary. 'Now?'

'What do you think I said?'

'Where will you go?' Mary was nonplussed, awkward, wondering just what situation she seemed to have precipitated and whether the woman was sick in the head.

Cath was impatient, she seemed to imagine Mary had come armed with an agenda in perfect accord with her own.

'I've got a place to go, I told you. My brother's.'

'Look,' said Mary.

'Oh, all right then,' said Cath, turning away. 'I'll walk or get the bus. It's only one stop, but I've got a few things to take.'

'Listen,' said Mary desperately. 'Do you want to make a complaint against your husband?'

'What would I want to do that for?'

'Then why are you leaving?'

'That's none of your business. Are you going to help or not?'

Mary thought of Shirley Rix. Shirley had been slow with explanations and the help had still come too late.

'I'll help,' she said. 'Forget the tea.'

The Eliots' small garden had become scrubland, resembling a poor football pitch after a long season without rain. Now it was swampy, the way Jane Eliot liked it best. She had added to the demise of the remaining flower-beds by jumping out of her bedroom window, conveniently on the ground floor at her own insistence. The route out of her window and round to the back door which led, via a corridor, back into the house, was one she could repeat again and again, flinging herself out from the edge of her bed, running back, doing it again, for no purpose other than a slight thrill. This evening, dressed in nightie, she paused in the twilight to rescue a remaining flower, without apology for having crushed the rest in weeks of indifference.

People dug in the ground and hid things. Her friend Susan had a dog which hid bones in their garden. Jane was in possession of stolen goods herself and, while the theft had been easy (from the bottom drawer of Daddy's desk, where he kept small surprises for them all, especially for Mummy), conscience had this way of creeping up. Jane loved perfume, always had to beg for it, as well as other grown-up indulgences, and she did not see why. So she had taken the biggest boxes she could find. The earth seemed a good enough place to preserve the contraband, ready for transfer to school at the end of these long holidays. While Mark and the others shouted over a game in the kitchen, Jane scrabbled with her hands at the soil below her window. Just as it was occurring to her that she would find it impossible to disguise all this dirt on her front and would have to invent something to explain it, she struck gold.

Not gold exactly, but a golden justification of very base metal. An old something or other; she could say she had been mining. Perhaps it was worth a fortune, and ugghh! Worms! She pulled the thing out of the hole she had made, dropped it and stood back, squinting in the dying light. It was a dagger, something like that, it had a handle like a sword and a metal sheath, rusty, unpleasant to the touch. Jane looked round, then moved three yards away and quickly dug another hole, a shallower grave for the Givenchy.

Then she carried the bayonet indoors and found she was wrong. Neither parent thought it was anything special and in no way did the discovery excuse the dirt. So she went to bed in mild disgrace and clean clothes. The bayonet remained in the kitchen. They were not alarmed: it could have been there for ever, although Emily remarked that the blade had been sharpened once.

Alistair suggested they could use it to poke the fire in winter. His parents had done the same. They did not listen to Jane when she said maybe it came from the man who had crept into the garden. The one who was scared of perfume.

It was a good tale to tell, raising the spectre of the bogeyman who no longer gained her the attention he had, but it was like all good tales. No-one believed you.

CHAPTER EIGHT

Pre-trial conferences. Ryan hated them. Going over old ground with a new barrister who pretends he understands it. Bailey, looking both aggressive and uncertain, and a timid young man from the CPS taking notes.

'This is the way I see it,' Bailey announced. 'No, more like the way I smell it. Feel it, if you like,' he added, noticing the expression on Ryan's face at the mere mention of intuition. 'Like I feel egg coming down all over my face.'

'Well I understand why you find it so unsatisfactory,' Alistair Eliot remarked. 'But it's too late, isn't it? I mean the way it's been delivered to me, your investigation is complete. Trial date set, only a month away. Trail gone cold and hardly time for further enquiries now. Of course it isn't entirely fair. There were three men involved in the fight, on either side. The three who came back to collect the money they'd lost had weapons: pool cues, a knife or two. The other three, including the dead man, Damien Flood, weren't armed, unfairly disadvantaged, you might say.'

Ryan considered the relative sizes of the men and the boys, and shook his head. Fights between drunks were never equal.

'Damien Flood doesn't seem to mind the disadvantage, according to one of his friends. He wades in, gets into a close scuffle with our defendant, who manages to hit him on the side of the head, and he reels back. His friends are so big that they've frightened one youth and disarmed another. They leave Damien, take up the chase. They catch the one who grappled with the deceased. With remarkable restraint, they merely slap him, find out where he lives and let him go. Then they go back and look for Mr Flood, who seems to have gone home. He is not where they have left him, slightly hurt, as they thought. They go to Damien's bedsit. No sign. They back-track through the leisure centre. Find him there. Call the police.'

Alistair shook his head. He was in formal role, sitting in chambers: a small room, shared with three others, crammed with books. Ryan considered a barrister ludicrous without wig and gown, found himself shocked at the sight of an obvious scorch mark on a shirt, noticed how the man's hair lay flat against his skull as though waiting for the headpiece. Then Alistair caught Ryan's scrutiny and smiled with such unfeigned sweetness that the other man blushed.

'Anyway, ' Alistair continued, 'because Damien's friends knew where the youth they had pursued actually lived, he was arrested. He has always refused to say who the other two of his gang were and is adamant none of them, bar himself, carried a knife. He's also adamant he only used it to inflict a scratch, but the evidence,' he glanced at a lurid photograph on the desk, blenched slightly, 'is clearly to the contrary.'

'A little flick knife,' Bailey murmured.

'Not enough to do damage like this, you mean?' Alistair asked gently.

'The pathologist says possibly, but only with considerable force. Since we don't have the actual knife, only one identical to the one the boy describes, who can say?'

We should have found that knife, Bailey thought. The boy said he chucked it away, can't remember where, but showed us an identical one he kept at home.

'In any event,' Alistair continued, 'it makes little enough difference. We aren't putting the case on the basis that this boy was totally responsible. We're putting it on the basis that our defendant went away and armed himself, on his own admission. He came back to the scene intending to do serious bodily harm. In the ensuing fight, a man was killed. We do not need to prove anything else, but the *intention* to do serious injury. If death results, even by recklessness, it is murder. That's the law. Murder does not necessarily involve an intention to kill. Even if his *compadres* were equally guilty, it does not make this one innocent of murder. What egg on face do you mean, Mr Bailey? It seems to me you have done the best you can.'

Surnames here. No first-name terms in this set of chambers, not like at home, laughing over the Eliots' kitchen table.

Alistair spread his hands. 'But,' he said, 'having told you I don't see this case as anything other than straightforward, albeit stuffed with dissatisfaction, leaving the defendant free to blame his absent friends, I must now tell you that I am walking away from it. The CPS agrees someone else should take over. We juniors are easily interchangeable, you know,' he added, noting Ryan's look of disgust. Fickle bunch of bastards, Ryan thought. They take on a brief and all that money, then they dump you in the shit almost at the door of the court.

'Yes, I understand,' Bailey was saying, giving Ryan a stern glance before relenting and explaining. 'Didn't I tell you, Ryan? Damien Flood's sister works for Mr Eliot's wife. It all gets a bit personal, see?'

All Ryan could see, from his position of discomfort, crowded up against the third desk in this room, was the top photo on the desk. Taken at the scene by flashlight. Damien Flood, sprawled against a tree, trousers undone, belly exposed. Not the belly, the contents, spilling out on the ground. Not a stabbing, an evisceration. Lights and liver like his granny used to boil for their pets, and for the first time in a case he had never really cared about, Ryan could see why Bailey was worried. That little punk on remand could not have done this, not without help. Could he?

A fly landed on the lurid colours of the photograph. Out of some kind of respect for the dead, Bailey flicked it away.

'I'm sorry about this,' Alistair Eliot said after the others had gone and they were left alone in the crowded room, sunlight streaming through. 'I didn't feel I had a choice. I've sat down outside a local pub and talked to a man who's a witness in the case, the dead man's sister is in my house every day . . . Can you imagine doing the trial, even as the junior, with Quinn doing all the talking and me the homework? I'd have to explain to poor Cath what was going on, wouldn't I, and then either she, or I, or Emily, would feel about as comfortable as a hair shirt.'

'There's no need to apologise,' said Bailey. 'Ignore my sergeant's sulking. Nothing lost. You only opened the damn file a few weeks ago and there's plenty of time for someone else to absorb it.'

'I need advice,' Alistair said suddenly, 'of a domestic nature.'

Bailey grinned. 'You're asking me? Why not try an expert?'

'You'll do. You know more about women. So far, I haven't breathed a word of this to Emily. I adore my wife, Bailey, you know I do, but I've got the feeling she'd smother Cath with kindness, counselling, etc. She'd be knocking on the door of the Spoon and Fiddle and dragging the husband out by his hair. You see, Emily always believes something can be done. About everything and everyone. I don't.'

'Nor do I. Is that your answer?'

'I hate keeping things from her, but how can it help? Would it be worthwhile, do you think, if I popped into the pub, I do quite often anyway, and just dropped a hint to Joe Boyce, I mean, something just to let him know I knew that he hits his wife? I don't know much about these things, more Helen's line, isn't it, but I've always imagined that if a chap knows someone else knows he's hitting his wife, it may limit him. For shame.'

'Or it may make him stop her coming to work for you.'

'Oh,' said Alistair, confused. 'I didn't think of that possibility. Dear God, what a privileged, sheltered life I lead.'

'There's something else,' Bailey said, wanting to comfort him. 'My sources are Ryan, via a lady in a domestic violence unit, strictly confidential, you understand? Your cleaning lady is dealing with her own problems. She's left her old man and holed up in the place where her brother lived. Her husband, according to her, does not know the existence of the place. It's on the same bus route,' he added irrelevantly, thinking of the convenience of the family Eliot. 'Does that make you feel better?'

'Yes, much. I still feel I should have a word with Mr Boyce.'

'Ah,' said Bailey. 'I thought I might set Ryan on him.'

Alistair looked surprised. 'Is that wise?'

Bailey sighed. 'I doubt it.'

'How's Helen?' Alistair asked, shaking himself, changing the subject with evident relief.

'Fine,' said Bailey, a shade over hearty. 'Very busy.'

Dear Cath, I'm sorry cleaning is a bit difficult today, because of the painter. He's only doing ceilings, I'm supposed to do the rest. If you could just clean what you can, and the kitchen windows. Suggest if nothing else, you sit in the garden and have a rest. If tendency to weed comes over you, don't resist. By the way, if you ever want to come here during the day, you know you are welcome.

That was early in the week. There had been a note in reply:

Dear Helen, I gave the painter a hand, hope that is OK. Will come back tomorrow afternoon and do some more if that is also OK. I like painting. Is £5 an hour all right? PS I know where there is a good carpet shop near me in Clapton. , It is on the 59 route.

OK? It was brilliant. Helen West's domestic talents included an ability to slap paint on walls, applying extra to gum up cracks, but it took a while to get going. It was an act of economic conscience to limit the decorator to the difficult bits: it did not follow that she relished the rest. So to find, along with Cath's poorly written note, evidence of the first coat covering the bedroom walls in a colour called golden white, was a discovery tantamount to the finding of treasure. There is nothing, Helen realised, quite as exciting as the sight of pristine paint. Beat sex, beat everything, and if Bailey chose to persist in stand-off mode, that was fine, too. He was welcome to sulk until it was all done, and with the unexpected bonus of Cath, it would take a week rather than a month. If Emily Eliot's curtain lady worked with similar speed, as promised, this would be a seven-day revolution. Then Helen kicked the rolled-up carpet in the living room. She had thought it would do. Cath's broad hint in the note she had left could not have been clearer.

It was such bland carpet, piecemeal from where the blood-stained parts had been replaced, and she did not want to think about that.

Cheap carpet, Clapton. Number 59. Take Cath. Good for her, she clearly likes this stuff, might also get her to talk. An outing. Two days off booked already. She shivered in anticipation. A trip to buy carpet had all the flavour of gun running. Cath's obvious energy with the paint meant she was well. No need for immediate concern, just a niggling doubt.

Damien Flood had moved around during his life. He had been dedicated to impermanence and achieved it through a measure of deceit. Putting down roots was anathema. Which was why a one-room flat at the top of a high-rise council block, easily obtainable even on a long waiting-list, because no-one else – not a pensioner or a mum with baby, or anyone who resented burglary, or had no stamina for the stairs – wanted such an inaccessible space. Damien did not mind a place where it took forty-five minutes on a bad day to put out the rubbish. He had another gaff, grace and favour of Mickey Gat: he had drifted between a dozen more in his thirty years of riches and penury. Cath said Damien had a death wish: he liked the high places from where he could fling himself, and he denied himself the anchors which would ensure survival, such as bricks, mortar and the love of a good woman. On the last point, there was less conjecture. Why settle for one woman, when you could run a string of them?

Not that he seemed to do that either, not in public. Cath could no longer remember his public persona, only that she had never seen him with any serious attachment. Nor could she quite recall him in any other setting but this one, from which a serious girl-friend, however besotted, and however low her expectations, would surely recoil. A single room, with mattress and armchair, a kitchenette at one end with a selection of other unmatched chairs abandoned round a white melamine table. A poster on the wall, shelves made with breeze blocks. A bleak bathroom. The whole place was drab, unkempt without evidence of heavy dirt, lived in by a man who washed his clothes and his person with obsessive care and left the rest to itself until just before it began to rot. No wonder the council had showed no interest in getting it back. Cath doubted if Damien's erstwhile landlords even knew he was dead. Someone had given her the contents of his pockets some time after he died; it might have been one of his friends, it might have been a policeman, but the packet included his keys.

She had given the Mickey Gat keys back straightaway, via Joe, but she never admitted having this set. As far as she knew she was the only visitor here when Damien was alive, and the escape route it provided was heaven-sent now, a sign of divinely orchestrated protection, evidence that Damien's soul might have gone to the right place. There was nothing about home she missed, apart from the telephone. On a wall in the living room, there was a hole where a socket might have been. Cath realised with a start that she had no idea how to get one connected. Then she shook herself. She was not going to stay here for ever. It was like living in a greenhouse far above the world, while she craved the spaces below, away from the milky light, the windows with nothing but view, the slight swaying in the wind and the movement of the water in the brown lavatory pan.

Cath closed the door softly behind her, moving in the early morning heat which ascended the building, like smoke up a chimney, towards the lift. Today, it worked. She felt safer than houses at this hour in the morning. No-one else seemed to recognise the light of day before noon, and only then, she thought, nose wrinkling in disgust at the smell and the graffiti, to go and get some booze, collect the giro, or admit the social worker. On the tenth floor, the door opened to admit a white mother and black child. Both cried softly all the way to the ground.

Cath got on the 59. She felt both tranquil and resigned. She had the nagging doubt that this would be the morning Joe came to find her at the Eliots'. He had left her in peace for three days, but Emily Eliot would surely help, surely tell the man Cath was taking a week off, something like that; Joe would not leave the Spoon for long in the morning, because he was frightened of Mickey Gat: it would only be a short call, and in the afternoon Cath would be safely cocooned in Helen's basement. There was enough to do there for the rest of the week and she wasn't thinking further ahead than that.

Jane Eliot greeted her on the doorstep. She was wearing a gold cardboard crown (courtesy of McDonald's) and her mother's old silk dressing-gown tied in a lump round her middle and still trailing on the ground over her bare feet. She put a finger to her lips, ushered Cath inside with the imperious gestures which seemed to confuse royalty with courtier, then stamped her foot angrily when Cath exploded with laughter. The little darling: she looked so sweet and so guilty and the sound of Cath's laughter, strange to her own ears, startled and amazed them both. Jane forgot where she was.

'What's the matter with you, Cath? You never laugh.'

She had all of a child's resentment against inconsistent adult behaviour. Cath gave her a hug, another upsetting action. The child smelled like a perfume counter.

'Well, I am today. Where's your mother?'

'Out. Dad had a day off work, so they said, sod everything, they were going out. Without us!' The indignation was profound, although little Jane had already decided there were ample compensations for paternal absence. It was something worthy of revenge. 'Mark is supposed to be looking after me,' she added. 'Mummy made him promise faithfully, but she didn't know about his hangover. He's gone back to bed. You'll look after me, won't you? We can play.'

'Where's your sister?' Cath asked, beginning to sense alarm as she looked upstairs and saw a trail of listing paper cascading down like a banner. Jane stamped her foot again impatiently.

'It's all in Mummy's note, silly. In the kitchen. She is staying with her stupid friend. They're going swimming.'

'And you,' Cath stated firmly, 'will drown in big trouble when your Mummy comes home.'

★

How much big trouble became apparent some little time later as Cath whistled through the long skinny house. Her own feeling of joy at being given responsibility, this accolade of trust and this freedom, was beginning to wane even before she reached Mr Eliot's study. There was so much to do in three hours, plus keeping Jane happy. Since she knew the futility of trying to wake a boy with a hangover, Cath did not attempt to rouse the trusted guardian, Mark. She judged the carnage wreaked by a younger and jealous sibling to be fairly thorough. But, above all, Cath who never resented work and was given this small element of control, wanted to honour everyone, prove her own worth. Happiness gave her energy. She wanted to protect the baby from a scolding and also succour the errant older brother; she wanted to be all things to all of them, because they loved her and she wanted to love them back. Onward Christian Soldiers.

At the door to the study, the room supposed to be sacrosanct, resolution failed. The child had scattered the papers. She had untied the bundles Cath had seen in there, bound with either pink or white tape. Some of the tape was round her wrists, a little more round her ankles: she was a gypsy princess, decked in scraps. Cath did not understand paper. She could read and write better than most teenagers, but she was confused by the quantity; knew she could only restore some semblance of order and felt a brief surge of pity for poor Mr Eliot, who worked so hard and was always so courteous.

Jane was downstairs, exhausted by her labours and mesmerised by the usually forbidden day-time TV. Cath began to sort and tidy. The room smelt of perfume, all at odds with the masculine air of the desk, the solid chair, the old pen-and-ink set and the anonymity of Alistair's computer screen. Cath moved with precision and speed, pulling papers into rough piles, not looking, but judging by familiarity of typescripts and creases in the pages to get them into some sort of order. She was coy in doing this, averting her eyes from the written word, until from the depths of the mess, she caught sight of her own name. Not Cath. Mary Catherine Boyce. Joseph Boyce, listed next in alphabetical order in the index. The rest of this bundle was more or less intact. Cath felt her heart shudder against her ribs. She began to read. Continued to read as her back rested against the wall, her legs splayed and her lips, ready to laugh again, mouthed the words.

There was so much about the aftermath of her brother's death she had not known. Joe had shielded her and she had welcomed it, believed him when he said it was better not to know, to forget everything as soon as possible. He was dead; nothing else had any importance. Joe had taken her to identify the body, a formal identification, Damien's lovely face so perfect. She did not understand the words of the doctor with all the initials after his name, but she understood the photos of a golden-haired man with his entrails falling on the ground. Cath clutched herself, feeling the rising tide of nausea, bit her lip, and carried on. Joe's statement was precise about times, emphatic about how he had left early in order to come home to her. Her statement contained the times he had told her to say. She had taken his word as gospel. Joe Boyce, saying how he loved his brother-in-law, but the man did not have time for him. Lies, all lies. Damien always had time; Joe had always envied him, that was all. Joe was such a liar.

'What are you doing?' said Jane from the doorway.

'Nothing,' said Cath, shuffling the papers so the photographs remained hidden. For God Almighty's sake, why didn't Mr Eliot lock his study door? Children could not help it if they were untrustworthy. Nor, at this moment, could she.

'Only there's a man at the door, asking for you. I said I didn't think you were here today, but I'd go and look. Are you here?'

The child was cunning. Cath wondered where she had got it from. She pretended to yawn.

'Oh, he must want your mother, selling something she doesn't want, I bet. If I come and talk to a man at the door, I'll have no time to play with you. Go and tell him you've had a good look round, 'cos you know I'm usually here, but your mummy is really cross because she's got a note from me saying I've gone away for a week. Ask if he knows where I am. Can you do that?' Cath winked, roguishly.

'Course I bloody can. What do you think I am, stupid?'

The child flounced. Little actress. Cath gave it three minutes, standing on the landing, listening for the dull echo of the front door closing, then went down.

'He went,' said Jane, with all her mother's authority. 'I asked him if he'd like to come in for a cup of tea, just to make it seem real, but he didn't want to.'

'Good girl,' said Cath, making her voice echo an indifference she did not feel. It could only have been Joe; he would have to try once, and she could not have faced him.

'I've got to tidy my room,' Jane announced. Cath was surprised; the effect made her calmer. Even a child was strong cnough to guard against Joe.

'Why's that, then? I thought you wanted to play.'

'That man at the door. He's the one who comes round when I'm messy, so he knows my room's messy now. We scare him off with perfume. Actually he only looked in the window once, but I tell everyone it was more than once, and he left something in the garden. Want to see?' She paused mid-flood. 'Daddy doesn't believe me. Do you believe me?'

'No,' said Cath, 'not a word of it. You've probably told fifty stories about that man, all of them different. What did he look like?' Oh, the shame of it. Joe coming round here and looking in windows like a thief, tainting this perfect house. How could he? But Cath thought more about Damien, haunted by the vision of him captured on celluloid in the study. I should take those photos away, Cath was telling herself. Take them away, if I dared, and hide them. No strangers should ever have seen Damien like that, all naked and ugly. It was shameful.

'This is what I found in the garden,' Jane was chanting, sick of subterfuge, television and anything short of exclusive attention. 'This thingy.'

She made a feint at Cath's toes with the sheathed, rusty bayonet. It looked as lethal as her toys. Cath regarded it with anger and horror. It was obscene for a child to brandish a knife in fun.

'I only think that man left it here, ages ago. Absolutely ages. Who else would leave it? Daddy says it's very sharp inside, though. Want to see?' Her eyes were full of teasing challenge.

Cath's hand was raised in sudden nervous rage, ready to slap. She brought it down instead, heavily on the girl's shoulder, shaking her roughly, ashamed of the action and the look of hurt she had caused. She turned the gesture into a clumsy hug, but Jane was not mollified. The hug turned into a pat: Cath struggled for self control, gained it.

'How lovely,' she said, still more sharply than she intended. 'Let's play with something else, shall we?'

Bailey stood with Ryan outside court number four, Snaresbrook. The outside of the building looked like a bishop's palace: the inside bore witness to extensive refurbishment. None of that old Victorian lavatory that Bailey rather liked and Ryan detested. It was modern, spacious and dignified, but nothing altered. By noon they were in their third hour of waiting their turn as witnesses in a case which had taken a year to come to trial: they had no idea how long they might wait and the one thing which united them was stoicism. Since they could not discuss the facts of an ancient episode of grievous bodily harm on a shopkeeper, they read their newspapers, *The Times* for Bailey, four-minute bursts with the *Mirror* for Ryan, who was harbouring, as usual, a sense of grievance unalleviated by Bailey's silence.

'I know what I was going to ask you, guv,' Ryan said, bored to death with scandal. 'You know yesterday? Going to see that Mr Eliot? Can you tell me something? Do all those barristers have rooms like that? I mean, a mess. I can't see how he'd ever find anything in there, let alone read it, but he had read ours, hadn't he?' Ryan had been dying to discuss this phenomenon since Bailey had abruptly abandoned him in the Temple; Bailey had forestalled him all morning.

'They don't have much space,' Bailey said. 'Eliot takes papers home, most of the time. I must remind him to give them back. What does it matter if they work out of chaos? As long as they get it done.' Ryan sighed with a theatricality Bailey found irritating, like many features of the boy, which made him ponder from time to time the random nature of affection between human beings. It remained so senselessly selective, not based upon virtues or admiration; it came out of the blue and landed him with loyalties often undeserved. He would have run through fire to rescue Ryan from danger without having any real idea why, especially at this moment. He put down the newspaper.

'And speaking of conferences with barristers, Mike, your manners were bloody awful yesterday. You were either sighing like a tragedy queen or grinning like a monkey, and the expressions in between ranged from pout to boredom.'

'I only grinned when he said there was nothing wrong with the case, didn't I? When he said he thought we'd done what we could. What's wrong with that?'

'Everything.'

'No wronger than him saying he couldn't take a case because it might risk his wife's cleaning lady. I never heard such crap.'

The doors of the courtroom opened. Three barristers in wigs emerged, followed in drabs by others without fancy dress. The barristers seemed to sense the brooding presence of two police officers and moved away.

'What's going on?' Ryan asked, enlivened by the prospect of movement, however minimal. Bailey caught the expression of ardent satisfaction on the face of the defending barrister, nodding with his opposite number, both in earnest conversation.

'It probably means the judge has got the hump and our brief is copping a plea to actual bodily harm.'

'But that bloke had a broken skull,' Ryan protested.

Bailey shrugged. 'So?'

'So,' said Ryan, without lowering his voice, 'the whole fucking system stinks. Wigs or no Wigs.'

'Sit down,' Bailey hissed. 'I was only kidding.'

Then one of the lawyers came towards him with an ingratiating smile, and he knew the joke was on them. He stared up at the vaulted ceiling of the magnificent *palais de justice* and tried to imagine it was a cathedral.

Helen and Cath stood under the white ceilings of Helen's flat. Decorator gone, job half done, Helen was turning round and round, as if she was staring at the ceiling of the Sistine Chapel.

'I think you've done enough, Cath. You'll be knackered.'

'No I won't.'

'Isn't it wonderful?' Helen murmured out loud.

'It's white paint,' Cath murmured prosaically.

Cath remained unscathed by paint. She seemed weary, preoccupied, but she worked with quiet precision. Helen had emulsion in her hair: her hands were stiff with it and a blister raised itself on her right forefinger.

'I've left him, you know,' Cath remarked idly.

'Oh. Would you like some tea?' What else was there to say? 'I expect he wants you to go back, does he?' she added.

'I expect so,' Cath shrugged. 'That woman you sent round was very helpful. Mary. She gave me a lift.'

It was on the tip of Helen's tongue to say she had sent no-one. Then she thought of interventionist Bailey, the man who never let anyone know what he was doing, and held her tongue. Cath had her own version of events: let her keep it.

'What are you going to do?' she asked gently. They were back to back in the kitchen, Cath cleaning a brush. The repeated shrug was felt rather than seen.

'I dunno. It doesn't much matter. Did you take down that address I gave you? The carpet place?'

Helen was beginning to realise the existence of a code. Cath could no more come out with a straight series of statements than she could fly over the moon. As soon as she had said anything personal, she needed to change the subject. The listener could not prompt or initiate, only hope for the thread to be renewed.

'Do you really think I need new carpet, Cath?'

'Yeah, if you can afford it, why not?' Cath gave a surprising, if grim, chuckle. 'Make the place really nice. Catch a man, that way. They like to be comfortable.'

'You sound like Mrs Eliot. She says the same thing.'

'I bet she does.'

They spent a lot of time, in between silences, talking about Mrs Eliot. Cath was never warmer or more animated than when talking about Emily, Helen realised. Mrs Eliot this, Mrs Eliot that, as if the woman were somewhere between goddess and patron saint. And a better role model than me, Helen thought. She often forgot, in her own milieu, how a career woman was not everyone's idea of a heroine. In Cath's eyes she was a slightly deficient spinster.

'Do you think I need her advice, Cath?'

'No more than I need yours. Are you going to get that carpet? Only if you want me to show you where it is, you'll have to come on the bus.'

'I've got paint in my hair,' Helen protested.

'Suits you,' said Cath.

She wondered if it did, this casual scruffiness which made her at one with everyone else on the bus, churning through unfashionable London. Down St Paul's Road, into Balls Pond, Dalston Junction, where the crowds hanging round the stops, newly risen from bed in the mid-afternoon, waited less for transport than simply for the sake of waiting. Into the nettlebed of Hackney, Helen silent, Cath, animated for Cath, treating her companion to a muttered commentary, given from behind the back of her hand as if it was confidential.

'They don't go out to work around here, not much, anyway. Don't know how they live, really. No self-respect. Look over there. That's the leisure centre and all they do is vandalise it, terrible. That's where my brother was killed in a fight. Don't worry, not far to go now. That's where I'm living now,' gesturing to a high-rise block on the left. 'Right on the top. They don't go to work from there, either. I bet you'll get a good bargain in this warehouse. I did, but Joe was sick on it. If they see anyone coming in with money, they'll fall over backwards.'

The code continued to invade this anecdotal account of Cath's life and times. First there would be a clue, a statement, a throw-away line, hidden in the midst of several sentences of banality, gems to be picked out of the dross. About how much she loved the Eliots, especially that Jane, how Joe did not know where she was in the afternoons and then, look at that dog, woman, shop, driver, tut tut. Some people got no respect, have they? This apropos of nothing, until finally, 'I hate this bus, you know, I do really. If Joe wants me back, he'll have to do something about this bus. And this is where you get off.'

There was nothing anyone could do about the bus. It moved of its own volition, snarling and wheezing, with a conductor suffering from a summer cold and seasonal indifference. It stopped and started, swallowed and disgorged. The engine throbbed; passengers shuddered in unison. A shambling drunk lurched on the bench seat downstairs, yelling at the window until the conductor yanked him up by the scruff of the neck without a word and he fell silent. Two overstuffed women, large enough to fill a seat each, sat in front of them, squeezed so tight that their laughter passed through acres of skin, loud and infectious. Amid a feeling of uncomfortable voyeurism, unused to travelling without a phallanx of commuters, Helen could see why Cath both hated and loved it. There was just too much life on an urban bus. Far too much. And that was all she understood.

CHAPTER NINE

Bailey looked at his watch; the unfamiliar action surprised him. Perhaps it was the fast-running clock which had confused him, wearing itself out for days with its frenetic telling of next year's time. He had cured the problem and the clock ticked in accordance with his watch, the hands crawling round the empty spaces of time at ordinary speed, and he now felt oddly disappointed. Real time, time without a purpose, hung heavy. It composed itself into units, each requiring a separate input of duty, pleasure, labour and necessity. He was clean, he was fed, he had done his work for the day, and unless he went to see Helen, the mending of another clock would be the last positive pleasure of the evening.

He sat on the enormous sofa, covered with tapestry cloth, the only spark of colour in the room, and surveyed his spacious domain with satisfaction. On balance, though, he preferred this room in winter, when artificial lights softened the harsher utilitarian edges and made everything glow. Looking forward to winter, and looking at his watch to dispel the restlessness induced by endless daylight, was surely a sign of depression. And he was not depressed, except by his own failures. He was simply at sea, armed with the engine of his own self sufficiency. Bailey, mid bottle of wine, decided it was too late to go to Helen now, he wouldn't be safe to drive.

He had himself and a book, a bottle and some music. No laughter, no discussion, none of life's non-essentials. He was sorry for people who could not cope on their own. He usually enjoyed it far too much.

Joe Boyce could not cope. He shivered and sneezed, could not catch his breath as he sat on the bus, felt as if his heart was jumping rather than beating. There were no fingernails left to chew. At other times he was hit by a peculiar lethargy and sat behind the bar with his mouth open, resembling, so Mickey Gat said in tones of ill-concealed disgust, some poor old geezer in the middle of a stroke. Mickey Gat, finding him thus on a Monday morning, was short on sympathy, the way she always was for anyone in her employment who could not work. Joe had no illusions about the profit motive and the rules of his employment, but Mickey's attitude hurt. It was one Joe had seen, heard, felt through his skin a thousand times before, condescension from the large person to the small, the officer to the non-commissioned, the boss to the wage slave, his father to himself. The hearty slap on the back, the smile, the jeering, all of it geared to stop him from doing what he wanted to do, which was weep.

'Women,' said Mickey Gat. 'Ungrateful, aren't we? S'pose she's a bit upset, is she? Did you give her that perfume or what?' Then roared with laughter. More boxes appeared in the back room of the Spoon and Fiddle. Another huge hand landed between Joe's shoulder blades, like a soft mallet being tapped against his spine, either as warning or solidarity, Joe did not know and could not have articulated a guess. Mickey did the dreadful business of tapping her nose. 'Mind you behave,' she said, roguishly, 'while your old woman's away.' Dear Mickey; so much one of the boys, she had become an honorary man.

When Mickey's grey Jaguar had slid away, like a sleek lion after a carnivorous lunch, Joe mustered his courage, and it was then, cutting the lemon clumsily so the juice ran round his bitten finger stumps, that he screamed. Anger had exhausted itself over the first few days. He had shouted and paced round the empty flat; he had examined the boxes in the attics, gloated over them, taken comfort from their bulk, made himself drunker than a skunk, yelled out of the top window, 'Good riddance!' while all the time the fear gripped his ribs. Joe Boyce cannot keep a wife. Joe Boyce cannot get it up. Joe Boyce retains nothing he holds dear, not a friend or even an enemy.

Now he sat with his head lolling, desperately sober after

Mickey Gat's bonhomie, unable to go for the bus which would take him home. Trade was slack: summer holidays. Today it felt like a personal insult, as if the drinking public at large knew what a failure he was and shunned him like a leper. Joe did not quite know if he should feel grateful for this, since, all of a sudden, Cath's defection seemed to mean that he had something to prove. Hard men, friends of Damien Flood, do not sit around weeping for wives. He was half asleep on his feet, too immobile by far to manage a yawn, wired up, and ready to spring, a jerky mess who was dangerous to know, when in came the man he called Colonel Fogey. Half cut at five in the evening. The fact that the old colonel, if indeed he had ever borne such a rank, was never in any condition other than half cut or quarter sober, did not improve his chances because all Joe could remember was Cath ticking him off for poisoning the old boy with cocktails.

'Attenshun!' the colonel announced as he swayed through the door. Sunlight meant nothing to a man steeped in India. Or so he said. Joe looked at him with the sourness of entrenched dislike, as he sashayed towards the darkest corner, humming. 'Shun!' he repeated, sitting with a suddenness which clearly alarmed him. The colonel had a figure like a frog, a trembling jowl; his shirt-tails hung out slightly before and aft, his pathetic linen jacket, worn ragged over the decades, seemed to bear signs of rust, while his trousers, pleated into permanent creases, bore ominous stains around the crotch.

'Beer, boy,' said the colonel, tapping the table and looking round the empty room for an audience, raising his patrician voice. 'Beer, old chap. Now!'

It was some dim remembered vision of the pristine cleanliness of Cath, the way she wiped vomit off the walls and ironed his shirts, which made Joe see nothing but red. Filthy old scroat, banging the table and issuing orders. No money to spend and nothing to offer but drunken platitudes in an upper-class accent, no memories but good ones, no voice but the kind which issued orders. Joe went towards the old man, bearing a half of strong lager. Carlsberg, the alcoholics' answer to the problem of sitting still. He poured it over the colonel. Then he crashed the glass on the edge of the table, leaving a jagged stump protruding from his fist. There was so much flesh about the colonel's face worth the mashing. Joe's hand trembled; he longed to plunge the glass into the smoothest part of the high dome of skin stretched over the forehead, could feel in advance the satisfying crunch of shards against such a bare expanse of bone. The colonel's terror, enough to cause hesitation, made his flaccid belly shake. The trembling moved from his wobbly thighs to his chest and then to his hands; Joe paused, closed his eyes, unable to stop. Then a hand fell on his shoulder. Another relieved him of the glass.

'Haw haw haw,' said a voice behind his back. 'Very funny, very funny indeed. Nearly had us all convinced, eh, old man?'

Joe stood, helpless. A male figure emerged from nowhere, clouted the colonel round the shoulders, and bent down towards him.

'A joke, sir, innit? Good, innit? Why don't you sit out in the sun, sir? Drinks on the house.'

Colonel Fogey was helped from his chair, led outside, his leader grabbing a towel off the bar as they went, talking all the time, like a burbling drain, not glancing back. Joe stood in a trance, looking at his own shaking fist, still seeing the lethal stump of glass. He had just about recognised Ryan, the cheerful man who had taken his statement all those weeks ago, fucking copper, nice enough, not that nice. His brain, shocked by the wash of violence, began to reel when he realised what he might have done. He registered the sudden sunlight streaming through the door, the presence of the other man, the sound of the colonel outside, giggling like the child Joe had met this morning, and a voice with a clean mint smell, familiar, without being bossy.

'How do I get the man a drink, guv? And another towel, if you would.' There was a pause in which he found himself responding, thrusting five towels towards Ryan's clean breath, holding a glass beneath the optic which poured whisky in singles, doubles and trebles. Whisky was the colonel's favourite whenever his pension allowed. Joe gave him a treble.

'That's enough, ta. Great.'

Joe watched this small-statured Boy Scout, of equal height but probably lighter than himself, whisk the glass away to the great outdoors. There was a distant murmur of traffic, nothing which threatened half as much as the imagined whisper of Mickey Gat's Jag over the cobbles. The world was taking some time to come back into focus. He had the same desire to cry that he had felt in the early morning, when he expected to hear the discreet rustle of Cath leaving the bed. Outside, the colonel had found a companion. There was an earnest sort of chat going on, punctuated by the old man's dreadful guffaws. He seemed to have fully recovered. His presence outside, drying out in the sun, stinking like a brewery, would keep custom at bay for an hour.

Ryan slid onto the stool opposite the bar with long-practised ease. Bailey had said the bill was on the house, also the taxi home. Ryan did not know the purpose of this luxury, but he might as well enjoy it. Joe swivelled his head round and reluctantly looked him in the eyes. He met nothing but a cheeky grin, sympathetic.

'Pint of bitter, please,' said Ryan, putting a note on the counter. It was clear he was not even going to press his advantage by demanding free drinks. The desire to weep was almost overpowering Joe. Not sobbing as such, simply a surfeit of tears, stored overlong and oozing out of the corner of his eyes as he pulled the pint and sat down again.

'I'm sorry about that,' he mumbled. He did not know if Ryan would assume he was sorry about the tears or sorry about the fact that he had almost taken the old boy's eye out.

'I didn't see anything,' said Ryan gravely, neatly covering both possibilities. They sat in silence for a moment. Ryan looked around the neat little snug of a bar, nodding approvingly. Joe Boyce liked that too. He was proud of the Spoon and Fiddle, never liked the implication made, however obscure, that the place was a shade effete, not a proper pub with music and all the trimmings, but a sort of club-like bar for the civilised of Kensington.

'Nice,' Ryan remarked sincerely. 'Very nice. Now, what's up with you? You look all in, mate, you really do.'

It was too much for Joe. Ryan's dimly remembered identity as a copper was all but forgotten. He poured himself a drink, blew his nose on a napkin, slumped.

'My wife's left me,' he said bleakly.

Ryan leant forward and touched him lightly on the arm.

'You and me, both,' he said. 'Don't tell me about it.'

So Joe told him.

At five in the afternoon, wearing a pristine white blouse, perfectly fitting skirt and a fair quantity of perfume, Mary Secura had sat in front of the desk of her divisional commander and been severely admonished for discreditable conduct. There was no particular sting in the tail, bar a reference to the fact that her next career move was under review and perhaps two years of domestic violence was long enough for anyone. He was kinder than she thought he would be, inclined to accept that the blame for Mr Rix remaining inside a fortnight longer than he might have done rested with the Crown Prosecution Service, who were easy to blame for everything. Mary was not sure what she had done to effect a relatively easy escape. She supposed it might have been her immaculate record, until the commander's over-warm handshake, almost culminating in an embrace at the end of the interview, indicated it might have been the perfume after all. She went back to the office and phoned Ryan for the celebratory drink he had promised, but he was out. So much for the return of favours. There was nothing for it but to go home. Back to the maisonette shared with Dave who would be on night shift. Great.

She went inside and shut the door behind her. Ryan would be home with the wife. She could have phoned her mother, but she only did that when she had good news. Everyone else had someone. Not her. It was not fair. She was the only person in the world at home with nothing to do. Then she remembered Mary Catherine Boyce at the top of her tower block, hiding, and, with a tinge of guilt, felt better and angry all over again.

Helen West's concrete floors were spattered with paint round the edges. She supposed designers got the desired effect of minimalist mess by accident. Magazines were full of illustrations of rooms resembling a wasteland, with a piece of lacy net twisted round a curtain pole, leaves on the floor and little else but an iron chair; scenes which suggested devastation. If she left the flat as it was, most of it thinly coated with the wash of golden white, she might win a prize. The current state would appeal to Bailey, not to her, apart from the carpet samples. They were in one-foot squares, leading from the front door into the living room, scattered further up the hall like stepping-stones over a stream, so that she found herself jumping from one to another. Footsteps were trailing home up the road: she could see varieties of feet passing the basement window, and felt the absurd desire to rush out and drag them in with the question, Look, tell me, which colour do you like best? Whatever she wanted they could deliver and fit by the end of the week. Cath was right. Cash buyers were greeted like lords. Stock without customers, the trader's nightmare. The stuff was so cheap, it could have fallen off the back of a lorry.

Just you wait, Bailey, just you wait.

She had insisted on a taxi, to drop Cath home and to carry the samples. Cath had not resisted. Past the leisure centre (which looked more like a prison or a warehouse), turn left, right and right again. Cath went, clutching her talisman bag. She had looked, suddenly, incredibly vulnerable. The thought of her going into that enormous block, outside of which gangs of children ran screaming, filled Helen with pity and frustration. Closing her own door behind her, spreading out her stepping-stones, she was glad to be alone. It was better than many a version of the same evil.

Cath thought there were few evils as bad. The lift did not work; she trod up twenty floors, pausing for breath at each landing. There were no open spaces in the block, it felt like climbing up the inside of a tunnel, the air becoming rarer with each fifteen steps. She could hear murmurings behind doors, steps rushing along walkways. She looked out of the glassed-in stairwell at the first, third, fifth floor, and then did not look again as the ground receded, intensifying a sense of remoteness from all which was real. How had Damien managed here? Nicely, she thought to herself, angry with him.

The top two floors were empty. Down a long corridor on the penultimate floor, there were the sounds of someone working, the whine of a drill and the thump of a hammer. Some of the doors were reinforced, amateur self-protection which could incarcerate as well as deter. Her feet crunched over a small quantity of broken glass as she approached the last flight and a wave of homesickness assailed her. Then she heard the echo of more feet and shuffling on the landing above. A cough, the sound of someone listening. She paused.

For a glorious moment she thought it was Damien, waiting outside his own front door for her to arrive, and it was that illusion which made her fly up the last stone stairs, her feet clattering, before, on the last step, she realised what a row she made, what a dream it was and how she had denied herself the possibility of retreat. She was suddenly afraid, but also, despising her own silliness, careless and aggressive, not bothered about who it might be. She also had the slight sensation, an instinct founded on nothing, that whoever waited there with such patience and lack of subterfuge, could mean no harm.

Mickey Gat was looking out of the window on the landing, her huge presence blocking out the light.

'That you, Cath?' she enquired pleasantly, turning back to the view. 'It ain't half a long way down there. Must take you half an hour to get all the way up. Got a cup of tea, love?' The shocking pink of the shell suit hurt Cath's eyes.

She did not speak or smile, merely fiddled with the locks and opened the door. There was still the numbing sense of disappointment that it was not Damien after all, and it was still too soon to wonder what Mickey Gat might want, or even feel a suspicion of her presence at all. Of course Mickey would have known all Damien's hidey-holes; it was natural she should, but less natural she should climb all those stairs.

'Not very cheerful is it, love?' she remarked as she sat on one of the ill-matched chairs at the table. 'I suppose you could make it nice, though. I mean, if you was planning to stay.'

The kettle, a cheap piece of tin, boiled quickly on one of two electric rings. Enough for a single person. Cath's packing from home, to Mary Secura's surprise, had included little else but cleaning equipment: bleach, Jif, cloths, window polish. Plus, as a sensible afterthought, a sliced loaf of the type which would last a week, margarine, tea and powdered milk.

She was at ease with Mickey Gat, always had been. Women were never a threat, however big. She had been used to a big brother, found a kind of gentleness which seemed to grow in proportion to human size. She had always known where she stood with Mickey Gat. Damien Flood's sister, was where. To be treated with respect on that account, but, like all other women, fundamentally unimportant and completely dispensable. Mickey Gat would never debate the point of whether a woman had a mind or clearly defined needs. She knew she had these features herself; for the rest, she was as chauvinistic as her fellow man and even more contemptuous.

'What can I do for you, Mickey? You didn't climb all the way up here for nothing.'

'And I didn't tell Joe where you might be, either,' Mickey said, cunningly.

'You were only guessing. I could have been anywhere. I got friends too, you know.' She thought of Helen West, the nice Secura girl, the Eliots; they gave her strength. A fragile energy, but still a help.

'I'm your friend,' said Mickey, as if injured by the prospect that she might ever need any other. 'I was Damien's friend. I loved that bloke, Cath. Just like you.'

Not quite like me, Cath thought. Fierce love it had been. The love for the only person who ever really mattered. No-one had loved Damien as she had done.

'So what do you want, Mickey?'

'I went to see your old man this morning, doll. He tells me you've up and left him. Well you must have done, mustn't you, or you wouldn't be here, would you?' Mickey laughed, shaking to a standstill as Cath's face gave no answering smile.

'Well, truth is, Cath, he's in a bit of a state. You'd be shocked, Cath, honest you would. I know he's not much of a man, but I mean, could you, do you think, reconsider?'

'What do you mean, he's not much of a man?' Cath retorted, stung into an immediate defence.

'I mean, he's only a man, Cath, not a saint. I wasn't criticising him, honest. We all have our ups and downs, don't we? You've got a nice home, Cath, you can't give it up just like that. I don't like seeing him in this state, Cath, really I don't. There's no telling what he might do. And he's a good-looking fella, you know. There won't be a shortage of takers, Cath, and I'd hate to see you left on your own. Damien wouldn't have liked that.'

Damien had not liked the idea of Cath being on her own. I can't always be with you, he'd said. You gotta find someone nice, Cath. I'll always be there for you, but this isn't the way to live, Cath; you need more than me to love. A woman on her own, Cath? C'mon, it just isn't on, is it? She could feel a great sinking of the heart. Damien had always been right. A woman on her own was an eyesore.

'You mean you want me to go back to a man who knocks me around, because if I don't he won't do his job properly? That's more like it, isn't it?'

Mickey spread her hands and the gesture seemed to fill the room. Her wedding ring winked. Honesty was always her policy when she could not get away with a lie.

'Well, that's part of it, Cath, to tell the truth. Blokes like Joe are hard to find, you know. I can't run that pub without him. He's the only one understands them kind of customers. And if he's knocked you about, well, I'm sorry, but it's better than him running off with someone else.'

'I've got a job,' Cath said fiercely. 'Two jobs, and I'll get more, see if I don't. I got people who need me.'

'Career woman, now, are we? Joe needs you, Cath. And you need Joe.'

It was true, she knew it was true, but she was not going to admit it.

'Tell you what,' Mickey continued. 'Give it a few days. He needs a lesson, right? You've got to show him who's boss, right? Make him treat you special. Then he's going to meet you, take you somewhere really nice for a night out, and you can talk about it. That's all I'm asking, Cath. Do it for me and Damien, won't you? How about next Monday? Meet him at the Spoon. I'll tell him, give him the evening off.'

Cath knew she had no choice. If she did not promise, Mickey would tell Joe where she was and Joe would haul her all the way down all those stairs by the scruff of the neck and no-one in this block of flats would even notice. Besides, as a compromise, it was not so bad. She liked the thought of Joe being in a state. She nodded.

'There's a good girl then.' Mickey smiled. One large hand disappeared into the pocket of the shell suit, pulled out a wad of notes and a box. Perfume. She could see it clearly. Fake Estée Lauder. When Damien worked for Mickey he had given her perfume every month. Joe had taken it away, like all gifts from Damien.

'Buy yourself a nice frock, doll.'

The price of supremacy: one hundred pounds in cash. A man needs a wife so he can do real work: other women are merely bought and sold. Mickey Gat lumbered to her feet and went to the door. As if in response to the authority of her presence and her demand for convenience, Cath could hear the distant whining of the lift, working again.

Emily Eliot suppressed the urge to slap her daughter. She could not bear the child whining. The need to slap a nine-year-old was not one she always withheld, although she had never administered a blow which could injure. A sharp hand was a good thing to have up your sleeve, catharsis for mother, humiliation for child, the ultimate in tame punishments, reserved for truly disgraceful behaviour. Which this was not, quite, and it did have some excuses. Children get you all ways, she had tried to explain to the few friends who were without progeny. They drive you to leave them for half a day, but cannot bear you having time to yourself; you have to make it up to them later and still they punish you.

Alistair had gone back into his chambers but he would be home again soon. No-one coming in this evening, so maybe dinner à *deux* and an early night? That was before she saw the study, but after she had understood that Mark's role in the supervision of his sibling had been to ignore her entirely. Raised voices, challenges, surly defences, accusations of ingratitude followed, also the banging of doors. On the sidelines, little Jane fumed. No-one had time for her. Not even Cath, who had become so preoccupied she put sugar in the lunchtime soup. The same Cath who had shaken her, almost slapped her and then refused to play. The insults had come thick and fast to Jane's pride and Cath's contribution was the worst. It was sunny, but Mark would not take her out. He said the light hurt his eyes.

All this emerged in a whine to which her mother paid scant attention. And when Jane was dragged to witness the carnage of the study, to which she had added, once Cath had finally woken Mark to resume control and left. She had done it, despite Cath's dire warnings, because she was fed up with Cath too, and the day's frustrations had reached the eye of their own particular storm. Not only was she being ignored, something she resented with all her mother's passion, but she was also going to be punished.

'Do you realise, you little horror,' Emily was saying, keeping her fists bunched against her sides and her voice ominously calm, 'just how long it will take your father to sort this lot out? Did you think of that, you selfish little . . .? Do you know how hard Daddy works, and do we have to lock doors to keep you out? I feel like locking you in.'

The recitation stopped at that. Emily was gazing at the open drawers of the desk, making a mental inventory. Presents lurked in there, wrapping paper, surprises, Alistair's own cache of things to be dispensed. By an unwritten rule, she was not supposed to raid this desk either, but she was, of course, familiar with the contents. Her eyes were riveted: Jane could see her mother deciding, perhaps a little too late to put it into effect, that this might be an occasion for a clip round the ear, after all. She saw the direction of her mother's gaze and a self-righteous cunning froze her expression for an unseen instant.

'What's the matter, Mummy? What did I do? Why are you shouting at me?'

'Because you . . .' The disingenuity of Jane's limpid gaze made her pause. 'You've made a mess,' she finished lamely.

'Mummy, I didn't, not really. I came in to get some paper, that was all, Mummy, I promise it was. Oh and I took some pens,' she added with convincing sheepishness, nodding towards the top drawer where Alistair kept the lurid marker pens vital for annotating papers. Emily remembered him saying he did not know how his profession would live without such pens.

'Cath told me off,' she added in hushed tones, scuffing the carpet with her sandal, 'because I'd been in before and she'd tidied up once already, she said. She chased me out, but then she stayed in here a long time, reading, I think. She told me to go and fix my own room, and I did, Mummy, I did. She was horrid today, Mummy; she smells of bleach. Shall I bring back the pens?'

'Get out of here. Go down and watch TV. Don't move.'

Emily stood in the centre of the room, somehow overwhelmed with disgust. She had an intense feeling of losing control. It could have been Jane's mention of that lingering, cheap-soap, clean-but-not-entirely-pleasant smell which so typified Cath, and which Emily had told herself explained her own aversion to being within inches of the woman in any closed space. A snobbish aversion, as slight as her turning away from the sight of Cath eating bread and butter open mouthed, but one which created a *frisson* of revulsion if she thought of Cath poking around among her things. The same reaction applied, only in intensified form, to the idea of Cath touching things personal to her husband. Emily could share her privacy if she chose; in his absence, Alistair had no choice, no-one to defend his domain except his family. Cath had no business putting her stubby fingers and her ever-so-humble body in this small and exclusive room, however messy it had been.

And besides, everyone in Emily's house had to be subject to Emily's control. They could be perfectly good or perfectly bad, but they had to accept rules. And they had to be nice to her children, who were the very stars of her existence. Emily allowed herself to seethe, aware that she was being a bit of a control freak, fanning herself into indignation because she should never have been out of her domain long enough to let anyone take charge of it. Her command of them all, her single-minded mission to find them the best people in the world, brooked no renegades and took no captives. Poor Alistair. Poor Jane, treated with such unfairness, even though she was being honest enough to admit minor theft and trespass; that was brave, wasn't it? Emily the mother ignored the fleeting glimpse of guile she had seen in her shamefully neglected child, cut out the sound of her whingeing, instead she concentrated on the empty drawers of Alistair's desk, and in her search for a culprit, allowed a horrible suspicion to develop.

It grew as she made a comprehensive search of the corners of Jane's room. The child would not have the imagination to hide perfume anywhere else, since no-one in this most open of households would condone deceit. Jane's ground-floor bedroom contained no secrets. The marker pens were scattered on her bed in a litter of scrunched-up listing paper, and Emily's fury curdled into more guilt. How could it have occurred to her to blame her darling child for emptying the perfume drawer and interfering in the privacy of the study, how could she? The sad logic pointed to Cath, left with responsibility, taking the chance to pry and steal, and, even worse, leaving darling Jane to carry the can. That is what people did when they were poor, acted poor, smelled poor, but it did not excuse such conduct or mitigate the betrayal. The anger rose, swelling against the new target. No-one crossed the boundaries of Mrs Eliot's house rules without dire consequences.

It was enough to ruin the evening. Mark went out, deciding that the best cure for the remnant of his hangover was to try again and the best cure for parental disapproval was to earn even more. Jane was subdued, sweetly affectionate, her sister merely sleepy. They were a family with all hysteria spent and the relaxation of Emily's half day off seemed a thousand years old. Instead of an early night, she and Alistair drank far too much wine, which rendered them sleepy and philosophical. He was worried, she had noticed it at lunch, where her own gaiety had disguised his preoccupation. She had mentioned over supper, well after Jane's hurried goodnight to her papa, about the devastation of the study, cured for the most part before he came home, drawers firmly shut. She didn't want to linger on the missing perfume, because she was not supposed to know, and because what she was going to do about it was her decision alone. She did not mention Cath, either, any more than he did. There was a story in the paper he read out to her. A man leaving his family to work as a missionary for three years, what did she think of that?

Not much, she said shortly, not if his children were still dependent, no, she did not think much of that at all: it made her frightened. She did not add that she already felt under threat, for her judgement, for everything.

Are people with families allowed no other loyalty? he asked. Is there nothing beyond that? He was thinking of loyalties to his clients, giving up on a case because it was too close to home. You could not abandon care of anyone else, could you, simply because you had children to protect?

Yes, you could, said Emily shortly. Your family came first: sod anyone else. That was the whole idea. And if he wanted to be a missionary, would he take Jane with him?

They did not talk much after that.

Give a man a drink and he will talk until he drops. Ask a man who can mix a cocktail to give you a demo, and there could be serious damage, so Ryan concluded. Joe Boyce could not only mix them with dizzying speed, using up his resentment of Mickey Gat by being free with her ingredients, he was also keen to sip. It certainly improved his mood. First he assembled a concoction he described as a Scotch Kiss.

'One fluid ounce best Scotch, blended, any kind will do, but the better the ingredients, the better the drink, one fluid ounce Tia Maria, half ounces Malibu and pineapple juice, skip the fucking pineapple and strawberry on the side. You can't make the same cocktails with Irish or Canadian, you know. What do you think?' All the measuring had been done by sleight of hand, a buzz of liquid slopping into blender with precise ease.

'I'm sorry, I think it's disgusting,' Ryan said.

'Go and give it to the colonel, then.' The old man still sat outside, bawling at passers-by. He accepted the slightly foaming glass with indifference. Ryan wondered if he was suffering from shock.

'I can tell what a man like you needs,' Joe was announcing from behind the bar, hands everywhere, sipping a single malt himself. 'Something simpler. I like anything based on whisky, myself. You got a preference?'

'Oh no,' said Ryan jovially. 'Whisky every time.'

'People have gone off cocktails, you know. Gone off most things I'm good at. Here, try this.'

Ryan sipped. He liked it. Bit sweet, but he liked it and by hell, it packed a punch. 'Yeah,' he nodded. This one would not go to the colonel.

'Think I'll have the same,' Joe mused, 'while I'm thinking. Rusty Nail, they call it, silly name. One ounce each of best Scotch, I mean best, and an ounce of Drambuie. They got separate cocktails for Japanese, you know. Get a few Japanese in here. Lovely people. All smaller than me, thank God. Now, what next?'

Ryan had been under the impression that cocktails, certainly those he had ever bought for women, were to be sipped, savoured and made to last. Joe's Rusty Nail did not linger long enough for rust to form. He was fiddling with an ice bucket.

'Straight Irish, two ounces whiskey, must be Irish, though for this one, I'm not quite sure why. Has to be aged for five years, the Irish, so it's much better. Two ounces of that, what a waste when I come to think of it, plus half ounce each of Pernod and curaçao, couple of dashes of bitter and maraschino. Some people love it.'

Ryan merely liked it. They gave the second to the colonel, who had commenced singing hymns as the light began to fade. A few homegoing customers braved his barricade, lingered briefly while Ryan and friend moved on to Whisky Sour, Boyce style. Whisky and lemon juice, without sweeteners, suited Ryan's taste best, but it could not beat the sweetness of the Glenfiddich which followed. Someone came in and expressed concern about the colonel. They got him a taxi, paid the fare in advance, and then, with a sigh, settled back where they were. Ryan kept offering to pay. To his secret relief, the barman just as consistently refused. The plant, situated to the left of Ryan's elbow, would never recover from his carefully spilled libations, but he had slid into the confidential stance, propping his head on his hand. Coming in here was like going on a building site, he had decided. If you did not have a hard head, you needed a hard hat. By anybody's standards, he had consumed a lot and the night, if not young, was youthful.

'Problem with my wife is, p'raps I should say was,' Ryan said, lying, but prognosticating on everything he knew about Mary Catherine Boyce, 'she got too independent. Got a job, see? I think when they use their heads, it goes to their heads. Everything they got in the fanny, well, that just dries up. She didn't like being touched, see, only she was wearing all these short skirts. To go to fucking work, I ask you. Should be ashamed, I told her. Scared to have kids, is what it was. Have kiddies and get dependent. Why fucking not? I asked her. It's me paid the fucking bills for five years, all for no fucking . . .'

Ryan had three children, the apples of his eye, fathered on a wife far more competitive than himself. He recognised the truth of that without a trace of guilt, and found a certain enjoyment in his new persona. After all, it did not really matter what he said. He was humble enough, and had done it often enough, to know that inebriated exchanges between men did not include the complicating factor of one really listening to the other. Women were different, and so was Bailey. He remembered Bailey with a rosy affection, forbore, wisely, to mention him. Joe was squinting at the ceiling. The tears had left his eyes, but his face was pink.

'Trouble with mine is all about her being fucked up by her brother.' Ryan wanted to sit up straight, remembered he should not.

'Wife's got a brother,' he volunteered. 'Fucking nerd. Comes round, tells me what to do.' Joe nodded.

'He told her what to do, all right. Or rather, he didn't. Didn't tell her what she should do. When she was about fourteen. Could be younger, she wouldn't say.' His head maintained a constant nod.

'You gotta be joking,' Ryan muttered. 'C'mon.'

'Nope. She got pregnant, right? Went wrong, it died. 'Course I didn't know till after I married the bitch, did I? Well, I knew she'd got this scar on her belly, an' I knew she wasn't no virgin bride, who wants one? Made me sorry for her, to tell the truth, I wanted to look after her. Only I didn't know he was the one should have looked after her when she was having it, poor cow didn't tell, there was no-one to tell 'cept him and what did he do? Nothing! Why didn't he look after her? Why didn't they get him home to stop some bloody doctor on duty for sixty hours making a fucking mess of it? She told me she wanted to die. And that fucking Damien, where was he? Learning to box in the fucking Army or something. Our hero. Everyone's hero. Wanker.'

'What could he have done?'

Joe's tears had somehow resumed, which meant a wet face, vivid with sincerity as he held a glass under a spiggot, one glass then another, banged both generous measures of best malt on the counter.

'Could have done?' Joe yelled. 'Could have done? Never mind what he could have done, what could *she* have done? She could have stopped fucking loving him for a start, couldn't she? And did she love him? Did she, all the time: Damien this, Damien that . . . Where the fuck was he when she was fucking needing him? Off the fucking planet, is where. Winning some tournament, is where. And she still thinks he's god, is fucking what. They were like that, those two.' He doubled the first two fingers on his left hand making a sign more of solidarity than obscenity. 'Like that,' he repeated.

'You mean, like that?' Ryan repeated the gesture with the fingers of his right hand. 'I mean really, like that?'

'He ruled our fucking lives, I mean really,' Joe said. 'Really. What he said went. My job, my gaff, my car. My woman.'

'Can't have been nice,' Ryan commented, still slumped.

'No,' said Joe, turning back to the optics. Amazing, Ryan thought, how his hands were so steady while the rest of his body jerked and twisted the way it did. Just amazing.

'It wasn't nice,' said Joe, with a turn of sobriety. 'It wasn't nice at all. I mean he introduced me to Cath, but I hated that fucker, you know? Hated him. Like fucking poison.'

'Give us another of that malt, will you?' was all Ryan said. He was already poisoned. May as well get worse. He needed something to cope with a horrible sensation of shock. Plus something he did not dare admit: pity for the man, and fear, plus a sensation of half truths not quite making a whole, a man talking in code.

He missed his wife and wished he was going home to bed.

CHAPTER TEN

It was soft and safe but the light hurt his eyes. There was Bailey, with an evil look, promising there were always means to make a man talk.

'What did he tell you, Ryan?'

'Leave me alone, will you? He told me some things, not everything. There was something more; something he wanted to boast about, apart from the cocktails. Something he was proud of, but guilty about. I don't know. He's done something heroic, that man, and he wants to tell. Let me sleep.'

'I think he's wearing his guilt in the wrong pocket. Guilty about the wrong things. Proud of the wrong things, too.'

'Were you always convinced he had something to do with killing Damien Flood?'

'Was I? Did I say so? It had to be someone full of hate.'

'Well, he knows about hate.' Ryan's eyes were closing: the lids felt like heavy coins.

'His sister might have hated. It was Damien's baby she had, when she was only a kid herself. There's a birth and death certificate with Flood's name on, I found them. Looked like Damien posed as husband. Who would know?'

Ryan opened his eyes. 'Oh Jesus Christ Almighty. Why didn't I think of that? Jesus. What a clever old man you are.' His eyes closed again. News of any kind, however exceptional, remained subject to other needs. He murmured to cover a kind of embarrassment. Bailey murmured back.

'Oh no, the sister loved him all right. But I don't think our Joe has any idea whose baby it was. I think he might have said.'

'Are you sure? . . . For God's sake, let me sleep.'

*

There was a roll of thunder: Joe twitched in his own bed, dreaming of glory. Technicolor dreams in rancid sheets: Damien Flood, the golden boy, covered in green blood. The same handsome Damien, adored by little Joseph Boyce, who had clung to his coattails, and then been presented with Damien's sister, like a gift from heaven, so comely, so sweet and so much in need of protection it would make a man of him and admit him to the inner sanctum of Damien's gang. Joe Boyce, showered with the stardom of that wedding, all his needs provided for: a job, a place; until, apart from the goods in the attics, his whole life revolved around Damien's hand-outs, Damien's contacts. And still his little wife did not really love him. Perhaps with that scar on her belly she could never let herself be loved, never believe it, but when it came to loving, she was just like the rest: Damien came first. Bastard.

So, in his dream, Joe took command. He came out of a cloud of memories, each more humiliating than the last, until the dream took over.

There they would be, a band of brothers, drinking away a good time. Only in the dream, Joe would not be the servant, the trooper for their colours, with alcohol the only bond between them, never equality, although he would still be the one who left to go home first. He would do that by choice, not because he feared to be left behind.

Damien would come out of the Gents, zipping up his trousers, then slap his arms round the shoulders of the other two men before walking out ahead of them, swaggering; the woman clearing up behind the bar following with her eyes the sight of his small buttocks and thick, blond hair gleaming gold against the white of his shirt before she turned back to emptying ashtrays. How can a man walk as he talked, slurred, but bouncy? The friends would be taller, lankier, neater and somehow less impressive; even from behind, Damien had a certain charisma. A little drunk, yes; as drunk as he ever was, never disorderly, ill humoured or loud, never a really dirty joke or piece of rudeness. He might have been going to seed a bit, but he did so with an element of youthful dignity and he had a laugh which echoed joy.

Joe could not shake away the dream. He had refined it, through a thousand half dreams, into a kind of visual reality, so that once he stepped out into the open, he could actually feel the chill of the air, damp with winter drizzle, or hear the distinctive sound of a diesel engine churning uphill as they crossed the road to the car park next to the leisure centre. It was dark in there. Joe, watching from the shadows of the trees, anxious, curious, wanting to go with them, knowing they should not have laughed at those lads, nor taken their money.

Then the three kids, snarling like cats, pouncing with such a lack of skill that Joe pitied them, empathised with their futile aggression; they were kittens, not tom-cats, so pathetic even with their broken pool cues, it was like setting flies to attack a wall, but there was nothing inevitable in this dream. So the first youth, the runt of someone's litter, a boy without facial features and bluish skin, sprinted forward, felled Goliath, and Joe was surprised. He almost leapt out from behind that tree and ran to Damien's aid, until the incubation of three years' hatred forced him to stay still. Eughh! He could see himself, covering his eyes and listening to the sounds: grunts, groans, fist on bone, short sharp screams, the same sounds of the power he could only ever exercise over Cath and only then with appalling shame. He felt hot, boiling inside his jacket, despite the cold of the rain around the bare trees of the park. When he removed his hands from his face, to the sounds of running footsteps, the stink of breath still reverberating, he could not believe that Damien, the immortal, was still there. They had both shifted places, him retreating, Damien staggering breathlessly into the dark of the park, lying down to rest against a tree, looking peaceful, presenting to any man who hated him enough, the perfect opportunity. Uncannily perfect, with someone in the wings, neatly poised to take the blame. In all his dreams, Joe was never without the satchel he carried, but in this dream, it contained the bayonet he had sharpened, brought along for no other purpose except to show it to Damien. Damien had said he was interested in all that stuff, but he wasn't and Joe never got a word in edgeways. Running feet, shouting in the distance; the flatulent sound of far-away bus brakes and the murmuring of the trees, a thunderous silence, Damien, groaning, but still oddly graceful.

Joe turned in his bed. At this point the dream was more day-dream than a vision of the night, the focus was clearer; he could hear words, although from a distance, voices without intonation or individuality. What would he say? Would he say, See this, Damien? See this? I brought it for you. See this? Watch Damien's eyes widen, his face, even with the graze on his forehead, taking on that look of familiar welcome. 'It's you,' he would murmur. 'Yes, it's me,' Joe could hear himself say as he stabbed him the first time, in the chest. He was so muscular there, it was as if he did not feel it. Then there would be Damien again, murmuring something like, 'No, no, don't,' as his great hands came out like a pair of pliers, and gripped Joe by the shoulders. 'Don't do this, Joe, please. What did I do wrong, Joe, please?' Too late to stop, the wrong kind of knife, sharp on one side, not a dagger, but a heavy blade, took all his strength to get it out, relieved at the lack of blood, standing back and wanting to retreat. And then a moment of terrible reality, when Joe could not think of a single thing which Damien had done to deserve this. The blood came out like a fountain and that toneless voice again, loud, almost a scream. 'Cath . . . Oh, my lovely Cath, save me.'

That was the point of perfect clarity, when the dream became completely sensuous. Joe, plunging the bayonet as hard as he could into the softest bit of belly, the part of Damien which showed how he had gone downhill, sloping into a suggestion of fat. Joe looking on with wonder as he saw himself using both hands to drag the blade from left to right and back, feeling the connection of bone, tissue soft and hard, and whenever Damien said, Cath, digging in further until he felt the spine and still the bugger would not die. The mess was extraordinary, the emergence of the contents of that tight abdomen something akin to a newborn child and the staccato, wailing sounds, more than similar. Cath, Cath: Damien still repeating her name, refusing to stop and refusing to die, until Joe could not bear the sound, yanked away his clumsy weapon from the groaning lump with the ever-open mouth, toppled with the effort, saw himself rolling over in the wet grass, away from the blood. Not looking back as he wiped the blade, stumbling away from that voice, still calling in the rain, hands clawing at the red raw spillage of life.

Joe landed on the carpet by his bed with his fists bunched against his chest, his body rigid. Then he opened his eyes to the smell of whisky vomit. A captive fly buzzed against the window. He made the experiment of trying to stand, pushing himself onto his knees, then straightening his torso, then levering himself to his feet with the support of the bed. Once upright he felt stable for a moment, then crashed sideways onto the mattress, and lay there staring at the ceiling. There was no thunder, except the reverberations inside his skull. The fly buzzed; the light through Cath's home-made curtains showed the features of early dawn.

It was a dream; a nightmare of glory. Only a dream. It could have happened like that. If they beat him, he would have to confess it had happened exactly like that; he would be terrified to confess, but proud of it, too. Then the evening before the dream came back to his mind in a series of slow images. Talking to the man in the Spoon. He had not boasted, he had only wept. The man had felt sorry, got him home safe and not on the bus either. So everyone was safe, now and for ever, but if the dream was true, why on earth was it that he could not remember what he had done with the bayonet? Dreams were untidy, short on practical details; that part remained blank, shocked into oblivion. Joe was as bitter as the whisky taste was sweet. No-one would ever come looking for him now. No-one would ever look at him and see the hero.

The mists had cleared. Ryan knew that coffee in the morning was not the best way to treat a surfeit of whisky the night before, but it was all he wanted and Bailey made the best. Ryan rose from his bed of pain on the couch with exaggerated groans, in fact feeling fine, all things considered, better than he supposed he deserved. The conversation of the early hours caused more confusion in his brain than the alcohol; in the meantime, he had been dreaming of women in violent, pornographic poses and it blurred his memory. Bailey was talking: Bailey could talk through a storm, flood or fire, without raising his voice. Ryan blinked hard, shook his head and looked round. The colours of the sofa on which he had lain attacked his eyes; everything else was light and bright. It was so clean in here, any smell must be his own, not dirt or dust. Thinking what a good little housewife Bailey was, and what an efficient host, did not cut him down to size. Or stop him talking.

'You agree with me, then?'

'Of course. About what?'

'About Joe Boyce being violent, out of control. Devious, dangerous.'

Ryan shook his head again. 'I didn't before. Thought he was a harmless little bloke who took out his frustrations on his wife once in a while, that's all. Until I saw him with the broken glass, ready to do some poor old sod in the eye for nothing more than speaking out of turn in the wrong accent. Yes, he's violent. More than average. Violent enough to do that kind of damage to Damien Flood.'

'And if his wife goes back to him, she would be in danger too?'

'Doesn't follow. He loves her.'

'He must have loved her brother once, too. And if it was Joe who did it, she'll remember something, won't she? When she's finally recovered from the death, she'll think of some niggly little detail. She'll remember how hubby didn't come home at quite the time she says in her statement. How he went straight to have a bath and left early the next morning with his clothes in a bag, something like that.'

'It rained,' Ryan remembered. 'It was raining when I got to the body.' His case, he thought bitterly; my case with minimal supervision from you. Bailey letting him spread his wings only to gum them later. Blood running away into the ground; the dead man's yellow hair plastered against his head.

Bailey made more coffee. 'Enough danger to the wife for you to get your PC Secura officially involved.'

'Are you going to arrest him?'

'Who?'

'Joe Boyce.'

'On what grounds? There's no more evidence than there ever was. Even if Mary Catherine Boyce told us interesting things, we'd be nowhere near.'

'So what's all this for?' Ryan yelled. 'Why have I got this bloody headache?'

'I needed to know, that's why. Do you need a clean shirt?'

Cath had not been allowed the luxury of open grief, but she had still been grieving, wandering in a daze, a constant fog, like someone high on tranquillisers, floating along at the same level as other people's knees, never quite able to raise her eyes or concentrate for more than a minute. Even in the Eliots' house, wandering from room to room to fetch something and forgetting when she got there what it was. Sometimes, sitting on the bus, she would find herself surprised at the sight of a landmark which she could have sworn they had already passed. Today, she could see it all clearly. Joe had not let her cry; when she had cried he had hit her and then cried himself as if to say, what about me, what about me?

Cath sat on the 59 in a state which approached contentment. Not happiness, Cath had long since forgotten what that concept was, but a state of anxious resolution which she felt called for some self-congratulation, although she could not say why.

Handling Mickey Gat, keeping a hundred pounds of her money, learning that Joe missed her? Better still, being left independently in charge of Mrs Eliot's household: that had been a source of pride, too. Proving indispensable to Helen West added some weight, although that was less important. Cath dismissed to the anterooms of her mind her own sojourn in Mr Eliot's study, although she was half-heartedly aware that it was the most important thing of all and would have to be disinterred, later. The immediate impact was clearer, because it brought a measure of relief. All those papers in the study could only mean that nice Mr Eliot (and, it followed, his wife) knew more about Cath than she could ever have guessed; knew about Damien, for instance, had some measure of what she had suffered and how brave she had been these last months, so that when she took the momentous step she would take this morning, of asking Emily for help, she would not have to begin at the beginning, because in the information stakes, she was halfway there. How kind and sensitive of them both to mind their own business. In the midst of all this concluding, planning, swaying with the bus, anxious, but confident, it never occurred to Cath that the first-name-only terms which prevailed in the relationship between cleaning lady and cash-paying employer made it unlikely that anyone would automatically connect her full name on a page with the Cath they knew, or that if they had, they might fail to tell their nearest and dearest. Cleaning ladies were treasures with telephone numbers; their full names, their identities, apart from idiosyncrasies, remained in a kind of limbo. The more reliable they were, the more anonymous.

The sun touched Cath's face through a smudged window; she thought briefly of what it would be like up in the eyrie in winter. Yes, explain, calmly and briefly, what her situation was and ask for help. How easy, and yet how difficult a concept that was, but it was not as if she was asking for much and certainly not for anything they could not give. She would like more work, enough to fill three afternoons a week, babysitting, anything they could arrange for her, with all their friends. Emily had fixed her up with Helen West, hadn't she? And there was surely more. Plenty enough to allow her to squat in Damien's flat until she could find something better. Mustn't overburden Mrs Eliot, though, she was a busy woman; ask Helen West later about things like dole money and all that stuff, or take up the offer of that friend of hers, Mary somebody. What a calculating customer she was becoming: she'd be making lists next. The Eliots loved her: she was family, they had often said so. Today, she would accept the accolade, break the habits of a lifetime. Ask for something.

With the bus moving into the smoother reaches of Knightsbridge, it all seemed simple.

*

She let herself in with the key, smelling the household warmth which was so different from the warmth of the sun, carrying scents of burned toast, soap, feet, and the promise of cheerful voices. She put down her PVC carrier bag, which she always carried regardless of need, and made for the hall cupboard and the Hoover. She always did that first thing, so as not to be seen to have to wait for some special instruction and in any event, there was never a day when this hall did not need cleaning. The house was silent: it seemed almost a shame to waken it into life with the bad-mannered noise of a machine.

Despite her activity Cath was anxious to reach coffee time. Emily Eliot was not. She waved over the noise of the Hoover, disappeared rapidly to the upper regions, put on her make-up and made a list. Ask Hormsbies to supper: frightful people, but their daughter gets on well with Jane and we've been there twice. Write to your mother and thank her for Mark's present. Buy new clothes for Mark, although he does not deserve it, must be his fault he's growing out at the knees, or has he actually cut those jeans? Emily threw her pen across the room. This was procrastination. Get on with it, woman, get on with it. There had never been a motto better suited to a wife: she should get the words emblazoned on a T-shirt.

'I want to talk to you,' she yelled, over the noise of the Hoover. Where was Jane, subversive, eavesdropping little brute with a passion for dirt? Ah yes, waiting for the friend who was coming for the day, and arranging her room in accordance with what said friend would find most admirable. Cath beamed at her, followed her meekly, while Emily felt irritated. Worse still, when Cath sat at the pine table in the kitchen, she fingered with evident, if critical, affection the surface she had scrubbed so often. Honey spilt at breakfast, a shower of crumbs left by Alistair, Coco Pops spilt by someone. Same old stains on the ceiling, food hiding in every crack.

'Mr Eliot's room,' Emily began, putting bread and butter on the table, fumbling with a jar of instant coffee.

'Yes,' said Cath. She grabbed a piece of bread, talked hurriedly with a full mouth. 'I was going to tell you about that.' She looked round, a trifle shifty, looking out for Jane, waiting to say how the child had only been looking for paper and was very sorry, and hadn't she herself put it all back more or less right? Emily looked at the open mouth, nauseated. On cue, Jane came sidling in. No hellos, just a sideways shuffle, clinging to the cupboards.

'Look what I found, Mummy.'

'Where?'

'In Cath's bag.' She held aloft a boxed bottle of Estée Lauder, White Linen. Mickey Gat's bribe, which Cath had dropped in there, intending to give it to little Jane, who liked that kind of thing. Emily got up and switched off the kettle. She put back in the bread bin the remains of the granary loaf which Cath ate with such relish, amusing the children who could not understand anyone who did not prefer biscuits.

'I think you'd better go, Cath. I'm sorry about this, but it's best all round.'

Cath stared dumbfounded. She had begun to laugh, her face contorted in a smile which would preface an explanation about how anyone was welcome to Mickey Gat's perfume, since none of it was real, despite the labels, and it wouldn't last five minutes on a camel, although it was still lovely if it was free; and there was Emily Eliot, fumbling in her handbag and handing her five twenty-pound notes, crisp from a cash machine.

'A week in hand,' Emily said, her voice as crisp as the notes. 'Don't worry about the Hoover, I'll put it away.'

Joe was right then, wasn't he? Joe was right about a lot of things, including people in big houses. Cath stood on the doorstep, clutching her bag. Her head seemed to be shaking with a life of its own, turning left and right, right and left like some weary old dog suffering from blindness. She had money in her fist, her bag on her arm; she had never left a house with such speed and she had no idea why. She wanted to sit on the steps which led down to the street, but the thought of lingering where the chill of their cruelty could contaminate her further moved her on. Wandering, she remembered to put the cash in her purse, the second one-hundred-pound bribe she had received in twenty-four hours: at this rate, she would be rich. Cath sat on a doorstep five doors down.

They knew, was why. The bad things as well as the good. With their clever wit and all their knowledge they had decoded it all. About she and Damien shoved out to care, shuffling around in the same bedsit when they ran away; the brother with convictions for theft, and the baby that never was. They knew everything there was to know about the potted life-history contained in the statement of Mary Catherine Boyce. And from the pinnacle of their omnipotence they had decided she was not worth the butter on their bread. Four hours a day, sometimes more, five days a week for a year, uncomplaining Cath would do anything, and she still wasn't worth a hearing. She found herself looking down the road which led into the mews where the Spoon and Fiddle sat; but resisted the temptation to walk down there, find Joe and say you were right after all. She had sat on cold stones for more than an hour: she was strong enough to move out of range, but all the morning's resolution was gone, leaving nothing but a residue of duty. The afternoon was promised; another hundred yards brought her to the number 59, and the golden yellow walls of Helen West who could not paint her own bathroom and did not have a man.

She had had enough of the PVC bag, too: Mrs Eliot had given it to her last Christmas. Cath prepared to shove it in the bin by the bus-stop, felt the weight at the bottom, looked inside instead. Resting on her umbrella was the wee bayonet Jane had shown her yesterday. Get rid of rubbish on the cleaning lady. Cath felt a moment of complete panic, but then it fell into perspective. There was no malice in the child, no knowledge, no accusation; only the contemptuous action of getting rid of something which disturbed her. Just like her mother, getting rid of clothes infected with moth. It was a gift of fate, nothing sinister in it, only contempt.

Bailey could not settle. He found himself in that vacuum created by useless knowledge which he could not share for lack of proof.

It would lie on his brain like indigestible food. No-one inside the police force wanted knowledge which led to nothing. He could tell the collator at the local nick to mention Joe Boyce on the files, brief each relief to watch out for him, but what good would that do? Bailey was angry with himself for setting a hare he could not catch; he had disturbed Ryan to the marrow of his bones, for nothing. There was no-one to save and almost no-one to tell. He sat at his desk, drumming his fingers, and looked out of the window into the back yard which steamed with heat and exhaust fumes. He heard laughter coming from next door and thought of his uncluttered home. Then he thought of Helen's.

Well, he seemed to have cut himself off from solace there. She would have given him a good objective analysis, would she not? Yes, in normal circumstances, but perhaps not when it was so close to home. Bailey knew he was refusing to give her the benefit of the doubt, knew that in some way he was on the brink of disaster with her, and that part of it was his own fault for saying he would not see her until the weekend, let her sort out her own household mess, leave him out of it. Selfish, yes, but she had agreed with it. She knew damn well his offers of help were half-hearted. Bailey did not like change. He disliked it, perversely, as much as he disliked staying still.

The leisure centre park where Damien Flood had died was no great distance from the police station where he had landed, peripatetic animal that he was, that morning. There was a monumental pile of papers on his desk: there were other more recent murders, but he could not let this last case lie. Somewhere soon, he would be moved on to new professional hunting-grounds, despite his own resistance, in the same way that life was going to shift Helen and himself into another gear. He wanted something settled before the revolution he could sense on the horizon, like the promise of a storm. And he did not want that boy convicted of murder when all he had done was a feeble attempt at revenge.

Walking round the perimeter of the park, Bailey found it difficult to imagine it in the depths of winter. There would be fewer places to hide. Trying to translate the appearance of a place into another season was like trying to look through binoculars the wrong way round. Now, in the afternoon, it was a vision of innocence. There was a small playground beyond the tennis courts; mothers sat with babies in prams, and if the peace was disturbed by shrieked commands, 'Val! Get down off there!' 'Danny, stop that, now!', often punctuated by imprecations not suitable for the ears of children, there was nothing sinister about it. It was a multicoloured scene of racial harmony, paralleled in the crowds on the tennis court, kids mainly, playing games without discipline, using this space like any other space. Animals herding, Bailey thought, making lowing sounds to one another, enjoying the sun.

He found the place depicted in the photographs he had memorised. The tree which had supported the body, the scrubbed grass around it leading to the cinder path. Cut through here and you got to the pub, go the other way and you came out almost next door to Joe Boyce. He had not realised the distances were quite so small; it surprised him, but there was nothing else to discover. He was not quite sure what he had expected. A bunch of flowers to commemorate the scene, perhaps, as if Damien Flood had been a fallen hero.

Whatever else he was, Flood did not warrant much status. No-one was going to erect a statue to commemorate every mugging in this place, but it seemed a good idea. A commemoration of victims, Bailey thought, amused by the idea. He went back to his desk and phoned Helen at hers. Out, he was told, in tones of disapproval. Day off, for painting her flat. Unavailable for comment.

They sat in the kitchen eating a scratchy and early supper, baked potatoes with cheese, salad, which Cath ignored in favour of bread and butter; no wonder she was starving, as well as plump. Helen was thinking how Bailey was perhaps wise to stay away, because a kitchen full of chaos was not conducive to trust, appetite, confidence or condolence, not as far as Catherine Boyce was concerned. The talkative Cath of yesterday was transformed into the red-eyed misery of today, energetic, yes; communicative, certainly not. Arriving earlier than expected, she gave her brief news and then said she would get on with the painting.

I'll speak to Emily, Helen had said, sick with fury; how could she do that to you? She did and you won't speak to her, Cath said fiercely. Please. After that, all Cath would discuss was carpets. She moved from one of the stepping-stones to another, nodding approval, making her own choice and then changing her mind, as if her battered ego was taking refuge in playing games, finally agreeing that Helen had chosen right. And if Helen West thought she might loosen up and discuss the intimate details of her life over a plate of bread and butter, Cath was not going to oblige. She had wanted to do that this morning, and look what happened then.

The silences were uncomfortable. Cath could feel Helen's disappointment and her helpless desire to make amends: it washed over her like a balm both prickly to the skin and comforting, until, within the strict confines of her ability, she relented. She spat out, in her own code, the conclusions reached on the number 59 from Knightsbridge to here. Conclusions formed while sitting on doorsteps which remained cold despite the sun, contemplating the death of still-unformed hopes.

'You see? It ain't no good at all, trying to do without a man, is it?' she burst out. 'No good at all. At least, as long as I had Joe, other people couldn't push me round. Still, I suppose I'll get used to it. I gotta get used to it, haven't I?'

Helen thought of Redwood, the tyrannies of work from which Emily Eliot was so immune, and frowned.

'Having a man never stopped anyone pushing me around,' she remarked.

Cath was not listening. 'I need something new to wear,' she announced. That sounded positive.

'Yes, you do,' Helen agreed, no longer surprised by the illogical sequence of Cath's announcements.

'Make me feel better. You always feel better if you try. Isn't that right?'

'Sure you do.'

'We're going out next Monday,' Cath stated flatly. 'Joe and me. For a chat.'

'Is this the first time you've left him?' Helen asked, sadly. Cath managed to shake her head and nod at the same time.

'Once before. That wasn't any good either. This time I gotta manage. Get myself looking nice, at least.'

Helen thought of leaving Bailey and all the times it had been on the cards, never more so than now, because their needs seemed to have become so incompatible. That was all any of them were, men and women both, nothing but a series of needs to be met by a series of ever-more-disgraceful compromises and, in the light of that, she realised how powerless she was to help Cath in any but the most small and practical of ways. People do what they will: you cannot make them trust or do what is best for themselves.

'Monday?' she queried. 'I suppose that's as good a day as any. Somewhere nice? Come on, Cath,' she was trying to be cheerful, finding it a strain, trying to break an unbreakable code. 'Tell me, what's your idea of a nice time? A treat?'

Cath looked down at her bread and butter, replaced the last morsel on the plate, held it captive there in case it should escape. She felt nothing but despair. She could not think of the last time she had been happy, apart from when she had lost herself in work, or, dawdling at the Eliots' kitchen table, had watched Jane in the garden; and that thought, more than anything, made her want to cry.

'I think,' she said, swallowing quickly, trying to emulate Helen's smile, 'I think my idea of a real treat is never again going on the number 59.'

'That doesn't seem much to ask,' Helen said.

She thought, in desperation, Is there anything I can offer to do which will help? Anything?

'Does your new place have hot water, Cath?'

'Not so's you'd notice. I manage.'

Helen imagined the vacuum of the weekend ahead. Wondered what a woman did at the top of a block on a sweltering Sunday.

'If you could help me part of Saturday, Sunday too if you like, Monday if you can make it, Cath, that would be great. We'd finish everything, gloss paint the lot. Hang the curtains, put everything back. I can't do it on my own. Then I'm sure I can get you loads more work, and anyway, there'll still be plenty to do here. The garden for a start. OK?'

It was the right kind of offer. Practical. Cath nodded with vigour. Helen wished she could like her. Find more in her own heart than a guilty kind of admiration. It was true what Bailey and Mary Secura both said in their separate ways. She did not understand.

CHAPTER ELEVEN

'Do you know what they print at the bottom of Crown Prosecution Service letters? They've got this printed line. It says, "Working for Justice". They must be out of their minds, printing that. What a nerve.' Mary Secura stared at her own hands holding the drink, noticed her bitten fingernails and hid them under the table.

'Helen West told me how she got a letter back from a bloke. Said he couldn't see how that line at the bottom of the letter had anything to do with the rest of it. Why don't we have something like that at the end of a letter from the police? You know, a little something to tuck inside the summons, like they give you with the big electricity bill, telling you it's all for your own good, really.'

Ryan smiled at Mary Secura's mockery. 'We used to have a recruiting slogan,' he said, 'years ago. "Dull it isn't." They put it on the bottom of posters in the Tube. Wasn't true, either. Another?'

Amazing how quickly his hangovers seemed to flee these days. Maybe that meant he was a real alcoholic instead of pretending, or it could have been that the two days spent in the bosom of his family since the last binge had effected a cure. More likely, it was the simpler pleasure of Mary's company, what with both of them grousing and putting the world to rights. Ryan would have preferred Mary with hair ruffled and no clothes on at all, but a man cannot be picky. Since that sight was not on the menu so far, he was perfectly prepared to make do with the company of a woman who felt as hard done by as he did himself. There were many routes to bliss: this was only one of them. No-one ever told you what a positive pleasure it was to sit down and moan.

'Think you'll do all right with Bailey,' he hinted. He was going to go on and add how he had put in a good word, but then avoided the chance to tell a downright lie that Mary was likely to detect. The two of them were having a pleasant evening and Ryan did not want to spoil it. PC Mary Secura was reeling from the discovery that her career was in the lap of the gods, who rated the weight of brain power and dedication rather less than perfume and a short skirt. She was remembering her admonishment, uneasily tempered by the overlong handshake, followed by the reaction of her policeman partner at home, who had acted as if she had laid a dozen men by lunchtime on a Monday: boiling with angry shock, wondering about the impact of her disgrace on his own career, all that shit. In the tide of these resentments, the face of Shirley Rix swam up like a picture of a drowned woman with her hair floating away, and with that image there swelled all the furious love Mary still felt for her chosen career and her chosen victims. Apart from the Rix incident, she had always played it by the book; now there seemed less point and she looked at Ryan with a greater appreciation of alternative methods for getting any damn thing done.

'It isn't just a job, Mike, is it? Not just nine to five, do what you can, surely not? Yes, it is, I can see it written in your face. Working for justice, hey? What a laugh. Last time I saw justice was a punch-up at a party where the right person got a fat lip.'

Ryan sipped his drink. Not a bad pub, not as nice as the Spoon and Fiddle, source of his last hangover. He thought he might take Mary there another time provided it changed hands as well as management, since a pub owned by huge Mickey Gat and managed by a bloke he might have fingered for murder was not a place he would take a respectable girl who was spoken for. He tried to recall what Bailey had said to him the other night, about the enormous pleasure of having a conversation free of double meaning, innuendo and at least three motives. A luxury too complicated for Ryan. Speaking for himself, he never had conversations like that, especially with women.

'How are you getting on with Mary Catherine Boyce?'

He waited for her to say she thought this was a social

conversation, but she didn't. Mary mixed business with pleasure, without noticing the difference. She took work home and also out for the evening like other people would a baby. She would be hell to sleep with, Ryan thought; she would talk about work in her dreams.

'Went to see her today, as a matter of fact. We had her husband in the Unit yesterday, claiming we'd kidnapped her. He'd been tearing the flat apart, he said, not a bad flat either, if you don't mind leaks, and he'd found one of our leaflets So we calmed him down, sent him to Everyman – clinic for violent men. But, of course, he'll never go. Cath's been out most of the week working, she says, and I know where, good for her, not many of our ladies work or even know how, even less their mothers, wish they did. So, we talked about getting her tenancy legal and we talked about getting benefits and I might as well have been talking to a brick wall, and then we talk about getting a solicitor so she can get a formal separation, and then, stone me, calm as a cucumber, she says she's going out with her old man on Monday, and what should she wear? I swear to God, I could've killed her. What do you do? I mean, what do you do?'

'Give up,' Ryan volunteered.

'Sounds about right. Not easy, but sure as hell, right.'

Ryan had never had an abstract passion for justice. It was some moving standard way out there on the horizon while he enjoyed his job for the freedom, the powers and the occasional moment of influence. He could feel such a moment coming on, right now. He could also feel the guidance of Bailey's philosophy, which had a rough translation along the lines of, if you obey most of the rules, most of the time and then have the patience to wait, you get them in the end. Ryan could see the advice in purely picturesque terms; an old family motto, carved wood around some old grizzled buzzard, which lent the whole idea a kind of respectability, although he himself had never quite got round to believing it. There was always a quicker way to work for justice.

'Listen to what I found out about that poor cow's husband,' he began. Ryan forgot, in the telling, that truth was a virtue, while conjecture was not; he revelled instead in this wide-eyed, female audience far younger and sexier than many who had made him cast discretion to the wind. All right, so Bailey and he, the other morning, had dreamt up a scenario which was more acceptable as an explanation for Damien Flood's murder than the one on record so far. The tale Ryan now told Mary included details of how he had checked with the Boyce neighbours, only to discover that Joe Boyce had indeed come home on the night of the murder much later than the times underlined in his statement and that of his weeping wife. Despite the row they made themselves, the downstairs neighbours knew that the Boyce partnership never took a bath at night, except this once, when one of them did and the bath leaked through the neighbours' ceiling. It was the first time that had ever happened, not a leak, the sort of flood you get with an overflow: someone had left the thing running, but would they come to court and say so? Never. They had only remembered because it was the day before Giro cheques and because of Joe's uncharacteristic humility the next morning when they mentioned it. Since then, he had reverted to type.

Ryan did not add that he had only got thus far by threatening a full-scale drugs raid, not in his power to activate, nor did he stress that these late and unreliable enquiries were ones he might have thought to make in the first place, soon after the death. Bailey would have done so, but Bailey, at the time, had three or four major enquiries. You could get to hate Bailey's example if you worked for him long enough, which in Ryan's case was not yet.

Mary Secura lit her fourth cigarette, smoking as if she only did it to make herself feel worse, a woman with a guilt problem, scratching it raw through amazement and outrage. In her company, Ryan came to share her frustration, it passed between them like a buzz. His story rendered her shell-shocked.

'He kills her brother and she's worried about what to wear on their grand reunion,' Mary murmured. 'If that don't beat all.'

There was a vision dancing before her eyes of going to the Boyce household, ringing the bell, standing back, waiting for the blood to come over the doorstep. Or going, as she had done once, to a house full of hungry blue bottles, swarming round a corpse. Cath would be one of those; the type of battered wife who goes on claiming love, ignoring the cut-off point, leaves, returns, leaves and returns until she is finally carried away in a coffin. And then the man pleads he was provoked.

'Don't suppose she has any idea of what Joe might have done,' Ryan suggested.

'Don't suppose you have much hard fact either,' Mary replied, but he could tell she was hooked. She could see Joe Boyce as a murderer all right. She could see all husbands as potential murderers; the job had got to her brain.

'You going back to see her again? Like, over the next twenty-four hours?' he asked.

'Could do, I suppose,' she said, stretching and yawning like a glorious, aerobic-exercised cat. Think of that in a leotard, Ryan told himself; better than no clothes at all, leotards.

'Fancy a curry?'

She seemed to recover herself, shuffle slightly like someone who had heard these unseductive lines before.

'What's your wife doing this evening, Mike?'

'Spanish class.'

'I thought,' she said as she swept up her good handbag from the table, planted a kiss on his forehead and stroked his cheek in a way which made him feel dizzy, 'she might have been home, ironing your shirts. You're a star, Mike. Thanks for the drink.'

Alistair Eliot went to the pub on his way home. He knew that he did not stop at the Spoon as a panacea, or even because two days without a professional cleaner had turned his house into a minefield of things on which the average man could break his neck. He stopped because he no longer wanted to get home, on account of a row with Emily which had passed all boundaries known before, and because if home was no longer a source of comfort, his conscience was worse. How could she have sacked that poor woman for stealing perfume? Perfume was simply not important enough to warrant such action against someone so loyal. In a proper job

Cath would have been given warning. His anger had been one of bewilderment, a disappointment in his wife, even before he remembered that Emily had not known exactly how unfortunate Cath was. It did not matter, he had said, who possessed the perfume hidden in his desk drawer; sacking Cath still stank. Poor Cath, he had kept on repeating to Emily's evident displeasure; poor Cath. She is not poor Cath. She smells, she's irritating, she has bad table-manners and she's a thief!, Emily had yelled, aggressive and defensive. A thief!

And you are scarcely better, he said gravely, to treat her in such a fashion without a second chance or any attempt to find out the truth, listen, evaluate or learn why someone who so clearly loves and reveres you should behave in such a way, for so little.

I gave her a hundred pounds and she took it, Emily flashed back. Isn't that what you lawyers call an admission? Only an admission of need, he replied: supposing you were innocent as charged, wouldn't you have taken the money? What finished it was when he told her of Cath's situation, bereaved of a close brother, beaten by an otherwise loving husband. To Alistair's amazement, Emily had said that made no difference at all. She was not duty bound to take on other people's problems; she did not want them in her house any more than she wanted carpet beetles. Which all explained why Alistair went to the Spoon, with some vague and woolly idea of doing good by explanation. Or parting with another hundred pounds, something along the lines of atonement by word or deed, in full recognition that whatever he did would be clumsy. It was a cloudy, muggy evening; the flowers in the window-boxes drooped, reminders of how everything comes to an end, even summer, slipping slowly past the sell-by date. Alistair sat by their suffocating smell.

Joe Boyce had watched his hesitant steps down the street as he stood by the mullioned windows polishing glasses. In contrast to the days before, his mood had become benign. He thought of Mickey Gat, in here yesterday, purringly kind, saying now, now, Joe, I got news for you. Joe had somehow forgotten to take offence at the fact that Mickey Gat knew the whereabouts of his wife while he himself did not: it seemed perfectly acceptable in the order of things, this female solidarity, a reminder that Mickey was one of them, after all. Condescending, yes, but also acceptable as long as Mickey Gat did not lord it, only said, humbly, that she was acting as go-between and wouldn't it be a good idea if the two of them started all over again? Joe and Cath, starting with a clean slate and a special night out, Monday? She misses you something dreadful, Mickey Gat said; she does, really, Joe, she keeps saying so, but you gotta behave these days if you want to keep a wife, and you gotta start as you mean to go on, so next Monday, evening off, show her the town. Joe nodded, sweating with relief, trying not to laugh when the paw produced perfume again. If only Mickey would not do that, forgetting the last time and the time before.

Over twenty-four hours, though, the facts got blurred and Joe's old arrogance began to surface. The prospect of next Monday evening had undergone a subtle change. It was no longer a gentle, tentative experiment in which he would treat his little wife like gold dust and let her know how much he cherished her; it was becoming instead a *fait accompli* in which Cath returned to him and said she was sorry, ready to come home and resume normal married life there and then. Joe decided he might accept her apologies, but then again, he might not. It was not himself who required forgiveness: it was her.

So Mr Eliot came at a good time. Joe Boyce was getting back into the driving-seat, feeling magnanimous and perfectly prepared to overlook the fact that a favourite customer had not been in for a while.

'Hello there, Mr Eliot! How are you? No, stay where you are, sir, I'll bring the usual.' Alistair was nonplussed by the bonhomie. Joe sat with him, the same old scenario, only this time with one of them deeply uncomfortable.

'I gather my wife wasn't working for your wife last week, Mr Eliot. She was staying with relatives, you see, I hope it wasn't inconvenient. Only one day, can't remember which, I forgot and called with a message for her, something I wanted her to get on the way home. I talked to your daughter, silly me. Cath will be back in harness, any time now.'

'Oh.' The expression made Alistair wince.

We are all at cross purposes, he thought, every one of us a little mad, each of us with a piece of puzzle in our hands, while the truth floats up there like that big, black raincloud. Alistair knew part of the story, Bailey knew something, Helen West another thing and this man on the opposite side of the table was in possession of his own version entirely. Alistair drank his token half pint and made small talk, thinking how you could not apologise to someone who was entirely unaware of anything deserving it, even less to a man who hit his wife. He rose to leave, giddy with confusion.

'Wait a minute, sir,' said Joe, tapping his finger to his nose, Mickey Gat style. 'Take home a little something for Mrs E, will you?' To Alistair's ill-disguised horror, Joe Boyce presented him with a box of perfume. Ma Griffe.

'Plenty of that in our house,' Joe whispered conspiratorially with a frightful wink. 'Not quite the real thing, if you see what I mean, but it does the trick with the wife.'

Alistair could only stammer thanks. He was even more bewildered. Why should Cath steal perfume when she had so much already?

There was a mirror in Damien's place: Damien would never have left the house without looking in a mirror, not even if he had been in a state of Saturday-night fever. Now Cath stood in front of the mirror, crying in the way she could only ever have done in private. Helen West had meant well: she had found Cath the promise of three jobs and kept her fully employed painting gloss paint on windows, making a new home, taking up those lovely curtains, keeping up a stream of chat, and then, with the usual carelessness kept for such gestures, doing what Emily Eliot did, turning out her wardrobe in Cath's direction. What made Cath weep now was not the pile of clothes she had brought home on the bus, but the thought that, unlike Emily Eliot, Helen West, whom she had rather despised, did not give away what was strictly surplus. She gave away her best things, only pretending they were no longer needed, when what she had done was select garments which would fit and look good on Cath's lumpy figure. Cath was finally moved by the subterfuge, and by that underground flat which did not sway with the wind, heat like an oven or reek with loneliness. She had the fleeting notion of asking Helen West to give her the cat, watch the silly woman hesitate for a moment and then say, Yes, of course, Cath, if you treat it nicely and you think it would help. She would, too, the stupid woman.

Crying made her deaf, until the knock on her door made her freeze. She heard shuffling steps outside, a firm rapping repeated. It was too late to put out the light and simply pretend she was not there. Cath shut her eyes in panic: it couldn't be Mickey Gat this time. What was it Damien had told her about what happened here when youths, high on glue or worse, broke in and found nothing to steal? They smashed bones, that's what; old people living here barricaded themselves in, burned to death when they could not get out. The knock was repeated, someone was calling her name, a female voice, soft, but demanding. Cath opened her door to Mary Secura.

'Just passing,' Mary remarked. Even Cath could tell it was a lie. No-one was ever just passing a place where you had to climb twenty flights of stairs.

'You look nice,' Mary remarked with unflattering surprise. So I do, in a way, Cath thought, turning back to the old wardrobe door which served as mirror. Nicer than usual in a cream-coloured blouse and a full skirt which twirled round her calves in a rich, dark floral print. She could only think of one thing at a time. She stripped off the blouse and dropped the skirt to her ankles, totally unselfconscious of her semi-nakedness. Mary Secura gasped, then coughed to hide it: she had seen worse by way of violent injury, but her eyes were transfixed by the scar on Cath's belly. Ugly, puckering, disfiguring in the minute it remained revealed, before Cath pulled a loose dress over her head, buttoned the neck and turned a circle.

'Not as good,' she muttered.

'You could get that scar fixed, you know, Cath, if you wanted. Wouldn't cost you,' Mary volunteered, casually.

'I don't want to, thanks,' said Cath, looking at her for the first time. 'It's mine. Think I'll keep it. Joe doesn't mind it.'

Mary was not listening. She was in another planet, hovering above the hemisphere, disorientated by the height, remembering how far away she had left the car which might not be there when she went back. She sat on one of the uncomfortable chairs, letting the handbag drop.

'Cath, how is it you can leave that man and even think of going back? I want to leave mine without ever going back.'

'Well, more fool you,' Cath said.

'I came to tell you something. About your man, Joe.'

'I know all about him.'

'No, Cath. You think you do, but you don't. What time does he normally come home? What time did he come home when he went out drinking with your brother?'

Cath was fussing with the dress.

'He always came home just before pub closing. Fridays, he went out. He usually gets time off on Fridays.' She was mumbling, looking slightly alarmed, staring at the mirror and seeing not herself, but the photo she had seen of Damien in Mr Eliot's study. The irritating voice of Mary Secura came from a distance: Cath wished she would simply go.

'Did he ever carry a weapon, Cath? Like when he was carrying money from the pub? Might have needed one sometimes. He was jealous of your brother, Cath, wasn't he?'

Cath undid the top buttons, turned in front of the mirror.

'We're going to have a nice time, Monday,' she chanted. 'Me and Joe. Talk things over. Mickey Gat said. Going out, we are, somewhere special. He promised.'

'Did Joe ever keep a weapon at home?' Mary continued inexorably. 'Up in those attics of yours? Something which could just about cut a man in half?'

'Who asked you here?' Cath shouted. 'Get out! Get out before I kill you!'

She gestured towards the window with a stubby finger, but the window would not open. She stood by the glass as Mary's voice continued. It was a long way down: Cath could feel herself wanting to jump, to float before she hit the ground, and still Mary went on talking.

'Out on the piss,' Bailey said, looking across the road. It was what Helen called his loud look full of challenge, the kind of look which would make anyone behave worse. She had long since decided she was a coward. If she met a mugger she would smile and say, of course, have my purse, in the same way she would pretend to laugh if she were teased. She would have skirted round the herd of half-drunk youths who jostled them on the pavement, and although Bailey also preferred stand-off to confrontation, the lines on his face did not indicate the same degree of acceptance. It was a Saturday night out: the place he had chosen to eat was rarely so crowded and the wait for a table irritated him. They should have been dining *chez* Eliot, but words had been spoken between Emily and Helen which had put the invitation into abeyance. Bailey could not understand why Helen did not simply shout down the phone, Emily you got this all wrong, in the same way he would have yelled at Ryan and then forgotten about it, but women were women, and their diplomacies a mystery. In pursuit of food, he had invited Helen well into his own territory, a terrain uneasy on the eye, ugly, craggy, uneven, good in parts, foul for the remainder, the restaurants not for the rich and famous, especially the latter, since no-one would know who they were.

The inside of Arrivederci made Helen sigh with pleasure: Bailey could watch her relax before her long, paint-stained fingers fluttered in indecision over bread and aromatic olives and then fished for a cigarette in guilty postponement of more fattening pleasures. When in this Italian ambience, one ate like a Roman; the plants were dusty and the proprietor a tyrant who could not stand small appetites. Persons who tucked his napkins under their chins, cleaned the dish of olives and ate the bread were served with alacrity.

I love you looking jubilant and greedy, Bailey wanted to say, and I am sorry for my evasions, equally sorry for yours this week. He thought they were up to date on Cath the cleaning lady, he had told her most of what he knew, including Cath in her high-rise flat receiving advice from PC Secura. He knew rather less of what Cath had been doing in Helen's house for most of the week. Since he had, as she put it, flounced away from the mess, access had been either unsought or denied, but all distractions forgotten, she was as sunny as the weather this Saturday night. Bailey placed his hand over hers, wanting to say something momentous, not as yet articulated; something which contained apology and declaration. She used the other hand deftly, to stroke the corner of his mouth.

'Black olive,' she said. 'You messy eater. Have you mended that clock yet?'

'Which clock?' He had thirty-seven clocks at the last count, not including sufficient pieces of clock to make five more, and he had still fallen into this strange habit of consulting his watch.

'The one which races us into the next decade.'

'I forgot to show you. Yes, I mended it, but it's given me a neurosis.'

He was hungry, not only for the food, but for the humour and the intimacy of trust she always offered, along with that heady formula of mutual respect. I have abused that mutual respect, he thought; she knows it and so do I. I have also abused the time-honoured tradition that if you do not keep on asking a woman to become your wife, she will find another man, or at least, another way of living.

The proprietor appeared, looked warmly at the dearth of bread. Helen opened her mouth to speak but Bailey looked at her warningly, in the knowledge that in this place you ate what the boss told you to eat. The moment for making an effort to say something personal was past. He felt it slip like the taste of garlic on his tongue, hid the biting sensation in a question.

'Listen, what exactly are you doing to your flat, Helen? Tunnelling for freedom? Knocking down walls?'

'I'm turning it into a brothel,' she said seriously. 'Grand

opening night next Tuesday, I think. Don't rely on a discount.'

He laughed, but his heart sank. Lamb, the proprietor had ordered. You havva the lamb and eat it all. His spirits lifted at the prospect. Bailey looked at the contentment of her face and wondered if it still had anything to do with his presence.

'How much did Emily Eliot help with all this interior design?'

'Think I can't do this kind of thing on my own, do you? She helped quite a bit, to tell the truth. You know Emily can't stand indecision. Go shopping with Emily and there's no hanging about, no luxuriating in choice. And she always knows someone who knows someone who gets things done cheap. It's an art. She's clever.'

'She wasn't very clever with Cath.'

Helen was silent. 'Do you know, I'm glad to be single?' was all she said. 'I'd hate to be a megalomaniac wife and mother. Mothers run a closed book. They shut the world out, close off anything inconvenient, as if being mum in charge of a family is so self-justifying, so sanctifying, they never need have a conscience about anything else. Some of them make me sick.'

Prejudiced, judgemental, politically incorrect, leaping onto a band wagon and waving a flag: the Helen he loved.

'You see them in shops and cars,' Helen continued angrily. 'Expecting everyone else to give way. Look at Emily. She'd put Cath in prison without a backward glance if it meant motherly peace of mind and, what's more, she wouldn't even regret it. She owes Cath nothing. Cath isn't family. Beware the family who say you're one of us. They never mean it.'

Bailey was enjoying this. 'We're talking about the survival of the human race,' he objected.

'No we aren't. It survives all by itself. Probably because people without families have to devote themselves to looking after those who have. And then get splattered all over the pavement and reviled for not being normal. I'm going on, aren't I? This lamb is good.'

'I wasn't wanting you to stop.'

'What irritates me so much is that people like Emily feel

superior and make me feel inferior. She has the right to pig-headed intolerance: I don't. Do you know what she said to me on the phone? She said . . .' Helen swallowed. 'She said she pitied me. If I had kids, I would understand.'

'Now that,' said Bailey, 'was unwise.'

Saturday was passing into Sunday. Upstairs in the flat where Joe Boyce lived, the air was stuffy underneath the eaves, lit by the streetlight and a moon the colour of milk. There were shuffling sounds from the attics: nervous laughter, whispers in the half light and sounds like the dragging of a body, something bumping downstairs from the top floor, slowly, pauses in between as one box after another hit each step in turn. Gradually, they grew bolder, less concerned about the noise. Pause, thump, pause, thump: unrhythmic but certain, repeated time and time again.

The neighbours downstairs turned off the music to listen, then decided to turn it on again lower, so they could hear at the same time as pretending they did not. They kept the door closed. Has he killed her then? one asked in a stage whisper; has the bastard finally done it? Mesmerised by the prospect, until they heard more muffled laughter and a sharp command from above their heads, herald of more shuffling, thumping on the lower stairs which passed their entrance and on out into the street. They turned the music up a notch and wished their front-room curtains did not hang in shreds with gaps in between they had never noticed before. The sound of removals did not mesh with the music, but the bass had more resonance than the footsteps going out into the road, laden, heavy. Had he killed her? Had he, the bastard who yelled at them for the noise but never turned it down himself when he belted his wife all round the kitchen? Had he really? Of all the half-stoned theories which passed across five sets of lips, not one included the suggestion that they should do anything other than listen. One of them had been drunk since noon; three others were slightly high and the fifth not a day over fourteen, with no wish to go home to mother. She shook, choked on a cigarette, drank the cider and looked for the darkest corner.

When she could no longer stand the suspense, she crouched by
the gap in the curtains and watched while the others watched her
watching.

She turned back, scorning them for their huddled circle and
exaggerated dread of a second visit from the police in one week.
They had done nothing wrong, had they? She danced across the
room in the same eerie light which lit the attics, put her thumb to
her nose. Naa, she said, nobody's dead. It's only all them boxes he
keeps getting delivered. He's only moving them out, doing a flit.
Or more likely, he's getting done over. They collapsed into giggles.
Nothing to worry about, but still she gazed back to the street
where the burglars, one of whom had heard Joe Boyce boasting in
a pub somewhere, loaded the van; and when it pulled away, she
waved, as if to say, take me with you.

Saturday had slipped away and with it, the word 'weekend', which
meant very little to Joe Boyce, the last passenger on almost the last
bus wheeling across London, with his head resting against the
cool of an upstairs window as the number 59 raced past empty
shops at one fifteen, rattling his anaesthetised bones, only just
keeping him awake. Fuck you, up yours, he kept on repeating to
himself, singing little snatches of songs for as long as he could
recall the words. 'Onward Christian Soldiers, marching on to
war' . . . 'Hit the road, Jack, ain't you coming back no more, no
more?' And somehow, 'God rest you, merry gentlemen', in
memory of the colonel who had been in this evening and treated
him as if he was lord and master. Oh yes, young Joe was on the up
and up, and then the bus turned the corner like a frantic sniffer-
dog on a scent and almost tipped him out of his seat. He was not
drunk, merely tipsy. *In vino*, as Joe had told the colonel, tapping
his own nose in the manner of Mickey Gat, does not always mean
in veritas, hey, old boy? Memory's not so good with drink aboard,
is it, old son, but didn't we have a good time the other night?
Rather, said the colonel, suddenly a trifle uncertain about why his
drinks were still generous, and, incidentally, free.

Not drunk, merely Brahms and Liszt, still capable of making

sweet music. Maybe Cath would be home, unable to wait until Monday because she really could not stay away. At home, sleeping like a baby. He could not think in anything but clichés and he was singing, 'Hello, Dolly' as he walked, not stumbled, up the stairs and saw the light on.

No double lock either, but the emptiness inside was like a punch in the stomach, repeated as he went from room to room, wailing, 'Cath, where are you?', his voice echoing from floor to ceiling. A joke, that was what it was, a joke, the house looking like this, rooms emptied not only of physical presence but of almost everything else too. There were table and chairs, carpet on floors, kitchen stuff, sofa, bed, all Cath's secondhand things. Nothing in the attics but drip-stained floors and the rubbish of packing.

There were old wardrobes in the attics, Cath again, but the doors which were formerly jammed shut by the weight of things piled outside them were now hanging open. In one of these, on top of listing floorboards, he found the last box of all. Damp to the touch, full of army insignia, his beret, three olive-coloured sweaters eaten by moth and three old bayonets, the last of the collection.

The white moon winked scorn through the window as Joe Boyce stood and wept for the loss of his only possessions and for the dreams which had gone into the acquisition of a thousand useless things. He wanted to plead with the thieves, then replaced his misery with bitterness. None of this would have happened if Cath had been at home, doing her duty. Then Joe became maudlin again, then bitter.

Wife, come home. He was nothing without her; felt he had loved her since the day he was born, counted on the fingers of both hands all the things she owed him.

And at last, sinking into sleep, he could remember where he would have put the other bayonet, the one in his dream. Upstairs in that cupboard. So the only good thing the burglars had done was to take it too.

CHAPTER TWELVE

Helen saw them through her office window, spotlit in the cruel gaze of early Monday morning. Something was going on.

On the other side of the road, secretary for supervisor number two (without spectacles), entered her own little box of a room, stage left. The secretary to number one (office Lothario, with specs), sidled into her own room at the other end of the floor. On each of their desks was a red rose faded by the weekend, the blooms variously disposed in a glass vase and a blue mug. Simultaneously, each woman adjusted the flower in its receptacle. Then for reasons unknown, both ladies moved from their cubicles and marched straight across Helen's line of vision to the opposite end of the floor. The meeting in the middle resembled a square dance and was obviously something of a mutual shock. They handled it well, smiling distant smiles and looking hell bent on important errands. Number two's secretary carried a sheaf of paper towards the copier standing next door to number one's office, while number one's secretary seemed destined for the fax machine. Once ten steps beyond the other, and hidden by open-plan screens, each raced into the other's room and began rummaging around in the desk. They made swift, unskilful searches, leaving a trail of fingerprints of which Helen did not approve. Then, each of them decapitated the red rose belonging to the other. Helen sighed. She could have told them that they both kept the cards given by number one, he with the specs and the scholastic air, in the top right hand drawer. Also, they both sat on his knee. Also, he took one of them out for drinks and promises on Wednesdays, the other, Tuesdays and Thursdays She could have saved them coming in early on Monday. All they had to do was wave and she would have answered in Morse code.

The two ladies passed again in the middle, heads high, no greeting this time. Other staff had arrived, filling up the space. One of the women was crying.

Helen turned her back to the glass, regretfully. The sun rose a little higher. The day was all but accounted for: two hours form-filling, the relentlessly stupid, bureaucratic curse of working for cut-price, ill-managed justice, then a funeral, then the last of home improvements. Not bad for a day off which Redwood would resent because it was summer and she did not have children.

It had taken some time to get Shirley Rix arranged for her passage from corpse to ashes. The husband had made a fuss, said he wanted horses with plumes, until he realised fuss meant money and he only got a small grant for a fiery consignment to mother earth. Mr Rix might have been as sad as Mary Secura, but his primary symptom was resentment. He sat on one side of the Chapel of Rest, still bearing signs of prison pallor among persons looking slightly tanned, his son sandwiched between himself and his own mother with a smattering of hunched family behind, while on the other side was Shirley's crowd, planning kidnap of the child and so full of hate they could scarcely say their prayers. The arrangement into combat zones was more appropriate to a wedding. Mary Secura, braced, but not motivated to keep the peace, bristled when Helen West slid into the seat beside her.

There was the disembodied sound of pre-recorded organ music and the sensation of being crushed by the queue waiting for the next one outside.

'What are you doing here?' Mary sniffed. 'What did you have to come here for?'

'Same as you. Showing respect.'

The place stank of flowers, the lingering perfume of exotic blooms, tributes in wreaths and hothouse bouquets. More sweetly from home-grown bunches of roses, sweet peas from allotments, backyard scented stocks predominating over sterile lilies.

'How did you know this was going on?' Mary hissed, her voice drowning in a languid hymn. Helen was wishing religious culture could catch up with the times: in a building with supermarket windows, it seemed odd to be playing music which belonged in a dark church.

'You told me. You phoned me and told me, last week. You barked, remember?'

'I still don't understand why you came.'

'I didn't want you to think I'd forgotten, that's all.'

They stood, filed out. There was a short, sharp squabble at the exit door, swiftly shushed into ominous silence. Shirley Rix's son ran to his maternal grandad, he was yanked back none too gently and began to cry. He was a beautiful boy, Helen noticed, eyes like brown saucers and hair like a smooth thatch. They all breathed better, dispersed more quickly out in the heat, while the next queue moved in. Helen and Mary Secura sat on a bench, smoking; they watched the rest climb into cars while an older man rearranged the flowers, as if looking for his own.

'That one over there,' Mary said, 'is under the impression he is Shirley's dad. He could be right. Shirley didn't think so. He wouldn't listen when she wanted help. You've seen the photos: what do you think?'

'Don't know, doesn't matter,' Helen said. 'But it did occur to me to wonder whether Shirley's gorgeous little boy is really the same blood as the man who reckons he fathered him. I mean, look at them. Not remotely alike. Shirley had quite a past, didn't she? I'm not examining her virtue, you understand, but if it ever came to needing to remove that boy from his dad's care, well it might help to question Papa's territorial rights. Can't hurt Shirl, can it? Suggest it to the family. DNA testing would prove it. Filthy thought.'

'Christ,' said Mary. 'I never considered that.' She shivered, not quite knowing why it was so uncomfortable to either like or admire Helen West, setting herself against it.

'You know DC Ryan, don't you? He told me you were beaten up once. By a bloke. Is that true? That how you got a scar on your forehead?'

'I bumped into something.'

Smoke wreathed upward through perfumed air.

'You came to this funeral for me, didn't you? You're watching me.'

'What's so important about you? I came for Shirley. In case no-one else did.'

'Oh fuck off. You're just like every other lawyer I ever met. A bloody liar, only you do it nicely. Got to be an angle, I mean, you've got to want something, haven't you? All right. I admit it. I've been to see your cleaning lady.'

'I never asked you to do that.'

It was in her throat to say that she did not actually know how to utilise police power to her own personal purpose, that the ambit of her authority was smaller than any of them dreamed and that she had spent two hours filling in forms to stress her role as cog in wheel; but sitting on a warm wooden bench, with a view of a garden full of mourners drifting round like blossom, she could also sense the futility of trying to turn prejudice into realism.

'Course you didn't ask me to see her,' Mary mimicked her voice. 'Not in so many words. Can't accuse you of anything so straightforward, can I now? Only it just happens to be Ryan, Bailey's sexy little errand boy, who comes down to me and asks the questions, doesn't it? Now is that coincidence or is it not? Don't answer, I don't want to know. How's the decorating, by the way? Does he like it?'

'Not in any way you would notice. He's scarcely seen it.'

'I gather from her, Cath Boyce I mean, that the place looks great and she's been helping a lot.'

'Yes, she has. Still does. I thought the best thing I could do was keep her busy and give her money. I don't think anyone goes to heaven on my counselling skills.'

Mary stubbed out her cigarette, grinding it onto stone with a neat heel.

'Cheap labour, isn't it? Still, I suppose it's better than no job at all. In answer to the question you meant to ask, your Cath seems fine. She got the long straw, after all. Such as, a man who hasn't yet got round to hitting her in the face, somewhere to go when she left and no kids for blackmail fodder. More than most of my ladies get in a month of Sundays. Not frightened either, our Cath.'

'Yes, she is. How can anyone not be frightened in her situation? She's left him anyway. I wish I knew when people should stay or when they should go, but I hope she stays away.'

Helen said this with regret. It seemed such an indulgence to let Bailey traipse across her memory: Bailey's distance, Bailey's removal from anything, his taciturnity, followed by openness, making her feel like an occasional convenience in his life, not an influence.

'I didn't say anything about Cath,' she began. 'I didn't come here to talk about her. Cath has her own willpower. I don't want to talk about Cath; I don't need to talk about Cath, I'm not even good on double motives—'

'Nor am I, but we all have to pretend we aren't, don't we?' Mary interrupted with a laugh so loud it fluttered the lilies. 'Anyway, I'll tell you what you want to know, in case you didn't already. Your cleaning lady is getting reunited with her old man this evening. Whatever he's done, she still loves him. So she's going out tonight, meeting him from work, all dressed up in her glad rags. From what I can see, you've even provided her with the frock; she showed me. Good gear you gave her, you gotta be made of money. Or guilty as sin to be giving away stuff like that. She says you haven't paid her.' Another drag of fresh cigarette. 'Haven't paid her for all the work she's done. Painting, all that.'

Helen was calm, growing calmer. Seeing Cath take home all those clothes.

'You're making this up as you go along, Mary. She's certainly cheaper than a decorator, but that wasn't why . . . What do you mean? Sure, I gave her clothes, that's my business, and I always pay her far more than she asks.'

Mary took no notice.

'Well anyway, she's going out with the little fucker tonight. The man might have killed her brother and she's going out with him like a virgin girlfriend, full of hope, outfit provided by the Crown Prosecution Service to save money all round, I ask you. Don't offer me a hanky while I cry, I've got my own.'

She was back into that big bag, diving deep down in there among the radio, paper handkerchiefs, the scarf, the notebook and all the detritus of a woman who carries her life around. The thing looked like a punch-bag, Mary could have flung it round her head and thrown it like a hammer, she was strong enough and sufficiently angry. Helen ventured one more question.

'Where is she meeting him? Cath, meeting her old man?'

'I thought you would know,' Mary spat. 'You probably made them a dinner reservation.'

Helen stood up, shook out her skirt: there were petals in the folds of the cloth. She thought of Cath, morose and uncommunicative the whole weekend, giving nothing away.

'Enough, Mary. Enough. If you can tell me how I can help Cath, I'll listen, but otherwise, not.'

Mary had fallen into silence, wanting to spit or apologise, the way she always wanted things too late, and then went on, making them worse.

'Advice? About Cath? Strikes me you already gave it. There's nothing you can do. She'll help herself to freedom, or she won't. Besides, you wouldn't want to stop her painting your windows, would you? Just don't interfere. You won't make it better. No-one can.'

Do not interfere. Bailey remarked this very English precept, which was honoured the length of the number 59 bus route, more so in the environs of Knightsbridge than in the neighbourood of Mickey Gat's pub, but still honoured. The failure to interfere, or even to offer information so that other people could interfere, was indigenous to the brickwork wherever he looked. In Mickey Gat's place, it was more a question of the punters not being good at framing facts or concerns into words. Greetings and jeers were often confused. Monday lunchtime was less than crowded; boredom made Mickey herself more than usually articulate.

'Where's your little friend, Mr Bailey? The one who has to go home to his wife, so she can wash his ears?'

'Day off,' Bailey smiled. 'Probably taking his kids to a park, so they can learn how to mug the others.'

'That's not nice talk, Mr Bailey. Sit down, will you? Nothing happening here.'

They sat, huge woman and slender man. With no-one watching, Mickey did not insist on the male ritual of making her guests drink. Both of them nursed orange juice.

'We haven't got this right, you know. We haven't got this right at all.' There was no need for Bailey to specify what he meant.

'Well, that makes a change, doesn't it? You don't often get things right, you lot. What's different now?' Bailey was quiet. Mickey's sigh was the last breath of a hurricane. She smelled wonderful. No fake perfume for Mickey.

'I loved that man Damien like a brother, Mr Bailey. Weren't a lot I could do for him though, except help him look after his own. So I got the flat for his sister and a job for the brother-in-law and I still take an interest, Mr Bailey. You can't stop taking an interest just because people get killed, can you? I dunno what you want to know. You just seem to ferret around. You even look like a ferret. My dad used to run them.'

'Just talk to me about Damien. Anything which comes to mind.'

As he spoke, Bailey was wondering idly how Helen would manage in a place like this. He was faintly surprised to conclude that she would manage very well. She would shake Mickey Gat by the manicured paw, cope with the extraordinary apparition without unfortunate comment, probably accept the perfume with a beatific smile and then offer to draft her will.

'I think they were all right, you know, Joe Boyce and Catherine. Damien worried about them, though. I mean Joe didn't want his wife to get a job, would you believe, but she went on about it until Damien told him, let her do what she wants, for God's sake, she ain't going to run away. So Joe agreed, but it had to be him found the job, somewhere near where he worked, so he could keep an eye on her, come home on the bus with her, that kind of thing, although I don't think it quite worked out that way. You know what I mean? He's so jealous, that Joe Boyce, he even went and looked in the windows of the place she works, one night, just to check. Silly bugger. He told Damien that, when he was pissed; Damien thought it was funny, so he told me. Last year that was, soon after she started. I suppose we all get jealous, don't we, Mr Bailey?'

Mickey leaned forward for her drink, tapped her nose. 'So I upped his hours at the Spoon and made it six days a week, of course. Gave him less time for mischief. He's all right, Joe, really.'

'Are you going to keep him on there?' Bailey made his curiosity sound mild and inconsequential showing no real signs of impatience, as if this information was incidental to what he might have wanted.

'Course I am, why not? He's reliable. Anyway, I thought of what Damien would have wanted. Best thing for his sister is for Joe to stay in work and her to stay where she is, with her old man. It's not good, a woman being on her own.'

'Oh, has she left him then?' He knew that perfectly well, but it was always wise to feign ignorance with Mickey.

Mickey nodded sadly. 'Yeah. She went to stay in Damien's gaff, but I've had a word with her. And him. So they're going out on the town tonight; I even gave her a bit of spending and him a night off. Women, you know, they sometimes make me ashamed. You know . . .'

'Yes, I know.' Bailey guessed what was coming next. 'Like cats, if you don't feed them.' Both of them stared at their unwanted orange juice, weighed down by their own wisdom. Bailey rose and stretched.

'So you don't know a single person who might have had it in for Damien?'

Michaela Gat shook her head, looked up at Bailey's height.

'Unless it was someone envied him. Damien was good at a lot of things, he was even ace at selling perfume down the market. He could do five hundred quid a day, could Damien. Dunno why Joe Boyce never wanted part of the action. He's a sensitive.'

'That must be why he hits his wife.'

Mickey shrugged herself to her feet.

'That's up to him, Mr Bailey. Shows he loves her.'

They were standing shoulder to shoulder. Mickey looked Bailey up and down as if examining a horse before a race.

'No, you're still in good shape, Mr Bailey, I'll say that for you. When you getting out of the police? You're wasted in there. We come from the same place, you and me, and look what I've done with my life.' She gestured the room, expansively. 'And then look what you've done with yours. I got a nice house in Wanstead, with a family and a swimming-pool, and you got fuck all. Shame, really. Let us know when you need a proper job. I could do with a useful ferret and I pay proper.'

With that accolade, they parted, Bailey smarting, despite laughing. It was a strange sensation to be pitied. Humiliating to be seen as the servant of another, and thus, a failure.

By mid-afternoon, the heat at the top of Bevan House was stifling. Mary Catherine Boyce had washed herself in cold water, although she had already taken a bath, courtesy of Helen West, before leaving that home for this. She had been tempted to stay there, change her clothes and go out for the evening, but it seemed a liberty which could only lead to well-intentioned questions, so she came home. Helen had given her too much cash, as it happened, but if she did not deserve it for pacifying the carpet men, getting up at dawn, Hoovering after they had gone and flogging back here on the bus in an afternoon of stifling heat, well, Helen would not grudge it.

Cath had dusted the mirror in order to feel better about her view of herself as she confronted it. She was so pale. Make-up, then: she had a little of that and Helen's bathroom cabinet had revealed a few supplies so clearly abandoned it was high time they were recycled. Cath did not have much skill with the art of *maquillage*, but a fingerful of eyeshadow and some carefully applied mascara made such a significant difference, she blushed at the sight of herself, emboldened to tackle the clothes. In the days when she loved clothes, she had preferred heavy coats, good woollens and colourful legs, not flimsy cotton. Summer was a time for girls; winter favoured women. Not bad all the same: black blouse, the cascading dark floral skirt, shoes with slight heel, all of her streamlined, taking the view of herself up from the tiny ankles, skimming full hips. Pity she had to take that little PVC bag with her in the absence of anything else convenient, but just as well. Joe might not be able to recognise her without it, and besides, it was fate which had given her something to carry in the bag.

She wished it was perfume, found herself searching Damien's one-time home in case he had some of it still hidden away, then shook her head in front of the mirror, chiding herself for the regret. What a terrible gift was perfume, always given by a man to make you wear it and please him, while you stank of blackmail; but in memory of long-past gifts, memory of Damien, she wished she could add a spray to her wrists as a kind of charm.

The bus would smell less sweet. She and Joe were going out on the town and she was going to act like a lady so she could be treated in the same way. In the heat of the afternoon, she walked slowly down the stairs, so as not to perspire, practising an elegant step as she turned left out of the central portico and made for the leisure centre in the near distance. There were always taxis cruising there.

When Helen opened the door to her own flat, her toes felt the tickle of new carpet. The front door moved across it stiffly, dragging on the pristine surface of deep gold. The door to the living room had been removed and left with a notice attached. All the rooms seemed slightly smaller, the ceilings closer, while her feet sprang as though on a trampoline, from room to room, before she kicked off her shoes in case they were dirty. Gold and blue, reflecting colours onto the white ceiling, even the kitchen painted, the window-panes mended and shining clean, the chipped surfaces polished within an inch of life and everything suddenly respectable. It felt like being given a prize, a parcel containing a ton of self-esteem, and for all that, it did not feel quite like home. There was the odd piece of furniture which looked as if it had strayed from the film set of some historical kitchen-sink drama into one of modern romance and, for a minute or two, she felt the same way herself. Outdated. The whole vision gave her the desire to comb her hair and tidy herself up a bit, just so she would match. Even the cat was infected. It came indoors via the flap in the kitchen wall and sat marooned on the floor, washing itself assiduously, then leaping onto the table, crouching with the close observation of a judge. The tail moved, sleek and ominous, while the cat cleaned her paws.

All right, Joe Boyce admitted to the colonel, I am, as a matter of fact, a bit nervous about the evening in hand. I mean, wouldn't you be? My wife walks out on me, leaves me to get burgled, decides to make it up in her own time while all I can think of is how we've lost everything. Everything, mate, I'm telling you, everything we ever wanted, including a whole lot of stuff I never even knew I had, see? Shameful, isn't it? Only she isn't ashamed, not her. They never are, are they, wimmin?

They were seated outside the Spoon. The flowers had the scent of decay about them; Joe had bombarded them with mineral water during the afternoon recess and the lobelia, in particular, seemed to resent it. Mickey had a man come and do the flowers, but the man's visits made no allowance for this kind of heat and Joe reckoned flowers had a thirst too, just like the colonel and himself.

You could talk all day to the colonel, Joe decided, provided he said nothing back, only made agreeable nods and grunts. He had done nothing much else since coming in here at three in the afternoon, cunning old bird to realise Joe was there, too, and just the company Joe needed. Somewhere along the line of the week's traumas, Joe was inclined to fuss the colonel like a dog so old and loyal the owner becomes impervious to the smell. The colonel had not moved in an hour: Joe had been in and out, recounting episodes of his own life with increasing indignation. Dear boy, the colonel murmured in receipt of each drink and each anecdote. Dear boy, how absolutely frightful for you.

His pose had become statuesque, if an egg-shaped body could ever be thus described, until, when Joe emerged with yet another

for both of them, he found to his surprise that the colonel had
leapt to his feet. Leaping was not his style; the effort made him
pant, his voice was both slurred and distinct and all the same his
heart was in it.

'Madam,' he said, 'charmed, I'm sure.' There was an attempt to
sweep a bow which almost turned into a curtsy. Cath helped him
back to his seat. She was bold as brass, sitting outside there as if
she owned the place, looking up at him, raising her sun-glasses;
Cath, in sun-glasses over painted eyes, smiling with a red mouth,
sitting with her legs crossed and her bag under the iron chair,
fanning herself against the heat. She looked a different woman: Joe
did not like to think that time spent away from him could have
done that.

'Hello, Joe. If you aren't going to say hello, do you think I can
have some water? I'm parched.'

Echoes came back to him . . . Joe, could you make me tea, I
hurt all over, Joe, please . . . He looked at her, goggle-eyed, unable
to move as she made conversation with the colonel. Nice weather,
isn't it? Yes, a bit hot, ma'am, but better than being cold, hey? Oh
yes, surely, I hate the cold, don't you, but what do you wear when
it's like this? The plants still drooping in misery behind them, as if
Joe had given them gin rather than water; Cath smiling like a
stranger, straight into the eyes of another old man. All that was
bad enough before Alistair Eliot walked by. Joe shot inside, thinking it was all too much to bear: it was as if his allies had all
gathered together to shoot him; his wife looking positively sexy, his
friend come by to reprove him, everyone looking at everyone
except himself, redundant amongst them all. Still the hanger-on,
not only at his own party but every other he had ever attended.

Alistair Eliot smiled at the duo outside the Spoon. They looked
like a nice old man and his daughter, he could see himself in that
role when Jane was grown up. He did not recognise Mary
Catherine Boyce in her smart outfit, although she stirred some
dim memory in his more than usually distracted state; she had
nothing to do with the Cath he had met so often in an overall.
Different women, different territory, however close. If he had had

a hat, he might have raised it. Joe watched him go with relief, Cath, with bitter hurt.

'You can go fuck off if you like,' Joe said to the young man behind the bar. 'Cos I don't think I'm going anywhere. My loving wife, see her, outside? She's come in to help. About time she helped.'

The young man shook his head, tempted but remembering the size of Mickey Gat.

'Can't do that, Mr Boyce. I got orders. You've got to go out.'

Sitting outside with the colonel, Cath watched her own expecta-tions fade. A posse of drinkers arrived out of their offices, chattering like starlings, ready to unload the day. The relief barman brought her water with lemon and ice, but Joe ignored her, until, after two hours in which her own immobility made her cold, despite the humid warmth, he came and sat down, sullen and silent. She placed a tentative hand on his arm, and then, jeer-ingly, he spoke.

'You look very nice. Planning on going somewhere special, were you?'

She felt for a minute as if her heart would break, smiled steadily, stroking his arm as if in supplication, and it was the sug-gestion of pleading in this action which finally mollified him, although he was already drunk. Drunk in the way Joe Boyce was at work, never quite showing it, simply possessed of a slight wild-ness.

'Come on,' he ordered. 'Off we go.' He marched down the street before her, letting her run behind. 'We'll find a nice pub,' he shouted over his shoulder, watching with approval her attempts to keep up. There had been the suggestion of tears in her eyes as she sat with the colonel: the unfamiliar mascara was blurred. The hard-earned dignity of her entrance was diminishing fast. Already her blouse felt creased, the armpits sticky and still she held on to her PVC bag. They got as far as two streets away, into an estab-lishment as far removed from the gentrification of the Spoon as was possible in the area. This one was full of tourists, young, impossibly handsome, brash and blond, girls in shorts grimacing at warm beer before they ordered more.

They stayed there for an hour, Cath on bitter lemon, Joe putting a couple more stiff ones down his neck, ogling the girls. Cath paid for the rounds without protest. Then they moved on, to another place, slightly worse and even more crowded. He led; Cath followed. Joe told her about the burglary, without otherwise volunteering much. He did not ask a single question about her welfare, what she had done, how she had been. She asked him if he had been eating properly and he said no. Her face grew stiff from smiling as Joe chatted to strangers in a long, almost ritualistic humiliation. In the last of four pubs, long after midnight, where drinking was still in full swing for a birthday party, Cath went to the Ladies and left him, via the back door.

The sky outside grew softly dark, then the rain stopped play for those bold enough to risk sitting out of doors in a London summer. Around Sloane Square, the cruising cars found other destinations and the streets shone with damp. In Emily Eliot's household, silence persisted. Jane was in her room drawing furiously on listing paper many hours after she was supposed to be asleep. Emily had long since gone to bed alone. Alistair was in his study, not exactly working, but staring at the wall, wondering about other trials rather than the one commencing tomorrow, worried about society, the universe, his household bills and any other subject but himself. He would have liked the oblivion of being drunk, to avoid having to conclude that there were times when he did not really like Mrs Eliot very much, even though he loved her.

Somewhere in the middle of a great deal of diffused guilt about what he might be doing wrong, Alistair saw himself walking past the Spoon earlier that evening, resisting the temptation to stop for a drink, noticing the old man sitting alongside that familiar face which had nagged him all the way home. Cath: he had it now, only it made the guilt so much worse. Of course it had been Cath, with that hunched way of sitting and that secretive smile, and he had ignored her. Alistair recognised the need to speak to some wise soul outside his family circle, to straighten out his own emotions. He could only think of Helen West or Geoffrey Bailey as those with the necessary degree of detachment to hear him out when he did not know what he wanted to say. He walked to his son's bedroom at the back of the house, noted that the window was wide open in the boy's absence. A lingering smell of cigarette smoke pervaded the room, explaining this sudden passion for fresh air; why didn't the boy just do it openly, instead of treating it as a clandestine pleasure? There were so many worse crimes, such as unkindness, brutality, dishonesty and wilful blindness.

The onset of rain made him feel better; he leaned out of the window. Down below, light shone into the garden from Jane's room, illuminating the churned earth outside her window. The perfume Alistair had accepted from Joe Boyce and failed, as yet, to show to his wife, burned a hole in the bottom drawer of his desk. He knew in his heart of hearts that his wife had acted on instinct, but he also knew that Cath, their victim, was not a real thief.

Cath could not move. Instead, she let two, three buses go by and stayed in the shelter, waiting for him. Joe Boyce had reached the point Cath had recognised on many an evening at home, all passion, all aggression spent, leading him into a state when he was as soft and floppy as a cuddly toy. Staggering to the bus stop, he was outrageously pleased to see her, affectionate, scarcely able to stand, the last remnants of recent memory gone. They stood beneath the awning with their bodies forming a triangle, he leaning into her, pressing against her for balance, while she braced herself against the shelter and let him slobber into her ear. 'Oh Cath, I'm sorry Cath, I do love you, Cath . . . why do you do this to me, Cath, why did you . . . I love you, Cath.' A litany going on, interrupted once in a while with a curse about the non-appearance of the bus. The ignominy of her evening no longer troubled her: she had money for a taxi, but did not search for it, she simply stood there waiting for the number 59, late night bus, to take them home as if she had known it would happen this way, all the time.

The bus stormed into sight, bottom half empty, top deck one third full. There were a few stares of disapproval as Cath pushed and shoved to get Joe upstairs and all the way to the front, out of harm's way, with him giggling throughout as if she was tickling him. She sat with his heavy arm around her shoulder, almost pushing her off the narrow seat, still murmuring, I loves you, Cath, you know I do, she shushing him as she would a child while the imperious conductor looked at their passes and ambled away, tongue clicking under his breath, shaking his head at the futility of the human race. And then, with a sigh, Joe slid towards the window and let his face rest against the pane. She had always marvelled at his capacity not only for instant forgetfulness, but also for unplanned, profound sleep. It was something she envied, rarely achieved and craved all the time.

Sleep softened the lines of his face, made his mouth seem generous rather than petulant. Cath stared ahead as the bus churned through the drizzle, past the deserted theatres of Shaftesbury Avenue where the lights gave promise of life still existing inside gambling parlours and slot machine arcades, the last resort of pimps, touts and those few still desperate for entertainment. In front of her eyes, night-time London took shape and showed shame: people bedding down in doorways, drunken revellers climbing on board for a few stops, restaurant waiters, the last to come out into the dark. By the time the bus reached Islington, it was almost empty again, ploughing a path east, rattling sleepy windows down narrow roads. Joe slid further down the seat, snoring. His hands remained crossed on his chest, his legs splayed, still allowing her no room for comfort. Cath turned. Behind her, near the top of the stairs, three other passengers also slept, one of them noisily. Joe's shirt had ridden up, exposing his belly. His trousers had slipped down as he stumbled up the stairs. Like his brother-in-law, he had grown soft in the stomach.

Cath leaned forward and kissed him on the cheek. I gave you the chances, she whispered. I gave you the chance to look after me, and you could not take it. I can't do anything else, my love. Then she felt inside the PVC bag and withdrew the bayonet.

Rusted, certainly, but sharpened again long after being ground to sharpness by some backstreet lathe, honed against stone, so that the blade was half the size it had been, whittled and ground to a shine. Damien had taught her how to do that, a long time since, when they had both learned how to make every single thing useful, even a bayonet. Joe or Damien, she forgot which: only men thought they knew how to sharpen a blade, something they learned in the company of other men.

She had her left arm firmly round his shoulder for balance as she plunged the blade into his belly. There was an inconsequential thought of how much more easily this could be done with a kitchen knife if such items were not, somehow, sacrosanct. As she plunged, with the same energy she applied to housework, she leaned closer, putting her hand over his mouth, the way she had done before when the conductor was looking, and dragged the blade towards herself, twisted, pulled it away, despite the resistance, then began again, left to right, systematically, the way she Hoovered stairs. The large sheet of thin polythene, pinched from Emily's dry-cleaned clothes and now used as a kind of apron, rustled as she twisted the blade for the second time. Cath had a passion for cleanliness and did not want to get dirty: the skirt was important. Joe's eyes opened wide; his mouth bubbled with spittle; he struggled in weak spasms. She held him tighter; she had muscles like an ox. From behind they looked like a couple adjusting themselves for amorous comfort. The little barks he made could have been those of a man fondled intimately.

Before the blood cascaded, Cath covered him with the jacket which had been half off his shoulders when he wailed his way to the bus stop. She wiped her hands on it first. She looked around again before tugging out the bayonet, amazed at the effort it took, mumbling under her breath about the inefficiency of the thing and at the same time examining the dark floral skirt and the black blouse for damage. There was little sign. The bus sailed past St Paul's Road and into Hackney. Cath waited for a moment, withdrawing from him fastidiously and carefully. She was a mile or so from home.

Fate had given her the weapon. She was governed by fate. A child had given her the knife. It was preordained.

When she alighted, five stops from the main terminal, surrounded and hidden by three teenagers in search of a club they had heard about up here which stayed open all hours, she looked like an ordinary little waitress coming home from a job rather than someone returning from a night out. She remembered not to open her mouth, set off for Bevan House. With the bayonet in the PVC bag, Cath walked smartly along the main streets, her little heels whacking the pavement in challenging sound. No-one stirred. No short cuts, no shrinking in the shadows. Walk proud: someone had told her that was the way for a woman to stay safe.

Halfway up the rising heat of the flats, wiping away the last of the mascara, blurred by tears into black channels round her mouth, she reminded herself how dangerous it was out there. Wept anew, because she had loved him.

CHAPTER THIRTEEN

Helen West was day-dreaming, playing several scenes over in her mind. Scene One: the door would open. Bailey would cross the threshold, gasp with admiration and fall at her feet. Scene Two: the pair of them hosting a party, without argument. Scene Three: herself, in this room, preaching hypocritically to Emily Eliot and Redwood about the joys of single life. Scene Four was the door opening again, but this time to admit a total stranger, a dependable-looking male with a chunky physique diametrically opposed to Bailey's own, carrying a bouquet of flowers as he murmured, What a lovely home you have, Helen; what exquisite taste; marry me tomorrow and never work again. Scene Five: even bigger bouquets. The next, possibly most realistic scenario, was the door opening yet again, Bailey waiting behind it, refusing to come in, while she ran across to welcome him and tripped on the new carpet. The last sequence was Bailey and herself sitting in the golden living room by the fire, like Darby and Joan. Then the film snapped.

Unable to make much sense of her own quixotic day-dreams, Helen was severely ashamed of them. Halfway through Tuesday evening, she had completed the final touches, added two new plants and some flowers in the kitchen. She was so impressed with the splendour of the flat, she had been tempted to phone Bailey and warn him that if he did not faint at the sight there would be dire recriminations, but that would spoil the surprise.

Day-dreams made her angry, they were yet another weakness. It was useless pretending she was not influenced by what she saw and read; she was not immune to the contagion of the romantic or the desire for security purveyed by mothers and magazines, even though experience had taught her to expect so little. Wedding bells were the music of the young. Helen did not want a solid

Emily Eliot style ménage, but she did not quite know how not to not want it either, or how to close her ears to the blandishments of marriage propaganda. So here she was, a grown-up woman, more emancipated than most, mistress of all she surveyed in an elegant apartment with real food in the kitchen, waiting for her man with all the subtlety of a street-corner prostitute.

Dear Bailey, save me from an evening of contemplating nothing but my bank balance. Even if the effort was not entirely mine, will you please, for once, compliment me? Even if you don't love me, admire what I've achieved.

He had a key. She had taken off the dirty track-suit suitable for dusting books and hanging pictures, wore a casual shirt in loud stripes, clean jeans cut off at the knee and bare feet, the better to enjoy the carpet. Even in her present mood she could not manage frills, and added only enough perfume to mask the smell of cigarettes and paint.

Bailey administered a peck on the cheek and walked straight into the kitchen, the one place in her whole abode which had altered the least radically. He opened the fridge, ignored the ample contents, pulled out a lager and leant against the wall with a sigh.

'What do you think?' she demanded.

'About what?' He was staring into the garden. 'Listen, has your cleaning lady been here today?'

It was not a request for information, more an aggressive demand, and he was refusing to turn round and face her. Or look beyond, into the marvels of the hall. The hectoring tone prompted rising anger, chill anxiety and a spontaneous lie.

'No. Why?'

Cath had been here, to Helen's surprise, when she herself came home. They had coincided for half an hour; not long, so not therefore, quite such a large lie. The encounter had not been pleasant; she wanted to forget it until later.

'Husband was killed. On the bus, late last night. They forgot to check everyone was off, parked it. Found him this morning. No wallet. I didn't get called in to identify him until this afternoon. We couldn't find her anywhere.'

He made it sound like an accusation. Helen leant against the kitchen table, appalled.

'How was he killed?'

'Stabbed. Thoroughly. He might have survived, all the same, if he hadn't lain there and bled to death. By the smell of his clothes and the vomit, he was as drunk as a skunk.' He slumped against the sink. 'I don't know why I thought she might be here. People tend to come to you, that's all. I should have gone to her place and waited. Someone's got to tell her. I don't particularly want it to be Ryan.'

'You know I thought for a minute you were going to say she had something to do with it. Killing him, I mean.'

He looked at her vacantly, his way of telling a lie. 'Why would you think that?'

'I didn't . . .'

'Good. I've got to go.'

'I'll just get my shoes. Wait a minute.'

Bailey swallowed the last of the beer and turned on her. 'You don't need shoes. What do you need shoes for? What do you think you're doing?'

'Going with you. Look, I don't love her, but for all I know, I'm the best she's got. Better than some great big copper standing over her saying, Madam, did you know your husband's dead? Wait for me.' She was hurrying out of the room, like one of the scenes from the day-dreams, tripped on the new height of the carpet, before he was holding her by the arm, roughly.

'No! I'm not taking you anywhere. I'm not. I don't want you with me, understand? This is work. I don't want you going to places I have to go to, right?'

'But I want to go. For Christ's sake, it isn't me who'll come to harm. What are you doing which can't take a witness? If you don't take me, I'll go by myself.'

'You don't know where she lives.'

'Block of flats on the 59 route. Top floor, I've seen the place.'

'Which block, which number flat? Don't be silly.'

She put her arm across the door, stopping him, suddenly calm.

'Listen to me for a minute. You're going to tell some poor perse-
cuted woman that her husband's dead. He might have been a
bastard and she might not be what I'd call a friend but she's valued
by me and she knows me, so why can't I come with you, even if I
only sit in your car? The only reason is you can't ever really let me
share the important bits of your life. You seem to want a dizzy
little bimbo you can park on a bar stool without the meter running. If you can't give a better excuse, you and I don't go
anywhere, ever again. Have you got that? I'll get my shoes.'

He shuddered, as if afflicted by cold. Helen felt the breeze and
heard the slam of the front door before she was halfway back
from the bedroom. She sat in the golden living room, ashamed of
her own state of ultimately guilty rage. Judgement day. She was
nothing but a little woman who ignored the world to paint her
house.

Damien Flood's place had been turned over good and proper.
There was a hole in the door to indicate where the lock had been
chiselled out in clumsy fashion, noisily and slowly. No attempt had
been made to resecure it: the damage was fresh. Inside, there had
been precious little to steal: no video-recorders, cameras, com-
puters, nothing to make the time spent worthwhile. There was a
token amount of wanton destruction, even that limited, as if the
childish burglars had grown tired: sugar and powdered milk
dumped on the floor, slices of bread scattered, a set of makeshift
bookshelves, put together out of planks and painted breeze-blocks,
dismantled, two mugs smashed. No faeces or graffiti; no statement of envy pertinent in a flat as bare as this; instead, Bailey
supposed children had used it as a temporary playground.

He noticed a print on the wall showing a bowl of daisies, a
theme echoed in two tea towels hanging over a chair, as if someone had once tried to give a touch of personality to the anonymity
of the place. Bailey felt his angry frustration die, felt only sympathy for the occupant. Wherever she was, life was pushing Mary
Catherine Boyce to the limit.

★

The pity had grown to outrageous proportions by the time he encountered the inside of the real home of Cath and Joe Boyce. A young neighbour from downstairs tried to close the door on him, as if he was a Jehovah's Witness come to save her soul. Yes, she had been out all day; she'd said so before, hadn't she? And the place had been burgled on Saturday night: is that what he had come about? They had all heard the man who lived there walking round and screaming when he came home. He had paced round, crying and shouting most of Sunday, none of their business.

Bailey went upstairs, put his shoulder to the door. It showed signs of fortification, recently destroyed by experts, gave to the slightest pressure. There was nothing inside to indicate burglary, merely a sense of emptiness which was all the more pathetic because the living room, kitchen and bathroom on this floor bore such signs of strenuous, penny-pinching effort. Daisy print on the wall here too; shelves constructed in the same way as Damien's. There was the detritus he might have expected from a primitive married man left on his own for a week, a few unwashed dishes, grime accumulating on the draining board, all at odds with a significant smell of bleach. Bailey picked up a tea towel, patterned with daisies, he noticed, and used it to cover his hands as he looked through an old kitchen unit, battered, lovingly painted with gloss at some point in a venerable life. Lying among the knives in the cutlery drawer was an old bayonet. Bailey lifted it out with the tea towel, and moved into the living area to find better light. The pattern on the towel, those clumsy shelves, the print on the wall, somehow shocked him more than the weapon in the drawer. Damien Flood's hide-away, Joe Boyce's home: both somehow dominated by the same, feminine touch.

Bailey tried to imagine the time it would take to sharpen such an obdurate piece of metal blade designed for the forceful thrust rather than the delicacies of surgery. Someone at some time had ground this blade on a lathe to obtain such a cutting edge, refined by resharpening again for effective use. There were marks on the side of the breeze-block shelving, Bailey remembered his mother outside the back door, sharpening a carving knife against the wall.

No-one had ever searched this house: Joe Boyce had never been a suspect. Bailey could not see why this savage bayonet had been left, even by Joe Boyce. Joe could have kept it sheathed among the military memorabilia above the bar of the Spoon, or taken to carrying it again after he had been attacked on the way home; murderers were always fools, and yet nothing quite explained either why it should be the cleanest and most incriminating thing in an otherwise greasy drawer, or the pervasive scent of bleach which hung around the sink.

Then there was a footfall from above him, a plaintive voice, calling down querulously.

'Is that you, Joe? I'm sick, Joe, make us some tea. I hurt, Joe, I hurt all over . . .'

The voice echoed, and the air was suddenly cold. The voice spluttering, repeated the refrain. I hurt, Joe, make us some tea. It was a refrain like a chant; finally, it unnerved him.

'Come on down,' he shouted.

Poor bitch; perhaps she was so attuned to obedience, she would have obeyed the summons of a thief, provided he was male. The step on the stairs was weary; the figure emerging into the stuffy room, slow and shambling.

'Hello,' Mary Catherine Boyce murmured without rancour or surprise. 'If you've come to take any more stuff, don't bother. Someone else has had it all. Joe's going to be ever so cross. I should have been here, you see, only I wasn't. I was somewhere else. It's so hot today. Someone took all the boxes.'

It was the plaintive voice of a little girl, driven to the thumb-sucking habits of adult dementia. Cath swayed slightly, sighed and went on speaking, with difficulty.

'Only I'm a little bit drunk, see? I got it on the way. I thought if it worked for him it might work for me, even if I hate the taste. And then if he hits me, p'raps I won't feel it.'

She was grinning inanely, puzzled, entirely naked, with her

hands crossed across her chest, her hair lank, her lumpy stomach folding over a puckered scar. She was shaking her head.

'It doesn't work, you know. I don't know why he ever thinks it does, does nothing for me.'

'I'm a police officer, Mrs Boyce. And Joe's dead.'

She began to wail, like an animal in pain.

He had no personal radio with him. The burglars had taken the fancy phone. There were enough reasons for him to ignore the formulae he should have followed, such as calling for help, getting in a female officer, all that. Instead, he turned his back on her, put the kettle beneath the tap and bellowed over the sound of running water and her desperate wailing.

'I'm making tea, love. Get some clothes on, there's a good girl.'

The pity had grown to a lump of gristle in his throat, choking. He was thinking of the lump of humanity, abused by his own kind, a pretty woman making herself revolting by being so pitiable. He was also thinking of Joe Boyce, rolling round on the top deck of an empty bus. Lying there and dying in his own vomit, perishing through asphyxia and blood loss, not from his clumsy wounds. Thinking too, how this woman had been a constant presence not in one home, but two. Would Helen's kitchen, or Emily's, ever sport tea cloths with daisies? As his mind raced, like his delinquent clock, he wondered how he would phrase his report to the Crown Prosecution Service, to lawyers like Helen, so removed but working in the interests of justice as far as they knew it, which was not as well as he. Thinking of the bottom line, insufficient evidence, or a plea bargain, plus all that destructive nonsense in between.

Helen had found the shoes and the car keys. This kind of car would be safe wherever she took it and since she felt as attractive as a leper, she was safe too. East. Away from gentrified houses and towards the urban edges of the metropolis. The number 59 droned past the end of the road; she followed it.

There was no sensation of following a star, like the three kings trailing through another kind of desert in pursuit of divine message, hope instead of despair; it was simply an alternative to doing nothing.

Light was fading at nine o'clock, diminishing with the slow reluctance which heralded the inexorable sunset of summer. Long shadows, heat stored in the brickwork, ragged flowers and brown grass between buildings, the trees of north London still green, the hedges of gardens still gallant. Helen did not feel self-conscious about following a bus. Late evening traffic was brisk and purposeful; no-one noticed. The bus itself skipped stops, skittish, like an antisocial cat. On paper, Helen knew these streets, some of them boasting real or faded glory, others history, others an ethnic dominance which was busy and brave in the dying light. Looking for landmarks, pausing, with the bus, parallel to playing-fields, watching a game of football on brown turf, moving forward again. She thought she would have been safer on the bus, without the shell afforded by a car, until she remembered Joe Boyce.

Major junction, red lights, where the youths came forward in a gang, threw water at the windscreen and began to wipe it off. Helen had no money, sat there revving the engine and on the change of lights jolted forward without payment. One shook his fist and yelled; the others melted back: wrong car. Hackney emerged through glass streaked with dirt and soap: the exhaust of the bus spouted blue smoke; and into the equation, as she saw where she was, came motorway signs, local signs, a distinctive pub and railway-station sign, and then the block Cath had pointed out emerged on the left. There was no-one behind to protest at her abrupt and ill-mannered manoeuvre towards it.

Top floor, Bevan House: that was where she was, strange Cath, and this was where a stranger parked a car. In between two other cars, one wrecked, the other in the first stages of renovation, Helen's car simply looked like a vehicle awaiting therapeutic attention. And this was where she walked on a sultry evening. Sauntered downhill, into a building, found a lift, pressed a button, waited in vain until someone ran past and rewarded her optimism with a two-fingered salute and a grin. She looked at the darkening flight of stairs to which he pointed. She knew these places on paper: she had a map of the city in which she lived, on paper. She could climb stairs, too.

She felt the scar on her forehead, she could never quite suppress the memories of fear and pain. She felt Bailey's contempt, and remembered at last what it was Cath had said. Going out as she was coming in, Helen somehow disturbed to find her back – yesterday had been the final day: Helen needed no more help than regular cleaning, Cath no more help than regular jobs. She had felt a sense of being taken over, something which had made her brusque, until Cath had said, humbly, she just had to see what it was like with everything finished. The sight of Cath, with a great big bin-liner, taking away left-over paint, without asking first, made Helen feel mean as well as angry. You didn't need it, Cath had said, all wounded and defensive; I thought you wouldn't mind. I'm going to do up our place, now I've seen what can be done with yours. No-one's going to interfere, this time. There had been no invitation and even less inclination to ask about Cath's grand night out with the old man. Emily Eliot did not know about that; Helen did not think anyone else did either, apart from Mary Secura, Bailey least of all. Big night out, special treat, the man drunk. Him coming home on the bus. Cath hated the bus. Cath knew when she took the paint that wherever he had gone, Joe Boyce was not coming home.

No-one had managed to find her, Bailey said. Because she had been hiding in Helen's flat until Helen came home, planning, getting the time wrong. And if Cath said no-one was going to interfere in her domestic plans this time, she could only have been referring to him. Him, the until-death-us-do-part man.

It was somewhere on the way back that Helen came to the conclusion that she would say nothing unless anyone asked. Even if Cath were guilty of collusion in a death, so be it. Even if it went completely against her principles and her belief in justice by the rules. Shades of Mary's bitterness. Mind your own business. Watch out for policy. The fact that in all her cases there had been one, potentially murderous, husband convicted out of the last dozen, with her watching Cath work up to new life without really offering help, standing in the sidelines, working in the interests of justice. About which they said, if it ain't broke don't fix it. Helen drove back to home, sweet home.

'I suppose she sent you, as well,' Cath said. 'She keeps on sending people.' The whine was still in the voice, the childish note gone with the tea.

'Who's she, Cath?' he asked gently.

'Helen. Lady I worked for. Decorating. Shan't go back there. She won't want me anyway. Very mean, that lady. Real slaver. Makes me work hard. Forgets to pay, have to fight for it.'

Bailey could not begin to equate this description of Helen with the truth, although he could see that Mary Catherine Boyce was in the kind of state where accuracy was unlikely and truth, if it emerged at all, would be accidental. It was the kind of accident he prayed for; truth, coming out of a side road before the driver noticed a wrong turning. He had underestimated her. Cath was accustomed to underestimation. It was a feature of her life, amounting to contempt.

'I don't like this tea much,' she grumbled. 'Did you put sugar in it?'

'Plenty. Cath, what was that bayonet doing in the kitchen drawer?'

'I couldn't throw it away, could I? I never throw anything away.' She looked at him as if the suggestion was vulgar.

'Oh I don't know. It's a good idea, sometimes, isn't it, throwing away things which aren't any use? Keeps the place tidy.'

She nodded earnestly, as if he had endorsed a long-held philosophy.

'But it's Joe's, you see. I was never allowed to throw away anything which was Joe's. I knew he had it, of course, even though he put it upstairs with all his other stuff. Burglars might have found it, left it out. He brought it with him last night. Showed it to me when we were in a pub. Told me I would get some of it if I didn't behave. We were supposed to go somewhere nice, but we didn't. He just got drunk.' She began to cry, a snuffling sound which produced moist eyes rather than tears. Bailey remained completely still.

'I ran away from him,' Cath said. 'I ran out of the last place the back way and went for the bus, only a bus didn't come. They never come when you want them. But he found me. He was cross. He got that thing out on the bus. I thought he was going to do for me. I was fighting him for it. I didn't scream, what would be the point and anyway, I didn't want anyone to see him, drunk like that. It slipped, went into his tummy. He was laughing. I didn't think he was so much hurt. I just thought I've got to get away and never come back, this time. Can I have some more of that tea, please?'

'You must have known you'd have given him a nice little scar, Cath. Like he gave Damien.'

'Yes,' she agreed, nodding vigorously, then clamped her hand over her mouth.

'And like Damien gave you, all that time ago?'

She was suddenly more composed. 'Oh, I don't know. That policewoman, Mary, she told me I could get that fixed, but I didn't believe her, not really.'

Bailey was silent, his mind running on again to the report. They would move him soon, he knew they would, to a life well above street level, full of endless reports. Reports which could not even begin to place reliance on what a suspect said under the unfamiliar influence of alcohol, without being given the formal words of caution. You do not have to say anything, but what you do say can be used against you. The woman talked in code.

'I think I sort of knew about Joe and Damien,' Cath continued chattily. 'You know, things Joe would let slip when he hit me. You and your brother, bad as one another, that kind of thing. He had to go, he would say: he can't do that to you, and not go. Thought he meant Damien not being around when I was pregnant. He never knew it was Damien's baby. I didn't know for certain how he'd killed Damien until I saw him with that knife last night. I kept thinking, why didn't he use a proper knife? But I don't suppose he could. I would have noticed if he took things from the kitchen. I knew when I saw that old dagger thing. He would never have used anything new. He couldn't. It would have spoiled it.'

Bailey poured more strong tea into her cup. Both were orange in colour. He ladled into it three teaspoons of sugar.

'Damien got you a fine scar on your belly, didn't he? Then Damien is cut apart, the same way you were. No anaesthetic though. Joe did that. Did you kill Joe for revenge, Cath? For Damien, or for all the beatings he gave you?'

'Kill him?' Cath was wide-eyed, shaking. 'Kill him? I would never have wanted to kill Joe. Didn't cross my mind. I loved him. I loved him. You don't seem to understand anything. Someone else killed him. I loved him.'

'We'll have to go, Cath. May take a while. Do you want to bring anything with you?'

She looked around in a state of total confusion.

'I can't, can I? It's all gone! and I . . . anyway, I haven't got a bag.'

Bailey led her out of the house with the deference of a ballroom dancing partner, his mind still running ahead, going into over-drive. Get this place watched and turned over in the morning. Nothing doing, been burgled by an expert. Formal interview under caution, get a woman to do it. Even halfway sober, Cath could clam up in response to sympathy, couldn't blame her, really. Yeah, she'd done for her old man just like he did for her brother, but what if she said nothing, said she'd gone home alone? What he knew already showed she'd left some pub or other long before Joe. It would be, at best, a formal prosecution, with a bit of public attention because it had all happened on a bus. They wouldn't even get near a conviction for manslaughter, not with a battered wife, not with this kind of history. Formal result. A fable of the times, discussed in newspaper editorials for a day. At least that little boy on a murder charge might not go down for long enough to really learn how. He supposed that was something of an achievement, the best he was going to get.

'One more thing,' he said once they were inside his car, while she patted and stroked the seat, like a pet. 'Did you keep on going with your brother Damien, making love to him, I mean, after you married Joe?' It was a casual question, ending with a click of seat belt. Nothing said in cars would do as evidence these days; there would be nothing he could do with the knowledge. Cath's eyes beneath the street light shone like pools of rain on a white pavement.

'Oh yes, whenever he wanted. He was my brother. He would have told Joe about how I used to sleep with him before if I didn't. Joe loved Damien, you see, and anyway, I loved Damien, too. Most of my life, see, he was all I ever had.'

She settled back, a child on an outing. 'So I never wanted it to stop, not really,' she continued. 'Not even when he came to meet me in the park. Sometimes he frightened me, doing that. He liked to play games. Hide-and-seek in the park, in the dark.' She giggled, softly. 'He liked that.'

Close on midnight, Alistair Eliot phoned Helen West. He was as far out of Emily's earshot as Helen was herself; still both of them spoke in low voices, as if afraid of being overheard.

'Sorry to bother you.' Alistair so often prefaced statements or requests with an apology.

'Alistair, don't do that. I'm having an argument with Emily, not with you.'

He sighed. 'Yes, I know. Me and you, both. About Cath. That's what I wanted to ask about. Look, I think one of us should go and see her. Emily says she never knew where she lives. Do you?'

Shame came back and hit her like a punch.

'No, I don't.'

'Well, I do,' he said triumphantly. 'I've found it on a set of papers. Do you think I should go and see her? I feel so guilty about what we did to her. And then I saw her last night, outside that pub her husband runs. I walked straight past. She was looking smart, but so sad, Helen, and I didn't even wave. I went back today. There was an old man outside. Told me Cath's husband had ignored and abused her, dragged her away, later. Drunk. I could have saved her from that, Helen. I could have saved her, and I just walked on by.'

Helen had a strong mental picture of Cath, truculent and defensive earlier on. Got a better picture than she had ever imagined of that grand evening out. She took a firm grip of the phone.

'No, Alistair, I wouldn't go and see her. Not yet. There've been a few developments.'

'Oh?'

'Theft, wasn't it? Perfume? Well, I doubt if Cath would ever steal anything new, but she would take something second hand. And she can lie. Probably only when she's driven to lie, but all the same . . .' Gabbling. Wanting this kind man to understand something without giving him any information which might enable him to understand. Trying to talk in code, like Cath. Like Bailey did to her so much of the time. Alistair was suddenly cold. He sounded both puzzled and sad.

'You're like Emily,' he said. 'You've been talking to Emily. You sound like our judgemental judges. No imagination. They don't always listen, either.'

There was a full glass of red wine next to the phone in the hall. Helen watched it topple, did not move as it seeped away into the old carpet.

CHAPTER FOURTEEN

On the tenth day of September, the charge against an eighteen-year-old boy was reduced from murder to one of affray and assault. The youth had grown fatter on remand: he was never going to play pool again. There was no member of the murder-victim's family in court to complain how this was a travesty of justice, and the family of the boy was too relieved to care. No public explanation was made, save a brief statement that the Crown accepted that there had been an intervening human cause in between the fight and the death; a man unconnected with this defendant in any way. Constructing a balance sheet which included almost six months in custody and a few minor convictions from the recent past, the judge gravely sent this miscreant down for a further nine months. An adequate gestation period, Bailey thought. In his pocket he had the letter picked up from his desk that morning, ordering his own transfer to penal servitude. From now on, he was handling complaints against police, and he would never be able to stop looking at his watch.

First thing in the morning, Cath lay in her own bed, curled like a snake in a warm burrow. A little snap in the air today: no incentive to get up. Better to lie where she was and open her eyes slowly, stroking her belly, moving her legs and arms to get the energy going, look around. This room was as far as she had got. She had painted the walls yellow, moved in the daisy print from the kitchen, bought, without a hint of guilt, a brand-new bed-cover the pristine white of snow. It was not the old alarm clock which had woken her, but this voice inside her head, Is that you? Is that you? Is this really you, lying idle?

Yes, this was the way she liked it. Bare and clean, like the living room. Mickey Gat said she was doing up the Spoon shortly, throwing out a set of table and chairs, as well as all the carpet. She did it each year, she said. Cath had told her, don't chuck the furniture: I'll have it. There was bound to be paint left over as well. Cath liked working in the Spoon: she was good at it, a quick learner. Mickey said, Yes, she would do. Better than Joe, as it happened. Mickey Gat knew all about women being better than men, especially if they had the guts to take over a man's job. Poor old Joe, always did have bad luck or judgement, but they had given him a good funeral. What a way to go. Some thug doing you in on the bus. Must be a loony, thrown out of one of those homes they kept closing down. Somehow, by an obscure and logical route, it came back to another version of 'them' and 'us'.

'We don't have to be friends,' Helen said carefully to Mary Secura. 'It isn't a necessary part of the arrangement and probably doesn't even help. But we have to be able to communicate. My boss says so.'

She grinned with a shrug as she spoke. Mary rewarded her with the ghost of a smile. There was more than a hint of the apology she could not bring herself to make. All that money Cath had. Of course Helen West had paid her. Mary was subdued, respectful even, she seemed to have lost some of the fire, like someone recovering from an illness. Despite the volatility of Mary in health, Helen was hoping that this convalescent state was temporary. The woman firing off in all directions was distinctly preferable. All Mary was thinking, in a state which bordered on guilt, still-remembered shock now overlaid with defensiveness, was how Helen West's ability to turn the other cheek was infuriating. Mid-thirties burn-out: that was Helen West. She did not want to be like that.

'This Rix case. I can hardly believe it. Shirley scarcely cold, and he's got another woman and the other woman has made a complaint. Incredible. He must be out of his mind.'

'It isn't the new woman complaining, it's her sister. And he had her before he got charged with hitting Shirl. Sort of a sideline, really. I've got a feeling Shirl found out. That was the first cut-off point, I reckon, with the kid the final straw. Not the beatings.'

'Well, we're going to need some corroboration. We can't run this on a medical report and a complaint from the sister. Hearsay, all of it.'

Mary shook her head. 'We'll have to wait for the repeat performance then, won't we?'

'Unless the victim gives us a statement, yes.'

'OK. Next?'

It was not much of a mystery why Redwood was instigating meetings between police and Crown Prosecution Service (in their offices, of course, God forbid his staff should go to police premises), at an earlier stage in the case. After that mêlée next door, the police were suddenly allies. He had waxed lyrical in a meeting. You will all have seen the fight in the offices over the road, he had announced to the assembly. At least, judging from the crowds at the windows, most of you did. Two women scrapping, pulling hair, biting, actually drawing blood. Men joining in, if you don't mind; you could hear the shouting from here. Some fool on our staff, a young blood whose name I shall not mention, went over the way, to help, he said, because a poor man in spectacles seemed to be getting the worst of it. He received a black eye for his pains, so you see, we must have a policy. Which is, if you do happen to see nasty things occur either at court or in your daily lives anywhere, don't intervene; call the police immediately. The police are made for this kind of thing; they smoothed the situation in no time. They are there to control breaches of the peace, not us. We work in the interests of justice, which is a very different thing altogether.

Redwood had not seen the crowd in his room stuffing handkerchiefs in their mouths to restrain ribaldry, Helen, doodling in a corner. She wondered if she would feel violent if, after the recent absence, she heard rumours of Bailey with another woman. Among a phalanx of men in grey clothing, Helen missed Bailey. Would jealousy, however futile, make her want to scratch the face of another woman? She had closed her own eyes and felt savage. Yes, it would.

Mary was gathering files and photos, stuffing the notebook back into the bulging handbag, looking for escape. She was uncomfortable with the proximity of so many lawyers padding about, bloodsuckers in uniform.

'Sit down a minute.' She sat.

'Cath killed her old man on the bus, didn't she? You were in on the interview as the only female officer she knew. Tell me.'

'Nothing to tell. I gave her her rights, told her she didn't have to say anything, and she didn't. No-one remembers her being on that damn bus. The conductor refuses to remember what day of the week it was. Witnesses in the last pub they went to said she left before him, a good half hour before, distressed because he was drunk, spilt whisky on her skirt. There isn't anything to say they even travelled together. She went back to her brother's place, went out next day as usual. Place got burgled. So she goes back to the old man. Again. Only he was dead already and the first she knew was when Bailey told her. That was when she showed him the knife.'

'Bayonet?'

'That's it. Been chatting to Mr Bailey?' A note of anxiety entered her voice.

'No. Not much. More guesswork, really. And your friend Ryan.'

'Who?'

'Never mind. Are you going to tell me what you really think?'

Mary remained seated, wanting to leave. Perhaps she did actually owe this woman something, for her own misjudgement. For the fact they had once got on so well and needed to do so again. And because she was Bailey's bird, and Mary still wanted to work for Bailey; but chiefly because she already seemed to know so much.

'It doesn't matter what I think,' she said. 'But yes, I think you could be right. She could well have killed him. Poor bitch. I also think it doesn't matter. He deserved it.'

'That bayonet . . .' Helen began, then stopped. She knew enough about that bayonet. Ryan, when bumped into accidentally in a court corridor, was always pleased to see her, assumed she knew everything Bailey would know, and chatted with an amazing lack of discretion. All about this crazy bayonet which Joe Boyce had hidden from his wife and Bailey had found in a cutlery drawer. What an odd place to put it.

'Any large knife could have done the damage to Joe Boyce,' Mary said flatly. 'Nothing suggests that the bayonet ever left the house, or that it was ever used at all, except by Joe Boyce. Cath said she would have no idea how to get such a thing sharpened. It would need to be done by a powerful grinder in the first instance, I suppose. Joe played with things like that. It simply moved into the cutlery drawer after Cath had left. Cath said it repelled her, all Joe's military stuff repelled her. Let's face it, every cutlery drawer has a murder weapon in it.'

She stood again, looked out of Helen's window to the workers opposite. 'Close, aren't they? At least offices are safer than houses.'

'If you say so,' Helen murmured.

'Did you complete all that decorating you were doing?' Mary asked by way of ending on a casual note. 'Yellow, wasn't it?'

'All over. How's life at home?'

Mary was halfway out of the door. 'Fine,' she said airily. 'Just fine. I thought about getting rid of dear old Dave, but it isn't worth the hassle. A woman on her own. You know.'

Mickey Gat levered herself out of the Jag, bounced across the cobbles of the Mews and into the Spoon. The place shone like a new pin, whatever one of those was, Mickey was not into needlework. Cath could get a fair old shine on that bar: you could see your face in it, and Cath's face wasn't the kind of mug to keep custom at bay. Mickey hadn't been so sure at first, but now she was. Cath turned exactly the right kind of blind eye to all the boxes of counterfeit perfume in the back room, too: she didn't even dust them. It was about the right time of year to start stockpiling for Christmas. Mickey was on her way to Harrods after this, to get a few ideas. She wafted indoors in a cloud of Poison, the real thing, not her own brand, and almost collided with an old gent coming out. He wore a cap, raised it. Mickey reckoned only people drinking half pints did that.

'You want to be careful with these old lags,' she told Cath. 'Sit around all day, take up space and don't spend nothing. We want them yuppy types, that's what we want.'

Cath shook her head. 'I know,' she agreed. 'But yuppy types like seeing the old ones hanging around, see? Gives the place a homey feel. Besides, some people won't go into a pub if it's empty. You need a couple of ornaments to fill up the corners.'

For a moment, Mickey did not know if Cath referred to the custom or the decor.

'Oh, yeah. Suppose you could be right. I'll have an orange juice.'

'I thought we could get a coffee-machine,' said Cath. 'People think it sobers them up, so they have a coffee, then they have another drink.'

'Steady on, girl,' said Mickey admiringly. 'Steady on. Think I'm made of money?'

She was looking at the takings. Not bad, not bad at all, for the tail end of summer.

It was time to mend fences. Alistair had said so. You can't just lose friends, he said: they are too rare and too valuable. Please, make it up and ask them for supper.

'Whoops!' Emily sighed, voice a little high, body a little drunk, deciding that this was all so difficult she deserved another drink. Her mind was full of fearful imaginings, something to do with this direction about friend Helen West who was, after all, very easy to look at, admired by Alistair in his distant way and mentioned twice, obliquely, in the last week or three. Better get in there first. It did not do for a dedicated wife to have her man distracted the way hers had been. Such men were like a viral culture looking for a new plant: there was no telling what they would let grow on them. Besides she did have a conscience, even if it was not troubling her.

Dear Helen,

    OK, I've been shitty and over the top and I was devastated to hear what happened to Cath's husband, but I do miss you. Can we have lunch or something?

There was a pause, writer staring into distance. No, that would not do. She'd have to make it longer, chat a bit, to bring Helen round. Let her know that life was going on at the usual hectic pace, try and get Helen involved.

    . . . Jane sends her love, to Bailey, little flirt . . .

Another pause, then Emily smiled and wrote with animation, the way she always could when describing children.

    . . . She is a flirt, you know. You have no idea how children play with the truth. We're thinking of setting up a courtroom in the kitchen, where we test one another for truth or fib! One person's evidence against another's, it's the only way! Otherwise, it's amazing what you believe when you want to believe it. I don't know how I could have believed so badly of Cath, except for the funny bad manners and the smell, like school lavatories after a wash, would you believe. School or prison, but you know more about those . . .

Helen supposed it had cost Emily some to write what looked like a long letter in the middle of her oh-so-busy life, but since Helen was not mother, housekeeper or any of that herself, simply an observer, she could read her personal mail whenever she pleased, and it did not please her to do so immediately. She had all the time in the world. Even when the letter was accompanied by a peace-offering to make up for Emily's rash judgement, which may well have helped Cath on her way to desperate violence. Helen felt that Emily Eliot did not quite deserve forgiveness and conciliation by return of post. Nor did she want to plough through a missive of family news, designed to charm her. The rest of the letter could wait. So could the gift accompanying it, a small box, soap, perfume perhaps.

In the evenings the room seemed to have slipped back into familiarity with sinister ease. There was extra fluff and a fine coat of gold dust on everything, which Helen could not quite bring herself to clean. No-one else was going to do it, she was quite certain of that. Somewhere, floating around London, there were two sets of keys, Bailey's and Cath's, but she had needed a new lock anyway.

The place was still remarkably different, impressive even. After a few weeks, surfaces no longer quite so pristine, a few spillages and a bit of neglect, she no longer felt the need to wipe her feet when she entered or comb her hair when she passed a mirror. Golden light came in at the kitchen window, twinkled on the slightly smeared wineglass. Dishwasher next. The fridge still panted like a thing in labour and worked with only moderate efficiency, no real problem at the moment, since there was so little in it.

Which would have been why Bailey came to call, homing instinct working overtime, plastic bag in hand as if he thought he could use food and drink as a password after all this time. She saw his feet from the street, wondered what he would do if she let him discover how his key no longer worked and knowing she would not make him wait, waved from the window and let him in.

Scene fifty-five, take five. Balley came in through the front door, tripped on the new carpet, righted himself and made an undignified entrance into the dulcet yellow wash of the living room, dropping the bag. The gasp was not quite one of astonishment, the words used merely the gentler obscenities uttered by someone who has just avoided falling.

'Christ Almighty. What have you done here? It's all clean. Yellow, is it?'

'I'm glad you like it,' Helen said. 'Nice of you to notice. You've seen it before, but I don't suppose you remember. Where've you been?' She spoke as if the absence had been hours, rather than far too many days.

He looked slightly hangdog, turned on his heel and made for the kitchen. She remained as she was. There was the sound of a cork popping, and more muffled swearing as he searched through reorganised cupboards. Her mood had been desperate, depressed, any kind of self-esteem notable by its absence; now she could feel herself lifting, like a balloon, the beginnings of laughter starting in her throat as she listened So much for pride. Back he came with a tray of glasses, fizzy stuff.

'What are we celebrating?'

'We aren't. Yet. And if we do, it'll be because of being alive and halfway sane. There's fuck all outside to celebrate.'

Silence fell. One of the things she had always loved about Bailey was his comfort with silence. It never bothered him any more than it did her, and he needed silence in order to find the right words.

'She killed him and you fudged it on paper. Is that what you were aiming to tell me?'

He looked up at her in surprise, took a large swig of the wine, and coughed.

'Yes and no. Well, no, that wasn't what I was going to say first. I was going to say, I think we ought to get married. We'll just lose one another if we don't get married. Only I've got this clock at home, started going at the rate of a day every hour again, and I can't stop it turning round until you do.'

'You're a liar.'

'No more than you. You lied to me about Cath being here the day after Boyce was killed. She told me, in the car. For all I know, you've got the life history of a bayonet at your fingertips and you wouldn't volunteer that, either. You would if you thought it was going to lead me in the direction of the right result. Which is not, as I see it, a wretched little cleaning lady with a wretched life to date, being put in prison for doing to her husband what he did to her brother. Even if it could be proved, which it can't.'

She nodded. The affirmation was reluctant, but definite. Two years ago, she thought, I would never have agreed. I have always believed in letting a jury decide. Why did I change? Guilt warps judgement, or is it arrogance? Perhaps we simply grow more alike, more cynical.

'I was going to tell you . . .' she began.

'Shh,' he warned. 'Don't. Clean slate from now on, all right? He was off, like a butler, for the bottle. She had large wine glasses; a bottle of bubbly lasted no time at all. Helen fingered the curtains next to her chair. All that effort and expense.

'I don't think you could live in the same place as me,' she called.

'I don't think so either. What's that got to do with anything? You can be married and not live in the same place. Bloody royals do it all the time. Provided we both know where the other one is and we get the hell out of it from time to time.'

'Sounds like a good idea, then. I should have asked you, a long time ago.'

He shot back into the room. 'Well if that's yes, thank God. I couldn't go through that again. You must be mad, saying yes.'

'You must be mad to volunteer.'

It was stupid and peculiarly embarrassing to be suddenly close to tears. He brushed the hair off her forehead, kissed the scar, withdrew and grinned his huge grin. She noticed he was trembling.

'You know, I've been sitting in my poxy flat, driving nails into my head, wondering if I ever get anything right.'

'Oh yes, you do. It's me who doesn't. I don't do anything right.'

He laughed, a reassuring crow of joy. 'Who says? Well, you just sit there and be a deep, dark goldmine, then. What do you want for supper? Not yet. Later.'

'Food would do nicely.'

'I could fix you a nice sandwich,' Cath said winsomely to the colonel. 'We was thinking of doing sandwiches, quality ones, you know. You can get this lovely bread round the corner.'

He shook his head, politely. 'So sorry about your husband,' he said, for the fourteenth time. He had been saying it in various tones of disbelief for the last ten days, once the penny dropped. The colonel had a particular penchant for widows, even when the newness of their regime in his watering-hole meant the drinks were no longer free. She was kind to him though, liked the company in the afternoons, she said, made him feel protective and let him nod to sleep in the sun while there was still a chance. Nights beginning to draw in round about now, he told her, as if she had never had cause to discover such a phenomenon for herself. Had he been terribly insensitive to tell her that the grieving time would be over and that one day, she would be able to think of marrying again? He could hear himself saying it, minutes ago, before she offered the sandwich, so he had not caused offence, after all. Busy Lizzies, busy dying. Something new in the window-boxes, heavy-scented stocks. Made him dopey.

Cath eyed him, nodding off. He probably had a bob or two in bricks and mortar, she decided, but, for all that, he was still a shade too old. She could not quite see herself taking off her clothes and showing her scars for this one, sweet though he was, poor old thing. Pretty deaf with it, still a good listener, even while he slept. She needed a good listener who could not hear, patted his freckled hand as his eyes closed.

'You don't understand, Mr Colonel, sir. You don't really, which is all to the good, 'cos it wouldn't be a tonic for your health if you did. Course I'm grieving. I loved him. Or at least, I sort of loved him. Only there's grief and grief, if you see what I mean. I loved Damien, you see. I loved him to pieces. I couldn't have loved anyone else like that. He gets me pregnant, leaves me in the club, lets me get on with it, I lose the baby and get this sodding great scar. I can cope with that, at the time, anyway, see? Though you can never look at yourself the same way again. You aren't worth shit with a belly like mine. Least, that's what it feels like at fifteen.'

She sipped a Bloody Mary. Two a day of those was more.than enough, plenty of Worcester sauce to give it bite, good for a girl. Better than lunch. This glass was cracked, she must remember not to use her muscles in the washing up.

'My one and only love,' she continued, dreamily. 'Sends money, comes home, looks after me, gets me the hotel job, and then, he gets me Joe, and Joe loves me. Does he ever? Till he finds out.

Well, he thinks he finds out about me still going round to Damien, only he daren't say, just hits me. I mean, I didn't mind marrying Joe, because a woman should be married, Damien was right, you've got to put up with it.' So comforting, talking to the colonel. Old men, with old-fashioned values, they understood so much. About respectability, status, all that. Not like these yuppies in the bar.

'I thought he was doing it for my own good, see? Damien, I mean. But what I couldn't stand was when I came to realise he was just shoving me off. He used to keep Joe in order if I complained; I mean Joe couldn't help it if he couldn't keep his end up and had to fight his way out, could he? He was like that, and he loved me. Would have done anything for me, me for him, too. But when he got worse, and I went round to Damien with bruises, well, Damien didn't like me with bruises. Sodding great scar, yes, but bruises turned him off. And him a champion boxer!'

She let out a snort of laughter. The colonel stirred. Cath picked up the cigar left in the ashtray between them, and stubbed it out fiercely.

'Dumping me. Used to take me out at least, but the boys were better fun. Dumping me, so I'd stand outside the pub and watch for him and Joe, mostly him. After all he'd done. And all I'd done for him. Wanted to offload me, get rid of me. I was the only one who really loved him, and he wanted . . . What time is it?'

The colonel moved in his sleep. 'I'm *so* sorry about your husband,' he droned. Cath seized his wrist, looked at an ancient watch, put the arm back carefully.

'That's all right, early yet. I used to watch the time when I waited. Had a watch: Joe smashed it. Joe comes out the pub, always earlier than the others in case they leave him behind, see? Comes home that night in two minutes round that track, fit bloke, Joe, but angry, see? Tells me there's going to be a fight, crashes out indoors. Falls fast asleep, he could always do that. I dunno what I thought. Save Damien, I thought, silly fool he was in a scrap. But then when I ran across the park, I saw the tail end of the fight. I saw Damien waltzing away from it scarcely hurt, a bit out of breath, causing all that fuss for nothing, sitting down by a tree, and then I thought, you bugger, and I knew what I wanted to do. Give him back that scar he gave me, is what. So I did. I loved him. He loved me. Simple. He was doing wrong, dumping me. I couldn't live, knowing that. He'd walk away from me like he did from that fight, leaving everyone else with the scars.'

She patted her own stomach, drew in her breath to flatten it.

'Course I knew Joe had that bayonet thing in his satchel; he always did, he was so proud of it, I knew where to look.'

She looked at the cigar butt with regret. Smoke would be nice, but thinking of smoking was the equivalent to dirty thoughts and she did not have any of those. Dirty thoughts were almost as wicked as anyone thinking she would steal.

'Wouldn't stop screaming,' she clicked her tongue in disapproval. 'Never had any self-discipline. Took for ever and made me sweat, I can tell you. Ever such a noise. Didn't matter; no-one listens round there, I don't even know why Joe woke up to come out and look, but he did. He was quite nice to me, after, ran me a bath; but being nice – being ever so protective, wanting to pretend he did it – didn't last. He really wanted to pretend he did it. I wouldn't let him hide that bayonet, though. I put it in the only place I could think of, a garden. Where else could I put it? Where else was I allowed to go? And I gave Joe his chances, I did, I really did; I wanted him to be like Damien, wanted him to try to be as nice as Damien had been once, when he loved me the way I loved him, but he couldn't. And I couldn't stop loving Damien, even though he was dead. Never lasts, does it?'

'What?' said the colonel.

'People being nice to you,' Cath shouted. 'Do you want that sandwich, or not?'

He was too old. What a shame. Otherwise, he would have been ideal.

During the course of the night, the wind blew. Helen had forgotten to undo the grille which covered the bedroom window. The sound of the wind was reminiscent of a wild animal rattling the bars. About that time, they got up and ate scrambled eggs. Supper had been bypassed; once there had been fading daylight to hide the sudden, self-conscious nerves. Now it was dark. Autumn had begun to blow against the panes.

'I could live without those,' Bailey said, pointing towards the grilles with his fork before it speared a piece of burned toast.

'You don't have to live with them.'

'Nope, not every day, but there are better versions. Double glazing, better-looking stuff than that. I can fit it. Nice curtains you've got. Are they new?'

'Don't you notice anything?'

'You. You, always looking like you, whatever you put on. That's what I notice. You could call it X-ray eyes, but I also like what you put on. I also like you. You could chuck me out tomorrow, I'd still think so. I'd like you anyway. Oh yes, even if you get frightened and even if you lie. You've always got a good reason. Something to do with being a good woman. More than I could say about being a good man. Get this egg off this duvet.'

She was spilling the stuff in the effort to cut the toast.

'Mary Secura thinks I'm a burnt-out case.' He choked on the coffee, the thought trickling across his mind about whether he should tell her about an appointment in Police Complaints. Settling on an answer.

'She doesn't listen to what you say. Doesn't sleep with you, either. Thank God. So how would she know? Doesn't egg travel?'

Boiled eggs go off like bombs, Helen remembered. Scrambled, they only need to go as far as carpet level to bring in a cat with an addiction to butter. She scooped up the rest on her plate.

'Were we right about Cath?'

He got out of bed and ushered the cat out of the room. Kicked the fresh-painted door with his foot.

'I think so. Why? Don't you?'

'We didn't have a jury in on this one, that's why. There should be a jury. Evidence, all the safeguards which should come before judgement day. It feels arrogant.'

He nodded gravely. 'I know. I think I know. There are exceptions. Come here. I don't like doubt. I can't stand it. Did you hear me earlier? I once thought that if you didn't marry me, I might die, still think it once a day. You want a jury? You want a deed poll?'

Sweet morning, swelling against the garden windows, insistent to be seen. The first hint of a chill and a big, black beetle marching a path to suicide on the way to the kitchen. Far too much light in here. Helen West, soon to be a married woman, swanned in there, gossamer clad, walking on air, tired as all hell, fit for anything. Including yesterday's post, something to read while the kettle boiled. She was proof against anything. Even circulars, and the remnants of Emily's letter:

. . . Well, while you've been battling in your version of the real world, I've been labouring away in mine, and there's quite a lot I have to eat humble pie about. Such as discovering that my youngest child is a pathological liar, but maybe we should just call her creative. You see, I never believed she was CAPABLE of stealing the perfume, but it was her, she buries it. Alistair found it when he noticed signs of digging and went out there to see if the silly child had hidden this funny old bayonet thing which had somehow gone missing. When you tackle Jane about lying, she's perfectly frightful! She just makes up something else! Yes, she'd taken the bayonet (admittedly she'd found it in the first place, so I suppose it WAS hers really), but Jane being Jane, she HAS to say that she was only giving it back to Cath, because she'd seen Cath put it there in the first place. I ask you! Now that was the worst lie of all, because she'd always said some ghosty chap had put it there, oh, she's impossible. Mind, I'm glad to be rid of the thing, it was awfully sharp, and she would play with it.

Sorry to ramble on, but life is not a bed of roses. I do miss Cath. The bayonet incident reminds me of one of many reasons why. I mean, she would get things done for me, on her way home; she always knew places to get things done. Got all the knives sharpened for me one day, something I suppose you can do in the East End easier than round here! All blunt again now, of course, and the kettle doesn't work. Now please don't mind if I ask a favour, but I know you, loyal old thing that you are, you might see Cath in her troubles. Could you give her back this perfume? I know now she never stole it. It's the best I can do as an apology. She must have brought it in with her on the day Jane found it in her bag. We know it can't be ours, of course, because it isn't the real thing . . .! That's what started us off, wondering about Jane.

Helen read with her hip propped against the work surface, found she had turned to face the wall with the corner of a unit pressing into her stomach, painfully. It was a rounded edge, but it hurt. So did the contents of the letter. She needed the concentration of that slight pain in order to think. Of Cath, and her unreal perfume, and her odour of sanctity. Secreting in a garden a knife she would know how to sharpen, the knowledge of which she denied. Why hide it if she did not know Joe had used it?

Because she had used it?

'No,' Helen said out loud. 'No, no, NO!'

She went back to the bedroom. They had promised each other they would break their habit of keeping secrets.

Bailey was still asleep. Sleeping the slumber of the just. To which she was no longer entitled.